FROM THE ASHES
Bon Marché, vol. II

Tor books by Chet Hagan

Bon Marché

From the Ashes

FROM THE ASHES

Bon Marché, vol. II

———————

Chet Hagan

———————

TOR

A TOM DOHERTY ASSOCIATES BOOK
NEW YORK

FROM THE ASHES

A TOR Book
Published by Tom Doherty Associates, Inc.
49 West 24th Street
New York, N.Y. 10010

Printed in the United States of America

First edition: September 1989

0 9 8 7 6 5 4 3 2

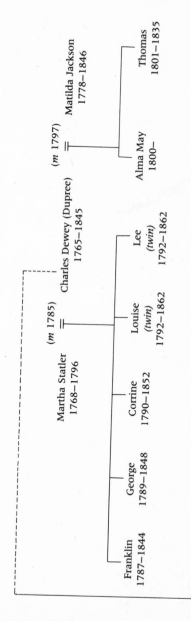

1

DEWEY GENEALOGY

Martha Statler
1768–1796

(m 1785)

Charles Dewey (Dupree)
1765–1845

(m 1797)

Matilda Jackson
1778–1846

Franklin
1787–1844

George
1789–1848

Corrine
1790–1852

Louise
(twin)
1792–1862

Lee
(twin)
1792–1862

Alma May
1800–

Thomas
1801–1835

(1797)
Angelica *(slave)*

Marshall Dewey
1797–

2

DEWEY GENEALOGY

Franklin Dewey
1787–1844

(m 1809)

Amantha Bolling
1789–1819

(m 1834)

William Bonsal
1792–

Carrie
1811–

Alvin Mussman
(divorced)

(m 1829)

Honey
1829–1845
(suicide)

Richard
1813–1819

Virginia Stoker
1820–
(divorced)

(m 1840)

Albert
1814–

Lillian Thomas
1825–

(m 1851)

Jefferson
1841–

Jackson
1843–1861

Carolina
1844–

Staunch
1845–

Lance
1852–

DEWEY GENEALOGY

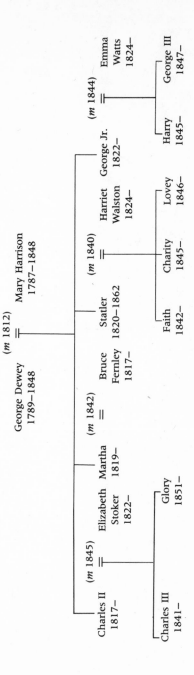

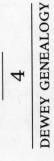

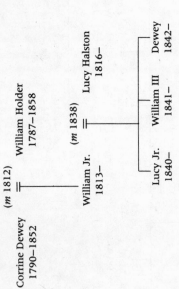

4

DEWEY GENEALOGY

Corrine Dewey
1790–1852

(*m* 1812)

William Holder
1787–1858

William Jr.
1813–

(*m* 1838)

Lucy Halston
1816–

Lucy Jr.
1840–

William III
1841–

Dewey
1842–

DEWEY GENEALOGY

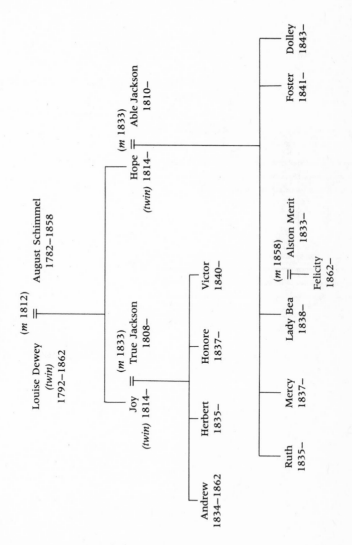

6

DEWEY GENEALOGY

Alma May Dewey $\overset{(m\ 1817)}{=}$ Nathan Ludlum
1800–ㅤㅤㅤ1792–1858

(divorced, 1822)

Prologue

CHARLES Dewey was dead.

The master of Nashville's Bon Marché stud had gone to meet his Maker and there were those among Dewey's friends who wondered how God would contend with him.

"The Lord will be glad to consign him to the Devil," one of his fellow horsemen suggested with only partial humor, "when He learns Charles intends to manage Heaven."

BOOK ONE

Until I reach that Sweet Day when I am
with my darling Charles once more I have
only one mandate: to keep Bon Marché
whole.
—Matilda Jackson Dewey, 1846

1

Green grow the laurel, all sparkling with dew,
I'm lonely, my darling, since parting from you . . .

BREVET Captain Albert Dewey, late of West Point, was disquieted and morose. Worse—he had begun to doubt his own worth, a new and alien thought for a young man who had been taught, almost from birth, that he had a gift from God to be someone special. That to be a *Dewey* was the best possible circumstance in the human experience.

But by the next morning I hope to prove true,
And change the green laurel for the red, white, and blue.

The poignant song, accompanied by the mournful wail of a mountain man's fiddle, drifted up to him from the campfires of the American army ringing Matamoros, Mexico. It added to his discomfort. Had he "proved true" in his first test under fire in this strange war? He was uncertain. But of one thing he was sure: the glory of battle, as preached in the classrooms at the United States Military Academy, was a lie. His instructors had engaged in sophistry, filling his brain with their subtle arguments about the grandeur of military engagement. It had been deceit, nothing but deceit.
Oh, God, how naive I've been!
Instead of being grand, the warfare he had seen thus far had been ill-planned, totally confused, and largely com-

manded by incompetents. His despondency told him he was one of those—a rank incompetent.

There had been no war when he came to what was known as Fort Texas, a hurriedly constructed, star-shaped earthworks redoubt on the Rio Grande River opposite the city of Matamoros. No war and, indeed, little thought there would be war. Mexico had been enraged by the admission of an independent Texas as the twenty-eighth state in the American Union. But no one in real authority in the army commanded by "Old Rough and Ready" Zachary Taylor believed there would be war. Mexican anger, everyone contended, would not, could not, be translated into fighting, given the disorganized nature of the Mexican government. Everyone said a show of American strength on the Rio Grande would be enough to deter the Mexicans.

"Everyone" had been wrong!

A Mexican army (under the command of General Mariano Arista, they would learn later) struck across the Rio Grande late in April of 1846 with a large force of cavalry, butchering an American patrol of sixty-three men. With such ease, it seemed. And then there had been fighting at a place called Palo Alto, little more than a meadow of tall, dusty saw grass; also on the low banks of a dry streambed the official reports would designate as Resaca de la Palma.

Brevet Captain Dewey's command was a hastily organized company of the volunteers who were pouring into Texas. His temporary promotion had come because he was a West Pointer and, as such, was expected to have the training necessary for the task of molding the "vols" into a fighting force. They were rabble. An unsavory bunch: adventurers, petty criminals, brawlers—almost all unwilling to accept discipline.

Nevertheless, he had tried.

He remembered it now as a series of searing vignettes not mentioned in his diary, because he found it emotionally impossible to put it into written words. But the memories remained and he could not erase them.

The May morning at Resaca de la Palma had been beautiful, the golden sunshine gleaming off the massed bayonets of his company. The exquisite fragrance of prairie wildflowers wafted along on gentle winds. His men stood before him, their lack of military unity reflected in the ragged ranks: some at attention, some at ease, some with partial uniforms, some with no uniforms at all. Yet, there was something mesmerizing about the moment. Maybe it was the beauty of the day. Maybe it was the company guidons snapping smartly in the breeze. Maybe it was Dewey's West Point orientation on the glory of battle.

Whatever it was, the captain felt the necessity to address his command. He sat ramrod straight on the back of his horse.

"Men!" he had shouted. "I am not going to ask you to be brave on this day, because to do so would only insult you. Only brave men would be standing there now in your ranks, ready to defend our flag—to safeguard the honor of our country!"

Huzzahs rose up from the infantrymen.

"But bravery does not require that you be foolhardy. Be calm. Be resolute. Keep in mind, men, when the roar of battle is upon you, that only a small proportion of the shots fired in combat are effective." Captain Dewey had even laughed at that point. "An old drill sergeant once told me that men shoot dreadful careless in battle—"

There were guffaws in the ranks.

"—But be not careless yourselves. Be sure of your shots. Make them count. And a benevolent God will see you through—to victory!"

"TO VICTORY!" the volunteers had bellowed in response.

In truth, there *had* been victory that day at Resaca de la Palma. But at what cost?

The benevolent God of whom the captain had spoken was represented on the other side as well. They had not faced a heathen horde; it had been a clash of two Christian armies, both worshiping the same Supreme Being. Had He looked away? Had He abandoned them both, in His disgust at what they were doing, to the forces of Hell? Albert Dewey believed so now, unable to drive from his mind the stark realities of what he had witnessed.

The enemy had been massed across a chaparral, raking it with grapeshot and musket fire, as Dewey's company led a flanking attack. A private—Dewey didn't know his name, but he was just a beardless lad—had been running alongside the captain's horse, screaming defiance at the Mexicans. Suddenly, his headlong dash was stopped by the impact of a musket ball full in the face, frozen for an instant in death before he fell. His blood had spattered Albert's boot.

And there was Sergeant William Gordon, who had been leading his squad in a charge on a cannon emplacement in the center of the Mexican line. They were only a scant ten yards from their goal when the cannon fired once more, the heavy ball striking the sergeant in the left leg, severing it at the knee, sending the limb flying grotesquely through the air. Before the fieldpiece could be reloaded, Gordon's squad overwhelmed the position, bayoneting the Mexican gunners, breaching the line. Captain Dewey had written a report to General Taylor recommending Sergeant Gordon be decorated as a hero. Posthumously.

When the Mexican line broke and a general rout was under way—the enemy throwing away weapons, dropping cartridge boxes, stripping off uniforms as if somehow making themselves lighter so they might run faster—Lieutenant George Seimanski, waving his sword cavalierly, exhorted his men to give chase. He tripped inadvertently, sprawling facedown on the turf. In the blink of an eye, a retreating Mexican lancer wheeled his horse, plunging his lance through his foe's back, pinioning him to the ground. One of the company's backwoods riflemen shot the lancer off his mount. Too late. The young officer's lifeblood nourished the wildflowers.

The Resaca de la Palma victory was bought in that manner. Two days later, the United States formally declared war, President James K. Polk saying in Washington: "The cup of forbearance has been exhausted." Still, more than a week went by before General Taylor chanced ordering his army across the Rio Grande to invest the city of Matamoros, as the regimental band gaily played "Yankee Doodle." General Arista had long since withdrawn his forces from the area; the opportunity to destroy them had been lost by the American delay.

In one sense, encampment at Matamoros was even worse for Brevet Captain Dewey than the battle. At least under battle conditions his disreputable, ill-trained volunteers were free to do what they did best—fight and kill. They adapted poorly to the idleness of camp life. Regular drills were impossible; desertions were commonplace.

Dewey sat now in his field tent, trying to compose a letter

to the mother of a dead regular soldier from Mississippi, one of the very few regulars in his company. Details of his death sickened Albert. On the night before, a whiskey-crazed volunteer had raped a Mexican woman in a house in Matamoros, stabbing the screaming woman to death in full view of her three terrified children. In the row that followed, Corporal Vernon Mayfield had tried to arrest the offender, who pulled a pistol and shot him dead, fleeing the scene. He was still at large and would probably never be caught.

Albert had written the date—"Wednesday, May 20, 1846"—and the salutation: "My dear Mrs. Mayfield . . ."

He had wrestled with his conscience before committing the first sentence to the paper: "I regret to inform you that your son, Corporal Vernon Mayfield, has given his life in the service of his nation."

Dewey groaned. As a company commander there would be more such letters to be done, inane and devoid of the detail that might reveal to the survivors the senseless nature of their losses. How many other lies would he have to tell?

The canvas flap of his tent parted, his Negro orderly entering, saluting smartly. The captain returned the salute lazily.

"A letter fer ya, suh."

"Thank you, Cephus." Reaching for it, his heart jumped; the address was in Virginia's hand. Dewey tore it open quickly, ignoring the orderly's departing salute:

> My darling Albert,
> We all miss you terribly, but no more desperately than today, because Bon Marché has suffered a cruel blow. I wish for some way to spare you this news, but I'm not clever enough to sugar-coat the reality of what I must tell you. Sometime during last night [the letter was dated Friday, June 12—more than a month earlier] your grandmother was stricken. The doctor tells us she has suffered a stroke and he says her condition threatens her life.

The captain cursed under his breath.

> She has lost the use of her limbs on the right side; also the power to speak properly. But, on a more positive note, Dr. Thompson assures us her heart is strong and that there are many examples of sufficient recovery from

strokes so that the victim can resume a long and productive life. Providence controls that, he says, and it is for that we all pray now, knowing your prayers will join our own.

Wanting to get this into the post immediately, I will add only that all of the children are well. Until that happy day when you shall return to them, and to me, I send my undying love.

Your adoring Virginia.

Albert kissed the letter. That had become a ritual for him. Kissing her letters, which she had touched, allowed him to imagine touching her, kissing her.

Then, he wept. Not so much because of the critical illness of his step-grandmother, but because of his frustrations. More than anything in life he wanted to be part of Bon Marché at that moment. The realization surprised him. When he was growing up there he had no ambitions to follow in his late father's footsteps as the Bon Marché breeding manager. Perhaps he had been too close to the plantation to fully appreciate it. He tried to remember why it was he had appealed to his grandfather, the founder of Bon Marché, to use his influence to secure an appointment to the United States Military Academy. His choice of a soldier's life, he mused, had been a terrible mistake, and not one easily corrected.

> *Green grow the laurel, all sparkling with dew,*
> *I'm lonely, my darling, since parting from you . . .*

Virginia's lovely face appeared before him, framed by ringlets of blond curls, just as he had seen her on their wedding day at Bon Marché. It had been more than a year since he had *really* seen her, when he handed her into a carriage at Fort Jesup, Louisiana, and watched her being carried away toward Nashville, their fourth child still nestled in her womb.

Would he ever see his new son, Staunch? Would he ever see any of his children again? Jeff and Jack, such proper little gentlemen. And sweet Carolina, a perfect copy of her mother. She had started to walk since they had parted, another important moment his military service had cost him.

Singers in the camp began again: "Green grow the laurel, all sparkling . . ."

"Damned song!" Dewey muttered audibly. "Don't they know anything else?"

It was a ballad so pervasive among the men of the American army that Mexican tongues, trying to sing it in derision, had corrupted the first two words, "green grow," into "gringo," a hard, double-syllable imagery of the invaders. *Gringo!* It had become a bitter malediction.

I'm lonely, my darling, since parting . . .

The captain left his field desk and his odious writing chores, tossing himself onto a cot in his despair, staring up at the canvas ceiling, permitting his thoughts to transport him to Bon Marché.

II

As the chestnut filly, Mattie's Darling, swept across the finish line, four easy lengths the better in the second and decisive heat of the match race, the Frenchman raised his glass to George Washington Dewey.

"I salute you, monsieur—the premier trainer at Metairie!"

Dewey acknowledged the compliment with a sober nod. "Thank you, Bernard." There was none of the exuberance one might have expected from a winner.

"If I continue to follow your horses, George," the Frenchman laughed, "I may yet recoup the family fortune before the meeting is ended."

"Let's hope you do." The trainer got to his feet. "You'll excuse us, Bernard . . . we have a dinner engagement." He reached out a hand to his wife.

Making their way to their carriage through the departing crowd at the Metairie Racecourse, they were stopped frequently by others offering congratulations on the filly's victory. Dewey was strangely annoyed by it all, and showed it. He was a stockily built man, with graying, thinning hair, his square-cut face capable of a terrible scowl, which was what he put forth as he pushed through the throng.

Once in the carriage, instantly put into motion by the top-hatted Negro driver, his wife chided him sharply: "Georgie, sometimes you can be quite rude."

"I just didn't feel like indulging the sycophants today."

"Sycophants? Certainly you can't put Monsieur de Mandeville in that class, and you were rude to him, too. That was a rather clumsy white lie about a dinner engagement."

Dewey laughed sarcastically. "The truth, my dear, of what I feel about the vaunted Bernard Xavier de Marigny de Mandeville would have been a good deal more clumsy, believe me. The man is an ass."

"Georgie!"

"And for God's sake, Mary, stop calling me 'Georgie.'"

She pouted. "You used to love it."

"Maybe I did. But I've grown up since then. In the event you're not aware of it, I'm fifty-six years old." There was an iniquitous grin. "Meaning that you, Mrs. Dewey, must be fifty-eight."

"Georgie! It's absolutely horrid for you to remind me."

The husband groaned.

Mary Dewey fell into a sullen silence as they drove through the bustling, humid city of New Orleans. A plumpish matron, she had been a beauty as a young woman; only vestiges remained. There was some compensation for lost beauty in the expensively stylish gowns she wore, and the lavish cosmetic attention she paid to her face. Still, she hadn't considered age a foe until recent months when George seemed to lose interest in her. That coincided with his first objection to the loving appellation of "Georgie." She had seen such erosion in other marriages, but never imagined it would happen in her own.

The carriage entered Chartres Street where the Deweys maintained a three-story brick town house. It stood as a reminder of another argument they had had, when Mary had insisted on the purchase of the property because it was in the center of the social life of the city. She understood that George might have been more comfortable remaining in the country, some ten miles north of New Orleans, at Nouveau Marché, the stud farm he patterned after his father's in Tennessee. But she reasoned he was working too hard there and it was time for George Junior, at twenty-four, to assume a management role in the family's breeding and racing enterprises.

Dewey, never able to deny his wife what she really wanted, had acquiesced in the matter of the fashionable town house. After that the elder George's life had become a series of daily carriage rides from Chartres Street to the Metairie track and back again, being involved with his horses only enough to be given unwarranted credit for their successes.

This day had been an example of that. It was George Junior who bred the filly they named Mattie's Darling, who broke her, and who brought her up to racing condition. The father had merely saddled her for the match, a ceremonial chore at best, and had accepted the accolades of his peers for having brought her to victory. It was an empty thing for him. His thoughts took him back to his days at Bon Marché in Nashville, when he had trained the dam of Mattie's Darling, a tough, hard-knocking competitor named Matilda in honor of his step-mother. Matilda, bred by his late father, carried the blood of the great Messenger.

Dewey recognized he was fortunate in having a son who would sublimate his own ego for the good of the family business. That both pleased and appalled him. He never would have been capable of such easy sublimation and he wasn't certain he welcomed it in a young man carrying not only his blood but his name. Somehow, he saw it as a weakness in Junior.

At that moment George Washington Dewey Sr. was sure of only one thing: his utter boredom. Bored with what racing had become for him, bored with Mary's constant social posturing, bored with the opera, with the theater, with the masked balls, with intimate dinners for effete Frenchmen claiming ancient titles and Spanish planters prattling about their wealth, with the incessant gossip about quadroons (who had tinges of Negro blood, as if it really mattered), and bored, too, with the ever-present quaintness of New Orleans. To him it would always be a suspect city; a foreign place, American only by the accident of geography.

When they entered the town house, George went at once to the drawing room, where he poured himself a liberal portion of bourbon. Downing it in one gulp, he sank into an easy chair, sighed deeply, and put back his head, closing his eyes.

Mary studied him for a moment or two. Then: "George, what *is* it?"

"I'm weary is all."

"It's Two, isn't it?"

The eyes opened. "What about him?"

"Georgie, sometimes you can be so damned exasperating!" Dewey sighed once more. "I thought we agreed we weren't going to hash over . . . well, the saga of Charles Dewey the Second again. Wasn't that our last word on it?"

"Yes, but—" She sat down opposite him. "I wish you'd make peace with Two. He's corrected his error, you know, by marrying the girl. And their son, after all, is our grandchild."

"He brought dishonor to the Dewey name."

"There are times when you can be such a hypocrite."

"So we're back to that again," he said bitterly.

"Yes, we are, because I can remember when he was sowing his wild oats how you used to laugh about it. 'A chip off the old block,' you'd say proudly."

"That was no excuse for him to be stupid about it."

Mary tried to keep anger from her voice. "It was you who always taught the children to be self-sufficient, to make their own choices in life. In sum, that was Two's only sin."

George smiled wanly, seeing a way to possibly redirect the conversation away from the subject of his eldest son. "I did, didn't I? Well, Mary, it seems to have worked out well for everyone but the man who gave the advice."

"What does that mean?"

"I'm talking about all this"—he made an all-encompassing gesture with his arms—"this artificial life we lead . . . this unrewarding mess—" He got to his feet, making for the bourbon bottle again. "Mary, I feel a lack of *reason* for my life."

"Georgie! You're frightening me."

He poured a drink, looking up at his image in the large, gilt-framed mirror over the mantel, not liking what he saw. An aging man stood before him, filled with doubts.

"When we were growing up at Bon Marché," he tried to explain, "my father put a challenge in our way every single day of the year. And we were expected to meet those challenges. I don't have that any longer."

There was a silence; she unsure of what to say, he caught up in his melancholy.

Suddenly, Dewey turned back to his wife, a decision made.

"I'll be catching the packet boat for Nashville in the morning."

Mary gasped. "Why?"

"I'm going back to Bon Marché to claim my inheritance."

"Your inheritance!"

"That's right. I was there at the beginning when Charles Dewey started Bon Marché. I played a role in building that estate—a major role, no one can deny. Now, from everything we are told in the letters, Mattie may be nearing the end of her days. It's time for me to take over, to assume my responsibilities."

"You're mad!"

"No, Mary, I've just come to my senses. Bon Marché is where I belong."

"New Orleans is where you belong," Mary said angrily. "Our roots are *here* now. My God, George, we've been here for more than a decade—"

He cut her off. "Three quarters of my life has been invested in Bon Marché."

"And have you forgotten why we came to New Orleans in the first place? How you were shunted aside at Bon Marché when your stepmother brought in those two cousins of hers to manage the estate? And how your father never lifted a hand to keep you there?"

"I made a mistake in not fighting then," George answered flatly. "I intend to rectify it."

"And destroy what you've built here? You have your own wealth now, your own farm, your own horses. Largely through your efforts the Metairie track was built and—"

"I can sell my Metairie shares to that Ten Broeck fellow. He's been making noises about wanting to control it."

"And Nouveau Marché?"

"Junior is already managing it, isn't he? He can have it all when I take over Bon Marché."

"And what about me, Georgie?" She seemed ready to cry. "Do you have a convenient way to dispose of me, too?"

"I'd hope you'd be with me at Bon Marché."

"And if not?"

"If not," he replied coldly, "you shall have this townhouse." As an afterthought: "And enough money to maintain yourself, of course."

Mary sank deep into her chair, weeping now. George stood away from her, watching her, making no effort to console her. Nor to further convince her of the rightness of his position. He had made his decision; she'd have to make her own.

It took her several minutes to bring her emotions under control. When she had, she rose and went to George's desk, where she rummaged through some papers before finding what she was seeking.

"Georgie, I've listened to you over the years," she said with determination, "extolling the virtues of New Orleans as a racing center. And I remember it was just a few weeks ago when you read me this—with great pride, as I recall it."

Mary searched through a copy of *American Turf Register and Sporting Magazine.*

"Here it is: 'The horses which run at New Orleans comprise the cracks of several states; the studs of Alabama, Tennessee, Mississippi, and not infrequently the Old Dominion, are annually represented there by their best and bravest.' Isn't that true any longer?"

"It's true."

"Then *why,* as one of the most prominent horsemen in New Orleans, would you want to leave here?"

"As the eldest surviving son of Charles Dewey I have my rights at Bon Marché."

"Your rights!" She laughed derisively. "You can't honestly believe Mattie Dewey is going to abandon her cousins after all those years they've been in charge of that plantation."

"That's exactly why I must press my claims now, *before* my stepmother dies."

Mary shuddered. "I want no part of Nashville."

"Well—" He shrugged. "I can only say I mean to have Bon Marché."

III

BLACK, scudding clouds maneuvered in the skies over Bon Marché like a fleet of ebony-sailed men-of-war, attacking the more than thirty-five hundred acres of the plantation with torrents of rain. For a moment there was an artificial night in the middle of the late June afternoon, and then broadsides of lightning made the night into instant day as the cannonade of thunder tumbled waves of crashing sounds one over the other.

A small carriage, its driver-passenger sitting open to the sudden storm, sped along the wide road leading to the Bon Marché main house, racing between white-fenced pastures now empty of the thoroughbreds for which the Tennessee farm was renowned. They had been removed to the safety of the big barns. The driver reached out, flicking a whip on the flanks of his lathered horse. Sweeping into the circular drive-way fronting the mansion, the carriage came to a sudden stop. A young man, carrying a black bag, leaped out, taking the steps two at a time to the veranda. Before he could knock on the oaken double door, it was opened by a Negro servant.

"Bad day fer drivin' in an open rig, Dr. Thompson."

"It is, indeed, Joseph," the visitor agreed as he entered the house. "The drive from Nashville turned into an adventure. There are trees down on the road all along the way."

The black man nodded, reaching for the doctor's soaked cape and dripping, broad-brimmed hat.

"Have someone take care of the horse, will you? I'm afraid I used him up."

"Yassuh."

Dr. Thompson looked down at his trousers clinging wetly to his legs. Grasping each knee of cloth, he flipped the trouser legs back and forth, sending little sprays of water across the polished entrance-hall floor.

"They's all waitin' fer ya in Miss Mattie's bedroom," the servant prodded him, not successfully hiding his dismay at the mess the doctor was making on the floor, a mess he'd have to mop up.

"Of course." He moved quickly across the foyer, mounting the curved stairway to the second floor. It was the third time that week he had been at Bon Marché. He feared now it would be his last. *Even the Deweys,* he thought, *are not immortal.*

Pushing open the bedroom door, the physician wasn't surprised to find the entire Dewey family in attendance around the bed of Matilda Jackson Dewey, all sober-faced, several of them weeping. It annoyed him somewhat that every time he came to Bon Marché he had to do his doctoring under the stern gazes of the assembled Deweys. Old Dr. Almond, whose own ill health had made it impossible for him to continue to minister to the family, had warned Thompson it would be that way, but the younger man was still uncomfortable with the situation.

"I came as quickly as I could," he explained quietly.

No one in the room spoke as they made way for him to get to the bed, where the daughter, Alma May, sat holding her mother's hand.

The doctor acknowledged her. "Miss Alma," he said as he took the hand from her to feel for a pulse in the wrist. Harry Thompson didn't understand why, but every time he was close to Alma May Dewey illicit thoughts about her coursed through his mind. He wondered whether other men experienced the same phenomenon.

Mattie Dewey's pulse was very weak, its tempo erratic.

"May I have a little hot water in a cup, please?" the doctor requested.

Alma May gestured to one of the black servant girls in the room and within seconds the cup of water was produced. The Deweys were used to such response. A gesture, a snap of the fingers, a meaningful nod of the head, were all commands they expected to be obeyed. Not just by their slaves. The family members were powerful people, at ease with leadership, accustomed to having their own way in all matters.

Reaching into his bag of medicines, Dr. Thompson brought out a bottle of dark-colored liquid, pouring a small portion of it into the water. He swirled the water around in the cup, mixing the medicine with it. It was nothing more than a tonic, a hoped-for mild stimulant for the languid heart; it wouldn't do any real good, but he had to administer something to the dying matriarch of Bon Marché.

"Miss Mattie," he said softly, lifting the patient's head from the pillow, "let's see if we can take a sip or two of this."

Mattie's eyes opened. There was a dull, unseeing vacancy in them.

He put the cup to her lips, tilting it so that a few drops ran into her mouth. She didn't swallow. Perhaps she could no longer swallow, or perhaps she couldn't comprehend she was supposed to swallow. The tonic dribbled out of her mouth and

down her chin. Dr. Thompson mopped at it with his handkerchief, then lowered her head to the pillow once more.

The eyes remained open, staring. The young man closed
the lids with a sure, gentle motion.

Conscious of his role as a surrogate for Dr. Almond,
Thompson reported, "In our consultations, Dr. Almond and I
have discussed the very real possibility that Mrs. Dewey might
suffer another seizure. After one paroxysm, it's not unusual
another will follow." He sighed. "That, I'm afraid, has happened. In lesser degree, of course, but—"

He looked around at the array of sad faces.

"She's very weak. Quite honestly, there is little more I . . .
uh . . . we can do."

"How . . . long?" Alma May asked hesitantly.

"I can't be certain. Hours, perhaps. Yes, no more than a
few hours."

2

THERE were ghosts there in the early-morning haze, in that brief, uncertain time between darkness and daylight. Yet, George Dewey was at ease; the spirits were familiar ones. He stood as dawn broke in the small grove of tulip poplars serving as the family's graveyard, head bowed as if in prayer.

But not in prayer. He was listening to the muted voices of Bon Marché, being carried back to an August day of fifty years earlier when, as a lad of six, he had come there with his father and his sisters and brothers. It had all been wilderness then. There had been no white-fenced pastures, no comfortable barns, no fields of sweet hay-grass, no training track, no game preserve, no great mansion. Not even any horses at first. All of that had come from the steadfast dreams and indefatigable labors of Charles Dewey, the very special man who was his father. Factually, not from his father alone. They had all played a role; all of the Deweys. The twins, Louise and Lee. And Corrine. And George himself. And his older brother, Franklin, who was among those at rest under the poplars.

His eyes were drawn to the fresh mound of clay, banked with floral tributes, at his feet. Yes, and Mattie Dewey, too; she had been important in the building of what was to be called *Bon Marché*—"Good Bargain." That couldn't be denied. When Charles had brought his motherless children to Tennessee from Virginia the strong-willed Matilda Jackson had filled a void for the elder Dewey, first as his lover and then as his helpmate, his partner, in making Bon Marché the most successful thoroughbred breeding farm in the "West."

George sucked in a deep breath, exhaling it slowly. He had been too late, arriving at the plantation from New Orleans in the middle of the night, to be greeted only by servants and to be told his stepmother had died. The funeral had been twenty-four hours earlier. If only he had been in time, George thought, to press his claim with Mattie, Bon Marché would be his at that moment. Was such an idea mad, as his wife had suggested? George believed not, even now. Mattie certainly would have recognized his position, as she drew her will, as the eldest surviving son of the founder and, as such, the logical one to guide Bon Marché's future.

He stared at his father's tombstone:

CHARLES DUPREE DE GRASSE DEWEY
1765–1845
Aide-toi, le ciel t'aidera

It was astonishing, really, how much his father had accomplished in his lifetime—a former cabin boy in the French navy who had never known his parents; whose very name was an invention of his imagination. And who had lived his full life under the guidance of the simple precept chiseled in the granite of his headstone: "Help thyself, and Heaven will help thee."

A voice broke his reverie: "Hello, Father."

George turned to find his firstborn son there, startled for a moment by how much, in the half-light, the young man resembled his grandfather. Charles Dewey II had the same light blond hair, the same intense hazel eyes, the same square-cut face, the same sturdy frame. And, like his namesake, the same look of self-assurance, of a measure of arrogance.

"Hello, Two," George replied, using the family nickname. There was no emotion in the greeting; it was an acknowledgment only. No embrace, no handshake.

"It's good to see you again, Father."

"Hmmm."

"I heard you had arrived during the night."

"Yes, and too late, I'm afraid." He nodded toward Mattie's grave. "It's seven days on the packet boats from New Orleans. But that's a lot better than it used to be on the Natchez Trace."

"Yes, it is." A pause. "Is Mother well?"

"Quite well. She sends her love, of course." There was no point in mentioning the bitter argument.

"And Junior?"

"He's doing an excellent job with the horses at Nouveau Marché."

"That doesn't surprise me."

"And your brother Statler seems content with his role as a rising young lawyer"—a wry grin—"especially in the light of his wife's fortune."

Two also grinned. "Statler always was a fellow who saw the best opportunity, and seized it quickly."

"Yes."

They had used up their conversational gambits; father and son with nothing to say to each other.

After a moment, Charles bent down, idly rearranging some flowers on the new grave. "We're going to miss her a great deal."

"I imagine so."

"It was through Mattie's insistence, you know, that I've started to work with the horses here."

"Oh?"

"Yes, you see, about six months ago she decided it was time to bring some younger blood into the operation. So I was asked, and so was Drew—"

"Andrew Jackson!" Shock showed on George's face.

"Yes."

"Good Lord! That boy can't be more than fourteen or fifteen—"

Two laughed uneasily. "He's twelve, Father."

"Which makes it even more idiotic!"

"Drew's very levelheaded and seems to have a natural talent for handling horses."

"So now you're an expert on horsemen," George commented churlishly.

"Cousin True seems to believe I'm doing quite well as the assistant trainer of the Bon Marché racing string."

What had been only derision up to that point now boiled into anger. "Cousin! True Jackson is *not* your cousin!"

"No, but—" Charles smiled broadly, trying to defuse the

anger. "Everyone calls the Jacksons 'cousin,' as Grandmother Mattie did. Cousin True . . . Cousin Able—"

"I see." *When I take over Bon Marché those damned Jacksons are going to be sent packing!* "And I suppose you're living here now?"

"No, Beth and I still live in the small house in Nashville. And we wish, while you're here, you'd come to visit us. And Charles Three, of course. He's never seen his grandfather, you know."

George didn't reply.

"We would hope, Father," Two went on slowly, "that you'll find it in your heart to forgive us. We know we caused you, and the rest of the family, some pain when we had Charles Three out of wedlock, but it was never a situation where you had a bastard grandson. Perhaps we made a mistake by not marrying before he was born, but he was always a child of our real love. And you'd love him, too, if you gave yourself the opportunity."

"We'll see," George muttered.

"We call him Buster," Charles chuckled.

George just grunted. There was another strained silence, broken finally by the son. "Have you had your breakfast?"

"No."

"Would you take it with me?"

"Very well."

As they walked toward the mansion, Two said: "I suppose you've heard Mattie's will is to be read this morning?"

"One of the servants mentioned it when I arrived. It never ceases to amaze me how much the blacks know about the family's business." Casually: "How do you think it'll go?"

"Oh, I don't think there's much doubt the Jacksons will be left in control of Bon Marché."

George stopped, angry again. "And what of the children of Charles Dewey? What of me!"

"I'm probably wrong," his son said quickly, anxious to placate him. "I have no knowledge at all of the contents of the will."

II

LAWYER William Holder was ill at ease.

While he was a nominal member of the Dewey family because he had married one of the late Charles Dewey's daughters, he was not one of them. He had never wanted to be one of them. When he married Corrine Dewey they had left Bon Marché to live their own lives away from what Holder believed was a thoroughly disreputable life-style: that of the horse-racing genre. Gamblers of that type appalled him. And Corrine never contradicted that attitude of her husband.

Now he was back because a year earlier, just after Charles Dewey's death, Mattie Jackson Dewey had come to him to draw up her last will and testament. Holder never knew why she had selected him as her lawyer; certainly, she had understood why he had stayed away from the Deweys. Perhaps she thought involving him in her legal matters would heal the breach between the Holders and the Deweys. If she *had* believed that she was wrong. Holder was still as adamantly opposed to the Deweys now as he had been when he had taken Corrine away from the plantation.

The lawyer recognized his presence there, the day after the burial of Mattie Dewey, might be resented by some members of the family. But that was of little concern to him; he had his legal duty to do. He sat at the large mahogany desk in the Bon Marché drawing room, the assembled Deweys before him, the pages of the will spread out for the reading.

Holder coughed nervously. "Before I begin with the disclosure of the details of this will, I want to add my own preamble. Less than two months after the death of Charles Dewey . . . uh, the elder Charles Dewey, of course . . . his widow came to me with a will she had written. I reviewed it with her, telling her that what she wanted to do was legally valid, and then going with her to the Davidson County Courthouse where the document was duly witnessed by myself and by the Clerk of Courts. Thus, what I am about to reveal to you is the *legal* last will and testament of Mrs. Matilda Jackson Dewey."

His eyes scanned the faces of those in the room. "I must also tell you that, in keeping with my lawyer's code of confidentiality, my wife, a stepdaughter of the late Mrs. Dewey, does not know of the contents of this document. Further, you should be aware that I never, at any time, made an effort to influence Mrs. Dewey's decisions on how she would dispose of the assets of her estate. Those decisions were hers alone. The words are hers alone, not mine."

Billy Holder tapped the papers. "Well . . . I imagine I can proceed now." Clearing his throat, he began to read.

"'From his first days on this land, Charles Dewey visualized Bon Marché as the finest estate in Tennessee. That was his dream when there were only a few acres, unfenced, untilled, unheralded, so to speak. In drawing my own will, as the inheritor of all of Bon Marché on the death of my beloved husband, I believe I owe a debt to Charles Dewey's dream. I told myself this: until I reach that Sweet Day when I am with my darling Charles once more, I have only one mandate: to keep Bon Marché whole. To leave it to other generations intact so that Bon Marché's greatness will not be diminished, but enhanced, in the years ahead.

"'It would be easy, as I draw this document, to simply leave it in equal shares to Charles Dewey's surviving children and grandchildren, making happy for the brief time it will take to read this will all of those who carry Charles Dewey's blood. There is a temptation to do that, loving, as I do, all of you equally. But reason tells me such a decision would serve only to fragment Bon Marché, to subject it to the certain contentions of a dozen or more individuals, perhaps destroying it.'"

The lawyer moved to the second page. In his audience, George Dewey smiled. His stepmother had more common sense than he had realized. There was only one conclusion he could reach: if she meant to keep it whole, Bon Marché was to be his alone!

"'I also feel it is incumbent upon me,'" Holder read on, "'to detail the reasons for my decisions, most especially those dealing with Charles's issue.

"'Charles Dewey's eldest surviving son—'"

George's smile grew broader.

"'—George Washington Dewey, with his family, is actively engaged in a prosperous horse-racing enterprise in New Orleans, and needs no further help from Bon Marché.'"

George's mouth gaped. His face flushed. He started up from his chair.

"You have a comment, George?" the attorney asked.

Glaring, George slowly sank back into his seat. "Go on," he snarled.

"'Corrine Dewey Holder, Charles Dewey's eldest daughter, having made her decision years ago to live apart from Bon Marché with her husband, a successful attorney, and their children, has never needed largess from Bon Marché.'

"Corrine and I will, of course, accept that evaluation," Holder commented pompously. He smiled at his wife before looking down at the document once more.

"'Daughter Louise Dewey Schimmel,'" he continued, "'as wife and partner of newspaper publisher August Schimmel, is wealthy in her own right. Louise's twin, Lee Dewey, has achieved a measure of fame as a successful writer and illustrator. Neither twin needs Bon Marché to survive; indeed, neither has exhibited a primary interest in the management of Bon Marché.'"

George glanced questioningly at his sister Louise, who soberly nodded agreement with what had just been read. Lee Dewey wasn't even in attendance, George noted for the first time.

The reading proceeded: "'That, then, leave two other children of Charles Dewey with whom to contend: the surviving daughter who is issue of my own marriage to Charles Dewey, Alma May Dewey Ludlum; and Marshall Dewey, a child of Charles Dewey by a Negro slave woman, Angelica (now deceased), but fully acknowledged as his son while Charles Dewey still lived.'"

Holder slid over the third page so that he could read it more easily.

"'Marshall, having made his own decision to absent himself from Bon Marché, nevertheless may have some need. Recognizing the peculiar, and perhaps difficult, circumstances under which he must live, I bequeath to him the cash sum of twenty-five thousand dollars, hoping he will view it as a fair settlement.

"'To our daughter, Alma May Dewey Ludlum—urging upon her a new sense of responsibility to replace a way of life I have often regarded as profligate—I leave one third of the total Bon Marché estate.'"

George sprang to his feet, his face livid. "See here, Holder, I think it's about time someone objected to this—this travesty!"

"Travesty, George?" Billy Holder was startled.

"You're damn right! It must be clear to everyone in this room"—George looked around wildly—"that a fraud is being perpetrated here! How do we know this nonsense is really the will of Mattie Dewey?"

Holder, angered, slammed his fist down on the desk. "This will has been duly witnessed by the Clerk of Courts of Davidson County!"

"Who could have been bought off!" George shouted.

"You give me offense, sir!"

"I damn well mean to, Holder!" He started toward his brother-in-law, his fists clenched.

"For God's sake, George," his sister Louise called out, "shut your stupid mouth and sit down!"

He whirled to glare at her. But her words, her *command*, had cowed him. Mumbling epithets under his breath, George returned to his chair.

The attorney drew a deep breath, struggling to keep his hands from trembling. He resumed the reading:

"'Recognizing the substantial roles played in the management of Bon Marché since 1833 by the brothers True and Able Jackson, and believing such mature management must continue for the well-being of Bon Marché, I leave one-third shares of the total estate to their wives, Joy Schimmel Jackson and Hope Schimmel Jackson, granddaughters of Charles Dewey, with the stipulation that their husbands continue in the management of Bon Marché for as long as is feasible.'"

"Just as I suspected," George snapped.

Holder ignored him. "'The three principal heirs, Alma May Dewey Ludlum, Joy Schimmel Jackson, and Hope Schimmel Jackson, are specifically prohibited from disposing of any portion of the Bon Marché estate (individually, or in concert) during their lifetimes. Nor may the managers of Bon Marché, True Jackson and/or Able Jackson (or their successors), make management decisions to dispose of any portion of the Bon Marché estate, save the necessary sale of horses or of any natural production of the plantation.'

"The final page," the lawyer announced.

"'While one might wish to control the destiny of Bon Marché in perpetuity, from the grave, I recognize the total impracticability of such a wish. Nevertheless, I urge upon my heirs, when they face the necessity of leaving a will, the keeping of Bon Marché in the hands of those through whose veins course the blood of the founder, Charles Dewey.

"'Now, I bid you all good-bye, leaving behind my love. I am firmly convinced, by acting as I have in this will, that I have done three things my late husband would have wanted for his dream. First, I have kept Bon Marché whole by bequeathing it to like-minded heirs who loved him; second, it remains in the hands of those carrying the blood of Charles Dewey; and, third, continued mature management is assured for the foreseeable future.'

"The concluding paragraph," Holder explained, "was added to the will, in Mrs. Dewey's hand, when it was witnessed before the Clerk of Courts."

He read again: "'Being of sound mind, and acting without duress, I, Matilda Jackson Dewey, do declare this to be my last will and testament, before God and the authorities of Davidson County, Tennessee.'

"It is dated July twenty-third, 1845, and, as already mentioned, is witnessed by myself and by Squire John R. Foster, Clerk of Courts, Davidson County." Holder glanced around the drawing room. "Are there any further comments?"

George Dewey was already stalking from the room. "You're not going to get away with this, Holder!" he shouted over his shoulder. "Not you, or any of your fellow conspirators!" He was gone.

The lawyer smiled weakly. "Perhaps we haven't heard the last of this. But the will is *valid,* and I congratulate those who have been given the task of taking Bon Marché forward to a new day."

The last was a statement lacking in candor, because he cared not at all what happened to Bon Marché. What had been true at the beginning of the day was still true at the end: Billy Holder may have married into the family, but he was never a Dewey.

III

GEORGE Dewey sat at dinner in the Nashville Inn, thinking it had become a rather seedy hostelry since his days in the city. His companion was an old friend, a former county judge named Benjamin Wright, now in private practice of the law.

"From what you tell me of your stepmother's will," Wright was saying to him, "I'm afraid any challenge of it would fail."

"Why is that?"

"Because you waited too long."

"What? The will was read only this morning. I couldn't have consulted a lawyer any more quickly than I have."

"Tell me this, George—when your father died, did you or any of your brothers and sisters challenge his will?"

The question perplexed George. "No," he answered hesitantly.

"You made no legal contention then that Charles Dewey's second wife shouldn't inherit his estate?"

"No."

"You didn't raise any question at that time about the quality of the management of Bon Marché by the Jackson brothers, your stepmother's cousins?"

"No."

"Or go to the courts with a proposal that you ought to share in your father's estate because you had made a substantial contribution to its growth through a good part of your adult life?"

"No! What the hell are you getting at, Ben?"

"What I'm getting at, old friend," the lawyer said evenly, "is that the time for you—individually, or jointly with your siblings—to have made a claim for a share of the Bon Marché estate was when your father died. Not now. You acquiesced, in the legal sense, to Charles Dewey willing the entire estate to his widow. By so acquiescing you put yourself on record as totally approving of your late father's actions. Thus, I can think of no judge who will *now* allow you to intercede in the estate, because you no longer have a stake in it."

"That's ridiculous!"

The lawyer shrugged. "Not so, George. It wasn't your father's estate any longer. It belonged lock, stock, and barrel to Mattie, and she was free to dispose of it as she saw fit. She might have left the estate, as just one example—and meaning no disrespect to the departed—to someone as reprehensible as a clandestine lover."

"You must be joking!"

"For your sake, I wish I were. But I'm not. You see, the courts will entertain a motion to overturn a will only if there is evidence of duress on the person drawing the will . . . threats to life or limb, or blackmail . . . something of that sort. Or if there is *evidence*—and I stress that word—if there is evidence criminal fraud has been perpetrated—"

"Of course there was fraud!"

"*Real* evidence, George."

"Everyone knows what a pompous ass that Billy Holder is."

Wright laughed heartily. "If pomposity could be equated with being fraudulent, we'd have damned few attorneys left to practice in Davidson County."

"I see nothing humorous about this!"

"And neither do I, my friend. But Mattie Dewey's will seems to have been drawn with great intelligence, with an effort to *preserve* an estate, not destroy it. You would have only one argument, and a rather shaky one, with which to go to court against it."

"Tell me, for Christ's sake," George demanded impatiently.

"You'd have to prove *need*."

"Oh—"

"Either on behalf of yourself, or for one of your heirs—your children. Perhaps even a grandchild."

Dewey was morosely silent.

"That's not a condition you can claim, is it?"

"No," George admitted. He toyed for a time with the food on the plate before him. Then: "So Mattie and the Jacksons have gotten away with it?"

"Those wouldn't be the words I'd choose to describe what has happened, but the will is valid, yes."

"Hmmm."

"Well, George," Wright said, getting to his feet. "I think we can consider this excellent dinner will adequately compensate me for my legal advice." He stuck out his hand.

George rose and shook the hand. "You know, Ben, I think what galls me most," he said quietly, "is the thought of Alma May now being the mistress of Bon Marché. She's such a . . . a . . . libertine."

Wright laughed again. "George, I've always enjoyed talking with you. Sometimes your choice of language is absolutely marvelous. *Libertine?*"

"Isn't she?"

"I suppose," he answered, continuing to laugh. "But I'll wager the Princess would be flattered with 'libertine,' when there are so many other more expressive words in the vernacular you might have chosen."

He was still chuckling as he walked away.

IV

ALMA May giggled coquettishly. "Have you noticed anything different about me tonight, Willie?"

"Different?" Her companion rolled over on his elbow, looking into her face. "No. But I can say you're up to your usual high quality of . . . well, entertainment."

"Indeed!" She punched him playfully. "Well, darling, I'm an heiress now—the matriarch of Bon Marché."

"Oh, that."

"That doesn't impress you?" she laughed.

"Not much. That 'matriarch' thing may be a little disconcerting, perhaps." He grinned. "But not intimidating in any way."

"It doesn't bother you, then, that I'm now as rich as you are?"

"No. As a banker, though, I might make a suggestion or two about investments. For example, rather than just keeping this suite of rooms you might want to buy the whole damn Nashville Inn."

Alma May's lighthearted attitude changed quickly. Her face went sad. "No, Willie, I don't think that's a good idea. As a matter of fact, I may have to give up the suite."

"Oh?"

"You see, in my mother's will," she continued in feigned seriousness, "she specifically requested I give up my profligate ways. To do that, the suite would have to go. And you, too, darling."

He studied the situation for a moment. "Not necessarily, Princess. There'd be another way not to be thought profligate and still maintain our convenient relationship. You could accept my long-standing proposal."

"And become Mrs. Wilfred Carstairs?"

"Exactly."

"But I'd never be sure, would I, whether you'd expect to be married to the Princess, as she is now, or the Heiress, as you might prefer her to be?"

"No, you'd never be sure." He laughed now. "Just as I'd never be sure you wouldn't welcome other occupants to these rooms."

"Well, then, we've come to an impasse, haven't we?" She reached for him, drawing him into her arms. "You do understand, darling, that what Mother made was a request. It wasn't an *order*."

"I understand that perfectly."

There was no more talk.

V

IT WAS a hot, humid morning on the Nashville Wharf, a rather grand designation for the graded, sloping, earthen bank on the Cumberland River where more than a dozen shallow-draft steamboats were tied up; long, swaying gangplanks serving as umbilical cords between the boats and the mother shore.

George Dewey, traveling bag in hand, stood amidst the bustling activity, fascinated as he watched the boat crewmen, the roustabouts, the draymen, the clerks, and the merchants going about their business in a confusing din. There seemed no order to it as, in one quarter, a huge pile of freight was being loaded aboard a boat, while just a few yards away muscular men were unloading another boat, creating a like pile of freight. On the street fronting the wharf (appropriately, Water Street), the solid row of substantial brick and stone buildings, headquarters for the wealthy merchants, stood as testimony to the fact that what was being done there represented Nashville's economic lifeblood.

The traveler checked his pocket watch, anxious to begin the return trip to New Orleans. He faced a long journey; some fifteen hundred miles on the twisting waterways of America's heart. Northward on the Cumberland into Kentucky, where the Cumberland joined the Ohio River; west and south on the Ohio to Cairo, Illinois, to be welcomed to the broad expanse of the Mississippi. And then south to New Orleans and home. *Home?* New Orleans was a place on the map, not home.

Home was what he was leaving now, with no thought of ever returning.

Out of the corner of his eye George saw him coming. Charles Dewey II hurried along Water Street, his gaze searching the busy scene. He began to run when he spotted his father.

"I was afraid I'd miss you," the son said breathlessly when he came up to him. "Beth was very disappointed when you didn't come to see us. I was, too, of course."

"I had some business to attend to," George replied lamely.

"I know you're upset about Mattie's will, Father, but I would hope it won't prevent us from—" The voice turned to pleading. "I want to be your son again."

George couldn't hazard a reply. It surprised him that his emotions were so close to the surface.

"Isn't there *some* way, Father?"

A sudden thought: "You could come with me to New Orleans."

"And do what?"

"Join Junior at Nouveau Marché. I'd deed the property over to both of you. You could be equal partners, Two."

Charles pondered his answer for a moment—not what he would say, but how he would say it. "I can't leave Bon Marché. It means more to—"

His father interrupted angrily. "You'd rather stay with those Jackson bastards?"

"Bon Marché isn't the Jacksons! I would think that you, of all men, would understand that better than anyone. Bon Marché is the spirit of Charles Dewey. And Grandmother Mattie didn't leave it to the Jacksons, she left it to that spirit. She made certain, it seems to me, that only those with Charles Dewey's blood would ever own it. Well . . . I not only have his blood, I have his name."

"And you think you're going to get Bon Marché someday?" George laughed sarcastically.

"If not me," Two answered soberly, "then my son—Charles Dewey the Third."

"You're a stupid fool!"

"No, Father, I'm not. If there's been a *fool* in all of this it's been yourself—"

George reached out quickly, slapping his face. "No child of mine speaks to me like that!"

Charles rubbed his stinging cheek. "You can strike me all you want," he said slowly, "but let me explain to you how big a fool you've really been."

"I don't want to hear any more of this!"

Two grabbed his father's shoulders in strong young hands, holding him fast. "You'll hear me, damn you! Just a few days before Grandmother Mattie was stricken, Cousin True talked to me about a plan he had. He wanted to propose to you an amalgamation of Bon Marché and Nouveau Marché—"

"There wouldn't have been any chance of that!"

Charles shook him. "Listen to me! An amalgamation of Bon Marché and Nouveau Marché, with an eye to expanding to Kentucky and New York. And he wanted *you* to be the managing partner of the amalgamation. He reasoned that he and Able would have plenty to do here at Bon Marché, and that Junior would handle Nouveau Marché. And that you would have the time and the ability, the experience, to put together the expansion. Then, suddenly, Grandmother became ill and it was all put aside."

He let go of his father's shoulders.

"I had every reason to believe," Two continued, "that True meant to talk to you about it before you returned to New Orleans. But you staged that idiotic demonstration at the reading of the will—" The young man shrugged.

"Why didn't you tell me this before?"

"When could I? You've been barely civil to me since you arrived."

George was without words.

"And now I want to say something else," his son went on. "Last night, when you failed to visit us, when you failed to come to see your grandson for the first time, I held Beth in my arms as she cried over the hurt. You called me a fool earlier. Perhaps you're right—because I was fool enough to believe, in spite of everything, that there still might be an opportunity this morning to . . . to be father and son again. I was wrong." He touched his cheek. "Now, as far as I'm concerned, Father . . . you . . . can . . . burn . . . in . . . Hell!"

He turned, striding off down Water Street.

"Two, wait—!"

Charles began to run.

A voice bellowed: "Passengers for the W. H. Harrison Upper Cumberland boat, all aboard! We cast off in five minutes! All aboard!"

Wearily, George Dewey reached down to pick up his bag. As he made his way up the narrow gangplank, it rocked crazily.

So, too, would his life.

3

"THE course is very firm," True Jackson reported to his assistant, "and I'm not certain that bodes well for us. I'd prefer to see it a little more yielding, especially in light of that problem with his left fore."

He nodded toward the big bay horse there, its lead rope held by his son Andrew.

Charles Dewey II smiled tolerantly. "I think, Cousin True, you're making too much of that leg. It showed no sign of soreness in yesterday's work."

"Hmmm, perhaps." A shrug. "Maybe what concerns me most, Two, is the competition, meaning that long-striding filly of young Wade Hampton's. He wouldn't have brought her all the way from South Carolina just for the exercise."

A black jockey approached, wearing the solid purple silks of Bon Marché and carrying his tack.

"Ninety-seven pounds, suh," the jock told Jackson.

"Thank you, Elmo. I appreciate your efforts in keeping the weight down."

"Yassuh."

As Dewey took the tack to begin the careful routine of saddling the horse, Jackson turned to survey the Clover Bottom course. His hands behind his back, rocking heel to toe, toe to heel, he appeared to be studying every blade of grass on the Nashville racing strip.

True Jackson seemed a humorless man, a factor contributing to the impression he was older than his thirty-eight years. Certainly, he was in no way handsome. His clothes never quite fit his portly frame, and he was balding—a few strands of hair running in errant patterns across his skull. Yet, there was something imposing about him; a stranger might have immediately concluded that here was the man in charge.

A detractor might have made a case denigrating his leadership position: that he was regarded as the "master" of the Bon Marché plantation only because his cousin Mattie Dewey had insisted on placing him on that course when he was nothing more than a struggling young attorney from Asheville, North Carolina; that the late Charles Dewey had taught him everything he knew about training racehorses, only to have the younger man supersede him in Dewey's declining years; that he had been elected president of the Nashville Jockey Club simply because he was of Bon Marché, and not because of any significant contributions he had made to Nashville racing.

True was aware there were a few who thought those things of him. Aware, too, that a few others showed him a strange resentment just because his name was Jackson. He *was* a distant cousin of the late President and he recognized Old Hickory was resented in some quarters; the blunt old man had had his enemies. On the other side of the coin, being perceived as a Jackson was important in Nashville, although True tried not to trade on it.

What was of primary consequence to him on this day was that it marked the first time he would campaign a horse without the dominating presence of Charles Dewey or of his cousin Mattie Dewey. If there had been reliance on their reputations for his well-being in the past, all that was gone now. Today he would have to be just True Jackson. On his own.

On his own. And at a distinct disadvantage, he believed, in the annual running of the Bon Marché Cup, the feature of the August meeting at Clover Bottom. He had entered a five-year-old son of Priam, out of a Bagdad mare, but he wished he had something else for the event. For one thing, the horse was named Charles Dewey (a last tribute to the founder of Bon Marché), and he desperately wanted to rid himself of that association in the public eye. For another, the bay, while it had always trained well, had not seen fit to win a race in four earlier starts. Even though its breeding was superb, there simply had been no correlation between the horse's training and its performance on the track, and True didn't know why.

He turned back to the thoroughbred, saddled now and being walked in wide circles by his son. He looked intently at the animal. Then to young Dewey: "You don't see a slight favoring of the left fore?"

"No, I don't." Two chuckled. "I'm beginning to think you're seeing a phantom ailment."

"Phantom?" True smiled for the first time, ever so slightly. "You may be right. Phantom? That's an interesting way to explain it."

"Riders up!" a steward bellowed.

Making a cup of his hands, Jackson boosted the jockey into the saddle. "Keep the filly in sight," he instructed. "That's the one you're going to have to beat. But don't use him up. Let's have something left for the second heat."

"Yassuh."

An afterthought, spoken in a low voice: "And keep an eye on that left fore."

The jock saluted him with the whip and dug a spur into the horse, urging it toward the starting line.

II

MAJOR General Zachary Taylor sat at a wooden field desk in the Matamoros house he had taken over as a command headquarters, sweat beading his rugged face. He looked the role of "Old Rough and Ready," the Indian fighter. Which is to say, he did *not* look like a major general of the United States Army.

He wore a soiled white shirt, nonuniform trousers of a type a frontier farmer might have worn, and ragged carpet slippers. His dusty riding boots were propped at a crazy angle against the side of the desk. If there was any military bearing about him it was totally destroyed by the wad of tobacco in his cheek. Also by the distinguishing mark of all addicted tobacco chewers: a suggestion of dark spittle on his lips.

Up to that moment, Brevet Captain Dewey had seen the general only at a distance, sitting his horse, Old Whitey, in a lounging fashion, eschewing a formal uniform in favor of a long brown coat and a broad-brimmed straw hat.

Dewey stood stiffly in front of him, offering a sharp salute, which Taylor saw fit to ignore.

"I want you to know," the general said quietly (the tone was *grandfatherly,* the younger man thought), "that we are much impressed with the hard work you're doing to bring that volunteer company into being."

"Thank you, sir."

The general waved a hand. "Sit down, please, Captain."

Dewey obeyed, but even while seated he appeared to be at attention.

"Relax, young man." Taylor smiled.

Albert tried to follow orders.

Zach expertly spat a stream of tobacco juice into the cuspidor at his feet, without seeming to look at it. "You come to me highly recommended, Captain. From Tennessee, aren't you?"

"Yessir."

"I sometimes wonder," Taylor said, chuckling, "what this army would be without Tennesseans. Your people are volunteering fools, it seems."

"There are a great many here from Tennessee, yessir."

"But you're a product of West Point?"

"I am, sir."

"Tell me a little bit about yourself."

"Sir?"

"Your personal history, Captain—are you married?"

"Oh, yessir, to a Nashville girl. We have four children." A slight pause. "I haven't yet seen my last son. He was born after we left Fort Jesup."

"Hmmm. My information is that your family is engaged in breeding racehorses, and that it originally came from Virginia."

"Yessir, my late grandfather brought his family from Virginia."

"Virginia is my birthplace, you know. Orange County."

Dewey nodded, wondering where the strange interview was leading.

General Taylor stared at the young man for a moment. "My reports tell me you're an intelligent officer, not given to foolhardy adventurism." He spat again.

Albert sat silently.

"You don't wish to comment on that?"

"I believe I'm a responsible individual, sir."

"Hmmm." The commanding general picked up a piece of paper from among many on his desk. "Have you ever heard of the San Patricios, Dewey?"

"No, sir."

The voice hardened. "The San Patricios—that's the Mexican name for them—are a breed of men not noted for honor. They're U.S. Army enlisted men, and some officers, who have gone over to the Mexicans, apparently lured by promises of land grants, rapid advancement in the Mexican army, and even Mexican citizenship."

"I see."

"Deserters! Out-and-out traitors!" There was anger now. "And enough of them to make it necessary for the United States Army to act decisively against them. To seek them out and punish them severely. To make an example of them—to discourage others who might be tempted to emulate them."

Taylor gestured with the paper. "You, Captain Dewey, have been chosen to put together a special corps of some fifty men to find some San Patricios, to conduct field courts-martial where you find them, and . . . to . . . hang . . . them!"

Albert was silent.

"Too tough for you, Captain?" The question was punctuated by another dead-center hit on the cuspidor.

There was a momentary hesitation. If Albert had been asked the question *before* he had experienced the cruel realities of war, there would have been no doubts assailing him. Now—?

Finally, an answer. Firmly. "No, sir."

"Good, good." General Taylor handed him a sealed packet of papers. "Those are your orders and your authorizations, signed, you will see, by the President of the United States. And by myself, of course. Mr. Polk is most anxious that this . . . uh . . . disease does not spread into an epidemic. You will be breveted a colonel for this mission."

"But, sir, I am already breveted a captain."

"That has been corrected. Upon acceptance of those orders you are commissioned a full captain."

"Thank you, sir."

Taylor waved away the thanks. "We believe it's important that the officer carrying out this assignment be recognized as at least a colonel. Now—your orders, you will find, give you considerable latitude. I urge you, Colonel Dewey, to choose your men carefully—"

"Volunteers, sir?"

"No, no! Select the best men you can. This task is too critical to leave it only to volunteers."

"Yessir."

Once more Taylor rummaged through the papers on his desk, finding the one he sought after a few seconds. "We have taken the necessary liberty of selecting four men to be members of your staff." He looked down at the paper. "Captain Walter Darnell of Mississippi, who has been Colonel Davis's adjutant. He will look after the administrative details for you. The legal niceties, if you will, of the courts-martial and what follows them."

"Excuse me, sir, is Captain Darnell a lawyer?"

"No, but he's much experienced as an adjutant. You will consider him your chief of staff."

"Yessir."

Another glance at the paper. "Also First Lieutenant Father Matthew Ryan, a chaplain. A priest, obviously. He will be responsible for the souls of the San Patricios you corral. Perhaps they won't merit such consideration, but we must be civilized, eh?"

"Uh . . . yessir."

"And then, two civilians," General Taylor went on.

"Civilians, sir?" Dewey was surprised.

"One is a doctor, a surgeon—Dr. Richard Carrothers, of Austin, Texas. He's been under contract to this army and I hate to have it without his services, but I suspect you'll have need of a doctor."

Albert nodded agreement, his eyes following Taylor's unerring aim at the cuspidor.

"And finally, because it's our desire to get word out about the apprehension and punishment of these blackguards, we have decided to allow a newspaper correspondent to accompany you on your mission."

Old Zach smiled, seeing the distress come to Dewey's face. "This correspondent, I'll venture, will meet with your approval. His name is Lee Dewey."

"Uh . . . he's my uncle, sir."

"So I've been informed. He's just recently arrived in Mexico and has our confidence."

The new colonel sighed. "I'll admit, sir, being more than a little disconcerted by all this."

"Yes, well . . ." General Taylor stood; so did Dewey. "From this point, Colonel, it's in your hands. You're to report directly to me, but I don't expect you to be waltzing in and out of here for every minor detail. Just find those traitors and rid us of them!"

"Yessir."

"The gentlemen I mentioned will be reporting to you within the hour."

"Thank you, sir." Dewey saluted smartly.

The salute was returned this time. "Good hunting, Colonel Dewey." And once more there was a dull thud on the brass cuspidor.

III

A BUGLE sounded calling nine runners to the post for the Bon Marché Cup as Alma May, on the arm of banker Willie Carstairs and trailed by four black servants toting large wicker hampers, hurried up to the Bon Marché entourage.

"Oh, God," she said apologetically, "we nearly missed the start." She winked. "But I wanted to make sure we had enough provisions for the afternoon." The Princess nodded toward the hampers.

"We've brought enough for an army," Carstairs said, laughing, "especially if the army is thirsty."

"Shush now, Willie. Everyone is partial to the Bon Marché bourbon." Alma May turned to True Jackson: "We also had to stop at the public pool to make a wager on Charles Dewey. Was a thousand imprudent, Cousin True?"

The trainer frowned. "It's a good deal more than I would have recommended." He had made no bet.

"Oh, dear—" She shrugged. "Well, I suppose we should make some kind of public demonstration of our support of the Bon Marché Cup, don't you think?"

"I suppose." True's attention went to the starting line.

At the post, assistant trainer Two Dewey watched as the bay son of Priam was jogged toward the starter, looking for any sign of tenderness in the left foreleg. He found none, but he couldn't dismiss the concern True had for what he considered a potential weakness in the thoroughbred. True's concerns, young Dewey admitted to himself, were rarely wrong. And a lot of hard racing faced the equine Charles Dewey.

The Bon Marché Cup was for four-year-olds and up, the best-of-three two-mile heats. It was a rich race, owners of the starters having posted five-thousand-dollar subscriptions, winner take all. Two was astonished when he had heard nine runners would start, especially in light of the knowledge that Wade Hampton II had brought his undefeated mare, Willing Woman, from Charleston in a caravan including four other horses destined to campaign at the Clover Bottom meeting. It was claimed Willing Woman, a huge animal, had a stride of twenty-seven feet. Her reputation had made her the clear favorite of the thousands at the Nashville course that day, at even money.

Two thought only three other horses rated consideration in the wagering: Colonel Baylie Peyton's Great Western, Bon Marché's own Charles Dewey, and, with an outside chance, Alexander Barrow's well-bred Herald, making his very first start.

The starter called the thoroughbreds to the line. All were behaved and the drum tapped almost immediately. Herald shot into the lead, getting two quick lengths on Great Western. In third position was a horse young Dewey didn't recognize, and then came Willing Woman, followed by Charles Dewey. The others stretched out in single file.

On the backstretch the first time around, the third-place horse faltered, dropping back rapidly. Willing Woman took its place, gaining ground on Great Western as the crowd roared its collective approval. The Bon Marché jock went to the whip to keep Charles Dewey on the mare's heels.

True Jackson groaned. "Too soon with the whip," he said to no one in particular.

The field stayed that way through the homestretch and into the second mile and then Willing Woman, with a sudden burst of speed, seeming to eat up distance with ease, took over second. Charles Dewey couldn't follow her.

But Herald stayed on the lead, two lengths the better. Into the backstretch once more, down its length, and into the turn for home, there were no changes: Herald, Willing Woman, Great Western, and Charles Dewey, the latter separated from the leader by eight lengths.

Whipping and yelling madly, the jockey aboard Herald kept him at the front. It seemed he was going to win it. But two jumps from the finish line, Willing Woman's superior stride prevailed. The stewards called her margin of victory "a head." It might have been less than that.

Uniquely, the five trailers of the field were all distanced, and declared out of the second heat.

True Jackson came up to his assistant. "She's a good one," he said quietly.

"She is," Two agreed.

Charles Dewey was cantered up to them, True's son taking the reins, the jockey quickly dismounting.

"The left fore, Elmo?" Jackson asked immediately.

"No trouble Ah could see, Mistah True."

"Hmmm." The trainer picked up the leg, running his hand over it, searching for heat, putting it down finally without comment. To his son: "Drew, have him rubbed down thoroughly, put a heavy sheet on him, and keep him walking."

"Yes, sir." The youngster directed several black handlers to follow his father's orders.

True looked over at the second-place finisher as other handlers were ministering to Herald, his muscular sides heaving, his dark bay coat lathered white. "That one's finished, I suspect." He chuckled uncharacteristically. "If any of us had any sense we'd withdraw now and let young Hampton have his money in a walkover."

He sobered at once. "You know, Two, if we were in some other town, and we weren't involved in the Bon Marché Cup, I'd take Charles Dewey out now. On his best day he's not going to beat that mare."

Fifty yards removed, Alma May was holding court as "the Princess," dispensing bourbon to all who stopped by, and sampling a good deal of it herself. "Maybe I ought to side with the female," she said to anyone who would listen, "but Charles Dewey has yet to run his best race."

There were a few who followed her inexpert advice at the public betting pool, not understanding it was the whiskey talking.

When the second heat was called, Herald was declared unfit by his owner to challenge Willing Woman again. Thus, only three would report to the starter; most of the bettors on the course rushed to further support the South Carolina mare, backing her down to one to five.

This time at the start, Great Western was inexplicably rank and when the drum sounded the horse was turned around in the wrong direction. By the time the jockey got him running straight the others, Willing Woman and Charles Dewey, were twenty lengths away. Wisely, Colonel Peyton signaled to his rider to rein in his charge, and it was a two-horse race.

Willing Woman's effortless strides took her to the front by three lengths.

"That ought to do it," True said under his breath.

Yet, as the race progressed through the first mile and into the first turn of the second, Charles Dewey had narrowed the gap to a single length. Turning into the backstretch, Elmo grasped the reins tightly in one hand, unlimbering his whip. He cracked it hard on the bay's rump and Charles Dewey shot forward, coming abreast of Willing Woman.

A great roar went up.

The Bon Marché horse put a nose in front.

Then—

The sound of it was like a rifle shot!

Charles Dewey bobbled crazily, pitching forward, crashing the jockey to the sun-hardened turf with a sickening thud. The great equine body followed, the horse thrashing madly in its pain, its terror.

By the time True and Charles ran to the scene, several of the Negro handlers had fallen on the thoroughbred, trying to quiet it. A jagged, splintered bone had torn its way through the skin of the left foreleg and the screams of the stricken animal had a strangely human quality.

"The gun," True said, holding out his hand to Two.

Dewey took a small Philadelphia Derringer, a single-shot .41 caliber, from his waistband, handing it to the trainer.

"Keep his head steady," Jackson ordered the handlers. He bent down to put the short muzzle to an ear.

Without warning Alma May was there, grabbing at his arm, shrieking at him, "No! Stop! Damn you, you can't do that!"

Jackson reacted angrily, trying to push her away. "This animal is in pain!"

She threw herself on the horse, her billowing skirt covering the head. "I won't let you! Not this horse! Not Charles Dewey!"

The thrashing of the thoroughbred intensified, its panic increased by having the skirt shut off its vision.

True gestured beseechingly to Charles, who went to the frenzied woman, grasping her arm. "Aunt Alma, please . . . there's nothing you can do for him."

She lashed out at him, striking him in the face with her small fist. In the end it took the efforts of Two, and Willie Carstairs, and a bystanding stranger, to pull the distraught Princess from the horse and wrestle her away.

Jackson quickly dispatched Charles Dewey, the sound of the shot echoing across the racecourse. So, too, the anguished scream of Alma May.

Andrew came running up, tears coursing down his face. "Father!" he cried to True. "It's Elmo . . . he's dead!"

"Oh, good Lord—"

He hurried the few yards, pushing his way through a knot of blacks huddled around the fallen jockey. Dropping to his knees, he cradled the tiny form in his arms. The head lolled; Elmo's neck had been broken.

The trainer gritted his teeth. "I knew that damned left fore would bring us grief."

Elsewhere on the Clover Bottom course the long-striding mare, Willing Woman, was loaded into a baggage wagon and vanned away, its owner forty-five thousand dollars richer.

IV

"Do you mean to tell me, Uncle Lee," Brevet Colonel Albert Dewey was asking, his incredulity unmistakable, "that there's been talk of Zach Taylor as presidential timber?"

"Quite a bit of talk, as a matter of fact," the newspaperman answered.

They sat at a modest dinner in the colonel's tent.

"By all that's holy, on what basis?"

"On the strength of his victories hereabouts," Lee Dewey reported. "When the news of the Mexican defeat at Palo

Alto, and then at Resaca de la Palma, reached the public, the American victory was greeted with the ringing of church bells in more than one town."

Albert laughed. "Victory? It was more a case of ineptitude on the part of the Mexican command."

"Ahhh, but that's not the way the people saw it. Old Rough and Ready had whipped the Mexicans and that was reason enough for celebration. There have been any number of community resolutions of praise for General Taylor, and one Louisiana delegation, I've heard, is on its way to Matamoros with a golden commemorative sword for him."

"But the presidency—?"

"One of the reasons August Schimmel sent me hustling down here," Lee said, "was to sound out Taylor on exactly that matter."

"And have you?"

"Uh-huh."

"What were his reactions?"

This time it was the newspaperman who laughed. "He . . . uh . . . well, he did *not* say he was disinterested. I asked him about his party affiliations, and he admitted he had never cast a vote in a presidential election. Then he added that if he *had* voted in forty-four he would have supported Henry Clay."

"So he's a Whig?"

Lee clapped the colonel on the shoulder. "My naive young nephew—Zach Taylor will be anything the political managers will want him to be. There's no doubt in my mind he's been bitten by the presidential bug."

Albert shook his head. "My God, Uncle Lee, everything about this mess is unreal. Take my new assignment, for example. I wish I could feel some pride in being given this task, but frankly, I approach it with a great deal of trepidation.

"And, in all honesty," he went on, "while it's very pleasant to see you again, I wish you weren't here . . . not this way. You're bound to lend credence to what I'm about to do with your words, and what I'm about to do isn't noble, you know."

"We're all slaves to what is perceived as *duty*," his uncle replied. "Me as a newspaper correspondent, you as a soldier."

"That's just it—I don't think of myself as a soldier anymore. I've seen enough unjustified death now for what is called honor, or patriotism, that I know I'm not a good soldier. And now I'm trapped into hunting down, and executing, some other Americans whose only crime is disagreement with the established military order."

Lee smiled wryly. "That's simplistic, isn't it? I'm sure your superiors wouldn't accept that characterization."

"Of course not. But that doesn't make it right in *my* eyes . . . in my *heart*." He sighed. "I think my only chance for sanity is to get this over with as quickly as possible and find some way to leave Mexico. Oh, how I long to be back at Bon Marché—"

The older man, seeing a way to move the conversation away from Albert's discontent with the military, asked, "What day is this?"

"Day? Why, it's August eighth—a Saturday."

"Just as I thought. The Bon Marché Cup was run this afternoon at Clover Bottom, and Cousin True was planning to enter Charles Dewey."

"How I'd love to have been there. Perhaps the day was nice and Virginia took the children out there, and she'll write to me about it."

"I'm sure she will."

"You know, Uncle Lee, it's only been in recent weeks that I came to the realization how . . . well, how *magnificent* the sport of horse racing is. There's a kind of purity about it, isn't there?"

Lee nodded agreement.

At that hour, some eleven hundred miles away, three men sat in the drawing room at Bon Marché, sipping sherry. One of them was True Jackson. Another was his brother, Able, the breeding expert, looking not at all like True's kin. He was handsome, prone to an easy smile, extroverted. The third man was much older; their father-in-law, newspaper publisher August Schimmel.

Their late-night get-togethers for sherry, and conversation, was a ritual of sorts. Schimmel and the late Charles Dewey had started it years earlier, and now Schimmel had revived it after the Jackson brothers came into control of the plantation. He liked to believe his age accounted for some wisdom that might profitably be passed on to the younger men.

"What's to be done with Alma May?" True asked. "Her demonstration on the racecourse today was abominable."

"Perhaps you're overreacting," Schimmel suggested. "After all, what happened to the horse must have been a great shock to her. An even greater shock when you consider the animal was named for her father—and she was very close to Charles, you know."

"No, no, it wasn't that kind of emotion." True snorted. "If you had been there you would have known—it was just plain drunkenness."

"And there was the added flaunting of her illicit relationship with young Carstairs," brother Able contributed. "He's fifteen years her junior! And they carry on, in public, like bitches in heat."

"An interesting analogy," the publisher laughed, "if somewhat biologically flawed."

No one else was amused.

"But she *has* been drinking quite a bit lately," Schimmel admitted. "As for Carstairs . . . well, he's a likable enough fellow. As a respected Nashville banker, he's a reasonably solid citizen, I have to say."

True took a sip of sherry. "Look, August, I'm not trying to put myself up as an arbiter of Alma May's morals. Willie may be a 'reasonably solid citizen,' as you say, but what happens if she ties up with a charlatan, someone who would see Bon Marché as a prize to pluck? My primary concern is the well-being of the estate, not the way the Princess chooses to lead her life."

"Maybe if *you* spoke to Alma May," Able suggested to Schimmel.

"God, no! That would be a mistake. She has listened to only one man and that was Charles Dewey. And poor Charles had his hands full with her most of the time." The publisher thought for a moment. "Suppose your wives took a hand in this? They're levelheaded young ladies." He smiled. "I know, because they're my daughters as well. Perhaps some female logic would bring Alma May to see . . . uh . . . to see—"

"The error of her ways?" Able said.

"Something like that," Schimmel answered, grinning. "In any event, propose it to them. It may give Joy and Hope roles in the estate—after all, those women *are* the owners of Bon Marché, while you two are merely the powers behind the throne, so to speak."

"It might help," True conceded.

"Yes, it just might," Able echoed.

Schimmel raised his glass. "Gentlemen, I propose a toast: to the ladies!"

"The ladies!" the brothers Jackson responded.

4

JOY Jackson's sitting room in what was known as the "Schimmel wing" of the mansion was feminine to a fault, decorated with frilly laces, muted and delicate colors, and elegant, though dainty, furnishings. There was no sign at all of a male—Joy's husband, True—sharing those quarters with her. Nor that children had ever set foot in the room, although Joy and True were the parents of four, ranging in age from twelve to six.

Joy's imprint on the place was total.

On this day she fussily directed three Negro maids in setting a table by a wide, open window, thin chiffon curtains moving lazily in the modest breeze of a late summer noon. The table shone with the iridescence of imported Irish linen, on which were placed translucent dishes of rose-patterned Josiah Spode bone china, and gleaming crystal from the Pennsylvania furnaces of "Baron" Stiegel, and tastefully simple and graceful utensils fashioned by the best of the Boston silversmiths.

"How lovely," her sister commented as she entered.

"Overdone, do you think?"

Hope Jackson inclined her head in brief thought. "It *is* a special occasion."

"And that's what worries me," Joy said. "We may be making it *too* special. I fear it will make us appear insincere."

Hope laughed. "I imagine you can never be too special for the Princess."

They were twins. Identical twins. At thirty-two, handsomely attractive. Like their mother, Louise, a daughter of Bon Marché's late patriarch, Charles Dewey, they were a bit too willowy to be thought sensuous. There was none of the appealing buxomness that marked other women of the Dewey blood. They were slim, tall, their faces without an identifiable flaw. Yes, attractive, but not sensuous.

Both were self-assured young ladies, born to money and raised in the atmosphere of Southern gentility—from their earliest days they were served by slave housemaids and grew up expecting service. Perhaps needing it to confirm that the Deweys were special. As with all of the Dewey grandchildren, they were liberally educated by a series of no-nonsense tutors; they spoke French, and read "good books," and talked knowledgeably of art and opera, although in Nashville fine art and grand opera were almost alien things.

Their similarity was skin-deep only. Joy, the eldest by several minutes, was sober, reserved. Dull, some thought. But in no way a dullard; she was intelligent and well spoken. Hope, in contrast, was brightly gay, quick to laugh, vivacious. And easily bored with talk of serious matters. Because their personalities were so drastically different they were not cursed by their twinness; people could tell them apart, after knowing them only briefly, very easily.

In an odd way they seemed to have taken on the colorations of their husbands. Joy was sober as True Jackson was sober; Hope extroverted like Able Jackson. But it wasn't the influences of their husbands mirrored in them; they had always been that way. When the courting process had begun, Joy was immediately drawn to brother True, and Hope to brother Able. There was none of the nonsense about the attraction of opposites.

Chattering was heard in the hallway outside the room. An adult's voice and a child's. Alma May Dewey swept in, holding the hand of a pretty, laughing little girl.

"We had a great ride," Alma May announced. "Didn't we, Lady Bea?"

"We sure did, Princess." The child giggled.

"Bea!" Hope chided her daughter. "She's your auntie Alma, *not* Princess!"

"Don't tell her that." Alma May groaned. "It has taken me weeks to get her to call me Princess."

Hope frowned, signaling to one of the servant girls. "Caroline, please take Lady Bea to join the other children for luncheon."

"Yas, ma'am." The black took the girl's hand, starting to lead her away.

"Bye-bye, Auntie . . . Princess," the youngster said gaily, waving her free hand.

Alma May wiggled her fingers at the departing child, winking at her.

"You spoil her outrageously," Hope said disapprovingly.

"Yes, I suppose I do." Alma May took a glass of sherry from a silver tray preferred by one of the servants. "It's just that she reminds me so much of myself when I was eight." She grinned. "I know you probably don't want to hear that, Hope, but there's a great similarity—if my memory isn't doing tricks on me. The same curiosity, the same enthusiasm for life, the same love of riding—"

She paused, becoming pensive. "If I had a child I'd want her to be like Lady Bea. You're very fortunate, Hope—and you, too, Joy—having the children you do."

Joy picked up a tiny silver bell from the table, ringing it. In an instant, other slaves from the kitchen staff came into the room, carrying dishes of food, scurrying about at their tasks. Alma May watched the activity, bemused. When the table was set, the three women sat down, and Joy offered a short prayer of thanks, one retained from her childhood.

Missy, Joy's personal maid, continued to hover about, but was dismissed by a wave of her mistress's hand.

Alma May's eyes followed the departure of the stolid old black woman. When the door had closed behind her, the Princess laughed. "So . . .it's going to be that kind of a get-together, is it? You don't want the servants gossiping about what's said here."

Joy, embarrassed by the directness of the words, looked to her sister for support.

"Auntie Alma May—" Hope began.

"Wait!" the older woman interrupted. "I'm not going to be able to sit through an afternoon of 'Auntie this' and 'Auntie that.'" She feigned a shudder. "When you two get a bit older you'll appreciate my aversion to that. So, call me by my name . . . or even Princess."

Hope giggled. "Agreed."

"All right, now what's all this about?"

"Well, Princess, when we decided to invite you to have this luncheon with us, Joy and I talked about it in some detail. We agreed we would not—indeed, we didn't think we could carry it off any other way—that we wouldn't try to . . . uh . . ."

"Beat around the bush," Joy contributed.

"Exactly. So, right off, you should know that all of this"— she spread her hands, indicating the luncheon preparations— "was suggested by our husbands."

"And we're distressed," Joy added hurriedly, "that we didn't have the courtesy to invite you before. As you know, there's always been a kind of . . . I don't know, an odd lack of socializing between the Schimmel and Dewey wings of this"—she smiled—"Bon Marché mausoleum."

"The big house is dreary sometimes," Alma May agreed.

"You see," Hope continued, "True and Able were distressed by what happened at the racecourse when Charles Dewey had to be destroyed. They felt your actions were— my, this is difficult!—were brought about because you may have had too much to drink."

Alma May nodded sagely. "I see. It appears we're going to have a frank conversation, but must we let this lovely luncheon get cold while we talk?"

She had broken the tension. They began to eat.

"And there's more," Hope went on, now less tentatively. "Our husbands contend your association with Mr. Carstairs is inappropriate and may bring scandal to the name of Bon Marché."

Alma May wanted to laugh, but she restrained herself. "And you two are going to bring me back to the path of righteousness?"

Hope giggled first at the humor of the uncomfortable moment. Then Joy. Within seconds the three of them were consumed with laughter.

Finally, wiping away the tears brought on by the laughing, Alma May said, "I can appreciate that, at times, my behavior may not win the approval of everyone. God knows, my mother didn't approve most of the time. You may remember she spoke of my profligate life-style in her will—"

Her nieces nodded.

"—but, I'm afraid, there's too much of the spirit of Charles Dewey in me to reform completely. However, I will give you this: I *should* be more conscious of the consequences of my love of Bon Marché bourbon. As for Willie"—she shrugged— "I want you to know that I'm not dead yet. I have an appetite for male companionship and I don't see, in all honesty, what concern others should have for it."

She had shocked the twins into silence.

Joy finally braved breaking it. "Perhaps more discretion—?"

"A point well taken." She reached out to pat Joy's hand. "You may report to your husbands that I will make every effort to repent." She chuckled. "Now, will that do it?"

Once more her candor brought a momentary silence.

"I appreciate how difficult this has been for you," the Princess said soberly, "but I recognize it was motivated by love."

"Oh, it *was*!" Hope interjected.

"And I think, too," Alma May pressed on, now in control of the conversation, "that this will bring us closer than we have ever been before. We *should* be close, you know, because sitting here at this table are the legal *owners* of Bon Marché."

She waited for the reality of that fact to sink in. "We three are the *future* of this plantation. Your husbands may manage it, and manage it well, but it is we—we who are the blood of Bon Marché, as your grandmother put it—who must guide the destiny of what Charles Dewey began."

The Princess had the total attention of the young women.

"And what do we know of Bon Marché? Do you know, Joy, how much cash there is in the banks and what plans True has for it?"

Hesitantly: "No."

"And you, Hope . . . do you know how many horses there are at Bon Marché, and what plans Able may have for the increase or decrease of that amount?"

"No."

"And what do I know of the estate? Do I know how many slaves there are? How many crops are to be planted? What repairs are necessary to the buildings? What plans there are for the physical expansion of Bon Marché?" She shook her head negatively. "I don't know the answers to any of those questions."

Alma May took a deep breath. "We not only have the *right* to know, we have the *responsibility* to know. Mattie Dewey left Bon Marché to us. *To us!* And our responsibility transcends the present day. We're charged with leaving a great Bon Marché to future generations. To your children," she added pointedly.

She dropped the intensity of her voice until it was barely audible; there was a new intimacy between aunt and nieces. "Now . . . as we accept this responsibility there are bound to be difficulties. There will be talk that we're attempting to establish a matriarchy. But think a moment about your grandmother. When Mattie Dewey lived she ran Bon Marché with an iron hand, especially in her later years. Even while her husband still lived. Indeed, it was she who made the decision to bring in True and Able—your husbands. Mattie was the soul of Bon Marché. If that led to a matriarchy, so be it. She left this estate to *us,* my dears. No one can quarrel with that truth."

The Princess slumped back into her chair, seemingly spent by the labor of her argument. "Joy," she said, "do you have any bourbon in this place?"

An hour went by, and more, in a babble of happy conversation about the future of Bon Marché. The sum of it was Joy being charged with learning the fiscal details of the plantation, Hope accepting responsibility for the equine interests, and Alma May left with the physical "being" that was Bon Marché.

There was a glow to it all, helped in no small measure by the number of toasts thought to be required during the August afternoon.

And there was a final one. "To Matilda Jackson Dewey," Alma May intoned, lifting high her glass of bourbon.

"To Grandmother," the twins responded.

II

IT WAS late night in the Bon Marché drawing room as the week came to an end. Time again for glasses of sherry and masculine conversation.

"Your advice, August," True Jackson complained, "about involving the ladies in the matter of Alma May has stirred up a hornet's nest. It was the Princess who took advantage of our wives' *tête-à-tête* to fill their heads with tales of their 'responsibilities' to Bon Marché." He groaned. "My God, Joy came to me *insisting* on reviewing the finances of the plantation with me."

His father-in-law smiled. "Did you show her the books?"

"Yes, I had little choice."

"Did she understand them?"

"I believe so, yes."

"Was there anything there you would have preferred that she not see?"

"Of course not!" The question had riled him.

August Schimmel shrugged. "Then no damage has been done, has it? Joy may even be of some help to you, now that she understands what's involved."

"Help!" Able cut in. "Hope, who now seems to have become an equine expert, had the temerity to chastise me for allowing the stallion band to become 'dormant,' as she puts it. Our studs have become too old, she says."

"Is she wrong?"

"Not totally," the breeding manager admitted. "But I wasn't ready to make any moves. Now, to keep my wife happy, I suppose I'm going to have to make a deal with that scoundrel Barrow to bring in Childe Harold. And Hope has started chattering about something called Vandal, and where she learned of that God only knows."

Schimmel chuckled. "No doubt she's taken to reading your racing paper . . . what's it called, *Spirit of the Times*? Or perhaps her mother has been bringing home the exchange copy of the *Kentucky Gazette*. You can't keep your wives isolated from what's happening in the world, you know."

"And the worst of all this," True added, "is that after their first meeting my wife was . . . tipsy. They'd been drinking toasts to each other with bourbon. And *now* there are to be weekly get-togethers of what they call 'the owners of Bon Marché.'"

"But that's what they are, aren't they?" The newspaper publisher's attitude had sobered. "I would have thought, from the example you had before you in your own cousin, Mattie, that you fellows would have understood the Bon Marché women are very strong individuals. Now that the whole thing's out in the open, I suspect it will have a salutary effect on the Princess. Perhaps now she'll see her own responsibility and—"

"Responsibility!" True snapped. "I've heard that word constantly for a week!"

"Live with it, gentlemen. It will be for the best."

Able snorted. "But your wife doesn't—"

"My wife," August interrupted, "while she may seem to be quietly uninvolved, runs not only me, but our newspapers. To be truthful, I'm grateful for it. You probably didn't realize it, being busy with your own problems, but your mother-in-law left three days ago for New Orleans to look into a newspaper we may acquire."

"Alone?"

"Alone."

"But don't you fear that—?"

"Louise is perfectly capable of looking after herself. She has a Deringer at the ready, if needed, and the ability to use it. I made sure of that."

Able smiled. "And *that's* the mother of my wife."

True remained sullenly silent.

III

"I'm sorry Georgie isn't here for dinner on your first night in New Orleans," Mary Dewey apologized lamely. "But he has many business interests and—"

"I understand," Louise said. "There'll be plenty of opportunities to talk to my brother. Right now I'm more interested in hearing from my nephews."

They sat at the dinner table in the town house on Chartres Street: the visiting Louise Schimmel, her sister-in-law Mary, and the two sons of George Washington Dewey who had remained in New Orleans—George Junior, the horseman, with his rather shy wife, Emma; and Statler Dewey, a young lawyer, with his vivacious, very pregnant Harriet.

There was a round of rather gay talk during the meal, centered mainly on the children of the young men. Perhaps too gay; the voices too brittle. Louise sensed an undercurrent of tension. Eventually, the conversation turned to the reason for her trip.

"The *Delta Recorder* has been advertised for sale," Mrs. Schimmel explained, "and August and I have always wanted an editorial outlet here in New Orleans. Before I left Nashville we spoke of the possibility of you, Statler, representing our legal interests in any purchase negotiations."

"I'd be honored, Aunt Louise."

"Do you know the current owners?"

"No, I don't," Statler answered. "But I believe Harriet's father does. He's a banker, as you are aware. Possibly I can get a line on the owners from him."

In time the conversation exhausted itself. Louise sighed. "I'm rather weary, Mary. Would anyone care if I retired now?"

Once more Mary was apologetic. "Oh, dear, I should have realized you'd be fatigued from the trip. I was hoping Georgie would be home before—"

"I'll see him in the morning," Louise said.

Statler was on his feet. "Mother, let me show Aunt Louise to her room."

He quickly led her up the stairs to a large, pleasant room, where the windows were open to the night air and the sounds of the street below.

"I wanted a moment alone with you," Statler explained quietly. "You see, we seem to have a serious problem here. Father—although Mother will never admit it to you—hasn't been home in a week. And she has no idea when he's coming home."

"And you don't know where he is?" Louise asked, showing her concern.

"Not really. For the past two days I've had several of my household boys searching for him, and they've come back with partial tales of gambling sessions and drunkenness—"

"Good Lord!"

"—but there are many places to which the blacks cannot go, of course." He grimaced. "I'd look for him myself, but this has been quite upsetting to Harriet and I'm worried about her . . . the pregnancy and all—"

"How long before the baby's due?"

"About three weeks."

"You're right, Statler. Your first concern should be for your wife. Uh . . . how long has this been going on with your father?"

The young man frowned. "It started when he came back from Nashville after Grandmother Mattie's death. He got off the boat quite drunk, and did nothing but rail about how he had been cheated out of Bon Marché."

"Yes, he made quite a scene at the reading of the will," Louise told him.

"It got worse as Mother tried to placate him. I was here one day when they got into a terrible row about Two. Apparently just before Father left Nashville, Two tried to reconcile their differences, and I gather it wound up being a rather bitter confrontation. Anyway, about a week ago he just left, and Mother withdrew into that strange shell. You heard her nonsense at dinner about Father's many business interests.'"

Louise nodded.

"I really don't know what to do to help her," Statler added, running a weary hand over his eyes.

"Maybe this isn't the best time for involving you in the *Delta Recorder* matter."

"No, I want to do that," the lawyer insisted. "Anything that gets Father off my mind for a few hours will be welcome."

IV

IT was on Canal Street, alive with the multilingual cacophony that distinguished New Orleans from other cities in the country, that George Dewey could have been found at that hour. In a fashionable, garishly decorated gambling salon, at cards with other gentlemen. Several of them he knew from the Metairie racecourse; his frequent companion in his altered life, Bernard Xavier de Marigny de Mandeville, was one of them. But the others were merely a blur of names, changing over the hours with the fortunes of the game: Bordenave, Sabatier, Peyrefitte, Trexler, Hummel, Velasquez, Shaughnessy, Longiotti.

To George, "damned foreigners"—the lot of the them.

He was staring at the cards in his hand, his eyes half-closed in a hooded manner. He held all diamonds, but only eight-high. A stack of chips was pushed to the center of the table, joining a mountain of others there.

"A thousand more, Bernard," he said.

"I will have to call you, of course."

"Of course," Dewey muttered. He laid down his hand. "A flush," he announced, "all *carreau,* as you say."

"Ah, mon ami, je regrette." De Mandeville laughed. "A full house, as you say. Knaves over tens."

George cursed under his breath. "Well, that finishes me. How much do I owe you this time?"

The Frenchman made a quick mental calculation. A shrug. "Twelve thousand, George."

"You'll take my note?"

"Certainement." He snapped his fingers, getting the attention of a Negro waiter. "A pen," he ordered.

When it was brought, George wrote the figure on a piece of paper, scrawled his signature and the date, and handed it to Mandeville. "Join me in a drink?"

"If I may pay."

"That was my intention," Dewey said, having to force his laugh.

As they made their way toward the bar George saw her enter the room. She stood on the foyer landing, three steps above the gambling floor. Her raven hair was fastened with jeweled Spanish combs, her fashionable gown was cut low in front, the décolletage revealing the sensual appeal of her figure. She toyed with a lacy fan as her eyes scanned the room.

Dewey touched his companion's arm. "Bernard?" he breathed, nodding his head in the direction of the woman.

"The octoroon?"

"How in the devil can you tell? Octoroon . . . quadroon—?"

"Octoroon signifies one-eight Negro blood, quadroon is one-quarter—"

Annoyed, George cut him short. "I know the definitions of the words, for Christ's sake! I mean, *how* can you know?"

"Ahh . . . that takes the skill of a connoisseur," the Frenchman answered licentiously.

"Do you know who she is?"

"Her name is Marguerite Cappevielle."

"And you're acquainted with her?"

"*Oui.*"

"Introduce me."

"But George—"

"Introduce me!" Dewey demanded.

"Very well." They moved to her. Up close she was even more beautiful. Her skin was flawlessly smooth. Not in the sense of cold marble, George thought, but with the soft, warm texture of a lovely lily. And nearly as white. And her eyes! *Good Lord, her eyes are violet!*

Bernard affected a small bow. "Mademoiselle Cappevielle, may I present Monsieur George Washington Dewey?"

"Monsieur," she said softly in recognition of him, touching the fan to her perfect lips.

George could do nothing but bow. He was awed into silence.

"Monsieur Dewey," Bernard went on, covering the awkward moment, "is the most prominent racehorse trainer in all of New Orleans."

"I am aware of Mister Dewey's reputation," she said, seeming to stress the use of the English form of address.

George found his speech. "You've been to the Metairie track?"

"On occasion."

"I regret I've never seen you there." He smiled. "I'm certain if I had I would not have forgotten someone so lovely."

"You flatter me, sir." There was an imperious flip of the fan. "If you'll excuse me—"

She left them standing there.

George's eyes followed her as she effortlessly made her way across the gambling floor to the faro table, where a chair was quickly offered to her by a dark-haired young man. He kissed her hand.

"That fellow?" Dewey asked.

"Richard Oubre, of the shipping family."

"She has . . . uh . . . a liaison with him?"

De Mandeville laughed loudly. "That kind *always* has a liaison."

George continued to stare at her. "Dear God!" he said softly.

"That kind," his friend added with some force, "can also be damned dangerous."

5

"IT seemed the wise thing to do," Louise reported to her husband, "to install Statler as the resident publisher of the *Delta Recorder*. Editorially, the property appears to be in good hands, but I wasn't impressed with the management available in New Orleans. So, when Statler expressed a strong interest in newspapering, I did what I thought was best. What *you* might have done."

"I'll admit to having a reservation about his age," August Schimmel commented soberly.

"But he's a very mature twenty-six. I became aware of that by the way he handled the details of the purchase." She looked at him quizzically. "Perhaps you're concerned with me bringing another Dewey into the business."

"Certainly not! I cast my lot with the Deweys a long time ago. Thirty-four years ago, as a matter of fact—when I first saw you, my dear." He leaned over in the bed to kiss her.

Louise acted out surprise. "Oh! Has it been thirty-four years?"

They both laughed.

"And all good years. With the acquisition of the *Delta Recorder* we're coming close to realizing our dream—a national chain of newspapers. One voice linking together all the regions of this burgeoning country."

His wife giggled. "Darling, you're beginning to sound like one of your editorials."

"Maybe so," Schimmel said, failing to continue with Louise's lightheartedness. "But the day is not too distant when everything between the Atlantic and Pacific oceans will be one mighty nation. And it will all come about because of what the gloomy nay-sayers are calling Mr. Polk's War. Well, they should all get down on their knees and praise God for what that Tennessee gentleman has done for the United States of America. He's already solved the Oregon boundary dispute, and when the Mexican War reaches its end, with our inevitable victory, we will have gained more territory than at any time since Mr. Jefferson's Louisiana Purchase."

Louise remained silent, knowing his peroration was not finished.

"We stand on the very threshold of greatness! Mark my words, my dear—*nothing* stands in the way of the United States becoming the greatest nation on the face of the earth!"

"Yes, darling."

"Oh . . . by the way, there was an astonishing dispatch today from your brother Lee, with marvelous illustrations. It's largely about Albert. He's Brevet Colonel Albert Dewey now, the commanding officer of a special force designed to track down and court-martial American army deserters. Turncoats who have joined the Mexicans. What adventures our young nephew must be having—!"

II

THEY rode westward in a long single file, fifty-odd horsemen in dusty blue uniforms. Hot and tired. Moving slowly in the general direction of Monterrey over dry, hilly, sterile country, seeing before them on the distant horizon the rugged barrier of the Sierra Madre Oriental Mountains.

Jokingly, they called themselves Dewey's Desperadoes, but the only thing really desperate about them was their frustration. Their commander rode to the side of the column, trying to keep out of the choking cloud of dust raised by the horses' hooves. On one side of him was his uncle, newspaper correspondent Lee Dewey; on the other, his chief of staff, Captain Walter Darnell.

"This is idiocy," Colonel Dewey complained bitterly. "It's been nearly a month now of chasing across this godforsaken landscape searching for . . . phantoms. That's what they are, Darnell. I'm beginning to believe all this talk of San Patricios has been a stupid invention."

"Oh, they're real enough," the captain insisted.

"Why? Because we've been given a list of deserters who *supposedly* have gone over to the Mexicans? Have we seen any of them yet?"

"No, but they're out there."

"I wish I had the same confidence in the military establishment you seem to have."

Two scouts approached them at an easy lope. One of them, a sergeant, rode to Dewey, saluting. "Colonel, there's fresh water up ahead—a spring-fed brook, running well."

"Any sign of hostiles?"

"Not now. But the way the ground is chewed up around the water I'd say there's been a cavalry unit there, maybe two . . . three days ago."

"Lancers probably," the colonel suggested.

"Yessir, probably."

Dewey turned to his chief of staff. "We'll make camp by the water and wait for General Taylor's main body. I want a hot meal for everyone tonight. See to it, Captain."

"Yessir." Darnell jammed a spur into his horse, riding off to make the necessary preparations.

"I have hopes," Albert said to his uncle, "that General Taylor may have some new intelligence we can use in our search."

Lee grimaced. "That would be welcome. My butt is sore."

It was the following afternoon before Old Zach's forces reached Dewey's Desperadoes. Albert waited impatiently for more than an hour before he and Captain Darnell were summoned to General Taylor's tent, where the self-assured officer lounged behind his field desk, his cuspidor at the ready, seemingly without a concern.

"Sir, our mission to track down and punish those American officers and men who have gone over to the enemy," the colonel reported with stiff formality, "has been singularly unsuccessful to date."

Taylor nonchalantly gestured to them to be seated. "No scoundrels at all, eh?"

"Not a one, sir."

"The likely reason for that," the general said, pushing a paper to Dewey, "has to do with the Mexicans having taken them off somewhere to train them together as a unit. I was about to send this latest intelligence"—he nodded toward the paper—"forward to you when I learned you had stopped here. It seems the San Patricios are now a brigade, or a battalion, largely concentrating on artillery."

Albert picked up the report, trying to read it.

"Apparently the individual deserters," Taylor continued, "were treated contemptuously by the Mexican soldiers, who were reluctant to fight side by side with them, and it was necessary to set them apart." He smiled. "The Mexican government may call them San Patricios, but to the common Mexican soldier they're no better than traitors. They call them *colorados*."

"*Colorados,* sir?"

"Yes, the 'red ones.' Our informants tell us that's because so many of them have red hair, indicating a large percentage of Irishmen among them." The general scowled. "That doesn't surprise me; the Irish never were very good at taking orders. Damn, I wish it were possible to have an American army without so many immigrants in the ranks!"

Dewey didn't comment, uncomfortable with Taylor's prejudices. He was remembering his French-born grandfather's own modest beginnings in his new country.

Instead: "I imagine, sir, now that it's know the deserters are a full unit, some other plan for their apprehension will have to be devised. My fifty men would be no match for a brigade."

"No, your group will stay together. In the days ahead my army will meet up with the San Patricios. When we do, and they are defeated, you, Colonel Dewey"—Zach looked at the other young officer—"and you, Captain Darnell, will still have to conduct the courts-martial and mete out the proper punishments."

He dismissed them with a wave of his hand.

III

His eyes followed her hungrily as she left the bed, stretching catlike and posing in front of the full-length mirror, admiring her own naked body.

"You're the most lovely thing I've ever seen," George Dewey said.

Marguerite Cappevielle turned back to him. "Is that what I am, George—a *thing*?"

"Yes," he laughed, "a thing of God. Your beauty would convert an atheist, convincing him that only a Supreme Being could have created you."

"An interesting thought," she commented soberly, "but wrong, I'm afraid."

"Oh?"

"My creation was hardly divinely inspired. A drunken Cajun for a father and a high-yellow whore for a mother—"

"Only proving the infinite powers of God."

The door of the bedroom opened and a large black woman entered, carrying a tray. "Breakfast, ma'am."

"Thank you, Angel," Marguerite said, not embarrassed by being found nude.

The maid gingerly set the tray on the end of the bed at George's feet, grinning at him.

"Angel, this is Monsieur Dewey."

The black woman nodded. "Pleased t' know ya, suh."

George smiled weakly, uneasy with the strange intimacy of the moment. *How many other men has she found in her mistress's bed?*

As the maid left the room, Marguerite explained: "Angel raised me. Fed me, clothed me. Found money, somehow, to get tutors for me." A pained expression came over her face. "Poor Angel . . . she wanted me to be a lady." A sigh. "She used to work for my mother."

"I gather that your mother is deceased."

"Yes." She poured coffee into the cups on the tray, sitting on the edge of the bed and handing one of the cups to Dewey. "Just so we can be finished with this . . . biography, my mother was killed by one of her lovers. A stevedore. He knifed her to death."

"Good Lord!"

She offered him a small pastry. "But all of that is of no consequence now. What's important now is that we . . . well, that we face what is fact." She leaned over to kiss his cheek. "I like you, George. You're kind and gentle and—"

He waited a few seconds for her to continue. When she didn't, he asked, "And what, Marguerite?"

"And it's foolish to think we can continue. My differences with Richard will be patched up and—"

"No! I won't allow you to go on with that Oubre bastard!"

Her sadness was reflected in her violet eyes. "That *bastard,* George, has given me everything I have . . . my clothes, my jewels, these rooms. Without him—" She shuddered.

"It doesn't bother you that he's a brute with you?"

"Everything has its price."

Dewey put his coffee cup back on the tray, taking Marguerite's bare shoulders in his hands, putting his face close to hers. "Listen to me, Marguerite—you don't have to pay that price! I won't let you. What you're concerned about are only material things . . . things I can give you." He paused. "I can also love you."

"You're a fool. Richard is a vindictive man."

"I've met men like Oubre before. I can handle him."

"And what of your family?"

"That's a matter that need concern only me."

She pressed close to him. "I *do* enjoy being with you, George."

"Only that?"

"Only that?" she repeated slowly. "I don't know. But I'll never know, will I, until we try?" She had made her decision, her commitment.

Dewey gathered the lovely creature into his arms. "Not too many weeks ago," he said quietly, "I was convinced I had lost the most precious thing in my life. Now I know I've found it."

IV

MONTERREY was a city situated on the broad flood plain of the Santa Catarina River and nestled in a protective embayment of the Oriental Mountains.

"A formidable fortress," Lee Dewey commented to his nephew.

"Yes." The colonel studied the terrain with the eye of a trained tactician. "It won't be taken without a lot of casualties."

"I imagine not."

"I wonder whether the San Patricios are holed up in there somewhere."

"We'll know soon enough."

"Soon enough" was three more days. Days of horror for Albert Dewey. Left with nothing to do but observe the fighting, by order of the commanding general, he and his men were spectators to more death than any of them could have imagined. They witnessed one Lancers' full charge out of the city, falling in great numbers on a unit of about forty American infantrymen, firing their big carbines at point-blank range, and driving lances through the backs of those who tried to flee. In just a few minutes it was ended; no American in the unit remained alive. Dewey was to write in his diary (dated September 20, 1846): "They killed without mercy."

Inexorably, over the trio of days, Old Rough and Ready gained the upper hand. One by one the forts within the city fell. And the individual houses. Each of those, built of stone and surrounded by four-foot-high stone walls, had been a miniature fortress; each was bought with blood. Finally, the remaining Mexican force fell back to what the Americans were calling the Black Fort.

Colonel Dewey and Captain Darnell, in a position of comparative safety several hundred yards removed, watched as the Americans stormed that last fort, to be met by determined resistance. Cannon in the battered pile of stone blanketed the attackers, alternating between grapeshot and ball. Those guns took a dreadful toll.

"Someone in that fort," Dewey commented, "is a top-notch artillery officer."

"American, do you think?" Darnell asked.

"More than likely."

General Taylor's artillery chief brought up more guns, pounding the fort with a withering fire.

Suddenly, two Mexican officers stood up on the parapet, holding their swords by the points, waving them wildly. A signal of surrender.

Sharpshooters brought rifles to their shoulders.

"For God's sake, don't fire!" an officer yelled.

The order came too late. A trigger had been squeezed. One of the men on the parapet was straightened up by the shot, then slowly fell forward, crashing to the stone courtyard below, his sword clattering beside him.

American troops cheered.

The second Mexican officer ducked behind the parapet, but still waved the sword by its tip. Within minutes, a group of American officers, under the cover of a white flag, entered the fort. Dewey and Darnell raced to the scene, dismounting to push their way through enlisted men jammed around the entrance. Happy, laughing men. They were alive.

Reaching the gate, the leaders of Dewey's Desperadoes were halted by a stern-faced sergeant, his musket leveled at them. "Only members of the surrender party can be admitted, sirs."

And so they waited. For a quarter of an hour, and then a half. A colonel appeared from inside the fort.

"Under the negotiated terms of surrender," he shouted importantly, "this garrison is to be allowed to depart peaceably! You are all ordered to permit their passage!"

The men stood dumbly, unable to believe their particular moment of hell had ended so ignominiously. There was barely a sound as the Mexicans started to come out, their hands held high over their heads.

And then came a non-Mexican, dressed in a green uniform not seen before, and carrying a banner blazoned on one side with a representation of Saint Patrick and on the other an Irish harp and the coat of arms of Mexico. The American soldiers began to mutter angrily, pressing forward. They recognized him for what he was: a deserter, a turncoat, a traitor!

"Stand back there!" the colonel ordered, drawing his sword.

Behind the flag-bearer, the second man in the strange green uniform wore the epaulets of a Mexican officer.

"My God," Dewey exclaimed, "that's Sergeant Riley!"

The officer turned to look at him, scowling, no sign of recognition on his face.

"Who is he?" Captain Darnell wanted to know.

"Sergeant John Riley—he was my drillmaster at West Point!" Dewey whirled on the colonel in charge. "Who in the devil gave the idiotic orders to free these men?"

"I act on authority of the commanding general."

"And I, sir, am under *direct personal orders* of General Taylor to arrest these men for desertion! I demand that you assist my men in carrying out those orders!"

"Old Rough and Ready himself, is it?" the colonel said sarcastically. "Well, sir, I was under orders to arrange the capitulation as I did."

"You damned fool!" Albert advanced on the colonel angrily, to be met by a sword point pressed menacingly against his chest. "Don't you understand that these men"—he jerked a thumb at the green-clad men walking past him—"are deserters from the United States Army? Traitors!"

"I have my orders." He kept the pressure on the sword point.

"I'll get Taylor," Captain Darnell yelled, taking off on a dead run for his horse.

"In the meantime, Colonel," the sword wielder said, "I suggest you restrain your temper."

"I'll have you up on charges, you stupid ass!" Dewey screamed at him.

Ten minutes passed as Albert fumed. Then fifteen. And twenty. Only a small group of enlisted men remained nearby (the others having gone to rejoin their units), amused by the impasse between the two colonels.

Darnell returned, walking the horse. "I wasn't able to see Taylor," he reported disconsolately, "but one of his aides told me there's been an armistice."

"What!"

"Well, more of a cease-fire, I suppose. As I understand it, there's to be no more fighting for at least eight weeks. During that time, neither army is to cross the summit of the Orientals." He pointed toward the nearby mountain range.

Dewey just stared at him, unbelieving. By that time all of the men of the San Patricio brigade had disappeared into the alleyways of Monterrey.

"Shall we end this melodrama now?" the erring colonel asked, lowering his sword from Dewey's chest.

Without another word Albert stalked away. His anger wasn't abated when he found it impossible to get an audience with Zachary Taylor, having to lodge his complaint with the general's adjutant.

"Sometimes in the heat of battle, Colonel Dewey," the adjutant said condescendingly, "mistakes are made. I regret one may have been made in these circumstances, but—" He shrugged his shoulders.

"It wasn't just a mistake—it was stupidity! We had the entire San Patricio brigade in our hands, but for that incompetent ass—"

"Ah, yes, Colonel Sawyer. A good man, if inclined to be a bit unimaginative."

"Unimaginative! Is that what you call drawing a sword on a fellow officer?"

"Again, Colonel Dewey, the heat of battle." He smiled.

Albert grunted, starting to leave.

"Colonel!"

Dewey turned back to the senior officer.

"I believe a salute is in order."

"Yessir." He complied.

"Sleep on it, Colonel," the adjutant suggested, returning the salute, "and it will all look different in the morning."

Albert tried to accept the gratuitous advice. He failed when he undressed for bed and found a speck of blood on his chest where the sword point had pressed through his uniform tunic.

He failed, too, when he thought of the good men killed that day by the accurate cannon fire of the San Patricios, under the command of his one-time drillmaster. *How many more are going to have to die now because Sergeant Riley was allowed to go free?*

His rage kept him awake.

V

CARRIE Bonsal, shaking her head in doubt, was reading the smudged stone proof she held in her hand:

Victory in Mexico, as inevitable as the next sunrise as 1847 dawns, ought not to be diminished by the unseemly, discordant congressional debate over the extension of slavery—yea or nay?—into the vast territory we are certain to gain at war's end.

Principal architect of the discord is a Pennsylvania congressman named David Wilmot (a profane and slovenly individual, we are led to believe), whose name is attached to a "proviso," offered as an amendment to every appropriations bill for the conduct of the war. The Wilmot Proviso is devilish mischief, insisting that "neither slavery nor involuntary servitude shall ever exist in any part of the territory" likely to be acquired from

Mexico. It is mischief because it can have no legitimate connection with the fighting of the war.

Whether or not the new territory, or portions thereof, will be free or slave should not, must not, be the primary issue at hand. Only one thing is truly important: the expansion of this great nation from one mighty ocean to another. If we allow antislavery forces their contention that slavery is "the moral issue of our times," all of the sacrifices of our comrades in arms in Mexico will be denigrated.

Slavery is an economic issue only and, as with all economic matters, it will right itself under the impetus of the growth of the country . . .

"Will," Carrie called across the office of the *St. Louis Challenger,* "have you read this editorial August wants us to run at year's end?"

"I have," her husband answered.

"It's sheer drivel," she said angrily, tossing the paper on her desk. "One more proof that August Schimmel is out of touch with reality there in his ivory tower at Bon Marché."

"He *is* the publisher of this newspaper."

"August Schimmel is only half-owner of the *Challenger,*" she replied firmly. "You forget that I'm the owner of the other half."

Will Bonsal sighed. "That's not something I'm likely to forget, my dear."

Carrie Dewey Mussmer Bonsal was the daughter of the late Franklin Dewey, eldest son of the founder of Bon Marché. When she was born in 1811 she was Charles Dewey's first grandchild. Spoiled, indulged, she was taught the strong Dewey full-life philosophy on the knee of her grandfather. Indeed, she had become the fifty-percent owner of the *St. Louis Challenger* when she was only nine, as part of Charles's investment in the newspaper enterprises of his new son-in-law, August Schimmel.

It had been only a trust arrangement at first, but when Carrie was twenty-three, and just divorced from the brutish Alvin Mussmer, son of one of the plantation's overseers, she went to St. Louis to look into her newspaper property. It was to be a catharsis only, everyone thought. It soon became more than that. She was the apprentice of editor Wilson Bonsal, then his lover, and then his wife. Bonsal was nineteen years her senior.

In the twelve years since the marriage little had changed, if the masthead of the *Challenger* was taken as evidence. August was still the publisher, Bonsal was still the editor. Behind that printed declaration, however, was the reality of Carrie's growing control of the newspaper.

"We're not going to print that," she said, nodding toward the copy of the Schimmel editorial on her desk. "It's a ridiculous assumption on his part. My God, doesn't August know the country's coming apart over this issue of the *morality* of slavery? If it were just dollars would anyone really get so passionate about it?"

She picked up the stone proof again, reading: "'Slavery is an economic issue only and, as with all economic matters, it will right itself under the impetus of the growth of the country.' What utter nonsense!"

"August isn't going to be happy if we don't print it," Bonsal suggested.

"And I'm not going to be happy if we do," she snapped. "What does he know of the views of the people outside of that tight little enclave in which he exists in Nashville?" Carrie grew pensive. "I wish Grandfather were still alive. He'd set August straight on the morality of slavery—" She stopped suddenly, her eyes gazing off to some distant place.

Her husband was quiet, knowing what she was thinking. And how painful were the thoughts. Carrie was remembering her daughter, Honey Mussmer, who had been left behind at Bon Marché with her grandfather. And who, as a sixteen-year-old, had hanged herself on the day of Charles Dewey's death, unable to convince the other members of the family that Charles's dying wish was to free his slaves.

"Anyway," Carrie said, picking up her train of thought as quickly as she had dropped it, "August has greater problems with his newspapers than a difference of editorial opinion here in St. Louis. His hopes for a united voice aren't going to mean much to him when this country splits in two. How's he going to speak with 'one voice' in Nashville, and Lexington, and Cincinnati, and Pittsburgh, and Chicago, and Raleigh, and in that new paper he's bought in New Orleans, and here?

There'll be no hope for a united voice in those diverse places. Not for long, anyway."

"You speak as if a split is inevitable," Will said.

"I wish you wouldn't do that."

"Do what?"

"Always play the devil's advocate in our discussions. It's all right, dear, if you agree with me occasionally. It won't make you less of a man."

"Damn it, Carrie—!"

She halted him with a raised hand. "Will, I love you. Just as important, I also respect you. But you know as well as I do, my darling, that this country is firmly set on the path to hell."

"I don't like to think of it as an inevitability," Bonsal said sadly.

"Nor do I—not really." She exhaled a deep breath. "But nothing short of God's intervention—a miracle, in other words—is going to save us."

There was a wry smile as she tossed the offending editorial into a waste bin. "And the last I heard, August Schimmel isn't God."

6

HARRIET Dewey was radiant, as all mothers are radiant when they hold in their arms their newborn babies. Propped up in her bed, wearing a lacy nightgown her husband had bought for her at an expensive New Orleans shop offering imported French items, the occasion was the introduction of her third daughter to the members of the family.

"Isn't she sweet?" Harriet cooed. She looked up at Statler. "I'm sorry, dear, for not giving you a son."

The father laughed. "A son? Don't you know it's said it takes more of a man to produce a daughter than a son? And if proof be needed—" He gestured to two darling little girls standing by the bed, awestruck by the miracle of their new sister.

Everyone chuckled: Harriet's parents, Raleigh and Carmella Walston, very proper pillars of New Orleans society; and Statler's, George Senior and Mary Dewey. Statler hadn't seen his father in nearly a month and he wondered how his mother had got him there. He sensed the uneasiness between the elder Walstons and Deweys. It had always been a factor in the relationship of the two families, but now George had become something of a pariah, his gambling and drinking episodes matters of public gossip.

"Have you selected a name, dear?" Mrs. Walston asked.

It was Statler who spoke. "Well, we already have a Faith and Charity, but Hope is not really available to us, in that I have a Nashville cousin by that name. We felt a second Hope would be too confusing."

"And so," Harriet added sweetly, "we've decided to name her for Grandmama. We're going to call her Lovey."

"Mother will be so pleased," Raleigh Walston said proudly.

His wife tried to hide her disapproval. In her view, her mother-in-law had always been a demanding bitch. She also had the constant annoyance of Raleigh referring to his mother in the present tense, even though the woman had been dead for nearly a decade. *Lovey?* It was so common.

"I think we'd all better get out of here," Statler said, "and let you get your rest, darling." He nodded to a housemaid standing by, who took the baby and placed it in a frilly crib next to the bed.

Statler kissed his wife, then led the way to the parlor, where a Negro butler had poured wine for a toast.

"To my daughter Lovey, and to my darling wife," Statler intoned.

The toast was drunk, followed by a few minutes of idle conversation, strained by the necessity of trying to bring George into it. Mary Dewey offered an excuse to leave and George trailed her through the door of the Carondelet Street house.

Outside, two carriages were parked: Mary's and the Walstons'. She looked up and down the street.

"You didn't come in your own carriage?" she asked.

"No, someone drove me here," George answered.

"Mademoiselle Cappevielle?"

Mention of her name startled him. He had no idea Mary had any knowledge of Marguerite. "As a matter of fact," he said as calmly as he could, "it was Bernard. After your message about the baby was relayed to me through him, he very kindly offered to bring me."

"And he'll be returning for you?"

George hesitated. "No, I asked him not to. I thought I'd come home with you."

"Why?" There was open hostility in the simple question.

"Because there's a lot we ought to discuss—"

"Ah, so you've grown tired of your colored whore!" She grinned malevolently. "Or she of you?"

"Please, Mary, this is not a conversation we ought to be having on a public sidewalk."

His wife studied him for a moment. "Perhaps not." She

made for her carriage, waiting for him to open the door for her. Inside, she sat as far away from him as was possible. They rode for a few minutes in silence.

"Well, George," she said finally, "this is not the public sidewalk."

"Mary, I know you can't fully understand," he began slowly, "how distressing the Bon Marché matter was for me. I had put great store in the idea that I would, at long last, be the master of Bon Marché."

"A stupid idea!"

"In retrospect, I suppose it was. But, stupid or not, I believed in it. And when it collapsed . . . well, I guess my reactions weren't very rational."

Mary said nothing.

"And I found I wasn't able to accept the rejection I felt in Nashville and—"

"Poor man"—her sarcasm was knife-edged—"he feels *rejected*. And he uses that as an excuse for abandoning his family, for public drunkenness, and for scandalous behavior with a black trollop!"

George wanted to defend Marguerite, but he had something more pressing to do.

"All of that is true," he said sheepishly. "I deserve your anger. But even the worst of fools can be contrite. And that's what I am now."

"Don't ask me to forgive you, George."

"I don't. All I ask is the opportunity to demonstrate my sorrow over my mistakes, and to try to make up for them."

Once more, Mary was silent.

"I hope the years we've had together will earn me that much consideration."

She nodded her head slowly, in thought. "Yes, perhaps the years must be considered."

"You married an imperfect man, Mary Harrison."

"Yes . . . I did." She permitted herself a slight smile. "God help me, I knew it from the start."

George reached over to pat her hand. She didn't pull away from his touch.

He sank back into the cushions of the carriage, contentedly, delighted with himself. He had not lost his touch for sincerity.

And he thought of Marguerite.

He thought, too, of his desk in the drawing room of the Chartres Street town house and the legal papers there he'd need to complete his plans.

II

"I'VE come to the conclusion," Mary Dewey wrote to her sister-in-law just after New Year's Day of '47,

> that age is more of a terror to men than it is to women. Men—especially successful men, it seems—see a certain immortality in themselves, and growing old threatens that belief.

Louise Schimmel smiled as she read the letter; there was more depth to Mary than she had imagined.

> Georgie, after having proved he can sow his wild oats for a second time in his lifetime, seems content once more. He has renewed interest in the horses and he has become a doting grandfather with little Lovey, who is such a darling baby. And just two days ago, we learned that George Junior and Emma are going to become parents again. Sometime in August, they say. I can't tell you who was more excited by the news, Senior or Junior.
>
> In sum, Louise dear, our problems have righted themselves, and Georgie has become more mature. Isn't that an odd thing to say about a man approaching fifty-eight? But it's true and the hurt I have felt is gradually passing away.
>
> If you'll pardon an indiscreet intimacy, I have become a wife again. (For God's sake, don't let August read this!)

Louise giggled.

III

RICHARD Ten Broeck was not a man George Dewey found easy to like. True, there was something imposing about him— he was tall and straight and his bearded face was handsome. Most people saw him as an exemplary gentleman. But his eyes told George something else. They were icy blue, seeming to have the ability to cut through anyone upon whom he gazed, exposing the innards. *Like a hunter gutting a deer,* George thought.

There was mystery about him, too. It was generally known that Ten Broeck had been a successful gambler on the Mississippi riverboats, and that he now managed the Bascombe racecourse in Mobile and the Bingaman track there in New Orleans. But of his background before all that, little was known. Not with any certainty. George had heard one rumor that Ten Broeck had attended the United States Military Academy for a few months, before getting into a brawl with one of his instructors and resigning from the academy to be free to challenge the instructor to a duel. Whether or not there had been a duel was not a part of the rumor as George had heard it.

Sitting across the table now from Ten Broeck in the Metairie clubhouse, and looking into those cold blue eyes, Dewey could believe there *had* been a duel and that the instructor was in his grave. Yet, in spite of the dislike he felt for Ten Broeck, George had sought him out because Richard Ten Broeck was exactly the man he needed at that moment.

It was mid-morning. There was no race meeting under way at Metairie, but the gentlemen of New Orleans still used the clubhouse for a meeting place. George had selected that hour because he knew there would be few others around.

"Mr. Ten Broeck, there aren't many secrets around a racetrack," Dewey began.

His companion nodded.

"And I'm led to believe you're anxious to become part of the ownership of Metairie."

Another nod, confirming George's statement.

"I am, as you probably know, part of the original investment group in the racecourse, through the aegis of the Canal and Banking Company, of which I am a director."

"I'm aware of that," Ten Broeck said softly.

"My percentage is for sale . . . uh . . . under certain necessary restrictions."

"How large a percentage?"

"Fifteen."

Ten Broeck nodded once again.

"I'm prepared to offer that percentage to you, sir," Dewey went on, "provided the sale of it can be kept confidential between the two of us for a period of at least six months. I'm emboldened to place that restriction before you because I believe you, too, would want to keep it confidential if your intent is to gain a controlling interest in the track." Dewey smiled for the first time. "It might be easier to obtain a controlling interest if it were not known you already owned fifteen percent."

The other man made no comment on that. "How much are you asking?"

"Thirty-five thousand."

Ten Broeck's head shook negatively, very slowly.

George fell back to his prepared second position. "However, if I have your assurance, as a gentleman, that the six-months confidentiality will be maintained," he added, trying to appear calculating about it, "I could let you have it for thirty."

There was a brief moment of silence.

"Agreed."

Dewey looked around the clubhouse to determine whether their meeting had attracted any special attention. When he believed it had not, he pulled a document from his pocket. "I have the transfer papers with me, which I will sign over to you when the cash is available. Could that be done promptly? Perhaps later today?"

"I can do it now."

Somehow, George wasn't surprised.

Ten Broeck drew a small leather pouch from his inside jacket pocket (Dewey noted there was a monogram in gold: RTB), counting out the money in large bills, sliding them across the table. George quickly scrawled his signature and the date on the papers.

"I thank you, sir," he said, surrendering the document.

The man with the cutting blue eyes came to his feet, touched his fingers to his hat in an informal salute, and walked slowly out of the clubhouse.

I wonder, George thought, *what my former partners are going to say when they have to deal with that bastard?*

IV

THE slaves whispered about it. Persistently—from the fields to the stables to the kitchen. Even the favored Negroes of the household staff, where some discretion prevailed, dared to repeat the whispers.

There was a curse on Bon Marché!

Its origin was being traced to the incident at the Clover Bottom track in the preceding August when the bay horse, Charles Dewey, shattered his leg. Terrible forces were unleashed, the blacks were convinced, when True Jackson pulled the trigger of his Deringer to destroy the stricken animal.

"Mastah Charles don' laik what Mistah True done to his hoss," they said. And they could cite ample proof of Charles Dewey's ghost stalking the plantation, exacting vengeance for the death of the thoroughbred carrying his name.

There *had* to be a curse. How else could the ill fortune befalling Bon Marché be explained?

Whispering began in the spring when five of the first eight foals of the 1847 crop were either stillborn or had to be destroyed because they couldn't stand and nurse. It intensified when Bon Marché Lass, a mare carrying the royal bloodlines of the legendary Boston, refused to accept her baby, making it necessary to employ a nurse mare. Other mares did occasionally reject foals, of course, but never the Lass. She had been a perfect mother for nine earlier foals.

And what of Vandal, the newest stallion at Bon Marché? Hadn't he gone crazy in the breeding shed, savaging a handler so badly that the poor black lad was a permanent cripple, unable to use his torn right arm again?

Then, early in July, there was what happened to the stallion barn. A lightning bolt from a thunderstorm set it afire. It burned to the ground. Only the quick intervention of the stablehands had saved the studs, although several of them suffered burns.

It was the next morning before discovery was made of a second lightning strike, one splitting the poplar shading the grave of Charles Dewey, and leaving a jagged burn mark across the face of his tombstone. The news spread like wildfire among the slaves. In hushed, fearful tones they repeated, one to the other: *"Mastah Charles is a-walkin'!"*

No black would enter the graveyard, most especially the two assigned to keep the graves green and flower-covered. Disgruntled white overseers had to assume that task.

It took True Jackson's accident, however, to turn the whispers into open talk. While making a routine inspection of a yet unnamed two-year-old, a son of Priam (as was the dead Charles Dewey), the colt "cow-kicked" him, breaking True's leg. His left leg! Just as it was the left foreleg of the equine Charles Dewey which had been broken.

True chafed under the enforced confinement to his bedroom, his splinted leg propped up on a stool piled with pillows.

Joy entered the room, carrying a tray. "Time for your sustenance, dear," she said cheerily.

Jackson frowned. "Don't you have enough to do these days without taking on the servants' duties?"

"I was always under the impression," she replied lightly, "that caring for my husband *was* one of my duties."

"You know what I mean. Where is that damned Caroline, anyway?"

"It seems that poor Caroline is . . . well, frightened of you."

"What!"

Joy laughed. "You, sir, whether you know it or not, carry the curse of Bon Marché."

"Oh, good Lord! Is that nonsense still going on?"

"With renewed vigor, it seems, since that horse kicked you and broke your leg."

True groaned. "I suppose we must allow them their superstitions, so long as the work gets done."

"They're all like children, really." His wife sighed. "I do wish, though, we'd see an end to this streak of bad luck we've been having. It's becoming depressing."

"And costing money. How's the new stallion barn coming along?"

"Just fine. You should see the Princess out there directing the work just like a—" She stopped abruptly.

True chuckled. "You were going to say 'just like a man.'"

"I was," Joy confessed, "but that wouldn't be accurate. The truth is she's handling it like the Princess, which is quite different from the way a man would do it. She cajoles, and she praises, and somehow seems to make fun of the hardest work. She's quite a woman, dear. Bon Marché is fortunate to have her."

"Hmmm."

"You don't agree?"

"It's just that, at times, Alma May gives me a feeling of uneasiness. She conjures up for me the apprehension contained in some words of Shakespeare: 'By the pricking of my thumbs something wicked comes this way.'"

"True! How dreadful of you!"

"Yes, I suppose it is." He winced as he moved his leg to find a more comfortable position on the pillows. "You can blame my ill temper on this damn leg. And on all that nonsense about a curse."

V

THE place was called Churubusco.

"It's an old Aztec word," newspaperman Lee Dewey was explaining, "meaning 'Place of the War God.' From the looks of it that's very apt."

"Maybe this is where we're finally going to meet up with the San Patricios," Chaplain Matthew Ryan suggested.

Those in Brevet Colonel Dewey's tent laughed, a reflection of their frustrations. For nearly a year the special fifty-man unit had been seeking to apprehend and punish the American deserters by hanging, as a deterrent to others who might consider serving under the Mexican flag. But their mission had been totally unsuccessful to that moment. Indeed, after the first few weeks, there had been little or no help from the army command. What had seemed such an urgent task at one time now held a very low priority.

Unknowingly, they had become victims of an internecine political scrap in which Major General Zachary Taylor and President James Polk were engaged. Taylor's announcement of his intention to seek the presidency in '48 under the Whig banner had led to him being pushed off center stage in the Mexican War by the Democratic commander in chief. Old Zach was isolated in northern Mexico, with the bulk of his command—Dewey's unit among them—sent southward to General Winfield Scott, to whom Polk had entrusted the final defeat of the Mexicans.

Colonel Dewey didn't even know whether his original orders, given to him by General Taylor, had any current valid-ity. Several efforts to see Scott, a vain and pompous soldier, had been turned aside by the general's overprotective aides. Albert had learned what a lowly status a breveted colonel had in Scott's eyes.

Thus, Dewey and his men had been mere spectators in the war; they had seen the fall of Veracruz, and Cerro Gordo, and Puebla, and, just a day earlier, Contreras, without once being engaged. But Dewey understood it was their very inactivity that was keeping his group together. The handpicked men were perfectly willing to stay as members of Dewey's Desperadoes—it was safe duty.

"This war has seen a lot of idiocy," Captain Walter Darnell, Dewey's chief of staff, was saying. "Here we are, chasing after Americans fighting as Mexicans, and the army has recruited a bunch of Mexicans to fight as Americans. Have you heard of the so-called Spy Company, Albert?"

"No."

"Well . . . as I get the story from someone on Scott's staff, there's a Colonel Hitchcock who has enlisted the services of a Mexican bandit chief named Dominguez. His band of cutthroats has been given uniforms, has been fully supplied, and are now unleashed on their fellow Mexicans. On one hand we're tracking down traitors, with an eye to executing them, and on the other hand we're *embracing* traitors. Where's the morality in that?"

Chaplain Ryan sighed. "If you seek morality in war, my son, you search in the wrong place."

Colonel Dewey nodded sad agreement. "You know, Father, a minute or so ago we laughed when you said you felt we might finally be going to meet up with the San Patricios. But that may make some sense."

He turned to Captain Darnell. "Yesterday, Walter, did you observe the accurate pattern of Mexican artillery fire at Contreras? In my view it was a repeat of what we saw at Monterrey—"

"The work of your Sergeant Riley, do you think?"

The colonel got to his feet, starting to leave the tent. "Come with me."

Outside, encamped in front of them, was the ten-thousand-man army of General Scott. Dewey pointed off into the distance.

"Across that lava bed," he said, "is the next point of major resistance. You don't have to be a military genius to know the Mexicans have fallen back along that riverbank. And that bridge there to the right"—his finger moved—"leads up to that walled—" Albert paused.

"That's the Convent of San Pablo," the newspaper correspondent volunteered.

"Well, it's a fortress, no doubt of that. If you were Santa Anna, Walter, and wanted to live to fight another day, what would you do?"

"I'd cover my retreat," Captain Darnell answered, "by making that convent as difficult as possible to breach. The defenders there would be ordered to resist to the last man."

"Exactly." Dewey clapped his hands together. "And I'll wager any amount you want that Sergeant Riley and his traitorous San Patricios are moving their cannon into the convent at this very moment. He means to make it costly for Scott to advance. And while he holds up Scott, Santa Anna will fall back, with what's left of his army, closer to Mexico City. Their situation grows desperate now and the San Patricios will, as you suggest, Walter, resist to the last man. They'll have no other option."

The colonel's face mirrored his determination. "That's why we're going to be right there when the Convent of San Pablo falls. This time, believe me, there'll be no cease-fire and Sergeant John Riley will *not* be permitted to walk away as he was at Monterrey."

"If he lives," Darnell suggested.

"Sergeant Riley has an instinct for survival," Albert Dewey replied sullenly. "And this time, gentlemen, we're going to be in the thick of it. Now, after a year, we're going to earn our pay"—there was a bitter laugh—"modest as it is."

VI

THE August heat and humidity at Nouveau Marché was debilitating. All of the horses had been brought in from the pastures to the comparative coolness of the barns. But neither the heat nor the horses were of primary concern on that day at the Louisiana plantation.

For on Friday, August 20, 1847, a second son was born to

George Junior and Emma (née Watts) Dewey, and his name was to be George Dewey III.

Grandmother Mary Dewey had engineered that with the shy and compliant Emma. Mary saw it as a way to further bind George Senior to the bosom of the family. If the young father had any reservations, he didn't voice them.

Now the Georges, Senior and Junior, strolled idly along a shaded lane of the farm, perspiration sticking their clothes to them.

"You know, son," the elder Dewey said, "we really don't give enough credit to our women. It must have been hell for Emma this morning, giving birth in this ungodly heat."

"She's not much of a complainer. Never has been."

"You're very fortunate," his father chuckled. "I can't honestly say that of your mother."

They walked in silence for several hundred yards more.

"Are you planning to add further to your family?" the older man asked.

"I think not, Father."

"Then it just may be that the third generation of Charles Dewey's family is in place." George Senior thought for a moment. "All in all, if my arithmetic is correct, there have been twenty-three great-grandchildren. He'd be damned proud of that, you know."

"Yes." Junior hesitated. "Father, there's been something I've been meaning to talk to you about. Bernard de Mandeville came to me at Metairie the other day and mentioned something about partial ownership of two of the colts I've been readying for the races. The Grey Medoc and the good one out of Beeswing, he said. I was at a disadvantage, since I knew nothing of it, so I didn't say much."

"Oh, damn, son, I'm sorry about that! I meant to tell you about it, but it must have slipped my mind. Bernard wanted to make an investment in several new horses, and I thought we might as well have some of his money. So, I sold him half of those two colts. Sort of spreading our risk, in a manner of speaking."

"I see—"

"And you don't approve?"

"I really don't disapprove, Father, of the general idea of

selling shares, but you might have asked me about the worth of them."

"Of course, and I apologize."

Junior waited for further explanation. When it didn't come, he asked; "How much did you get, Father?"

"Fifteen hundred each."

The young man's eyebrows arched. "De Mandeville got a hell of a bargain."

"You think so?"

"I *know* so," Junior said forcefully. "If you had asked me I would have put a value on the Grey Medoc at twice, maybe three times that, for a half share." He grimaced. "And Beeswing's foal may be the best we've had in years. Quite honestly, Father, I question the wisdom of selling any part of that colt, and especially for fifteen hundred."

"Well . . . Bernard is an old friend," George Senior replied unconcernedly, clapping his son on the shoulder, "and it won't hurt to do him a favor. He's done many for me."

"Are there any more such deals I ought to know about?"

"No, no. As I said, Bernard is an old friend." He shrugged. "That's all there is to it, Junior."

He was lying.

7

THE acrid smell of gunpowder and the cloying stink of death hung heavy in the air at Churubusco. Cannon fire from the massive-walled Convent of San Pablo enfiladed the slowly advancing forces of General Winfield Scott, raking across the American ranks. And taking a terrible toll.

Colonel Dewey and Captain Darnell sat their horses next to the bridge leading to the convent road, their small unit screened from the artillery rounds by the bank of the river.

"I'd swear to God that's Riley up there," Dewey said, gritting his teeth.

"Those certainly aren't Mexican gunners," Darnell added.

For more than an hour Dewey's Desperadoes had been pinned down in their position, spectators once more. But now they sensed their long search was coming to an end. Their anticipation was a living thing, their anxieties transmitted to their horses, which neighed and pranced nervously as the cannon barrage seemed to become one solid, hellish noise.

American artillery, brought forward at great cost, pounded the stone fortress from end to end. Relentlessly; answered in kind by the guns of the convent.

"It seems to me," Darnell shouted to Dewey in the din, "that the fire from up there is slackening."

The colonel nodded.

Then, with an eerie suddenness, the bursts of cannon fire from San Pablo ended. More slowly, the American guns fell silent, too. There was no sign of surrender shown from the convent, but it was clear to all the battle was finished.

"This is it," Dewey said. Turning in his saddle, he raised

his right arm high in the air to his men. "Hoooo!" He shouted, spurring his horse into a gallop.

Dewey's Desperadoes raced up the road to the convent, dashing through the wide, arched gate into a courtyard. A scene of horror assailed them. Bodies lay everywhere; green-clad bodies—the Americans of the San Patricio Brigade. Others, many fewer than the dead, stood about dispiritedly, without apparent leadership.

"Round up those survivors!" the colonel ordered loudly. "Line them up against the east wall!"

His men went into action.

From a cellar in the corner of the courtyard there emerged perhaps a dozen frightened monks. "Father Ryan," Dewey called, "take care of those people."

The colonel rode in a slow circle around the enclosure, looking down at the bodies, searching for a man in an officer's uniform. For Sergeant John Riley, late of the U.S. Military Academy. And not finding him.

Out of the corner of his eye he saw an American brigadier general ride through the gates, followed by perhaps a hundred infantrymen. Dewey went to him immediately; he wanted no interference this time.

"Sir," he said, saluting smartly, "I am Colonel Albert Dewey, detached from the army of Major General Zachary Taylor on special orders from the President of the United States." He reached into his tunic for his papers.

"And what orders are those, Colonel?" the general asked wearily.

"To apprehend and court-martial deserters from the United States Army." Albert swept an arm around the courtyard. "What you see here, sir, are the remains of what is known as the Mexican San Patricio Brigade, manned entirely by deserters."

The brigadier made no attempt to read Dewey's orders. He simply glanced about, watching the men rounding up the survivors.

"What do you intend to do with them, Colonel?" he asked.

"I'm to try them and hang them, sir."

"Seems reasonable," the senior officer said, grinning. "Will you need our help?"

"Some of these, under strict court-martial procedures, may

not qualify for hanging. It would be helpful if you could leave some men to take charge of those who will remain as prisoners."

The general bellowed over his shoulder. "Lieutenant!"

An infantry officer rode forward.

"This is Lieutenant Benjamin Wilson, a good man." To the young officer: "Lieutenant, select twenty-five men to stay with you to assist Colonel Dewey here. The rest will withdraw with me."

"Yessir."

"Is there anything else you need, Colonel?"

"No, sir. You've been very helpful. May I know to whom I'm indebted, sir?"

"Barnstable. Brevet Brigadier General Amos Barnstable of Massachusetts."

"You're far from home, sir."

"Yes, and damned unhappy about it, too! Now, if you'll excuse me, Dewey, I'm anxious to get back to the rest of my command. I haven't been out of these boots in three days." He saluted lazily and wheeled his horse, riding out of the courtyard.

Chaplain Ryan hurried up to Dewey. "Albert, from what I can gather from their lingo, the priests say there was an officer hiding in the cellar with them."

"Riley, I'll bet!" Dewey dismounted. "Have them show me where."

One of the priests nervously led the way down a flight of perhaps a dozen stone steps and into a long corridor, ill-lighted with candles stuck on protruding stones along its length. The priest stopped, pointing down the corridor.

Dewey drew his pistol. "Sergeant John Riley!" he shouted, the words echoing. "You're under arrest by order of the President of the United States!"

A laugh came back to them, and then a figure appeared in silhouette some twenty yards away. "The President, is it? Old John Riley has come up in the world, it would seem."

He walked toward them slowly, the shadow becoming a reality. His face was haggard, but he smiled broadly as he came up to the colonel, stopping when he saw the leveled pistol. "Well, now, Cadet Dewey, you lied to me. 'Tis not the President at all."

"Then you recognized me at Monterrey?"

"I did that, laddie, but there wasn't time then to renew acquaintances." The grin grew wider. "And look at you now, Cadet, a colonel you be. But breveted, I'll bet, so's they don't have to give you a colonel's pay."

Dewey scowled, standing sideways and gesturing Riley past him with his weapon.

"'Tis just like the United States Army, you know," Riley went on, "giving titles but no money."

"Shut your mouth, Sergeant!"

"Ah, but laddie, you're talking to *Colonel* John Francis Xavier Riley, Mexican citizen and landholder. An equal, you might say. A person due some respect."

"Respect! What the hell do you know about respect?"

They came out into the open, blinking in the late-afternoon sunshine. Riley looked around disconsolately. "Well, all I can say, Cadet Dewey, is that the Americans paid dearly for our few dead."

"You bastard! You'll hang for this, Riley!"

The onetime drillmaster at West Point turned to face Albert. "Not so fast, Cadet—"

"Colonel to you!"

"Not so fast, Cadet Dewey," Riley repeated slowly. "Under the rules of U.S. Army courts-martial, you can't hang me, you know. I didn't leave American service during wartime. I was long gone *before* war was declared."

"I'll hang you anyway!"

Riley looked steadily into Dewey's angry eyes. "No, you won't, laddie. Your kind follows the rules."

II

IT was well into the night before the confusion at San Pablo Convent was sorted out. Dewey's men held seventy-five prisoners, all Americans and all presumed to be deserters. John Riley admitted there had been two hundred and sixty in his brigade; they counted one hundred and seventy-eight dead.

The other seven? Riley laughed. "Well, Cadet, they're deserters from the deserters, I guess."

"What I can't understand, Riley," Albert said, "is why you persisted when you knew the situation was hopeless. Why take all these dead?"

"Laddie, when men face the hangman's noose it doesn't make a hell of a lot of difference, does it? We'd be fighting yet if we hadn't run out of powder."

Captain Darnell tried to keep accurate records of those buried that night, laid in a common grave dug by the prisoners under the watchful eyes of the musket-carrying infantrymen of Lieutenant Wilson. Chaplain Ryan and three San Pablo priests were busy for hours with their Catholic rituals.

"I don't intend for these courts-martial to be strung out for days," Dewey told Darnell. "I want them finished quickly, and the sentences carried out just as quickly."

"I suggest to you, Albert, that after the trials we turn the traitors over to a higher command for the executions."

"That may prolong it for weeks."

"It may," Darnell admitted, "but are you willing to sign the hanging orders for this many men?"

Albert shuddered. "No, Walter, I'm not." The reply was barely audible.

At first light the next morning the courts-martial began. Colonel Dewey and Lieutenants Ryan and Wilson were the members of the court, Captain Darnell prosecuted, and Sergeant Riley was allowed to put up some kind of defense for his men.

It went quickly, efficiently. "There's something brutal about all this speed," Darnell whispered to Albert at one point during the proceedings. Colonel Dewey made no comment.

Before darkness fell again, all seventy-five had been tried. Fifty were deemed to be traitors, deserters in the time of war. They were to be hanged. Six were acquitted on the grounds that they had been captured and forced into the San Patricios by Riley and his men. Nineteen others, including Riley, were found to have deserted before war was declared. Their punishment was to be flogging and branding, plus imprisonment at hard labor for the duration of the war.

The outdoor trials ended, Dewey turned to his captain. "Walter, have the farrier prepare a brand."

"What do you intend to do?"

"I intend to carry out John Riley's sentence."

"Aren't you being irrational in this matter of Sergeant Riley?"

"You have your orders, Captain," Albert replied coldly.

With the San Patricios lined up across the courtyard, and with Dewey's and Lieutenant Wilson's men drawn up in formal ranks, Riley was tied to a post, his back bared. The colonel sat his horse, his sword drawn, counting the fifty lashes of the sentence meted out by a muscular young sergeant who wielded a cruel bullwhip.

There was no sound from the tough Irishman as the whip laid open the flesh of his back in bloody strips. But Riley turned his head so that his gaze met that of the colonel. He glared at Dewey during the entire ordeal. Albert, in turn, didn't flinch from the fiery eyes.

". . . forty-nine, fifty." Dewey shifted in the saddle. "Regulations require that all found guilty of desertion carry the deserter's brand," he intoned for all to hear, "to be placed on the cheekbone, as near as possible to the eye without jeopardizing sight." He nodded to the farrier.

With trembling hands, the blacksmith lifted the brand from the coals, moving the white-hot *D* to Riley's face, pressing it into the flesh.

Colonel Dewey's onetime drillmaster screamed in agony.

The farrier fell back, dropping the brand.

Albert stared down at Riley. Then: "Damn it, man, you've got it backwards! Heat the iron again!"

"Colonel, wait—!" Darnell called out.

"I'll have quiet in the ranks!"

With many of the men looking away, the branding was repeated.

"You bastard!" Riley shrieked. "I'll see you burn in hell!"

"Dr. Carrothers, see to that man," Dewey ordered. To Darnell: "Dismiss the men, Captain." Reining his horse, he rode out of the courtyard.

An hour later, his uncle found him sitting in the dark, his back against the stone wall of the convent.

"Captain Darnell is very distressed," Lee Dewey reported.

"No more distressed than I," Albert said quietly. "That man deserved to be hanged. He was nothing but a murderer of American soldiers."

"That's a very fine distinction to be making in wartime, Albert," the newspaperman commented. "Darnell sees the second branding as an act of vengeance, unbefitting an officer of the United States Army."

"And you, Uncle Lee, what do you think?"

"I must confess I agree with him."

"An act of vengeance?" the younger Dewey sighed. "Yes, I suppose it was." He paused. "In the morning I intend to turn the command over to Walter, and then I'm going to ride north to give my final report to Taylor. After that, I'll resign my commission."

"He won't be able to accept it in the time of war," Lee said.

"The war will be over before the year is out."

"Most likely it will."

"By then I hope to be on my way back to Nashville. Back to Bon Marché . . . where I'll try to forget this day."

"God grant that you can, Albert."

He did ride north in the morning to report to General Taylor the completion of his special assignment. And what he would learn of the fate of the remaining San Patricios would come in dispatches written by his uncle. Twenty-five of them were hanged at a place called San Angel. And twenty-five more at Mixcoac.

"The gallows at Mixcoac," Lee wrote, "were positioned with a view of the storming of Chapultepec Castle by American troops. As the Mexican flag on the castle came down, and the Stars and Stripes were raised, the condemned deserters, to a man, raised a great cheer. The traps were sprung, the cheers dying in their throat."

III

MARGUERITE drew on a filmy negligee which did little to hide her sensual body. George Dewey, stretched out on the bed, his hands locked behind his head, watched her. Enjoying her.

She smiled at him warmly. "I have something to show you, George."

"And how much is this going to cost me?" he laughed.

"No, nothing like that. It's a . . . well, you have to close your eyes."

"Oh, it's *that* expensive, is it?"

"George," she giggled, "it's no more than a bauble. But you have to close your eyes first."

When he had complied, Marguerite went to her wardrobe, got out a small box, and brought from it a tiny, gold-colored half-mask, trimmed with frilly lace and shining with gaudy bits of colored glass. She put it on, looking into the mirror. Satisfied with what she saw, she went to the bed, standing over him.

"You may look now."

He stared at her for a moment. Then he laughed. "Mademoiselle Cappevielle, I believe. I'd know you anywhere."

"Do you like it?"

He didn't know what he was supposed to say. "It's an attractive mask, but what—?"

"Next week there's a *bal masqué* and I thought we'd—"

"No!" he cut her off sharply.

"But, George, we never go out anymore." She pouted. "And I see you so seldom these days. Once . . . twice . . . a week, and then only in there." She pointed down to the bed.

"Marguerite," he said softly, "I thought we agreed we'd be discreet."

"Yes, but it's been so long—"

"And it will be only a little while longer, my dear, until I get my affairs in order." He caught her hand, pulling her down to him. "And then we'll be together for the rest of our lives."

"But not just in these rooms." The voice was demanding; it was not a tone he had heard before.

"No, not just in these rooms. I promise you that. I *guarantee* you that."

"I did so want to go to the ball."

"There will be plenty of balls, dear, believe me." He kissed her.

After having a parting sherry together, Dewey dressed and left his mistress's rooms. Her little pouting session was dismissed from his mind.

But Marguerite went almost immediately to her secretary, beginning to write a note. She pondered over it, glancing oc-

casionally at the mask, taking time to find the right words.
When she finished writing, she called out: "Angel!"

The black maid appeared.

"I want you to deliver this to Monsieur Oubre." She held
out the note.

Angel's mouth gaped. "Miss Marguerite—ya sure?"

"Do you have trouble with your hearing?" the woman
asked angrily.

"No, ma'am."

"Then do what I tell you!"

IV

ALBERT Dewey, dressed in newly purchased civilian clothes,
was about to board a steamboat at New Orleans. He had
thought of spending some time at his uncle George's, but the
vision of Virginia and the children intruded. He had booked
passage on the first available boat.

A ragged Negro lad, hawking newspapers, drew his attention.

"Over here, boy," Albert called. He tossed him a penny.

Boarding the boat, Dewey leaned on the rail, reading the
latest report of his uncle:

Mexico City, Sept. 14, 1847—General Winfield Scott, in
elegant full dress and accompanied by a colorful squad-
ron of dragoons with gleaming drawn swords, rode into
Mexico's capital city this morning at the head of his victorious American army.

Mexican citizens crowded rooftops and windows to applaud and cheer the . . .

Albert wondered whether Captain Darnell had witnessed it.
He hoped so.

General Scott and his staff took quarters in the national palace, on the top of which the Stars and Stripes
were already flying. An immense crowd of blanketed
leperos, the scum of the capital, were congregated in the
plaza as the commander in chief entered it. They pressed
upon our soldiers and eyed them as though they were
beings of another world. So much were they in the way,

and with such eagerness did they press around, that General Scott was compelled to order our dragoons to clear the plaza. They were told, however, not to injure or harm a man in the mob—they were all our friends!

On entering the palace, General Scott at once named General John A. Quitman, of Mississippi, as governor of Mexico—a most excellent appointment . . .

Albert read it all, then dropped the paper into the Mississippi, watching it drift away on the current. As he wished his memories of Mexico would drift away.

8

A LIGHT, early-morning October rain misted over the Cumberland River as the long, luxurious packetboat *Talleyrand* knifed through the waters, driven by huge sidewheel paddles. Albert Dewey was packing his traveling bag in one of the comfortable cabins when he heard the engines shut down, followed by shouts of the crewmen as they prepared to bring the heavy, shallow-draft boat to dock at Nashville.

He flinched involuntarily when the bass-voiced steam whistle let loose a sustained wail, setting up a reverberation that rattled the glasses in the cabin's cupboard. Quickly he closed the bag, stepping out into the passageway. Albert drew his woolen greatcoat tightly around him against the humid chill of the day. But he smiled; nothing was going to spoil his return. He was home!

He made his way the few yards to the starboard rail, facing Water Street, scanning the busy dock area for any signs of his family, hoping the letter he had posted on his way to New Orleans had arrived in time to tell them he was coming. Even with the noises of the docking activities, he heard the shouts. It was his aunt Alma May he saw first, her animated jumping up and down drawing his attention.

And by her side was Virginia. *Sweet Virginia.* He strained his eyes to see her lovely face, but she was bundled up against the cold dampness. She held a little boy in her arms. *That has to be Staunch!* And around her stood three other children. He could make out little Carolina easily enough, and the lad next to her, waving wildly, was Jackson. Soberly contemplating the scene was six-year-old Jefferson. *Good Lord, how tall he's grown!*

As the *Talleyrand* drifted toward the bank, he could recognize the others in the crowd. His mother-in-law and father-in-law, and Aunt Louise Schimmel, and his cousins Joy and Hope, with their husbands, True and Able Jackson, and several of their children. And cousin Charles Dewey II and his family. And . . . and . . . it seemed the entire family was there to greet him.

There was a sharp jolt as the boat ran aground and stopped. Albert waited impatiently, his heart beating in a strange fluttering way, as the crewmen ran out the gangplank. Once it was in place, he raced along its length, making his way through the confusion of piled-up freight to sweep Virginia into his arms.

He kissed her lips, her cheeks, her eyes. Caught up in the tight embrace was the little boy, who whimpered slightly and then burst into a howl. Laughing, Albert took the child from Virginia, holding him at arm's length, studying the son he had never seen.

"I'm your daddy, Staunch," he said, an emotional sob catching in his throat.

The howl grew louder.

"You're a stranger to him now," Virginia said, taking the baby again and hugging him, petting him to end the crying. "It'll take a little time, dear."

"I suppose." He turned his attention to the other children, embracing Carolina and Jackson simultaneously, kissing them.

When he moved to Jefferson, the lad stuck out a hand for shaking. "Welcome home, sir," he said formally.

Tears ran down Albert's cheeks. "Thank you, son." He shook the tiny hand. "I suppose at six, a young gentleman is past kissing and things like that?"

"Yes, sir." Jeff studied him soberly. "Where's your uniform, Father?"

"In my bag, son, where it's going to stay."

"You're not going to be a soldier anymore?" The boy seemed disappointed.

Albert tousled his hair. "No, Jeff, I'm not. I've found there are more important things in my life—and they are all here right now."

It was time then for the others, setting off a round of kissing and embracing and handshaking.

"I was going to enlist the town band to welcome you," Alma May told him, "but Virginia dissuaded me."

"Thank God for that," Albert laughed.

"But I *am* planning a big party at Bon Marché to honor our returning hero."

"No, Princess," her nephew said with some force, "I don't want that, either. There was nothing heroic about what I did in Mexico."

"But—?"

"That's past. I mean to keep it in the past."

Alma May grinned, patting him on the cheek. "Very well, Albert, we'll talk about it later."

The rest of the day was euphoric, in one sense, for Albert. He spent many hours with his children at the home of Virginia's parents, where they had been staying while Albert was away. After they had been put to bed—and after Albert had made some special effort to ingratiate himself with little Staunch—there was the obligatory dinner with Brian and Maybelle Stoker, his parents-in-law.

There had always been some distance between them; the Stokers had not really approved of their daughter marrying a soldier. But now Albert tried to close that gap.

"Father Stoker," he said, "has Virginia told you I've resigned my commission?"

"She has," Stoker answered, "and I've been waiting for the right moment to tell you there will be a post at the bank open for you. You are, after all, well educated, and—"

"Excuse me, sir," Albert interrupted, "but I've been contemplating my future in a somewhat different manner."

"Oh?"

"Yes—and I wasn't prepared to discuss it right now." Albert sighed. "I wish we could save this for another time, until I've had the opportunity to discuss it with Virginia." He reached over to squeeze her hand.

"Of course," Brian said in his stuffy manner. "But you

should be aware that this area is booming and the greatest growths will be in banking."

"I appreciate that, sir."

It was an uncomfortable moment for him. After dinner was concluded, and after Albert and Brian had smoked a cigar and had a whiskey together, Albert and Virginia were finally allowed to retreat to their bedroom.

He embraced her as soon as the door was closed behind them. "Oh God, Virginia, it's good to hold you again. You'll never understand how much I've dreamt of this moment." He kissed her wildly and she responded. But when he began to caress her and make an effort to begin to undress her, Albert sensed a stiffness in his wife.

"What is it, darling?"

Virginia moved away from him, going to the full-length mirror in the corner of the room and fussing with her blond curls. "It's been more than two years, Albert," she said quietly.

"Yes, it has," he laughed. "And your soldier is home from the wars."

"I've been thinking of this moment, too, dear"—she turned to him, her face flushed—"and . . . and . . . you're something of a stranger to me."

"What the devil—?" He felt his anger rising; he fought against it.

"Please understand, darling, that I've been without a man since—" She stopped, burying her face in her hands. "Oh, dear, that sounds dreadful!"

Albert went to her, taking her hands in his, kissing her roughly. "I'm your husband, damn it, and I don't need the coyness of our wedding night."

"Albert!" She began to cry.

He dropped her hands. "Oh, hell," he muttered. Going to the big wardrobe, he began to undress, taking time to carefully hang his suit away. Then he stripped off his outer clothes, walking disconsolately to the bed and slipping his naked body between the sheets. He closed his eyes.

Albert could hear her moving about the room, sobbing softly. He knew she was undressing. He also knew the passion he had felt during the long day would not be returning to him that night. Finally, she slipped into the bed beside him, brushing a kiss against his cheek.

"Am I being the bitch?" she whispered.

"You are," he replied coldly.

She was sobbing again. "I love you so much, Albert, but you know it has never been easy for me. There are times when I wish I had the convenient . . . virtue of your aunt Alma."

What the hell does Alma May have to do with it? he wanted to ask. But he kept silent.

Virginia touched her hand to his. Several moments went by. "Can't we talk, Albert?"

"About what? Virtue?" He immediately regretted the sarcasm; that wasn't making the situation any better.

Once more there was a long silence before she spoke again. "Perhaps we could talk about Father's offer."

He wanted to laugh. Everything was so ludicrous only laughter seemed warranted. Instead: "All right, Virginia, we'll talk about your father's offer." He raised up on his elbow, looking down into her beautiful face. "The answer is going to be no."

"But why? It's such a fine opportunity."

"Because I'm going into the horse business. With Bon Marché."

She frowned. "Will that be wise, dear?"

"I believe it will." The conversation was closed.

He shifted his body away from her, putting his head back on the pillow, closing his eyes. He kept telling himself to go to sleep; unsuccessfully. When the steady rhythm of her breathing told him Virginia had fallen asleep (Albert *hated* her for that!), he quietly left the bed, pulling on a robe, and made his way through the darkened house to Brian Stoker's den. There he opened a bottle of bourbon, pouring himself a liberal portion. He settled down into a deep easy chair, thinking of the salacious Mexican women he had missed having because of his wrongheaded fantasies about Virginia.

You're a fool, you know. Why do you let her do this to you? You could go back up there and demand—! No. She's your wife, not some compliant whore. Be patient. You've been patient before.

Albert groaned. Finishing the bourbon, he trudged up the stairway.

Virginia found him in the morning, asleep in a chair by Staunch's crib. She loved him for that.

II

"WHAT's the phrase, John?" George Dewey Sr. asked lightly. "Seeking flexibility? That's what I'm doing—seeking some flexibility with my money."

He sat in the office of the Canal and Banking Company, signing mortgage papers on Nouveau Marché and the town house on Chartres Street.

Banker John Westminster nodded. "It's intelligent, at times, to utilize your cash for other investments. The equity in those properties gives you that opportunity."

"Hmmm." *Opportunity.* George liked the sound of the word.

Going to the large vault in the office, the banker counted out several dozen packets of money. Putting them into a small leather case, he handed the money to Dewey. "Use it well, George."

"I fully intend to, John." Soberly, but grinning within himself, George left the bank, climbing into his roadster carriage, and whipping the horse into action. This was going to be a very special day.

Over the past several weeks he had been methodically turning his assets into cash: the fifteen-percent interest he had held in the Metarie racecourse, the partnerships he had sold in his horses, and now the mortgage on his two pieces of real estate. In all, he had accumulated more than two hundred thousand dollars. Even with his outstanding gambling debts, he still had more than enough to complete his plans.

He drove slowly, saving the city. For the first time New Orleans seemed magic to him. And why not? Everything he wanted was now his. He turned onto Bourbon Street, passing the French Opera House and stopping in front of an awninged dress shop. Vaulting out of the carriage (*how young he felt!*), he marched into the shop.

The French proprietress greeted him warmly. "Ah, Monsieur Dewey, you're early. She's still being fitted."

George shrugged. "I have nothing but time, madame."

"You're going to like what we've done."

"I'm sure I will." He moved about the tiny shop, idly picking up swatches of cloth, studying them, and then putting them down again. More than fifteen minutes went by.

"Monsieur," the French woman called to him. George turned as she was pulling aside the curtain separating the front of the shop from the workroom in the rear, and Marguerite swept through, twirling about to show off her new gown.

Dewey's mouth gaped. Not because of the gown—he barely noticed that—but because of her beauty. The voluptuous figure, the jet black hair, the creamy smooth skin, the violet eyes; every time he saw her she took his breath away. And especially on this day.

"Do you like it, George?" The pleasant modulation of her voice matched her physical perfection.

"Wonderful." He beamed. "Most wonderful!"

"It meets with your approval, then?" the shopkeeper asked.

"Of course. How much do I owe you, madame?"

"One hundred and fifty, monsieur."

George counted out the money. Turning to Marguerite: "Leave the gown on, dear. We have a special place to visit."

"But, George—"

He handed a small card to the proprietress. "Deliver her other clothes to this address." Without another word, he extended his arm to Marguerite, guiding her out of the shop.

"George, where are we going?"

"You'll see soon enough." He grinned at her, helping her into the roadster.

As he cracked the small whip over the horse's back, Marguerite laughed. "So this is to be a guessing game?"

"It's a good deal more than a game, Mademoiselle Cappevielle," Dewey replied seriously.

They drove in near silence. George would permit only talk of matters of little consequence—the weather, idle gossip of the city. Finally, he turned the carriage into Prytaneum Walk.

"I've always loved this street," Marguerite said enthusiastically. "The houses are like . . . well, like little jewels. Are we visiting someone here?"

"Yes, we are."

He stopped in front of a two-story frame house distinguished by the five unique Gothic arches that set off the front of it. Colorful rose-hued shutters dominated the large windows, contrasting vividly with the light blue with which the main part of the house had been freshly painted. A gleaming white picket fence surrounded it all.

"It's lovely," she said. "Are we acquainted with the owner?"

"Intimately." He leaped to the sidewalk, extending his hand as she alighted from the carriage.

Marguerite giggled. "And you're not going to give me a hint about who lives here?"

"A hint?" George laughed. "Very well—it's the most important person in your life."

"But who—?"

"No more hints." He opened the gate for her, leading the way to the porch, and banging the brass knocker. The door opened immediately, a large black woman giving her impression of a curtsy.

"Welcome, Mademoiselle."

Marguerite's violet eyes opened wide. "Angel! What are you doing here?"

Dewey couldn't restrain his happy laughter. "This, my dear, is your new house."

"But . . . but . . ."

"Angel moved everything from your rooms this morning while you were busy with the fitting."

Marguerite threw her arms around his neck, kissing him wildly. "Oh, George, it's so lovely!"

"It's merely a setting for your beauty."

"And it's *mine*?"

"Ours," he said.

She took a half-step backward. "Ours?"

"I've left Chartres Street. I intend for us to live here together."

"Oh—"

Dewey frowned. "That doesn't please you?"

"It does . . . it does . . ." she answered quickly. A pause. "It's just that it's so sudden, George."

"I know. But I wanted to surprise you."

Marguerite laughed. "You have, darling. More than you can imagine."

He took her on a quick inspection of the fashionable little house, ending in the spacious bedroom where her clothes had been put away in one wardrobe and his in another. She turned in circles, slowly, taking in every aspect of the room.

"I hope," she said softly, "all of this doesn't bring you grief."

"How could it do that, with you here?"

She frowned. "I was thinking of Richard."

"Why?" he asked, suddenly distressed. "You've ended it with Oubre, haven't you?"

"Yes, yes . . ." The frown continued. "It's just that he can be such a violent man when he believes—" She stopped to change the course of her words. "When he hears of this . . . of us . . . I'm fearful of what he might do."

"Why should he do anything?"

Marguerite forced a little laugh. "You're right, George. I'm sorry I brought up his name in this . . . special place." She went to him, taking him in her arms, kissing him with passion. "This is a special place, isn't it, darling?" She gazed about the bedroom, a teasing expression on her lovely face.

"Very special."

"Then I suspect we ought to prove it." She began to undo the bodice of her new gown.

George Dewey grinned. It was going to be just as he had imagined it. And to hell with all the others. With those hypocrites at Bon Marché. With Mary. Most especially, to hell with that ass Richard Oubre.

III

ALBERT Dewey sat in the Bon Marché drawing room with True and Able Jackson. Uneasily, believing now he had placed himself in the embarrassing position of begging. He had come to the plantation to find himself a place in the running of Bon Marché, convinced such was due him as a grandson of the late Charles Dewey.

"Colonel, we much admire, of course, your heroic service in behalf of our nation—" True Jackson was saying.

Albert grimaced. "Please, True, the military title isn't valid anymore. I've resigned my commission. And I'm a bit tired of everyone trying to make me out a hero. I wasn't."

"Your modesty is noted," True smiled. "But you mustn't denigrate your service, Albert."

Young Dewey shrugged.

"*But*"—the contrary conjunction fell heavily on Albert's ambitions—"this is not the best of times to consider association with Bon Marché. Truthfully, we've had a very poor year, both in breeding and at the track, and—"

"The blacks keep prattling about a curse on Bon Marché," Able interrupted, chuckling.

The older Jackson silenced him with a glare. "What I'm trying to say," True went on, "is that a position is not open commensurate with your abilities."

"Or the lack of them," Albert interjected.

"I make no such evaluation," True continued stolidly. "It's just that a proper position for a gentleman is not now available."

Alma May swept into the room at that moment, dressed in a modish riding habit, cracking her whip against her boot as she walked. "I just now heard you were here, Albert."

The men stood as she went to Albert and kissed him on both cheeks. "I ought to be angry with you, dear nephew, for scuttling my plans for a party in your honor. There are precious few excuses for a party here, and you've robbed me of a great deal of fun." She laughed.

"Princess," Albert said, laughing with her, "if you really need an excuse for a party we'll put our heads together and invent one."

"I shall hold you to that." She gestured for the men to be seated. "Now . . . I seem to have interrupted a rather serious discussion." She sank down on a divan opposite them.

"We were explaining to the colonel . . . uh . . . to Albert," True told her, "how difficult it would be to find him a proper position at Bon Marché, especially in light of our recent reverses."

"I see." Alma May contemplated that for a moment. "Cousin True, perhaps our *reverses,* as you call them, are partly due to some reluctance for experimentation."

True's face showed her remark had offended him.

"What ails us, it seems to me," she pressed on, "is that we

have become stagnant. We have withdrawn behind the stone walls of Bon Marché while the rest of the world is reaching out, conquering new frontiers, as it were."

"Our mandate," True challenged her, "is to preserve the resources of Bon Marché."

She cracked the riding crop against her boot. "*You*, sir, don't have the mandate!" The voice was hard. "My mother's mandate belongs to the *owners* of Bon Marché. And, because it does, we believe there must be an expansion, not a retrenchment."

There was not another sound in the room; it was as if the others had stopped breathing.

"I know it distresses you when I express myself in such a forceful manner. But here"—she nodded toward Albert—"we are given the opportunity to take Bon Marché in new directions. It occurs to me that with the availability of Albert's talents we might consider the possibility of establishing a *second* stud farm."

There was a startled gasp from True.

"In Kentucky, perhaps," the Princess added.

"Such a move," True said slowly, "would require a great deal of capital."

"It would, yes. But it would also make available to Bon Marché new bloodlines, new markets, new opportunities to make money."

"Or lose it! You'd have to convince me it isn't a gamble."

Again the riding crop came down hard against the leather. "A gamble? Damn it, True, don't you understand that everything Charles Dewey did was a gamble? Without risking something, Bon Marché would not exist today for you to toy with."

Albert came to his feet. "Perhaps you'll allow me to withdraw. This is not something I ought to—"

"Sit down." The Princess spoke softly, but she had given a command.

Her nephew regained his seat.

"There is on the market," Alma May reported, "a seventeen-hundred-acre property at Lexington. For reasonable money in today's climate. There's a good, solid house on it, three well-made barns, some fencing already, and good water. There's the added feature—depending on what the future brings—of the availability of additional acreage. Ideal for a new thoroughbred nursery. For what could be, with some imagination—with some gamble, if you prefer that word— *Bon Marché Lexington.*"

"You seem to be very well informed," True said with some sarcasm.

"I am. It really wasn't very difficult. The exchange of a few letters, the employment of a Kentucky agent to evaluate the property—standard business practices."

"You might have told us this before," Able contributed.

"There was no reason to tell you, given the belief that no management was available." She smiled at Albert. "There was no thought, quite honestly, that Albert might become available for such a project. Now that it seems he would be, there's no reason not to consider such an expansion."

True was frowning. "And how much . . . uh . . . *gamble* do you see in this?"

"Approximately a hundred thousand."

"Impossible!" True was shocked. "We simply don't have that additional resource at this time."

"I'm aware of that." The Princess was having a good time now. "But if we assume a portion of the investment, perhaps Albert could—"

"I have very little cash," he cut in.

Alma May grinned. "Ah, but your wife does, doesn't she? Or she could free some"—the grin grew into a laugh—"with the aid of your good offices, from her father."

Hesitantly: "Yes . . . perhaps."

"There!" She stood up quickly. "The possibility exists for a Bon Marché Lexington. Imagination, gentlemen. I'll get the papers I've accumulated, and you *men* can work out the details."

She left the room as she had entered it. Flamboyantly, with the riding crop beating a rhythmic tattoo against her boot.

IV

"WHILE the Mexicans seem to be dragging their heels in the negotiations," August Schimmel wrote in the first 1848 issue of his newspaper,

9

A CROWD jamming into the offices of the *Nashville Monitor* watched with astonishment as the strange little device on a desk clattered unintelligibly, finding it difficult to believe the young man sitting there was actually receiving a message from as far away as Louisville.

However, he *was* writing down letters hurriedly as the clattering continued, and the letters were rapidly becoming words.

August Schimmel, excitedly leaning over the young man's shoulder, was reading those words aloud: "'This is . . . Louisville . . . Kentucky . . . and my name . . . is Henry . . . O'Reilly.'"

Schimmel looked up at the spectators, beaming.

"'On this . . . momentous . . . occasion . . . I send . . . my good . . . wishes and . . . compliments . . . to all of . . . the people . . . of Tennessee.'"

The young man, his fingers dancing on the instrument, made some clatter of his own.

"What did you send in return, Jake?" the publisher wanted to know.

"I said Mr. O'Reilly has our thanks," the operator answered, "and that the people of Tennessee send their fondest regards to our neighbors in Kentucky."

"Marvelous, marvelous!" Schimmel enthused. "Ladies and gentlemen," he said, louder now, "you have just seen history made. I respectfully suggest that you make note of this date: Tuesday, February twenty-second, 1848. You'll be able to tell your grandchildren that you were present at the inauguration of telegraph service to Nashville."

"How does it work?" someone in the crowd called out.

August laughed. "Well, I'm not an authority, but in the most simple terms, an electrical current is sent through wires strung from one city to another, and by the use of the sender"—he pointed to the instrument—"that electrical current is interrupted for specific intervals according to a code developed by Mr. Samuel F.B. Morse, whose invention this is."

He looked at a young lady standing in front of the desk. "What is your name, miss?"

"Nellie," she giggled. "Nellie Rimby."

"Jake, let her hear what her name sounds like in the code."

The operator, in just seconds, clicked out the name.

"That don't make no sense," a skeptic yelled.

"Perhaps not, but I can assure you that what was tapped out there was 'Nellie Rimby.' Maybe Mr. Jacob Arnold, who will be the *Monitor*'s telegrapher, could explain the code to you."

The young man grinned, pleased to be in the spotlight. "Well, you see, the Morse code is built around a series of dots, dashes, and spaces. Now, with the dot, the key here is depressed for about one twenty-fourth of a second. A dash is about three times longer—three twenty-fourths of a second. And when you know the code for each letter, it's pretty simple."

"Show me," the skeptic insisted.

"Certainly. This is an *A*." *Dot-dash*. "And a *B*." *Dash-dot-dot-dot*. "This is an *S*." *Dot-dot-dot*. "Every letter has its own symbol. Punctuation, too. This is a question mark." *Dash-dot-dot-dash-dot*. "Now, when you're sending those letters you keep them separated by using intervals, or a space, between them."

"Anyone as proficient as Mr. Arnold with the code can send, or receive, as many as thirty words a minute," Schimmel added. "What all of this means is that we will be able to receive news dispatches from anywhere there is a telegraph line with great speed.

"The day is not too far distant when we will be receiving dispatches on the workings of our government in Washington.

On the same day, you understand! And we will see in our lifetime, I will predict, similarly swift dispatches from the capitals of Europe."

"How they gonna get a wire strung across the ocean?" the skeptic demanded.

"I'm sure I don't know, sir," Schimmel chuckled, "but I'm certain it'll happen."

An old woman near the desk, who had not changed her somber expression during the entire demonstration, spoke now: "The whole thing 'pears ungodly to me."

"Not so, madam," the publisher replied. "We must believe that God guided Mr. Morse in his invention of this wonderful instrument. We mere mortals are, after all, only tools of the Almighty."

She contemplated Schimmel's contention. "God don't hold with this kinda nonsense." And she pushed her way through the crowd.

II

CHARLES Dewey II was envious of his cousin Albert. For Albert, who had already had the grand adventure of serving in the Mexican War, now was going to another adventure as the master of the family's second horse farm: Bon Marché Lexington.

Spring was just arriving and Alma May had an excuse for a lavish party, one designed as a farewell for Albert, Virginia, and their four children. They were to leave in a few days for Kentucky and a new life.

Two and Albert stood together, sipping champagne, watching the dancers in the spacious double parlor which had been stripped of its normal furnishings to make way for the several hundred Nashvillians who had been invited to the gala.

Albert laughed, nodding toward the crowd. "The Princess is in her glory at something like this."

"I've never known anyone," Charles added, "who seems to enjoy life more."

"I'd say our aunt squeezes every bit of juice out of the fruit of life."

"My God! My cousin waxes poetic."

"To the contrary," Albert said with some embarrassment. "I have to confess that I read that somewhere."

"Nevertheless, it's apropos. That fellow she's dancing with now," Two asked, "is he known to you?"

"Not to anyone, apparently. Oh, I know his name is . . . ah . . . ah . . . Wheeler—I believe that's it—and that he's some kind of drummer. But where the Princess met him, or how, no one seems to know. But . . . there he is."

"To the consternation of Willie Carstairs, I'll bet."

"No doubt." Grinning, Albert nudged Charles, indicating the lone figure of Carstairs leaning against the wall, sullenly watching Alma May and the stranger gaily whirling to the sound of the music.

"Poor Willie," Two said. "It must be difficult to be in love with the Princess."

"I suppose." Albert was suddenly sober-faced. "Yet with her, at least, you must know your love isn't going to be rejected."

Charles glanced at him questioningly. They were not only close as cousins, they were also brothers-in-law, Albert being married to Virginia Stoker, and Charles to Virginia's younger sister, Beth.

"This move to Kentucky," Charles asked carefully, wondering whether something was amiss with Albert's marriage, "does it please Virginia?"

"Of course. Without Virginia's help with our stiff-necked father-in-law there would have been no money—" He paused. "You know that I've invested seventy-five thousand in this Kentucky venture? Or should I say Virginia has invested it with the acquiescence of her father?"

"So I've heard."

"I intend to work very hard to return that investment as soon as possible. I don't want to spend the rest of my life answering to Brian Stoker, or to any doubts Virginia may have about my abilities."

Once again, Two was concerned about the bitterness evident in Albert's words. "Well, certainly that's not a problem I'll ever have—answering to Stoker, that is. He barely speaks to Beth or to me. We're still paying for our youthful indiscretions."

"He hasn't accepted Charles Three yet?"

"No. But, then, neither has my own father. Poor little lad. He'll never know the love of grandparents."

Uncharacteristically, Albert put his arm around his cousin's shoulders. "You'll find, Two, that you'll survive. At the risk of sounding like a much older man, I'll tell you there'll be other disappointments in your life and you'll learn to live with them." He squeezed the arm tight. "The Deweys, after all, are a sturdy stock."

Beth Dewey came up to them, smiling sweetly. "I've given you two young gentlemen enough time to solve the ills of the world. Now, if I may, Albert, I'd like to borrow my husband for a little dancing. It is a party, you know."

She pulled at Two's arm, guiding him into the flow of dancers.

"Serious talk?" she asked.

"Yes and no." He frowned. "Are Virginia and Albert having problems?"

"Why do you ask?"

"Just a kind of undercurrent in Albert's words. A suggestion of trouble."

Beth pulled him closer to her, whispering in his ear. "Virginia is having . . . uh . . . having difficulties adapting to Albert's return."

"But that was *months* ago."

"I know," his wife sighed, "but she's been unable . . . well, unable to satisfy him."

"She spoke to *you* of this?" He knew the sisters weren't close.

"Uh-huh. In desperation, I think, having no one else to take into her confidence. On the evening of his return things didn't go well. Virginia was . . . shy, it seems."

"Shy?" Two had to swallow a laugh.

"I was trying to be discreet. Anyway, it has been tense with them ever since."

"That explains it."

"Explains what?"

"In speaking of Aunt Alma's apparent latest conquest"—he nodded his head toward the Princess who was still dancing with the stranger—"Albert said something like, at least with Alma May a man knows he's not going to be rejected."

"My sister is such a damned fool!"

"She's fortunate she has good, solid Albert as a husband."

"I'd certainly never give you the opportunities she's giving Albert."

"You mean, you think I'd . . . *stray* under similar circumstances?"

"Wouldn't you, Two?"

"This is much too profound a conversation to be having while dancing."

"You haven't answered me."

Two smiled at her. "I haven't answered you because that's not a problem we have." His voice took on an intimate tone. "Remember the first time we were together?"

"Even if I wanted to forget it," Beth replied easily, "I'd always have little Charles before me as a reminder."

They both laughed heartily.

Albert, witnessing their levity, envied his cousin.

Two young Deweys, each envying the other. For totally different reasons.

III

"I SWEAR to you," Able Jackson was saying, chuckling in the midst of a dishearteningly somber discussion, "I'm beginning to see some merit in the slaves' talk of a curse."

August Schimmel chuckled with him.

But not True Jackson. "Our reverses," he said angrily, "are not a subject for humor!"

April had lengthened into May, May into June, June into July. The racing season was fully under way in Nashville and the fortunes of Bon Marché were in steady decline. Twenty-three horses had started without a win. It was the principal topic at the late-night sherry session in the mansion's drawing room.

Schimmel tried to placate his concerned son-in-law. "True, you've been in horse racing long enough to expect some reverses occasionally. It's the nature of the beast, isn't it?"

"Of course it is," True snapped. "But our losses here are being magnified by the further drain on our resources of that experiment we've begun in Kentucky. We're stretched much too thin to suit me."

"Oh? Young Albert isn't doing well in Lexington?" Schimmel asked.

"I don't mean to imply that. He seems to be organizing Bon Marché Lexington in an able manner. But the truth of it is, we can't expect to see any money from Kentucky for the first year or two. It's all going out, with nothing coming in. While we anticipated that, we didn't anticipate we'd not be able to win with the Bon Marché horses in this area."

"The fall yearling sales ought to bring in some cash," August suggested.

True groaned. "That's just it—we're going to have to forgo the fall sales. Albert is going to need some stock from here, and Able"—he nodded toward his brother—"is going to need some additional blood for the breeding shed. It's better now that we keep what we've got."

A silence fell among the three men, who concentrated on their glasses of sherry. There were times in those discussions when the quiet periods were just as important as the flow of words. This was one of them.

Eventually, Schimmel spoke again. "Some more positive news, gentlemen. We're beginning to hear a great deal of excitement from the west. In the past week or so we've received dispatches about major gold strikes. One at a place called Sutter's Mill on the American River in northern California has stirred the adventurers."

"Adventurers!" True grunted derisively. "That kind of thing isn't going to help us."

"Perhaps not directly," August said, "but the opening of the Pacific west, now that we've acquired it through the Mexican War treaty, is going to have a great impact on our entire nation."

"Maybe," True replied.

"No, sir, not *maybe*. I submit to you that there is a parallel with what is happening in the far west and what took place here in Tennessee, when Charles Dewey came to this 'west' to seek his fortune." Schimmel's voice rose with his enthusiasm. "True, there'll come a time when you will look to the opportunities offered in California."

"Good Lord, August, don't we have enough expansion with our Kentucky matter?"

"Mark my words, gentlemen, you've only just begun your growing."

"And with growth comes what?" True asked testily. "We'll

have nothing but power-grabbing and dissension. It seems I can't read an issue of your newspaper, August, without seeing some kind of declaration, pro or con, about the expansion of slavery. God, I wish the rabble-rousers would keep their mouths shut on that subject! Those who talk the loudest know the least about it. And everyone, it appears, freely talks of *fighting* to secure the aims of their point of view."

"Speaking of that," Able interjected, "I've been approached by several of Nashville's leading citizens concerning the possibility of organizing a company of militia—"

"The ultimate madness!" his brother interrupted.

"I think not, True. There may come a time, if I read the tempers correctly, when militia will be needed to defend our . . . well, our way of life."

Exasperated, True turned to Schimmel. "Will you tell this fool that nothing good comes from a resort to arms?"

The newspaper publisher thought for a moment. "Ordinarily, I'd agree with you. Yet there are numerous examples in history to suggest there are times when a ready militia has some merit."

True was on his feet, his face flushed. "I've heard enough for one night! I hope the morning will bring some sense to both of you. Now, if you'll excuse me, I'm going to bed, hoping all your wild speculations won't keep me from getting a night's sleep." He stomped from the room.

"Sometimes True can be quite intractable," Able commented.

"Hmmm." Schimmel drained his glass. "Don't be too harsh on your brother. He's a man of great strength and when that strength is needed True Jackson will come to the mark." A pause. "Are you seriously considering association with this militia effort?"

"I was until this little discussion." He smiled wryly. "Now, I'm certain True won't hear of any Bon Marché investment in it."

"If it's money you need, I might have some available."

"You mean that?"

"Yes, and I don't know why." Schimmel's face was sad. "I would hope that militia won't ever be needed. But it might, God help us, be necessary . . . just to keep us whole."

IV

"FATHER, I need to talk to you," George Dewey Jr. said, his embarrassment evident as he stood before the elder Dewey, who was seated at a table in the Metairie clubhouse with Marguerite Cappevielle.

"Fine, this is as good a time as any. Sit down, son."

"It's confidential, sir."

"I have no secrets from Marguerite."

Young Dewey nodded. "Well, Father, some other time then." He walked away.

George sighed. "Will you excuse me, dear?"

"Of course."

Leaving the table, George hurried after his son, catching up with him and grabbing his arm. "You were rude, you know."

Junior frowned. "I suppose it's because I'm not in the habit of discussing family business with my father's mistress."

George gritted his teeth, fighting against his rising anger. "And I'm not in the habit of allowing *you* to run my life. Now . . . what is it you wanted?"

"What I wanted is to try to find out what the hell you've been doing with our horses." His own anger was on the surface. "You sold partnerships to Bernard de Mandeville and I could understand that, in light of your long friendship with him. But now I find out that I've been training horses, in other partnerships, for Turner and Martinez and Wells and Chinn. Even Ten Broeck, for Christ's sake!"

"Those are perfectly legitimate business dealings. I told you once and now I'll tell you again—I am merely spreading our risks."

"Our risks!" Junior winced. "You must think I'm stupid. You're giving away half our income. What risks are those bastards assuming? I've been winning, haven't I?"

"Yes, and that's fortunate," his father said. "But you know as well as I do that luck can run out."

"Luck has very little to do with a successfully run stable."

"You're naive, son."

"I suppose I am," Junior said. "Or I *was*. But not any longer, Father. You need the cash to support that whore, and you're perfectly willing to ruin our estate—"

"It's nothing like that at all," George insisted heatedly.

"No? Then why sell your interest in Metairie? And why mortgage Nouveau Marché? More risk-spreading, is it?"

Dewey was shocked that his son had learned of his dealings, but he tried to maintain an outward calm. "Just business, Junior. And none of it yours, I might add. You forget, young man, that *I'm* the master of Nouveau Marché, and not you. And, until you are, I suggest you stay out of all this!"

Junior glared at him momentarily, shrugged, and left his father standing there.

For an instant, George thought of going after him, of trying to apologize for his outburst. But he didn't.

As he approached the table where he had left Marguerite he saw Richard Oubre there, seated close to her, holding her hands, engaged in an intense conversation. He stood watching them for a moment, looking for any sign that Marguerite objected to Oubre's presence. She seemed not to.

His gut knotted. The doubt he had never been able to shake about Marguerite and Oubre now overwhelmed him. His temper, already irritated by the confrontation with Junior, exploded. He rushed up to them.

"See here, Oubre," he shouted, "I'll thank you to leave Mademoiselle Cappevielle alone!"

Surprised by the sudden appearance of George, Oubre jumped to his feet, knocking over his chair as he did. There was a look of disdain on his handsome face. "And if I don't, Dewey?"

"I'll see to it you're thrashed!"

Oubre's loud laughter drew the full attention of the others at tables nearby; most had already been eavesdropping on the unfolding drama.

"George, please don't—" Marguerite said.

"And *you*"—Dewey snarled—"you shut up!"

"Old man," Oubre said with ridicule, "you're nothing but an empty tub, making a lot of booming noise, but with nothing inside you. Is it *you* who's going to thrash me?"

"If need be!"

"George," Marguerite pleaded with him, "don't be goaded by him."

"Take her advice, old man," Oubre grinned, "or you won't have enough energy left to service your little filly."

Dewey smashed a fist into his face, knocking the younger man sprawling against an adjoining table, sending dishes and glasses smashing to the floor. Several women screamed. Very slowly Oubre pulled himself to his feet, making an act of brushing off his clothing. A hand went to a stinging lip; the fingers came away bloody.

"Sir," he said, loudly so that all might hear, "I am left with no choice but to demand satisfaction. If, indeed, you are gentleman enough to—"

George cut him off. "Name the time and place, sir!"

"Someone will be in touch with you." Oubre strode away, dabbing at his cut lip with a silk handkerchief.

"You've made a terrible mistake, George," Marguerite said, her voice quavering, as he sat down at the table with her.

Dewey stared into her wide violet eyes, sucking in deep breaths as he sought to control his anger. Finally: "My mistake, it seems, was in trusting you."

She leaned close to him, touching his hand. "George," she whispered to him, "I made no objection to Richard coming to the table because I didn't want a scene—"

"And I'm supposed to believe that?" He was forcing the words through his teeth.

"Yes, George, you are."

There was a silence as he continued to stare at her, as if trying to get inside her head. To tap her brain for the truth.

"George, whatever you may believe now, I beg you—don't accept his challenge. Send him an apology."

He shook his head negatively.

"He means to kill you." Marguerite's voice was now steady, without emotion.

Dewey affected a smile. "If so, I die for good reason."

In just those few moments, those scant, tortured seconds, he had sorted it all out in his mind.

Marguerite had betrayed him with Oubre!

Faced with that conclusion, living or dying was of little consequence. He just didn't give a damn.

V

"August, I *must* go back to New Orleans," Louise was saying excitedly, waving the telegram she had received from Mary Dewey.

"No, I won't allow it," her husband said with determination.

"But it's *family,* August!"

"And it's George's family who ought to deal with it."

"Yes, but—"

"I'll make arrangements," Schimmel told her, "for Two to make the trip. It's his father, after all, who has got himself in this dueling mess."

Louise began to cry. "Oh, God, George has become such an utter fool. And poor Mary—"

Schimmel took her hands. "Darling, I'll do anything I can to help, but I insist that you not go. Perhaps a little money spread around in the right circles on the docks will get us a packet boat which will be able to cut a few days off the trip."

"Wouldn't it be faster to go overland?"

"I don't see how. For Two to ride, we'd have to arrange for relief horses—" He shrugged, indicating the impracticability of such a plan. "No, the boat, if I can charter one, would be the answer."

His wife sighed. "I suppose you're right. I'll wire Mary that Two's on the way. That might give her some hope."

"And don't forget," Schimmel added, "Junior is there with her. And Statler, too. And he has the resources of the newspaper if it's of some value to him."

On Chartres Street at that hour, Mary Dewey was tearfully arguing with George Junior. "What you want to do amounts to abandonment of your father!"

"My father has abandoned *us*—don't you understand that? And I'm not going to find myself and my family ruined because of his insanity."

Mary's weeping had silenced her.

"Mother, listen to me," Junior said quietly, but with resolve, "we're going to be inundated with creditors when Father is killed—"

"Junior!" Mary screamed.

"I'm sorry, Mother, but this is not a time to deny fact. Richard Oubre is an experienced duelist. He's younger than Father; he's a better shot, he's quicker." A slight pause. "And when . . . . when it's over, the creditors are going to take everything we have. Everything! Farm, horses, town house . . . *everything,* Mother."

"Can't you stop him?"

"I'm not so sure I want to."

Mary's tear-stained face showed her shock.

"Anyway, Statler is out now trying to stop him," Junior went on, regretting the hurt he was bringing to his mother with his words. "But Father isn't going to be deterred. He's lost all reason over that . . . whore." He got to his feet. "In the meantime, Mother, I'm going to do what I have to do."

VI

JUNIOR'S brother stopped his carriage in front of the Prytaneum Walk house, hurrying to the door and banging with the knocker. The black servant, Angel, responded.

"I'm Statler Dewey," he announced. "I must see my father immediately."

"Mastah Dewey ain't here," the maid replied, "but Miss Marguerite's to home."

"Then I'll see her." Statler pushed his way into the house.

Angel scurried away. It was only a moment or two before Mademoiselle Cappevielle appeared in the foyer. Statler had never seen her before; even under the strained circumstances he found her startlingly beautiful. There was even a thought about understanding how his father might have been captivated by her.

"May I help you, Monsieur Dewey?" she asked in her sensuous voice.

"My father—do you know where he is?"

"I have no idea."

Statler didn't believe her. "Damn it, woman, I have to stop him from this foolishness! Now, *where* is he?"

"I appreciate that you're upset, monsieur, but I don't know where he is."

The son let out a long breath, wondering how she could appear so calm. "Do you approve of this duel?"

"No."

"Then why don't *you* stop him?"

"I can't."

"Or won't!" he said accusingly.

"I can't," Marguerite repeated. "I've already tried, monsieur." The reply was strangely lacking in emotion.

"Don't you know that Oubre will kill him?"

"Yes."

"Yes! Is that all you can say? Doesn't the prospect of his dying . . . *reach* you in some way?"

"I shall miss him."

Statler glared at her. "You're a cold bitch!"

"Monsieur, what do you know of me?" she replied. "Do you see me as beautiful?"

"Yes, of course—"

"Do you recognize that I'm well educated?"

"Mademoiselle, I don't see what this—"

She cut him off. "Or do you see me as a whore?" For the first time there was a hint of emotion.

Statler hesitated.

"You have no idea what it's like to live in *this* skin! From the time I was only fourteen, to this present day, the people of *society*"—she spat the word—"have seen me as only one thing—a woman with a few drops of Negro blood running in her veins. And because I was also more than passably attractive, they would allow me to be cast in only one role. There are many euphemisms for that role; you may choose your own. But if I am a 'cold bitch,' as you say, it's only because the good people of New Orleans have made me that way."

Statler found himself intimidated by her candor. "Uh . . . I meant no disrespect—"

"Of course you did! Why should an octoroon whore have any respect in your life? Especially one who has caused your father to leave his family and act the public fool. Well, I didn't entice George Dewey. He sought me out. And he's been kind. Yes . . . that's the proper way to put it: he's been kind."

"Do you love him?"

She thought for a brief moment. "I have repaid his kindness."

"Only that?"

"Only that, Monsieur Dewey." The reply was softly spoken. Perhaps sadly.

"Isn't there *any* way you can dissuade him from this foolish dueling?"

"No. Your father . . . and Richard Oubre . . . must finish out their attempt at what they call 'honor.' They make believe they're fighting over me." She laughed. "What dishonesty! They'll shoot at each other because Richard is cruel, and your father because he wants to die."

Young Dewey gasped. "He *wants* to die?"

"Didn't you know that?" she asked, once more emotionless. "I don't pretend to understand everything that goes on in his mind, but I know that life has lost its meaning for him. Why? I'm not sure. Perhaps there was a betrayal in his family—"

Statler thought of the dispute over the Bon Marché ownership.

"—and now, to add to his despair, he believes that I have betrayed him, too." She raised a hand to stop Statler's question.

"Whatever bedevils George," Marguerite went on, "he wants to drive out those demons by dying. It's as simple as that. And if he faces Richard on the dueling field, he *will* die."

"Yes," Statler sighed.

She drew herself up, thrusting out her breasts, smoothing out her gown nervously. "Now, if you'll excuse me, Monsieur Dewey, I have to finish packing."

"You're leaving here?"

"Unlike George, my motivation is to survive."

"With another . . . lover?" he asked bitterly.

Marguerite Cappevielle shrugged her shoulders. "Survival, I've learned, has its own dictates."

10

THERE was a certain madness in the air.

If George Dewey Jr. had ever contemplated what might be the worst time of his life, he would never have imagined what had transpired in the past few days. And if he had permitted his mind to question his actions he surely would have wept.

Three days earlier he had come close to weeping.

Then, under gloomy, rain-laden clouds reflecting the mood of the day, he had bid farewell to his wife, Emma, and their two small sons. He had seen them drive away from the plantation in a carriage, under the care of overseer Will Stabler and a black housemaid.

They were heading west to Baton Rouge, and then would turn northward with dead aim on the river port city of Natchez, Mississippi. Stabler carried five thousand dollars with him, nearly all of Dewey's available cash. But enough, Junior believed, to accomplish what he meant to do. Perhaps it would have been more convenient to do it at Baton Rouge, but young Dewey wanted to be clear of the state of Louisiana before he carried out the second part of his audacious plan. He also considered that there would be fewer questions asked in Natchez, a freewheeling city noted for its tolerance of shady dealings. Dewey understood that honorable men, if such actually existed, would not do what he was doing.

Two days earlier, forty-seven of the slave farmhands, each leading a thoroughbred horse, had filed out of the Nouveau Marché plantation, following the same route set for the carriage. And one day earlier, a van carrying four blooded stallions, representing the soul of Nouveau Marché, had also left.

"Hurry!" Dewey shouted now to his remaining blacks, "I want to move out within the hour!"

Nouveau Marché, under Junior's management, had always been a calm, happy, reasoned place. But no longer. It was the scene of feverish activity: open farm wagons were drawn up in a line and household furnishings, clothing, tools, tack, farm supplies, and food were being piled into them.

It was a Thursday and his plan, undertaken in desperation, required haste. Should his father die in the duel set for Saturday, Junior wanted to leave nothing behind for the inevitable pack of creditors. His ultimate goal was to reach Nashville with all of the movable assets of Nouveau Marché intact.

The creditors be damned!

"Is everything loaded?" he called out.

"Yassuh." The reply came from several quarters.

"Then hitch up the dray horses and let's get moving!"

Enoch, a burly black man he had known all his life, ambled to his side. "It ain't easy to leave, Mastah George."

"No, it's not."

"Seems a shame t' leave all this . . . fer the vultures."

"Hmmm."

"'Scuse, Mastah George," the slave said hesitantly, "but do ya wannah put a torch t' it?"

Young Dewey's eyes took in the whole of Nouveau Marché: the handsome mansion his father had built, the array of neat horse barns, the fenced and carefully tended fields.

Torch it? An evil thought, but one in keeping with what I'm doing. Those bastard creditors, who took advantage of the weaknesses of Father, would deserve to find nothing more than ashes.

But he shook his head from side to side. "No, no," he said quietly. "We'll just leave it, Enoch, and remember how happy we were here."

"Yassuh."

"Have everyone move out."

"Yassuh."

Junior mounted his horse, turning it slowly in tight circles, surveying Nouveau Marché for the final time. He permitted a few tears to dampen his cheeks, but the rest of his emotions were held in check.

Without another word, he rode to the head of the line of

wagons, waving his arm to start them forward. The pain in him told him to scream in anguish. He didn't. He was a Dewey and the Deweys had the strength of pride.

II

IN the darkness two hours before dawn, the small lugger, its oddly shaped, four-sided sails catching the breeze, eased into the wide, mud-brown Mississippi, propelled away from New Orleans by the combined impetus of the wind and the inexorable current. Downriver it moved slowly; its destination was the Bayou Barataria.

There were five passengers: a Cajun fisherman on the sails, another at the rudder, and three *gentlemen*—sullen-faced George Washington Dewey Sr., his distraught son Statler, and the only man aboard who seemed to be enjoying himself, Bernard Xavier de Marigny de Mandeville. It was not a comfortable craft, being utilitarian only. They were crowded together in the tiny boat, and nearly overwhelmed by the persistent odor of rotting fish.

It would be an hour, perhaps longer, before they would reach their destination, and Statler Dewey was determined to use that time to try again to dissuade his father from his deadly adventure.

"Father, what good purpose will be served by this duel?" he demanded.

The elder Dewey sighed. "When you think about it," he replied softly, "what good purpose is there in life?"

Exasperated, Statler turned to the Frenchman. "Bernard, as I understand the ridiculous Code Duello, isn't it the duty of the seconds to try to negotiate a settlement before a duel?"

"Oui." There was a slow Gallic shrug. "And I have tried, but both parties insist on upholding their honor."

"Honor!" He laughed derisively at the absurdity of it all. "What honor is there in one man killing another over a . . . a . . . colored whore?"

"How dare you say that of Marguerite?" his father snarled.

"I dare say anything that will stop this idiocy!"

There was a small silence. When George broke it, the others had to strain to hear his words. "You know nothing of the joy she brought to me. That woman . . . for a short time at least . . . gave meaning to my life. And without her—"

"She's going to stand by your side this morning?" the son interrupted.

"I've forbidden her to come."

Statler's sarcasm was cutting. "Forbidden her to come! How can you even suggest that she would have? Do you know that she's already moving out of that house you bought for her? That she's more concerned with her own survival than with what might happen to you? That she's even now seeking another paramour to support her?"

"Shut your foul mouth!"

Again, the son turned to de Mandeville. "For God's sake, talk some sense to him, Bernard!"

De Mandeville's only reply was another shrug.

Statler lapsed into silence, running through his mind what he would do when they got to the dueling ground. *Perhaps Richard Oubre will listen to reason. Maybe money will buy him off. Failing that—?* The younger Dewey plotted his course of action.

Wind and current carried them along the western edge of the river. On the shore they could see only the black, eerie shapes of the dwarf oaks and cypress and palmetto trees that pushed out of the swamp. There were the occasional cries of night birds and the gentle swish of water under the flat bottom of the lugger.

Suddenly, from de Mandeville: "There! A light!"

All eyes turned to see a lantern hung on a cypress, feebly lighting the way into a watery channel of the bayou.

"Couldn't you have selected a more remote location?" Statler asked caustically.

"Ah, monsieur," the Frenchman replied, "a duel, unhappily, can no longer be a public event. Here we need have no fear that the New Orleans authorities will interfere. Indeed, it was here in Barataria that Pierre and Jean Lafitte operated with . . . impunity, shall we say?"

"Well, I guess it makes some kind of perverse sense to bring this madness to a pirate's hangout. But tell me, Bernard, what good is all this so-called test of honor if no one witnesses it?"

"But *we* shall witness it, young sir," de Mandeville answered. "And so will Monsieur Oubre's party. Honor doesn't need a crowd."

Statler muttered an epithet. "You have an answer for everything, don't you? But don't you see how utterly stupid all of this is? This artificial code of dueling is a sham, Bernard. It's a set of rules to cover the cruel actions of fools!"

"Someone has written—I can't recall who it was, but he was French—that 'an infinity of wise things are conducted in a very foolish manner, so there are some foolish things conducted in a very wise manner.'"

"And the latter characterizes dueling?"

"You could say that."

The lugger pushed through a growth of water hyacinth. There was a slap on the coffee-colored water, indicating the flight of an alligator from the intruders. And then the bottom of the boat scraped against something solid, coming to a slow stop.

"Our journey is ended," de Mandeville announced. He shouted into the darkness: "Hello!"

A lantern showed, being waved back and forth as it came closer. Statler could make out the form of a young man as he approached the lugger. "De Mandeville?" he called out.

"*Oui.*"

"Come ashore."

The lantern was held high to light a path through the swamp foliage, as de Mandeville leaped nimbly from the boat, offering a hand to help George Dewey to the shore. Statler followed, his shoes squishing in the swampy soil. The two Cajun fishermen pulled their lugger higher on the land, falling into single file with the others.

They walked perhaps two hundred yards before coming into a clearing ringed with cypress dripping moss, where five or six additional lanterns lighted a group of three men—one white, the other two black.

De Mandeville made the introductions. The man who had met them with the lantern was Ronald Oubre, younger brother and second to the aggrieved party in the duel. The other white man, of course, was Richard Oubre himself.

"May I speak to Mr. Oubre?" Statler asked.

"But of course."

Statler went to the shipping heir, guiding him away from the others. "Mr. Oubre, I'd be a poor son if I didn't make an effort to stop this duel. Is there any way to influence a decision against it?"

Oubre scowled. "I was publicly humiliated when your father struck me at the Metairie clubhouse."

"Oh, come now, Oubre—was it really that serious?"

"It was, sir."

"But it was an argument over a . . . a—"

"You mean to say 'whore,' Mr. Dewey?"

"Yes," Statler admitted.

Oubre smiled for the first time. "Marguerite's obvious talents are not the issue here. What is at issue is simple enough: your father attacked me without provocation. In public. I had no choice, Dewey, but to demand satisfaction."

"And you'll get satisfaction by killing my father?"

"I will, Mr. Dewey. I certainly will."

"Would money dissuade you, Mr. Oubre?"

The smile grew broader. "How much?"

"Ten thousand dollars."

Oubre guffawed. "I wager that much on the turn of a card."

"Twenty thousand."

"You have a lot to learn, Mr. Dewey. Honor cannot be bought."

"Except with blood."

"If you wish to see it that way." Oubre started to walk away. "We have had our little talk." He looked up through the trees. "Dawn is upon us."

A soft light was beginning to filter through the thick foliage as Oubre returned to the center of the clearing, standing face-to-face with George Dewey. Ronald Oubre opened a case in which two large-bore dueling pistols lay on royal blue velvet, offering it to the elder Dewey to make a choice. George simply pointed to one of them, and de Mandeville took it from the case, hefting it to test the balance. Richard Oubre took the other weapon.

The seconds—Ronald Oubre and Bernard de Mandeville—went through the ritual of loading the pistols, and then de Mandeville took a coin from his pocket. "Your choice, sir," he said to Ronald as he spun the silver piece into the air.

"Heads."

The coin landed on the turf. Both seconds bent over to look at it. "Tails," the Frenchman said. "I shall instruct the duelists."

He placed a stone at one end of the clearing and quickly paced off twenty strides, marking the end of his walk with another stone. "Gentlemen, take your places, please."

George Dewey went to the stone at the western end of the clearing, facing the sun. That appalled Statler; his father had chosen the least advantageous position. Richard Oubre walked with determination to the stone at the eastern end. Both men carried their guns with the muzzles facing the ground. Statler noted that Oubre was left-handed.

"Gentlemen, please pay attention," de Mandeville commanded. "I shall say 'fire,' and then will count to three. At 'three' you may raise your weapons and fire at will. Is that understood?"

"Understood," Oubre said firmly.

George simply nodded.

As de Mandeville backed off to begin his count, Statler strode forward to put his body squarely between the two duelists. "I will *not* permit this to happen!" he said purposefully. Everyone stared at him in disbelief.

"Monsieur Dewey," de Mandeville said, "you are interfering with a matter of honor."

Statler folded his arms, staying his ground.

There was the sharp click of a pistol being cocked. "Monsieur, I suggest that you move now"—de Mandeville leveled a gun at the young man—"or I shall be forced to shoot you down."

"You wouldn't dare!"

"Ah . . . but I would." He grinned as he aimed carefully at Statler's head. "And without compunction, monsieur."

Statler's arms fell by his side. After a moment of tortured indecision, he slowly stepped backward, out of the line of fire.

"Gentlemen, hear me," de Mandeville instructed. "Fire! One . . . two . . . three!"

Oubre's left hand came up quickly. He squeezed the trigger.

The reverberating sound of the shot panicked birds from the trees and the clearing was alive with their voices.

George Dewey, who had never raised his gun at all, staggered backward as the heavy ball smashed into his chest, a deep red stain seeping quickly through his coat. After a second or two, he collapsed in a heap.

For just an instant, everyone was frozen where they stood. Statler moved first, rushing to his father, dropping to his knees, feeling for a pulse. Oubre's shot had been true. Gently, the son closed the elder Dewey's staring eyes.

Statler looked up at de Mandeville standing over him. "Has honor been served now?" he asked bitterly.

"It has."

"And you, Oubre," Statler screamed in his agony, "has your honor been—?"

Only then did he realize the Oubre party had vanished into the dense bayou. He was left with nothing but his grief. As he wept over the dead man it came to his mind that his father had said not a single word there in the clearing. He had been mute in facing his death. Mute and deliberately inactive; George Dewey Sr. had never intended to use his weapon.

Marguerite Cappevielle's words came back to him: "Whatever bedevils George, he wants to drive out those demons by dying."

De Mandeville directed the Cajun fisherman to carry George's body to the lugger. And he reached down to help the distraught son to his feet.

Statler fought to stem his tears. "Tell me, Bernard, would you really have shot me down?"

"Ah, my young friend, so that you are not wracked with that doubt for the rest of your life, I can assure you that I would have."

"And it wouldn't have bothered you?"

"Not in the slightest, monsieur."

Statler felt nauseous. "All in the name of preserving the rites of honor, I suppose?"

"Exactement."

III

On the afternoon of his father's death, unknown to him as fact but perceived to be a reality, George Dewey Jr.'s odd caravan of horses, wagons, and slaves crossed the Louisiana border into southern Mississippi.

By relentlessly pushing forward with his wagon train, Junior had linked up with the two other elements of his escaping entourage: the van carrying the four stallions and the blacks leading the bulk of the Nouveau Marché thoroughbreds.

It was nearly four o'clock when he called a halt outside a small village just a mile or two over the border.

"We'll stay the night here," he told the elderly slave Enoch. "Have the women prepare a meal. As substantial a one as they can. Tomorrow, we'll try to reach Natchez."

"Yassuh."

Junior sank wearily to the ground, stretching out the muscles of his body, gazing up at the clear blue sky. And thinking of Emma and his sons, safe now, he believed, in Natchez, awaiting his arrival.

Had his father been killed in the duel? Perhaps Statler had found a way to intercede and have it called off. Junior hoped for that. But whether or not there had been a duel didn't change what he had to do. Had he stayed at Nouveau Marché his father's creditors would have taken everything. Eventually, all of Nouveau Marché would have fallen into other hands: the property, the horses, the slaves.

This way, at least, I'm saving something.

His rambling thoughts conjured up a picture of his mother. She had always been such a gay, full-of-life woman, appreciative of the many good things that came her way. Maybe a bit vain and, at times, inclined to spend money foolishly, but she was a *good* woman, a good mother. The past year of his father's irrational behavior, though, had turned her old, had made her bitter. Junior wanted to understand his father's actions, but he couldn't. They made no sense to him at all.

Enoch stood over him. "Mastah George, there's food now. Ham an' some greens."

"Good, good." He pulled himself to his feet, his muscles aching. Walking to the circle of slaves gathered around a hastily built fire, he accepted a plate of food.

He made an announcement. "We're some thirty miles from Natchez, and, if all goes well, we'll be there before sundown tomorrow." He paused. "I know that some of you don't really understand what's going on, but what we are doing is necessary."

He looked around at the sober black faces. "I'd like to offer a prayer." He gazed heavenward, beginning hesitantly: "Dear God . . . protect this band of . . . souls as we leave behind an old life and move to the beginning of a new one. And keep us safe in Thy glory. Amen."

There was dead silence in the circle. The faces stared at him. So much had happened. So swiftly. And now this. Never before had they been privy to a prayer by the master of Nouveau Marché. It was bewildering.

IV

THERE were no tears from Mary Dewey. She sat stiffly on the divan in the drawing room of the Chartres Street town house listening to her son Statler give his report on the duel in the Bayou Barataria.

"I don't believe there was any pain, Mother," he said. "He was killed instantly."

She nodded understanding. "And where is he now?"

"We've taken his body to the mortuary."

"And was that . . . was Mademoiselle Cappevielle with him when he died?"

"No, Mother."

"So much for love," she said sardonically.

A silence fell in the room. Four people were there: Mary, Statler, another son, Charles Dewey II, who had rushed from Nashville but had arrived too late, and Bernard de Mandeville.

It was the Frenchman who spoke finally. "Madame Dewey, I want to express my sincere sympathy in your time of grief. I want you to know that if there had been any other way, I would have made every effort to guide George in that direction. Unfortunately—" He shrugged.

"And with that little speech, Bernard," the widow said softly, "you expect to be absolved of all blame in this matter."

"Madame, had it been in my power—"

She cut him off sharply. "It was your evil influence, de Mandeville, that turned my husband into—" She stopped. "But what's the use—he's dead now, isn't he?"

"George was my friend," the Frenchman said defensively.

"So I thought." A small smile came to her face. "Bernard,

I recall defending you at one time when Georgie characterized you as a pompous ass. I didn't realize then how correct he was. Or how far off the mark he was."

De Mandeville contemplated a reply, but thought better of it. He made a small bow. "Madame . . . if I may be excused." He started to leave the room. At the doorway, he said, "Statler, may I have a word with you?"

Young Dewey joined him in the hallway.

"Your mother is upset, of course," de Mandeville said unctuously.

Statler made no comment.

"There's a small matter of which you should be aware, Statler. Your father left behind . . . uh . . . some obligations . . . some debts. And when the estate is settled those obligations will have to be recognized."

"He owed you money?"

"Yes."

"This seems hardly the time to go into that," Statler said heatedly. "The man is not yet in his grave."

"Obviously, I regret the necessity of bringing this subject to your attention, but—"

"How much did he owe you?"

"Well . . . twenty-seven thousand dollars."

"What!"

"Plus, of course, the shares in the horses. I am a fifty-percent owner of several of the Nouveau Marché horses. Seven of them, to be precise. But your brother George Junior knows of that."

Statler stared at him in disbelief. "Father never would have sold partnerships in the horses."

"Regretfully, he did. And not just to me. There are several other gentlemen in New Orleans who advanced him money in exchange for shares in horses."

The son let out a deep breath. "How deeply does this go, Bernard?"

"Mademoiselle Cappevielle was an expensive diversion."

"How deep, damn it!"

"To the best of my knowledge, he also took mortgages on his properties"—a sweeping gesture of the hand—"this town house and Nouveau Marché itself."

Statler groaned.

"I regret that I'm the one to bring you this news, but I do hope that my claims will be given proper priority . . . when you have the time to settle the estate, of course."

"If what you say is true—"

"It's true."

"—then you may have a long wait for your money."

De Mandeville smiled. "I would guess that the remaining assets of Nouveau Marché will cover it all."

"Leaving his widow with nothing!"

"Ah, but she has her family, doesn't she?"

Statler made for the street door, jerking it open.

The Frenchman strode through the doorway, turning to bow again. "Good day, Monsieur Dewey."

The door was slammed shut.

11

SUNDAY morning in New Orleans was always a lovely time, especially in the affluent quarters of the city where the wealthy, insulated from the poverty and racial deprivations of the majority, could appreciate the melodic harmonies of uncounted church bells. At once deep-throated and soprano-voiced, the message of the bells was one of hope and promise. But in many alleyway hovels they were merely the noise of a God who seemed to prefer those who could fill the collection plates and the poor boxes.

On any other Sunday morning the bells might have been welcome at the fashionable Chartres Street town house of one George Washington Dewey Sr. But on this morning their tolling had a funeral tone, for the master of the house was newly dead, ignominiously cut down in a one-sided duel in which he had chosen not to raise his pistol.

The bells woke the departed Dewey's eldest son, Charles Dewey II, who groaned and stretched in the strange bed, touching the form of his younger brother Statler. It had been years since they had slept side by side. The town house was not their home; in happier times they had grown up together in the luxury of their grandfather's Bon Marché stud in Nashville. And then they had gone off to make their own lives. Now, in grief, they were as one again.

Statler also stirred.

"Mornin'," Charles mumbled.

Statler sat up in the bed. "What a night! I saw it all again, Two, in a most graphic nightmare."

His brother looked at him sympathetically. "You must believe that time will dim those images."

"I hope so."

There was a gentle knock on the bedroom door. It was opened to admit the Negro butler. "Breakfast, gentlemen," he said with the proper formality of his station.

He carried a huge silver tray on which there were two silver pots—one with dark, strong coffee, the other with hot milk. *Café au lait* served in the French manner. There was an array of tiny hot French pastries, and a plate of fresh fruit on a bed of shaved ice: giant strawberries and thin slivers of several kinds of melon. Somewhat ceremoniously, he poured the coffee and milk simultaneously into translucent china cups.

"Is our mother up yet?" Statler asked.

"No, suh. Ah told Naomi to leave her sleep so long as she could."

"That's wise. Thank you, James."

The black man bowed his way out of the room.

Two sipped at the steaming brew. "Perhaps because it's Sunday we may get a day of respite before the . . . sins of our father descend on us in full force."

"Hmmm." Statler bit into a pastry. "But if what de Mandeville told me yesterday is true, I'm afraid we won't have to wait long before we hear from a host of creditors."

"Do you doubt de Mandeville's story?"

His brother shook his head. "No."

"Did you have any warning of what Father was doing?"

"There were hints only, Two. When he took up with that Cappevielle woman, I knew he was spending a lot of money, but—" He shrugged.

"Have you heard anything from Junior?"

A shocked look came to Statler's face. "Oh, Christ—Junior! Stuck out there at Nouveau Marché, he probably hasn't heard of the outcome of the duel. How could I have been so stupid?"

"That makes two stupid Deweys," Two said, quickly taking his share of the blame for the oversight. "We'll have to have James send one of the boys to Nouveau Marché to tell Junior what has happened."

They began to dress hurriedly.

The sounds of the persistent metallic bang of the door knocker came up to them.

"Who the devil would that be?" Statler asked.

"Maybe we were too quick in believing the vultures wouldn't be circling on a Sunday."

They heard the butler coming up the stairs. Two opened the bedroom door.

"A gentleman to see ya, suhs. Mistah John Warminster."

Two looked questioningly at his brother.

"A banker," Statler explained. "President of the Canal and Banking Company."

"And so it begins," Two groaned. He addressed the butler: "Tell Mr. Warminster we'll be with him presently. And James, send a messenger to Mr. George at Nouveau Marché to tell him what has happened."

"Yassuh."

The brothers finished dressing and went down to the drawing room where they found a fat, little man, his hands clasped behind his back, contemplating the portrait of George Dewey Sr. hanging over the fireplace.

"Warminster," Statler said.

The banker turned to face them. "Statler, when I heard last night of your father's . . . uh . . . misfortune, I was, of course, shocked. Uh . . . and grieved. I'm sorry to call on you so early on a Sunday morning, but I wanted to offer my services in any way I could. George was a fine man . . . a fine man, indeed. And, it goes without saying, a dear friend."

"I don't believe you know my brother," Statler said. "May I introduce Charles the Second?"

Warminster came forward to pump Two's hand. "I regret having to meet you under these unhappy circumstances, young man. Nevertheless, I'm pleased to know you. Your father spoke of you often."

Two just stared at him, knowing the banker was lying.

Statler took up the conversation. "We appreciate your condolences, Mr. Warminster, and we shall tell our mother of your concern." The words were meant to dismiss the visitor.

"Yes, well . . . I can understand what a shock this must have been to Mrs. Dewey—" He turned to look again at George's portrait. "If you will indulge me for a moment more—"

Statler nodded.

"Uh . . . were you aware of your father's business dealings?"

"To a degree."

"Then perhaps you know that the Canal and Banking Company, of which your father was a respected director, recently agreed to . . . uh . . . underwrite mortgages on his real property."

The sons said nothing.

"Uh . . . this is most difficult, sirs, but . . . uh . . . necessary under the unique circumstances." He took a deep breath. "The company holds mortgages on this house"—he gestured with a fat hand—"and on the Nouveau Marché plantation."

"To what extent?" Two wanted to know.

"On both properties, a total of one hundred and ten thousand dollars and—"

Statler interrupted forcefully. "We'll deal with that, sir, at the proper time."

"Yes, yes . . . of course. But . . . uh . . . there is the reality, you will appreciate, that in recent months your father had rather lavishly—how shall I put this?—had undertaken a lifestyle in which he expended considerable sums of cash and—"

"And you fear you'll not get yours."

"Please understand my position," Warminster said, taking a handkerchief out of his pocket to wipe a sweating brow. "If the stories of your father's . . . uh . . . excesses . . . are factual, then the company—to protect its business investments—will face the unpleasant duty of having to foreclose on the properties on which the company holds mortgages."

Two was angry. "Were you thinking of doing that this morning, Mr. Warminster?"

"No, no, no . . . please understand that I—"

"Perhaps I should awaken my mother and tell her that she'll have to vacate the premises immediately?"

"Please, sir—" the flustered banker objected. "I was merely trying to acquaint the heirs with the facts . . . uh . . . in the event I might be of some assistance in these troubled times."

"And now you've done that, Mr. Warminster." Two called out: "James!"

The butler entered the drawing room immediately, carrying the visitor's hat. "Yassuh?"

"Our guest is leaving, James," Two said pointedly.

"Yassuh." The hat was handed to Warminster.

"Well . . ." the banker said. "Once more, my condolences." He bowed. "Your servant, sirs." And he followed the black man to the door.

"So," Two said to his brother, "it *has* begun."

Statler exhaled loudly. "One hundred and ten thousand!"

"And only the beginning, I'm afraid," Two added. "Only the beginning."

II

THE young black rode hesitantly toward the Nouveau Marché mansion, gazing around in disbelief. Ever since he had crossed the boundaries of the plantation he was uneasy. There were no horses in the pastures. And no workers in the crop fields. And there was an eerie silence, broken only by the yapping of a hound scampering across the vacant acres in pursuit of a rabbit.

Something was wrong. The boy was frightened.

"Hello!" he called out. There was no answer. As he came up to the steps of the mansion he remained on his horse, his eyes searching for any sign of activity. "Hello!"

Tentatively, he slid out of the saddle, slowly mounting the steps and dropping the knocker on the huge double doors. The sound of it echoed through the empty house.

"Mastah George!" he shouted. "Mastah George, is ya in there?" He got no reply, although he waited several moments for it.

Retreating, he made his way to the brood-mare barn, which was nearest the mansion, to find nothing inside. No horses, no tack, no water buckets, no grooms, nothing in the oat bins. There were only the empty stalls from which the manure had not been mucked.

"Damn!" he said aloud to himself. And then he turned and ran to his horse. He meant to leave this ghostly place as quickly as he could. As he mounted, he heard another rider approaching on the main lane and that frightened him even more. He kicked his animal into a gallop.

"Hey, boy!" The voice was loud and authoritarian. "Hold up there!"

The slave reined to a stop, turning his horse to face the intruder, his heart pounding in his chest.

A white man, dressed in a stylish habit, rode up to him. "Do you work here, boy?"

"No, suh. Ah works at the house on Chartres Street."

"Then what are you doing here?"

"Ah come to deliver a message to Mastah George—that his daddy's dead."

The white man, scowling, lounged back in his saddle. "Is anyone here?"

"No, suh. Not a soul."

"Where are they?" the man demanded.

"Ah don't know, suh. All Ah know is they's gone. Ain't nobody or nothin' here."

"Stay right where you are!"

"Yassuh."

He watched as the white man rode from barn to barn, dismounting at each building to look inside. As the inspection continued it was evident the searcher was becoming more and more angry. Finally, he rode back to the slave.

"Boy!" he shouted at him. "Are you sure you don't know where they've gone?"

"No, suh, Ah surely don't. Thet's gospel, suh."

The man glared at him. "You going back to Chartres Street?"

"Yassuh, Ah gotta tell 'em—"

"Let's go, then!" The white man whirled his horse, spurring him furiously.

The young slave followed in his dusty wake.

III

"DAMN it, Dewey, don't tell me you don't know what's happened out at Nouveau Marché!" Richard Ten Broeck shouted at Statler. "How can you *not* know what your brother has done?"

"I'll thank you, Mr. Ten Broeck, to lower your voice," Statler demanded. "I don't want you upsetting Mother."

"She'll be a damned sight more upset when she learns that

her son has made off with everything at Nouveau Marché. *Everything,* I tell you—horses, equipment, wagons, slaves. There's nothing there!"

"Thet's right, Mastah Statler," the black boy confirmed. "Jest ain't nothin'. Ah think the house's empty, too."

Statler and Two just stared at each other.

"Mr. Ten Broeck," Statler said, "I can't give you an explanation. But I am curious about what concern it is to you."

"My concern, Dewey," Ten Broeck growled, "is that a dozen of those horses your brother seems to have spirited away are my property. Do you hear that—*my* property! And he's stolen them!"

Statler sighed. "You, too, eh?"

"What the hell does that mean?"

"It means there are other partners in the horses . . . well, one more that I know of for certain. Yesterday, Bernard de Mandeville claimed to own a fifty-percent share in seven of the horses, and he suggested there were similar deals made by Father."

"The others don't concern me. I want mine."

Two laughed; it was an involuntary reaction to his despair. "Everyone wants their pound of flesh, Mr. Ten Broeck. But there's little we can do to satisfy you."

"There's nothing funny about this. Find that damned brother of yours!"

"We have no idea where he is."

"Well, you'd better find out! You have until tomorrow morning, sirs. After that, I'll let the law handle you all."

As the door closed behind the angry horseman, Mary Dewey entered the drawing room. "It seems your father has left us in quicksand," she said wearily.

Her sons came to her solicitously. "You heard all that, Mother?" Two asked.

"Yes." She sat in a chair near the fireplace, the portrait face of Charles Dewey Sr. gazing down at her. "I didn't mean to eavesdrop," she said apologetically, "but, then, that gentleman was quite loud."

Statler sank down on the floor in front of her, taking her hands. "I'm sorry, Mother. We had hoped to spare you all this."

She smiled at him. "I'm a strong woman, dear. I've had to be."

Statler drew in a deep breath. "Mother," he began hesitantly, "the situation is very bad."

"I know."

"It's not just Mr. Ten Broeck, Mother. There are other—"

"I know it all," she interrupted.

"What?"

"The day after your father had that . . . imbroglio with Oubre at Metairie," she explained slowly, "Junior came to me with chapter and verse of what Georgie—I'm still doing that, aren't I?—of what your father had done. He told me everything: about the mortgages, about the partnerships he sold in the horses, about the sale of his share of the racetrack—"

Her sons were speechless.

"And Junior wanted to . . . well, thwart your father by making off with everything at Nouveau Marché."

"Then you know where Junior is?" Two asked.

"I must assume he's carrying out his plan," she sighed. "He's taking everything to Nashville. To Bon Marché."

Two clapped his hands together in delight. "Isn't that marvelous?" he chortled. "My brother is going to beat the creditors!"

"Is he?" Mary asked sadly. "I'm afraid he'll only postpone the inevitable." A tear ran down her cheek. "And what's really distressing is that Georgie has left everything on your shoulders—as the heirs."

Statler winced. "A fine lawyer I am. A will never crossed my mind until this moment. Do you mean to tell us, Mother, that *you* aren't his heir?"

She shook her head. "Several years ago"—Mary looked up at Two—"even before Charles Three was born . . . I prevailed on your father *not* to leave everything to me, but to draw a new will that would provide for equal shares for all our children. And now—" She was weeping.

Statler squeezed her hands. "Mother, we'll come through this all right," he said reassuringly.

"Right," Two added. "We'll just have to make the best of the situation."

"Where is the will, Mother?" Statler wanted to know.

Mary pointed to her husband's desk.

Getting to his feet, the young lawyer-publisher went to the desk and pulled open a drawer. A perplexed expression came to his face. Another drawer was opened. And another.

"It's empty," he reported. "There's nothing at all."

His mother stared at him. "But—?"

"Of course," Statler said, "Prytaneum Walk!"

"What's that?" Two inquired.

"Father's . . . uh . . . other house." He glanced at his mother apologetically. "His papers must be there. Two, I think we ought to go over there and find what we can."

"And I'll go with you," Mary said.

"No, Mother—"

"I'm going!" she said firmly. "I have a right to know how he spent his last days."

IV

THE sun, its dying light diffused in myriad shades of pink and red, was falling to the horizon west of the Mississippi as the Nouveau Marché caravan slowly came over a grassy knoll to see the splendor of Natchez spread out along the bluffs overlooking the river.

"Natchez," George Dewey said idly to the giant black man walking beside him. "We've made it, Enoch."

"Yassuh, we surely has."

For more than a mile, George had been walking his horse, needing to stretch his legs and to ease his sore butt.

A rider approached them at a gallop, whipping wildly. As he came up to them, they could see he was a lad of no more than twelve or thirteen.

"Are you Mr. George Dewey Junior?" he called out as he brought his mount to a sudden stop.

"I am."

"Mr. Will Stabler has sent me out to look for you," the boy reported. "You're now on the property of Hope Farm and Mr. Stabler has made arrangements for your party to stop here. He asked me to bring you to him."

"And where is Mr. Stabler?"

"At Connelly's Tavern, sir. A ten-minute ride from here."

George vaulted onto his horse, looking around. To Enoch: "Turn the horses out into that pasture there." He pointed. "And then see that everyone has a meal. And I don't want anyone wandering off."

"Yassuh, Mastah George."

"Lead the way, son."

The lad kicked his horse into action, speeding away. Dewey, however, followed at only a moderate rate, causing the youngster to rein in his horse, whirl about, and come back to him.

"It'll be more than ten minutes at this pace, sir," he said.

"That's all right, son. There's no great hurry anymore."

As they rode along, the boy said proudly, "I've been helping Mr. Stabler make ready for your arrival."

George grinned at him. "And very efficiently, I'll bet."

"Yes, sir. I know every inch of Natchez and just about everybody who lives here. Good and bad."

"A valuable asset."

"Mr. Stabler pays well."

"Does he now?" Dewey laughed.

In a short time, after passing several opulent mansions (*Cotton money*, George thought), a large frame building loomed up in front of them, dominated by two long galleries across the front, supported by slender posts.

"That's Connelly's," the young man announced. "It was there, sir, that the American flag was first raised over the lower Mississippi Valley. Back in ninety-five, when this area was still Spanish."

"You *do* know a great deal of this area."

"More than most, Mr. Dewey."

As they approached the tavern, George saw his overseer hurrying down the steps from the lower porch, waving to them.

Dewey returned the wave, spurring his horse to quickly close the distance between them. He slid off the animal to enthusiastically shake Stabler's hand.

"Is all well, Will?"

"Just fine. All arrangements have been made."

"And Mrs. Dewey?"

"She's putting the boys to bed."

Disappointment clouded George's face. "Then we're not leaving immediately?"

"No, no. Not until tomorrow morning. It wouldn't be wise to try to move the horses and all the wagons down the steep street to Natchez-Under-the-Hill in the dark. Further, you wouldn't want to have your family down there after sundown."

"It's a devil's broth down there at night, sir," the boy interjected from the saddle.

Stabler nodded. "It's that and more. I daresay there's no greater collection of cutthroats and scoundrels and gamblers and brawlers anywhere on the Mississippi."

"That's true, Mr. Dewey," the young man added. "Murder is so common there we don't hardly mention it anymore."

"As you can see," Stabler laughed, "young Mr. Postlewait has been an invaluable source of information. I don't know what I would have done without him."

"Postlewait, eh?"

"Yes, sir. William Mercer Postlewait. Most folks call me Bold Billy."

"Well, Billy," George said, "why don't you ride back to where my party is waiting and tell them I said to bed down for the night. Ask for Enoch."

"That big buck?"

"Yes."

A whip cracked on the flank of the horse and Billy was away at a gallop.

"Where'd you find him?" George asked.

"He lives in a small room here at the tavern."

"His folks own the tavern?"

"No, he's an orphan. For four or five years now, as I understand it. The tavern people keep him around because he's so damned useful."

Dewey chuckled. "There doesn't seem to be much doubt of that. Tell me, Will, what has transpired here?"

"I've leased the largest cargo steamer I could find—the *Belle Amie*. Passenger accommodations are crude, but there'll be room for the horses and the baggage. But it costs four thousand."

George shrugged.

"And with Bold Billy's help, I've uncovered an agent who

will be willing to buy the rolling stock—the carriage, the van, the wagons—just before we cast off. If we're lucky, we may get a thousand back on those."

"Seems reasonable," Dewey commented. "Now, I want to see Mrs. Dewey."

"She's on the second floor—room 211."

George sprinted up the stairs, opening the door without knocking, startling Emma. "Darling!" She rushed to him, falling into his arms. "I was so worried, dear."

"We had an uneventful trip, though tiring." He kissed her. "Where are the boys?"

"In the next room. Asleep, I hope."

They tiptoed in and George looked down at his sons for a long time. Harry was nearly three; George III was only a baby, not yet a year old. "Such innocence," the father whispered. "They have no idea of the terrible events of these past few days."

"Thank God they don't."

Emma led George out of the room, carefully closing the door behind her.

"Do you have any word of your father?" she asked.

"None."

She sighed. There was nothing more to say about that. "Are you hungry?"

"No, just exhausted." He sprawled out across the bed. Emma came to him to pull off his boots.

"Are we doing the right thing, George?"

"We're doing the only thing left to us to do." He closed his eyes, seeming to fall asleep immediately. Gently, lovingly, Emma finished undressing him.

V

PENSIVELY, Mary Dewey stared at her husband's clothing hanging in a wardrobe in the Prytaneum Walk house. She reached out to touch one of his jackets, a handsome English tweed she had bought him in London. On their honeymoon.

"Thirty-six years," she said aloud.

There was no one to hear her; her sons were in another room searching through a desk for their father's last will and testament.

Thirty-six years. That damned English tweed is indestructible. Georgie was always so handsome in that coat. And he wasn't like other men who ran to fat when they grew older. He kept his physique. Maybe if I had— No! I'm not going to stand here blaming myself and making excuses for him. He was always attracted to other women. What was the name of that creamy-skinned bitch in London? "Lady" something or other. That's humorous, I guess. They were all "Lady" something or other. But he always came back to me. I can't say we didn't have fun in London, because we did. I wanted to stay, but he had to get back to his precious Bon Marché! How I hated all that pretense about being "a Dewey," as if God gave them some special reason for existing. The other Deweys never knew about all of Georgie's escapades. Maybe I should have told them. No—they wouldn't have believed me. If I'm going to be honest, I didn't want to believe it myself. I loved him; oh, God, how I loved him! I thought he was the most wonderful lover— That's funny, too. Maybe he wasn't that wonderful. How would I know? I never had anyone to make comparisons with him. Perhaps I should have. I wonder whether he made comparisons? Did he speak of me to Lady—what the hell was her name? Did he talk about me when he was with that octoroon? He probably did. And maybe they laughed about me. Why don't I admit it? Georgie was a sonofabitch!

She slammed shut the wardrobe door.

In the other room, Statler Dewey held up a sheaf of papers. "Here it is, Two. The last will and testament of George Washington Dewey Senior." He studied the document briefly. "Christ, Two, this is brand-new. It's only a week old, dated the day after he had that fight with Oubre at the racetrack."

"Is it valid?"

Statler flipped to the last page. "It was drawn by James Balsom—he's a reputable New Orleans attorney—and it's witnessed by a magistrate of the parish. It's legal all right."

His eyes raced over the pages. "And listen to this: 'I leave all of my worldly goods and possessions, without exception, to Mademoiselle Marguerite Jeanne Cappevielle—' Do you realize what that means, Two?"

"It means our father was a bigger fool than I thought he was!"

"Maybe not," Statler chortled. "If Mademoiselle Cappevielle is the sole inheritor of Father's estate, she also is solely responsible for the *debts* of that estate!"

"What?"

"As though underscoring that fact, Father had the attorney list all of the assets *and* all of the debts"—he shuffled through the pages—"in carefully precise detail." He tossed the will to his brother. "See for yourself."

Two took several minutes to go through the document. "Good Lord," he said soberly, "the total debts are in excess of a quarter of a million dollars."

In the bedroom, Mary idly opened the door of the second wardrobe. The faint odor of perfume came out at her.

So, that's the smell of you, is it, Mademoiselle Cappevielle? It's pleasant enough, I'll admit that. Did Georgie choose that scent for you? And where are you now? In whose bed?

Her sons came into the room and Mary rather sheepishly closed the wardrobe door, as though she had been caught in some indiscretion.

Statler explained to her what they had found and the implications of the will.

Shock registered on her face. "Do you mean to tell me that whore owns *my* house?"

"It doesn't make any difference, Mother," Statler insisted. "One way or another the house is lost—to the creditors."

"But it's still my house and now she owns it!"

"For a day or two only, Mother. Once I make sure Attorney Bascom files the will for probate the whole house of cards will collapse. True, the house will be gone, but none of us will be responsible for Father's debts. Those will all fall on Marguerite Cappevielle. Don't you understand that?"

"I understand one thing," she said bitterly. "Georgie gave *my* house to that whore." She began to cry.

Two took her into his arms. "Statler and I feel, because the next few weeks will be very trying for you, that you ought to get away from New Orleans. I want to take you to Nashville. We could take a boat tomorrow—"

"I hate Nashville," she snapped.

"But Junior will be in Nashville with his family. And Martha is there—and you haven't seen your only daughter for a long time." Two grinned. "And you'd have Charles Three to spoil. We'd have a family reunion, Mother, until this whole mess blows over. Then, if you want to come back to New Orleans—"

"Your father still has to have a proper burial," she said stubbornly, "and that's my responsibility."

"We both thought," Two said hesitantly, "that it might be well to take his body back to Bon Marché and have him buried there. With his father and his brother."

She sighed. "I guess Georgie would like that."

"He would, Mother." Statler took her arm. "Come, let's get out of here."

They were nearly out of the room when Mary Dewey turned and walked resolutely to George's wardrobe. She opened it again and took the old English tweed coat from the hanger. Draping it over her shoulders, she pulled it tight around her.

And she was warmed. As Georgie's arms had once warmed her.

12

SEPARATED by three hundred miles of twisting, shoal-laden, demanding, unforgiving waters, the Mississippi River towns of New Orleans and Natchez were as different as the two sides of a coin. Yet, like the faces of a coin, one did not exist without the other; they were joined in an alloy of dependence on the waterway that had birthed them. What the river did to one it did to the other.

Thus, on that chilly, early December Monday morning they were both blanketed by a river-borne fog that seemed determined to hold off the day. Workers on the docks at New Orleans could not see fifty feet from shore. In Natchez it was just as bad, and the denizens of that narrow, muddy riverside shelf known as Natchez-Under-the-Hill groped through the murkiness, unable to see even halfway to the top of the three-hundred-foot bluffs above them.

To those named Dewey in both towns the capriciousness of the weather carried a personal connotation. In New Orleans the fog was a properly somber shroud under which to carry the mortal remains of George Washington Dewey Sr. In Natchez the gray mist was a portent of news still unheard, of fear that the elder Dewey *might* be dead.

But in both places, the Deweys were on the move, impelled by the foolish sins of that one man.

II

"Hooo, lads, take care of that! Easy now—" The voice of the captain of the *Natchez* boomed out on the New

Orleans docks as six hands wrestled the heavy, ornate oaken casket up the gangplank. Mary Dewey, in widow's black, stood watching, leaning heavily on her son, Charles Dewey II.

When the casket was stowed on the lower cargo deck, and was being covered by a tarpaulin, Charles gestured to the captain. He was a giant of a man, one obviously used to having his own way; as he approached them, though, he solicitously removed his hat.

"Captain, may I present my mother," Two said. "Mother, this is Mr. Tom Leathers, the master of the *Natchez*."

Leathers nodded, his bearded face properly sober. "Ma'am, I'm sorry we're not able to comply with your wish to have your husband . . . with you in your cabin. As I told your son, the doorways of the cabins are not wide enough to—"

"I understand, Captain," Mary said.

"But be assured the casket will have proper care."

"I'm appreciative, Captain."

Leathers looked out over the river. "I'm afraid this damned—excuse me, ma'am—this fog is going to delay our departure a bit."

"Long enough, Mr. Leathers, for me to send a telegraph message?" Two asked.

"Oh . . . yes, sir."

"Mother, why don't you and Naomi"—the son nodded in the direction of the Negro maid who was with them—"go aboard and get comfortable in your cabin? I want to see whether I can't get a message to Junior."

"But we don't know where he's gone."

"He certainly hasn't gone overland with that entourage," Charles contended. "We can guess, then, that he's thinking of going by steamer—from either Baton Rouge or Natchez. I'll send a message to both places in hopes of finding him. He ought to know what has happened."

The widow nodded in agreement. Captain Leathers offered his arm, taking her aboard the boat.

III

IT WAS called Silver Street for no apparent reason, but it was little more than a wide, muddy path leading from the high bluffs of Natchez down to the busy dock area on the riverfront. The street offered a dangerously precipitous route to Natchez-Under-the-Hill, one difficult enough just to walk. But George Dewey Jr. and his overseer, Will Stabler, had to try to move more than a half-hundred horses and a dozen heavily loaded wagons down the slope.

"The last thing to go down will be the horses," Junior ordered. "I don't want them standing for hours aboard that boat while we load the other stuff. They're going to be panicked enough with all this strange activity. So . . . we'll put the horses aboard just before we shove off."

"That's wise," Stabler agreed.

Junior looked down the steep incline. "Block and tackle, do you think?"

"Yes, I've already instructed Captain Purcell on that score."

Young Dewey looked around. "Then where in the hell is he?"

The overseer shrugged, sighing. "I'll find him. Billy!" he called out to the Postlewait boy. "Come with me."

Slipping and sliding in the mud underfoot, Stabler and Bold Billy made their way down to the dock area. At the tied-up *Belle Amie,* Stabler asked a crewman: "Captain Purcell aboard?"

Sullenly, the crewman pointed to a shack opposite them. "In O'Brien's."

Stabler cursed under his breath, hurrying to the saloon. Inside, he and the boy faced a bedlam. It was jammed with riverboat riffraff, laughing and shouting and swearing. In one corner someone was playing a concertina, and several disreputable couples were trying to dance.

There was a sour odor to the place. A persistent, clinging smell suggesting *evil* to the Nouveau Marché overseer.

"Captain Jubal Purcell!" Stabler shouted over the din.

"Aye, mate!" a bellow came back to them. At the rough-hewn wooden bar, where a fat whore was draping her arm over his shoulders, Purcell raised an arm high in the air. "Over here!"

Stabler and Billy pushed their way through the throng to get to the captain.

"My God, man," the overseer said in disgust, "you're drunk!"

"Naw, naw, mate," Purcell said, laughing, the resonance of it rumbling up from his ample belly, "just havin' meself a eye-opener, ya might say."

"Well . . . let's get going. We have to bring those wagons down from the bluffs."

"Aye." The captain drained his glass, shrugging the whore away from him. "Now, hear this," he yelled, "the lads of the *Belle Amie*—heave to! 'Tis another day, lads!"

Grumbling and curses followed the announcement, but perhaps a dozen men made for the door. Several of them were stumbling drunkenly.

Stabler shook his head. "We're in for an adventure, I'm afraid," he said to Billy.

The lad grinned at him. "Some of these fellas, Mr. Stabler, can't work at all if they're sober."

IV

RUMBLING bass notes of the steam whistle of the *Natchez* bounced along the New Orleans docks, causing several carriage horses nearby to rear up in panic, as the three-hundred-foot riverboat slipped away from its berth nearly two hours behind its announced departure time. Most of the fog was gone, but its residue clung to the water like gray cobwebs hiding some ancient secret in a dank basement.

Charles Dewey II stood in the pilothouse with Captain Leathers, watching the pilot expertly maneuver the big boat to the center of the river and then point it northward. Below, two giant engines throbbed, sending their power to the two-story-high side paddle wheels. In turn, the wheels cut into the Mississippi, churning the water against the splash guards in a continual flood.

"A fine vessel," Charles commented.

The captain nodded appreciatively, looking at his pocket watch. "I apologize for the delay, Mr. Dewey. We'll make up some of the time in the run to Baton Rouge. With luck, we'll be there by . . . oh . . . seven-thirty tonight."

Dewey raised his eyebrows. "Ten hours only?"

"Hmmm. I've done it in less. And when I get to build the

boat I have in design, it'll have more speed. *Natchez II* will be a coal-burner. Bigger than this one . . . more grand, you might say."

Leathers's pride in his boat was evident. And Dewey could understand that. The *Natchez* was luxurious. Even opulent. It was richly furnished with solid rosewood pieces; cushions on the chairs were covered with heavy crimson satin. The main cabin, which also served as the dining room, boasted velvet carpets; its walls were decorated with huge mirrors. The fretted ceilings were etched with gold leaf. And there were stained-glass skylights. The cabins could accommodate two hundred; the lower deck had room for two hundred and fifty steerage passengers. There were the amenities of a fine hotel: a barber shop, bathrooms, a bar for gentlemen which featured numerous gaming tables for their amusement. At dinner, two hundred could be accommodated at one time, and service was on Limoges china. A musician played on a grand piano at mealtimes, seated in front of the largest of the plate-glass mirrors at one end of the gallery.

"Will you and your mother take luncheon with me at my table?" the captain asked.

"That's kind of you, sir." Dewey frowned. "But I don't believe Mother is up to being sociable at this time."

"Of course. But if you need anything to make her trip more . . . ah . . . bearable, Mr. Dewey, you need only ask."

V

MUSCULAR backs strained against the ropes as the last of the Nouveau Marché wagons were being let down the steep, muddy slope of Silver Street. Several hours had been consumed in lowering the other wagons to the docking area at Natchez, where the contents were being stowed aboard the cargo steamer *Belle Amie*.

It had not been a pleasant few hours. Captain Purcell's crewmen—all white, strangely, when most of the riverboat crews on the Mississippi were black—sweated side by side with the slaves of Nouveau Marché. And with more than a little resentment. Epithets and slurs were common as the hard work continued.

At one point George Dewey Jr. said sharply to Purcell:

"Wouldn't it be a lot easier, Captain, if all this cursing would cease?"

Jubal glared at him. "Me crew's the best on the river . . . *sir*. Maybe ya oughta look to them damned lazy niggers!"

Young Dewey chose not to continue the dialogue, fearing it might contribute to more delay. Natchez had to be put behind him as soon as possible.

Now, as the heaviest of the wagons, the one carrying the Deweys' household furnishings, was being lowered down the hill by a makeshift block-and-tackle device, a worn rope snapped. Suddenly, the loaded wagon was careening down Silver Street on an erratic course, as both boat and crewmen and slaves scattered to keep out of its path.

Its journey lasted only seconds before it smashed into a shack at the bottom of the street, caving in a wooden wall. Several women, in various stages of undress, scrambled out of the wrecked building, followed by their unhappy male customers.

"Jesus Christ!" Captain Purcell roared, clearly delighted with the turn of events, "ya done broke up a crib, Mr. Dewey!"

Junior half slid down the muddy street. "Is anybody still in there?" he demanded of one of the frightened whores.

"No, but no thanks to you, you stupid bastard!" she screamed at him. "Look what ya done to my house!"

Chortling, Purcell gathered the woman into his big arms. "Now, Sally, me darlin', don't take on so. Mr. Dewey here is a proper gentleman an' I be sure he figures to pay ya for the damage." He looked questioningly at Junior.

"Yes, of course," he muttered. To his overseer: "Take care of it, Will." Dewey's attention was turned to assessing the damage to his furniture.

Stabler and Bold Billy wrangled with the prostitute about the loss. After some minutes of that the sum of fifty dollars was agreed upon, although Stabler believed the payment was exorbitant.

Junior directed several of the slaves: "Pull out of this mess what you can. And don't discard the broken pieces. Put them all aboard the boat." A large mahogany headboard for a bed had been badly split, several large standing mirrors had been smashed (somehow the frames remained intact), and several chairs were little more than kindling. The wagon, he figured, was a total loss. The slaves moved quickly to follow his orders.

"Not a word of this to Mrs. Dewey," George instructed Stabler and Billy. "I'll explain to Emma later. Right now, I just want to get out of here. Start bringing the horses down."

With a slave leading each blooded horse, a long line of equines started down the street. By this time, the denizens of the Natchez docks were nearly all involved as spectators, jeering and making jokes about the Dewey caravan. Junior tried to ignore it all.

At the boat's gangplank, another problem arose. The first horse balked after setting his forefeet on the gangplank and finding it a frightening, swaying monster. Another three quarters of an hour was consumed by the building of a wider, more substantial gangplank for the skittish animals. The slaves did all that work; Purcell's crewmen contributed nothing.

But the loading of the horses went swiftly after that as they were led aboard and carefully tethered in narrow stalls which had been nailed together a day earlier. In all, Dewey was taking fifty-one horses to Bon Marché, including four stallions.

One of those presented a final obstacle. He reared wildly when the black handling him tried to lead him onto the strange gangplank. A second effort to put him aboard also failed.

"Blindfold that horse," Junior called out, "and let's have several boys at his rear." The blindfold worked, although the stallion was quivering and was quite lathered before he was secured in his stall.

"I'll go fetch Mrs. Dewey," the master of Nouveau Marché announced. "Let's have everyone aboard, because I want to get away immediately."

He raced up Silver Street to Connelly's Tavern, where Emma, his two sons, and a Negro nursemaid were waiting. Junior took three-year-old Harry into his arms; the black woman carried the baby. On the way down Silver Street again, Junior tried to explain to his wife what she'd find aboard the *Belle Amie*.

"It's a cargo boat, dear," he said, "with very limited accommodations. There's only one cabin, but Captain Purcell has given that up for you and the children."

"I'll make do, George," Emma said softly, trying to pick her way around the worst of the mud of the street.

At the boat, they found Stabler and Bold Billy wrangling with the agent who had agreed to buy the rolling stock: wagons, van, and carriage.

"Now he's offering only six hundred," the overseer reported angrily. "Two days ago it was a thousand."

George shrugged. "Take what he offers, Will."

He guided Emma and the nursemaid up the gangplank and to the upper deck to the captain's cabin. It was a small, filthy enclosure with one cot like bed covered with dirty, smelly blankets.

"It'll only be for a few days," Junior said apologetically.

"I told you, dear, I'll make do."

Young Dewey left the cabin to make his way to the pilothouse.

"Steam up, Captain?" he asked.

"Aye."

"Then let's go."

"Aye." Purcell reached up to pull the cord on the steam whistle. It let out a high, piercing scream. From the lower deck came human shouts and the panicked cries of a horse in distress.

"What the hell—?" Dewey ran out of the pilothouse and down the ladder to the lower deck, to find a stallion—the one blindfolded to bring aboard—thrashing wildly in its stall, one of its forelegs hung up over the wooden side.

From Stabler: "That damned whistle—!"

"Ease that leg down," Junior called to the blacks. "And let's have enough hands in there to calm that animal!"

His orders were followed immediately, but the worst had already happened. The left foreleg had been broken. Junior groaned. "Do you have your gun on you, Will?"

Stabler produced a pistol from his waistband and Dewey dispatched the stallion with a shot directly into the ear. Everyone stood around for a moment in stunned silence.

"Let's get this body to shore," Dewey said quietly, seemingly about to weep.

As the heavy carcass was being dragged off the *Belle Amie,*

Billy Postlewait ran up the gangplank waving a piece of paper. "A message for you, Mr. Dewey, from the telegrapher."

George Junior took the paper, read the few scrawled words, and groaned deeply. "The end of a perfect day," he said bitterly as he handed the message to Stabler.

The overseer read it: "'Regret to inform you Father died instantly in duel. Mother and I en route Bon Marché.'" It was signed by Two. "I'm sorry, George."

"Yes, well—" A sigh. "Tell Captain Purcell to get under way. And without that damned whistle!"

Bold Billy and the agent who had bought the Nouveau Marché rolling stock stood on the muddy bank watching the *Belle Amie* back out into the current on the Mississippi. The youngster smiled broadly, waving to the Dewey entourage.

He turned to the agent. "I told you he'd accept any price because he was anxious to get away."

The agent nodded, grinning. "And now, I suppose, you want your share?"

"You damned right!" the boy answered, the voice hard. "You saved four hundred, and my share is two."

"You're a scoundrel, Billy." The agent counted the bills into Postlewait's hand.

Clutching the money, Billy waved again at the *Belle Amie,* pointed northward now, carrying what remained of Nouveau Marché.

VI

CAPTAIN Tom Leathers of the steamboat *Natchez* had been as good as his word. The delayed run from New Orleans to Baton Rouge had been accomplished by seven-thirty that evening. The handsome boat had eased into its berth there, to discharge passengers, pick up new ones, unload cargo and take on other cargo, and replenish its supply of wood for the huge boilers.

Charles Dewey II sat at dinner with his mother in her cabin. They could hear the sounds of the docking activities as they ate.

"Captain Leathers tells us we'll be in Baton Rouge in only an hour," Charles said. "Would you like to go out on deck and get some air after dinner?"

Mary shook her head disconsolately. "I don't know why I'm so tired, Two. Certainly, I haven't exerted myself at all today, but I still feel exhausted."

"It's mental exhaustion, Mother."

"I suppose."

"It'll be only a few days to Nashville and then you'll be able to get your strength back."

She smiled weakly. "I never imagined I'd ever be returning to Nashville. I've always hated it, you know. But now—" She sighed. "I have a poor choice, it seems: Nashville, which I despise, or a return to New Orleans where my bridges have been burned, thanks to Georgie."

"Nonsense," Two insisted. "Time is forgiving. After this mess blows over you'll be able to return to your friends, if you wish. Of course, you could always stay in Nashville with us. Beth would like that. So would Charles Three, I'm sure."

"We'll see." Mary had ended that part of the conversation. "After Baton Rouge, what next? Natchez?"

"Yes." Her son referred to his pocket watch. "We'll probably be arriving there in the middle of the night, and then there's a long run to Memphis—a bit over three hundred miles. There'll be a layover in Memphis. Perhaps you'll want to do some shopping there?"

"Perhaps."

When the dinner was concluded, Two excused himself. He thought he might have a drink in the bar. But he stood by the rail of the upper deck for a long time, watching the activity of the stevedores below him. He was still there when the *Natchez* got under way again. By that time he wanted only to sleep, retiring to his own cabin.

VII

MARY Dewey was awakened by the noise of the arrival in Natchez. She wondered whether her son George Junior had been there. And the more she thought of the audacious actions of Junior the more she came awake.

She heard the engines of the steamboat thump into action once more and she felt the gliding sensation of the vessel moving out again. After the obligatory whistle blasts the boat grew quiet, with only the rhythmic churning of the paddle wheels coming through to her. From across the cabin she could also hear the steady, deep breathing of her sleeping maid, Naomi.

Mary started to count to herself. Slowly, from one to sixty and then over again. And again. And again. She kept a mental tally of the passage of the minutes that way. When she reached forty-five she slipped quietly from the bed, rummaged through one of her bags in the dark, and found Georgie's tweed coat. Putting it around her to partially cover her nightdress, Mary quietly opened the door and went out on the deck. It was deserted at that hour.

Cautiously, she made her way down to the cargo deck where she had to make certain she didn't step on any of the sleeping steerage passengers. Mary found the casket containing her husband's body. It sat at the rear of the boat, covered with a tarpaulin, in a somewhat isolated island of space. It seemed none of the steerage people wanted to sleep close to it.

She stood over the bulk of the casket for a moment, staring at it.

Georgie, she thought, *I'm on my way to Nashville and you know how unhappy that makes me. I suppose I should be grateful that Two and the others want me there, but I would rather have stayed in New Orleans, no matter what happens now. They're going to bury you at Bon Marché. Their belief is your soul will know that and rejoice in having returned to Bon Marché. But I'm not so sure. I wish I had the faith to believe a soul survives. I don't know—it all seems so illogical to me. There's one thing I do know though, Georgie. I love you. I hate what you've done to me, but I love you. And I don't really want to be anywhere without you.*

Mary bent down, gently kissing the covering over George's coffin. She sighed. And then she moved to the stern rail. For a long time she watched the water rushing away from under the *Natchez*. There was another deep sigh. After looking around to determine whether anyone on the cargo deck was observing her, and satisfied that no one was, she hoisted herself over the railing.

Mary Harrison Dewey, a New Orleans widow of sixty-one, drawing the English tweed tightly about her, dropped the few feet into the cold, murky current of the Mississippi River.

13

To Alma May Dewey, Christmas Day of 1848 was not just an excuse for a party, although that certainly was a convenient element of it. But the Princess also saw it as a time of *healing,* one beautiful day that might ease the hurt of recent developments, that might cleanse away the ill fortune seeming to infest Bon Marché.

She remembered how her father had always placed special store in Christmas. "It's a time of unlimited hope," he used to say to her. "A time when the troubles threatening to overwhelm us are placed in the proper perspective. How can you read the story of the glorious miracle of the first Christmas and not realize all else palls in insignificance? Some theologians will argue that Easter, with its victory of the Resurrection, provides mankind with its greatest hope. But not to me. Easter, when you think about it, also speaks of treachery, of pain, of dying. And do we really see ourselves being role players in the holy drama of Resurrection, being whisked away from our earthly torment by a band of angels? I doubt that most of us do; I certainly don't. On the other hand, the birth of that humble baby, who was to grow into the most significant figure in all of recorded history, is the real symbol of man's hope. We have all been babies, not unlike Joseph and Mary's child, and we can believe we're all mirrored in that infant. If such a mean beginning can lead to such ultimate glory, then what prevents us, patterned in His image, from contemplating just a small measure of personal accomplishment on this earth? That's *true* hope, Princess."

Alma May had frequently disagreed with her opinionated

father. On the subject of Christmas, however, they were of like mind. From her first recollection of a Christmas Day the occasion had filled her with wonderment. It wasn't just the gifts and the yuletide merriment. It was so much more than that. There was a genuine restorative warmth about the season, a sense that all wrongs could be set right, all evil transformed to good.

As a small child she had been sung to by the Negro nursemaids; improvised songs about that special baby's birth, songs that were never sung the same way twice. But songs of such tenderness, such *belief,* that Alma May, cradling a doll in her arms, could imagine being under the gaze of farm animals in a crude stable, with radiant angels standing guard. She found glory and comfort in those moments.

Like the late Charles Dewey the daughter's faith was a personal thing, rarely enunciated, and taken into a church infrequently. The father lived every day of his life under an assurance he was guided by a *spirit.* God? Dewey never made such a claim. But, without question, a special spirit. *Of* God, if not God himself. From that grew a distinct Dewey morality, an ethic, a way of life. Unique, but strong. Alma May tried to perpetuate it by copying it.

As 1848 drew to a close Bon Marché *needed* Christmas. The year had seen the dueling death of George Dewey Sr., the subsequent suicide of his wife, Mary (made more terrible by the failure to recover her body from the waters of the Mississippi), the uprooting of the family of George Dewey Jr. with the debt-ridden demise of the Nouveau Marché plantation in Louisiana; all of that was added to the declining fortunes of the racing enterprises of Bon Marché itself.

The Princess mused about the fortunes of '48 as she sat in her suite of rooms and made her final plans for Christmas. At least one nagging problem had been solved earlier in the day—the final disposition of the contentions involving the Nouveau Marché horses. For a time, it had been a nightmare, begun only two shorts weeks earlier. The details were still fresh in her mind—

II

GEORGE Dewey Jr. clucked to the horse drawing the borrowed carriage, asking for more speed as he saw the familiar stone walls marking the outer reaches of Bon Marché. He had grave doubts about the quality of welcome he would receive. So did his wife.

"We should have sent a message ahead, George," Emma said.

"Perhaps." He frowned. "I suppose I mean to present them with a *fait accompli,* giving them no choice but to accept us in some manner. Certainly, there's no way we can just wander aimlessly, like gypsies."

Within the hour, the *Belle Amie* had docked at Nashville, drawing a big crowd of onlookers as George and Will Stabler unloaded the thoroughbred horses, and the large band of Nouveau Marché slaves, sixty-eight in all. From a steamship agent, George had borrowed the rig he was driving now. Emma was holding the baby, George III, in her lap. The older son, Harry, was in the rear of the carriage with a black nanny.

The youngster spoke: "Is this where we're going to live now, Father?"

"We may be."

"Is it a nice place?"

"I was born here, Harry." Junior gazed around at the carefully tended pastures, his practiced eye studying the horses grazing there. "Yes, it's a very nice place. Your great-grandfather Dewey was the master of all this."

Ahead he could see a figure in one of the smaller pastures working a young horse on a long line. As they drew closer, Junior recognized True Jackson, who looked up as he heard the carriage approaching.

True's mouth gaped. "My God!" He tossed the line to a Negro handler and ran to the fence adjoining the road. "George! Where have you come from?"

Young Dewey brought the carriage to a stop, vaulted out and hurried to the fence, extending his hand. True shook it vigorously.

"We've just arrived from New Orleans," George reported. "Father has been killed in a duel."

"Yes, we know," Jackson answered soberly. "Statler sent a message on the telegraph."

"Well, sir . . . what you see here"—he gestured to the carriage—"is the vanguard of what remains of Nouveau Marché.

At the Nashville docks there are fifty horses, the Nouveau Marché hands, and what we could carry of our personal belongings."

True just stared at him.

"It's such a mess," Junior went on, "that it's not explained simply."

"Yes, yes, of course." True climbed over the fence, going to the carriage, stepping up to kiss Emma on the cheek. "Let's get you all to the house. You must be exhausted."

Emma smiled wearily. "It's been an adventure, Cousin True."

In the Bon Marché drawing room, George Junior told the entire tale to a stunned audience: both Jacksons, their wives, Joy and Hope, and Alma May.

Able found it difficult to comprehend the extent of Junior's actions. "Do you mean to say you've made off with *all* of the horses and *all* of the slaves and—?"

"Everything that wasn't nailed down," the young man said wryly.

"And the creditors of whom you spoke?"

"I imagine they'll be on our heels."

Able exhaled a deep breath. "We're in for some trouble."

"Nothing we won't be able to handle," Alma May insisted supportively. "I don't know that I wouldn't have done the same thing." She grinned. "I'll bet my father would have."

In sum, it was the Princess who convinced the others of the rightness of Junior's escapade. Two days later, when a lawyer arrived representing the interests of the combined creditors, a hard bargain was hammered out. Quickly dismissed was the contention that Marguerite Cappevielle, as sole heir of the elder Dewey's estate, was responsible for its debts.

"Even if we accept that the mistress was Dewey Senior's legal heir, which we don't," the lawyer said coldly, "the fact remains that his son made off with assets of the estate, removing them from Louisiana—assets legally the property of the creditors of Dewey Senior." He shrugged. "I would hope we don't have to take young Dewey's *criminal* actions to a court of law."

Out of that came a difficult compromise; *very* difficult in light of the strained finances of Bon Marché. It was agreed Bon Marché would "purchase" all of the horses and all of the slaves for one hundred and fifty thousand dollars. There was also to be an additional payment of fifty thousand for what was called compensatory damages.

It was two hundred thousand dollars Bon Marché didn't have, but Alma May prevailed on banker Willie Carstairs to take a mortgage on the plantation in that amount.

True Jackson had last-minute doubts. "There's never been an encumbrance on Bon Marché before."

"Would you rather that a grandson—or maybe *grandsons*—of Charles Dewey go to jail over this?" the Princess snapped.

"No, but—"

"We *gain* something from all this, you know. We're adding fifty horses to our stables. And all of good bloodlines, I think you'll agree."

"Yes."

"And we add to the hands at Bon Marché—"

"I'm not convinced we have use for those additional slaves," True responded churlishly.

Alma May ignored that point. "And we also gain the services of a very fine young trainer."

True nodded, knowing Alma May meant to have her way. Knowing, too, she had already worked her will on Joy and Hope. With the three "owners" of Bon Marché in agreement, there was little True Jackson could do to upset the compromise.

The rest of the transition was quickly accomplished. The body of George Dewey Sr. (brought aboard the *Natchez*) was buried in the Bon Marché cemetery next to his father and his brother Franklin. There was only a brief commitment service. No tears were shed. What was necessary was done.

Franklin's house on the corner of the plantation nearest the Richland Creek, which had stood vacant for years, was re-opened. Slaves from Nouveau Marché swarmed over it, readying it for the new tenants—the family of George Dewey Jr.

Alma May turned her full attention to Christmas. And its healing.

III

TRADITION was served at Christmas. Charles Dewey's tradition largely. On the morning of the day before Christmas

Alma May had gone out into the woods with a representative body of slaves to find and cut a yule log. On Christmas Eve, then, it was ceremoniously lighted in the drawing room as Lee Dewey—the great-grandchildren of the founder gathered around him—read the story as told by Saint Luke:

"'And it came to pass in those days, that there went out a decree from Caesar Augustus, that all the world should be taxed . . .'"

The yule log snapped and crackled in the fireplace. Alma May, who had been studying the rapt attention of the children, looked up at the portrait of Charles Dewey hanging over the mantel. It seemed that he, too, was looking at the children. The Princess felt safe, just as she had been on Christmas Eves past when she had nestled in her father's lap as he had read those same words.

And when the reading was done this time, and the black nursemaids herded the children off to bed, Alma May busied herself pouring sherry. When she had finished, the butler passed the glasses on a large silver tray.

The Princess raised her glass. "To Christmases of another time," she said soberly, "and to the loved ones who were with us then."

The toast was drunk. Many eyes were wet.

IV

PERHAPS the rest of Christmas might have been regarded as an anticlimax, even though Alma May staged a lavish ball at Bon Marché on Christmas Night, a time when she was clearly in her element as "the Princess."

She dominated the scene as she had intended. Although she was forty-eight, there was not a more beautiful woman in the room. Her auburn hair, her flawless ivory skin, her voluptuous figure, suggested a much younger woman. So, too, did her indefatigable energy; it seemed she was determined to dance with every gentleman present.

At one point during the evening a knot of those gentlemen, fortified by Bon Marché bourbon, stood in conversation about the number one topic of the plantation: racehorses. True and Able Jackson were in the center of the group. Their younger assistants, Charles Dewey II and George Dewey Jr., were on the fringe of the gathering which included half a dozen of the leading campaigners on the Tennessee racing circuit.

"I swear to you," True was saying, made unusually ebullient by the liquor, "Bon Marché is on the threshold of a whole new era. We are most fortunate to have on our staff now George Dewey Junior, whose fine work in New Orleans must be familiar to you all."

He went on for several minutes about the accomplishments of young George, until it became embarrassing to the newcomer. He leaned over to his older brother, whispering: "That's the whiskey talking, Two."

Charles II grinned at him. "Whiskey or not, the accolades are well deserved," he said softly.

But Junior was still concerned about the impression being left that he was trying to replace his brother as the assistant trainer at Bon Marché. In truth, it was an impression making a mark on Two as well.

Sometime later, while dancing with his wife, Beth, they whirled past Alma May, who waved at them gaily.

"The Princess certainly is a great party-giver," Beth commented. "This is a wonderful affair."

"For some maybe," Two grunted.

His wife chuckled. "What does that mean, Mr. Dewey?"

"It means I'm not going to have the opportunities I had anticipated here at Bon Marché."

"Oh?" She realized he was being serious.

"I think, Beth, that Junior is going to be the heir apparent. True seems to believe so. And, if I'm to be honest, my younger brother has a great deal more experience as a trainer than do I."

"That's strange talk for a man who has told me he's going to be the master of Bon Marché."

"That was before Junior showed up."

She leaned into him, kissing him. "I won't listen to any such self-deprecation. You're twice the man your brother is."

"The source of that comment is prejudiced."

"Admittedly, but accurate nevertheless."

"I love you, Beth." He pulled her closer to him. "No man has ever had a more loyal wife. But you have a blind spot. Unlike you, I'm aware of my shortcomings."

"That's . . . that's . . . well, that's horseshit!"

Two laughed heartily. "I suppose that's the final, definitive word on the subject. Want another champagne?"

"Why not? It's a party, isn't it?"

It was well past two A.M. when the last guest at the Christmas Ball had left Bon Marché, and Willie Carstairs was sprawled across the bed in Alma May's suite, watching her undress.

"May I say that for a woman of your age you're quite well preserved?"

"You may not!" the Princess snapped, feigning anger. "A woman of my age, indeed! Aren't you aware that mature women make the best lovers?"

"Uh-huh, I'm aware," Carstairs chuckled. "And mature women are the most appreciative, as well, if we are to accept the wisdom of Benjamin Franklin."

"There's a certain truth in that," Alma May admitted.

She stood in front of a long mirror, admiring her reflection. "You know, Willie," she said shortly, "I truly believe I'm more beautiful now than I was at twenty-five." She had managed to say the words without appearing to be vain.

"I didn't have the pleasure when you were twenty-five. After all, I was only ten."

"You're better off knowing me now," she commented candidly. "I was a terrible *bitch* at twenty-five."

She went to the bed, sitting next to him, starting to undo his cravat. "It may be a presumption on my part, but I did think you were going to stay the night."

"I am." He arose, starting to undress. "Were you pleased with the party?"

"Very much so. Christmas is very special, you know. And I think it points, this time, to a great year ahead for Bon Marché."

"I can think of one way to make it greater."

Alma May laughed. "You're awfully transparent, darling. You're going to talk of marriage again."

"Uh-huh."

"Let's not."

"But now I think I have a better argument. As the holder of the mortgage on Bon Marché I can foreclose if I'm rebuffed."

It wasn't a threat, of course, and Alma May didn't see a

need to banter with him. "I really *do* see a whole new era for this place—a growth that would make Father proud."

Willie, ready for bed now, came to her, reaching for her, taking her into his arms. "Once more, Princess, marry me."

"No, Willie."

"Bon Marché comes first?" he groaned.

"Always, my dear, always."

BOOK TWO

San Francisco is a robust town, growing
at a mad pace. But it is clear it will
soon be a great city and I mean to make
the Dewey name a major factor here—
and in all of California.
—Charles Dewey II, 1849

14

"READERS of this newspaper are aware," August Schimmel wrote in his first editorial of 1849,

we would have much preferred to have had the astute Henry Clay as the Whig candidate for the presidency in '48. But the party managers thought otherwise, choosing instead a candidate believed capable of uniting the diverse elements of the Whigs and, in the broader sense, capable of being elected to the presidency.

The ultimate wisdom of the Philadelphia convention is clear before us. General Zachary Taylor, the hero of Buena Vista, will take his awesome oath of office in a few short weeks.

There are lessons to be learned from the presidential campaign just past. One is this: though there have been regional contentions within the Whig Party, i.e., the so-called Cotton Whigs and the poorly named Conscience Whigs (whose aberrant consciences do not allow them to see the dangers of their abolitionist ravings), Taylor's selection and victory are proof that men of goodwill can put aside their prejudices for the well-being of the nation as a whole. And a second lesson: the south, as a region, cannot elect a President. Democratic candidate Lewis Cass won the South and lost the election.

The voters have spoken clearly. They've chosen a patriot over contentious politicians, a man who can be expected to carefully recognize the problems of both regions and choose a course for America, not pitting North against South, nor favoring South over North.

We would hope that General Taylor's coming to the presidency will still all talk of disunion. It's a bastard word, not worthy of parental acceptance by either North or South.

II

NOT since the heyday of Andrew Jackson had there been such an enthusiastic crowd gathering on the banks of the Cumberland River awaiting the arrival of a steamboat. On this morning—it was Wednesday, February 7—the air was bitterly cold. But the weather did nothing to chill the warmth of the Nashville reception for President-elect Zachary Taylor. Nashvillians felt a special closeness to the presidency. Andy Jackson had held it for eight years, changing the office, molding it in his own image. And now Taylor, recognized as a frontiersman even though he had been born in Virginia, would be replacing their own James Knox Polk, who, with Jacksonian ability, had distinguished himself in the President's Mansion. Party affiliation aside, Zach Taylor did no violence to their beliefs about what a President should be.

There was a prolonged blast on the whistle of the boat bringing Taylor to Nashville. A mighty roar went up and the town band struck up a discordant version of "Green Grow the Laurel"; lips of the horn players were sticking painfully to the icy brass instruments. Newspaper correspondent-illustrator Lee Dewey, a member of the official welcoming party, winced. He had heard the song so often during the Mexican War that he had hoped never to hear it again.

Another whistle blast, echoing off the stone and brick facades of the merchant headquarters on Water Street, and then Taylor's boat came to a stop on the docking bank. The gangplank was quickly run out. And there he was—Old Rough and Ready, his lined face stern, the hooded eyes piercing, his nearly white hair in studied disarray.

"Company . . . attention!" Able Jackson bellowed from the back of his horse and the inexpert ranks of the new Nashville Militia company tried to follow his orders.

Taylor was in civilian dress, a greatcoat buttoned tightly against the cold. "General" Jackson, the militia commander, felt a momentary embarrassment, dressed as he was in a rather gaudy uniform delivered only a day earlier by one of the city's best tailors.

Lee Dewey stepped forward, extending his hand. "Nashville is pleased to have you, General. Uh . . . excuse me . . . Mr. President."

Taylor smiled, pumping the hand. "Well, Dewey, it's a different scene than the last time we crossed paths in Mexico, eh?"

"Yes, sir, it is. Happier."

"Indeed, indeed. And that nephew of yours—what's happened to him?"

"Albert's in Kentucky," Lee reported, "running one of the family's horse farms."

"Hmmm. I suspect he'll do well in that venture. Colonel Dewey was an excellent officer in an organizational sense. Yes, a good officer, but not a good soldier. Perhaps he had . . . well, too active a conscience for the hard realities of soldiering."

Lee decided not to prolong their conversation, quickly introducing the other members of the welcoming committee before guiding Taylor through the throng to a waiting carriage. He was to be driven to the capitol to be honored by the governor and the Tennessee legislature.

Newspaper publisher August Schimmel stood off to one side, watching it all. His time with Taylor would come later, when the President-elect would be at dinner at Bon Marché to be questioned by Schimmel's editors brought into Nashville from newspapers in St. Louis, New Orleans, Lexington, Pittsburgh, Chicago, Cincinnati, and Raleigh. Schimmel had arranged all of that weeks earlier in an exchange of correspondence with Taylor's aides.

Not only was it to be a golden opportunity to determine what kind of a President the old Indian fighter would be, but it would also enhance the importance of his newspaper chain.

IV

"Suppose we start, Mr. President," Schimmel said, "by asking you how you visualize the upcoming Taylor administration."

The dinner at Bon Marché was concluded and the party had

adjourned to the drawing room, where bourbon was being served.

"Well, sir, I believe there's a simple reply to that," Taylor said easily. "As you know, I'm a Whig—but not an ultra Whig. I will not be a President merely of party. I will endeavor to act independently of party domination. I'm determined to administer the government untrammeled by party schemes."

Schimmel smiled weakly. What Taylor had answered had been said many times during the campaign; in truth, those words were virtually the only ones he had spoken during the entire campaign.

"Could we be more specific?" Schimmel asked. "The burning question, of course, is the expansion of slavery into the newly won territories—"

"Yes, it is," Taylor cut in, "and, frankly, it's disturbing that there's so much heat generated by that argument. You may recall, Mr. Schimmel, that the Whig convention saw fit not to saddle its nominee with a platform from which there could be no retreat."

Carrie Dewey Bonsal, at the meeting from the *St. Louis Challenger,* spoke up. Her sarcasm was undisguised. "Might not the lack of a Whig platform suggest that there are too many opposing factions within your party for agreement on common principles?"

Old Zach looked hard at her. "Young lady," he said, "Whig principles and my principles are well known, and are one and the same. There can be no doubt that we rest our beliefs on the Constitution. Indeed, in less than a month I'll take the oath to 'preserve, protect, and defend' the Constitution. And I intend to do that with all of my being."

"That's admirable, General, but—"

"I will maintain," Taylor pressed on, "to the extent of my ability, the government in its original purity. To adopt as the basis of my public policy those great republican doctrines which constitute the strength of our national existence."

"Fine words," Carrie snapped, "but what do they mean?"

The President-elect looked to Schimmel pleadingly, seeming to ask the publisher to give him relief from Carrie's persistence.

"Perhaps Mrs. Bonsal is inclined to be a bit . . . well, argumentative," Schimmel said, smiling slightly, "but she seems to want to know what all of us here want to know. Permit me to state it quite simply, sir: what will be your position on the expansion of slavery into the new territories?"

Taylor drew a deep breath. "All legislative powers are vested by the Constitution in the Congress, are they not?"

"Yes."

"And, constitutionally, it's for the wisdom of Congress to regulate matters of *domestic* policy."

Schimmel was incredulous. "Then you intend to leave to the Congress this thorny matter?"

"I'll look with confidence, Mr. Schimmel, to the . . . uh . . . enlightened patriotism of that body."

"But . . . Congress is shot through with more factions . . . than . . . than . . . Mrs. Bonsal has suggested for the ranks of the Whig party."

The old general waved a hand imperiously, brushing away that suggestion. "Congress is the body to adopt measures of conciliation as may harmonize conflicting interests."

"Oh, dear God!" Carrie moaned.

Taylor glared at her.

Schimmel, himself appalled by the pomposity of the President-elect, looked around the drawing room for other contributions.

The editor of the *Chicago Clarion* coughed nervously. "General Taylor, you are yourself a slaveholder, are you not?"

"I am."

"Then isn't it reasonable to expect that you will align yourself with that point of view when you're in the Presidency?"

"The question, sir, is insulting!"

"My apologies, General," the Chicagoan said. "Allow me to put it another way. Should the Congress in its 'enlightened patriotism'—I believe that was the phrase you used—elect to expand slavery into the territories, would you welcome such a move?"

Taylor contemplated the question. "While your implication is still offensive, sir, I'll give you an answer. Any action by Congress that would tend to perpetuate the Union would be welcome to anyone who truly loves his country."

"I see. And should the Congress *not* elect to give free rein to the extension of slavery—?"

"As long as I'm in the Presidency I will unite with the coordinate branches of government to preserve the Union. And zealously, with my every breath, I might add."

The Chicago editor grimaced; Taylor's nonanswers were irritating. But he tried one more question: "I take it, then, that you're opposed to any talk by other slaveholders of disunion."

"Disunion is an abhorrent thought!" He looked at his watch. "I believe I should return now to my hotel. I leave Nashville very early in the morning."

In a flurry of "thank yous" and "good-byes" President-elect Zachary Taylor left Bon Marché. Behind him he left a disheartened group of journalists, disappointed that the general's views on whether or not slavery should be taken into the territories still eluded them.

"Do you really think he intends to let Congress try to settle this issue?" Carrie Bonsal asked.

"I don't think there's much doubt about that," the Chicago editor replied.

"Then let's hope there's at least one statesman in the Congress."

"I believe there is," Schimmel said firmly. "His name is Henry Clay."

V

THE next morning August and Louise Schimmel had a private breakfast with their nephew Statler Dewey, who had come to the Taylor meeting in his capacity as the resident publisher of the *New Orleans Delta Recorder*.

"I'm afraid I didn't make much of a contribution to last night's discussion," Statler said apologetically.

August laughed. "Given the lack of political acumen in our President-elect, I don't imagine any other contributions would have made much difference."

"No, I suppose not." He toyed with the eggs on his plate. "I wanted to talk to you two in confidence because I have a rather serious personal problem."

"How may we help, dear?" Louise asked quietly.

"Well, you see, the George Dewey matter—the aftermath of the duel and the problems with the creditors—simply won't go away. Oh, the estate mess is finally cleaned up, but the gossip continues. Hateful gossip, really. I could probably live with it if I were alone in it. But too much of it has fallen on Harriet.

"The stories of Father's dalliances with that Cappevielle woman just won't die. I suppose it's just too ripe a scandal. Anyway, that scandal has caused Harriet to lose some of her closest friends, or acquaintances we thought of as friends. There are no social invitations at all anymore, and when we attempt to go out on our own—to a restaurant, or the theater, or the opera—there's the continual spectacle of whispering and sniggering behind the fans of the women and the gloved hands of the . . . *gentlemen.*"

Statler sighed. "And now the mail has started. Obscene mail, with the sickest language you can imagine. Some of it even suggests . . . well, that Harriet might enjoy some—" He stopped. "Aunt Louise, I can't repeat for your ears some of the suggestions made. But be assured the situation is horrible for Harriet."

Louise put her hand consolingly on Statler's.

"We've decided we must leave New Orleans and, as of now, I'm submitting my resignation. I know this is going to put you in difficulties regarding the management of the *Delta Recorder,* but—"

"Where will you go?" Schimmel asked.

"I don't know."

"Were you thinking of continuing in the newspaper business?"

"Yes. But I can always open a law practice. We've spoken of Texas—"

August interrupted him. "There'd be an opening for you here in Nashville."

"What?"

Schimmel looked at his wife apologetically. "We haven't had an opportunity to discuss anything like this, dear, but"—he grinned—"I think we'll be of like mind on this. I'm sixty-six years old, Statler, and fully aware of human frailties. I think now is the time for me to turn over some management duties to a younger man. You, for example."

"August, I'm flabbergasted."

"You needn't be. You've done a good job—an excellent job—in a short time in New Orleans. Given a couple of years under my direct tutelage, I think you might be put in a position to eventually succeed us." He looked at Louise. "If you approve, dear."

"Of course I do." She was grinning broadly. "I certainly do." She sobered. "Our daughters, you know, Statler, are not involved at all in the newspaper business. Their lives are totally wrapped up in their husbands and in Bon Marché. August and I have several times talked about what would happen to the business if anything should—" A shrug. "Those human frailties August spoke of."

"I can't tell you how happy this makes me, Aunt Louise. And Harriet will be *delighted*—more so than I, perhaps."

Schimmel stood, shaking Statler's hand. "It's decided, then. Find us some interim management in New Orleans and come to Nashville as soon as it's convenient."

Statler laughed. "Tomorrow won't be too soon for Harriet."

"Well, we are pleased, too," August said, clapping him on the back, "to have you as the general manager of the Schimmel Newspapers."

15

THERE was an atmosphere of renewal at Bon Marché, consistent with the annual revitalization of soil and spirit by the arrival of spring.

Slave carpenters had finished the refurbishing of Franklin's old home to accommodate Junior's family, and there was talk among the blacks that they'd move next to work on a new house for Statler and Harriet Dewey, one that would overlook the Bon Marché deer park. Older blacks looked upon the arrival of the two young Dewey families as a good omen, when good omens were most needed.

But it was in the foaling barn where the promise of spring was most deeply felt. Of the fifty thoroughbreds George Dewey Jr. had spirited away from New Orleans, twenty-four had been mares heavy in foal. In the first week of March eight of them had dropped their burdens—five colts and three fillies. All were sound. To masters and slaves alike it was ample evidence the "curse" of Bon Marché had dissipated.

Junior was delighted, too; his life had taken on new meaning.

"I realize those foals are now the property of Bon Marché," he said to breeding manager Able Jackson, "but I hope my association with them will allow me to suggest names for this crop."

"I don't see why you shouldn't name them," Able replied.

"Well, I've always wanted to use a system—and my father thought it foolish—utilizing the Greek alphabet; Alpha, Beta, and continuing on."

"Agreed," Able said. "It's a fine idea. It'll also solve the problem I always seem to have in finding suitable names."

That evening, then, Able sat down at his desk to begin a letter to *The American Turf Register*. His spirit was ebullient and he approached the writing in a manner much less formal than he usually used:

My dear gentlemen,

This, I suppose, is the acknowledged center of the racehorse region. Bloodstock here is all the go. To be without it is to be out of fashion and destitute of taste. We have been fortunate enough to secure a new supply of the real grit, which, by and by, it is our intention to increase.

Since it is a custom to bespeak names in your valuable journal, I am emboldened to claim for a large group of them all at once—the Greek alphabet, from Alpha to Omega, inclusive. The first eight (through Theta, then) are claimed for the following list of 1849 foals.

Able carefully noted the breeding of the newborn thoroughbreds with the Nouveau Marché bloodlines. The first three letters were assigned to the trio of fillies: Alpha, Beta, Gamma.

He had a strange premonition about the latter name as he prepared the letter for posting. Gamma? There was a strength about it, something special in it.

"Gamma," he said aloud to himself. He liked the sound of it.

II

ALBERT Dewey was near exhaustion. Responsibilities of the burgeoning Bon Marché Lexington farm consumed his every waking hour. Since he had come to Kentucky there had been months of days in which he had not had eight hours sleep. More often it was four or five. Only on rare occasions, six.

While he was able to bring from Nashville four blacks with horse experience, the rest of his hands, purchased hurriedly at the slave market in Lexington, were not what he had been used to at Bon Marché. In theory, slave trading (meaning the importation) had become illegal. In practice, because demand remained, the flow of new blacks from Africa was continual. Because of his inexperience in the art of buying slaves he had acquired too many newly arrived off the boats.

Further, he had been unsuccessful in securing good white overseers. Seven had already come and gone; some just leaving without warning or explanation, and several having to be dismissed because of cruelty or incompetence. And the two he had now were in the latter category; they also would have been fired if he knew where to find decent replacements.

Manpower demands in Lexington were high. Both slaves and overseers of quality were difficult to find. What distinguished Lexington from Nashville was its almost total preoccupation with racing horses. Nashville boasted many fine horse farms, of course, and was a principal racing center, but it was not the equal of Lexington, where horse farm bordered on horse farm, and where the talk in the streets of the town was single-mindedly equine.

Albert struggled now to maintain his footing on the steeply pitched roof of his main barn. Several recent rainstorms had proved the inadequacy of the old roof. What was most annoying was that he was up on the roof himself, trying to complete the repairs. It was hardly fitting duty for the master of Bon Marché Lexington. Yet his predicament mirrored what was wrong on the farm. Nothing seemed to get done. He had hoped to build a new foaling barn, and it had been started. But for weeks now no work had been done on it and little more than the foundation and the studs of one wall were in place.

A rider approached up the lane and Albert cursed under his breath. He didn't need any interruptions at this point.

"Hello!" the rider called as he spotted Albert on the roof. "Could you direct me to Colonel Albert Dewey?"

"You've found him," Albert replied, no hint of humor in his voice.

The expression on the face of the young man on horseback showed his surprise. "Well, Colonel," he shouted up to him, "one of your neighbors, Mr. Jacob Harper, has suggested it might be worth my while to speak to you."

Albert didn't want to stop his roof repairs. "For what purpose?"

"Employment."

Dewey dropped his tools, shinnying down a ladder.

Dismounting, the visitor shook Albert's hand. He was thin and tall, with sandy hair, dark brown eyes, and a boyish countenance. In his early twenties, Albert guessed.

"Colonel, my name is James Orr. *Doctor* Orr. I'm a veterinarian seeking a position—"

"Excuse me," Dewey interrupted rudely, "I have no position for a veterinarian and probably not enough money to pay one properly. I'm in need of more basic help"—he gestured to the barn—"to fix leaky roofs, to keep fences in repair, to relieve me of some of the everyday drudgery."

"Oh?" Orr's disappointment, and his companion lack of comprehension, was evident. "From what Mr. Harper told me you have a growing operation here. Of some merit, he said. I thought perhaps—"

"Mr. Harper is too kind." The words had a bitter edge. "What I have here, Dr. Orr, is too damned much work. *And* twenty-six blacks, of whom not a half dozen are worth their keep. *And* two stupid whites who claim to be overseers."

Orr looked around quizzically. "I don't see—"

"My temper is out of sorts today. They're"—he smiled for the first time—"avoiding my immediate company for the moment."

The young man laughed.

"So you can see, Dr. Orr, that I really don't need the luxury of a veterinarian."

"Mr. Harper says you have animals with fine bloodlines."

"I do. And I've been trying to get several of them ready for the spring meeting at the Kentucky Association track. But—" He shrugged. "By the way, now that you're here—and I *will* pay your fee—I'd like you to look at a four-year-old I have. He's lame. But it's strange. I'm really not sure he's lame, if that makes any sense to you."

"Let's have a look at him."

As they entered the barn, Albert said, "From your accent, I'd guess you're a Scotsman."

"Yes, from Edinburgh. As a matter of fact, I studied at Edinburgh University. Two years ago I came to America, convinced that opportunities were greater here."

"And they haven't been?"

"Let's just say I haven't yet found what I've been seeking."

"This is the fellow," Dewey said, moving to a stall door. He reached in to gently play with the ears of a docile bay horse. "He was training extremely well, and then suddenly . . . how do I explain this? . . . I thought I spotted some lameness. Then, not. But the . . . fire had gone out of him."

"Hmmm." The vet opened the stall door, going in, pushing the animal away from him so that he could step back and observe it. In just a few seconds, he said, "The right fore, eh?"

Albert's eyes opened wide in surprise. "Yes. How did you know?"

Orr ignored the question. Picking up the right foot, he pressed his fingers firmly on the soft cushion of the frog; the horse tried to jerk the foot away from him. "Some heat," he muttered. He placed the foot down in the straw on the stall floor, continuing his observations. "The course where you work him"—Orr went on, not looking up—"it's extremely firm, I imagine."

"It is. Hard, even. We've had little rain recently." Albert showed his annoyance. "I ask you again—how did you know?"

"You notice how he holds that right leg," the veterinarian said, "how it's set out in front of the left, resting on the toe, the fetlock and knee flexed?"

"Yes."

"Well, Colonel, that's a classic symptom of navicular arthritis. That and the heat and tenderness of the frog."

Dewey was perplexed. "I've never heard of that."

"Not many have," Orr said quietly. "Or, at least, not many recognize it for what it is. It's an insidious thing. And generally obscure. Before most horsemen notice its onset the animal is dead lame and the ailment is ascribed to other things. Falsely, of course."

"Specifics, please."

Orr nodded, beginning his explanation slowly. "Navicular arthritis—it's called that in British veterinary circles, although it isn't an arthritis at all—defines what, in the final form, is inflammation and caries of the navicular bone in the foot, probably induced by repeated bruising—"

"Wait a minute—*caries*? My medical vocabulary is limited,

but doesn't that mean a progressive deterioration of the bone?"

"Or the teeth, yes."

"Damn!"

"An apt reaction." The young Scotsman wasn't trying for humor. "What happens, because the navicular bone is being constantly bruised, on hard turf mostly, is that a corrosive ulcer is in play on the bone."

"Oh, my God!"

"And it can only get worse."

"You mean there's no cure?" Albert felt nauseous.

"Cure? No. Were this a lesser horse I'd recommend it be put down immediately. But with a son of Priam, I think it valid to institute a treatment procedure which might save him for stud."

Once more Dewey was startled. "How did you know this is a Priam?" He gestured toward the horse.

"Priam stamps his progeny unmistakably. I saw several good ones by him racing in England. Indeed, I was there at Epsom Downs when he won the Derby."

"That's not possible," Albert insisted. "Priam won the Derby in 1830—nineteen years ago—and you can't be more than—"

"I was a lad of sixteen, attending the races with my father, who was—and is—a horse sales agent."

"But that means . . . no, I can't believe you're thirty-five years old."

Dr. Orr grinned. "Ah, yes, the boyish face. It has its drawbacks. Yet, it does seem to have a salutary effect on the ladies."

"I'll bet." Albert frowned now. "There'll be no racing for this son of Priam?"

"I'm afraid not. We can institute some surgery, rasping away the wall of the heel and blistering the coronet with Spanish-fly ointment. And we can make sure he's turned out on wet, soft pasture only. But the basic deterioration will continue. Gradually there'll be stumbling, a seeming stiffness in the shoulders, a stilty walk, profuse sweating if he's worked even a little bit."

"With pain?"

"Indeed. Intense pain. If you decide to put him to stud, I

suggest the cutting of the nerve to the fetlock to reduce the pain."

"Isn't that drastic?"

"The whole damned thing is drastic, Colonel Dewey. But there are no reasonable choices with this ailment. Eventually, no matter what is done, he's going to have to be put down. But with some care, he ought to give you a couple of crops. Maybe even three."

Albert shook his head in disgust. "What I can't understand is why I didn't notice this earlier."

"That's a peculiarity of navicular disease. It progresses quite far before *any* lameness is seen. And then it seems to disappear. He may be lame one day, and seemingly sound the next. Or, he may be lame for a week, only to have a remission for a similar period of time. Of course, a veterinarian regularly in attendance might have—" He shrugged. "But, then, the end would have been the same."

Dewey groaned, going to the colt and patting his neck. He was using the time to think.

"I'd like to try to save him for stud." A sudden thought struck him. "This navicular thing isn't hereditary, is it?"

"Not to my certain knowledge," Dr. Orr answered. There was a slight grin. "Which means I'm not sure."

"I want to try it anyway."

"Very well. I'll start with him in the morning if that suits you, Colonel Dewey."

"It does. And please, the military title is a thing of the past. The name is Albert."

"And my friends call me Jamie."

"Fair enough. Now, Jamie, will you take dinner with my wife and I?"

"I'd like that, if it's not an imposition on Mrs. Dewey."

"Believe me, she'll welcome the opportunity for some conversation with a male other than myself."

Dr. Orr wondered whether he was correct about the note of despair he detected in the remark.

III

HARRIET Walston Dewey was a young woman of ambition. She liked to believe her ambition was channeled into the career of her husband and the well-being of her daughters. But there was a lot of "self" in her makeup, nurtured in her upbringing as the only daughter of a prominent New Orleans banking family. Her marriage, some nine years earlier, to Statler Dewey had been a product of that ambition. There was love in the relationship—she was almost calculating about that—but Statler represented to her something beyond passion. He was handsome, young, of a wealthy family, and he was *not* of the old New Orleans families; not French, not Spanish, not of mixed origin. It was almost as if she were bringing new blood into the city's social structure. Statler was somehow different—solid, but different, fresh, exciting.

She saw something else in him, too. His ambition matched her own. Together, they could be something special. Her wealth and social standing, matched with the Dewey horse-racing fortune, could place her at the pinnacle of the New Orleans social world. That it had not worked out, because of the scandal generated by Statler's father, was only a momentary setback to her. Now that she was in Nashville, Harriet viewed those tragic months just past as an opportunity; an opportunity she meant to seize.

She knew how to do it.

As Statler and Harriet prepared for bed in their cramped temporary quarters in the Bon Marché mansion, she said to him, "That piece of land by the deer park is going to make a lovely setting for our new home."

"Hmmm." Statler was studying a sheaf of reports on the finances of the Schimmel Newspapers.

"I've been giving some thought to what the house ought to be."

"Uh-huh."

"You're not listening to me, darling."

"What?" He looked up from the papers. "I'm sorry, dear, I've been trying to make sense of these reports. You mentioned something about a house—"

Harriet smiled at him. "Not just a house, Statler, but a proper setting for the future owner of the Schimmel Newspapers."

He laughed. "Aren't you being a bit premature? I'm merely a salaried employee of August Schimmel."

She went to where he was seated at a small table, putting

her arms around his neck, kissing the top of his head. "I don't like it, darling, when you make light of what you're doing."

He turned, pulling her into his lap, cradling her, enjoying the smell of her. "I'm not making light of it. It's just that there are no guarantees I'm going to be the heir apparent—"

"But that's implied, isn't it, by August and Louise designating you as general manager?"

"Yes, I suppose it is."

She kissed him. "Well, then, I think we ought to give some serious thought to what kind of house we're going to build at the deer park."

Statler chuckled. "Why do I get the feeling you've already made that decision?"

"Am I that transparent?"

"Uh-huh."

She snuggled down into his lap. "Well, I *do* have a confession, Statler. I've been in touch with the architect Adolphus Heiman—"

"Oh?"

"—and some preliminary drawings he's made arrived in the post today."

She sprang up, running to the wardrobe, taking out a roll of sketches and spreading them out on the bed. Statler joined her, looking down at the plans soberly.

"It's to be an Italianate-style house incorporating classical elements . . ." Gaily she went through the details: the grand salon highlighted by six Corinthian columns across the expanse of it, parlors on each side of the salon for lavish entertaining, a master bedroom suite consisting of the bedroom itself, a parlor, a library, and a drawing room "where you can entertain gentlemen and business associates, darling." Also a dining room, three large bedrooms on the first floor for guests, a gallery above the salon, reached by two wide stairways, to accommodate living quarters for their three daughters, plus additional bedrooms for their guests; Carrara marble fireplaces . . . bronze chandeliers . . . French blinds . . . gold leaf on the cornices . . . Venetian glass in the windows . . . classic statues on the parapet of the roof.

He let her go on, unwilling to stem her enthusiasm.

"And in the rear of the main house, darling," she said, "a separate building for the household staff, where the kitchens will be, of the same exterior design as the mansion. A carriage house, of course, of similar design. And formal gardens with fountains and gazebos—" Harriet took a deep breath. "Isn't it *marvelous,* darling?"

"And for a marvelous price, I'll wager."

"It will be the finest house in all of Davidson County!"

"No doubt. But how much?"

"Well," she said hesitantly, "Mr. Heiman estimates the total cost will be three hundred and eighty-five thousand, but—"

"My God!" Statler gasped. "There's no way I could afford that. I am, as I mentioned before, a salaried employee of the Schimmel Newspapers."

"But there's my trust fund, darling—"

"No!"

"And I'm sure Daddy will allow me to have it for such a worthwhile project."

He laughed. "Daddy will think you're out of your mind."

"But if he releases the money—?"

"Don't you think it's a bit pretentious? Bon Marché already has a Princess, you know."

Harriet wrinkled up her nose. "Alma May has let Bon Marché get rather dowdy, don't you think?"

Statler sighed. "Am I going to have any peace over this matter?"

She put her arms around him, drawing him to her, kissing him with purpose. "I want this house for *you,* darling. I want you to be the most important man in Nashville." She jabbed at his ego. "Don't you want that?"

He didn't reply immediately. He was visualizing himself as the master of that grandiose house. It was a pleasing thought. "Do you honestly believe your father will release the trust?"

"Yes."

"Well, if he can't deny you, how can I?"

IV

IT HAD been a difficult decision for Albert Dewey, but one, he believed, of necessity. Some may have viewed what he did as a moral act. It wasn't. Bon Marché Lexington had simply not prospered with its slave labor. The work wasn't getting done to his satisfaction. He took his blacks to the Lexington slave market, all twenty-six of them, and sold them.

It had not been a pleasant experience. He winced as he watched the buyers, most of them agents for plantations in the deep South (the cotton and rice planters), pulling mouths open to check teeth, and pinching arms and legs to find out how muscular the blacks were. There was a crudeness in all that, setting his stomach to churning. And yet, it had only been a business decision. Perhaps others found the Negro labor adequate. He had not.

The sale completed, Albert sat at his desk, composing a letter to send to Bon Marché, trying to explain his actions—

In Nashville, True Jackson was not a happy man.

For the third week in succession Alma May had intruded on the gentlemen's sherry-laced discussion period in the Bon Marché drawing room. At best, True felt, it had a dampening effect on the openness of the conversation. At worst, the woman always seemed to dominate the discussion, to insist on the rightness of her views. It annoyed True even more that brother Able and his father-in-law, August Schimmel, seemed to welcome the contributions of the Princess.

Now, on this night, there was a second annoyance: a letter from Bon Marché Lexington with which True disagreed on all points.

"I seriously question," he was saying, "the need for the employment of a veterinarian, especially in light of the still strained finances there in Kentucky."

"Albert's no fool," Alma May interjected. "He's obviously doing what he believes will enhance the Lexington operation."

"He's doing more than that," True snapped. "In essence, he's taken this young Scotsman—and how do we know he's what he says he is?—in as a partner of sorts. My God, he's turned the heart of the operation, the racing stable, over to this stranger, as Albert dallies with his plan, as he puts it"— he looked down at the letter he held—"'to rid the farm of its dependence on the uneven qualities of the labor of the blacks.' And so, immigrant Irishmen are being brought in. Even Germans—"

He halted his tirade in embarrassment. "Of course, August, I don't mean that as a slur on those of German origin."

Schimmel laughed. "Of course you don't, True. But I can see some merit in what he's doing. If he's had difficulties with the black labor available there—"

"There are no such difficulties here," True interrupted.

"Hmmm. Perhaps not." The newspaper publisher's tone changed. "But maybe Albert is in the van of changes that will become inevitable. Whatever defense can be made of the employment of slaves to maintain this plantation, or any other, it must be clear that the situation is an artificial one. Charles Dewey recognized that a long time ago. How long can we safely rely on the blacks as a ready supply of labor?"

"Are you siding with those damned abolitionists?"

"I didn't say that, True, and don't put words in my mouth!" The discussion had been heated to the boiling point. "I stand opposed to the efforts of the abolitionists to dictate terms to the South. But, damn it, the idea that we can continue to maintain our economy on the backs of those people is a dangerously false one. Worse, it's a demeaning one. You must sense that, too, True."

"I'm not sure I do," the elder Jackson brother answered sullenly. "Look around Bon Marché. What would happen to us should the blacks be suddenly removed?"

"That's just it—it shouldn't be *sudden*. But we have to recognize that we *must* gradually change to a labor force working for wages, one that is far more stable than the blacks."

True threw up his hands in disgust.

"It seems to me the strengths of the Northern region are brought about by the employment of *free* men," August went on. "Fifty years ago, I'll admit, there would have been no Southern economy without the ready supply of slaves. But that's not true any longer. Other labor—perhaps better labor—is now becoming rapidly available with the increases in immigration."

Schimmel stood up to make his point, his hands clasped behind his back. "Blind insistence that there is only one way—the slavery way—will be the death of the South! The *death*, I tell you!"

There was dead silence in the drawing room.

When Schimmel spoke again, the voice had become calm. "What Albert Dewey is doing in Kentucky might well be the most significant move he'll ever make in his life. It might be a course, Cousin True, which Bon Marché ought to consider emulating."

True shook his head, convinced of only one truth. "Such a thing will not happen so long as I hold the reins of Bon Marché in my hands."

Holding the reins did not necessarily equate to ownership of the carriage. And another silence prevailed, because it was clear True had challenged the legal holders of the plantation with his intractable statement. Both Able and August believed Alma May, who had been strangely quiet, would rise to meet that challenge and were surprised when she didn't. Maybe even a little disappointed.

"Circumstances are different here in Nashville and in Lexington," she commented with uncharacteristic composure. "Albert will just have to be allowed to pursue his own course in Kentucky. And here"—she paused for an instant—"we must rely on the experience of tradition, as long as it gives strength to Bon Marché. We'll know soon enough if weaknesses develop. If they do, we'll deal with them at that time."

The Princess drained her glass. "My father would have been stimulated by tonight's discussion." She stood, preparing to leave. "In the end, gentlemen, it all comes down to this: Bon Marché's well-being is the only thing that matters—and the rest of the world can go to hell!"

True Jackson permitted himself a small smile.

V

DID the words spoken at that late-night meeting motivate what happened at the Gallatin races? Perhaps obliquely, in that they reinforced True's stewardship of Bon Marché at a time when the finances of the plantation were seriously overextended. It was a cash-poor estate for a number of reasons: the funds expended for the expansion into Kentucky, the money spent to buy off the creditors of the late George Dewey Sr., and the inexplicable decline in Bon Marché's "racing luck" in the '48 season.

Alma May's contention that "the rest of the world can go to hell" may have emboldened the normally cautious True Jackson, taking him beyond the limits of his prudence.

In any event, the Bon Marché racing entourage traveled the

forty-odd miles of the Cumberland Road, generally following the course of the river northeastward, to take on the back-country horsemen at the Gallatin races in the first week in April. Although only those few miles separated the two communities, Nashville and Gallatin were worlds apart. By 1849, Nashville had taken on some polish, a necessary adjunct to being the state capital. But Gallatin prided itself in having retained the tough frontier spirit.

Gallatin horsemen liked nothing better than to see the Jackson brothers' sleek, highly bred Bon Marché racing string coming up the road. It represented to them the outside world and an opportunity to prove the superiority of the methods employed with their hard-knocking horses. Indeed, a year earlier, the Bon Marché runners had been soundly beaten at Gallatin, and the natives welcomed the chance to do it again.

What was not known, at first, by most of those attending the '49 meeting was that a new era was under way at Bon Marché. It was personified by one George Dewey Jr., handling the thoroughbreds spirited away from New Orleans—horses not seen before in those rural precincts. One of those, a Louisiana-bred called Bayou Boy, was entered in the Gallatin Cup; a stern test in that it was the best-of-three heats, each heat contested at three miles.

Bon Marché had a second entry, the home-bred Vandal's Pride, saddled by the farm's other young assistant trainer, Charles Dewey II. But the strategy for the Cup race, outlined to both George and Two by True Jackson, was that Vandal's Pride, expected to draw considerable support from the bettors, was to be the stalking-horse for Bayou Boy, setting an artificial pace in the early stages of the first heat so that Bayou Boy could come off the pace to run down tired horses.

True's plan had two purposes: one was to win the Gallatin Cup and its liberal purse; the second was to take advantage of the wagering patterns he anticipated to accomplish a betting coup. Bayou Boy, not known there, could be expected to go off at high odds and True meant to take advantage of them.

Two Dewey objected: "Vandal's Pride is a legitimate contender for the Cup. If we've got to have a rabbit, why not make it Bayou Boy?"

"Because, lad," True explained patiently, "Bon Marché

needs a substantial score. I ask you: how many race purses did we win last year?"

"There were none," young Charles admitted.

True shrugged. "Given that sad reality, we can't afford another financial disaster in forty-nine. It's for the well-being of Bon Marché, Two."

"You speak of a 'substantial score.' May I know what that is?"

The older man grinned malevolently, whispering his answer: "A Bayou Boy win could give us something in the neighborhood of seventy-five thousand."

Two was shocked. "You've been busy, Cousin True." The sarcasm wasn't hidden.

"I won't deny that. But I've only done what is necessary."

Two looked to his brother for comment, but George Junior was strangely silent. "I see. And the second heat, Cousin True? Am I expected to sacrifice Vandal's Pride in that one, too?"

There was a hesitation. "The first heat results will have to dictate what we do later."

Disconsolate, Charles Dewey II nevertheless decided to go along with the plan. He told himself he had little choice in the matter.

The entire Bon Marché entourage was on hand for the running of the Gallatin Cup. Princess Alma May, in the company of Willie Carstairs, presided over the family picnic. Joy and Hope Jackson were there, too, with all of their children. Also the wives and children of the young assistant trainers, George and Two. The newspaper branch of the family was fully represented: Louise and August Schimmel, Lee Dewey, and Statler and Harriet Dewey, with their three daughters. For Harriet, it was a new beginning, free of the cruel gossip that had plagued her in New Orleans.

"This is . . . uh . . . quaint," she commented to her husband, gazing around the country racing grounds.

"It's certainly not Metairie in New Orleans," Statler grinned.

"Thank God for that!" Harriet, buoyed by her enthusiasm, threw her arms around Statler's neck and kissed him soundly. "I, for one, intend to enjoy *these* races."

And most of the Deweys did enjoy the races. Charles Dewey II was not one of them. When it came time for the Gallatin Cup, Two sullenly saddled Vandal's Pride and then drew his jockey away from the others to give him his instructions.

"Dick, I want you to trust me on this," he said to the black boy. "I want you to get the lead immediately. Use the stick on him, if you have to, to go to the front—three, four lengths."

The jockey's surprise showed on his ebony face.

"And hold it as long as you can," Two went on. "But it's very important that you not use him up. If Bayou Boy challenges you at the end, let him by—" He thought for a moment. "If he can get by. But the most important thing is to set the pace in this first heat, and have something left for the second. Is that clear?"

"Yassuh." But he was disturbed by the instructions.

"I'm well aware, Dick, that Vandal's Pride is best off the pace. But not this first heat."

"Yassuh."

"Riders up!" a steward bellowed.

Trainer and jockey went to Vandal's Pride and Two boosted him aboard.

"I need a second heat," the trainer said forcefully.

The black rider nodded his understanding.

Fourteen went to the post, all well behaved as they approached the barrier. The drum tapped and they were off. Dick followed his instructions to the letter, screaming and whipping as he took Vandal's Pride to the front, quickly opening up a five-length lead.

"Now, settle him in," Two said under his breath. As if the jockey heard him, the whip was put away and he took a firm hold on his horse as the lead was maintained.

True, pleased with what he was seeing, said to his young assistants, "The public pool let Bayou Boy go off at twenty to one. I've got a thousand wagered there, as well."

George Junior stared at him. "Even with that artificial pace, I'm not sure my horse can come off it to win."

"He'll win," True said confidently. "Believe me, he'll win."

The first mile was covered in a brisk 1:54 by the leader.

"Good, good," True chortled. "He's dragging the others with him."

Vandal's Pride's five-length lead had shrunk to three and a half by the time the field had entered the backstretch in the second mile. Turning for home the second time, the lead was down to two lengths. Bayou Boy was running easily in seventh place, saving ground on the rail. Time for the second mile was 1:56, to True's delight.

As the horses swept into the first turn of the third mile, a runner appeared on the flank of Vandal's Pride. By the time they straightened into the backstretch for the last time, Vandal's Pride had been caught.

"Save him, save him," Two breathed.

Bayou Boy, in full stride now, was moved out to make his challenge, quickly taken into sixth place and then fifth. Around the turn he ducked into the rail once more, passing two others on the inside for third. Two, though, was not watching his brother's horse. His only concern was what Dick was doing with Vandal's Pride, and Dick was following orders. He was hand-riding the colt, saving him, yet keeping him from being distanced.

In the homestretch, the two leaders, having accepted the challenge of the artificially quick pace, were faltering. Bayou Boy, in a clear path on the rail, shot through, taking command with seventy-five yards to go, winning easily.

Two raced to Vandal's Pride as he crossed the finish line in eighth place, grabbing the halter and beaming at Dick. "You did well," he said to the jockey.

The black lad slid out of the saddle. "If we come off the pace, Mistah Charles," he said soberly, "we win this race."

"I know." He examined the legs of the lathered animal. "Was he laboring?"

"No, suh. We jest too quick early, that's all."

Two patted him on the back. "But he'll race again, Dick." To the handlers who had come up: "Put a sheet on him and walk him. Keep him moving. And no water until I say!"

He made his way back to the happy collection of Bon Marché supporters. When the initial excitement of the victory of Bayou Boy had played itself out, Two drew True Jackson aside.

"All right now, you've won your wager," he said sternly, "and I'm not going to sacrifice that horse again."

True's mouth dropped open. "The wager wasn't for the heat," he explained, "it was for the race. For the Cup. Didn't you understand that?"

"I didn't, no."

"We will have to win another heat to collect."

Two scowled. "You're asking a lot, Cousin True."

"Not for myself," Jackson insisted, "but for Bon Marché."

"It's always for Bon Marché, isn't it? There are days when I wish the plantation could voice its own wishes." He turned to walk away.

Charles II didn't return to his family. Instead, he made his way through the crowd and into a wooded area several hundred yards from the racecourse, where he dropped down and propped himself against a tree. The first heat was rerun in his mind and he saw again the dishonesty of it. He huddled there alone, debating with himself.

When the field was called for the second heat, eleven answered the steward. Three had been distanced in the first heat and declared out of Cup competition. Once more he saddled Vandal's Pride, satisfied with his condition. And once more he counseled the Negro jockey.

"Off the pace this time," he said quietly. "If you're third or fourth at the end of two, you might have enough left to win it."

"Yassuh, we will."

"Then, good luck." He smiled as he helped the boy into the saddle. "And whatever happens—thank you, Dick."

"We win it, Mistah Charles."

Two winked at him.

Again the start was clean. But this time there was a new pacesetter as Dick settled Vandal's Pride in the middle of the pack, running stride for stride with his stablemate, Bayou Boy.

"What the devil's going on out there?" True Jackson demanded.

Two frowned. "I suspect that first heat took too much out of him."

"We *need* that pace!"

"Then somebody else's horse is going to have to set it."

When the first mile was run in 2:03, True was moaning, "Too slow, too slow."

Two made no comment, his eyes fixed on Dick, who had unlimbered his whip as the field swept into the backstretch for the second mile. The jock showed the whip to his mount, then flicked it lightly against its neck. Vandal's Pride responded, not with a sudden burst of speed, but slowly, inexorably. From sixth place he began to pick up horses. Bayou Boy's rider, unsure of what was happening, followed.

In the run down the homestretch for the second time, Vandal's Pride was third on the rail, with Bayou Boy lapped on him, a half length behind. They went into the third mile that way and down the backstretch without a change of position. On the third turn, Dick's whip cracked and Vandal's Pride lunged forward as the jockey guided him to pass the leaders, brushing Bayou Boy as he did.

In five strides, Vandal's Pride put his nose in front. Bayou Boy, bothered by the brushing contact, tried to challenge, but couldn't make up the ground. Whipping rhythmically now, Dick drove his mount to the finish line, increasing his advantage with each jump. Bayou Boy was third, beaten four lengths.

Two ran to the side of the winner. "No matter what you hear from now on, Dick," he instructed, "you're to try to win the third heat."

"Yassuh." The black boy was grinning.

As expected, True Jackson was livid with anger. "Not only have you jeopardized the wager," he snarled at Two through his teeth, "but you've also put The Cup in doubt!"

"You're so caught up in your scheme," Two said sarcastically, "that you forget The Cup is already ours. The third heat will be a match race—between the two winning Bon Marché horses."

"Yes, yes, of course," True sputtered. He fought to control his temper, finally putting a hand on Two's shoulder in a gesture suggesting repair of their differences. "And now we must concentrate on the wager, mustn't we?" He forced a smile. "Seventy-five thousand for a Bayou Boy win—and that's a lot of money."

The rest was an anticlimax; the real drama had already been played out. As Two knew he would, the elder Jackson insisted on giving the final instructions to both jockeys. Two didn't even listen. But he was content in the knowledge that there was one other honest man there: a tiny black lad named Dick, who might yet frustrate the master of Bon Marché.

When the drum tapped for the third heat, Bayou Boy assumed a slim lead. And through three grueling miles he held on to win the Gallatin Cup. But by just half a length. The strain of having set the false pace in the first heat had taken its inevitable toll on the gallant Vandal's Pride.

In a sense, it had all come out right. True Jackson had replenished the coffers of Bon Marché. And the vaunted all-purple silks of the plantation had been carried across the finish line in victory once more.

Yet Vandal's Pride had been sacrificed. The thoroughbred wasn't the only victim of the betting coup. It had taken its toll, too, on Charles Dewey II.

16

BETH Dewey was frightened.

The anger and the companion despair she saw in the pleasant young man she had married was something new, something foreign. What Two was proposing to do was so radical she couldn't fully comprehend it. The pretty wife knew only that she had to try to find a way to dissuade him.

"California?" she cried. "You can't be serious, Two."

"Deadly serious," he said with quiet determination.

"But over a . . . a . . . *misunderstanding* about a wager on a horse race?"

His face was sad. "Of all people, I thought you would understand."

Beth put her arms around him, kissing him. "I believe I do, darling. If what True Jackson did was dishonest, I can appreciate your concern. But to consider . . . fleeing to California—?"

"Not fleeing, Beth. We'd just be . . . hell, I burned my bridges at Gallatin. It's not possible for me to work with True anymore. Junior will be the fair-haired boy now and I'll be a pariah." He shook his head. "No, we need a new place, a *clean* new place, to begin again. And California offers the best opportunities."

"But there must be other places of opportunity."

"Like what?"

"Kentucky, perhaps. You could join Albert there."

Two's chuckle broke the soberness of the moment. "I suppose you'd enjoy spending the rest of your days in such close proximity to your sister?"

Beth also laughed. "No, I confess the prospect of putting up with Virginia day after day is a bit overwhelming."

"Then Kentucky isn't the answer, is it?" Her husband shrugged. "Getting involved in the problems of Albert and Virginia seems no better than my tenuous situation here."

"But—California, Two? How could we do that? It's such a long way. And the money—where would we get the money to start over again?"

"I'll work it out," he assured her.

II

IN Lexington in those same hours, Albert Dewey was telling himself the same thing: *I'll work it out.* But his relationship with Virginia seemed not to improve. Jamie Orr's arrival at Bon Marché Lexington had helped for only a few days. The young veterinarian's charming manner had thawed his wife for a time, but now she was regressing to the coldness her husband found so inexplicable. And so maddening.

Albert had hopes, though, that the opening of the race meeting of the Kentucky Association (more formally, the Kentucky Association for the Improvement of Breeds of Stock), with its attendant gay social life, would permit Virginia to emerge from her strange cocoon. She had, under Albert's persistent urging, bought a new gown for the ball to follow the first day of racing a week hence.

As they prepared for bed, Albert said, "The word is that the spring racing ball is *the* social event of the year."

Virginia sat before the mirror of her dressing table, soberly brushing her hair, silently counting the strokes she gave her gleaming tresses, which were the color of cured young tobacco leaves. Perhaps it was an odd blond hue, but it fit Virginia admirably, enhancing her beauty. She didn't answer Albert as she continued her methodical brushing.

He watched her from the bed, remembering how he had felt when he first met her in Nashville. Remembering that he had never seen a more beautiful woman. He still believed so, but now he recognized beauty alone was not enough for him.

"I think the ball will be a good thing for us," he said. "Once you're into the social whirl, you'll feel more content with your life here in Lexington."

She stopped the brushing and stood up, her clinging night-gown sensuously outlining her firm figure. "Do you think I'll be acceptable in local society?"

"Of course you will!" The question had startled Albert. "What a strange thing to ask."

"Perhaps."

She went to the bed, sliding between the covers, positioning herself stiffly by the side of her husband. He kissed her on the cheek.

"I'm not exactly the outgoing social type, you know," she said quietly.

"Nonsense—"

"No, I recognize that," she insisted. Virginia turned to face him. "And I recognize that you believe so, too."

He laughed. "What a conversation to be having. What is this, self-denigration time?"

"No." The voice was very soft, emotionless. "No." She sighed. "It's not that at all. It's just that—well, I find it difficult to be like other women."

"I don't want you to be like *other* women. I fell in love with *you*. I want *you*, not other women."

He reached for her, pulling her into his arms. She responded, nestling down, seeming to relax. He fondled her, cupping a breast in his hand. Virginia strained against his touch. A hand roamed down, catching the hem of her gown, starting to pull it up.

"No!" Inexplicably, she pulled away from him. "No!" She began to cry. "Dear God—"

Albert groaned. Angrily, he pushed himself from the bed, drawing on his gown, making for the door.

"Albert! Don't go!" It was a command.

"Why? So you can continue to make a fool of me?"

"*Please* don't go. We have to talk." She was struggling to stop her sobbing.

His hand on the doorknob, he turned to look at her. "Talk! It seems a bit too late for that."

"Please!" It was a cry for help.

"Very well." He shrugged. "Talk."

"I have to say some things"—she sucked in a sob—"while I have the courage." She wiped her tears on a corner of the sheet, sitting up in the bed. "It's not going to be easy for me, Albert. It will help if you let me speak without interruptions."

Her husband nodded.

"When we first met," Virginia started quietly, "I thought you were one of the nicest, one of the most considerate, men I had ever known. Admittedly, I didn't have much experience with men, but that's the way I thought of you." The words were flat, delivered in almost a monotone. "When you asked me to marry you, I didn't react, I'm afraid, like a giddy, love-sick girl."

Albert remembered.

"Instead, I considered that you were a kind young man, with whom I could be at ease. But"—she hesitated—"I accepted your proposal for one important reason—you were in the military. Oh, it wasn't because of any romantic notion I had about soldiers and heroes. It was because—God, forgive me!—your career would keep you away from me for long periods of time, limiting those times when I'd have to be . . . intimate with you."

He exhaled deeply, feeling ill.

There was a sob again. "I married you, Albert, because it was expected of me. In my parents' eyes I would marry a fine young man, have children, and be content. What they didn't know—" Weeping halted the words; it took her several moments to regain her composure. "What they didn't know was that the very idea of being with a man was repulsive to me. I convinced myself that such an unnatural feeling would go away once a man made love to me. It didn't. God help me, it never has."

Virginia's crying overwhelmed her now. Disgusted, Albert went to the window, gazing out, seeing nothing. His growing anger was blinding him.

"I think . . . I think"—she sobbed—"I *know* I'm telling you something you already suspected. You must understand I love you for . . . being patient with me. I love you, too, for being the good father you are. But . . . I . . . I . . . don't love you in any *normal* way. The terrible truth, Albert, is that I can't force myself any longer to . . . to give myself to you. I . . . just . . . *can't!*"

Her weeping now had become hysteria. As Albert listened to the sound of her the full import of what Virginia had confessed enraged him. He had been betrayed! And he remembered their wedding night when their marriage wasn't consummated; and the day he returned home from the Mexican War when she had pleaded for time because he had become too much of a "stranger" to her. And those other times—

"Jesus Christ—all these years!" he screamed at her as he turned away from the window. "All these years . . . and four children . . . and all that time you've been . . . you've been . . ."

"A fraud," she whimpered.

"A fraud?" He laughed in an ugly manner. "Worse than that! I can't even bring myself to say it. And . . . now . . . what do you expect of me?"

"Nothing. If you want a divorce, you shall have it." Again, she wiped her eyes on the sheet.

"And what of the children?"

"I'll do whatever you want."

"What I want?" He felt crazed. "What I want is a wife—!"

Her fingers toyed with a corner of the blanket, her eyes following the movements of the fingers as if they were important. "I think I should leave in the morning."

"Yes," he said coldly. "And before the children are awake. I don't want them to know of this. I don't want them *ever* to know of this!"

"Of course."

It all seemed so unreal to him. A horrible fantasy. With just those few words they had made a final decision on their marriage. And on the children.

"Good Lord," Albert Dewey sighed, "what a stupid fool I've been."

He left the bedroom then, closing the door firmly, hoping the act would shut her away from him. As he went down the stairs toward the first floor, intent on getting a bourbon, a curious feeling of relief came over him. And then guilt because of it. He sank down on the steps, groaning in excruciating pain.

III

It wasn't "gold fever" infecting him. He was certain of that. Charles Dewey II had read the increasingly lurid newspaper stories of pristine streams paved with gold and of men made as rich as Midas overnight, but his decision to head out to California was based, in his mind, on more solid ground: the West represented a new beginning for him, just as the "West" of Tennessee had offered the opportunity for a new start to his grandfather, his namesake, some fifty-three years earlier.

If there was to be gold at the end of the voyage, it would be a peripheral thing, because Charles intended to "be in business," to establish himself as a responsible citizen; as a leader, if need be, of one of the key states in the burgeoning Union.

It was on that basis Nashville banker Willie Carstairs saw fit to finance young Dewey's dream. Carstairs looked upon it as a solid investment and the collateral was Charles's integrity. Indeed, it was his integrity in the matter of True Jackson's betting coup which made it necessary for him to leave Bon Marché and strike out on his own.

Two had studied the ways of getting to California and his choice of a route seem preordained. Overland, via Conestoga wagons in huge trains, was the most popular way. But it was slow and not without hazards. While he was thinking about it he read the account of one gold-seeker, who had written to a newspaper: "Instead of turning up the golden sands of the Sacramento, the spade of the adventurer is first used to bury the remains of a companion." By sea, there were the sailing ships—some of them fast clippers—rounding South America at Cape Horn and then heading north to San Francisco. But it was a voyage of seventeen thousand miles, one requiring the commitment of six to eight months of time, and often longer.

To Charles, then, the best way was the shortest way—by ship to Central America, across the mere seventy-five miles of the Isthmus of Panama to the Pacific, where another ship would take him to San Francisco. The agents of a New Orleans-based shipping company, with whom Dewey exchanged letters, assured him California would be reached in six to eight weeks. *Why would anyone go any other way?* he wondered.

As he stood now at the Nashville docks, waiting to board a steamboat for New Orleans, he had in his pocket a message informing him that he would leave New Orleans as a passenger aboard a vessel of the United States Mail Steamship

Company, which would take him to the Panama port of Aspinwall. There, an English-speaking guide would take him across the Isthmus, and once in Panama City, he'd have passage on a reputable sailing ship bound for San Francisco. He would be in San Francisco by the end of July.

There was no big send-off for him at Nashville. He wanted it that way. His wife, Beth, was there, and his proud eight-year-son, Charles III. He planned to send for them once he was established in California. "It'll be just a few months, darling," he had told Beth the previous evening, "before we're reunited again."

At the docks also were his aunt Alma May and Willie Carstairs.

"I'm going to miss Bon Marché," Charles admitted as Alma May kissed him good-bye.

"You don't have to leave," the Princess told him. "I can always use my influence to patch up the differences with True."

"No. I suspect I would have made this move eventually anyway, regardless of the circumstances prevailing at Bon Marché." He turned to shake hands with Carstairs. "I'll do everything in my power, Willie, to make your investment pay off."

The banker laughed. "Two, my boy, you never would have gotten the money if I had thought otherwise."

Charles bent down to his son's level, holding him at arm's length to look into his face. "You're to look after your mother, son."

"Yes, sir," the little boy answered soberly. And then he fell into his father's arms, hugging him mightily.

Finally, there was a farewell to Beth. He kissed her gently, grinning at her. "I'm afraid if I kiss you with more passion," he whispered to her, "I won't want to leave."

"We'll keep the passion until later, then." She struggled to hold back her tears.

"Agreed."

Without another word, he picked up his traveling bag and hurried up the gangplank, standing at the rail just staring at them. The gangplank was raised and the sidewheeler's giant engines throbbed to life. As the boat began to back away from the dock, Charles waved.

He called out: "Until California and—"
The wail of the steamboat's whistle drowned out his words.

IV

CAREFULLY reining the double-hitch drawing his phaeton, Albert Dewey maneuvered his way through the hodgepodge of carriages crowding the infield of the Kentucky Association track, hoping he could still find a place in the shade under one of the large trees. He had not intended to be there at all; Virginia had been gone less than a week and his mood was foul. But the children had been promised a picnic on the first day of the race meeting, and Albert's guilt (he had lied to them about why their mother had left) compelled him to produce the picnic.

Eight-year-old Jefferson had told him: "If we have the picnic, Father, we can tell Mother all about it when she gets back. That way she won't think she missed anything."

The childish logic, based on Albert's story that Virginia had merely been called to Nashville because their Grandmother Stoker was ill, left the father with no escape. Now, the children—Jefferson, Jackson, Carolina, and Staunch—bounced about happily in the rear of the phaeton, demanding from the Negro housemaid, Susan, knowledge of the contents of the picnic baskets.

Albert found a place in the shade and delegated to the black woman the responsibility for the well-being of his children, going off in search of Jamie Orr, who would saddle the runners representing Bon Marché Lexington on that day. It was an important moment, after all: the first competitive appearances of his horses. He had designed new silks, taking the royal purple of his late grandfather's stable and crosshatching it with bands of gold.

"Too gaudy, do you think?" he had asked Orr.

"For racing silks?" the young Scotsman had laughed. "There's no such thing as *too* gaudy."

Dewey pushed his way through the throng gathering for the inaugural 1849 races, finding Jamie chatting amiably with an elderly gentleman and a young woman.

"Ahh, speaking of the devil," Orr said, grinning, as Albert approached. "Mr. Thomas, I'm pleased to present the master of Bon Marché Lexington, Colonel Albert Dewey."

Use of the military title brought a frown to Dewey's face.

"And Albert, this is Mr. Raynall Thomas, a breeder from nearby Georgetown. And his daughter, Miss Lillian."

Albert shook the man's hand, bowing slightly to acknowledge the young woman. "I've heard of your farm, Mr. Thomas. You've had some good runners come out of there."

"Yes, we've been most fortunate. But truthfully, Colonel, I'd rather talk about your employment experiment. Dr. Orr has been telling us that you've got rid of all your blacks."

"Except for some old retainers on the household staff, yes."

"And you've replaced them with Irishmen?"

Albert grinned. "Well, not all Irishmen—two are Polish, one's a Hungarian, and four or five"—he looked to Orr for confirmation—"are German. All recent immigrants."

"Five Germans," Jamie said.

"And all have been placed on wages?" Thomas asked.

"Yes. We have seventeen in all right now, including two jockeys, and they've replaced twenty-nine blacks."

"Equally?"

"Absolutely. They're fine workers, and our costs are no greater."

"Amazing." The older horseman shook his head. "How are the jocks?"

"One of them, Mike Murphy, came to us with some experience in his homeland. The other, Shamus Ryan, is being schooled by Dr. Orr and seems to be coming along very well."

Raynall Thomas soberly contemplated what he had been told. "If you succeed in this, Colonel Dewey, you may start a revolution in the Southern horse business."

"That's not my intent, Mr. Thomas. I'm concerned only about my own farm. What others choose to do doesn't bother me at all."

Jamie excused himself to saddle the Dewey entry for the first race.

"I'm afraid I've taken too much of your time, Colonel, with my questions," Thomas said apologetically. "I do have something I need to do, and I trust you'll excuse me." He gestured to his daughter.

"Am I expected to be polite again," she asked petulantly, "while I listen to those same tired stories of your cronies?"

Her father scowled. "Come, Lillian," he said quietly. It was an order.

"Perhaps Colonel Dewey and I could watch the races together and I might be able to enlighten him on some of the local lore." She smiled sweetly.

"Lil, that's enough!" Thomas snapped. To Albert: "Unhappily, my wife died some fifteen years ago and I fear I've done a poor job in raising my daughter. I hope you'll accept my apologies for her forwardness."

"Apologies aren't necessary," Dewey replied. "I'd be happy to have Miss Thomas as my companion. Her local lore might be instructive." *Why am I saying this?*

The young woman immediately laid a firm hand on Albert's arm.

The father grimaced. "Be forewarned, Colonel—my daughter likes to have her own way." He tipped his hat and was gone.

"Do you like to have your own way?" Dewey asked, chuckling.

"Always."

"In that case, your father's warning is welcomed."

He studied the young woman as they sought out a vantage point to watch the first race. Her figure was boyish, firm, although there was no doubt of her womanliness. Her pretty open face was framed by bright chestnut curls, and her eyes were green—a delicate green like the first leaves of spring. And while she talked incessantly, the talk was witty and charming, spiced with a candor he admired. Albert found himself comparing her with Virginia, and that disquieted him. There was no question this woman didn't have Virginia's buxom beauty, but what was the motive for comparison? Was it important enough for him to care how they matched up, or didn't match up?

As they watched the initial race—a two-mile "dash" for maiden four-year-olds—Lillian Thomas was not like the other young women nearby. There was no squealing and no jumping up and down in feigned excitement; Miss Thomas watched the race intently, appearing to analyze it.

Albert's horse came third, beaten a decisive six lengths, but

at least Bon Marché Lexington had been in the money in its
first effort.

"I think you might have got second," she said, "if your boy
had moved on him earlier."

"You do, eh?"

"I'm sure of it, as a matter of fact."

He laughed. "I'm pleased to be in the company of such an
expert."

"Don't laugh at me, Colonel," she said sternly. "I *am* expert. I'd be a trainer if all these"—a sweep of the arm indicated the crowd—"would forget that I'm a woman."

"My apologies."

"Accepted." She squeezed his arm.

Albert led her to where the children were having their picnic and watched Lillian charm the youngsters as he had been
charmed.

When they went to take in the second race, he said,
"You're very good with children."

"Thank you."

He sensed a sadness in her then, as they found their way to
the rail once more.

"Are you attending the ball tonight, Colonel?"

"Please," he replied, "it's not 'Colonel' anymore. My military career is in the past and I want to keep it there."

"That's a mistake, you know."

"Oh . . . how so?"

"In this society, a military title is looked on as something
important. It gives you an entrée into certain advantageous
circles. If I were you I wouldn't throw away the 'Colonel' so
easily."

"I'll take that under consideration, Miss Thomas."

"Now, will you answer my question—are you attending the
ball tonight?"

"No. We . . . uh . . . I was going to attend, but I've
changed my mind."

"Your wife's not well?"

"I . . . uh . . . don't have a wife." He immediately regretted having said that. "Truthfully, I have a wife . . . but we are
being divorced."

"I see. So a wife, or the lack of one, is not the reason
you're not going to the ball tonight."

"No."

"Would you consider being my escort?" she asked boldly.

Albert sighed. "Under other circumstances, perhaps." He didn't want any verbal sparring with her. "My wife left our home less than a week ago, and my mood is something less than gay. I wouldn't even be here right now if I hadn't promised the children a picnic."

"The ball will do you good, Colonel."

He grinned. "I doubt that."

"Why don't you try it? You might find I'm right."

"And you're always right—"

"Often enough."

Dewey hesitated.

"Father and I are staying at the Phoenix Hotel. You may pick me up at eight."

He shrugged. "Well, I can't say I wasn't forewarned about you. Very well, eight o'clock it shall be."

Albert's decision to accept her invitation was a mistake. Attendance at the ball only served to intensify his memories of Virginia. Their last bitter moments coursed through his mind, bringing back those feelings of despair he had known on the morning she left Bon Marché Lexington. He recalled, too, the momentary happiness she had felt when he had shown her the new ball gown. Worse, he remembered how much he had loved Virginia, and he found himself resenting Miss Thomas's attentions to him.

After an hour: "Lillian, I must apologize. This is not working out." He tried to smile, making light of it. "I'm afraid you've been wrong in this instance; the ball is *not* helping my . . . well, our separation has been too recent and—"

"You want to leave, Albert?"

"Yes."

"Then we shall leave." There was no recrimination in the statement. "If you'll escort me back to the hotel—"

"Of course."

"—we'll simply write it off as a failed experiment."

"I feel bad about having ruined your evening."

She smiled at him. "Colonel, in no way have you ruined my evening."

There was little talk as they returned to the hotel. She spent the silence cataloging her perception of him: he was stolidly good-looking; his face perhaps too square-cut to be thought beau ideal; his dark blond hair might have been less unruly if he paid more attention to it; his hazel eyes were clear and without hint of deception. In sum, she found him kind, vulnerable perhaps, virile, and *desirable,* recognizing that most people would not use the word in association with a man. *Desirable?* Lillian Thomas decided it fit Colonel Albert Dewey admirably.

When he walked her into the crowded Phoenix lobby, and bowed a good night to her, he was pleased that she displayed no coyness.

"Thank you, Albert," she said matter-of-factly. "Another time, no doubt."

"Perhaps."

17

Two Dewey had not expected that his journey to California would be one of luxury, but not even a nightmare of the most horrendous proportions could have conjured up the village of Chagres in the Central American state of New Granada. Some also called it Panama.

It was designated as a port on the Atlantic coast of the Panama Isthmus (someone had told Dewey it was discovered by Columbus in 1502), but sandbars at the mouth of the harbor made it impossible for any ship of size to enter. Thus, the United States Mail steamship, on which he had sailed from New Orleans, put in at the more open port of Aspinwall, some eight miles removed from Chagres. That had all been a surprise to him; at no time during his careful plan-making had anyone told him he'd have to find his own way from Aspinwall to Chagres. Yet, it was in Chagres he had to be, because it stood at the head of the Chagres River, the trans-Isthmus waterway that would take him southwest to the Pacific, where a sailing ship would be waiting to carry him to San Francisco.

Several hours were consumed in arranging for a mule and a guide to take him to Chagres and it cost him twenty-five dollars—a fee he thought outrageous. Worse, the mule was sore-legged and Charles had to walk a good part of the way along a swampy jungle trail, constantly batting at mosquitoes and other biting insects for which he had no identification. In the four hours it took to cover the eight miles, sweat soaked through his clothing in the 100-degree-plus humid heat. When he finally got to Chagres he found himself wishing—for one petulant moment—that he had stayed at Aspinwall and had taken the mail boat back to civilization.

For Chagres was a stinking hellhole, no more than a collection of mean huts in a semicircle on a narrow, filthy beach of sorts. He was astounded at the number of people he found there; several hundred Americans milling about, trying to arrange passage to Panama City on the Pacific side. There was a maddening cacophony of loud voices in several languages, all of them seemingly angry in the fetid heat.

Charles quickly abandoned his guide and mule to search out one Juan Melendez, a man known to be the agent for the New Orleans shipping company with which he had made his travel arrangements. But Melendez was not easily found in the bedlam existing there. Carrying his heavy bag, picking his way carefully to avoid the fecal matter (human and animal) that seemed to be everywhere underfoot, he pushed his way through the throng, stopping every few seconds to ask someone: "Can you direct me to Señor Juan Melendez?"

Sometimes he got an answer—always negative—in American accents. Other times, when he addressed someone he thought might be a native, the reply was a blank stare. Either way, Juan Melendez was fast becoming a myth.

Charles found himself at a shaded spot near the river, one less crowded, and dropped his bag to the ground, mopping the sweat from his face. He itched all over. The flies and the mosquitoes had feasted on him. He stood there disconsolately, trying to reason out a way to find the agent and get on his way to Panama City.

A tall, muscular, bearded man stood watching him for a moment, and then approached him. "I gather you're looking for Señor Melendez?" The accent was East Coast United States, New York or New England, perhaps.

Dewey smiled for the first time in hours. "I am, indeed. Do you know where he is?"

"I do, sir." He extended his hand. "The name is Roger Weatherford. From Connecticut."

"Dewey—Charles Dewey, from Nashville, Tennessee." The hand was shaken vigorously. "If you can direct me to Melendez, I'd be most grateful."

"Yes . . . well," the man said slowly, "that's what I was hoping."

"What?"

"You see, Mr. Dewey, I've been following you around through this Hades for the last twenty minutes or so, trying to find the gumption to approach you. Finally, I decided I might exchange something I know for something I need."

"I don't understand—"

"You want to find Melendez—*need* to find him, I'd guess. And maybe you'll find him without my help. Then again, maybe you won't, because he'll take off downriver and he won't be seen in these parts for a week, or perhaps longer. In the meantime, you'll have to accept the hospitality of Chagres." He laughed.

"Go on," Two said, annoyed that the stranger wasn't getting to the point.

"So, I'll take you to Melendez right now, if you'll show me your gratitude by giving me three hundred dollars."

Dewey's mouth dropped open. "Of all the arrogant—!"

"Don't be too quick to chastise me, sir," the man interrupted, "until you've heard the whole story."

"Then go on and get it over with." His anger was on the surface.

"You see, I left my farm in Connecticut, determined to seek my fortune in California. The lure of gold, you know. Very carefully, because I'm a prudent man under normal circumstances, I put together the money I'd need for the trip. I left New York on a bark and arrived here . . . let's see . . . eighteen days ago now, with a letter introducing me to Señor Melendez, who was to see to my passage on the Chagres River to the Pacific, and thus aboard a ship to San Francisco. But when I met our Señor Melendez, I was informed the price had gone up. Considerably. Unless I pay him three hundred dollars more, he told me, there'd be no boat down the river and no sailing ship to California."

"That's despicable!"

"So it is, especially since I don't have the extra three hundred. And I've spent more than two weeks in this paradise searching the faces of the newcomers, looking for one I might approach—for a loan. And that, sir, is why I approached you."

Dewey shook his head in disbelief. "Well, let's just find this Melendez and have it out with him. I, too, had a commitment made to me on price and I don't intend to be made a fool of!"

"He has a black heart, Mr. Dewey."

"I've dealt with blackguards before."

"Not in these circumstances, I'll wager." He looked into Two's eyes. "Do you have the extra money?"

"I may," Dewey answered cautiously.

"If you do, you'll be able to do business with Melendez. Otherwise, not."

"We'll see. Now, where is he?"

"I'm sorry, Mr. Dewey, but I can't tell you unless I have your assurance you'll help me."

Charles was silent for several moments. "Don't you have enough money to return home?"

"Yes, barely. But return home to what? I've already sold my farm and—" The words trailed off in deep despair.

Dewey walked a few feet away from him, gazing into the yellow-green water of the Chagres River, debating his move. *Is this fellow genuine? Or is he a charlatan? And if he doesn't help me find Melendez, will I be stuck in this godforsaken—?*

He turned back to the farmer. "Very well, Mr. Weatherford, we have a deal." He offered his hand.

Buoyed by the decision, Weatherford quickly led him along the riverbank, some five hundred yards to a rickety dock where a large dugout boat was tied up, the rear half of it shaded by a piece of canvas stretched over four poles. Under the tentlike cover lay a swarthy man, apparently asleep.

"Señor Melendez!" Weatherford called out.

"Sí." He turned over, opening one eye slowly to look at them. "Ah, Señor Weatherford. Back again, eh?"

"This is Mr. Charles Dewey from Nashville," the farmer said. For an instant, Two felt foolish; finding Melendez had seemed so easy. But he had made the agreement with Weatherford and he intended to carry it out.

Melendez sprang to life, leaping out of the boat in one fluid move to stand before them on the dock. "Señor Dewey," the agent said, flashing a smile, "I have been expecting you." He stuck out his hand.

Charles didn't shake it. His face was stern. "Mr. Weatherford tells me that you've arbitrarily raised the prices—"

Melendez interrupted him. "Oh, please, Señor Dewey, let's not have a tiresome argument. So many seek gold, señor, and I would be a poor businessman if I did not—how you say?—profit from that, eh?"

"But there are those like Mr. Weatherford who had put all their resources—"

Once more there was an interruption. "The sad stories I have heard too much, señor. I am not a priest, I don't offer solace. My business is to get men to California. If some can't afford it, that's no fault of mine, is it?"

Dewey stared at him in disgust. "You're a reprehensible man, Melendez."

"That is true, señor," he smiled. "But I have boats, no? And so many want them. Will you leave in the morning, Señor Dewey?"

Charles sighed. "Yes . . . both of us."

Melendez was surprised. "So, you . . . uh . . . invest in Señor Weatherford's future?"

"Yes, if it's any of your business."

"It is not, señor." He shrugged. "I'll have the money now."

"You'll . . . have . . . the . . . money . . . Señor . . . Melendez," Charles said deliberately through gritted teeth, ". . . when . . . we . . . get . . . to . . . Panama . . . City!"

The agent studied Charles's livid face for several moments, then shrugged again. "I will trust you, Señor Dewey."

"I would hope so." Two turned on his heel and strode away, Weatherford hurrying to keep up with him.

"Jesus Christ," he laughed, "that was wonderful! I swear, you had that bastard cowed!"

"Hmmm. Where do we spend the night?"

"I have a little spot in the jungle I've been using," the farmer said apologetically. "If you cover yourself with a blanket, head to foot, you might not get eaten alive by the night bugs."

"The best accommodations in Chagres, I take it?" Charles grunted.

"Just about, Mr. Dewey, just about."

II

Staunch Dewey, nearly five, was a precocious youngster with a perception far beyond his years. He sat now at dinner with

his family at Bon Marché Lexington, staring at the pretty
young woman who shared the table with them that night.

She was laughing at something his father had said when he
interrupted, his childish soprano cutting through the sounds of
gaiety. "Lillian, are you going to be our mother from now
on?"

There was a dead silence.

"I think your question is a bit premature, Staunch," she
answered.

"What does that mean?" the lad demanded.

"Well, the word 'premature' means 'too soon.'"

"Oh." Staunch pondered that soberly. "Then it doesn't
mean you're not going to be our mother."

Albert Dewey held up a stern parental hand. "I think we've
heard enough on that subject, young man."

"But *everything* has a mother," the boy insisted. "I mean,
the foal has a mother, and the baby robin, and the young
raccoons—"

"Enough, I said!"

"—and we don't have a mother anymore, do we?"

"Yes you do," Lillian Thomas answered, glancing at Albert, her eyes asking him to permit her to reply. "It's just that
she's not here right now."

"But she's not coming back, is she? I mean, I heard Susan
tell Henry that this morning. So we don't have a mother anymore."

"Perhaps the servants are mistaken, Staunch," Lillian said.

"They certainly are," the father said forcefully. "And now
that we've covered that subject, it's time for you all to go to
bed."

The children obeyed, the three boys, Jeff, Jack, and
Staunch, shaking their father's hand in a manly manner, and
little Carolina kissing Albert as she hugged his neck.

As they were almost out of the room, Staunch turned and
said, "I wouldn't mind if you were our mother, Lillian."

"Me, too," Carolina added.

"To bed!" Albert pointed a finger menacingly.

He was clearly embarrassed by the incident. Leading Lillian
to the drawing room, he went to the cupboard to pour whis-
keys for them. But he said nothing.

"You're going to have to deal with it, Albert," she said.

"It's difficult to know what to say to them."

"Admittedly, but now that the children have raised the subject it makes it a bit easier, doesn't it?"

"Maybe." He carried the glasses of whiskey to the divan, sitting down beside her. "And what do I say when they ask whether Lillian is going to be their new mother?"

She giggled. "You answer however the spirit moves you."

Albert sipped the liquor. "Lil, I find you very attractive and I enjoy, more than I can say, your company, but—"

"You don't see me as a wife."

"Don't make it any more difficult than it is," he said with annoyance. "At this stage in my life I don't see *anyone* as a wife."

"That lays it on the line, doesn't it?"

"Lil, I'm sorry—"

"No need to be, Albert. I shouldn't tease as much as I do. Truthfully, I don't see anyone on the horizon as a husband, either."

"Oh?" He seemed disappointed.

She smiled at him, laying a hand against his cheek briefly. "My dear friend," she said, "you can't have it both ways, you know. You can't say, in your manly manner, that you don't see anyone as a wife, and then appear to be hurt when someone suggests they may not see you as a husband."

"I did do that, didn't I?"

"Yes, Albert, you did."

He looked at the clock on the mantel. "I think I should be getting you back to Georgetown."

"It is getting late."

"Hmmm."

"I really hate to have you drive me all the way out there, and then think of you making the long return trip alone."

"I don't mind, really. I enjoy having you here."

She sighed. "I shall have to make other plans for my transportation the next time I'm invited to dinner."

"Another drink before we leave?"

"No, thank you." She hesitated. "But I tell you what I would like—I'd like to stay the night."

His face mirrored his surprise.

"You do have a place for me?"

"Of course."

"All right, then I'd like to stay. I want to see how you work that young Childe Harold colt in the morning. I may be able to give you some hints on how best to bring him along."

"Jamie Orr will like that," Albert said. "He seems taken with you."

"And you're not."

Dewey laughed. "I always seem to be saying the wrong thing."

"You make it very easy for a perverse woman to 'fun you,' as the local farmers like to say. But I do apologize; I do it entirely too much." She set her glass on an end table, moving close to him, her body touching his. "The truth, Colonel Albert Dewey, is that I care not at all about the Childe Harold colt, and even less about whether your Scotsman is 'taken' with me or not. I asked to stay because I want to be with you."

He kissed her then.

III

DAWN broke steaming hot at Chagres. It had rained during the night—in a deluge. Two had never seen such a volume of water pouring from the sky in such a short period of time. He and Weatherford had been soaked through; the natural tropical canopy under which they had tried to sleep gave them no protection at all. But there must have been some sleep because Dewey had the impression he had come awake as the hot tropical sun, burning orange, appeared suddenly in the sky.

He was miserable. There was no other word to describe his condition. He itched all over—a maddeningly persistent itch. And when he scratched through his clothing his fingers found hard swollen lumps. Quickly, he stripped off his shirt to find his torso covered with the lumps, most of them oozing secretions.

"My God, look at this!" Dewey said in alarm.

The Connecticut farmer nodded. "Chiggers," he commented flatly. He opened his own shirt to show Two similar eruptions on his flesh, some of them bloody welts from the scratching.

"What the devil are chiggers?"

"Damned if I know," Weatherford admitted, "but they're some kind of mites. Kin, I guess, to the ticks we have back home. But worse."

Two grimaced. "What can we do about them?"

"Nothing. I've been here long enough to know that. We just have to put up with them until we get the hell out of here."

Dewey groaned. Picking up his dripping blanket and his gear, he left the canopy to step out into the bright sun, spreading out his blanket and his shirt so they might dry. The sun worked no such miracle; the all-pervading humidity of the place kept them damp. Finally, Two put his shirt back on and it was immediately saturated with his sweat.

As he folded his blanket, he said, "Good Lord, there's mold growing on this!"

"Uh-huh. And it'll be on everything else in your bag, too. If you've got any metal in there, that'll have some kind of fungus on it, I'll bet."

Two was disheartened. "I don't even want to look."

Carrying their gear, they made their way to Juan Melendez's dock, to find four sullen-faced Cuña Indians, nearly naked, loading provisions into the big dugout boat.

"They don't seem to be bothered by chiggers," Dewey said quietly.

Weatherford laughed. "Maybe those critters don't like their stink."

Melendez appeared, carrying two rifles, double belts of ammunition crossed on his chest. "Good morning, señores," he called gaily.

"Are you expecting trouble?" Two asked, concerned about the weapons.

"No, no, Señor Dewey." The Spaniard grinned. "It's just that Melendez is a cautious man, especially when carrying such distinguished gentlemen as yourself. Put your bags in the cabin there"—Juan pointed aft in the boat where the canvas was stretched on the four poles—"and we'll get going just as soon as the others arrive."

"Others?"

"*Sí*. Six others—all seeking the *oro y plata*." He grinned again, as if the search for gold and silver was a foolish thing. "You, Señor Dewey, do you expect to get rich in California?"

"I don't know, but I'm not after gold."

"Oh . . . what then? Adventure? Or perhaps you're leaving behind a broken affair of the heart?"

Two resented the questioning and didn't answer. He went to the boat, stowing his baggage under one of the two benches on either side of the "cabin," thinking about how crowded it was going to be with eight adults in there.

At that point the others arrived and Dewey was surprised to see that one of them was a woman. Melendez made the introductions hurriedly. Four of the six were from New York City; Two didn't retain their names. The other two, husband and wife, were from Philadelphia: Mr. and Mrs. Amos Martin. The young woman's name was Julia.

"We're on our honeymoon," Martin volunteered. "And I must confess this isn't quite what we had in mind. Still—a new life awaits us."

Mrs. Martin said nothing, but Two noted that she appeared ill. Her face was flushed and her eyes were feverishly bright.

"Let's get aboard," Melendez ordered.

The passengers crowded under the canvas. Dewey and Weatherford sat on the bench opposite the newlywed couple. Next to Two was an obese gentleman (his name was Robert Mercer) who wheezed when he breathed, and who seemed to sweat even more than the others. The situation under the canvas was, in a phrase, extremely uncomfortable.

"How long to Panama City?" Two asked.

"Four . . . five days, señor."

Dewey was shocked. "But it's something less than seventy miles, isn't it?"

"*Sí.* But it's jungle, you know. And it's the distance we have to go on mules that slows it."

"Mules?"

"*Sí.* The river . . . it is not all . . . uh . . . hospitable."

The passenger from Tennessee groaned, cursing himself for not having asked those questions before. *But even if I had I'd still be going.*

The Indians poled the boat away from the dock into the swift current of the Chagres. The craft had no rudder and the poles were constantly in use.

Within minutes, it seemed, what was the civilization of the village of Chagres disappeared. The jungle closed around them, a green canopy so dense it enveloped them. No sense of direction remained; there was only the unrelieved green. Even the reference point of the sun was blotted out. It was as if they had drifted into a dream world—a nightmare world—where there was no north or south, no east or west. And, most frightening, no apparent escape.

Dewey had expected that the rain forest would be alive with sound. It wasn't. There was an eerie silence about it all; only the rush of water under the boat made a noise. And the steady buzz of the cloud of mosquitoes. But even those sounds were muffled. It got so that the occasional call of a bird—always far off—was welcome.

The silence infected the passengers; there was no conversation among the miserable, sweating travelers. They were like prisoners in an alien place. A hell, perhaps, where their accumulated past sins were being reckoned. And where the punishment for them was made more terrible because it was unknown.

IV

SATURDAY, June 16, 1849—[Charles Dewey II wrote on the damp pages of his journal.] We are now only a day, according to Melendez, from Panama City and the Pacific coast. All are exhausted, dirty, smelly. Several of the New Yorkers, Mr. Mercer notably, are afflicted with some sort of stomach ailment, unable to keep down any food. What remains of the provisions put aboard at Chagres is now crawling with maggots. Poor Mr. Weatherford, unable to control the scratching of his multiple insect stings, has now had many of them become infected; there are open sores on much of his body. Why the rest of us have escaped similar affliction, I do not know.

Mrs. Martin has become desperately ill with swamp fever; I fear for her life. At Melendez's last jungle camp, he had some quinine cached and that seems to have helped her a bit. No one speaks of it in those terms, but she may not survive this terrible ordeal.

Melendez may be the most reprehensible man I have ever known. It has crossed my mind several times that he ought to be killed; God help me for such thoughts! But without the Spaniard, I know, we would never get out of this. Tomorrow morning we are to leave this final camp—in a dugout again after three days on mules—to cover the final miles to Panama City.

And then on to California, breathing the clean sea air of the Pacific!

Dewey had hoped to make a journal entry for every day of his trip, but it had not been possible. Several times he had simply fallen into an exhausted sleep before he could write. But it didn't matter; his mind would always retain the details of what he had been through.

He closed the journal now, but had no desire for sleep. It was only several hours till dawn and the thought that the new day would bring him to Panama City kept him awake. Blowing out the small oil lamp, he sat in the darkness of the vermin-infested shack Melendez called a camp, hearing the deep breathing of the others.

There was a slight moan, and a few whispered words of consolation, and he knew it was the Martins—those two young people trying to survive the first weeks of their marriage. He thought of Beth, and little Charles, and he wondered how he'd get them to California.

Certainly, they can't come this way!

18

It was late afternoon when the dugout was poled to a dock at Panama City. In the distance could be heard the booming surf of the Pacific Ocean crashing against the beaches. To Charles Dewey II it was a marvelously exhilarating sound. He stepped out of the dugout, turning to help Amos Martin lift his wife out of the boat. She was too weak to walk and they laid her gently on the dock.

"Find a carriage for this woman," Two demanded of Melendez. "She must be taken to a doctor immediately."

The Spaniard shrugged. "If there is a doctor."

"Certainly there must be a doctor in Panama City."

"Perhaps. Perhaps not. It all depends on who has left to join the gold rush since I've been here last."

"Well, do *something*, for God's sake!" Dewey shouted at him. "And do it quickly!"

"First, Señor Dewey, we have some unfinished business." He held out a hand. "The money, señor."

"No, Melendez, first the name of the boat."

"Of course." He grinned. "You will leave for California on the bark *Emily*."

"When?"

"As soon as she is ready. A day or two, perhaps."

"Wait, you scoundrel! I want to know for sure!"

Julia Martin, lying in the sun on the dock, moaned. Charles turned to look at her. The jaundiced face, the skin stretched like parchment over her cheekbones, frightened him. He felt guilty, too, about his haggling with Melendez while she was suffering.

"Very well, Melendez. How much?"

"As agreed, señor, eight hundred. Five hundred for the original passage, three hundred for the . . . uh . . . bonus. And if you still intend to be Señor Weatherford's patron, then three hundred more."

Reluctantly, Dewey drew his money pouch from his bag, counting the mildewed bills into the Spaniard's hand. "Now, find a doctor! Immediately!"

It took an hour before a doctor was located and before Mrs. Martin was bathed and put into a clean bed.

The doctor, an American with the ironic name of Blessing, was not optimistic. "She's very weak," he told the husband. "Very weak, indeed. And the fever has—" He stopped, the import of his words painfully clear.

It was only then that Dewey, with Weatherford, set out to investigate the ship that would take them to San Francisco. They made their way to the harbor to find the bark *Emily*.

Not a single ocean-going vessel was in the harbor. Not one!

"Jesus Christ," Weatherford cursed, "where are all the ships?"

Two grimaced. "Once more, Roger, our friend Melendez—"

Panama City, they found soon enough, was crowded with Americans like themselves, all awaiting passage to California. Hundreds of them, perhaps thousands. The main thoroughfare, Calle de la Merced, was jammed with American-owned hotels, and American-owned saloons and gambling parlors, and American-owned whorehouses—all catering to those afflicted with gold fever. Calle de la Merced was a madhouse. It was well after dark when they learned, after making numerous inquiries about Juan Melendez, that he was merely an agent for an American named Cabel Starnes, who owned one of the larger hotels, The California House.

Once more, Dewey felt the fool. He had come all this way from Nashville, and had endured the rigors of the trans-Isthmus passage, without really knowing with whom he was dealing. And it angered him again.

Starnes, when they found him in his hotel, was a portly man, dressed in the highest fashion, jeweled rings on all of his fingers, and a permanent smile fixed on his florid face. That

smile annoyed Two as he told Starnes of their dealings with
Melendez.

"Well, let's just see," he said agreeably. A large ledger was
produced from under the counter in the lobby. "Dewey, eh?"
he asked as he flipped it open.

"Yes. And Weatherford, too."

A stubby finger traced down the page and then the page
was flipped. There were pages upon pages of names. Finally:
"Ah, here's Mr. Weatherford. Yes, yes, all paid in full. For
the bark *Emily*."

His search continued. Two pages later he also found the
name of Charles Dewey. "Yes, Mr. Dewey, all is in order."

"I thought, perhaps, Señor Melendez might not—"

Starnes laughed loudly. "He's not a man who inspires a lot
of confidence, is he?"

"Hardly," Dewey answered.

"But he does his job."

"We've been to the harbor, Mr. Starnes," Two reported,
"and there's no *Emily* there. No ships of any kind, for that
matter."

The fat man closed the ledger. "Yes, well, that's one of the
disadvantages of my service. Uh . . . not all of the vessels
leaving here return, you know. Crews often jump ship when
they get to San Francisco. The lure of gold is very powerful.
I've been told the harbor of San Francisco is a sea of masts of
abandoned ships."

Dewey frowned. "Then you don't know whether the *Emily*
will return?"

"If you wish a guarantee, no. But the captain is a very
strong man and he manages to keep a crew together. Of
course, each trip, it seems, the bonuses paid to crews are
greater and, therefore, sometimes . . . uh . . . adjustments
must be made in the price of passage."

Weatherford spoke up. "Do you mean I might have to
come up with *more* money?"

"That's always a possibility."

"Jesus Christ!"

"Yes, well . . ." Starnes shook his head sadly. "I'm afraid
I'm portrayed as a villain in many quarters of Panama City,
but I'm merely an agent for the captains. If they charge more,

I charge more." For the first time the voice grew cold. "This is not a charitable enterprise."

"Can you give us a guess, Mr. Starnes, about the *Emily*?"

"Maybe tomorrow," he said easily. "Or next week. Or next month."

"And in the meantime—?" Two was disheartened.

"The services of The California House are available to you."

"For how much?"

"Ten dollars a night."

Weatherford whistled through his teeth.

"Of course, if you two are friendly enough to share a room," Starnes went on, "I could offer a special rate of fifteen for both of you."

Dewey laughed now, seeing humor in the madness of Panama City. "Mr. Starnes, you've found your gold field right here, haven't you?"

"That's true," the man confessed. "Very true, indeed."

Two booked the room. The California House even offered the availability of a bath; for two dollars each. Dewey, as he soaked in the hot water, thought what a luxury being clean was; it was not something that had ever crossed his mind before.

The room was comfortable. As they went to bed that night, after applying a soothing lotion to their many insect wounds, Roger Weatherford expressed his gratitude for Two's friendship.

"Charles, I'm keeping a complete record of everything I owe you. You'll have every cent back. Maybe it'll take me some time, but I want you to know that I'm not one to live on charity."

"It hasn't been charity, Roger."

"I know you don't look at it that way, and I appreciate that." He paused. "I know now that a true friend is worth more than all the gold there is in the world."

II

FOUR days later, the Pacific Mail Steamship Company's vessel dropped anchor in the harbor at Panama City. Hurriedly,

Charles wrote a letter to post to Beth—the first opportunity he had had to communicate with her. He told her he had arrived safely on the Pacific coast and was merely awaiting the ship that would take him to San Francisco.

> While it has taken a bit longer than anticipated for this voyage [he wrote], time has not weighed on my mind. There have been a few adventures, but nothing that can't wait for another time to be told. Please tell August I'll write the article he wanted about the trip when I get to San Francisco. If you find the time, also go to see Willie Carstairs and say I am clear in my mind now about a business to undertake in California, one that will certainly make his investment in me most worthwhile. Details will have to await my arrival in San Francisco.
>
> Now, all my love to you and to Buster. Being away from you for this protracted time merely reinforces the extent of my love for you. If you should not hear from me for a few weeks, or longer, do not worry. I am extremely well and more enthused than ever about our future in California.

Rumors sped through Panama City that passage on the mail ship could be had for premium rates. One story suggested that it was a thousand dollars, another said it was two thousand. Dewey considered for a brief moment trying to leave on the mail ship, but the thought was discarded for two reasons: one was that he didn't think it wise to deplete his cash that much; the other had to do with Roger Weatherford. He saw in the Connecticut farmer something he admired deeply; he had no desire to abandon him. There would be a time, he was sure, when Weatherford would be a great asset to him.

Thus, the steamship left without them, but perhaps a dozen more goldseekers, with affluence enough to meet the inflated costs, were able to escape Panama City on her. How much had they paid? Dewey didn't know; the truth was a fragile commodity in Panama City.

A week went by. And another. And another. Dewey and Weatherford chafed under the enforced imprisonment in that humid Hades. Yet, their friendship prospered; it was only that which kept them sane. Just when it appeared they might never be able to reach the goal of California, the bark *Emily* was seen entering the harbor. There was a great hue and cry at The California House, where Cabel Starnes was accosted by hundreds from whom he had taken passage money. For a time there seemed a real fear that his life might be endangered (certainly a number of desperate men made the threat), but Starnes maintained a certain good humor, if not an attitude to satisfy all.

"Gentlemen!" he bellowed from behind the registration desk to the mob assembled in the hotel lobby. "Please hear me!"

Some semblance of order was achieved. "The *Emily* will sail at dawn carrying two hundred and fifty of you."

There was angry grumbling; obviously, some would be left behind again.

"But the captain of the *Emily* tells me he knows of at least two other vessels en route to Panama City at this moment." There were some cheers in the lobby as Starnes smiled.

He held up his ledger for all to see. "I have here the list of all of you who have paid for passage. You will be permitted to board her tomorrow in the order in which you deposited your money. Those here longest will go first."

The fat man coughed nervously. "There is one matter with which we must deal. The captain informs me that, because of the bonuses he has had to pay to keep his crew, there will be an additional . . . uh . . . fee."

"You're a goddamned thief, Starnes!" someone in the crowd yelled, bringing the accumulated anger to the boiling point.

"Please! This is not my doing. The crewmen get more and so must I." He sighed. "I will call out the names of tomorrow's passengers. Come forward when you hear your name, prepared to deposit two hundred and fifty more—"

As one, the mob howled.

"You bastard!" a bearded giant near the registration desk screamed. He drew a pistol, leveling it at Starnes's chest.

Suddenly, another man crashed a heavy club down on the giant's head. He fell like a sack of grain, his head split open. From Dewey's vantage point it seemed certain the man was dead. Others near him fell back.

With no concern for the fallen man, Starnes went on: "Come forward when you hear your name, prepared to deposit two hundred and fifty dollars more. You will be given a boarding pass signed by me. At dawn tomorrow you will bring that pass to the dock, present it to me, and you will be rowed to the *Emily*." He looked around, the good humor erased from his face. "Is that clear?"

Angry grumbling continued, but no one seemed willing to further challenge the hotelkeeper's authority. The body of the earlier protester was still there, the blood from his crushed head congealing on the rough wood.

"Elijah Simmons—!" Starnes began.

Some didn't answer the roll call; no doubt they didn't have the extra money. Perhaps a hundred names were called before Starnes shouted, "Roger Weatherford—!"

With Dewey at his elbow, Weatherford pushed through the crowd to the desk.

"I don't want to cause any fuss," Roger said quietly, not wanting others to hear, "but I'm traveling with Mr. Dewey and he has to go, too, on this ship. Indeed, if he doesn't go I won't have the money. He's paying for me."

Starnes looked at Dewey. Two nodded agreement, and the hotel owner shrugged. "I can't separate two men with such a vital . . . uh . . . economic link, can I?"

He watched as Two counted out the five hundred dollars, handing over two of the precious boarding passes and checking their names off in his ledger.

"Benjamin Harkins—!" The reading of the list went on.

Two and Roger retreated to their room.

"That Starnes is an evil man, Charles," Weatherford commented.

"In a sense, I suppose he is. But the circumstances here dictate there has to be at least one Cabel Starnes."

"Maybe," the farmer said, unconvinced.

They began to pack their bags for the final leg of the voyage. Dewey groaned. "Good Lord, everything I own is covered with mold."

"The Panama crud," Weatherford laughed.

They went to bed and had been there perhaps an hour, in uncertain sleep, when there was a knock on the door.

"Who is it?" Dewey called out.

"Starnes."

It was Weatherford who was out of the bed first, going to

the door and jerking it open. "Not one goddamned dollar more, Starnes—!"

The hotelkeeper grinned at him. "The purpose of my visit, Mr. Weatherford, is the direct opposite of what you suggest. I am able to offer *you* some money." He entered the room.

Two sat on the edge of the bed; Weatherford stood scowling in the middle of the room.

"Gentlemen," Starnes began, "the boarding passes you hold for the *Emily* have taken on increased value since earlier this evening. I'm prepared to buy them back from you, giving you a profit of fifty dollars each."

"Why?" Dewey demanded.

"Because, sir, there are . . . uh . . . unfortunates who were not on the list who are offering premiums—"

Weatherford cut him off. "You pay us three hundred dollars for the passes and resell them for what?"

Starnes shrugged. "I would, of course, add a fee for my services. Admittedly, you could . . . uh . . . market the boarding passes yourselves, but there are some risks in that. I heard just a half hour ago that two . . . uh . . . gentlemen entered into such heated negotiations that one, unhappily, killed the other." The fat man sighed. "Sadly, there are two hundred and fifty places on the *Emily* and perhaps a thousand more willing to take . . . uh . . . considerable risks to be one of those two hundred and fifty."

Dewey stared at him. "And every time a ship comes in, this happens, I'll bet."

"Unfortunately, yes."

"To your profit?"

"Ah, but my profit has its very real dangers, Mr. Dewey."

"Dangerous enough for you to consider leaving on the *Emily* yourself?"

Starnes roared with laughter. "One measures his dangers, sir. Be killed over a gold-mining claim in California, or be killed here engaging in . . . uh . . . more *certain* profit-making. Given that choice, I prefer the more . . . uh . . . comfortable circumstances here in this tropical paradise."

Two, who had never gotten to his feet, said now: "I'd like to continue this fascinating conversation, Mr. Starnes, but I am quite weary. Our boarding passes are not for sale."

"In that case, thank you for your time"—he made for the

still open door—"and be assured that you have my wishes for a pleasant journey." He was gone.

Weatherford closed the door after him. "What a reprehensible sonofabitch!"

"Hmmm. We'll talk about that in the morning." Dewey stretched out on the bed. "I really am tired."

19

ALL of the dementia that was Panama City was concentrated the next morning at the harbor. Under a blazing sun and a humidity approaching one hundred percent, several thousand men milled about, sweating and cursing, to witness the departure of the bark *Emily*. She stood out in the harbor, her sails still furled, an American flag hanging limply from the midmast, a seemingly placid island in the midst of turmoil.

The lucky two hundred and fifty who had boarding passes for her had difficulty forcing their way through the mob. Every step they made was accompanied with offers to buy the boarding passes.

One man grasped Charles Dewey's arm, pleading: "Mister, five hundred dollars for your pass!"

"No, I'm sorry," Two said, trying to pull his arm free.

"It's all I have." Both hands were holding on to Dewey.

"If you offered a thousand, I wouldn't take it," Two tried to explain.

"Is that what you want? A thousand?" the desperate man asked hopefully. "You'll have it! I'll sign a note for it . . . I'm good for it, I promise . . . and in California I'll—"

Dewey wrenched himself away, looking neither right nor left as he pushed to where Cabel Starnes stood at the end of the dock, surrounded by a dozen toughs, guns in their hands.

"It's sad isn't it, Mr. Dewey," Starnes commented, "what men will do in the grip of gold fever?"

Two didn't reply as he handed the two boarding passes to the hotelkeeper. Dewey and Weatherford were directed into a longboat, manned by muscular rowers. In just moments the boat was filled and was moving across the harbor toward the *Emily*.

As they came up to her, Two said to his companion, "She's small, isn't she?"

"About what I expected," Waterford answered.

"But two hundred and fifty passengers—?"

"She's going to be crowded, no doubt of that."

The longboat bumped into the wooden hull of the *Emily*, and as the crewmen held the boat fast, the passengers climbed up several rope ladders to the deck. The act exhausted Two. Once aboard, he dropped his bag, leaning heavily on the rail.

"Are you all right?" Roger asked with concern.

"I've felt better."

"Well, when we get under way, the sea breeze will revive you."

"I'm sure you're right."

They stood at the rail watching the three longboats shuttling back and forth across the harbor, bringing to the *Emily* her complement of passengers.

After two hours, the last of the boats drew near. Weatherford pointed a finger. "Say, isn't that young Amos Martin?"

Two squinted into the bright sunlight. "I believe it is. But I don't see Mrs. Martin."

Neither one wanted to say what was in his mind. As Martin came up the rope ladder they moved to meet him, Weatherford extending a hand to boost him aboard.

It was Dewey who asked the question that had to be asked. "How is Mrs. Martin?"

"Julia's dead—"

"Oh, good Lord!"

"—sixteen days ago." The young man turned to look at the shore. "She's buried back there in that . . . that—" A sob ended the explanation.

"I'm so sorry."

"There are times," Weatherford added, "when God's will is hard to understand."

Martin stared at him. "God's will? God abandoned this hell a long time ago. No," he said bitterly, "it wasn't God. Only the Devil could devise a scheme that gave me enough money for one passage, but not enough for two. If Julia had lived"—

he shrugged—"Satan would have confined us to this earthly purgatory. God? I doubt He exists anymore."

II

THE *Emily* was a sturdy little bark commanded by a muscular, taciturn gentleman named Fuller, whose face had been leathered by a thousand suns and uncounted winds and whose only evident badge of office was the formidable revolver thrust into his waistband. Even without a uniform of any kind, he was clearly the master, addressed deferentially by the crew as *Mister* Fuller, a mode of reference quickly adopted by the passengers. If he had a first name it was not made known to those who had just come aboard.

Under Fuller's sure commands the ship came to life. The anchor was raised and men scrambled aloft to set the square-rigged sails on the foremast and mainmast. Sails were rigged fore and aft on the mizzenmast and the *Emily* began to move slowly in what was little more than a calm. There was just enough breeze in the harbor to ease her away from Panama City into the Golfo de Panama, heading almost due south to the open Pacific.

With favorable winds the *Emily* might be at San Francisco in three weeks.

It didn't take Dewey and Weatherford long to learn that she was badly overcrowded. Sleeping quarters, if such they could be called, consisted of a few benchlike structures only roughly approximating a bed; basically, it was expected that the passengers would mostly find places on the floor of the hold, spreading blankets to try to sleep cheek by jowl with their neighbors. Immediately, Two and Roger decided not to stay in the hold, making their way to the aft deck to stake out an informal claim on a few feet of space to lay out their blankets.

"I'm in no mood," Dewey said, "to be a prisoner in that smelly hold."

Weatherford agreed with him. "There's no telling what manner of affliction you might catch there, too." He said it in a bantering manner, but he was concerned about the flush he saw in his companion's face.

Two sank wearily to his blanket, propping himself against the rail, taking his notebook from his baggage and trying to compose his thoughts. "July 6, 1849," he wrote. "We are away from the pestilence of Panama City finally, but I fear I have brought some of it with me. A fever grows in me, even though I try to ignore it. I feel light-headed at this moment, hoping that the sea air will revive me."

He stared at the page for a moment, sighed, and closed the book, returning it to the baggage. He closed his eyes.

Weatherford was watching him. "Are you unwell, Charles?"

"Hmmm."

Roger got to his feet. "I'm going to find the doctor."

Two laughed, opening his eyes. "A doctor? That's a luxury I'm afraid the *Emily* isn't going to provide."

"Of course there's a doctor! No captain could, in good conscience, undertake a voyage with so many people without a doctor."

He hurried away, asking half a dozen sailors about the whereabouts of a doctor before he was finally directed to the crew's quarters.

"He's down there somewhere," his informant reported. "Name's Herring—Rufus Herring. Says he's a doctor." He laughed derisively.

Weatherford was still hearing that laugh when he found Dr. Herring stretched out in a string hammock, eyes closed, breathing deeply, his exhaled breath reeking of whiskey. Roger shook him. The hammock rocked, but Herring's eyes remained closed.

"Dr. Herring!" Weatherford shouted into his ear.

Slowly, the eyes came open. "Good Lord, man," the doctor mumbled, "you trying to wake the dead?"

"It seems necessary to do that, doesn't it?" He was disgusted by the drunken man. "My friend has a fever."

"So soon?" Herring groaned. "I hoped . . . I had . . . seen the last of it." He made no effort to get out of the hammock.

"He's on the aft deck, and he needs your help."

"Needs . . . my help—?" The drunken words were almost incoherent. "They . . . all need . . . my help. What they need . . . my good man . . . is God's . . . help, and he's on . . . holiday." He closed his eyes once more.

Weatherford grabbed him, shaking him violently. The unstable hammock tilted, spilling the doctor's body out of it. But before he crashed to the deck, the farmer caught him, easing him down.

"Very well . . ." Dr. Herring said in his semistupor. "I suppose I'll have . . . to come with you." He was seized with a paroxysm of coughing.

In spite of that, Weatherford pulled him to his feet, wrestled him away from the crew's quarters, up a short ladder, and out onto the main deck. The exertion had him sweating profusely.

Blinking in the bright sunshine, the doctor protested, "My God . . . it's daylight!"

"Of course it's daylight—it's approaching noon."

"Wasn't when . . . I last went to . . . bed."

A strong hand on the doctor's arm delivered him, finally, to Dewey's side. Herring reached down to place a hand on his brow. After a moment: "My good man," he muttered, ". . . you may be suffering from the ague."

"You mean malaria?" Roger asked.

"Malaria . . . ague . . . jungle fever . . . marsh fever . . . swamp fever—" He shrugged drunkenly. "Your friend may have it."

"But you're not sure?"

The doctor's ruddy face twisted into a smile. "Dear sir . . . you see before you . . . a fallible vessel." He gestured grandly. "More's the pity." Suddenly, he turned away from them, leaned far out over the rail, and vomited. Without another word he stumbled away, wiping his dribble on his sleeve.

"I'm sorry, Charles," Weatherford said in his despair.

Dewey grinned weakly. "Don't concern yourself. I don't need a doctor. I'll be all right. Fresh air and sunshine—" The words ended there in uncertainty.

Angrily Roger sought out Captain Fuller, chastising him for the condition of the ship's doctor.

"I'm aware of Dr. Herring's shortcomings," the master said evenly. "The truth is that there isn't an able doctor left in San Francisco. They're all out seeking gold. Herring would be doing that, too, I imagine, if he could stay sober long enough."

"But . . . what good is he!"

"Not much, I'll admit. But he's the best I could do." It wasn't an apology, but simply a statement of fact.

Disconsolate, Weatherford returned to Dewey, who tried to reassure his worried companion.

"I'm feeling somewhat better," he said, "and I'm certainly not going to accept that man's diagnosis. Believe me, Roger, I *don't* have malaria. Why, I'm even a bit hungry."

Their first meal aboard the *Emily* was almost as shocking as the condition of the doctor. There was no way, aboard the overcrowded ship, to serve the voyagers in any formal manner, so it was accomplished by the sailors carrying food— fruit, bread, pieces of cold boiled beef—along the rows of passengers as everyone just grabbed at it.

"I fed my swine better than this," Weatherford grumbled.

"But your pigs," Two smiled, "weren't on the *Emily*."

III

A FAIR wind rushed the bark northward, its sails full and straining. The speed they were obviously making through the waters of the Pacific heartened Two and Roger. As the sun met the horizon and night came, a myriad of stars (more stars than the Nashvillian had ever seen) appeared against a jet black, moonless backdrop of infinite vastness. The day's heat was dissipated. Already the memories of the time wasted in the dissolute precincts of Panama City were fading; the human mind's natural defenses against recalling too much that was abhorrent came quickly into play.

They ate again, Dewey confining his meal to a lone piece of sweet tropical fruit without identification, and then prepared to bed down on the aft deck. As were all other parts of the ship, that area was crowded. When Two and Roger stretched out under their blankets, their bodies touched others. In the closeness there was an unhealthy odor on the *Emily* not wafted away on the clean ocean breezes.

Weatherford, normally a sound sleeper, was awakened by what he thought was someone shaking him. It took him only a moment to realize the "shaking" was Dewey's profound shivering, accompanied by the loud chattering of his teeth. Roger was genuinely frightened.

"Charles," he half whispered, "what is it?"

"I'm so . . . damned . . . cold." The answer came with difficulty, made almost incoherent by the tremblings.

Roger's hand touched Charles's fingers and they were icy. He sat up, removing his blanket and placing it on Charles, tucking the edges of it close around the body. He reached out to put a hand on Dewey's forehead, finding it also clammy.

"I'm going to fetch Dr. Herring," he said.

"No, no," Two pleaded weakly, "I don't want him." A pause. "The extra blanket is already making me feel better." That last was a lie.

Weatherford's anxiety pained him. He wanted to do something for this man he had known for only a brief time, but who had become a dear friend. He would have gladly assumed Dewey's illness had it been possible. Now, however, he could only sit by him in a passive, sympathetic role.

Time sped along and faint light began in the east. As it grew Roger could make out Dewey's face. The pale, dead-white skin frightened him anew. And the shivering and teeth chattering seemed to take on a violence of sorts.

"Oh, hell—" Dewey moaned.

"What?"

"I've . . . passed my . . . water." His eyes opened. "Like a . . . torrent, Roger."

"Perhaps the ague, or whatever it is, is breaking." He tried to appear hopeful.

"Perhaps." He closed his eyes again.

As the light increased, and as Weatherford watched him, a change took place. The shivering stopped and the whiteness of the skin turned to a vivid flush. Once more the farmer put his hand on the friend's brow. It was burning hot now, but there was no sweat. Roger thought it was sand-dry. Dewey's breathing had become shallow; there was almost no sign of it.

"Charles?" Weatherford whispered.

There was no reply.

Louder now: "Charles?"

Again, no reply.

Roger came quickly to his feet, hurrying toward the crew's quarters. Dr. Herring, whatever his shortcomings, was his only hope. But he hadn't gone more than a few yards before he saw the doctor, in the company of Captain Fuller, bending over another man lying on the aft deck. As Roger approached them he saw the same violent shivering with which Dewey had been afflicted.

"My friend," Weatherford said, single-minded about Charles's illness, "is very sick. Please come immediately."

The doctor looked up at him. "In a moment," he replied. "There are others, too." He was sober.

The captain straightened up, laying a hand on Roger's arm. "The damned jungle fever," he said. "We have to contend with it on every trip." He sighed. "It does seem worse this time, though."

"What can be done for it?"

"We have plenty of quinine," Fuller assured him. "It controls the worst of it."

Weatherford waited impatiently for Dr. Herring to finish with the other man. When he had he pushed him along toward Charles. Dropping to his knees the physician felt the hot brow.

"Hmmm. How long has he been like this?"

"Only briefly. He was cold and shivering for several hours."

"Uh-huh." Herring went into the small chest he had with him, taking out a dark bottle, pouring some white powder into his hand. "Prop him up," he ordered. Roger complied.

Opening Dewey's mouth with one hand, the doctor dribbled the powder in with the other. Then, he put a small silver flask to the patient's lips, pouring liquid in to wash down the powder. There was no indication that Charles knew what was happening, but he did swallow involuntarily.

"Should he have whiskey?" Weatherford demanded.

"It's water, lad," the doctor answered, smiling slightly. "Whiskey has other . . . uh . . . medicinal uses." He gestured to Roger to put Dewey down again. "Now, when he starts sweating," he went on, "come for me right away. He'll need more quinine."

"And in the meantime—?"

"In the meantime"—the doctor shrugged—"a prayer or two might be in order. From the looks of things I'm going to need all the help I can get."

As the Connecticut farmer sat by Dewey's side, and as the sun rose, sailors under the direction of Captain Fuller began

to cordon off the aft deck. Those who were well were moved
to other areas of the ship, and the aft section became Dr.
Herring's hospital. Weatherford counted thirty-seven men under his care.

It was almost noon when Charles began to sweat copiously.
He became animated, jerking and rolling from side to side in
a kind of delirium, moaning softly.

"Doctor!" Roger called urgently across the deck.

Herring came to them, once more dosing Dewey with salts
of quinine. This time the patient seemed more conscious of
what was going on, but the eyes remained closed and there
were no words from him.

"And now what?" Weatherford wanted to know.

"Now we wait." The doctor moved to another unfortunate
passenger.

Sweat drenched Dewey's clothing as surely as rain would
have. His companion marveled at the amount of perspiration
continually pouring from his body. Going into his baggage,
Roger pulled out a shirt, tearing it into large pieces, using
them to tenderly mop the sweat from his friend's face.

For several hours it went on that way, hours made more
terrible for Weatherford when he watched the sailors sew a
body in canvas and drop it into the ocean. With no ceremony,
no appeal to a supreme being for eternal mercy. And not just
once, but three times during the afternoon.

Sometime past mid-afternoon, Dewey's eyes opened.
"Roger?" he moaned.

"I'm here, Charles."

"God, I'm weak." The sweating was subsiding.

"You've had a long siege of it."

"How long?"

"Oh . . . twelve hours. Maybe a little longer."

"Lord!" He took a deep breath. "Prop me up, will you? I
don't seem to be strong enough to do it myself."

Dewey's recovery seemed miraculously fast. While he remained weak, and his muscles ached, he told Weatherford he
felt well. He even asked for something to eat; bread was
brought for him.

When Two complained of sitting "in his own stink," Roger
stripped off his clothes, bathed him with seawater brought up
in a bucket, and redressed him in fresh clothing retrieved

from the baggage. They even laughed because everything in the bags had the musty smell of Panama City mold.

"I'm going to wash all of it," Weatherford promised him, "and hang it in the breeze to dry properly."

"You've done enough already, Roger."

"Nonsense."

"No, really." He thought for a moment. "You saved my life."

"Don't be foolish. Dr. Herring's quinine saved your life."

"I saw it, Roger," Dewey said quietly.

"What?"

"Death. And it wasn't terrible at all, you know—"

His friend cut him off. "You were delirious."

"No, it was more than that. I was walking down a long tunnel, bathed in the most refreshing light. Brighter than the sun, but not hot. And at the end of the tunnel there stood a man beckoning to me. An angel, I remember thinking. It *was* a man, but as fair as a woman, and with a smile that was so . . . comforting. There was music coming from somewhere— the most beautiful melody I've ever heard, but not really played on instruments. I can't describe it to you. And I was content as I walked along, seeming to have no weight; all concerns were lifted from me." He stopped, frowning.

"What happened then?"

"I don't know. I have no memory of anything after that feeling of total contentment. I suppose I was pulled back from it." Those last words were sad.

Weatherford said nothing.

"If it was death I saw," Dewey added, "I now know that it's not something we need fear."

IV

FEAR, however, remained a constant companion as the *Emily* sailed ever northward toward the goal of San Francisco. Dr. Herring, alternately sober and drunk, had only limited success in his struggle with the malaria outbreak. Every day there were more dead sewed into canvas and dropped into the waters of the Pacific.

Forty-eight hours after Dewey thought he was recovered, he was stricken again, a victim of the same terrible cycle of shivering cold, then hot, dry burning, and then profuse sweating and delirium. Perhaps not as severely as before, but nonetheless debilitating.

"Malaria's like that," the doctor explained. "You're going to have small bouts for the rest of your life—on and off."

"Will it threaten life?" Weatherford wanted to know, concerned for his new friend.

Herring smiled, taking time to screw the top off his silver flask so that he might have a taste of whiskey. "Sir, the very act of living," he answered with solemnity, "threatens life."

Had it not been for the tragedy of the malarial deaths, the voyage of the *Emily* might have been thought of as idyllic. Near perfect weather had blessed them; they sailed through only two heavy rainstorms. On the twenty-second day after leaving Central America—the date was Wednesday, August 15, 1849—the little bark entered the wide, accommodating bay of San Francisco in bright morning sunlight.

Dewey and Weatherford stood together at the rail gazing at the clutter of buildings of the California community, scattered haphazardly on the flatlands and on several of the hills rising up from the bay. Before leaving Nashville Dewey had read somewhere that San Francisco, until only recently called Yerba Buena, was a village, a hamlet. What he saw before him now, however, was no village; it was a booming city.

They tried to count the spars of the abandoned sailing vessels in the harbor, the crews having deserted to the goldfields. An exact count was impossible, but the number was large, ranging into the hundreds.

Captain Fuller ordered the *Emily*'s anchor dropped.

"Well, Charles, a new life."

"Yes, I suppose so," Dewey mused. "But I remember reading a poet—the words have stayed with me, but not the name of the author. Anyway, in embracing this new life, perhaps we should consider this warning:

> *Nothing is new; we walk where others went;*
> *There's no vice now but has its precedent.*

In just a few hours they would discover the great truth of that.

20

In mid-June, Nashville was in public mourning.

James Knox Polk, the eleventh President of the United States, died in his mansion in the city. He had ended his labors in the seat of national government only seventy-four days earlier.

Publisher August Schimmel, near tears as he composed the obituary for his *Nashville Monitor,* wrote:

Mr. Polk gave his life for the nation he loved, just as certainly as does the warrior in battle.

Once looked upon by the political cynics as a mere shadow of another stellar Tennessean, Andrew Jackson, Mr. Polk may have been little known nationally when he first took office. But in only four years his stature grew, we submit, to rival that of Mr. Jackson in our country's glorious history.

Faced with problems the Founding Fathers could not have imagined less than seventy-five years ago, James K. Polk met those problems with courage and integrity. Our debt to him must be acknowledged in glowing terms when his accomplishments are recalled.

Schimmel capsuled them: revision of the troublesome tariff laws, establishment of an independent treasury, settlement of the Oregon boundary dispute, reannexation of Texas, and the opening of public lands to settlers.

All of those things he promised when he came to the presidency; all of those things he did, giving his life in the doing.

Lesser men, who daily trumpet their dissatisfaction with one public issue or another, might benefit from the example set by Mr. Polk. He was not a man given to great public pronouncements; he did not speak, he acted. It is to be hoped that rhetoric will be softened, that talk of disunion—from both Northern and Southern precincts—will cease.

And that those contending forces, in remembrance of a great President, will rededicate themselves to the one cause for which James Knox Polk made the ultimate sacrifice: the Union!

"It seems to me, August," True Jackson chided the publisher, "that you make out Jim Polk as a saint."

"Politically, he may have been." Schimmel sipped his sherry in the Bon Marché drawing room.

"Hmmm, perhaps. But the same situation prevails today as when Polk was elected. The North continues its attacks on . . . uh . . . Southern institutions, meaning to overthrow them with force, if all else fails."

Schimmel frowned. "'Southern institutions'? Since when have you adopted that euphemism for 'slavery'?"

"Very well, I'll say it—*slavery!*" True was angry. "I'm just so damned sick and tired of always being portrayed as some kind of an ogre—"

"By whom?"

"By your damned newspapers!" True shouted at him. "I can't understand why you must continue to reprint that slander from the likes of the *New York Tribune.*"

The publisher sighed. "Because, True, our differences are never going to be reconciled without a thorough understanding of what those differences are."

"That's pap!"

"It's the truth."

True got to his feet, walking toward the door. "Well, your truth and my truth are two different things these days."

As True departed, Schimmel turned to his other son-in-law, Able. "Each day, it seems, True gets less . . . well, less reasonable."

"Perhaps I shouldn't tell you this," Able started slowly, "but True has been corresponding with Calhoun's people, and they seem to have convinced him that there's a need for calling a Southern Convention to take up the question of secession."

"You're not serious?"

"I am. And, to tell you the truth, I'm half convinced on that score myself."

"Able! Why?"

"Because it's becoming painfully obvious those Northern abolitionists will settle for nothing less than Southern destruction. If it comes down to that—we'll have to go our own way."

"That would mean war—!"

Able shrugged. "That's a phony assumption, I believe. The abolitionists are like all cowards—bluster, but no stomach for fighting."

"I can't believe what I'm hearing," Schimmel groaned. "My own sons-in-law talking like . . . like . . . idiots!"

"We didn't think you'd understand," Able Jackson said in a matter-of-fact manner. "After all, you're not—" He stopped.

"Not what?"

"Well . . . truthfully, not a native-born American. Not a Southerner . . . not really."

Schimmel was shocked into silence.

"I hope you don't take that the wrong way, August," Able added, weakly apologetic.

"Oh, no, I won't take it the wrong way, young man." His tone was icy. "I grasp your meaning *perfectly*."

II

GEORGE Dewey Jr. was swept with a rush of euphoria as the light cocking-cart sped along the road to Nashville, the high-stepping hackney moving proudly in a rhythmic gait. It was a perfect end-of-June day, clear and clean, pleasantly warm without the humidity normally associated with the area. And the just completed spring meeting at the Clover Bottom racecourse had clearly signaled the return of Bon Marché greatness. He had sent nine winners across the finish line in the plantation's solid purple colors, including a straight-heat win in the newly instituted Nashville Jockey Club Gold Cup. That success—the best racing season in nearly a decade—buoyed George, proving his worth as the Bon Marché trainer.

Further, True and Able Jackson, busy with other enterprises, were giving him more and more authority in the running of the plantation. He could visualize the day when it might be "his." Now, on this lovely morning, he was on his way to Nashville to meet the coach from Lexington, bringing his cousin Albert for a discussion on how best to coordinate the breeding and racing interests of the two thoroughbred nurseries—another indication that a new grandeur for Bon Marché was in the offing.

Honestly, George Junior had some doubts about Kentucky. As he drove along, lightly flicking the whip over the hackney's head, he was recalling the brief conversation he had with his aunt on the preceding afternoon.

"Albert's arriving from Kentucky tomorrow," he had told Alma May. "Do you want to be in on our meetings?"

"No, no"—the Princess had waved a hand imperiously— "you do what you think is best for the Kentucky operation."

"It may not be that simple, Aunt Alma. Albert's investment in Bon Marché Lexington came from Virginia's estate, you know, and now that they're divorcing it may be that we'll have to find the money to buy her out."

Alma May nodded. "We have the resources, don't we?"

"Yes, if the Bon Marché owners want to continue in Kentucky."

"Does that mean, George, that you don't think it's wise to continue there?"

Her nephew hesitated. "The horseman in me tells me that it is. But Albert has been so damned preoccupied with his problems with Virginia that—" He paused.

"What?"

"Well . . . he's let a lot slide."

The Princess pondered briefly. "Albert's a good man, don't you think?"

"He is."

"I'm glad we agree on that. You handle it, George."

"I'll do my best."

When he had said those words concern about Bon Marché Lexington still loomed large in his mind. Now, less than twenty-four hours later, the perfectness of the new day washed over him, cleansing him of his doubts. He truly admired Albert—although they had never really been close—

but he would have preferred someone like his brother Charles II in charge of the Kentucky farm. But if Albert's talents weren't those of a natural horseman, George believed he could guide his cousin sufficiently to make the Kentucky plantation profitable. It would never rival the original Bon Marché, but, then, no horse farm in the country could claim to do that.

George drove his rig to the front of the Nashville Inn just as the Kentucky public coach arrived. Vaulting from the cocking-cart, he hurried to the coach, pulling open the door, seeing Albert there.

"Welcome again to Nashville, Cousin!"

Albert smiled, getting out and shaking George's hand vigorously. "It's good to be here."

"Get your baggage," George ordered, "and we'll be off."

Albert, however, turned back to the open coach door, extending his hand to help a chestnut-haired young lady to alight.

"George, may I present Miss Lillian Thomas of Lexington?" To the woman: "And this, Lil, is my cousin George Dewey Junior."

"Mr. Dewey"—she grinned at him—"it's a pleasure, indeed."

"Uh . . . yes . . . uh—" He forced a smile. "Truthfully, I hadn't anticipated that Albert would be bringing a guest. I've arrived, I'm afraid, with only the cocking-cart, hardly a vehicle for a lady. If I had known . . . well, I would have brought a more suitable rig."

"Don't concern yourself, George," Albert said lightly, "we'll make do with the cart, won't we, dear?"

"Yes, of course." She recognized George's annoyance. "I'm to blame for this, Mr. Dewey. At the last minute I insisted on coming along. Perhaps I shouldn't have."

"No, no . . . it's quite all right. But the cart will be most uncomfortable."

Albert laughed, clapping his cousin on the back. "It really doesn't matter, George."

They crowded themselves and the baggage on the small cart, George clucking to set the hackney in motion. During the drive toward Bon Marché, Albert presented a running account of his days at the plantation, and Lillian responded gaily. George was sullenly silent.

As they reached the stone-wall boundaries of Bon Marché, their attention was drawn to several hundred men, marching in a pasture in an approximation of military drill. Able Jackson was seated on his horse, waving a sword, giving orders.

"What the devil is that?" Albert asked.

George brought the cart to a halt. "That, Cousin, is the Nashville militia company. And you recognize, of course, General Able Jackson?"

"General!" Albert guffawed.

"Yes, somebody had to be the general," George answered without enthusiasm. "A good deal of Able's time these days is spent in that . . . pursuit."

"But what's the purpose of it?"

"Readiness. There's more and more talk, you know, about disunion."

Albert sobered. "The ultimate folly!"

George nodded agreement. Then he chuckled. "Perhaps you'd like to give them a hand, *Colonel*?"

"What I'd like to do is give General Able a boot in the ass!"

His cousin cracked the whip. "In that case, we'd better go on."

They had gone no more than four hundred yards when Albert said: "George, what's that by the deer park there?" He pointed to a host of slave masons laboring on what seemed to be a growing house.

Once more the cart was stopped.

"That is my brother Statler's new home," George explained. "To hear Harriet tell it, it's going to be the finest house in all of Davidson County. And I don't doubt it—the story is that she's spending some three hundred thousand on it. Maybe more."

Albert whistled in astonishment.

"It's one of the benefits of marrying a wealthy woman, Albert."

"Uh-huh." Albert was silent for a moment. "Sometimes those benefits can be burdens."

The whip cracked again.

"Harriet's calling it Beau Monde. To the blacks working on it it's simply 'the castle.'" George chuckled. "I guess they're both right—it's to be a castle that illustrates my sister-in-law's version of a beautiful world."

As they swept into the curved driveway in front of the mansion, the Bon Marché trainer said, "Our aunt Alma May will be pleased to see you, Miss Thomas. And I'm sure she'll find accommodations for you."

The Princess did greet the unexpected guest effusively, taking her to her quarters, trailed by a housemaid who carried the woman's baggage. George guided his cousin to the drawing room.

"I have the feeling," Albert said, "that you don't approve of Lil's presence."

The butler brought coffee for them.

"That's nonsense," George replied. "I'll admit, however, that I don't see how Miss Thomas's presence is going to help your . . . well, your negotiations with Virginia."

"I shouldn't think it will make any difference at all."

"You're still married to Virginia," George reminded him.

"Legally, not emotionally."

"But if she should know of . . . this woman, it might color her decision on what to do about her interest in the Lexington property."

"Virginia is in no way vindictive," Albert assured him.

"Still—" George shrugged.

In the guest suite of the mansion, Lillian turned around slowly, admiring it. "This is truly lovely."

"Thank you," Alma May said.

"You know, I think I know you all so very well. Albert spent the entire coach trip telling me all about you. With great admiration, I should add."

"And *we* admire Albert, too."

"That's evident," Lillian commented. "I know how much he appreciates the support you've given him in these . . . difficult times for him."

"Hmmm." The Princess studied her. "I've always been known for my candor, Miss Thomas, and this doesn't seem the time to change. Are you planning to marry Albert?"

Lillian laughed. "To the point, eh? Albert said you'd be like that."

"That's the way I am," Alma May replied. "But you haven't answered my question."

"Marry Albert? Tomorrow, if he'd have me. But the truth—although he can't admit it—is that he's still in love with Virginia. She's hurt him terribly, but his love for her is going to die slowly. I understand that, even if Albert doesn't."

"It's a difficult situation for you, then?"

"No, Miss Dewey, it's not. I take what Albert gives me—gladly. I don't need to be married to Albert to be with him, you know."

"I see. Those are brave words, Lillian . . . may I presume that informality?"

"Please."

"And I am Alma May."

"You're called the Princess, I'm told."

"I am, indeed. And now that we've got that out of the way . . . you use brave words, but I suspect you fear he'll return to Virginia if she gives him the opportunity. And you came along because you want her to know you're here. You want your presence to scotch any chance of a reconciliation."

Lillian didn't reply immediately. "You're very perceptive, Princess."

"I've had many years to hone that skill. Far be it from me to interfere in romance"—Alma May's words turned hard—"but Albert's visit here, Lillian, is necessary to negotiate the final settlement on the Lexington property. Any interference in that may cost Albert—more exactly, may cost Bon Marché—many thousands of dollars."

"Albert led me to believe you intend to buy her out."

"We do. But on our terms, not hers. If she's aware of your . . . uh . . . attraction to Albert, it may suggest to her that she ought to strike a harder bargain. And if that doesn't occur to her, it certainly will to her father."

Lillian sighed. "Then I've made a mistake."

"You have," Alma May agreed. "And I'm going to have to ask you to be discreet . . . to stay here at Bon Marché and not let it be publicly known that you've accompanied him from Lexington."

The visitor thought for a moment. "Very well, Princess, I'll be your prisoner." She laughed.

"Good. It should only be for a few days, and the jail is comfortable." Alma May grinned naughtily. "Shall I have the servants move Albert's bags in here?"

"Do you mind?" Lillian asked, obviously not embarrassed by the suggestion.

"Mind? Then Albert didn't tell you *all* about me. Of course I don't mind."

III

Two days later, Albert sat stiffly in a chair in the parlor of the Nashville home of Brian Stoker, Virginia's father. Tension permeated the fashionable room as Stoker, Albert, and Willie Carstairs, representing the interests of Bon Marché, waited for Virginia to be present.

"Good morning, gentlemen," she said as she came in. She was not alone. A plain-faced, full-figured young woman, whose most compelling feature was her wide, dark eyes, entered behind her.

"May I present my friend Maude Royalton," Virginia said easily. There followed the obligatory round of introductions, after which the two women sat together on a sofa, the younger woman taking one of Virginia's hands in both of hers, squeezing tightly.

Stoker, who remained standing, seemed to think a further explanation was necessary. "Miss Royalton is a daughter of one of our bank directors and has been most supportive of Virginia in these . . . uh . . . troubled days. I'm sure no one will object to her presence."

No one said anything.

"Well . . ." Stoker said, thrusting his portly body forward, his hands clasped behind his back. "As pleased as I am to have another banker here"—he nodded toward Carstairs—"I would have thought, Albert, that your interests might better be served by a lawyer."

It was Carstairs who answered. "In a very real sense, Brian, I'm here with Bon Marché's complete power of attorney. Miss Alma May thought my presence might be called for because our business deals with fiscal matters."

"Yes, of course." Stoker rocked back and forth. "I don't wish to prolong this . . . uh . . . unhappy matter any more than necessary, but Mrs. Stoker and I—Mrs. Stoker apologizes for her absence; she's not feeling well this morning—we thought, being opposed to divorce as we are, that Albert and Virginia ought to make another effort to reconcile their . . . uh . . . their marital differences."

Albert blanched. "Is that what *you* want, Virginia?"

Her eyes were fixed on the hand being held by the Royalton woman. "Yes." The reply was no more than a whisper.

"So, I suggest to you, Willie," the father went on, "that we allow these young people to withdraw to discuss, as husband and wife, whether there isn't some way—"

"Albert will have to speak for himself on that score," Carstairs interjected.

"If that's what Virginia wants," Albert answered, getting to his feet, "I must abide by her wishes."

His wife, though, made no move. Maude Royalton leaned over to whisper something to her, then kissed her on the cheek. Virginia rose, not looking directly at Albert, and led the way out of the room.

When they were our of earshot, Stoker asked: "Are you privy, Willie, to what has caused this breakup?"

Carstairs looked questioningly at the young woman. "Perhaps Miss Royalton will want to—"

"I'll stay, Mr. Carstairs," the woman said firmly.

"Very well." He answered Stoker's question: "I have no idea what caused the differences between Albert and Virginia. I'm not sure I want to know."

Wearily, the father sat down. "Her mother and I have tried to speak to Virginia of this, but she has refused to give us any details. It was only last night I learned of what may have intruded on their marriage."

"Oh?"

"Yes. One of our servants, in speaking to a Bon Marché black at the market, learned that Albert arrived from Lexington in the company of another woman. Miss Thomas is her name, isn't it?"

"It is," Carstairs confirmed. "But it's my understanding Albert didn't meet her until after Virginia voluntarily left Lexington."

"But this may indicate a pattern of . . . uh . . . dalliances. Perhaps we don't know all the truth of his behavior."

"And maybe we should consider it none of our business."
Willie glanced at Maude Royalton, who smiled at him.

In Virginia's sitting room, Albert was trying to restrain his
anger. "I don't see what's to be gained from this so-called
reconciliation effort, do you?"

"Father wants it." Virginia sat with her eyes lowered, her
hands folded in her lap.

"Well, I don't and I resent his meddling."

His wife was silent.

"We might as well get back to the parlor. I have no desire
to simply waste my time."

She laughed, surprising Albert. "I think we're going to have
to waste enough time in order to convince Father we tried."

"That's ridiculous!" he snapped.

"Yes, I suppose it is. But a few minutes won't hurt."

Albert strolled to the window, looking out onto the Nashville street, watching people and carriages go by, straining his
eyes to see whether he could recognize anyone. He tired of
that game quickly; sighing, he started to walk across the room,
mentally counting the number of steps he was taking. He noticed a miniature of the Royalton woman on an end table, went
to it and picked it up, seeming to analyze the plain face.

"Miss Royalton seems to have assumed a prominent role in
your life," he said.

"She's a dear friend."

In his mind, he tried out several ways to ask another question about their association, then abandoned the idea. He
sighed once more, resuming his pacing.

"Are the children well?" Virginia asked.

"Quite well."

Again there was a silence and Albert returned to the window,
staring out. Just as he was about to call an end to the charade,
Virginia spoke: "Father tells me you've taken a lover."

Albert wanted to laugh; the situation had become black
humor. He just glared at her, wondering why she had raised
the subject.

"Have you, Albert?"

"Yes, if you must know. Now, can we get this matter over
with?" He started for the door.

"Is she . . . uh . . . uh . . . agreeable?"

He couldn't believe what was going on. "Agreeable? Don't you mean, does she enjoy being with me in bed?"

"Sometimes, Albert, you can be quite crude," she said prudishly.

His anger boiled over. "I believe you're *mad!*"

Virginia began to cry. Albert groaned, clenching his fists, squeezing shut his eyes so he wouldn't have to see her. He felt ill.

In the parlor, Stoker was saying: "Mrs. Stoker and I have been discussing our grandchildren."

"That's not a matter for discussion here," Carstairs contended.

"The whole marriage must be considered."

"No," Willie insisted. "We're here because *there is no marriage.* For God's sake, Brian, let them end it with some dignity."

The father was back on his feet, rocking to and fro. "Now, you must understand that Mrs. Stoker and I feel strongly about the grandchildren, and—"

Suddenly, from Maude Royalton: "Stop it, damn it! I'm sick of this hypocrisy! I'm not going to have Virginia come back in here and be a party to this stupid wrangling!" She turned to Willie. "How much is Bon Marché offering for Virginia's interests in the Lexington property?"

"A hundred thousand."

"That seems fair. Have you drawn up papers she's to sign?"

"I have." Carstairs quickly withdrew the document from his jacket pocket.

A stunned Brian Stoker regained his voice. "See here, young lady—!"

"I speak for Virginia," the Royalton woman said coldly. "She'll think, as I do, that one hundred thousand is reasonable and she's going to sign that paper. And you, Brian, will keep your mouth shut!"

Stoker was sputtering in anger as husband and wife came in, as if on cue. Maude hurried to her, taking her hands, and then embracing her, whispering to her. Virginia's head nodded. She walked to the desk, where Willie hurriedly spread out the agreement.

"I'm unalterably opposed to this!" Stoker growled.

Virginia hesitated, looking to Maude.

"Sign it, darling," the Royalton woman said.

Virginia complied. Albert signed as well, and Willie and Maude Royalton witnessed the document. Willie folded the paper, returning it to his pocket. A gesture to Albert and they both left the Stoker home.

Outside, Carstairs chortled, "Jesus Christ, that Maude Royalton is a wonderful bitch!"

Albert made no comment.

"Without her, we'd still be arguing with Stoker."

"Hmmm."

They entered their carriage and were driven away.

"Do you think those two are—?"

"Damn it, Willie, will you drop it!"

They left the streets of Nashville and were on the road approaching Bon Marché before anyone spoke again.

"Well, Albert," the banker said, "you're free to marry Miss Thomas now."

Young Dewey turned to him slowly. "Yes, I suppose I am," he sighed. "But it's not going to happen—with Lil, or anyone else."

Willie laughed. "I hope you won't be offended, my lad, if I tell you I don't believe you."

IV

"SAN Francisco must be seen to be believed," Charles Dewey II wrote to his wife.

> But it won't be complete for me until you, my darling Beth, and little Charles, join me here. I hope that in the spring, and certainly no later than next summer, we will make that a reality. Exactly when, and by what mode of transportation, will have to be the subject of another letter.

He sat at a writing desk in his room at the Palmer House, the best hotel the crude city had to offer, trying to organize his thoughts. He was still weak from his bout with malaria, but he was feeling better every day. He and Roger Weatherford (they shared the room) had surveyed the town and had agreed that what Two wanted to do held promise for a most profitable business.

I intend to be rather lengthy with this dispatch [he continued], so that it might serve several purposes. I hope you will be willing to show it to August, so that he might excerpt portions of it for the article he wanted. I hope, too, that Willie Carstairs will see it so he is made aware of the fine business opportunities available to me—to us—here. By sharing the letter you will relieve me of the necessity of writing it a second, or a third, time.

Dewey wrote only a short paragraph about the voyage on the *Emily,* unwilling to tell his wife of his illness and not wanting to alarm her with tales of those who died on the trip.

This is a brawny town; a city, really, of perhaps some twenty thousand, although the population seems to fluctuate wildly. But the size of it, and its vitality, is quite remarkable when you consider that just two years ago less than five hundred lived here in a village called Yerba Buena. Even just a year ago the population hadn't reached a thousand. Then, of course, the news of gold strikes north of here was disseminated and the present insanities ensued.

While I cannot verify these figures (I suspect that no one keeps records), I am told that as many as forty thousand have arrived thus far this year at the San Francisco port, and that perhaps thirty thousand reached the area on the various overland routes.

Most spend only a few hours here before going to seek their fortunes in the goldfields. But those who "stick" in the city are offered all the enticements of the flesh and of Lady Luck. Gambling abounds here—everywhere. Without actually counting them I can say without fear of contradiction that saloons outnumber residences; every saloon offers some form of gambling. There is no clock in force here; the saloons are open every minute of every day. The larger establishments—including the Palmer House where I am staying—have drawn the professional gamblers, who pay large fees to the proprietors for exclusive rights to ply their trade in those quarters. I am led to believe the gambling gentleman who operates the Palmer House games of chance pays an annual rent of

$60,000 for the privilege. We must assume it is a profit-
able venture for him.

For everyone here seems to gamble: public officials,
judges, gold miners, ranchers, even clergymen, sad to
relate. Gambling is clearly the number one business and
the number one vice. I say number one because vices
abound. While there are a few families here, the majority of the women are of the demimonde class, drawn by
the gold just as certainly as are the gamblers.

People talk of little else but gold. Men here speak of
dollars as easily as we in Nashville used to talk of pen-
nies. And what truth is there in all those stories of men
becoming fabulously wealthy overnight? You can hear
several such tales every hour here, but I, myself, have
not yet met such a fortunate fellow. Oh, I imagine some
must exist, but my own personal observation is limited to
the unhappy citizen who arrived last night at the Palmer
House with a chamois bag filled with gold dust, un-
earthed at God knows how much labor. He lost it all on
a single turn of a card in a poker game. Was he disconsolate? Hardly. He roared for a whiskey, poured it down,
and then shouted for all to hear: "By Jesus, there's more
where that came from!"

Physically, San Francisco is not at all attractive. It has
grown, mushroomlike, on the peninsula overlooking the
commodious bay. The land is virtually treeless; only low,
dry shrubs exist on a soil that is basically sandy. And
there is almost no flat land. The peninsula distinguishes
itself by being hilly; some of the city has already been
built on very steep slopes. Every building (without exception, I believe) is of wood, making one wonder what
would happen should fire break out.

The streets, if such they can be called, are narrow
strips of land between haphazard rows of buildings.
Some are so narrow as to prohibit passage of wagons. It
rained during the night, turning the loose, sandy soil into
a river of mud, some of it quite deep as my filthy boots
will attest. In only a few places are the streets planked.

Politically, these Californians—native and immigrant—are free-wheeling. There's much talk of statehood, without concern about what might be happening

in the nation's capital three thousand miles away, of which they have little news and are seemingly uncaring. There are newspapers—The *San Francisco Alta* and the *Placer Times* key among them. But they talk almost exclusively of local matters. Right now the principal concern seems to be the lawless gangs roaming the streets in the blackness of night (there are no exterior lights, from what I have seen).

The newspapers print any and every rumor of big gold strikes, apparently without seeking any confirmation. It is no exaggeration to say that money is a madness here. It is shorn of the values I had previously placed on it. Here in the Palmer House, when service is required, a gratuity of as much as fifty cents is not unusual. Common draymen can earn thirty dollars a day! A decent meal (and such is hard to find) costs five dollars, and more. The cheapest of boots sell for thirty dollars and they are hardly serviceable. Decent boots cost a hundred! Somewhat surprisingly, there is a theater here, but I haven't yet investigated what it offers. I have been told, however, that a private box can be had for fifty dollars!

No doubt there are fortunes being made in the goldfields. There can't be all that smoke without some fire. But it is clear to me that the real fortunes are not being built on gold; not directly, at least. Gamblers seem to be the most direct beneficiaries, but so are other businessmen catering to the needs of the gold seekers. I first became aware of that in Panama City when I ran into a scoundrel named Starnes, who is profiting greatly by providing hotel accommodations and transportation to San Francisco for those crossing the Isthmus.

But Starnes probably would not believe what I could tell him now, after less than a week in California. The most common items are bringing five or ten times, and more, their Eastern prices. In the goldfields eggs fetch a dollar apiece. Flour is two dollars a pound, tea four dollars a pound, sugar two dollars a pound, a loaf of bread in the mining country is worth a dollar and a half. A fresh tomato is priceless—and is being paid for with gold dust.

Hardware is of great value: shovels, picks, sledges,

rakes. So, too, are explosives. You need only set a price to find a buyer.

I start this next on a new sheet of paper, dear Beth, so that it can be for the eyes of yourself and Willie Carstairs only. Under no circumstances do I want what follows from this point to become a part of August's article.

With a friend I met on the Isthmus crossing (his name is Roger Weatherford, late of Connecticut, and I believe him to be a scrupulously honest man), I have begun what is called the Dewey Trading Company. With the cash resources brought with me, we have already acquired two sturdy wagons and two teams of mules, and Roger is out now making an effort to get them filled at farms in the area with fresh produce. Then the wagons will be driven to the goldfields and the produce sold. We might expect a profit of three or four hundred percent!

In the meantime, I am gathering together labor to build a warehouse and a pier on the north shore of the bay. That will probably exhaust our initial capital, Willie, but we should be able to get along with the profits made on produce until we can move into the next phase.

For that, Willie, I am asking you to have blind faith in my judgment. I'm urging you to put together, as soon as is humanly possible, a train of heavy wagons to bring to me overland as many shovels, picks, sledges as they can hold. And as many barrels of black powder as seems prudent to haul. Also cooking pans and pots, boots, clothing, hats; anything of that type you can think of. Don't forget tenting material. And nails—good nails are very scarce here.

And guns! Any and all variety of guns, with plenty of attendant ammunition. The revolving pistol I carry—for which I paid eleven dollars in Nashville—I could have easily sold for seventy-five dollars last night.

I'm recommending that the teamsters on the wagon train be hired as employees of the Dewey Trading Company, with promises of good-paying jobs when they get to California. The wagons and teams can be used by the company when they arrive.

Once you have arranged that, contact shipping agents in New York or New Orleans and contract for a shipload of similar supplies, adding barrels of flour, salt, sugar, good whiskey. Well-cured lumber, too. And try to find several large baking ovens; opening a bakery here would be most profitable. Make certain you lease a fast ship for the trip around Cape Horn. Speed is essential, either overland or by water. And, for God's sake, don't ship anything via the Isthmus!

I know you must think me mad, Willie, but I swear to you with all my honor that an additional investment of a half million now will bring a return of ten times that much! I have carefully thought out several policies for the Dewey Trading Company, which I intend will have permanency. Send only quality materials; I want the Dewey Trading Company to have the finest of reputations. I also intend to risk a small of the whole on credit, making several deals, as seems prudent, to advance supplies to several gold seekers in exchange for a percentage of their eventual gold claims.

Now, my final recommendation (my final idiocy, you will probably say). Come to California yourself! An experienced banker in these surroundings could become a Midas. Opportunities are everywhere: in land, building construction, shipping, and banking itself, of course. I realize you may not want to leave your comfortable surroundings in Nashville, but a man of means can be comfortable anywhere.

Two took another sheet of foolscap to finish the letter:

And now, darling Beth, I must close. There is much still to be done today. I long for the time when I can hold you in my arms again and prove, once more, my profound love for you. I imagine you must think I'm engaging in fairy tales with my grandiose plans, but they're based on the solid realities of what I've found here.

San Francisco is a robust town, growing at a mad pace. But it is clear it will become a great city and I mean to make the Dewey name a major factor here—and in all of California.

I promise, my dearest one, you shall be a queen here, and Charles Dewey III a prince.

21

AUGUST Schimmel hated doubt. Self-assurance was his armor; doubt rusted it. Now, however, as he sat at his desk at the *Nashville Monitor,* the flickering oil lamp tiring his eyes, he was assailed by doubts, distressed by the weakness they suggested.

More and more in recent weeks he had been working into the night at the newspaper, no longer able to engage in what had been a major element in his life—the sherry sessions in the Bon Marché drawing room with his sons-in-law. ("Solving the ills of the world," the late Mattie Dewey had once said.) Alienation from True and Able Jackson, over disputes about the direction the South should take, was complete. They were barely civil to each other these days, merely nodding in recognition when their paths happened to cross at the plantation.

Schimmel recognized his differences with the Jackson brothers only mirrored the more profound growing alienation between North and South over what ought to be done with the new territory acquired in the Mexican War. Every dispatch received at the *Monitor,* every reading of exchange newspapers from other communities, told him his beloved Union was being strained at the seams. *His Union?* Could True and Able be right? As one who had not been native-born, could he really present himself as a valid spokesman for the Union? That was the worst doubt.

Everywhere he turned he was presented with the reality of the number of people—many of them thought to be responsible leaders—who spoke openly of armed conflict to settle the differences over the extension of slavery. Abolitionists, of course, were the most intractable; they saw no other course but to destroy the South to end slavery. He could discount those views as being held by ignorant zealots. But he couldn't discount all those other heated disagreements.

Hard-liners on both sides seemed to welcome the idea of war. John C. Calhoun, he of the fiery eyes and lionlike mane, a man who had once been Vice President and who now was the spokesman for the uncompromising Southern viewpoint in the U.S. Senate, had recently said that "the alienation between the two sections has already gone too far to save the Union." Reflecting Calhoun's strongly held views, the Sumter, S.C., Banner had editorialized: "The only remedy which would free the South from Northern oppression is the secession of the slaveholding states in a body from the Union and their formation into a separate republic." Similar sentiments were coming from Northern newspapers. Schimmel had, only that day, read in the *Cleveland Plain Dealer*: "Rather than see slavery extended one inch beyond its present limits we would see this Union rent asunder!"

And now the Nashville publisher was faced with the fact that, within his newspaper family, there was acceptance of the inevitability of a schism in the Union. He was studying a memorandum written to him by young Statler Dewey proposing a plan that, on the face of it, seemed reasonable, even prudent. But its underlying theme was the acceptance of a divided nation.

Schimmel read it again:

The time has come, I believe, to consider the increasing difficulty of maintaining a newspaper chain with properties in both the South and the North. Were there a conflict (which does not seem beyond the realm of possibility) you, as owner of the Schimmel Newspapers, would face the loss of considerable capital investment in perhaps half of your publications.

It is not difficult to project that should there be war, your Northern newspapers might be seized, or lost in some other way, just because your chain is based in the South. Certainly, it would be difficult (if not impossible), under wartime conditions, to maintain any control—either editorial or fiscal—over Northern properties from headquarters in Nashville.

Therefore, I propose to you the possibility of seeming to divest yourself of the Northern newspapers by the establishment of two distinct divisions; two separate companies, if you will, one "owning" the Southern publications, the other "owning" the Northern newspapers. I am certain we can find a competent publisher to be placed in charge of the Northern papers; a gentleman who would run them for you, and keep them whole, during the course of any conflict.

(Even if there is no conflict, this course might be prudent for any number of business reasons. I question whether your "one voice" editorial policy can long be maintained in these heated days. Please do not view this as opposition to the "one voice" policy. Like you, I am firmly committed to resisting all talk of disunion.)

To complete my proposal, I recommend a Northern division encompassing the *Chicago Clarion,* perhaps anchoring the new company; *Cincinnati Bulletin; Pittsburgh Observer;* and *St. Louis Challenger.* In the Southern division, continuing under the direct guidance of the Nashville office, would be the *Nashville Monitor, New Orleans Delta Recorder, Raleigh Clarion,* and the *Kentucky Gazette* in Lexington. On that latter property, it might be argued that no one can safely assume that, were there disunion, Kentucky would side with its Southern neighbors. I'm of the view, however, that Kentucky is too Southern to resist association with a new republic of the South.

Please do not believe I have any ambition in making this proposal. I have no desire at all to leave Nashville; I intend to stay here, whatever may happen. Thus, if you decide to engage in such a split of newspapers, I would not be interested in association with anything but the Southern division, continuing under your leadership.

Schimmel smiled at that, not totally content with the idea that young Statler was devoid of ambition. He wanted him to be ambitious; Statler's youthful ambition was necessary to assure the growth of Schimmel Newspapers.

The publisher leaned back in his chair, contemplating the memorandum. Minutes went by. Finally, he leaned forward, taking a sheet of paper and dipping his pen into the well.

"Statler," he wrote. "Your proposal is one of merit. It confirms to me that I made the correct decision in appointing you as the general manager of the Schimmel Newspapers. However, I would prefer, for the moment, not to act on it. I pray that no future developments make it necessary for our newspapers to split. North and South. Nevertheless, I thank you for your perceptive evaluation."

He scrawled his name on the reply, blotted it, and wearily carried it across the office, dropping it on Statler's vacant desk.

As he drew on his topcoat, preparing to end his long day, he hoped he'd never have to think of the proposal again.

II

WEARY beyond anything he had ever known, Two Dewey drove the empty wagon, emblazoned with the now dirty red lettering, DEWEY TRADING COMPANY, down the wide, dusty main street of Sacramento. Following in his wake was an identical wagon driven by Roger Weatherford.

For three weeks they had been on the eastern reaches of the American River, seeing for themselves what madness the rush for gold was generating. They had sold everything they had in the wagons—fresh produce from vegetable gardens south of San Francisco—in just two days. They had also sold a half dozen shovels and three sturdy picks they had managed to acquire in San Francisco, and, quite literally, the clothes off their backs. Which is to say that at one remote gold camp, peopled by fewer than a dozen men, Dewey had sold a spare pair of pants to a fellow whose own trousers had been reduced to tatters by the rugged work of searching for gold. The price? Three ounces of gold dust, or the equivalent of forty-eight dollars. When the trousers were new, in Nashville, Dewey had paid three dollars for them.

They learned soon enough that they could have sold themselves naked—boots, pants, shirts, hats, socks, underwear . . . everything could have been marketed at exorbitant prices—if they had chosen to do so. At another stop, in a rapidly growing collection of crude shacks the inhabitants called Hangtown (it was in the foothills of the Sierras), Weatherford *did* sell the small Bible he carried. For fifteen dollars, a dozen times or more its worth. The man who bought it, morose and slightly drunk, complained, "I'm going crazy in this godforsaken place without something to read. Hell, I'll even read *that*." He jabbed a finger at the Bible and Roger parted with it.

Thus, Dewey and Weatherford had learned something else. Books were going to be a valuable adjunct to their trading company. Even outdated newspapers, they realized, had resale value in the goldfields. ("When we get back to San Francisco," Charles had said, "we'll make a deal with the newspapers there to take their unsold newspapers off their hands." He had grinned. "Maybe at no cost to us.")

The produce they had carried in the wagons, and the few supplies, had represented a cash outlay of just over $600. But as they drove through the streets of Sacramento, crowded with fortune hunters on their way to the golden streams north and east, they carried in their pockets some $4,200—a profitable increase of seven hundred percent! Better yet, they had visited gold camps after the wagons were empty to take orders for future delivery. In Two's diary the pages were filled with orders, for all manner of supplies, exceeding $50,000! Everything they had visualized was true, and more so. They were about to make the *real* gold strike.

What they had also learned was that digging for gold, or panning for it, was capable of providing a good day's pay for a hard day's work. Some of the adventurers *were* becoming wealthy. Around a place called Auburn, a few of the men were digging out $1,500 worth of gold between sunup and sundown. Most, however, were fortunate to realize an ounce of dust a day—sixteen dollars worth. Not much when you considered a shot of whiskey of uncertain quality cost a pinch of dust. That was a lot if the bartender had big thumbs.

Returning to Sacramento now, Charles and Roger were intent on setting up a branch of the Dewey Trading Company there, closer to gold country. They hoped to find someone to run it for them before they returned to San Francisco.

They drove their wagons up to the front of the newly constructed City Hotel, which fronted on the confluence of the Sacramento and American rivers. It was a unique frame building, three stories high, with a balcony running around three sides of the third story. Next to it was a livery stable.

The partners unhitched the four mules, leading them to the stable.

"I want them bedded down for a couple of days," Dewey instructed the stable's proprietor. "And give them the best feed you've got."

The stable owner tilted his head to one side, studying the strangers. "Five dollars a day," he said, "for each animal."

Dewey let a discordant whistling sound escape through his teeth, showing his disapproval of the announced rates.

The man shrugged. "If you don't wanna pay it, mister, you don't have to leave the mules here."

"And I imagine," Two laughed, "there are no other livery stables in town."

"They wasn't when I got up this mornin'."

"In that case, sir, you've got the mules."

When they entered the lobby of the City Hotel they learned that a room, in which they would have to double up, would cost them ten dollars a day. Each.

Two winked at Roger. "Well, that's reasonable—twenty dollars a day for the mules, twenty dollars a day for their masters. What could be more fair?"

But the room to which they were assigned on the third floor was large, comfortable, clean, with a door leading out onto the balcony. There was also a welcome bath at the end of the hall, with steaming hot water provided at the cost of a dollar a bucket. They were grateful for it.

Bathed, and in clean clothes, Dewey and Weatherford sat on the balcony, their feet propped on the railing.

"I imagine we ought to get something to eat," Two suggested.

"Not right away, Charles," Roger said pleadingly. "I just want to sit here for a bit on a seat that's not bouncing up and down."

Eventually, though, the pangs of hunger moved them. As they ate in the hotel's restaurant (the meal was excellent), Dewey spotted a newspaper abandoned on a table next to them. He reached over to retrieve it, glancing at the front page.

"Well, I'll be damned!"

"What?"

"California is a state. Listen to this." Two read aloud:

"'Delegates meeting at Colton Hall in Monterey have proclaimed for statehood, writing a constitution for California, and declaring the state free. A petition will be sent to the Congress in Washington seeking admission to the Union.'"

"That's good news," Weatherford grinned.

"It is, indeed."

"I don't imagine your Southern leaders are going to be delighted with slavery being ruled out here."

"There probably isn't a hell of a lot they can do about it," Dewey chuckled. He had no residual feelings as a Southerner. "California is presenting them with a *fait accompli.*"

III

YET, there was no *fait accompli* recognized by hard-line Southerners, feeling themselves betrayed by Virginia-born, slaveholding President Zachary Taylor, who had sent his own emissary to California to urge its citizens to put in place a stable government.

California's decision to bar slavey unleashed the beasts of contention. From Mississippi came a call for a Southern Convention in Nashville "on the first Monday in June next, to devise and adopt some mode of resistance to Northern aggression."

August Schimmel was appalled. His newspapers, every one, printed his editorial reply to the Mississippi alarum:

> These dangerous men who would meet in Nashville would have us at war over a dispute that properly lies in the Constitutional purview of the Congress. It is not war that will solve our problems, but debate and compromise in the councils of the House of Representatives and the United States Senate.
>
> This move of radical men, who say they wish to familiarize the public mind with the idea of disunion, is one of wildness and irresponsibility. One is tempted to say there is nothing but downright silliness in this project of a Southern Convention. Still, we warn it cannot be willed away by simply calling it silly.
>
> These gentlemen (and what an aberrant word that is in this context!) display the inherent weakness there is in the Southern psyche. They would play at being Cav-

aliers, a race distinguished for warlike and fearless character, a race renowned for gallantry, chivalry, superior intellect. They are none of these. Instead, they are backward children playing a dangerous game fit only for idiots.

They prattle that the Southerner has more aptitude and genius for war than does the Northerner; that the South has better generalship, better horsemanship, better marksmanship, more honor. They speak as if that alleged superiority is justification enough to throw down the gauntlet. But it takes no genius to pull a trigger and render another lifeless. The gun has no conscience, and in the South today, the men who would wield the guns in a conflict to rend the Union have no conscience, either. They do the work of the Devil and are beyond redemption.

It is sad that Nashville, which can be justly proud of the role it has played in building this great nation, is now to be the scene of the dishonor the Cavaliers would call a Southern Convention. It is to be hoped that the citizens of Nashville, if these blackguards dare show their faces here, will drive every TRAITOR of them into the Cumberland River!

Anger consumed True Jackson. Rolling up his copy of the *Nashville Monitor,* he strode purposefully to the Bon Marché stables, ordering a black handler to saddle a fast horse. Then, whipping the animal mercilessly, he dashed to Nashville, using up the horse and not caring about it.

At the newspaper office he vaulted from the horse, banging recklessly through the door, and hurling the newspaper onto the desk in front of editor Schimmel.

"This time, August," he shouted, "you've gone too damned far! I demand that you retract this!"

Schimmel had expected such a confrontation. "Oh," he said calmly, "something offends you?"

"You know damned well what I'm talking about! It's an insult to every *true* Southerner!"

"Hmmm." August got to his feet. "You surprise me, Son-in-law. I didn't mean it to be an insult to any *true* Southerner. I meant it to be an insult to the idiots who would come to

Nashville advocating an end to the Union. Those kind deserve nothing but my contempt."

Jackson, his face livid, leaned over the desk, the words being forced through his teeth. "It was I who urged the Southern Convention to come to Nashville."

The publisher shrugged. "I suspected as much."

"Then I'm an idiot, I suppose?"

"You are."

"And a *traitor*?"

Schimmel laughed at him. "You know, I searched my vocabulary for a stronger word. Unhappily, sometimes the English language is deficient in vitriol." The laugh died. "'Traitor' was the strongest word I could find. But you're worse than that, True, and it sickens me to think that a daughter of mine goes to bed with you every night."

"You give me offense, sir!"

The reaction was a weak smile.

"I demand satisfaction!"

August spread his arms wide, making a target of his chest. "Why go through the charade of a duel? Why don't you just draw your gun and shoot me dead now? Or does that offend your sense of honor?"

In one swift movement, True went to his waistband, a Deringer appearing in his right hand.

Statler Dewey, a witness to the confrontation from his desk nearby, leaped to his feet, rushing between the two older men. "For God's sake, Cousin True, put up your weapon!"

Silent seconds went by as True Jackson glared at the young intruder. Then, the gun was put away. "Another time," he muttered. Striding from the newspaper office, he mounted his still-lathered horse, and rode away.

Statler exhaled deeply. "He means it, you know, August. He means to kill you."

"No, lad," Schimmel replied, clapping his associate on the shoulder. "He needs the dueling field to satisfy what he thinks of as his honor. And I, of course, have no intention of dueling him."

"I wish I could believe it's that simple."

"Believe it," the publisher said. "There'll be no murder. A coward needs the Code Duello for his justification."

IV

Louise Schimmel wept. "To leave Bon Marché after all these years—"

"You don't have to go with me," her husband said. "I understand what Bon Marché means to you."

"Stop it! Don't you dare suggest I'd choose Bon Marché over you!" She fell into his arms, the weeping consuming her.

Developments were swift. August and Statler worked out the details of young Dewey's plan for dividing the newspaper chain into two divisions—North and South. The Northern publications, they agreed, would be run by Schimmel from Chicago under the banner of Schimmel Newspapers. The Southern division, to be newly designated as Dewey Publications, would have Statler as the publisher.

Both men were to have autonomy over their divisions, but it was solemnly agreed that one editorial policy would prevail—the newspapers would continue to stand for the Union.

"In these critical times," August said, "it's going to be even more important that we have adequate coverage of the Congressional debate. I'd like to send Lee Dewey to Washington on a permanent basis. It's about time we considered Lee's age—he's fifty-seven now—and let him retire from chasing around the country from one disaster to another. I think he might welcome settling down comfortably in Washington."

"Agreed," Statler replied. "We're going to need his maturity there."

That was business, settled dispassionately. But August and Louise still had to contend with the sad duty of telling their daughters, Joy and Hope, of their decision to leave. There were many tears. But the twins understood there was no other choice for their parents. Or for them.

Joy, between sobs, spoke for them both. "I hope you don't think we don't love you because of this . . . this . . . terrible dispute. We do. And we'll continue loving you. But our husbands—"

"Your families must come first," Louise said resolutely. "There's no way your father and I would want to split you from your husbands. You two, and our grandchildren, mean too much to us to . . . to—" She couldn't continue. The tears she had tried to hold back gushed forth.

August went alone to report to Alma May.

"I admit to you, Princess, that I feel like a schoolboy tattling on a naughty companion," he told her. "But you, of all people, have a right to know the truth of what is happening at Bon Marché. I submit to you that the attitude of the Jackson brothers is a dangerous one."

"Did True really draw a gun on you?"

"He did."

"The stupid fool!" Alma May paced around her sitting room. "I don't want to see you and Louise go. You've been too important a part of Bon Marché over the years. But I can appreciate that you think your position has become untenable here. If your heart dictates to your brain in this matter, I can understand that, too, because Charles Dewey often allowed his heart to guide him."

"My God, Princess, don't put it on that footing! This is not a matter of the heart in any way. It's a great deal more serious than—"

She interrupted. "But August, perhaps you've missed a very important point. Bon Marché is a Southern plantation, run by Southern people. Why does it seem so strange to you, then, that the attitudes of True—and Able, of course—are Southern?"

"It's exactly those regional attitudes that will eventually bring us to conflict," Schimmel insisted. "There's a hardening of position I don't like—an intolerance for compromise of any sort. If True and his ilk are allowed to have their way at this Southern Convention, there'll be war! We shouldn't be pro-Southern, or pro-Northern. We *must* be pro-Union. It's the only attitude that will save us."

"Perhaps the day will come when the choice will have to be made—North or South—"

"God help us if it does."

"—and where will you stand then?"

"Exactly where I've always stood," he replied fervently. "For the Union."

Alma May nodded and there was a brief silence. "When are you planning to leave?"

"Not until the spring. I don't want to inflict the rigors of winter travel on Louise."

"That's wise, of course." She smiled. "Perhaps by spring-time you will have changed your mind."

Schimmel shook his head. "That's not likely."

That evening, the Princess met with True and Able Jackson—without the two other "owners" of Bon Marché, the twins, Joy and Hope. They talked for several hours, seriously and without rancor. Bon Marché at large was not privy to what was discussed at that meeting. At the end, she poured each of them a large portion of Bon Marché bourbon, getting to her feet, and lifting her glass high.

"To the South!" she intoned.

"To the South!" the brothers Jackson responded.

They touched glasses and the sitting room rang with the bell-like sound of good crystal.

22

THE Princess understood theater. She knew how to select the proper stage, had a feeling for the characters, and was conscious of the need for plot. In that context, then, it was not surprising she chose her New Year's Eve party, welcoming 1850, to debut her latest drama—a tale she was sure was peopled by players the audience would perceive as villain and hero. And with a juvenile lead, as well.

The timing was right, too, because the family members and guests who attended the party in the double parlors of Bon Marché were all aware of the growing tensions within the Dewey ménage. It was no secret that True Jackson had drawn a gun on publisher August Schimmel, and as the story circulated, it had become more lurid with each retelling. What seemed so strange about it, though, was the lack of reaction—in a public sense—from Alma May.

The midnight hour had come, with its toasts and kisses and well-wishings, when Alma May drew the curtain.

"Ladies and gentlemen," she called out, silencing the large gathering, "I have an important announcement to make—a fitting one, I believe, at this time when we have come together to look forward to a new year, a new beginning." She beamed. "Effective immediately, George Dewey Junior, a grandson of the late Charles Dewey, will be the manager of Bon Marché. All of it!"

There were some gasps in the parlors, then a smattering of applause, as heads turned to seek out George. Eyes stared at him, trying to divine what were the thoughts behind his sober demeanor.

The Princess waited for quiet to return. "At the same time," she went on, "I am also delighted to announce the designation of Andrew Jackson, a great-grandson of the founder and the bearer of a proud Tennessee name, as the stud manager and trainer of the Bon Marché racing stables."

Excited, shocked whispers circulated through the crowd of party-goers. *Drew Jackson was a lad of only fifteen!*

Alma May raised her hand to indicate she wasn't finished. If there had been any doubts about who controlled the destiny of the plantation, they were dispelled by her imperious attitude.

"Mr. True Jackson and Mr. Able Jackson," she said, "who have served Bon Marché well for some sixteen years, will go on to other pursuits consistent with the well-being of Bon Marché. I'm sure you will all agree with me when I say that my father would have approved of these happy changes."

She signaled to the orchestra and the music for dancing was resumed, the Princess gliding across the floor in the arms of Willie Carstairs.

Animated conversation about the "happy changes" dominated the final hours of the party. The most persistent contention was that the Jacksons had been sacked by Alma May because the husband of her half sister Louise had been insulted so grievously that the Schimmels now found it necessary to move away. It was noted by many that Louise and August had absented themselves from the New Year's Eve festivities.

"Alma May has always been at odds with the Jacksons," one matron whispered to a knot of her contemporaries. "Why, I can remember when she publicly . . . well, you all know what happened that day at Clover Bottom when True destroyed her father's horse—the one named for Charles?"

The others nodded, also recalling the incident.

"She certainly is clever," another matron commented. "What was it she said? True and Able would go on to 'other pursuits consistent with the well-being of Bon Marché.' There's no doubt what she means—she's sending them packing!"

Among the horsemen at Bon Marché that evening the consensus was that George's managership of the plantation would be a felicitous change. *But young Drew Jackson as the trainer?*

They were astonished by that. While it was a fact he had served some apprenticeship under his father, True, the lad was hardly a seasoned horseman.

"Count your blessings," one racetrack veteran chortled. "Alma May's folly is going to make it a lot easier to win against the Bon Marché horses."

A second horseman shook his head negatively. "I can't believe she intends that Drew will be the trainer permanently. I think it's a case of just marking time until Two Dewey can be brought back from California. Hell, I can't imagine why the Princess let him go out there in the first place."

It was three A.M. before the party ended. As Alma May turned away from the door after bidding farewell to the last guest, she grinned at Willie: "Bed, darling?"

"Would you mind if we took a small walk first? It's a clear night and I could use some fresh air."

There was no objection from the Princess. Bundled up against the chill of the first morning of 1850 they walked slowly, hand in hand, along the path in the general direction of the deer park. There were no words at first; not until they came to the fence surrounding the park and they leaned on it, idly watching the docile bison grazing.

"Well, you've done it again," Carstairs said quietly. "Your little announcement was like a bombshell."

"It wasn't intended to be that," she replied. "It was just something that had to be done—a natural progression in the growth of Bon Marché."

"Natural progression?" he mused. "A good phrase. I think I'll borrow it for an announcement of my own."

"Oh?" She snuggled against him, comfortable with him. Not only as a lover, but as a friend. Alma May studied him now. He was certainly a handsome man: tall, strong, his clear brown eyes reflecting his honesty. She admired him deeply. Maybe she even loved him, although *love* was not a subject they permitted between themselves.

"But before I make my announcement," Willie said, "I have a question for you. You won't find it a new thing—and I wish I had kept count of the number of times I've asked it. Anyway, the question is, sincerely asked once more, will you marry me?"

The Princess sighed. "Dear, sweet Willie—so persistent."

She brushed a kiss across his lips. "No, darling, I won't. I don't wish to be married again. But we don't *need* to be married, do we?"

"I suppose not." The words were spoken hesitantly.

"And now, what's *your* announcement?"

"There's been a letter from Two," he began slowly. "A most enthusiastic letter—" He told her all of the details of young Dewey's California plans.

"I told you an investment in him would be worthwhile."

"You did, and I'm grateful for that." He paused. "But I haven't told you everything. Two strongly recommends that I come to California myself—that there is a need, and great opportunity, for an experienced banker there. I believe him to be correct."

Alma May was silent.

"I've made up my mind to act on his recommendation. I'll leave in March with a wagon train of supplies, taking Beth and little Charles with me."

"And if I accepted your marriage proposal?" she asked, the question barely audible.

"I'd stay."

Alma May put her arms around him, holding him tightly. After a long moment: "Then I'm glad I've turned you down—again. You should go, darling. It's a great opportunity." She sighed. "I'll not deny that I'm going to miss you. But when I look ahead I can't see that you have any other choice. I'm fifteen years older than you, Willie—"

"That doesn't mean a thing."

"—and if we continue this way you'll wind up with an old woman you'd learn to hate."

"Never!"

"No, you would," she insisted. "You're only thirty-four. If you wait, this adventure . . . this opportunity . . . is going to pass you by. You'll always wonder whether you made a mistake in staying with me."

"I love you, Princess," he said.

She put her fingers lightly against his lips. "It's not love, Willie, it's passion. And speaking of that—" She started toward the mansion, tugging at his hand.

He allowed himself to be pulled along, as she laughed gaily, girlishly. Halfway back to the mansion, he said: "I asked the butler to have my carriage brought around before we started on our walk. I can't stay tonight."

The laughter stopped. There was not another word spoken. When they got to the big house the carriage was waiting for him. He got in and the black driver cracked his whip. The sound of the wheels on the gravel path was thundering in Alma May's ears.

And she wept.

II

"I CAN'T believe what's happening in Nashville," Albert Dewey was saying heatedly, tossing aside a telegram from Alma May. "I think everyone there has gone suddenly mad."

Lillian Thomas, seated in the drawing room at Bon Marché Lexington, smiled at him. "Families do have a way of falling out, Albert."

"No, this is more than a falling out," he insisted. "This is a revolution. A genuine changing of the guard."

"And you don't like the new guard?"

"It's not that, exactly. My cousin George, I imagine, will manage Bon Marché admirably. In a way, I might be better off dealing with him than with True Jackson, who is such an intractable man." He hesitated. "Still . . . the sudden changes do make me wonder about my situation here, about whether the Nashville financial support will continue until I can get this farm on its feet."

"Why don't you offer to buy out their interests?"

Albert laughed bitterly. "With what?"

Lillian studied his handsome face. "I may have a solution."

"Oh?"

"I have some money from my mother's estate—"

"No!" he cut her off angrily. "I don't want another financial commitment from a . . . a . . ."

"Were you going to say 'wife,' Albert?"

"No. I was going to say I don't want another financial commitment I can't meet."

"I see." She grinned. "Suppose I offered some help with no commitment asked or implied."

"No."

"I mean, no commitment in a wifely sense."

"I know what you mean," he said churlishly. "I appreciate what you're suggesting, Lil, but the time has come when I must be my own man."

"And not beholden to some *mere* woman, eh?"

He frowned. "You have a way of being damned exasperating at times."

"Oh, God, I'm doing it again! My father has been warning me for years about my flippancy. I promise, dear, I'll stop it, as of this moment."

"Don't make rash promises you can't keep," Albert chuckled.

III

PRIDE was evident. What only three months earlier had been a disorganized, dispirited group of Nashville citizens, barely able to keep in step with the tattoo of the drum, marched now in string-straight ranks, smartly following the orders of their corps of officers.

The Nashville Grays, a company strong in the chill of the January afternoon, drilled back and forth across a broad pasture at Bon Marché, resplendent in new uniforms: gray tunics trimmed in red piping and closed with brass buttons, gray pants, white vests, ruffled shirts, black shoes, gray flat-topped caps with more red trimming.

Officers were even more grand. Their trousers were scarlet, their tunics trimmed in gold, their cockaded, crescent-shaped hats topped with gray feathers tipped in red, their swords sheathed in gleaming black leather. The mounted command staff—a brigadier general and two colonels—wore high black cavalry boots, shined to mirror brightness.

It may have seemed to a casual observer that there were an inordinate number of officers; in addition to the brigadier general and the colonels there were three majors, four captains, and half a dozen lieutenants—a ratio of one officer for every sixteen men. Yet, that spoke to the reality of organizing a volunteer militia company. When publisher Schimmel withdrew his financial support after splitting with his sons-in-law, General Able Jackson had no recourse but to seek money elsewhere, awarding rank commensurate with contribution.

The general's brother, True Jackson, sat in his carriage by

the pasture fence, soberly watching the demonstration, but involuntarily tapping his foot to the music of the Negro musicians, two fife players and two drummers. He wasn't fully convinced of the wisdom of the militia companies (this one and dozens of others springing up in North and South), but he wasn't willing, either, to arbitrarily dismiss the possible future importance of them. While he had once opposed such citizen military organizations, he saw now that the day might come when they would be needed.

Every day there were more angry exchanges between the two regions of the nation: in Congress, in publications, in letters from leaders of both areas. Few spoke of compromise, of peace.

The Grays were drawn up at parade rest in front of their commanding officer. Able grinned, tipped his hat to them in a casual nonmilitary manner, and bellowed, "Com . . . pan . . . nee . . . dis . . . missed!"

Still smiling, the citizen general wheeled his horse, dashing to the pasture fence, where he vaulted from his horse.

"This activity is making you spry," True called to him from the carriage.

"Full of life, no doubt of that. For the first time in a long while I feel . . . well, fulfilled." He leaned on the fence. "Are you off on your survey?"

True nodded. "My boat leaves in an hour." He checked his pocket watch.

"Then you've heard from Yancey and Rhett?"

"Yes, and DeBow, as well. I'm to see him in New Orleans."

"That's grand!" He saluted his brother. "And, if you find the time, I'd appreciate it if you'd get me some information on the militia companies in New Orleans. I'm particularly interested in the activities of the Continental Guards and the Orleans Grenadiers."

"I'll do my best." True gestured to the black carriage driver and the horses were whipped into action.

As the wheels began to turn, Able shouted, "God speed, Brother. The South needs your strength!"

IV

LEE Dewey was shocked by the appearance of Henry Clay. The Washington correspondent of the Schimmel-Dewey papers sat in the packed gallery of the United States Senate, looking down into the red-carpeted well of the chamber, as Clay rose to seek recognition from the presiding officer. The six-foot-tall Kentuckian—a man many, but not enough, had thought ought to be President—had always been thin, but now he appeared frail, even older than his seventy-odd years. His face was pinched and sunken. Dewey wrote in his notebook: "Obviously ill."

Clay cleared his throat, an act that led to a paroxysm of coughing. But when he finally started to speak, the voice was strong, determined.

"I hold in my hand," he announced, showing a sheaf of papers, "a series of resolutions which I desire to submit to consideration of this body. Taken together, in combination, they propose an amicable arrangement of all questions in controversy between the free and slave states, growing out of the subject of slavery."

The newspaperman wrote swiftly as Senator Clay outlined his proposals. The first called for swift admission of California to the Union without any Congressional stipulation as to slavery. *He knows the people have already made California free,* Dewey thought.

The second resolution dealt with the territories of New Mexico and Utah, with Clay urging establishment of territorial governments without provision either for introduction or exclusion of slavery. Dewey scrawled: "Congress challenged to allow ultimate choice of people there."

On the matter of Texas, the Kentuckian urged a settlement of boundary disputes in which the state would give up some of the land it claimed, but which rightly ought to be in the New Mexico territory. But the federal government, he went on, ought to assume the debts of Texas, recognizing it as fair compensation for the loss of duties that might be collected were it still an independent nation. "Horsetrading," Dewey wrote, underlining the word twice.

Clay called for an end to slave trade in the District of Columbia. (Only two days earlier Lee had written a story about the sad spectacle of manacled slaves being paraded through the streets of the nation's capital.) But the senator, carefully and slowly, stipulated that slavery in the District would not be prohibited so long as it continued in Maryland, or until Maryland and District slaveholders agreed to accept compensation for its abolition. Dewey jotted down three words: "Sop to South!"

The Kentuckian was coming to a close. He urged the enactment of a stronger fugitive-slave law, pointing out that Northerners must return runaway slaves to their owners. He recognized constitutional principle, and wanted others to, as well, when he said Congress "has no power to prohibit or obstruct the trade of slaves between the slaveholding states, but . . . the admission or exclusion of slaves from one into another of them, depends exclusively upon their own particular laws."

There was no bombast in what he said, no appeal to the gallery for emotional applause. Clay noted, with great sadness, that he had never addressed the Senate when it was "so oppressed, so appalled, so anxious."

He spoke of those who would advocate disunion and war. "I implore them to pause—solemnly to pause—to conjure at the edge of the precipice before the fearful and disastrous leap is taken into the yawning abyss below which will inevitably lead to certain and irretrievable destruction. [*He's begging*, the newspaperman thought.] I implore, as the best blessing which Heaven can bestow upon me upon earth, that if the direful and sad event of the dissolution of the Union shall happen I may not survive to behold the sad and heart-rending spectacle."

Lee Dewey hurried from the Senate gallery, half running to the telegraph office. The story, it seemed, wrote itself:

Washington, D.C., Jan. 29, 1850—Senator Henry Clay of Kentucky, ailing and distressed, has laid before the United States an omnibus bill of resolutions aimed at compromising the various contentions between North and South over the issue of slavery.

In the most statesmanlike presentation of his illustrious life as a public servant, Senator Clay pleaded with contentious representatives of both regions to pause solemnly at the "yawning abyss below," an allusion to all of the discussion of disunion and war which grips this capital city.

It can be expected that Mr. Clay's resolutions will engenger much debate in the weeks ahead from the most vociferous of the champions of both North and South attitudes. Observers in the Senate today noted that the leading spokesman for what is regarded as Southern intransigence, Senator John Caldwell Calhoun of South Carolina, was not present in the chamber to hear the Kentuckian's proposals. Numerous sources here report Senator Calhoun to be grievously ill, and he may not be able to . . .

V

Two Dewey whooped with delight, waving the letter like a flag.

"Beth and little Charles will be on their way soon! And Willie Carstairs is coming with them!"

He sat in his room in the Palmer House with Roger Weatherford, after a long, tiring day of work on the San Francisco waterfront warehouse of the Dewey Trading Company.

"And listen to this." He read: "'On Saturday, February second, the *Orleans Trader* sailed from New Orleans bound for San Francisco. I've leased the entire ship and am enclosing a manifest of her cargo.'"

He glanced at the manifest. "My God, Roger, he's shipping it all—tools, gunpowder, flour, sugar, salt, firearms, and . . . and . . . even our bakery!" Two tossed the document to his partner. "It's all falling into place."

"I'm pleased for you, Charles," Weatherford commented soberly.

"For *me*? You ought to be pleased for yourself, too."

"Oh, I am. I just hope we haven't oversold your banker friend."

Dewey laughed. "Willie Carstairs isn't a man who *can* be oversold. No, his enthusiasm for all of this just proves that we're on the right course."

"Hmmm."

Two studied the letter some more. "If the *Orleans Trader* left on the second of February, then it ought to be here by October, wouldn't you think?"

"Yes, I suppose so."

"And Beth and Charles Three will be here by that time.

They'll have to be through the Sierras before the first snow."
A startled look came to his face. "Oh, God—!"

"What?"

"I've got to have a house for them, Roger. A proper house.
All of our other work has just driven that out of my mind."

Weatherford smiled at him. "There's time to build a
house."

"But it has to be special. I owe that to Beth." He pondered
over it for a moment. "Something on the hills above the
town. That land above Market and Mission streets . . . what
are they calling it?"

"Nob Hill," Roger answered.

"That's it—we'll build a house on Nob Hill!"

23

EVENTS moved swiftly—for the Deweys and the nation; unfolding human drama reduced to scratches of the pen from the humidity of Washington City across the American continent to the warmth of the California sun.

From newspaperman Lee Dewey:

Washington, Mar. 4—A gravely ill Senator John C. Calhoun came to the well of the United States Senate today, swathed in flannels and with barely enough movement to show he still lived, to hear his reply to Senator Henry Clay's regional compromises read by Senator George Mason of Virginia. The roar of the old South Carolina lion was silenced, but the bite of his strong views remained.

Calhoun challenged Clay's proposals on every point, contending he had "believed from the first that the agitation on the subject of slavery would, if not prevented by some timely and effective measure, end in disunion." Mr. Clay's measures, he said, did nothing to change his view: government by and for one section was being established.

The Founding Fathers, Senator Calhoun contended, had established a confederate form of government, not a consolidated Union. The national government had "delegated" powers only, the States retaining their sovereignty. He characterized the Constitution as the rock against abuses from both sides. But when the Constitution no longer protects all, the South Carolinian wrote in his address, and when the central government becomes an agent for one interest to oppress the citizens of a state, secession is a right . . .

Letter from Willie Carstairs to Alma May Dewey:

Independence, Mo., March 5. My darling Princess. Have arrived here safely with Beth and little Charles Three to find a situation I can only describe as fantastic! Perhaps it's not yet mayhem, although it threatens to be that if I do not keep my wits about me. Thank God I took your advice and brought those Bon Marché blacks with us, because, without them, there would have been no way to unload our supplies from the steamboat. Other labor, when it is available at all here, is unrealistically costly. But we have unloaded and have established a "camp" of sorts on the western edge of Independence.

"Outfitting" is the big business here and, indeed, I could sell everything I've brought here—immediately and at a good profit. But if Two is correct (and I have no doubt that he is), then what we intend to take to California will bring even greater profits there.

There are no available hotel accommodations here, nor any private housing of any kind, and we are "living"—crudely, for my tastes—in two small tents. Beth is uncomplaining and Charles Three is absolutely delighted with the adventure. It seems we will not be able to leave here for at least a month, but I'll need the time to arrange for wagons (it'll take sixteen, it seems) and the attendant mules and/or oxen. Manpower is going to be the principal problem, and thank the Lord once more for the Bon Marché hands . . .

Dispatch from Lee Dewey:

Washington, Mar. 7—Senator Daniel Webster, reaching the apex of his justly praised oratorical skills, stood today before the United States Senate and supported Henry Clay's proposals to end contentions over the extension of slavery.

"I wish to speak today," Senator Webster said, "not as a Massachusetts man, not as a Northern man, but as an

American . . . I speak today for the preservation of the Union. Hear me for my cause!"

Political observers in this capital city view Webster's championing of the Clay "compromises" as a sign that most of them will be passed by the senatorial body. But Senator Webster chided Southern leaders who speak of secession as a redress of their differences, as Senator John C. Calhoun had done three days earlier. He scorned the possibility of secession without strife.

"Sir, your eyes and mine are never destined to see that miracle!" Mr. Webster intoned. "There can be no such thing as a peaceable secession." . . .

Letter from True Jackson to his brother, Able:

New Orleans, March 15. Dear Brother: If I did not believe so strongly in the Southern cause, I would be deeply distressed today. James DeBow declines to attend the Nashville Convention, claiming a lack of time because of his editing duties on *DeBow's Review.* William Yancey, given the opportunity to keynote the convention in light of his oratorical skills, likewise has declined. So, too, has Edmund Ruffin, sending me a rather curt note in which I detect, reading between the lines, a denigration of the Tennessee efforts on behalf of a greater South.

Yet, my journey has not been a total failure. Robert Barnwell Rhett received me graciously in the offices of the Charleston *Mercury,* quickly accepting the invitation to take a leading role in the convention and promising to light up the Nashville sky! Let's hope he can light up the entire Southern sky, now darkened, it seems to me, by Henry Clay's damned "compromises."

When I return I shall also be bringing with me considerable information on the militia activities, as you requested. There's even more than we had imagined, indicating a Southern resolve to fight, if that's what the North decrees. . . .

Diary entry by Charles Dewey II:

March 21—Attended with great pride the inauguration today of the first governor of the new state of California.

And glory be, he's a native of Tennessee, born in Nashville, no less, in 1807. Governor Burnett and I (his full name is Peter Hardeman Burnett) had a few moments on this busy day to reminisce about Nashville and I found him a gentleman and a solid legal mind. Certainly, it will not harm the future of the Dewey Trading Company to have such a ready ally in the Sacramento government . . .

August Schimmel editorial in the *Chicago Clarion,* March 30:

News received yesterday by telegraph of the death of South Carolina Senator John C. Calhoun may have a profound effect on the United States and its future. While we are not ready to accept one contention we've read that Mr. Calhoun's death was "the interposition of God to save the country," we are of a mind to suggest to other Southern leaders that the old lion's single-minded call for secession ought not be emulated.

What we should contemplate today, in the wake of this sad news, is that Mr. Calhoun served his nation well: as a member of the House, secretary of war, twice the Vice President, secretary of state, and as a United States senator. That he was certainly wrong on the question of secession should not be allowed to diminish the fact that he was a public servant of stainless integrity. The Lord God, we submit, must have welcomed him with open arms . . .

Letter by Harriet Walston Dewey to her parents in New Orleans:

Nashville, April 1st. Dearest Mommy and Daddy: Beau Monde is rapidly nearing completion, so much so that it seems safe now to plan the initial social event—a soiree to honor the delegates to the Nashville Convention in June . . .

II

CHICAGO was an uncertain thing to August Schimmel. It was a city, that much was a legal reality, but what kind of city? Even though he had owned a newspaper there for nearly a decade, he had never visited Chicago before he found it necessary to leave Nashville. The resident editor had been both publisher and editorialist of the *Chicago Clarion,* with Schimmel's control being limited to what he could impart through his long, instructive letters.

But now he was there, brought to the city on the southwest corner of Lake Michigan by his wounded pride—a pride, he thought now as he stood at the window of his hotel room and looked out onto Chicago streets, which might have been better served by not succumbing to his sons-in-law's goading. Without doubt, he had been grievously insulted by True and Able Jackson, his tenure at Bon Marché made intolerable. *Intolerable?* Maybe that was too strong a word; the realization did nothing to assuage his fear that he had made a mistake in leaving.

In just over a month, August had concluded he didn't like Chicago. It was simply too much city for his tastes, with its cindered streets, its unpleasant urban smells, and the apparent inability of Chicagoans to talk about their community without braggadocio. True, Chicago had made amazing strides since 1835, increasing in population from some 3,200 to almost 30,000—bigger now than Nashville. And it was a fact that the Illinois and Michigan Canal, linking Lake Michigan with the Illinois River and, thus, with the Mississippi, was making Chicago a major inland port. Even the railroad builders, that strange new breed of men, seemed to view the city as a future transportation hub. Yet, with all of that, Schimmel's discontent with Chicago grew daily.

For one thing, he wasn't happy at all with the condition of the *Clarion.* Seeing it from a Nashville vantage point, the newspaper had been a modest profit producer. But now that he was on the scene, he quickly realized the *Clarion* was the weakest of the five newspapers in the city, slovenly edited and poorly printed. Part of the problem was editor Ben Worrell, a man too comfortable with his whiskey. He'd have to be replaced. By whom, August had no idea. Just as important, if the *Clarion* was to survive, there would have to be additional capital investment for new presses, something he had not anticipated.

Also disconcerting was that Chicago simply wasn't Nashville. There was no gentility in the city; there was little of the mind-expanding he had known in the frequent gathering of gentlemen at Berry's Bookstore, where literary excellence was appreciated, where the exchange of ideas provided intellectual stimulation.

Worst of all, however, was the attitude Chicagoans had about Southerners. He was in the city only a day or two before he found he was looked upon as an alien. Not because of his German heritage—Chicago had many such immigrant citizens—but because he was *from the South*. All the problems of the nation were being laid at Southern doorsteps. There was a strident, intractable attitude about the South, only a part of it because of slavery. That the *Clarion,* and his other newspapers, had a pro-Union editorial policy, seemed not to count for much. He was a Southerner—and suspect. It saddened him that there appeared no room in Chicago minds for compromise; regional contention was stronger here than what he had recognized in the South. And when Chicagoans expressed pro-Union sentiments they saw the Union as perhaps better off *without* the South. Pro-Union to these people meant only pro-North!

Schimmel sighed, turning away from the hotel window, looking at his wife seated at a small writing table, composing a letter to their daughters.

He manufactured a chuckle. "Are you finding it difficult to come up with Chicago virtues to write about?"

"Not at all," Louise replied easily. "I'm telling them about some of the houses we saw today."

"And the exorbitant prices asked for them?"

She stopped trying to write, studying his unhappy face. "My . . . we are in a foul mood, aren't we?"

"With good reason," her husband growled. "I wish I knew what the devil to do about the *Clarion*'s editorship."

Louise grinned at him. "If you feel it necessary to get rid of Worrell, I have an easy answer for you. *You* take over the editor's job—an occasional editorial gives you precious little to do—and stop blaming yourself for being here in Chicago and not in Nashville."

"Don't you miss Nashville?"

"Of course. But I knew I would from the beginning. And I also knew I'd have to *adapt* to Chicago. What surprises me is that *you* didn't know it." She rose from the desk, going to him, putting her arms around him and kissing him. "If you stopped brooding about the *Clarion* and got to work on it, you wouldn't have time to feel sorry for yourself."

"I suppose I'm doing that," August admitted.

"Yes, dear." She kissed him again, going back to her letter writing.

"After all, there's no reason I shouldn't be able to edit the *Clarion* and take care of the management duties for the chain at the same time."

"Yes, dear."

"I'm not a doddering old man, for Christ's sake!"

"No, dear."

III

As far as the eye could see the vast Kansas Territory prairie on both sides of the wide Platte River was black with buffalo, a great herd moving slowly, grazing, its mass seeming to sway slightly as if reacting to the gentle breeze. Even the approach of the huge wagon train did nothing to disturb the stolid brutes.

There were eighty-seven wagons in the train, seventeen days out of Independence, Missouri, traveling easily along the flat terrain of what was known as the Oregon Trail, just south of the Platte. In the van were the sixteen heavily laden wagons of the Dewey Trading Company, all drawn by mules, and all but three with black teamsters from the Bon Marché plantation of Nashville, Tennessee.

At this point on the trail—hardened by the travelers who had gone before them—it was wide enough for the wagons to proceed three abreast. Beth Dewey and nine-year-old Charles Dewey III sat next to the Negro man driving one of the trading-company wagons in the first row (nearest the cooling river), not disturbed by the interminable dust cloud raised by the train. Those near the rear were not so fortunate.

Willie Carstairs sat his horse next to Beth's wagon. "Well, Buster," he called to the youngster, "what do you think of that?"

Young Charles's eyes were wide in awe. He was aware the animals were buffalo; there were four of them in the deer park at Bon Marché. But the sheer number of them was astounding.

"How many do you think there are?" he asked.

"Oh, quite a few," Willie grinned. "Tens of thousands, I'd guess."

"Who owns them?"

It was Beth who answered. "They're God's creatures, son."

"Oh."

A rider came up to Carstairs, a sturdy man whose face was nearly lost in a bushy beard. He was the wagonmaster; a well-recommended fellow the banker had hired in Independence to get the trading company's supplies through to California. The other wagons had joined the train for safety's sake and to share the costs of the journey.

His name was William Tyler Mason; he called himself Ty.

"Nearly time for camp," he said stoically, glancing at the fading light in the sky. "There's a grove of ash up ahead 'bout a mile. Tell your drivers to start drawin' up there."

"Very well."

"I'm puttin' out some hunters to get us a half-dozen or so bison. 'Bout time we have a feast, eh?"

"Won't the shooting . . . uh . . . stampede them?" Beth asked.

"No, ma'am. They's kinda stupid beasts. They'll just sorta mill around the ones what fall. It ain't no trick to shoot buffalo, ma'am."

And it was as Ty Mason had said. The hunters had an easy time of it and it didn't take long for seven buffalo to be killed, dragged into the night's camp by several teams of mules, butchered, and consigned to the huge fires Mason's men had begun in the grove of trees.

In a sense, it had been somewhat of an idyllic trip up to that time, the train moving inexorably west with no untoward incidents to slow them. A week earlier they had camped at what was known as the Loup Fork of the Platte, near a Pawnee Indian village, and all of the lurid tales of Indian raids on wagon trains seemed so much silliness. The Pawnees crossed the Platte to beg—for food, bits of clothing, anything the travelers were willing to part with.

They were sad people, Beth Dewey thought. She gave one of the women an old gingham skirt, which was taken with no show of emotion at all. Charles Three's efforts to converse with them failed totally. They came, they begged, and went back across the river to their village.

"How do they live, Mr. Mason?" Beth asked.

"Like you seen, ma'am," the wagonmaster chuckled. "They's just beggars."

"But don't they hunt, or grow crops—?"

Mason shook his head negatively. "Since the wagon trains come along regular like, they don't gotta. They learned soon enough that if they beg they can exist, an' that's 'bout it."

The camp on this night was much as it had been every other night. Someone always seemed to unlimber a fiddle, and there was dancing and singing. But now, for the first time, there were buffalo steaks—large and succulent.

The tenderness and the sweet taste of the meat surprised the Dewey woman. "Why . . . it's almost like veal," she said to Mason.

"Yes, ma'am. If we was closer to butcher shops in a city, I'd figger to make a good livin' with 'em."

The clear, moonless sky was an ebony blanket over them, sprinkled with more stars than most of the travelers had ever seen. As Willie Carstairs prepared to bed down he saw a pinkish light on the far western horizon.

"Ty!" he called to the wagonmaster, "that glow in the distance—?"

"Prairie fire," Mason replied laconically.

Willie was concerned. "Aren't we likely to be running into it tomorrow?"

"Naw, naw, Mr. Carstairs, that's two, mebbe three, days off. It'll burn itself out 'fore then."

IV

BEAU Monde was ablaze with light—inside from a host of new Boston-designed brass oil lamps and outside from dozens of specially made torches which lit up the lavishly landscaped grounds next to the Bon Marché deer park.

On this first day of June, 1850, a Saturday, Harriet Walston Dewey was likewise radiant in a shimmering gold-fabric gown imported from France, distinguished by its daringly low décolletage. Glitters scattered in her modishly coiffed brunette hair caught the light from the huge crystal chandelier suspended above her in the wide entrance hall, spraying out tiny bits of refracted colors as she greeted her guests.

Beau Monde, Harriet's castle, her beautiful world, was making its debut and, in a very real sense, so was Harriet. Nashville was seeing her for the first time as a fashionable hostess as she confidently presided over a reception for the delegates to the Nashville Convention of Southern leaders.

Not everything was perfect, however. Several of the first families of Nashville had declined her invitation to attend the soiree—for properly political reasons. But it was really because there were not a few in Nashville who regarded the upcoming convention as dangerous nonsense and wanted no connection with it, not even in the context of what was regarded as Nashville's premier social event of the year.

Then, too, Alma May Dewey, the mistress of Bon Marché, had swept into Beau Monde, noisily and slightly intoxicated, on the arm of one Barton Danbury, a man regarded as one of Nashville's most prominent gamblers and a dedicated roué. Alma May hadn't told Harriet she would be escorted by Danbury, a social faux pas, Harriet believed. Worse, the Princess was now firmly planted in the center of the Beau Monde salon, completely surrounded by men, laughing coarsely as she entertained them with a recital of risqué stories.

"I wish you'd speak to your aunt," Harriet whispered to her husband.

"And tell her what?" Statler Dewey asked. "To behave herself?"

"That would be a good start!" His wife was angry.

"Oh, come on, Harriet," he chuckled, "there's no one going to change the Princess after all these years."

"She may be a princess at Bon Marché, but *not* here!"

Harriet turned to the door once more, the smile returning to her face, as the last of the guests arrived and were properly greeted.

In spite of the defections of some prominent Nashvillians the large salon of the new mansion was crowded and, Alma May excepted, it was a sedate gathering. The music of a string ensemble, positioned on the balcony overlooking the salon, permeated the room, giving it the tone Harriet had sought. Busy with her social amenities, the hostess soon forgot about the Princess's disruptive entrance.

Harriet paid special attention to a guest Statler had told her would be the most important delegate at the convention: Robert Barnwell Rhett, the editor of the Charleston *Mercury*.

He was an intense, self-assured man and he stood now in the center of a group including True Jackson and his wife, Joy; Able Jackson and his wife, Hope; Harriet and Statler Dewey; and several other Nashvillians.

"Tell us, Mr. Rhett," Harriet asked sweetly, "what you hope to accomplish in the Nashville meetings."

"Simply put, Mrs. Dewey," he replied, "it is my hope we'll be able to prepare the Southern mind for the inevitable."

"And that is?"

He seemed surprised by his hostess's question. "And that is, my dear lady, a confederacy of the Southern states separate and apart from the debilitating influence of the Northern states. For much too long we have tamely acquiesced, until to hate and persecute the South has become a high passport to honor and power in the Union! A Union, I might add, which in no way serves the Southern cause."

One of the other men spoke up. "Secession—and that's what you're advocating, is it not?—can only lead to war."

Rhett sighed. "Ah, that's the cry, isn't it? We're supposed to believe that the South, should it secede, will bring us to war. But will the North take that last dangerous step? I doubt it. And, even if it should, what matter? The South is superior in military skills—"

The Nashvillian cut him off. "So I keep hearing, Mr. Rhett, but I fear it may not be true. Do you honestly believe that a few posturing militia companies can be the equal of the established United States Army and the industrialization of the North?"

"See here, Carbaugh!" General Able Jackson snapped, "The militia companies you seem to deprecate so easily will be in the front line, ready and willing to make the sacrifices necessary to preserve our Southern way of life!"

"You mean your large slaveholdings here at Bon Marché," the devil's advocate retorted.

"Gentlemen," Harriet said soothingly, "I hope that we're not going to fight a war here tonight." She laughed.

"Our hostess is right," Rhett offered. "We can ill afford to quarrel among ourselves. We ought to leave that to the public press, which seems determined to make light of the South's problems." He looked directly at Statler. "Didn't I read in your newspaper, Mr. Dewey, that the convention we are about to undertake was characterized as 'silliness' and that those calling for a Southern Convention were . . . let's see if I can recall the exact words . . . were 'backward children playing a dangerous game fit only for idiots'?"

"Uh . . . yes . . ." Statler replied uneasily. "That particular editorial was written by a senior associate."

"Damned traitor!" True Jackson muttered.

Rhett picked up quickly on the split in the ranks of the Dewey family. "Your senior associate—that would be August Schimmel."

"Well . . . yes," Statler admitted.

"It's my understanding Mr. Schimmel is now in Chicago and that you, Mr. Dewey, are managing the Southern papers."

"That's true."

"Then, certainly, our convention ought to rate fair coverage from this quarter."

Before the embarrassed Statler had time to answer, Alma May and Barton Danbury came up to the group. Somewhat reluctantly, Harriet made the introductions to Robert Rhett.

"It's a pleasure, Mr. Rhett, to meet the man," Danbury grinned, "who is going to have a role in winning ten thousand dollars for me."

The visitor wrinkled his brow. "I don't understand."

"Well, you see, sir, some fool just gave me four-to-one odds on twenty-five hundred that the convention would amount to something. And I bet it wouldn't."

"See here, sir—" Rhett's face clouded.

Harriet looked pleadingly at her husband for help.

"What do you say, Princess," Statler interjected, grinning broadly, "that you let me get you a champagne?" He took her arm.

"Damned good idea," Alma May slurred.

Statler led her away from the group, the gambler following.

Harriet smiled sweetly at Rhett. "Sir, this *is* a party. Will you honor me with a dance?"

"Delighted, ma'am." He whirled her in among the dancing couples.

Harriet Dewey sighed lightly, vowing never again to have a soirée in the context of a political event, as she had done on this evening. That was not at all what she wanted for her Beau Monde, her beautiful world.

V

In the final accounting, it must be assumed Barton Danbury won his bet. The Southern Convention *did* get under way on the following Monday in the McKendree Methodist Church, *and* Robert Barnwell Rhett did "light up the sky" with his oratory, as he had promised True Jackson he would.

In addressing the convention, Rhett let it be known to all that he favored, he advocated, disunion.

"Let it be that I am a traitor!" he roared. "The word holds no terrors for me. I have been born of traitors, but thank God, they have been traitors in the great cause of liberty, fighting against tyranny and oppression. *Such* treason will ever be mine whilst true to my lineage!

"Be not cowed by the Northern interests, my friends. Others before us have struggled successfully for their independence and freedom against far greater odds. And, if must be, we can make one brave, long, last, desperate struggle for our rights and honor, ere the black pall of tyranny is stretched over the bier of our dead liberties!"

He paused at that point and smiled. "To meet death a little sooner or a little later, can be of consequence to very few of us. And we must send to the North a message from this place: DISUNION is the dearest and holiest word to the brave and the free. The South must rule herself or perish!

"If a Confederacy of the Southern States could *now* be obtained," Rhett trumpeted, "should we not . . . deem . . . it . . . a . . . happy . . . termination?"

Aside from the South Carolinian's bombast (however genuine may have been the sentiments), little else happened at the convention sessions. Only nine states had appeared at the meeting, and some of the delegates were not front-rank individuals. After several days, when nothing substantial was accomplished, the convention was adjourned with a call to meet again in six weeks.

The community of Nashville seemed not to care at all about it. Taking his cue from that attitude, Statler Dewey's stories of the convention were brief and evenhanded. He did no editorializing on it and decided that a vitriolic anticonvention editorial telegraphed from Chicago by August Schimmel was overkill, not printing it in the *Nashville Monitor*.

In the meantime, daily reports from Lee Dewey in Washington indicated clearly that Henry Clay's proposals for compromise of regional differences were passing in Congress, even though the debate was bitter at times.

Then, late on the evening of Tuesday, July 9, President Zachary Taylor, Old Rough and Ready, died of what the doctors called cholera morbus, brought on by having stood bareheaded in a blazing sun at an Independence Day celebration and following that with large quantities of iced drinks. The hot-cold combination made him ill—unto death, as it turned out. Vice President Millard Fillmore, frightened by the knowledge of how ill-prepared he was for the responsibilities of the presidency, locked himself in his Willard Hotel room to spend a sleepless, worried night.

Yet, Fillmore's succession seemed somehow fortunate. He was not a man who was likely to upset the delicate balance of Clay's compromises. While he was on the record as regarding slavery as an "evil," he had also said it was an evil with which the national government ought to have nothing to do. He had said: "By the power of the Constitution that question is vested in the several states where the institution is tolerated. If they regard it as a blessing, they have a constitutional right to enjoy it. And, if they regard it as an evil, they have the power and know best how to apply a remedy."

When the Southern Convention met again in July in Nashville the influence it might have had had been dissipated. It did pass some resolutions, one asserting the right of secession, and another calling the compromise measures unsatisfactory.

But everyone knew the statesmanship of Kentucky's Henry Clay had turned the nation away from the gates of sectional war, and most of the convention delegates went home feeling they had wasted their time.

Statler Dewey, for one, gave the end of the convention less space in the *Monitor* than he did to former Tennessee governor Neill Brown's imminent appointment to the post of U.S. minister to Russia. "Secrecy and mystery characterize everything done there," Brown had told young Dewey in an interview.

24

BETH Dewey wrote another number in her diary: 93.

It seemed impossible—only ninety-three? In her mind and in her aching muscles she was being told it *had* to be more than just ninety-three days since their wagon train had left Independence, Missouri. But the neat order of the pages of the diary, containing more adventure than she had thought possible in her young life, confirmed the number. And what was still ahead? Wagonmaster Ty Mason had told her that morning they would reach their goal by September 15. That meant sixty-two *more* days to Sacramento. An eternity!

The date was Monday, July 15, 1850, and they were camped in the Great Salt Lake Valley, marveling at the community the sturdy and sober Mormons were building there. Marveling, too, at the vast expanse of the strange and forbidding lake. It was the second day of their camp there, Mason having decreed that both humans and animals—the mules and the oxen—needed rest before venturing across the searing, lifeless landscape Ty had said was the "Forty-Mile Desert," on the other side of which would be the Sierra Nevada Mountains, the last barrier to California.

The whole trip, it seemed to Beth, had been a series of barriers, some more compelling in her memory than others. As she idly paged through her diary now, her thoughts traveled backward.

To the measureless acres of blackened earth they had crossed after a prairie fire, the residual smoke stinging eyes until sight seemed lost, and the ashes blown up by the prairie winds choking them and making their faces as black as those of the slave teamsters from Bon Marché.

To the days they had spent, bruised shoulders pressed against the giant spokes of the wagon wheels, pushing, pushing, pushing to free the wagons from hub-deep sand or mud.

To the terror inherent in the steep descents on which they had to use block-and-tackle to lower the heavy wagons down the nearly perpendicular, rocky cliffs, the wheels double-locked against the inexorable weight. One such descent—and Beth hadn't even written down the name of the place (had she even known what it was?)—was particularly painful in memory. One of the Dewey Trading Company wagons, loaded with picks and shovels, had broken loose, crashing down nearly five hundred feet, killing one of their Negro teamsters.

To the indiscriminate nature of the cholera which struck some of the members of the wagon train, wiping out an entire family of seven from Pennsylvania; the name "Fenstermacher" was noted in the diary. Beth Dewey herself had dug the grave for the youngest member of the family, a baby girl born during the trip. It hurt her so to place the tiny flaxen-haired infant in the ground and cover the sweet, innocent face with prairie earth. She couldn't bring herself to toss in the dirt with a shovel; instead, she knelt by the hole, dribbling the earth in through her fingers. Gently, so as not to bring further pain.

And yet, there was some good moments, too. She recalled the exhilaration they had known when a scout came back with the news that Fort Laramie was dead ahead. And she remembered how kindly they had been welcomed there by the outgoing French trappers who worked for the American Fur Company and who all seemed to have Indian wives. And there was the beauty of the prairie made gay by a profusion of red, white, and yellow flowers. And the majesty of eagles soaring high over snow-covered western peaks.

Beth sighed, closing the diary, looking across the campsite to where her son was in earnest conversation with the wagonmaster. When they had left Nashville Charles Three was a pampered little boy. Now, at ten (they had celebrated his birthday on the way) he was self-assured, bronzed, muscular, looking so much like his father.

She ached inside when she thought of Two. Lord, how she

wanted him! Beth would have given her soul at that moment just to hold her husband in her arms.

II

DISPATCH from Lee Dewey to the Schimmel/Dewey newspapers:

> Washington City, Sept. 9—The United States Senate today put its stamp of approval on the admission of slave-free California as the thirty-first state of the Union. President Fillmore is expected to immediately affix his signature to the California statehood bill, as he has on other bills in what is now being called Senator Henry Clay's "Great Compromise of 1850." . . .

In Chicago, publisher August Schimmel gleefully began an editorial:

> The storm clouds of disunion, which have hovered threateningly over the nation, are dissipating rapidly under the enlightened wisdom of the U.S. Senate and President Millard Fillmore, who has been, these newspapers must admit, somewhat surprising in his statesmanlike role . . .

That evening in Nashville, as he read the telegraphed editorial, Statler Dewey had some doubts about how rapidly the storm clouds were disappearing. Like Schimmel, he was heartened by the passage of Clay's compromises, but he was also aware that other newspapers in the South weren't as sanguine about developments in Washington as was the Schimmel/Dewey newspaper chain.

Statler recognized the Great Compromise was just that: a *compromise,* but one masking the crisis between North and South. Only that day he had read an editorial in *The Spirit of the South* which perhaps told the greatest truth about what was happening:

> The present apparent prosperity of the South is one of the causes of whatever there may be of reluctance among her people to advocate resistance; because there is plenty to live on, because we are out of debt, and cotton brings a good price, many are in so good a humor and so

well satisfied with themselves and things around them as to shut their eyes to the future in the consoling reflection that the future cannot hurt them.

Young Dewey was of a mind to write his own editorial along those same lines; the future, he feared, was foreboding. Nevertheless, he handed August's editorial over to the typesetter.

"This will figure prominently," he instructed, "on the first page of the next edition." And he hoped Schimmel's optimism would prove valid.

III

TRY as she might, Beth Dewey could not dispel the nightmare she had experienced in the last three weeks. The wagon train was now on the friendly soil of California, traveling parallel to the American River, having passed Sutter's, and moving easily toward Sacramento.

But the memories of what she had been through remained vividly with her. There was still the stink in her nostrils of the hundreds of decaying bodies of oxen, horses, and mules scattered along the trail across the great desert, a stench which was suffocating in the oppressive heat. And then there had been the debilitating contrast of the bitter cold experienced in crossing the difficult Sierra Nevada Mountains, with blinding snow making every foot traversed a cruel test of will.

It was the morning of Sunday, September 15—155 days out of Independence—and Beth was reflecting on it all. The Dewey Trading Company had been fortunate; it had lost only one wagon and one life. But, in sum, seventeen wagons in the train had been lost or abandoned; some cargo had been discarded, as well. No less than twenty-one new graves dotted the path they had taken. The oxen and mules and other livestock rotting along the way went uncounted.

An outrider approached at full gallop. "Sacramento City!" he called to wagonmaster Ty Mason. "Four . . . five hours ahead!"

Beth reacted immediately. "We'll stop here for an hour, Mr. Mason," she ordered.

"Ma'am, I think we oughta just press on."

"No," she said firmly, "we'll stop. I need a bath and some

fresh clothes." She smiled disarmingly at him. "I don't intend to face my husband in this condition."

The wagonmaster, annoyed, looked to Willie Carstairs, who nodded his agreement to stopping. Mason shrugged, riding along the length of the train announcing a one-hour halt to "prepare for Sacramento."

Beth bathed in the waters of the American (making sure that Charles did, too) unconcerned about the propriety of her nudity. Carstairs, who also bathed fifteen or twenty discreet yards downstream from her, couldn't help but look at her, admiring her firm body, gleaming wet. *Two's a fortunate sonofabitch,* he thought. And he thought, too, of Alma May.

The baths completed, Beth opened a trunk in the lead wagon, removing a new gown she had bought in Nashville for that very moment. She slipped it over new, modish feminine underclothes, also purchased with an eye to her reunion with Charles. There was a new suit for Charles Three, as well.

"I want your father to see us in the best possible light," she told her son. "And for today, at least, I want no lurid tales of the trip. There'll be time enough for those stories. Today, I want him just to be glad to see us, without concern for what we might have been through."

"Yes, Mother." The boy contemplated her soberly. "May I show him the Indian artifacts I've gathered?"

"Yes, of course. But I want no talk of hardships. Do you understand?"

"Yes, Mother."

The wagon train started up again, the hours passing swiftly. As the community of Sacramento came into view, Beth Dewey reached into a purse and put some fragrance in her hair.

The next two hours represented a mélange of emotions, of laughter and tears, as Two Dewey and Roger Weatherford greeted the wagon train. There had to be time to unload the trading company's wagons at the newly built warehouse on which was emblazoned in huge red letters: DEWEY TRADING COMPANY.

"My God, Willie," Charles exclaimed to Carstairs, "this stuff represents a fortune for us! Like no fortune I've heard of coming from the goldfields."

"It is really that good?" Willie asked, believing Two might be exaggerating.

"That good and more! And when our ship sails into San Francisco harbor next month we'll be men of great means. Cocks of the walk, Willie, cocks of the walk!"

And then, at dusk, Charles and Beth were alone in their room in the City Hotel. Two held her tightly, kissing her with intense passion.

"Oh, Lord," he breathed, "you'll never know how much I dreamt of this moment. And it's strange—nothing is different from the dreams, not even the smell of you."

Beth smiled. "You're not the only one who has dreamt."

"Was it difficult, darling?"

"There were only miles," she lied, "each one bringing me closer to you."

"Little Charles seems to have prospered from it all. I'm astounded how much he's grown. He's every inch a young man."

"He's every inch his father. And if his father persists in all this talking—" Beth giggled.

Slowly, lovingly, he undressed her, savoring every second, kissing each area of white-pink skin as he exposed it.

Beth Dewey didn't hurry him.

IV

ALBERT Dewey and Lillian Thomas were caught up in the crowd gathered in front of the Phoenix Hotel in Lexington, being pushed and pummeled as they tried to make their way through the happy throng. Every church bell in town was being rung, and colorful rockets were lighting up the early October night sky. A huge bonfire in the street was roaring as the coach arrived and a tall, lean old man stepped out to receive three long cheers.

Senator Henry Clay had arrived home. His compromise work in Washington was done and the nation had been drawn back from the brink of war. Here was a hero who deserved the adulation.

"Speech! Speech!" someone screamed and the crowd took up the persistent chant.

With difficulty, Clay pushed his way into the Phoenix Hotel

to reappear on the hotel balcony and the cheers rent the night in even greater volume than before. The senator smiled broadly at the audience below him, raising a thin arm and pointing a finger to somewhere off in the distance.

"There lives an old lady," he said, trying to be heard, "about a mile and a half from here with whom I have lived for more than fifty years, whom I would rather see than any of you."

He grinned, bowed gracefully, and was gone, to be spirited to a carriage in the rear of the hotel, from whence he could travel to his Ashland plantation.

Albert and Lillian left the crowded street to find their own carriage. Once in it, and pointed in the direction of Bon Marché Lexington, Albert asked, "That old lady of whom he spoke—?"

"The former Lucretia Hart," Lillian told him, "the daughter of Colonel Thomas Hart. She brought her fortune to the marriage and, in a sense, she brought him into the privileged society of Lexington, opening the doors for him, so to speak."

"Hmmm." Albert thought for a moment. "Why do I have the impression that he seemed so sad? I mean, here he was, being *loved* by that crowd, and it all seemed to make him . . . well, melancholy."

"There's been a lot of tragedy in his life. They had six daughters and all died in their early years. And a son, Henry Clay II, who was expected to follow in his father's footsteps, was killed in the Mexican War. At Buena Vista. By any chance, Albert, did you know him?"

"No."

"And another son, as I understand it, is insane. In an asylum here, I believe."

"Yet, he does have the adulation of the public, doesn't he? And apparently the love of a woman?"

"He has that, yes."

Albert reached over and took Lillian's hand. "I've been thinking a lot about that kind of thing recently. That whatever may be my problems or my shortcomings, they would be somehow lessened if I had the love of a good woman."

Lillian was silent.

"Do I, Lil?"

"What?"

"Have the love of a good woman?"

"Are you referring to me?" she teased.

"Damn it! You know I am."

"Yes," she said slowly, "I love you, Albert."

"Then perhaps we ought to get married."

"There are times, darling, when I think you're the least romantic man I've ever met."

Albert reined in the horse, stopping the carriage, taking Lillian into his arms and kissing her. "Is that better?" he asked.

"Somewhat."

"Then, you will marry me?"

"What a left-handed way to ask me." But she grinned. "Yes, darling, I will—if you'll answer just one question."

"Certainly."

"What the hell took you so long?"

V

NASHVILLE in the early fifties was prospering, as the whole of the South was prospering. Every day seemed to bring a new revelation of its muscular growth. It had a railroad now, although modest in its beginning, called the Nashville and Chattanooga. A locomotive, dubbed The Tennessee, had been unloaded from a steamboat from Cincinnati to great public fanfare. And the streets of the capital city were being lighted by the soft glow of gas lamps, the gas generated from coal at a newly built plant.

The Dewey family, too, prospered along with the community. Racing income had never been greater, with what amounted to domination of the racing cards at Clover Bottom and Cumberland Downs and Franklin and Gallatin. The successes gave the lie to the skeptics who had predicted the "boy trainer," Drew Jackson, would bring disaster to Bon Marché.

The lucrative yearling sale was reinstituted at the plantation and George Dewey Jr., the master of Bon Marché, was looking to the promises of the future. He talked to the railroad builders about the possibility of eventually running a rail spur into Bon Marché so that he might ship horses northward for sale, perhaps as far away as New York.

From Bon Marché Lexington, where Albert Dewey had a

new bride, came regular reports of increased racing fortunes, enabling the Kentucky farm to show its first profits.

And from California there was no end of startling news about the golden future of the Dewey Trading Company. While communications from California were months in arriving, the letters always seemed to be filled with new ventures, new capital invested, new fortunes made or about to be made.

Charles II had written to his brother George Junior:

There's horse racing here now, perhaps not of the quality of that in Nashville, but not bad, either. I've put some money into San Francisco's first formal track, which we call the Pioneer Course. It is the intent to emulate Eastern racing and we operate under the rules of the Union Jockey Club of New York. Further, I'm a partner in a racetrack venture in Sacramento, where the trading company has other holdings.

What would you say, George, to the possibility of sending me some young fillies of good blood? They might be sent by sailing ship (I can't imagine them coming overland), and while it may be risky, I think it worth the gamble. Bon Marché would be fully recompensed, of course, for the bloodstock and the shipping costs. Don't concern yourself with the amount of money expended. Just give me something good. A dozen fillies, with strong brood-mare potential, would not be too many.

While I don't yet have a farm on which to put them, Beth and little Charles are searching for a property we might acquire so that we can get away, eventually, from the constant boisterousness of San Francisco.

The same post brought a letter to Alma May from Willie Carstairs, a long, chatty communication in which he told of the Dewey-Carstairs partnership acquiring a newspaper in San Francisco and starting another from scratch in Sacramento.

Nearly every waking hour [he wrote] is consumed by business of one kind or another. Our bakery, now that the ovens have arrived by clipper ship, supplies more than half of the bread for this city. And the First Bank of San Francisco, open less than a month, is doing brisk business. Two wasn't wrong about this place.

There was a poignant paragraph telling the Princess how much he missed her, and then he added:

I've met a woman who does, I'll admit, fascinate me. She is Consuela Sepulveda, daughter of a fine old California Spanish family. Her father, Don Andreas, is deeply involved in horse breeding (among other things) and the reality of California society is that the old Spanish families are of great influence. While she is not like you in appearance—she is dark and her figure is petite— she nevertheless reminds me of you. She's educated, strongwilled, and, yes, sensuous.

I realize that suggests some intimacies between us. Nothing could be further from the truth. The Spanish social code is most rigid and my contacts with her to date, involving only the exchange of a few harmless sentences, have been confined to meeting in large groups at one community gathering or another. Whether or not a relationship can grow from that I do not know. There is the very real complication of the Catholic church in all of this; I'd imagine her Catholicism might be a barrier to anything but a polite exchange of pleasantries.

Then, too, whether or not a relationship can grow will depend a great deal, I suppose, on the perceived integrity of the Dewey company. The Spaniards make much of honor, of integrity—in business as well as personal matters. And, my darling Princess, I'll answer the question I know is in your mind: given half an opportunity I intend to be a suitor.

Alma May swore under her breath.

25

STATLER Dewey felt the fool. A decidedly angry fool at that moment. In a sense he had helped to manufacture the dilemma in which he now found himself, being buffeted in an unruly crowd in front of the Adelphi Theater, his clothes wet through by a steadily falling rain, his boots caked with the mud of the streets. And worse: a matron had just jostled him in a most unladylike manner, knocking his hat from his head. It was there on the ground somewhere, no doubt trampled in the black muck underfoot.

And all because of a damned soprano!

Dewey realized that his resentment should not be directed at the soprano, but rather at her manager. For the singer was the renowned Jenny Lind and, as he had been telling the readers of the *Nashville Monitor* for weeks, Miss Lind was the greatest cultural phenomenon of a decade.

He had reprinted many of the reviews of the performer's triumphant seven-month tour of the United States, beginning with what the *New York Tribune*'s music critic had written of her American debut the preceding September: "Jenny Lind's first concert is over, and all doubts are at an end. She is the greatest singer we have ever heard and her success is all that was anticipated from her genius and her fame."

Indeed, it was immediately after reading the *Tribune*'s lavish paean that Statler (goaded by his wife, Harriet) had written to the singer's manager, one Phineas Taylor Barnum, suggesting Nashville as a stop on Miss Lind's tour. His action had a three-fold purpose: he hoped to bring such a universally acclaimed artist to his city, he wanted to impress Harriet with his growing influence, and he sought to have the concert booked into the Dewey Theater, owned by the Bon Marché estate and little used in recent years.

After a spirited exchange of correspondence with Barnum, Dewey could announce in the *Monitor* that "the Swedish Nightingale" would give a performance in Nashville on Monday, March 31!

Not in the Dewey Theater, however. Barnum had written: "I am certain you will understand that the greatest songstress in the world deserves the very best accommodations for her superb talents. Being informed it boasts the second-largest stage in the whole of the United States, I have selected the Adelphi Theater for M'lle Lind's Nashville appearance."

Disappointed, Statler nevertheless appreciated Barnum's position. And the fact that the family theater had not been chosen did not diminish the publisher's enthusiasm for the event.

On that rainy Sunday morning, though, when Miss Lind arrived at the Nashville Wharf on a packet boat from Cincinnati, Statler began to have doubts about his enthusiasm. For one thing, the soprano was whisked away in a closed carriage, surrounded by a large entourage of sycophants, to the private home of railroad builder Vernon Stevenson, because the public accommodations of Nashville were thought not adequate to her station. Dewey got only a fleeting glimpse of her, but enough to realize the demure, doe-eyed woman pictured in the lithographs he had reproduced in his newspaper had been an exaggeration of the *real* Jenny Lind. She was a good deal more . . . well, *sturdy* than the lithographs suggested and not as fair of face. At first he thought she was rather plain; then, trying to be fair, he settled upon the word "comely" to describe her facial features.

Then, too, he was somewhat appalled by the large number of drummers who disembarked with Miss Lind. Perhaps a dozen of them, loudly directing the unloading of many crates in which, he was to learn, were all manner of commercial products carrying the soprano's name and likeness: Jenny Lind pin boxes, Jenny Lind needle cases, Jenny Lind colored lithographs, Jenny Lind dinner bells, Jenny Lind candelabra, Jenny Lind paper doll sets, Jenny Lind gloves, Jenny Lind scarves, Jenny Lind riding hats, Jenny Lind perfume, Jenny

Lind ladies' fans, and even Jenny Lind cigars, packed in multicolored boxes on which naked cherubim held up a framed portrait—greatly enhancing her beauty—of the singer.

All of that cheapening of the Jenny Lind image was disconcerting enough. But when he met with P. T. Barnum at the Nashville Inn, Statler Dewey was soured totally. Barnum greeted him enthusiastically. At first.

"Ah, Dewey," the showman said, coming forward while grinning broadly, offering his hand, "we meet at last. I want you to know how grateful I am for your help here."

"I only wanted this event for the good of my city."

"Of course, of course. As it should be. Jenny has . . . well, sir, she has been a blessing to America. Not only is she a great singer, Dewey, but she gives us all her intrinsic worth of heart and delicacy of mind."

The newspaperman nodded. He wasn't quite sure just what that meant.

Barnum reached into his coat pocket. "To properly express my gratitude," he said, "I want you to have this." He handed *one* concert ticket to Dewey.

The ticket was taken hesitantly. "I would hope that I will be able to *purchase* others, Mr. Barnum, in that there are a number of my family anxious to hear Miss Lind, including—"

"I can appreciate that."

"Including my wife," Statler added meaningfully.

"You'll be able to get tickets at the auction."

"Auction?"

"Yes, starting at noon today—after worship services in the city—there's to be an auction of all available tickets, and some limited standing room, in front of the Adelphi Theater. My agents are making that known now to pastors in the city so that they might inform their congregations."

"An auction in this weather?"

"You'll find, Dewey," Barnum chuckled, "that inclemency of weather won't deter anyone from enjoying this once-in-a-lifetime experience. For that's what it is, you know. One opportunity to hear the most glorious voice in the world."

"Hmmm." Statler was remembering stories he had read about the auctioning of Jenny Lind tickets in other cities. A hatter in New York paying $225 for a ticket. A Providence banker paying $650. A Bostonian bidding $625.

"Nashville isn't New York, you know," he tried to explain, "or any of those big Eastern cities. I'm afraid you'll find Nashvillians a bit more conservative with their money, Mr. Barnum."

"On the contrary, Dewey," the entrepreneur grinned. "Size or location of a community has nothing to do with the appreciation of beauty and genius. I've become expert at gauging what people will be willing to pay to indulge that appreciation." He puffed out his chest. "I am willing to wager, sir, that the auction for tomorrow evening's tickets will bring in . . . oh, eight thousand dollars."

Statler's mouth gaped open. "But that averages out at about fifteen dollars a ticket!"

"A bit more, actually."

"Believing that, then, perhaps you will sell me what tickets I need for fifteen dollars each."

Barnum shrugged, his face sober. "I really can't, Dewey. That wouldn't be fair, would it? The auction, I've learned, is the only democratic way to make sure that those who want to hear Jenny have that opportunity, regardless of their station in the community. If I made an exception for you because you are the editor of the local newspaper, then where would I stop? Could I turn down a member of the clergy? Or, for that matter, could I turn down a prominent political leader—the governor, let's say?"

"No, I suppose not." The reply was disheartened.

Barnum clapped him on the shoulder. "But I'm sure you'll have no difficulty at the auction, sir."

Statler sighed. "In our last exchange of letters, we discussed an interview with Miss Lind. I'd like to arrange to do it this afternoon so that—"

"Oh, good Lord," Barnum interrupted, "did I promise that?"

"Promise? No, not in that sense, but—"

"As this tour continues, Dewey," the showman cut in again, "Jenny becomes more and more tired and I must see to it that she gets her proper rest so that she has the strength to perform. She gives her all in her concerts, you know."

Statler nodded.

"I honestly believe, though," Barnum went on, "that she

has by now answered every conceivable question, and if you'd like to see my collection of clippings perhaps you can—"

The publisher had hurried from the Nashville Inn then, angry and frustrated. By noon he was standing in the crowd, in the rain, in front of the Adelphi, waiting for the ticket auction to begin. He needed ten tickets (nine more than he had) because he had made a great show of insisting that the adult members of the family be his guests at the Lind concert. If he felt the fool now—wet and miserable as he was—what would it be like if he returned home with a single ticket in his hand? If the tickets were going to sell for $15, perhaps the expenditure of $135 was little enough for him to save face with Harriet and the others.

Barnum's agent—a young man, dandy in dress—appeared in the doorway of the Adelphi Theater, bellowing so he could be heard. "I know you want to get out of the rain, so let's start without preliminary. You are to bid on tickets for a once-in-a-lifetime experience—a performance by the glorious Jenny Lind!"

That damned Barnum's words, Statler thought.

"We'll start with the box seats."

"Fifty dollars!" someone yelled out.

Startled, Statler turned to identify the bold bidder, recognizing an aide to the governor. He groaned.

"That's the way to begin," the young man grinned. "Do I hear more?" There was silence. "Very well, we'll move to a second box seat."

"Fifty dollars!" the governor's aide shouted again.

There was a sick feeling in Statler's gut. "Seventy-five!" he responded, not believing it was his voice he was hearing.

"One hundred!" the governor's man insisted.

The agent looked to Statler, who motioned negatively.

"And a third box seat?" the young man said.

There was a momentary pause. Apparently the governor had the two tickets he wanted.

"One hundred!" Statler said, determined to get his tickets and end the matter. He went unchallenged. But the pattern had been set and the auctioneer knew it. He singled out the newspaperman for special attention as box seat after box seat was offered. Statler, when he had his last ticket (and had paid out $900), pushed his way out of the crowd. As he walked to his office across the street, he heard another ticket being sold for $35.

You are a fool! And he hoped it never got back to the family how much he had really paid for them to hear Jenny Lind.

II

THERE was a light tap on Alma May's sitting room door. "Come!" she called out.

"'Scuse me, Miss Alma," the butler, Joseph, said as he entered. "There's a gentleman waitin' to see ya."

"Oh? Who is it."

"He sez his name is William Smith."

"William Smith? I don't believe I know the gentleman."

"He claims it's most important, ma'am."

Alma May sighed. She was trying to finish a letter to Willie Carstairs and the interruption was an annoyance. "Oh, very well, bring him up."

In just a few moments, Joseph reappeared at the sitting room doorway with the visitor. He was broad-shouldered, his modishly long hair graying, his well-cut yet jowly face set off with thick glasses and a bushy mustache. He was dressed in a rakish manner, his striped suit not of the fashion preferred by the gentlemen of Nashville.

"Mr. Smith, ma'am," the butler announced.

The man stepped into the room, grinning. "Hello, Princess," he said softly.

She stared at him. Then, sudden recognition: "Oh, my God! Nathan? Nathan Ludlum?"

"The same." He came to her quickly, taking her into his arms, trying to kiss her.

Alma May broke away from him, gesturing to dismiss the Negro servant, and closing the door when Joseph had left. "Where in the hell did you come from?" she demanded, angry because she knew the blacks would be gossiping about her visitor in just a few minutes.

"I'm in Nashville with the Jenny Lind entourage," he explained. "With Barnum."

"There are actors appearing with her?"

"No, no," he laughed, "I'm a drummer. Or a commission

salesman, to use Barnum's phrase. I sell Jenny Lind gee-gaws." He reached into the inside pocket of his jacket, bringing out a small fan. "A genuine Jenny Lind ladies' fan," he said, extending it to her, "just for my wife."

"Former wife," she snapped. "A long, long time ago."

"Twenty-nine years, to be exact, Princess."

Ignoring the proferred fan, she sat down, pointing to another chair. He sprawled in it, lightly tossing the fan into her lap.

"You might as well have that," he said. "Actually, it's quite a rare thing. It's one of the very few signed personally by the great Lind. You'd be astonished at what some would pay for it."

"I suppose I would." She laid the fan aside on a small table next to her chair without examining it. "Now, let's get to it: what do you want, Nathan?"

"What I've always wanted—*you*."

Alma May laughed sarcastically. "Please spare me the insincerity. We never had more together than some youthful passion. And that wore out rather quickly."

"I loved you, Princess, and—"

"Enough! I no longer have the patience for your lies."

There was a brief silence in the sitting room.

"I went by the Dewey Theater an hour or so ago," he said. "It's not used much anymore."

"Yes, I know. I asked around about it. And what I learned got me to thinking that the Lind tour is coming to an end, and that I might be well served to stay here in Nashville to reopen the Dewey. It's a good house, Princess. And a new repertory company could—"

"There's no way that's possible!" She couldn't imagine having him around again.

"Oh?" He grinned once more. "I also learned, by asking judicious questions, that you haven't remarried, and that you're now the owner of Bon Marché."

"Part owner," she corrected him.

"And it occurred to me, now that you're the vaunted mistress of Bon Marché, that it might not be consistent with your new station to have it publicly known that our marriage, brief as it was, came about only because of your fraud—because of your faked pregnancy."

"Nathan," she sighed, "you're pathetic as a blackmailer. Who would believe you?" She gestured at him in a derisive manner. "Look at you—you're a cheap, seedy drummer of no consequence. Not only are you a pathetic blackmailer, but you were also a pathetic actor, a pathetic man."

His face flushed. "You'll be sorry you said that, Princess."

"I doubt it. I believe you know your way out."

Alma May made a show of turning to her letter writing again, dismissing him with her disinterest.

Nathan stormed out, slamming the door behind him.

She dipped a pen into the inkwell. "Willie, you'll never guess who was just here . . ."

Alma May had nearly finished the letter when Lady Bea, a daughter of her niece Hope Jackson came into the room. Lady Bea, a beautiful child of thirteen, was one of her favorites.

"Good afternoon, Auntie Princess," Lady Bea said, bending down to kiss Alma May's cheek. Her gaze fell on the fan on the table and she picked it up. "What's this, Auntie?"

"A genuine Jenny Lind fan," Alma May chuckled. "Signed by the great woman herself."

The youngster fanned it open, studying one side of it and then the other. "I can't see where it's signed."

The Princess took the fan from her, also looking for a signature. There wasn't one.

"Well, I suppose that's just someone's idea of a joke, darling. A feeble joke."

My God, he's even more pathetic than I thought.

III

FOR a time on the last evening of March of '51 Statler Dewey thought perhaps he hadn't overpaid to hear the voice of Jenny Lind, the Swedish Nightingale. And for a time, also, he even forgave P. T. Barnum his flimflammery in the promotion of her national tour.

The Bon Marché contingent of ten sat enthralled in two boxes overlooking stage right, stunned into silence by the sheer beauty of the tones of her soprano voice, understanding—even though most of the repertoire was foreign to them—that they were in the presence of greatness.

As the concert began, and maestro Julius Benedict's baton brought the orchestra to life, Jenny captivated them, holding them fast, from the first notes of "Casta Diva" from Bellini's opera *Norma.* There was a purity in the sound of her, an ease that produced gorgeous tones without forcing. It all seemed so effortless.

And suddenly Statler saw her as physically beautiful as well, the white-gowned singer as she was depicted in the lithographs, and not as the somewhat dumpy and plain-faced woman she really was. There was a magic to that transformation, the newspaperman thought, and he wondered how he was going to put it into words for the printed page.

Then came Meyerbeer's trio from *Camp in Silesia,* in which Jenny was accompanied by two flutes, and Harriet Dewey began to weep, reaching over to squeeze her husband's hand emotionally. Statler looked around at the others in his party to find Harriet was not the only one so moved. Even the somber True Jackson dabbed at his eyes with a handkerchief, trying to pretend he wasn't doing it at all.

It was while Miss Lind was engaging them with a medley of Scandinavian songs that the spell was broken. A young black from Bon Marché rushed into one of the boxes, breathless and sweating profusely from what had obviously been a hard ride. He bent over Alma May: "Come quick, Miss Alma! The big house—it's burnin'!"

Hope Jackson stifled a scream. "The children! What of the children?"

"Don' know, ma'am," the boy replied. "Ah jest come quick as Ah could."

As the Bon Marché group hurried out, annoying some of the concertgoers near them, an errant thought came to Statler's mind. *Nine hundred dollars! Wasted!* He silently cursed himself for having had it.

IV

DREW Jackson, only seventeen, fought against the panic growing in him, making him ill. The young horse trainer was directing the slaves in a long, snaking bucket line, extending to the Richland Creek, but he knew they were losing the battle against the flames which were inexorably consuming the

Bon Marché mansion. Even the moderate breeze of the evening—and it was no more than that—was fanning the fire, spreading it to the entire rambling structure.

When he saw the red tongues locking through the roof over the "Schimmel wing" of the mansion he knew all would be lost.

An eerie scream caught his attention and he had difficulty determining where it was coming from, the gray-black smoke billowing up from the building obscuring his vision. It took him perhaps half a minute, as the screaming continued, to discern his mother's personal maid, Caroline, hanging halfway out of a third-floor window.

"They's babies up here!" Caroline was shrieking. "They's babies up here!"

"Some of you fellows over here!" Drew bellowed, and the steady rhythm of the bucket line broke down as six or seven of the black males abandoned their stations, rushing to his side.

"Hurry!" Caroline screamed again. "They's babies up here!"

"How many?" Drew yelled up to her.

"Three! Deah God—!"

"Drop them down!" young Jackson ordered. "Just hang them out the window and drop them down. The boys'll catch them."

Caroline disappeared from the window for an instant and flames could be seen reflecting in the window glass. And then the maid reappeared, Dolley Jackson, the youngest daughter of Drew's Aunt Hope, in her arms.

"Make a tight circle, boys," Drew said to the slaves on the ground, "so you can catch her. And, damn you, make sure you do!" To Caroline: "Swing her out away from the building and just drop her!"

Little Dolley shrieked as Caroline, holding her by the forearms, swung her out with one mighty heave and let go of her. Strong black arms caught the terrified child.

When Drew looked up again, Caroline had positioned thirteen-year-old Lady Bea, another of Hope's daughters, on the sill. The youngster was crouched there, looking down, frozen in place.

"Push her!"

Caroline obeyed and Lady Bea came plummeting down, her fall stopped suddenly by the catchers, although two of them were knocked to the ground by the impact of the heavier child. She was sobbing uncontrollably, holding up her right arm, a strange bend in it. It was broken.

Almost before the blacks could be ready again, Caroline had young Foster Jackson also hanging out of the window, ready to drop him.

"Let him go!"

Foster, too—a slightly built lad of ten—came hurtling down, to be caught safely.

"Sweet Jee-sus—!" Caroline screamed as there was a sudden burst of flame through the open window, setting the maid's dress on fire.

As she was beating at the flames with her hands, Drew shouted: "Jump! Jump!"

Caroline seemed not to hear him and then, in an awful moment, she disappeared from the window, the night air rent with her agonizing shrieks. Suddenly, it was quiet; even the noise of the roar of the flames seemed to diminish for a moment.

Drew Jackson turned away from the stricken faces of the slaves and vomited.

But he knew that was only a respite, only brief seconds taken away from his responsibilities. Wiping his mouth on his sleeve, he ordered his younger brother: "Herbert, round up all the children and make sure we have them all out." And he gave similar orders to the butler, Joseph, to account for all of the household blacks.

By the time the carriages arrived from Nashville, from what was supposed to have been a gay evening of entertainment by Jenny Lind, all was lost. The futile bucket line had been discontinued and it had been confirmed that only the brave Caroline had been a flesh-and-blood casualty.

There was nothing for any of them to do, and the Dewey family members and their slaves stood stunned and watched the Bon Marché mansion being consumed by the fire. When the roof fell in with a mighty crash, Alma May Dewey, the Princess, sank to the ground, weeping as she had never wept before.

And she wondered again whether the soul of her father was

a ghostly presence, whether the man whose labors had built the great house would know of its destruction.

IV

THE first day of April dawned bright, clear, and warm—an ideal spring day belying the terrible thing of ashes now spread before the owners of Bon Marché. The mansion was nothing more than a blackened pile of rubble, little wisps of smoke still curling up from some of it.

Alma May and her nieces Joy and Hope Jackson—after having spent the night at Beau Monde—disconsolately examined what remained of their home, watching several of the blacks picking through the ruins. No one wanted to mention that they were looking for the body of Caroline.

"How's Lady Bea this morning?" Alma May asked of Hope.

"She didn't get much sleep last night," the mother replied, "after the doctor set the arm. But this morning she seems rather . . . well, *proud* of the cast. It's kind of a badge of courage, you might say." Hope frowned. "But it's Dolley I'm worried about. She's done nothing but cry about Caroline."

"The young are resilient," Alma May commented quietly. "It will all pass."

A moment of silence fell among them and then Joy asked: "How could this have happened? Joseph tells me there were no fires laid in the fireplaces last night. There was no need for them, it being such a mild night."

"We'll probably never know," the Princess replied. But she had a theory she was reluctant to enunciate. She was certain in her mind that the fire had been deliberately set and that the arsonist was Nathan Ludlum. Lacking even a shred of evidence, however, she decided to keep the suspicion to herself.

"What we really need to consider now," she said, "is how long we're going to accept the hospitality of Harriet. Certainly, all of us can't intrude ourselves on Beau Monde for too long a time."

"What do you think we ought to do?" Hope asked.

"It seems we have several options. You and your husbands might want to build your own homes now for your families. And perhaps it's time for me to consider a modest little place for myself."

A small grin came to Hope's face. "But those aren't options you're considering seriously."

"No," Alma May admitted. "I'd prefer to see Bon Marché rebuilt, even grander than it was before. I think my father would have wanted that. And Mattie, too."

Joy laughed. "Hope and I knew you were going to say that, especially the part about 'even grander.'"

"Then you both agree?"

"Yes," the twins said in unison.

The Princess clapped her hands together as Charles Dewey used to do when a major decision had been made. "Very well. Then I think we ought to seek out a proper architect—someone of the talents of William Strickland, who's building the state capitol building."

"*That* grand?" Joy asked.

"Absolutely! The new Bon Marché must be the finest in all of Tennessee!"

V

PERHAPS it was a snare of self-delusion, believing what was false and disbelieving what was true, but the denizens of Bon Marché were willing to accept Henry Clay's compromises of 1850 as "a final settlement" of the differences between North and South, as President Millard Fillmore hoped all Americans would. Even when the author of the compromises, denied happy retirement with his "old lady" at the Ashland plantation, died in Washington in June of '52, the myth of the permanency of his work persisted. And as the fifties raced along, Bon Marché embraced, too, the reassurances of Fillmore's successors, two other gentlemen who contended dark clouds did not a maelstrom make.

In coming to the high office in '53, Franklin Pierce saw the days ahead as a time when "no sectional or ambitious or fanatical excitement may again threaten the durability of our institutions or obscure the light of our prosperity." Even four years later—after a pro-Southern mob had sacked Lawrence, Kansas, and after a brooding John Brown had surfaced as an abolitionist avenger to murder Southern sympathizers at a place called Pottawatamie Creek, and after "bleeding Kansas" might have been considered to be a glance into the looking glass of the future—bachelor President James Buchanan told the nation: "Time is a great corrective. Political subjects which but a few years ago excited and exasperated the public mind have passed away and are now nearly forgotten."

And why not believe them? The decade of the 1850s was one of unprecedented affluence and influence for Bon Marché in all its reaches. The future stretched out before them as a bright, shining opportunity, in which success would beget more success and wealth would be piled on wealth.

Yet, not all of the Bon Marché community so believed. "General" Able Jackson persisted with the regular drills of his Nashville Grays militia, convinced they would be needed. And his brother, True, continued his travels throughout the South, consorting with the anti-Union firebrands many considered to be traitors. But the Jackson brothers were more and more looked upon as "old fools," if not worse.

From Chicago, too, August Schimmel continued to warn in his Northern newspapers of the South's warlike tendencies, tied, as they were in his view, to the need to preserve slavery. His was an unending editorial harangue that put him at total odds with the publisher of the Southern division of the family's newspapers, Statler Dewey.

But with all of the machinations of True and Able Jackson, and with Schimmel's growing alignment with Northern abolitionist views, the Dewey family did not see those things as being of any real significance. After all, the Jacksons and Schimmel were *not* Deweys; while they had married into the family and might be regarded as part of it, they were not *true* Deweys.

The Deweys, for their part, were arrogantly indifferent to anything but themselves. In California, Charles II and Beth became the parents of a second child, a daughter named Glory, born in Bon Marché West, Two's new thoroughbred nursery on 550 acres some twenty miles south of San Francisco at Point San Pedro, overlooking the Pacific Ocean. And when word came from Kentucky that Colonel Albert Dewey and his wife, Lillian, had had a son, Lance, it was merely further proof of the Dewey permanence. Indeed, even the loss of one of them—Corrine Dewey Holder, eldest daughter of Charles Dewey the founder, died of "the fever" in the winter of '52—did not occasion a long period of grief. In the

end the proper thing was done: Corrine was buried in the
tulip poplar grove at Bon Marché, reunited with the family in
death.

Mourning could not long be part of the Dewey baggage.
Nor could the political "truths" of the times. Too many marvelous things were happening.

Perhaps Statler Dewey mirrored the attitude of them all
when he welcomed 1858 with a glowing *Nashville Monitor* editorial:

> No city in the South is more justly celebrated for its in-
> telligence, morality, and courtesy to strangers than is
> Nashville. Its Sabbaths are quiet and orderly, and its
> pulpits and churches well filled. Its schools are burgeon-
> ing; its citizens are intellectual and well read.
>
> We are a city of nearly 25,000 now, and while our
> growth in wealth and population has never been very
> rapid at any time, it has nonetheless held an even, on-
> ward progress in such physical and moral wealth as forms
> the basis for permanent prosperity.
>
> Manufacturers and capitalists from abroad are looking
> to Nashville as admirably suited for a manufacturing city.
> Nashville is growing rapidly in every interest essential to
> its becoming soon one of the great cities of the Union;
> the Union, in turn, grows with a vitality unparalleled in
> modern history.

He might have mentioned, although he did not, the final
touches being put into place on the new Bon Marché. For
Alma May, ever conscious of her role as "the Princess," had
now set May first as the opening date of the new and glorious
mansion on the plantation, one that would certainly eclipse
the Beau Monde of her nephew and his wife, Statler and Harriet.

It had been seven years in the building since that tragic
March night of '51 when the old mansion was reduced to
ashes. Seven years were three more than she had originally
planned, but many changes were made in the initial concepts
of William Strickland—each one more grand and more costly.
Strickland had often been angered by Alma May's demands,
and because of the hours and days she took away from what

was his more compelling work on the state capitol building. His death in 1854 removed his genius from the project.

The Princess didn't care. It was to be her monument, not an architect's. She had worked her will, too, on the twin nieces who were the other owners of Bon Marché, adroitly turning aside the protestations of Joy and Hope Jackson as the costs of the mansion soared. In time the startling rumor circulated through Nashville that a million dollars were being expended on the work. The rumor was false, by double the amount and more, but Alma May let it stand uncorrected.

It served her position in society to be thought the matriarch of a million-dollar "palace." She told herself it was just compensation for the sacrifices she had made for Bon Marché, a conclusion given more weight when word arrived from California of the marriage of Willie Carstairs to his Spanish "princess," Señorita Consuela Maria Teresa Sepulveda.

On that particular evening, in the privacy of her temporary quarters at Beau Monde, Alma May Dewey decided to permit herself some rare moments of morose self-pity, aided by Bon Marché bourbon. She intended it to be only a temporary thing: a few tender recollections of the love she had known with Willie.

The second bourbon was already in the glass when there was a light tapping on her door. "Yes?" she called out tentatively.

"It's Statler," a male voice answered. "May I see you for a moment?"

"Of course."

He entered. "I'm sorry to disturb you at this late hour—"

A flick of her hand dismissed the necessity of an apology.

"I've just come from the newspaper office," her nephew said. "And there is some news that may . . . uh . . . be disturbing to you." He hesitated.

"Go on," the Princess said, annoyed by his failure to get to the point.

"Late this afternoon the sheriff was called to Willoughby's tavern—that disreputable place north of the city on the road to Gallatin." Statler hesitated again.

"And—?"

"There was a brawl and a man was killed. It was Nathan Ludlum."

Alma May took a sip of the bourbon. "Well, I can't say I'm surprised. Considering the type of man my former husband was"—she grimaced—"it's strange someone didn't kill him earlier."

"It doesn't make you sad?"

"Sad?" The Princess smiled. "Not at all. I'm glad the bastard is dead. It's even fortuitous in a way, considering that tomorrow we're going to celebrate the beginning of a *new* Bon Marché, after Nathan burned the first house."

"There's never been any proof," Statler suggested.

"But there's never been any doubt in my mind." Her voice was hard. "He destroyed the first Bon Marché. I know that with a certainty, proof be damned! And now it's finished, isn't it?"

"Yes, I suppose it is." He excused himself and left the suite.

The Princess poured another stiff bourbon and thought of the men in her life: the evil Nathan and the loving Willie. And those others; she thought of the word "transients." Now she would dismiss them all and think only of the bright future she had engineered for something she loved above all else.

Bon Marché!

26

It seemed an omen. Saturday, May 1, 1858, dawned as a sparkling jewel in a setting of the myriad colors of spring; a precious thing it was.

Alma May stretched contentedly in her bed at Beau Monde, trying to recall whether she had ever been more delighted at being alive. She thought not, especially when she contemplated she had spent her last night at Beau Monde, her last hours as a "guest" of Statler and Harriet Dewey. She grinned, imagining Harriet might be having similar thoughts at that moment, as pleased with the imminent departure of Aunt Alma May as the aunt was in leaving.

The Princess didn't feel her fifty-eight years; she was suddenly twenty again, certain of her beauty and sensuousness, vowing that when she retired that evening in her own lovely suite at the new Bon Marché she would not be alone. She had no idea with whom she would be spending her first night there, but it would be with someone exciting and vital, someone who could confirm her youthfulness, someone to share her joy—and enhance it. Alma May laughed out loud at the prospect.

Ringing the small porcelain bell on the night table to summon a servant with her breakfast, she got out of the bed slowly, padding barefoot to the window to look out on the deer park below. A man strode along there, rapping his riding crop against highly polished boots in the rhythm of his walking. Alma May knew immediately who it was and it added to her exhilaration. Charles Dewey the founder was once more surveying his domain. It didn't frighten her that it was a ghost she saw, because she was always conscious of her father's presence on this place.

She wondered whether he knew of the special race meeting to be held that afternoon at the Clover Bottom track, the principal event being the newly created Charles Dewey Memorial Invitational Stake for four-year-olds-and-up at two-mile heats. *But of course he did!* She reached out her hands to the window, thinking to raise it and call to him. She didn't, though, not wanting to startle him. So, she just watched him walking along, the crop beating its tattoo, as he turned and made his way along the wooded path leading to the Bon Marché mansion.

"You're going to love what I've done, Daddy," she said softly.

There was a light tap on the bedroom door. "Come," the Princess called as she turned away from the window.

"Beautiful day, Miss Alma," said the Negro girl who entered with a breakfast tray.

"Yes, indeed, as beautiful as a day can be."

II

"I TELL you," August Schimmel said heatedly, "that damn Dred Scott decision was, and is, an abomination. It just proves how far removed the majority of the Supreme Court is from the will of the people."

"What arrogance," True Jackson snarled at him. "You always were a pompous ass, August, seeing yourself as a spokesman for the *people*. How dare you?"

The younger Statler Dewey was uneasy in the role of the peacekeeper in this bitter family argument. He had been fearing it for days, ever since he had heard that August and Louise Schimmel would be on hand for the opening of the new Bon Marché. He stood now in a knot of family members at the Clover Bottom racetrack, a sober gathering of Schimmel and his angry sons-in-law, True and Able Jackson, along with Carrie Dewey Bonsal and her editor husband, Wilson Bonsal, who had come in from St. Louis.

"I believe," Statler said, reflecting what had been his conservative editorial position, "we must find some middle ground in the Dred Scott matter. While it may be the Su-

preme Court was too broad in its contention that Negroes
can't ever be U.S. citizens, it's very clear that slavery had
constitutional sanction and that the Scott boy couldn't be declared a free man just because he had been taken by his master to a free state for a time. Illinois, in this case."

Schimmel groaned. "Once a slave, always a slave, eh?"

"In one sense, yes," the younger man answered. "Unless
his master takes the steps necessary—signing the legal man-
umission papers, in other words—for him to be considered a
free man."

"But don't you see, *damn it,* that under this ruling by Chief
Justice Taney and his cronies a Negro, even though legally
declared free, is *not* free because a man of color has no legal
standing in our federal courts? Even a free black in the North
is not free, if we are to accept Taney's tortured logic."

Carrie Bonsal spoke up. "I agree with Uncle August. The
court majority showed a total lack of responsibility in declaring the Missouri Compromise unconstitutional—"

"That's a strange attitude," True cut in, "for someone who
runs a newspaper in St. Louis."

"Not so," Carrie countered. "Our neck of the woods is a
tinderbox. Fragile as it was, the compromise had some dampening effect. I don't want to see anything done to further en-
flame the situation, and this ruling has certainly done that.
The minority opinion of Justices Curtis and McLean was a
good deal more reasoned."

True shrugged. "Nevertheless, it was a *minority* opinion,
and unless someone repeals one of our basic precepts the majority is what counts. God help us if that changes."

Schimmel laughed bitterly. "For once I find myself in
agreement with you. And that offers one solution to this Dred
Scott travesty—change the majority."

"To the Republicans?" True spat the word.

"Exactly! A Republican President in sixty will assure a victory for the will of the majority . . . and maybe a shift in the
Supreme Court . . . and the majority—no matter how much
you rail about this issue—wants to see an *end* to slavery!"

"I can assure you, August, that the South will *never* accept
a Republican President. Never!"

"Then you're a liar, as well."

"What!" Jackson's face reddened in anger.

"You profess to defend majority rule, but only so long as the majority feels as you do. That's hypocrisy at its worst!"

"See here, August, I don't have to put up with your insults, and unless you apologize I'll—"

Fifteen yards away Louise Schimmel stood with her half sister, Alma May, watching the animated conversation with growing alarm. "I was afraid of that," she said, nodding toward the angry group. "August promised me he wouldn't get into a political argument, but—" She sighed deeply.

The Princess grinned. "Let me take care of it." Smiling sweetly, she strode toward the debaters, the riding crop she carried lightly and rhythmically beating against her skirted knees in the manner of the ghostly vision she had experienced early in the day. "Gentlemen—" she said quietly, as she came up to them. "May I suggest that your . . . uh . . . discussion is not in keeping with the reasons we've all gathered here for these few days?"

"August is being his usual *impossible* self," Able Jackson said churlishly.

Alma May's grin persisted. "And you two"—her crop brushed lightly across the coat fronts of the Jackson brothers—"haven't contributed to the discontent, I suppose?"

"These are vital issues, madam," Able answered defensively.

"Damn you!" The Princess's face turned hard. "And *especially* you, General Able. Your daughter is getting married this weekend. And *your* granddaughter—" She glared at August. "And *your* niece." Her vitriol was aimed now at True. "And the lot of you stand around here howling at each other like tomcats on nightly prowl!"

The men were chagrined.

"And this is also the weekend," Alma May went on heatedly, "when we pay homage to the great man whose dream we plan to rededicate with the new Bon Marché. And I won't have it despoiled by your stupid tempers. Am I understood?"

The group began to disperse.

"May I have a private word with you, Cousin True?" the Princess asked. She led him away from the others. "Now, sir, I'll have that Deringer you have tucked into your waistband."

"See here, Princess—!"

"Right now, True! I'm not going to be witness to any . . . uh . . . unfortunate accidents this weekend."

Reluctantly, Jackson handed over the tiny weapon, which Alma May quickly dropped into the pocket of her riding coat. As True turned to walk away she placed a hand lightly on his arm.

"True, don't believe that I don't share your concern for the future of the South in these troubled times. But you and Able and August aren't going to solve our problems by brawling for the next several days. I want this to be the happiest of times."

"Yes, of course."

Alma May's eyes misted over. "I saw Daddy this morning," she reported, "walking along near the deer park, making certain all was well." She stopped, brushing a tear from her cheek.

True stood silently.

"And I do so want everything to go well, if not for all time—that would be too much to ask—then just for these few days we're all together. I'm asking you to put aside your differences with August, to make a public show—"

"Now wait a minute!"

"—to make a public show of unanimity. Act it out if you must, but *please* do it."

"You're asking a great deal."

"I suppose I am. But if you can't do it for me, or for Lady Bea on the eve of her wedding, then do it for the memory of Charles Dewey."

True Jackson waited a few seconds before answering. "All right, I will."

The Princess squeezed his arm. "Now, don't you have some duties as the steward of the Memorial Stake?"

III

THE first heat of the special race honoring the late Charles Dewey had already been run when the family of Colonel Albert Dewey arrived from Kentucky. Their coach was begrimed by the road and the horses were lathered.

Alma May rushed to greet them. "Albert, where have you been? We expected you yesterday and have been worried sick about you."

"Broken down on the road," her nephew replied apologetically. "Not once, but twice. Same wheel both times. And let me tell you, I've found I'm not much of a mechanic."

The Princess cooed and fussed over the children. "Poor darlings, you spent the night on the road?"

"*Three* nights, actually," fourteen-year-old Carolina told her.

"We never did make the connections with the taverns where we had hoped to stop," Albert explained.

"But it was *fun,* Auntie Alma," Carolina giggled.

"I'm sure you thought so," Alma May laughed. She glanced at Carolina's brothers. "But I can see you had plenty of protection. My God, Albert, how they've grown!"

"Yes, they've become young gentlemen."

"Let's see if I can remember the ages." She pointed to the eldest son. "Jeff—seventeen, right?"

"Yes, ma'am," he said soberly.

"Which means that Jack is fifteen, Carolina fourteen, and Staunch is . . . well, twelve?"

"Thirteen, Auntie Alma," the lad said proudly.

"Of course." She tousled his hair. "And the baby is—?" Alma May playfully peeked at Lance Dewey who was trying to hide behind his mother's skirts.

"Already six. Can you believe that?" the mother replied.

The Princess kissed her on both cheeks. "It's good to see you again, Lillian. Why do we let so many years go by without personal contact?"

It had been a rhetorical question and Alma May's attention was drawn to a handsome man who had just straightened up from his examination of the legs of the carriage horses.

"I don't believe you've met Dr. James Orr," Albert said in a formal manner. "Dr. Orr, may I present my famous aunt Alma May."

"Ma'am." He bowed to her.

"Well, well," the Princess said appreciatively. "I had no idea Albert's veterinarian was such an . . . imposing gentleman." Her eyes scanned him from head to toe.

"You're too kind, ma'am."

"Not at all. And let's drop the 'ma'am,' shall we? I'm Alma May. Or Princess, if you wish."

"And my friends call me Jamie."

"As I shall," she said with a smile. "Jamie? I like that. Now, you'll have to excuse me for a moment. I'm to play the role of the honorary starter of the second heat of the stake. And if I'm any judge of horseflesh, it'll be the last heat, too. There's a bay gelding from Memphis that has devastated the field. I'm certainly glad we didn't have a Bon Marché runner in today." Alma May winked at Dr. Orr, turned quickly and was gone.

Jamie watched her walking across the infield of the track. "Albert, I think you lied to me about your aunt."

"Oh?"

"You said Miss Dewey was a woman in her fifties."

"She is."

"That's not possible. She's so . . . so . . . *vital*."

Lillian laughed gaily. "The Princess, Albert, seems to have the makings of another conquest."

"You *are* exaggerating her age, aren't you?" Jamie demanded.

"No."

"Amazing . . ." Dr. Orr said to no one in particular. "Absolutely amazing."

IV

"WELCOME to the queen of Tennessee plantations," Alma May was saying again as she greeted yet another guest at the opening of the new Bon Marché. "May I present my grandniece Miss Lady Bea Jackson, and her fiancé, the Reverend Mister Alston Merit?"

The Princess was in her element, grandly welcoming her guests, the center of all attention. And those who had been invited to the premier social event of the year (perhaps in several years) were astonished by the elegance of the mansion. On arriving they had gazed, awed, at the regal Greek revival structure, a porticoed home for the Deweys dominated in front by huge, square limestone columns, cut from the Bon Marché quarry and laboriously moved to the site by the straining muscles of dray horses and black men, their sweat mingled. The house was of brick, also manufactured on the property by slave artisans, covered by gleaming white stucco etched with an attractive fleur-de-lis pattern reflecting the

French heritage of the founder. Two substantial, perfectly balanced, three-story wings extended out from the higher central portion of the building. Visitors could believe what they had heard: that the mansion boasted forty rooms.

Inside, there was even more grandeur. A wide, gracefully curving stairway was the main feature of a broad entrance hall. Underfoot there was marble laid in alternating black and white squares like a giant chessboard. The plastered walls on both sides were painted with colorful, lifelike racing scenes, many of the great horses of Bon Marché's history easily identified by the horsemen among the guests.

Off the foyer were double parlors, either one big enough for a modest ball, and each with two fireplaces with lovely mantels in the classic Adams design, and flanked by floor-to-ceiling French mirrors, the gold leaf on the frames reflecting the light from massive crystal chandeliers overhead. The parlor to the right as the guests entered was called The Dewey Room, so identified by a tastefully small engraved brass plaque fixed in the white-enameled woodwork of the door frame. Displayed in the room were new portraits (the originals had been burned in the fire) of Charles Dewey and Matilda Jackson Dewey, one over each mantel. On the left, the parlor was designated as the Bon Marché Room, offering the portraits of Alma May Dewey and her twin nieces, Joy Schimmel Jackson and Hope Schimmel Jackson—the trio of current owners of the plantation.

There were no furnishings in the central hall, or in the two parlors, save many colorfully embroidered and gilded Louis XV chairs lining the parlor walls, and a large circular table in the foyer on which were displayed liquors and liqueurs and champagne among large blocks of ice carved in the forms of swans and deer and horses. The table was also piled high with hors d'oeuvres, from tasty cubes of the much-admired Bon Marché ham to venison (from the deer park) to imported caviar. The rooms were to be fully furnished after the inaugural ball; for this night, though, there was to be ample space in the parlors and the entrance hall for dancing. The Louis XV chairs were for those who sought a respite from the dancing.

Orchestras played for dancing in both parlors, each under a different conductor but miraculously coordinated in playing the same tunes simultaneously. It was something on which the

Princess had insisted, not wanting a cacophony of two orchestras in competition, and understanding that one orchestra, no matter where it was placed, would not be heard
well enough in all three venues. The hired maestros had told
Alma May that what she wanted was impossible; for the mistress of Bon Marché nothing was to be impossible. Thus,
there were three days of rehearsals of the two orchestras,
punctuated by much argument and screaming. In the end,
though, the impossible had been achieved.

For nearly an hour and a half the Princess had stood at the
head of the receiving line exuberantly greeting nearly five
hundred guests. When the ordeal was over—and she seemed
as fresh as she had been when she started—a mere nod of the
head brought a servant, in crimson velvet livery, with a glass
of champagne. As she sipped the wine, she sensed someone
watching her intently. Turning slowly, she saw Albert's veterinarian grinning at her.

She walked to him. "You find me amusing, Dr. Orr?" she
asked lightly.

"No, not amusing, Miss Alma," he replied, still smiling.
"'Fascinating' would be a more correct word. I can tell you
without fear of contradiction that I have never seen—not in
Edinburgh, not in London, not in New York, not in Philadelphia—a more charming hostess than you."

The Princess laughed, pleased with the compliment. "Your
accent, Doctor . . . uh, Jamie . . . brings back many fond
memories. My father's dearest friend was Scottish. A teacher.
Perhaps you knew him—Andrew MacCallum?"

"No."

Alma May shrugged. "Of course you couldn't have known
him; he was of another generation. But the point is that the
Scottish accent is most agreeable to my ears. I find it . . . uh
. . . almost titillating."

Jamie guffawed.

"Especially," she went on coyly, "when it flows from such
an attractive package."

"You're a great tease, Princess."

"No, that's not true." She moved closer to him, dropping
her voice to a whisper. "I *never* tease."

The orchestras had begun a waltz. "In that case," Dr. Orr

said, taking her empty glass and placing it on the round table, "I think we should dance."

They danced that dance and several more before other gentlemen claimed the attention of the Princess. Dr. Orr went to join Albert Dewey and young Drew Jackson, the stud manager and trainer of Bon Marché.

"Drew here and I," Albert told him, "have just made a wager of a hundred dollars concerning your future."

"Is it worth that much?"

"Oh, yes. Drew says I'm about to lose a veterinarian. That before the time comes for us to leave, Alma May will have convinced you to stay here and not return to Kentucky."

"Good Lord!"

"Obviously, Jamie, my money has been placed with an eye to the well-being of Bon Marché Lexington. I'd hate to lose you to the charms of my aunt."

"You gentlemen," Orr said with some sarcasm, "have certainly read a lot into a couple of dances."

"It's not the dances, Doctor," Drew explained, "it's knowing the Princess. I can tell that she'd like to have you here permanently"—he grinned wickedly—"and not just for your professional status as a veterinarian."

"Drew, you might as well pay my employer the hundred dollars now. You're either hallucinating or you're hopelessly drunk."

"Neither, Jamie," young Jackson laughed. "I'm both sober and in command of my mental faculties. The wager stands—its outcome still to be determined."

V

It was well into a new day when the last of the guests departed, declaring to the mistress of Bon Marché that they had never been witness to a more pleasant party. Even the two maestros, having spent the long evening in their strange synchronous musicale, came to the Princess and thanked her for the unique opportunity.

As the musicians left, Alma May dismissed the servants. "Put it right in the morning," she told the butler, "after everyone has had some sleep."

Taking an unopened bottle of champagne from the circular table and two crystal glasses, she slowly made her way to her suite in the new mansion, tired but still buoyed with enthusiasm over the special evening.

She also dismissed her personal maid. "I'll get myself to bed," she said. "And don't bother to wake me with breakfast in the morning." The black woman hurried out.

Alma May dropped her gown to the floor of her sitting room, also shedding her corset and her petticoats and her lacy underclothes, leaving the garments strewn across the room. In her bedchamber she stood in front of a long mirror, admiring her naked body, running her hands slowly over her breasts and down her flat abdomen. She smiled, pleased with herself.

She went to a large wardrobe and got out a filmy nightgown, drawing it on. And then she moved to her dressing table, seating herself there, unhurriedly and ritualistically letting down her auburn hair and brushing it. Finished with that, she went to the bed, turning down the covers, patting out an imagined lump from the down pillow. Slowly she walked to the room's far wall, where a handsome drape covered most of it, and she drew back the drape, revealing not a window but a door. She knocked on it.

"Jamie," she called softly.

"What?" The sleepy reply was uncertain.

"It's Alma May," she said. "May I come in?"

"Uh . . . yes, of course. Give me a moment."

She could hear him scurrying about, probably looking for a robe. In a few seconds: "I'm decent."

The Princess opened the door and drew back another drape on the other side, revealing his room.

He seemed startled. "I thought you knocked on the hall door. I had no idea the drape hid—"

"I had this house built for my accommodation."

"So I see." Jamie grinned at her. She was beautiful in the half-light of the moon's illumination filtering into the room.

"Everyone is gone," she said, "but I'm not near sleep and there's at least one bottle of champagne remaining. Will you share it with me?" She gestured toward her bedroom.

"Certainly." He came through the door. The fragrance she wore enhanced her sensuousness.

She went to the table next to the bed where she had placed the bottle, handing it to him. "Would you open it, please?"

He did, filling each glass, giving her one, at the same time proposing a toast. "To the new Bon Marché."

Alma May repeated the words, took a sip of the wine, put down the glass, and sat on the edge of the bed. "Sit by me."

He did, thoroughly bemused. "You know, Princess, Drew Jackson has wagered a hundred dollars with Albert that you'll ask me to stay here as the Bon Marché veterinarian and that I'll accept."

She smiled coyly. "Would you do that if I asked you?"

"No."

"Then we don't have to speak of it again, do we? We can go on with what we both want without fear of complications."

Dr. Orr groaned. "Have my feelings about you been that transparent?"

"They have, and I was hoping I hadn't misread them."

"You didn't." Jamie reached over, taking her into his arms, kissing her. The Princess pulled him down on the bed, returning the kiss feverishly. There was only a momentary pause in their passion as they removed their nightclothes.

"You're a startling woman," he whispered to her. "A genuine vixen."

"Hmmm—"

"And if I had known about that door behind the drape, I'd have knocked first."

She giggled now as she crawled beneath the covers. "And if I hadn't answered?"

"You would have."

"I'm not so sure I'd want such a self-assured man around here all the time." She kissed him. "Poor Drew," she laughed, "he's lost a hundred dollars."

"His instincts were right, though," Jamie said. "He sensed we were both—" There was a pause.

"In heat?" She laughed more gaily.

"Something like that."

"Well, Dr. Orr, if that be true, don't you think we've talked enough?"

"Absolutely." He blew out the candles on the night table, getting under the covers with her.

As they made love she thought of Willie Carstairs and hated him for having left her.

27

THE night before there had been five hundred guests at the Bon Marché ball. Now, on a bright, comfortably warm May morning there were nearly a thousand on the grounds of the plantation to celebrate the wedding of Lady Bea Jackson and the Reverend Alston Merit. It was to be an outdoor ceremony under a lavish bower of flowers built by the slaves.

In truth, while the wedding was the *raison d'être* for the large gathering, a good many of the guests had other reasons for being there. Some, who had not been fortunate enough to be present at the ball, came to see the new mansion. Others, horsemen from the area, were present to inspect two new stallions being added to the Bon Marché stud barn and to witness an experiment that only a breeding farm of the size and affluence of Bon Marché would dare to undertake.

On the broad lawn, waiting for the wedding ceremony to begin, Dr. Jamie Orr was in earnest conversation with George Dewey Jr., the "master" of Bon Marché.

"I must confess, George," the veterinarian was saying, "that I have grave . . . uh . . . misgivings about your experiment. Taking fifty yearlings as far as New York in railroad cars may be too much for them."

"Yes, I know," George replied soberly, his brow wrinkled. "We've been schooling them for weeks, leading them in and out of the cars, leaving them standing in the stalls there for several hours each day. We're trying to get them used to those strange surroundings."

"And when the cars move?"

"Honestly, Jamie, I don't know what to think about that.

I'm hoping there'll be no panic. I've moved horses on a river-boat, but, somehow, that might be a smoother ride than we can count on here. But we're going to have sufficient handlers in the cars to try to keep them calm—one boy to every two horses."

"That's wise. How long are you going to keep them in the cars?"

"No longer than twenty-four hours at a stretch," George reported. "I've made arrangements all along the way to have pastures ready to accommodate the horses for a day or two each time we stop."

"Well . . . if you're successful," Dr. Orr said, "you're going to revolutionize the horse-selling business. Bon Marché breeding ought to bring high prices in New York."

"Exactly." George was grinning broadly.

Elsewhere on the lawn, Alma May came upon Drew Jackson. "By the way, Drew," she said, "I'm afraid you've lost your wager."

"What?" He was startled.

"Dr. Orr will not be staying at Bon Marché as the resident veterinarian."

"Oh—"

"You may have been correct about our need for such a competent addition to the staff. It's just that you were wrong about the motivation that would keep Dr. Orr here."

"Aunt Alma, I meant no disrespect."

"Of course you didn't." She was smiling. "But in the future, young man, I suggest you not bet on what you think might be my private . . . well, desires. You'll lose a lot of money if you persist in that."

The orchestra at the wedding bower began to play.

"Come," the Princess said, "your cousin is about to be married."

Drew Jackson offered his arm to Alma May, wondering who it was who told her about the wager.

II

IT was a busy day at Bon Marché. The wedding ceremony and a lavish luncheon served to the throng on the lawn took up half of it. When the newlyweds left for their honeymoon trip to Charleston, the attention turned to the plantation's new stallions, Jack Malone and John Morgan. There were many "oohs" and "ahhs" of appreciation as they were led in wide circles on the lawn, and in less than an hour, their breeding books had been filled.

That was followed almost immediately by the arrival of the locomotive to be coupled to the cars that would carry half a hundred of Bon Marché's highly bred yearlings to New York for sale. Horsemen from all over the counties of west-central Tennessee were there to watch George Dewey Jr. load the young horses.

"Careful, boys," he said quietly to his black handlers, "just do it easy. Don't excite them. Be calm."

Half of the yearlings were loaded without incident. Then a nervous filly balked, rearing up, neighing loudly in fright.

"Lead her away," George ordered, "and keep the others coming."

When all were on the cars except for the filly, they tried again with her, but once more she protested wildly.

"Try a blindfold on her," Jamie Orr suggested.

But that effort just seemed to intensify her panic. When the filly tossed one handler to the ground with her thrashing about, George said, "Take her back to the barn. We'll go without her." To Dr. Orr: "Damn! I figured her as one of the best we had to offer. She's out of Gamma, from the bloodlines I brought here from New Orleans. And Gamma was the first champion I had at Bon Marché."

"Bad luck," Jamie commented.

"Maybe not." George smiled wanly. "If she stays here young Drew may win a lot of money with her eventually."

Quickly then George shooed his family—wife, Emma, and his two young sons, Harry and George III—into the new "living car" built for them. Bunks had been installed, and a kitchen, and other amenities of a home. The master of Bon Marché meant to be comfortable on the long trip.

He turned to Alma May: "You'll be getting regular reports, Princess."

"Godspeed, George."

For just a moment it seemed to Dr. Orr that there was a secret understanding of some kind between the Princess and her nephew. Something portentous.

Dewey waved to his fellow horsemen, pulling himself into the cab of the locomotive. "All right, Mr. Johnson," he said to the engineer, "let's get under way. And smoothly, please. We're carrying my future."

As the spectators watched, the train moved along the Bon Marché spur slowly. It cleared the boundaries of the plantation and was switched to the main tracks of the railroad and then disappeared from sight.

"A big undertaking," Jamie said to Alma May.

"Yes." A pause. "Yes, indeed, a big undertaking." She changed the subject. "Now, Jamie, when does the Kentucky party leave?"

"Albert wants to be underway at four." He consulted his pocket watch. "In a half hour."

She took his arm. "Come, walk with me a bit." When they had gotten clear of the others, she said, "I'm going to miss you, Jamie."

"And me you."

"I've been thinking," she went on, "that maybe Drew was right. Maybe I do want you to stay."

"And cost Albert a hundred dollars?" he chuckled.

She frowned. "Be serious for a moment. We seem somehow to be kindred souls. We might be very good together."

"No, Princess, it's not that way at all. Please don't be offended by this—but I'm just a diversion. It's not me you need, it's just . . . someone. Isn't that the truth?"

"Yes," she confessed, "and isn't that terribly sad? Here I am at fifty-eight, when I ought to be a grandmother, bedding down men who are young enough to be my sons. I ought to feel degraded by that, but—" She stopped.

"But you're not."

"No, I'm not. God help me, I feel a certain pride in being able to attract men at my age."

"That's because you're ageless, Princess."

"Am I?"

"Uh-huh."

"And will I be at *sixty*-eight?" she asked plaintively.

"At any calendar age," Jamie insisted.

"Even if you're lying to me—"

"I'm not."

"—it doesn't make any difference. I had a chance once to

be the wife of a good man—Willie Carstairs—and I turned him down." She sighed. "Because Bon Marché has always been my true lover. And always will be."

"I'm aware of that."

Their apparently aimless walking had brought them to the Richland Creek and they sat on the bank, Jamie holding her in his arms. There was no more talk as they simply watched the quiet waters flowing by. It was a brief respite only. After consulting his watch once more, Jamie helped her to her feet and they walked, hand in hand, back to the mansion. Again, silently.

Albert Dewey's coach had been brought around to the Bon Marché entrance, the Kentucky contingent boarding after a round of handshakes and kisses. Dr. Orr was the last to board. He held Alma May's hands briefly.

"Ageless, eh?" she asked softly.

"Without question," he replied, climbing into the coach and closing the door.

A whip cracked and the team of horses surged forward.

The Princess sighed, turning in a small circle to survey that part of Bon Marché immediately before her. A pleasant, loving, *small* episode had just ended. What saddened her now, in that moment, was the fear that the future, clouded with the contentions between North and South, would no longer have a place for pleasant, loving, small episodes.

III

TRUE Jackson recognized he was in the presence of greatness. The man who had once been the master of Bon Marché, and who now viewed horse racing as a mere frivolous diversion unworthy of a genuine Southern patriot, sat in a hotel room in Montgomery, Alabama, on a too hot, mid-May afternoon of 1858 and listened to the voices of the future. His future, he was certain, and the future of his beloved Southland as a whole.

True believed he was the equal of the other men in the room; equal in intellect, fervor, resolve. Yet, there was a hidden, nagging doubt about how he measured up against those others whom he regarded as the heroes of the true South. So, he spoke little. One reason for his reticence might have been that he agreed so thoroughly with what they espoused; he could find no quarrel with what they were saying, no flaw in their arguments.

He studied them. Edmund Ruffin of Virgina: slight, frail, strangely shy in a sense, but whose pen spoke with the lightning strikes of truth. Southern truth. Robert Barnwell Rhett of South Carolina: born Smith of New England forebears, but a disciple of the great Calhoun and now the influential editor of the *Charleston Mercury*. William L. Yancey, planter, editor, and lawyer from Dallas County, Alabama. He was also a friend of John C. Calhoun; an orator of superb talent, capable of swaying the masses. He stood out like Saul of old, someone had said, above all who spoke.

Those three, True, and others had come to Montgomery to participate in a commercial convention, but most recognized the real reason for their gathering. A local newspaper's contention was that "every form and shape of political malcontent is here present, ready to assent to any project having for its end a dissolution of the Union, immediate, unconditional, final." Neither Ruffin, nor Rhett, nor Yancey, nor True Jackson saw need to issue a denial.

"Gentlemen," Yancey intoned, "our duty is clear. We must fire the Southern heart, instruct the Southern mind, give courage to each other, and at the proper moment, by one organized concerted action, precipitate the cotton states into a revolution!"

"Hear! Hear!" Jackson called out.

Yancey grinned. "I would hope, Mr. Jackson, that your enthusiasm is reflected in your state. Tennessee, it seems to me, now sits firmly on the fence."

"Not so," True insisted. "There is a strong residual sentiment for an independent South."

"Ahhh, but can you motivate it, Jackson?"

"With time. And money." The Nashvillian hesitated. "It seems to me that now is the time to organize further, to have a banner around which we can gather advocates for that independence."

Rhett nodded. "A point well taken, Jackson. Hmmm? A rallying point, eh?"

"Yes."

"Perhaps a union of our own?"

"Yes, certainly."

Ruffin spoke up. "An organization, then, to be composed of committees of . . . uh . . . safety in all the cotton states." He looked at Yancey. "As you said, friend William, something to fire the Southern heart." He thought for a moment. "Perhaps we might call it . . . well, the League of United Southerners."

It was done quickly; agreement was unanimous.

"And my brother and I can pledge," True Jackson added, "a purse capable of financing much of our work."

"How large a purse?" Yancey wanted to know.

"Oh . . . large enough, I imagine. A half million, perhaps. Yes, let's say that." He added grandly: "Like those earlier revolutionaries, gentlemen, the Jackson brothers are prepared to pledge our fortunes and our sacred honor to the cause."

The others were impressed. True had made his mark in that august company. He was exhilarated by the acceptance he felt.

IV

"AND that's the plan—what do you think of it?" George Dewey Jr. asked the man he recognized as a friend if not as an uncle, although that's what he was. George was addressing Marshall Dewey, a light-skinned Negro who was the bastard son of Bon Marché founder Charles Dewey and a slave woman named Angelica. They sat at dinner in a small tavern hard by the National Racecourse at Newton, Long Island, where they had come to discuss the imminent auction of the Bon Marché yearlings. But now the Nashvillian had changed the subject.

"I'm greatly surprised, of course," Marshall replied soberly. He was a ruggedly built man in his early sixties, a slight graying of his black hair the only hint of his age. Otherwise, there was a much younger look about him. "Surprised because you're involved in it, George. I've always thought of you as a hidebound Southerner, unwilling to become . . . well, an adopted Northerner, so to speak."

George nodded. "It's true that I would have preferred to stay in Nashville. But the Princess's arguments for an expansion of Bon Marché were most . . . compelling."

"And surprised, too," Marshall went on, "because this seems a poor time for such an investment. I mean, with the unsettled condition of the country and all."

"Alma May believes—and so do I, I suppose—that if there is a war, both Nashville and Lexington might be caught in the middle of it. A Bon Marché here, then, would save some of our breeding stock for a later time." George shook his head. "But I think all this talk of war is confined to a few malcontents, and the majority of the people, North and South, won't allow war to happen."

Marshall frowned. "That last seems like a rosy attitude."

"Perhaps. Nevertheless, part of Bon Marché is to be here in the North now—whatever the eventual outcome. War or no war. The Princess has made the decision and I must be party to it." George sighed deeply. "You can't know, Marshall, the extent of her . . . power, not having been at Bon Marché for so many years—" He paused questioningly.

"Forty-nine years," Marshall replied. "I was only twelve when my . . . father allowed Andrew MacCallum to take me with him to Princeton. And Alma May was even younger. What? Nine or ten?" He smiled. "Even then she was called the Princess. Of course, I saw her again in twenty-three when she came to New York with the Bon Marché racing string. Young Carrie was with them, too. But since that time my knowledge of Alma May has been very much second- or third-hand."

"Well, she's in charge now. And she runs Bon Marché very much in the same manner as Charles Dewey. There are days when I think she's the feminine equivalent of Grandfather . . . uh, your father. Self-assured and willing to take a gamble. And I think we both agree there *is* an element of chance in all this."

"Yes. I'm a bit surprised that Alma May could get the approval of the Schimmel sisters—or should I say the Jackson sisters?—for this plan."

George sighed again. "She didn't. As of this moment, the decision to establish a Bon Marché breeding and racing farm in New York is known only to the Princess, myself, and now you. Of course, my wife knows. But the Jacksons were no consulted—not the nieces, nor their husbands."

"Increasing the risk."

"Somewhat," George admitted.

Marshall shrugged. "Well, it's of no concern to me. I've never been thought of as a part of Bon Marché, that much is clear."

"But you *have* been," George said insistently. "Mattie recognized you in her will."

"With a few dollars, yes." He thought for a moment. "I'm not ungrateful, George. But I'm just a simple horse trainer, nothing more. And I'm certainly not a part of Bon Marché. Not when my father lived and not since."

"The Princess has instructed me to change that." George was speaking slowly, deliberately, now. "You are to be an equal partner in Bon Marché East—for that's what we mean to call the new farm—you as racing manager and me as . . ."

"As master?" Marshall asked, filling the pause.

"Well . . . yes."

"George, my friend, as incomprehensible as this may be to you, I cannot, *will not,* accept the offer. I have made my way all these years without Bon Marché, a life which now has only a few more years probably. I would be foolish to accept a *master* now."

The vehemence of the light-skinned Negro's words was shocking to George. "Good Lord, Marshall, it was never my intent to suggest myself as your master. The choice of the word was inadvertent. I'll be the manager of Bon Marché East, that's true. But you'd manage the racing interests. There would be no thought of master and . . . uh . . . servant."

Marshall affected a wry smile. "I have lived for more than sixty years with one reality. I'm a Negro. Light-skinned, to be sure. Half-white. But a Negro . . . a nigger, really . . . in the public eye."

"Not in mine," George insisted.

"Perhaps. But your good intentions will not change what the public sees. You, as a white Southerner, will always be seen as the master of Bon Marché East, and I will always be the servant, to use your word. I haven't been that for a long time and I'm jealous of what personal respect I've built for myself. I'm not willing to change it now, as tempting as the offer may be."

"I just don't understand."

"If I could give you this skin, George, you would."

The younger Dewey studied his grandfather's disaffected son. Finally: "Alma May is going to be disappointed."

"Only for a moment or two."

"You're not being fair about this, Marshall."

The older man shrugged, indicating the subject had been exhausted. "I would think the Bon Marché bloodlines are going to sell briskly at your auction. I'll probably bid on one or two myself—if I have enough money."

"I'd be glad to sell you a couple at private treaty," George offered.

"No, no," Marshall answered firmly. "I'll take my chances at the auction ring. I want no favors from Bon Marché."

V

August Schimmel was not well. In his mid-seventies now, he had driven his own carriage from Chicago to Springfield to attend the Illinois State Republican Convention sessions. His wife, Louise, had protested vigorously.

"You have a competent correspondent in Springfield," she said. "Why do you feel it necessary to be there yourself?"

"There are times in a newspaperman's life," her husband answered, "when he has an opportunity to be a part of history, to be personally present at a momentous turn in the road. My gut tells me this will be one of those times."

"August!" Louise was clearly angry. "Momentous? For God's sake, what can be momentous about the nomination of yet another candidate for the U.S. Senate?"

He had grinned sheepishly. "I don't know for certain, that much I'll admit to you. But something is poking me in the ribs to go. Call it instinct, if you will—"

"*Idiocy* is more like it!"

The publisher laughed. "You may be right."

"And don't think I'm being humorous about this. Your health won't allow such a strenuous trip."

"Hmmm."

"And I suppose you haven't replied to Statler yet."

The old man screwed up his face. "No, and I'm not going to. Young Mr. Dewey will just have to content himself with what he already has. He's *not* going to take over the Northern newspapers and be given a bigger platform to spread his disunion poison. I regret every day that we turned the Southern publications over to him."

Louise sighed. "August, darling, please . . . you're seventy-six years old! There are days when you can barely drag yourself out of bed. If you don't want to think about yourself, then consider me and your daughters."

Schimmel reached for his wife, folding his arms about her, kissing her cheek. "Sweetheart, don't you understand that no man dies while there's still a mission to be undertaken?"

And so he had gone to Springfield, feeling somewhat foolish about his talk of "mission," and feeling less well than before, wondering whether he was just being a stubborn ass.

He had filed his story about the Illinois Republicans unanimously nominating former U.S. Representative Abraham Lincoln, a Springfield lawyer, to oppose the popular incumbent, Stephen A. Douglas, in the '58 U.S. Senate race. No other candidate had been considered. Now August sat in the House of Representatives' hall in the Illinois statehouse, a notepad on his knee, as Lincoln arose, tall and cadaverous in appearance, to deliver his acceptance speech.

The voice was not impressive. It was too high-pitched, too twangy in accent, to even suggest statesmanship in the speaker. He did little more in the first paragraphs than outline what had been the government policy on the slavery issue over the past four years.

Such policy, he said, "was initiated with the avowed object, and confident promise, of putting an end to slavery agitation. Under the operation of that policy, that agitation has not only *not ceased,* but has constantly augmented. In my opinion, it will not cease until a crisis has been reached, and passed.

"A house divided against itself cannot stand.

"I believe this government cannot endure, permanently half *slave* and half *free.*"

Schimmel wrote furiously on his notepad, knowing at that moment why his instincts had brought him there.

"I do not expect the Union to be dissolved," Lincoln went on, the words delivered in the manner of a summation to a jury. "I do not expect the house to fall—but I *do* expect it will cease to be divided.

"It will become *all* one thing, or *all* the other.

"Either the opponents of slavery will arrest the further spread of it, and place it where the public mind shall rest in the belief that it is in the course of ultimate extinction; or its advocates will push it forward, till it shall become alike lawful in *all* the States, *old* as well as *new—North* as well as *South*."

Lincoln warned that under "the present political dynasty . . . we may, ere long, see . . . another Supreme Court decision declaring that the Constitution of the United States does not permit a State to *exclude* slavery from its limits," adding that such a decision was all slavery lacked "of being alike lawful in all the States." And the divided house, he told the convention delegates, would become all free only by having a government whose leaders saw slavery as *morally wrong*.

Applause for the new Republican senatorial candidate could still be heard as Schimmel hurried out to the telegraph office, composing his opening sentences in his mind. Once there he wrote: "Springfield, Illinois, June 16, 1858—Special to the Schimmel Newspapers . . ." August paused for a moment in thought, adding, "and the Dewey Newspapers." He reasoned he might as well send it to Statler Dewey, because the young man just might print it full for Southern eyes, if for no other reason than to hold the Republican up to ridicule.

A keynote of American political history was struck tonight [Schimmel wrote], a clarion call for morality ringing clear, when Springfield attorney Abraham Lincoln enunciated a great truth in the current debate over the slavery issue: "A house divided against itself cannot stand . . . this government cannot endure, permanently half slave and half free."

Mr. Lincoln, who will oppose incumbent U.S. Senator Stephen A. Douglas, told the Republican delegates . . .

Page after page filled under the veteran editor's racing pen. He was strangely buoyed, forgetting the weariness he had known and the unwell feeling that had been with him for months. As he left the telegraph office there was a jauntiness about the way he walked. He decided not to spend another night in a Springfield hotel, but to retrieve his horse and carriage from the livery stable and begin his return to Chicago immediately. Louise would be pleased to have him home sooner than expected.

Some miles out of town on the road leading north, the Schimmel carriage stopped, the horse bending its neck to graze on the grass by the roadside. Every so often the carriage moved ahead a few feet as the horse sought a new patch of grass. How long it was there could only be guessed at, but it was nearly dawn when two farmers halted their wagon to investigate.

"Hooo, neighbor!" one of them called out. "Ya need some help?"

There was no reply.

One of the men vaulted from the wagon, approaching the carriage cautiously. He looked in at the passenger, believing him to be asleep. "Neighbor?" he said loudly. Schimmel's horse snorted. The farmer reached in to touch the inert figure, the reins still held between the fingers.

Startled, the farmer turned back to his companion. "Hell, Arnie, ya better fetch the sheriff. This feller's dead!"

VI

CHARLES Dewey II sat disconsolately in his carriage at the Pioneer Racecourse in San Francisco, listening to the cheers of the spectators.

"Damn it," he said to Willie Carstairs, "that foolishness isn't racing!" He gestured to what was happening on the track. "It's merely a stupid exhibition. What does it matter if Johnny Powers is able to ride a hundred and fifty miles in less than seven hours? He's not doing it on anything worthwhile. I mean, his mounts are nothing more than wild mustangs— grass-fed, ill-groomed, never having seen the inside of anything like a decent stable."

Carstairs chuckled. "You're a bloodstock snob, Charles."

"Perhaps." Dewey frowned. "But I didn't invest money in this track to see it misused for this kind of . . . of . . . circus." He shook his head. "God, there are days when I wish I were back at Bon Marché, where *real* racing is conducted."

"And where you were poor, Two."

Charles smiled now. "I can always count on you, Willie, to bring me back to reality. Have you heard from Bon Marché lately?"

"The Princess still writes, although with less . . . well, with less intimacy since my marriage."

"At least she's still your friend, Willie; most women would not be, you know. I heard from the East today," he went on, removing a letter from his jacket pocket. "From Aunt Louise in Chicago."

"How are things there?"

"August has died."

"Oh, good Lord!"

"And she's struggling with a decision about what she's going to do with the Schimmel newspapers. It seems that Statler wants to bring the Northern publications into his Dewey Newspapers chain and Louise has doubts about agreeing to that."

Charles unfolded the letter to read: "'I'm certain, dear Two, that August would not have wanted me to turn over the papers to Statler. Yet, I don't think I can keep them going on my own; I don't really want to. I want only to return to Bon Marché and spend my final days with my daughters and my grandchildren. I don't have August's dedication to publishing. While he lived I was perfectly willing to sublimate myself to his needs, but now . . .'

"There's more, of course, but the ending may be the most worrisome." Two read again: "'I've always valued your opinion and I ask you now—what shall I do?' I was never aware that my opinion had such value in the past. What makes it so compelling all of a sudden?"

"Your opinion, my friend, has more value since you've become the wealthiest member of the family," Carstairs replied matter-of-factly.

"And wealth is equated with wisdom?"

"Always."

"Hmmm. I *do* have an idea, but it depends on—" He hesitated.

"On what?"

"On your cooperation. Have you been reading the *Nashville Monitor*?"

"Yes, I get it regularly. Very late, but regularly."

"What do you think of it?"

"Gross nonsense, mostly," Willie answered. "More and more Statler's spouting the insanities of those barnburners who want to see the Southern states leave the Union. I suspect the Jackson brothers have worked their will on him."

"And if he gets his hands on Schimmel's Northern papers he'll spread that nonsense?"

"Without a doubt."

"Then what I want to propose to you, Banker Carstairs," Charles said in a conspiratorial manner, "is that we thwart my young brother and buy the Schimmel Newspapers ourselves."

Willie thought for a moment. "What would we be taking on?"

"The *Chicago Clarion, Cincinnati Bulletin, Pittsburgh Observer,* and Schimmel's half interest in Cousin Carrie Bonsal's *St. Louis Challenger.*"

The banker shrugged. "We ought to be able to afford a reasonable offer for that package."

"Then it's done?"

"Done." Carstairs shook hands with his partner. "And I think we'd be well served if we had Roger Weatherford go East to manage those properties. Can we spare him?"

"He's been a farmer, not a newspaperman."

"Ahh, but he's totally honest and loyal, and he's adapted quite well to the business world with the Dewey Trading Company."

Charles nodded agreement. "Very well. Maybe with Roger gone my son will see the need to pay more attention to the trading company. I don't believe he's been at the docks for weeks—and Weatherford keeps making excuses for him. Charles Three seems only to want to spend his time at the horse farm."

Willie laughed heartily. "Why do you find that so strange? He's a Dewey, after all."

"Yes, but I want him to understand that our businesses are what make the horse farm possible. Racing here is a mere diversion, and not a business as it is back home. My son has got to prepare himself for his proper role in the family. And that's with the trading company."

Carstairs laid a consoling hand lightly on Charles's arm. "Two, don't push him too hard. The lad's only seventeen. When his time comes he'll be ready. I've never yet known a Dewey who wasn't able to come to scratch."

A great roar went up from the crowd at the racetrack. Two groaned. "I suppose that sound means that Johnny Powers has completed his ride and has won his wagers. It's too bad that all that energy is wasted. It occurs to me that if he could ride horses at that speed in a straight line going somewhere some good might come of it."

"Is there a kernel of an idea in that remark?"

"No, no," Dewey said. "I suppose I'm just being malcontented. Still, wouldn't you think those Young Turks could find something better to do than simply ride a relay of mustangs round and round to no good end?"

BOOK THREE

I wish you could ride over Bon Marché and
see the rich, deep green sea of verdure,
high as my head, waving in the bright sunshine;
it is so suggestive of "peace and plenty" one
can scarcely realize that stern war, in all
its sad reality, is around and about us.
—Joy Schimmel Jackson, 1862

28

ALL that was right with Bon Marché and the Dewey family—
the continuing success of the Nashville racing string under
young Drew Jackson, Colonel Albert Dewey's rapidly expanding breeding operation in Lexington, a promising beginning of George Dewey Jr.'s Bon Marché East in New York,
the vast wealth being accumulated by Charles Dewey II in
California—was in vivid contrast to what was happening outside the Dewey orbit. For the nation could be likened to a
runaway wagon plunging headlong down a steep hill, the
horse having bolted from the shaft, the brake pad burned
away, facing a certain grinding crash among the boulders at
the bottom of the precipice.

While the plunge was to consume the days and weeks and
months of two more years, to some there seemed a lightning-
strike suddenness to it all. Not to the Deweys, however. Arrogance born of a belief they were somehow favored above all
others served to shield them from the inevitable reality. Yet,
the shield would prove to be porous, unable to protect them
from the truth of the times. Like it or not, favored or not, the
Deweys could not halt the plunging wagon.

II

LEE Dewey, the Washington correspondent of the Schimmel
and Dewey newspapers, cracked his crop across the flank of
the lathered horse, asking for more speed. He was racing to
Harpers Ferry, where the Potomac slashed picturesquely
through the Blue Ridge, for his own look at—and perhaps an

interview with—the man who may have fired the first shots of a war between North and South.

All of the elements of high drama had coalesced at the little town on that mid-October day of '59. Rabble-rousing abolitionist John Brown had brought a small "Provisional Army" to strip the federal armory at Harpers Ferry and then, instead of taking the opportunity to flee, had staged a pitched battle with U.S. Army troops from behind inadequate barricades in a firehouse. Brown was captured by Colonel Robert E. Lee, scion of one of Virginia's first families. The symbolism of such a confrontation, Dewey knew, would not be lost on his readers.

Sketchy telegraph reports reaching Washington had told of one of Brown's sons being killed and the leader himself grievously wounded. The reporter galloped into Harpers Ferry, hoping he would not be too late, heading for the armory where he surmised Brown would be held.

No one challenged him as he strode into the armory's office, to find Brown on the floor with another of the insurgents, covered with some old bedding. It was immediately evident Brown's wounds were not life-threatening. He was smaller than Dewey had imagined; stories of him originating in Kansas had suggested a man of some considerable stature. *"Wiry" describes him better,* Lee thought. He saw keen, restless gray eyes and wild hair with a grizzled beard. Brown's face, hands, and clothes were smeared with blood. Lee sought a sign of madness; he found, instead, a strange calmness in the prisoner. Perhaps a resignation, a willingness to accept his ultimate fate.

An interrogation was under way when Dewey walked in and he recognized some of the gentlemen in the crowded room: Senator J. M. Mason of Winchester, Virginia; Congressman Clement Vallandigham of Ohio, and Congressman James Faulkner, who lived only a few short miles from Harpers Ferry. Dewey pressed close, bringing out his notepad, writing swiftly.

"Can you tell us," Mason asked, "who furnished money for your expedition?"

Brown's answer was quietly defiant. "I furnished most of it myself. I cannot implicate others. It is by my own folly that I have been taken. I could easily have saved myself from it had

I exercised my better judgment rather than yield to my feelings. I should have gone away, but I had thirty-odd prisoners, whose wives and daughters were in tears for their safety, and I felt for them. Besides, I wanted to allay the fears of those who believed we came here to burn and kill."

"If you would tell us who sent you here," Mason went on steadily, "who provided the means—that would be information of some value."

"I will answer freely and faithfully about what concerns myself—I will answer anything I can with honor, but not about others."

Congressman Vallandigham insisted: "Mr. Brown, who sent you here?"

"No man sent me," Brown snapped, seeming to weary of the single-minded theme. "It was on my own prompting and that of my Maker, or that of the devil, whichever you please to ascribe it. I acknowledge no master in human form."

"Did you get up the expedition yourself?"

"I did."

The Ohio congressman shrugged and Senator Mason resumed his questioning. "What was your object in coming?"

"We came to free the slaves, and only that."

"And you use that to justify your violent acts?"

Brown stared at the senator for a moment. "I think, my friend, *you* are guilty of a great wrong against God and humanity, and it would be perfectly right for anyone to interfere with you so far as to free those you willfully and wickedly hold in bondage. I do not say this insultingly—"

Dewey thought the apologetic tone was oddly out of place.

"—but I think I did right and that others will do right who interfere with you at any time and all times. I hold that the golden rule, 'Do unto others as you would that others should do unto you,' applies to all who would help others gain their liberty."

There was a brief pause and Lee Dewey dared to fill it. "How many men in all had you?"

"I came to Virginia with eighteen men only, besides myself."

Dewey was shocked. "What in the world did you suppose you could do here with that amount of men?"

"Sir," John Brown said wearily, "I don't wish to discuss that question here."

"But how could you hope to—?"

Brown cut him off. "Perhaps your ideas and mine on military subjects would differ materially."

Lee nodded. "Perhaps. Brown, do you consider this a religious movement?"

"It is, in my opinion"—the voice was stronger now—"the greatest service a man can render to God."

"Do you consider yourself an instrument in the hands of Providence?"

"I do, sir."

"If you have anything further to say," Dewey added, "I will report it."

"I have nothing to say," the prisoner replied hurriedly, then thought better of it. "Only that I claim to be here carrying out a measure I believe perfectly justifiable, and not to act the part of an incendiary or ruffian, but to aid those suffering a great wrong. I wish to say, furthermore, that you had better—all you people of the South—prepare yourselves for settlement of that question that must come up for settlement sooner than you are prepared for it. The sooner you are prepared, the better. You may dispose of me very easily. I am nearly disposed of now. But this question is still to be settled—this Negro question, I mean. The end of it is not yet."

III

ON December 2, John Brown was hanged, becoming a martyr to the abolitionist cause. More than one Northern newspaper proclaimed editorially: "John Brown Lives!" Popular author Ralph Waldo Emerson wrote that Brown "made the gallows glorious like the cross." To many, the crash of the national wagon along the boulders at the bottom of the hill was now imminent.

But in Nashville in the December weeks following the hanging of Brown, publisher Statler Dewey tried to put aside the real fear he had felt when reading Lee Dewey's accounts of the drama, trying to dismiss Harpers Ferry from his mind as he worked on the publication of the 1860 *Nashville City and Business Directory*. For Statler, Nashville was to be his only reality. He recognized the influence he had allowed True and Able Jackson to impose on the Dewey Newspapers—the hard-shelled pro-Southern editorial policy he had pursued for months on end—had cost him ownership of August Schimmel's Northern newspapers; had robbed him of the opportunity to be a great *national* publisher. There was nothing he could do about that now (his brother Charles II had seen to that), but he could, perhaps, make up some lost ground by distancing himself from the Jacksons and taking a cue from what he clearly recognized on the Nashville scene.

Nashvillians, it seemed, were more interested in talking about the new McGavock and Mt. Vernon Horse Railway Company, the city's first trolley car, than of disunion. That subject had become a bore. A new political conservatism seemed to be at play in both the North and South, with politicians from each region continuing to seek more compromises aimed at preventing an open conflict.

Indeed, so many grand things were taking place that to consider a schism in the Union was regarded as foolishness in many quarters. The new railroad bridge over the Cumberland River—built for the Louisville and Nashville and the Edgefield and Kentucky lines—was being touted as the engineering feat of the century. It had four spans totaling seven hundred feet; the two end spans were fixed, but the two center spans were designed to be turned aside to permit the passage of the big steamboats with their tall and ornate smokestacks. Then, too, there was the wonder of the new Tennessee Capitol Building, open now, a woodcut of which was to grace the cover of Statler's city and business directory.

The directory was a chronicle of the wealth and well-being of Nashville; a steamboat yard, a brickyard, several foundries, four millwork and furniture factories, three patent-medicine companies, a factory producing artificial limbs, a carriage builder, a boot and shoe factory, two tobacco factories, three breweries, four insurance companies, and several banks and hotels, including the under-construction grandest hotel of all, to be known as the Maxwell House. Not present in the city directory was the fact that the rapidly growing city could also boast no less than sixty-nine houses of prostitution.

In a sense, Statler put whorehouses and disunion in the same editorial bag; both subjects were regarded, as 1860 approached, as unfit for inclusion in the pages of the *Nashville Monitor* and the others of the Dewey Newspapers. Early in January he had an editorial printed in all of his Southern publications: "The times require that we be perfectly cool, or as cool as we can be, putting aside rashness and passion."

Rashness and passion? Those were the traits of his cousins-by-marriage, the Jackson brothers, and the young publisher reasoned that he, and the South, would be better served by not being allied with the barnburners. And like Statler Dewey, others with that family name thought it best to be "perfectly cool."

IV

THE din set up by the small army of workmen nailing up the wallboards of the newest warehouse of the Dewey Trading Company, dockside in San Francisco, caused Willie Carstairs's head to ache. He stood watching his partner directing the feverish activity; Two was in his element, "at home" in the noise of growth.

Willie frowned. At times the unbridled ambition of the younger Dewey worried the banker; Charles seemed to have a *need* to have more, to physically see the tangible signs of his successes. Two had told him once that his accomplishments, his money-making, brought him "the same rush of emotions I feel when I'm making love." Studying him now, Carstairs could believe it.

But the expansion project was exciting and was indicative of their mutual gains. The heavy redwood boards making up the walls of the warehouse had been cut in their own sawmill north of Sacramento. The very nails being used had been fashioned in their own wire mill, Charles having insisted on importing the latest machinery from England. And the new dock extending out from the warehouse into San Francisco Bay was necessary to provide more mooring space for the additions they had made to the trading company's fleet of sailing ships, most of them acquired for modest prices from owners who had virtually abandoned them in the harbor to go search for gold.

Carstairs approached his partner, putting his hands over his ears as Charles saw him. "How do you stand all this noise?" Willie shouted to him.

"Isn't it marvelous?" Dewey was grinning.

"Hardly," Willie yelled. "Could we find a quiet corner?"

Charles gestured to the leather case Carstairs carried. "More papers to sign?"

Willie just nodded.

They left the warehouse and walked a hundred feet or so along the dock, finding two packing crates on which to sit.

"There are some days," Two said in a joshing manner, "when I believe half my life is made up of signing my name on something."

"The necessary appurtenances of doing business."

"I suppose." Dewey scrawled his signature as Carstairs placed the papers down on a packing crate. The task done, Carstairs stuffed the documents back into his case.

"Oh, by the way, Charles," Willie said, "do you recall that conversation we had sometime ago at the racecourse, when Johnny Powers was astounding the crowd with his riding prowess?"

Two shook his head negatively.

"It was the day we decided to buy the Schimmel newspapers."

"Ahhh, yes, *that* I remember."

"You said then that if Powers would ride his speedy mustangs in a straight line to somewhere something good might come of it."

"Uh-huh."

"Well, someone's doing it."

"Doing what?"

"The freighting company of Russell, Majors, and Waddell," Carstairs reported, "is beginning in April a service of fast relay riders to carry the mail from San Francisco to St. Joseph, Missouri—the western end of the railroad lines. They're claiming the distance will be covered in just eleven days."

"But that's twice as fast," Charles said in astonishment, "as the fastest stagecoach. Maybe more so."

"Exactly."

"Relay riders, you say?"

"Yes, they're establishing remount stations every ten miles, the riders to quickly change to fresh mounts at each station. And each rider is to cover thirty miles as fast as he can."

"With what bloodstock?" Two wanted to know.

"Indian ponies, mostly. That's why they're calling it the Pony Express."

"Hmmm?" Dewey sat in thought.

"They might be looking for investors," Willie suggested tentatively.

"No, no. I'm not interested. I'm a gambler, but not a fool. There'll be no profit in it." He grinned at his partner. "Do I disappoint you, Willie?"

"I did think you might be excited by the idea."

"I admit to being intrigued," Charles said, "but I'd much rather we'd consider a stake in the telegraph."

"But that's at least two years away. I don't imagine we'll have telegraph service of any kind until late in sixty-one. Maybe not until sometime in sixty-two."

"And when we do," Two said forcefully, "the so-called Pony Express will be out of business."

"True enough."

"Even after the railroads span the continent, Willie, the telegraph will still be making money." Dewey clapped his partner on the back. "In the meantime, I'm not so sure I welcome the quick news from the East. Every time we do get word from that quarter it's more of that insane talk of disunion. Hell, there are even some secessionist voices being raised here in California. What madness!"

Willie nodded agreement.

"I suspect that our remoteness is eventually going to be to our advantage," Charles added, "in more ways than we can now divine."

V

AT the Fashion Course on Long Island, George Dewey Jr. watched with undisguised admiration as the big bay horse was put through his work. He smiled as the animal suddenly switched from a gallop to a trot, seeming to go just as fast as before. The Negro jockey fought him to switch the gait and Thomas Doswell's Planet, of Bluefield Stud of Virginia, finally returned to the wanted gallop.

George had heard of binary horses—those capable of racing in either a trot or a run—but he had never seen one before. Yet, it wasn't the dual gait that impressed him most; it was the five-year-old's magnificent record. Two days earlier, in what had been hoped would be an epic North-South racing encounter, Planet had been challenged by only one Northern horse and had distanced his opponent. It was his twenty-seventh win in thirty-one starts, and he had won on all sorts of tracks: Petersburg, Richmond, Savannah, Charleston, New Orleans, Mobile, Ashland, Augusta, and now New York. He had earnings of more than $69,000 carrying Doswell's all-orange silks, replacing the great Peytona as America's leading money winner.

Doswell was leaning on a rail watching his champion work out in the early-morning light, and Dewey approached him.

"Excuse me, sir," the transplanted Nashvillian said, "my name is George Dewey Jr., of Bon Marché East. And I want to compliment you on your fine animal."

"Thank you." The Virginian shook George's hand. "Dewey? Any relation to the late Charles Dewey?"

"He was my grandfather."

"Oh, of course. Bon Marché—now I make the connection. I didn't realize there had been an expansion to New York."

"A modest one only, sir." George nodded toward the horse on the track. "May I ask, Mr. Doswell, what plans you have for him?"

"Plans?" Doswell smiled. "Right now I'm just going through a regimen of light work to let him down a bit before we start the arduous trip back home. After that—?" The owner shrugged. "I may take him back to Charleston next year to gain some revenge for two earlier losses we had there."

"Do you plan to take him to stud?"

"Not quite so soon, I hope. He's perfectly sound and I can look forward to three or four more seasons of racing, perhaps."

"If there is racing, sir," George said.

"Yes, there is the possibility, isn't there, that racing will suffer because of our regional political differences?"

"A possibility, certainly. But as you must, Mr. Doswell, I hope not."

"Hmmm."

"Because I must believe in a peaceful future, sir, I admit to you that I have designs on your horse as a possible stud in my barns."

Doswell seemed alarmed. "You mean you wish to buy him?"

"I do."

"That won't be possible, Mr. Dewey. Planet is not for sale." The words were hard.

"I can understand that you'd be reluctant to part with him, but maybe if the pot is sweet enough—"

"No." The Virginian shook his head vigorously.

"He's won nearly seventy-thousand for you, hasn't he?" George pressed on.

"Yes, not counting the wagers I've won on him."

"Therefore, Mr. Doswell, I think it proper to offer you a duplicate of that amount to acquire him."

Doswell's eyebrows twitched. "You mean seventy thousand?"

"Yes, sir."

"Some might consider that a princely sum," Doswell said quietly, "and I thank you for offering it because it is proof of the esteem to which he is held by others. But I cannot sell him."

"I'm also prepared to offer a half share in all his winnings over the next two seasons—"

"No."

"—and the placement of a thousand-dollar wager in your behalf every time he starts."

"No."

"And when he goes to stud," George continued, "I'll reserve for you fifty percent of the bookings."

Doswell laughed heartily now. "By God, Mr. Dewey, you are persistent! You've made it difficult, I'll admit, but the answer must still be no."

Dewey sucked in a deep breath; he had one more card to play. "If there is trouble between the states, sir, I submit to you that Planet might be safer here, away from the possible . . . uh . . . locations of contention, as it were. I would promise you, as a gentleman, that I would keep him safe, no matter what, moving him to Canada if necessary."

"No, I cannot." Doswell's answer was without equivocation. "He was foaled at Bluefield, where I have his champion dam, Nina. Whatever happens, Mr. Dewey, I *must* return him home."

George sighed. "I understand. I hope that I—and you, of course—shall see him run again . . . that differences between North and South can continue to be mediated on the racetrack."

"So do I, young man, so do I."

VI

THERE was to be no racetrack mediation, the presidential elections of 1860 ending all such hopes. Abraham Lincoln's victory unleashed the strongest emotions in both regions. Robert Barnwell Rhett's Charleston *Mercury* gleefully proclaimed: "The tea has been thrown overboard. The revolution of 1860 has been initiated." In Nashville, Statler Dewey found himself with a hard choice and made it as a Southerner. He instructed his fellow editors in New Orleans, Raleigh, and Lexington to reprint the entire incendiary Rhett editorial.

At dinner at Bon Marché Lexington, Albert Dewey angrily tossed aside a copy of the *Kentucky Gazette*. "My cousin has totally gone over to the madmen," he growled. "All of this talk of war. My God, don't they realize the folly of that?"

"But if there is war, Father," his son Jack asked, "where will we stand?"

"Stand?" Albert seemed shocked by the question. "We'll stand right here—defending what is our own, defending Bon Marché Lexington."

"But won't we owe some allegiance to the South?"

Albert's eyes rolled up to the ceiling as if seeking some divine guidance. "Listen to him, Jamie," he said. "Seventeen years old and speaking of allegiances!" To Jack: "Young man, as far as this family is concerned there will be no war. I've seen war, Jack, and it solves nothing. Nothing! It is cruel, wasteful, inhumane. There's no glory in it, if that's what you imagine. No man of any intelligence would ever consider war as a solution for anything."

"But if Kentucky decides—?"

Albert cut him off. "Kentucky will have no role in this insanity—not so long as I have a breath in my body to oppose it!"

The meal ended in sullen silence. The master of Bon Marché Lexington and his veterinarian retired to the drawing room for bourbon.

"Don't you think you were . . . well, a bit too hard with the boy?" Dr. Orr asked.

"No, I don't."

"But I suggest to you, Albert, that if there is war your views might not prevail."

Dewey shook his head firmly. "You're wrong. My sons are not of a rebellious nature. They will follow my lead."

"And if not?"

"Jamie," Albert sighed, "I must tell you that you're trying my patience. I'd really be grateful if we could change the subject."

VII

ON December 20 of 1860 the telegraph at the *Nashville Monitor* brought the news that the political firebrands of South Carolina had taken the state out of the Union. Secession had become a reality. In January of a new year, Mississippi also seceded. And Florida and Alabama and Georgia and Louisiana.

On February 8, 1861, the Confederate States of America was born in Montgomery, Alabama. And the next day—it was a Wednesday—Alma May Dewey pushed her way through the excited milling crowd filling the streets around the courthouse in Nashville. There was animated talk about the leaders of the new Confederacy: Jefferson Davis had been named President, Alexander H. Stephens was Vice President. The Princess took her place in a line of men snaking into the courthouse to vote on a plebiscite: should Tennessee also secede?

She was there representing not herself but Bon Marché. Charles Dewey's dream was the only thing motivating her. She was not concerned about the Confederacy, or the Southern "crusade," or even Tennessee. On that morning, as she arrived in Nashville in her jogging cart, she had sent identical telegraph messages to Lexington and New York: "Whatever happens now," she told Albert and George Dewey, "you have only one duty, the preservation of Bon Marché."

No one paid any particular attention to Alma May until she reached the courthouse doorway. There a uniformed guard blocked her way. "What do you want, lady?" he demanded roughly.

"To vote, of course."

"You know women can't vote."

The Princess glared at him. "Sir, I am the mistress of Bon Marché!"

"I don't give a damn who you are, lady, you can't come in and vote."

She put her hands against his chest and shoved mightily, causing the surprised guard to take a step or two backward. She tried to skirt around him to gain entrance to the polling precinct, but other male hands grabbed her, hustling her away from the courthouse, the strong-arm methods accompanied by numerous epithets.

For the first time in her life she wanted to be a man.

Her anger about being turned away didn't abate until the next morning when she learned that Tennessee had narrowly defeated the plebiscite, largely because of the strong pro-Union vote in mountainous East Tennessee where there was no plantation economy and almost no slaves. Somehow, the Princess felt justified; a majority had voted as she would have—for the Union. Hers would not have been a political vote; as she had told her nephews in Kentucky and New York, the only worthwhile cause was Bon Marché. In her view, the Union offered the best hope for that.

Yet—

On March 4, Abraham Lincoln was inaugurated President of the United States of America, maintaining that it remained an indivisible Union. Correspondent Lee Dewey reported the Republican's words to the family's newspapers: "In your hands, my dissatisfied fellow-countrymen, and not in mine, is the momentous issue of civil war. The government will not assail you. You can have no conflict without yourselves being the aggressors. You have no oath registered in heaven to destroy the government, while I shall have the most solemn one to 'preserve, protect, and defend' it."

Just a little more than a month later—on Friday, April 12—as the first uncertain light of dawn poked at the horizon to the east of the Federal Fort Sumter in Charleston harbor, and as naval ships sent by Lincoln to reprovision it stood off, a Confederate mortar shell arched high into the dark sky and exploded over the fort. The time was exactly 4:30 A.M.

A gleeful True Jackson, standing with hundreds of others on the Charleston Battery, was witness to the glorious moment.

The symbolic runaway wagon plunging headlong down a steep hill had crashed at the bottom, splintering into nothing but kindling; kindling from which a mighty blaze would be brought forth. Alma May Dewey understood that as she paced the Dewey Room in the Bon Marché mansion, ordering her mind.

She spoke aloud to the portrait of her father. "I swear to you, Daddy, your Bon Marché will be perserved. I swear that"—she paused as she felt his presence there—"to your spirit."

29

COLONEL Albert Dewey was weary in every muscle. He sought a more comfortable position by shifting his weight in the saddle, but was unable to find it. Albert was returning from Frankfort where he had spent four days, almost without sleep, arguing the cause of the Union with Kentucky legislators. Texas and Arkansas and North Carolina and Virginia had now declared for the Confederacy. But Tennessee had not, and neither had Kentucky. He was not alone, of course, in his argument, and if one thing had come clear to him it was that his state was about evenly divided, pro-Union and pro-Confederacy.

What worried him most was that Kentucky was becoming an armed camp. As he had ridden through Lexington he had seen militiamen drilling in the streets, volunteers for the Union cause on one side of the street, volunteers for the new Confederacy on the other. The makings of bloody conflict were there with only the narrow width of the street separating them. *How long can it continue like this?* he asked himself.

As Albert approached the familiar acres of Bon Marché Lexington he stopped for a moment and studied the barren mares in one of the fenced pastures. He was struck with the thought that the animals grazed in a contentment belying the furor of the times. And he wondered when again the mares might be bred, when again his plantation would pursue the peaceful business of breeding and racing. Racing had been suspended in Lexington; no one seemed to want to continue with what now seemed a frivolous diversion. Albert and Dr.

Jamie Orr had decided to breed only a dozen of the better mares, understanding there was no market now for young horses but not wanting to quit all breeding. "After all," Albert had said, "this is still a horse farm."

He spurred his mount, urging it into a light canter, wanting to get home for a bath and a good night's sleep. As he approached the gateway of Bon Marché Lexington he saw two of the hands, armed with muskets, patrolling the entrance. That, too, was indicative of the times. Somewhat reluctantly he had armed all of his farm workers—the immigrant Germans and Poles and Irishmen he had hired to replace the slaves he had sold—fearing an outbreak of hooliganism. Fearing, too, that his vigorous pro-Union sentiments might trigger some pro-Confederacy reprisals against him. Perhaps the burning of his barns. Or, worse, an attempt to harm his family.

Albert acknowledged the hands as he trotted through the gate: "Good afternoon, boys." They tipped their hats to him. He had gone only fifty yards toward the main house when he saw his eldest son, Jefferson, running toward him.

"Thank God, Father, you're back!" Jeff called to him.

Albert reined in the horse. "What's wrong?"

"It's Jack and Staunch—they're gone!"

The father groaned as he slid out of the saddle, his legs aching. "Gone where?"

"To Charleston. At least that's what they said in the notes they left."

"Oh, good Lord!"

"They said they were going to join the Confederate army. And I imagine they left while you were away because they knew you would forbid them."

Albert squeezed shut his eyes as if in pain. "How long ago?"

"Two days. Jamie and I rode out trying to find them, but we had no luck."

"Damn!" Albert's anger was very real. "Damn those young fools!"

Jeff nodded. "Lillian . . . uh . . . Mother is distraught."

"I can imagine." He started to lead his horse toward the mansion. "And you've heard nothing from them since they left?"

"No, nothing."

The master of Bon Marché Lexington exhaled a deep sigh. "I hope, young man, that *you're* not contemplating such foolishness."

"No, sir."

"Good." He put his arm around his son. "We must pray that God keeps your brothers safe."

"Yes, sir."

They walked in silence for a moment or two. "They're nothing but boys," Albert said finally. "Jackson is only seventeen and Staunch just fifteen." It seemed the simple recital of those facts startled the father. "Just boys . . ."

II

IN Nashville, True Jackson, having returned from the drama in Charleston, put all his efforts into bringing Tennessee into the Confederacy. He was appalled by what he regarded as stupid lethargy within the state government. Governor Isham Harris's attitude angered him.

"My God, Governor," True told him, "you must act! You cannot allow Tennessee to remain in the damned Union!"

"You're offensive, Jackson," the governor snapped back, his face going crimson. "I've already made it clear to the secretary of war that Lincoln's call for seventy-five thousand Southern volunteers for the Union army is *not* acceptable here. I've told him Tennessee will not furnish a single man for the purposes of coercion, but will—"

"I know all the political rhetoric," True cut him off churlishly, "but in the meantime our state remains in the Union!"

Governor Harris set his jaw. "Zealots like yourself, Jackson, who are not answerable to the will of the people, always have simple answers for complex problems. Tennessee remains in the Union today because the people want it that way. Like you, sir, I see our future with our Southern brothers. But the people don't want it right now—the plebiscite has told me that much. And I remain a servant of the people."

"The people can be led in a different course by a man of courage," True insisted.

Harris glared at him, determined to ignore the insult. "In

time, perhaps," he answered. "But right now John Bell and his associates are circulating an appeal for peace and a reunited country."

"Bell's an old fool!"

"John Bell, Mr. Jackson, is one of our most respected statesmen. This area voted overwhelmingly for him in the presidential election."

"I was for Breckinridge," True snorted.

The governor made no comment.

"You may sit idle if you wish," Jackson went on, his ire a self-perpetuating thing, "but I can't. I'm risking a half-million dollars of my own fortune to arm men to fight for the Confederacy. For the South!"

"I applaud you for that, sir, but I am charged—by my office—to act within the laws of the state."

True left the governor's office then, vowing never to return. For a few moments he considered seeking the support of John Bell, to redirect Bell's views, but he reasoned he had no time for such frustration. He headed, instead, for the office of the *Nashville Monitor,* where he worked his will on Statler Dewey.

The next issue of the newspaper carried True Jackson's broadside:

SOUTHERN PATRIOTS!
ENLIST NOW!
Join the glorious battle
for your freedom from
Northern tyranny. Uphold
the sacred Southern cause.
TO ARMS!
LIBERAL ENLISTMENT BONUSES!

His brother's name was affixed to it: General Able Jackson.

Whether it was the Jackson influence in the community, or whether it was more directly the exigencies of the times, Governor Harris called a special session of the Tennessee Legislature late in April, citing "an alarming and dangerous usurpation of power by the President." What came out of it was a second plebiscite on whether or not Tennessee would join the Confederacy.

It did, by a margin of better than two to one, with East Tennesseans making up most of the forty-seven thousand-plus who voted to stay in the Union. Only briefly did Alma May consider making another attempt to cast a ballot in the plebiscite; in the end, she decided not to repeat the humiliation to which she had been exposed almost six months earlier.

True, while buoyed by the voters' decision, was nevertheless not totally satisfied. "I think it's a disgrace," he told the family members at dinner that night, "that Tennessee is the last to embrace the Confederacy."

On Friday, June 17, 1861, then, with Able Jackson's Nashville Grays militia parading proudly to the Capitol hill, the United States flag was lowered from the Tennessee Capitol Building to be replaced by the rebel emblem of the Confederate States of America.

III

OVER the years, Alma May Dewey had kept a diary, but as a sometime thing. There were vast gaps in it, accounting for the times the Princess had become bored with writing in it. Now, however, with the war a real threat to the well-being of Bon Marché, she took it up again, believing that, in the years ahead, a future steward of the plantation might find some value in what she would put down.

Her first new entry—dated June 18—was a reflective one:

I suppose I should have been moved yesterday when I saw the United States flag lowered from the capitol building. Daddy, I'm certain, would have wept. And who's to say he did not? But I did not—could not. What I felt was only a sense of relief that the issue is closed. Tennessee's commitment is now complete; the Jackson brothers can get on with their crusade. What I feel today is isolation, because my world must now shrink to the confines of these acres. I cannot, as can the males of the family, ride off carrying dreams of adventure and heroics. Isolated, yes, but not without duty. My task is clear: Bon Marché first. Forever! I pray fervently that Tennessee's choice does not, in the day ahead, conflict with the stewardship of my sacred trust.

Just how much Bon Marché and its people would be involved in the Tennessee commitment to the Confederacy was noted in diary entries as the days unwound with dizzying swiftness.

On June 20 she wrote of Able Jackson's Nashville Grays marching out to link up with other volunteer forces pledged to defend Tennessee. What might have been a joyous moment was almost the exact opposite. No bands played and the faces of the new soldiers were somber. Determined. Indeed, it was a strange-looking company of men. Half of them were uniformed as the Nashville Grays, representing those who had been drilling under "General" Able for many months. The others—the new recruits, the farm boys and mechanics and brewery workers and "toughs" of the Nashville taverns—wore what they always wore. But they all brought their own muskets and shotguns; some carried sidearms and some even wore swords, and they tried to march off in some semblance of military cadence to the beat of the drummer boys.

Accompanying the Grays was a new company of cavalry, a hundred strong, put together by True Jackson's sons—Herbert, aged twenty-six, and twenty-one-year-old Victor. All were mounted on Bon Marché thoroughbreds, fine blooded horses bred for racing and now destined for sterner duty. Herbert had been appointed the captain of the company; Victor, a lieutenant. But like the late recruits of the Grays the cavalrymen were not standardly uniformed. Something distinguished them, however; all had been recruited from the many horse farms in the Nashville area and were superb horsemen. They had been born to the saddle.

In all, five great-grandsons of Charles Dewey went off with Able's forces. In addition to Herbert and Victor, the only son of Able and Hope Jackson, twenty-year-old Foster, rode side by side with his father, meant to be his aide-de-camp even though he had been given no special rank. Somewhat surprisingly, there were also two grandsons of the late Corrine Dewey Holder (Charles Dewey's eldest daughter): William Holder III, twenty, and Dewey Holder, nineteen, marching out with the Grays as privates in the ranks.

Alma May recorded:

Able had hoped to be appointed a brigadier general by the governor, but was instead breveted a colonel. True rages that politics denied his brother his rightful rank, but Able—less volatile, these days, it seems—apparently is satisfied. He is most pleased with the commissioning of his nephews, Herbert and Victor. I made certain all the young men directly of Bon Marché were well mounted before leaving, and had servants by their sides, pleasing their mothers. The same offer was made to the Holder boys, but they declined; the Holders still tend to stand off from Bon Marché, as did their grandmother for so many years. My heart goes out to Joy and Hope, who are now being asked to sacrifice so much—their husbands *and* their children. It might have been worse, especially for Joy, if I had not interceded . . .

"I'll not permit it, Drew," the Princess said sternly. "Bon Marché needs you now more than ever—more, certainly, than does the army."

"But there's no racing here anymore," the young man protested, "and there will be little need to engage in much breeding. So what's the point in my staying?"

"Because, no matter what happens, we *must* maintain Bon Marché. The way things are going you'll be the only man we can count on."

Drew Jackson grimaced. "Any *real* man wants to be in the fighting!"

"Any unselfish man," Alma May countered, "will see the need to hold his family's estate together."

"You'll do that," he insisted. "I know that much. And you'll have all the blacks here to—"

"Do you love your mother?" the Princess interrupted.

"Of course."

"Then think of her, if not Bon Marché. Is it right to expect that she should see *all* of her sons go off to the war? Aren't Herbert and Victor enough?"

Drew was angry. "I'm the one who should be the captain of that cavalry unit. I'm the oldest, and twice the horseman Herbert is."

"There'll come a day," Alma May went on quietly, "when

all of the imagined heroics will be ended, when the guns are laid down, and when Bon Marché will be all that remains for those of Dewey blood who fought. While we pray that nothing will befall the others, mustn't we look realistically to the future? Your duty, Drew, is here."

"I suppose." He was not totally convinced. "But Father will still be here."

Alma May permitted herself a slight smile. "True Jackson, if the truth be told, has a mistress—the Confederacy. Do you honestly believe your father is concerned anymore with Bon Marché?"

"No," he admitted.

"Then, who?"

Drew shrugged. "Very well, Aunt Alma, I'll stay. But if the day ever comes when—"

She took the young man in her arms. "You won't be sorry, dear," she said, "that you've made your commitment to Bon Marché."

IV

IT WAS on July Fourth of 1861—an ironic date in that for the first time in Alma May's memory there was no lavish Independence Day observance at Bon Marché—that she noted in her diary: "Albert writes in anguish about Jack and Staunch. He has word now that the boys are en route to Virginia with Hampton's Legion."

30

LEE Dewey was boiling with discontent as he urged his horse to maintain a steady, ground-covering pace through the moonlit darkness of the warm July night. He was traveling along the Little River Turnpike of Northern Virginia, heading west and a little south toward Fairfax Court House. He had hoped to make the trip five days earlier when Brigadier General Irwin McDowell's army had marched out of its encampments at Arlington and Alexandria, bands playing and guidons snapping, to challenge a large body of Confederate troops massing at Manassas, hard by a creek called Bull Run. McDowell had let it be known that he would authorize newspaper correspondents to travel with his headquarters staff, leaving an understanding that prior approval had to come from the War Department. It was there that Lee ran afoul of an overzealous captain.

"I note, Mr. Dewey," the captain had said, "that you're a correspondent for several Southern publications."

"Yes—the Dewey newspapers."

"Your newspapers?"

"No, I'm an employee only," Lee explained. "Just as I'm an employee of the Schimmel Newspapers, which are published in several Northern cities."

"Then your loyalties are divided," the officer suggested.

"Loyalties?" Lee was becoming annoyed. "My loyalty, Captain, is to the truth."

"Northern or Southern truth?"

"I wasn't aware that truth had boundaries." But Dewey realized the bantering with the young officer could lead to no good. "I'm a newspaper correspondent who has worked in Washington for a good number of years. My reputation is well-known to the leaders of this community. If I *must* take this matter directly to the secretary of war, Captain, I won't hesitate to do so."

"Yes, well—" The captain started to write on a paper in front of him. He stopped to look up at Lee. "Do you understand the uniform requirements for newspaper correspondents, Mr. Dewey?"

"What?"

"General McDowell requires that correspondents with his army wear white uniforms."

"For what reason, if I may ask?"

"The general feels white uniforms for correspondents will attest to the purity of their character."

Laughter burst from the newspaperman.

"You find General McDowell's requirements humorous, do you?" the captain asked angrily.

"I mean no disrespect," Lee replied, continuing to chuckle. "It's just that I appreciate the general's sense of humor. You don't believe McDowell is serious about those white uniforms?"

The captain just glared at him.

"My God—you do!"

The officer stood up. "I have other duties, Mr. Dewey. I suggest you come back later."

"When? An hour? Two hours?"

"Tomorrow, perhaps. Or the next day."

"See here—you can't put me off that way!"

The captain picked up a dispatch case from his desk, spun on his heel, and left Dewey standing alone in the office.

Now, after being delayed for the better part of a week— after McDowell's men had already been engaged in several minor skirmishes in Virginia; minor, though blood had been spilled—Lee Dewey had an official-looking paper in his jacket pocket and was on his way to the general's headquarters, wherever they might be. He wore no white uniform, but rather a serviceable wardrobe he might have worn while deerhunting. He knew, after having covered the Mexican War, that one dressed on the battlefield as if all of life was a camping-out experience. But not in uniform, white or otherwise.

It wasn't the uniform matter that bothered him now, nor even the captain's question about his "divided loyalties," but his anger grew with each mile covered as he became more and more aware of the sheer idiocy of his having wasted days wrangling over permission to be with McDowell's army. For traveling on the turnpike with him were hundreds of civilians: ladies and gentlemen in fancy carriages, rigs with beautifully groomed matched pairs of high-stepping horses; and farm wagons drawn by sturdier equine stock and carrying whole families—fathers, mothers, children, no doubt aunts and uncles and cousins, too. And they had no War Department sanction to be there, nor had they sought any. They knew of the McDowell departure—it was hardly a secret in Washington—and now, Sunday dawning and relieved of their jobs and chores for a few hours, they were all rushing into Virginia to see the fun, to unpack picnic lunches, and be witness to a quick end to the war, to see the Southern rebels routed, and to carry the glorious memory of it through the years ahead to their grandchildren.

Just how prevalent was that belief was made clear to Lee when he stopped at Padgett's Tavern along the way to rest his horse and perhaps drink an ale. The tavern was crowded and the Virginia proprietor was gleefully serving the patrons he had never expected to have. The newspaperman recognized a New England congressman in the press of people and approached him.

"Well, Dewey," the politician shouted over the din, "you're going to have quite a tale to write, eh?"

"I'm astounded, sir, that . . . so many believe a battle is such . . . entertainment."

"And so it shall be, my friend. The rebels have brought this melodrama on themselves, but it's McDowell who'll fashion the denouement, making quick work of their treason, believe me!"

"It may not be that simple."

"The rebs don't have an army," the congressman insisted. "They're little more than a gathering of rabble."

Dewey's scowling face reflected his doubt.

"I don't believe you know my wife, Dewey." He turned to the pretty, smiling blond woman by his side. "Evelyn, darling, this is Mr. Lee Dewey, a newspaper correspondent."

"Oh, isn't that exciting," she gushed. "Have you ever seen a war before, Mr. Dewey?"

"I have—in Mexico."

"But this one isn't going to be . . . uh . . . as trying, is it? I mean, those backward Southerners can't be expected to—"

Dewey, having heard all he wanted to hear, interrupted. "Ma'am, you should know that I was born in Virginia and grew up in Tennessee."

"Oh!" Her hand fluttered to her mouth as she recoiled from him. "Then you're . . . you're—"

"An American," Lee snapped, turning and pushing his way out of the tavern.

Now, an hour later, after pausing briefly at Fairfax Court House to learn that McDowell had established his headquarters in the little village of Centreville, Dewey was on Warrenton Turnpike, sharing space on the road not only with the civilians from Washington but with part of McDowell's supply train as well.

He came upon a group of those supply wagons, perhaps a dozen of them, pulled off the road and parked in a field, the six-mule teams standing stolidly in their full harness and the teamsters gathered around a small fire, passing bottles of whiskey. Their drunkenness was quite evident.

Dewey recalled the congressman's remark about the Confederates being a "gathering of rabble," and wondered whether the truth was that both armies had their ample share of rabble. McDowell's army was made up largely of ninety-day recruits, toughs from the city streets and farm boys seeking a lark and even that shadowy criminal element of society seizing an opportunity to kill and be applauded for it, some in training only a few weeks, some only days in uniform, not even long enough to learn their facings. What will happen, he mused, when some officer commands "Right wheel!" and his troops, under fire, turn in confusion in all directions? Was this motley army being sent into battle too soon because Lincoln had been forced into hasty action by the almost daily cries of the Northern newspapers: *On to Richmond! On to Richmond! On to Richmond!*

The problem was that the way to Richmond, the acknowledged heart of the Confederacy, was blocked by a rebel army firmly in place at Manassas Junction, and commanded by the flamboyant Brigadier General Pierre Gustave Toutant Beauregard, the hero of Fort Sumter. Ironically, McDowell and Beauregard had been classmates at West Point—class of 1838—and both had served honorably in the Mexican War. Now they followed different flags.

Dewey wondered, too, whether McDowell faced battle without a key ingredient in any general's arsenal—the element of surprise. Certainly, there was no secrecy left in McDowell's movements. Lee presumed agents for Beauregard rushed to Manassas with the news when the first of McDowell's army left the encampments. Maybe even before they moved. But even if Beauregard had no spies in the national capital—an unlikely development in that Washington was basically a community of Southern sympathizers—then, unquestionably, once the Federal army was fully on the road any number of Virginians along the way would have served as informants for the Confederate general. Sadly, even spies and Southern patriots weren't necessary; the general public *knew,* attested by the hundreds who hurried along the road to be spectators.

Another thought startled Dewey. General Irvin McDowell and his men were enemy invaders of Virginia on this Sunday morning.

Enemy? Invaders?

The words were strangely foreign to Lee. For the first time the full impact of what was about to happen came clear to him. He was to witness one American army in deadly combat with another American army. It brought pain to him behind his eyes; real, stabbing pain.

His heel kicked his mount into a faster pace. Centreville lay dead ahead in the early light of dawn. To his ears came the unmistakable distant sound of gunfire. *The skirmishers are out,* he thought.

II

JACKSON Dewey stretched his cramped legs, the muscles protesting as he did, trying to find a comfortable position on the makeshift straw bed on the hard board floor of the railroad car. It had been almost thirty hours since the train had left Richmond, heading northward in the general direction of

Washington City. There had been little sleep as the train crawled along, alternately stopping and starting with great jerks. Word was that their destination was a place in northern Virginia called Manassas Junction, some twenty scant miles west of Washington, where they'd link up with a greater army under Beauregard. The pain in his legs caused him to moan slightly.

"Not sleeping?" a voice next to him in the darkness whispered.

Jack chuckled lightly. "Hell, no. And you?"

"Don't think I slept at all," his younger brother, Staunch, answered. "Or maybe I did. I don't know whether I've been dreaming or my mind's running away with me, but I've been seeing pictures of Lexington. And Father."

"Hmmm."

"Do you think we'll ever see Father again?"

"Of course we will."

"Will he ever forgive us for running away?" There was a hint of a tear in the question.

Jack reached over to touch his brother's arm. "Don't go soft on me now, Staunch. In the end, Father's going to be proud of us. Just wait, you'll see."

The young men, Jackson not yet eighteen and Staunch just turned sixteen, were members of Hampton's Legion, an elite infantry corps of six hundred trained and financed by wealthy South Carolina planter Wade Hampton, scion of one of America's first families. His grandfather, the first Wade Hampton in the dynasty, had been a captain in the Revolutionary War and a brigadier general in the War of 1812. The Dewey boys, having heard Hampton's name mentioned frequently in the horse-racing stories told by their father, sought him out in Charleston after leaving Bon Marché Lexington, and Hampton, recalling the Dewey name fondly with some racing stories of his own, made a place for them in his Legion—as infantry privates. They were grateful for that; grateful, too, that Hampton had not asked whether they had their father's permission to leave Lexington. Jack and Staunch had been in training for a month before they realized they were going to be paid for their adventure; eleven dollars a month in the new Confederate money.

The train shuddered to another stop. There were the

sounds of the venting of steam and a loud blast of the engine's high-pitched whistle. Suddenly, the door of the boxcar was rolled back, letting in the early morning light.

"This is it, boys!" a sergeant roared. "Manassas Station, Virginia! Fall out for company inspection!"

The Deweys' car, and the others of the train, emptied quickly, Jack and Staunch double-timing to the ranks of B company (there were six companies in the Legion), pulling on their knapsacks. Colonel Hampton sat astride his gleaming chestnut thoroughbred gelding, ramrod straight, watching his Legion assemble. He was an imposing figure; a decidedly handsome man, with clear, deep-set eyes capable of boring through any miscreant in the ranks. He wore a full black beard, his hair was long over the ears, and both beard and hair were attractively curly. There was a studied arrogance about him; there was no doubt that he was a man accustomed to leadership.

By his side was his second-in-command, Lieutenant Colonel B.J. Johnson, also mounted on a blooded horse—a large mare of dark bay color with nearly matched white stockings. With them was a third officer of the rank of brigadier general. Whispered questions about him coursed through the Legion: "Who is he?" "Is it Beauregard?" Some insisted it *was* the commanding general; others thought that unlikely. Whoever it was, and it was never revealed to the men of the Legion, there was a brief conversation with Hampton and Johnson and the general rode off hurriedly.

Immediate commands to move forward were given. The Legion was headed toward the persistent sound of the rattle of musket fire, punctuated by the heavier thumps of artillery. Hampton's Legion, just minutes off the train, was being thrown into the fighting.

"It must be going badly if we're being used right away," Staunch said nervously.

Jack laughed, partly to reassure his brother and partly to calm his own fears. "Or the opposite," he suggested. "Beauregard's probably got the Feds on the run and we're just being asked to mop up." But he didn't believe it.

III

THE day had grown oppressively hot. Quickly so, once the early morning mists had burned away. And the roads were tinder-dry. As Lee Dewey approached Centreville he could see a cloud of dust suggesting troop movements. It didn't surprise him that there would be such activity because the noise of the fighting had grown louder as he came closer to McDowell's headquarters. What did dumbfound him, when he came abreast of the troops, was that they were moving *away* from the battle. A large force it was, perhaps of regimental strength, and not marching in any military cadence. It was just straggling along, in twos and threes, the men laughing and chattering.

The correspondent stopped one of the officers, a major, seemingly as unconcerned as were his men. "What unit is this?" Lee asked.

"The Fourth Pennsylvania."

"But the fighting seems to be behind you, sir."

"Well, I reckon it is," the officer shrugged. "You see, mister, we're going home because the men's time's up. We've had three months of this kind of work, and that's quite enough of it."

The major touched a hand to his cap in a ragged salute and moved on.

In only a few minutes the bewildered Dewey was in Centreville. It wasn't much; just a few frame houses and one stone church, which Lee recognized was being used as a makeshift hospital. The military had overwhelmed the village. Supply wagons were everywhere. And uniformed men— mostly officers—were scurrying about importantly. He made his way to McDowell's tented headquarters, showing his official permission to be there to a major seated behind a field desk on which numerous maps were piled. The officer nodded approval of the permission paper and handed it back.

"I just passed a unit identified to me as the Fourth Pennsylvania," Dewey said, "and was told they're retiring."

"Those bastards!" the major snapped. "The general pleaded with them last night to stay, but they wouldn't. And the worst of it is that we've got other ninety-dayers who are also coming up to their final days, some of them in the next twenty-four hours. God knows how many will desert us."

Lee asked for, and was given, a briefing on the military situation of the moment. The officer, using one of the large maps, pointed out the known disposition of the Confederate defenders. "Generally speaking," the major said, "the enemy is arrayed along the western side of Bull Run"—Dewey noted how twisting the creek was—"and in superior strength, most likely. We know now that Joe Johnston's army escaped the Shenandoah and have been arriving on the Alexandria and Orange Railroad. We know, too, that Hampton's Legion arrived this morning from Richmond, also in cars. So what was bad enough yesterday with Beauregard, is worse today."

"The strong points?" Dewey wanted to know.

"Here at the Stone Bridge at the Warrenton Turnpike," the major replied, stabbing at a point on the map. "General McDowell, though, hopes to flank that position by using one or more of the numerous fords on Bull Run." He indicated another position on the map. "At last report, the general is approximately here, personally rallying the men. But the rebels fight desperately. That's not to say, you understand," he hurried on, "that there's any doubt in the Federal ranks about the ultimate victory."

"I understand." But Lee had caught a nuance of doubt in the major's words. He continued to study the map. "An observation point, Major?"

For the first time the officer smiled. "If you don't mind company, Dewey, here at Cub Run, running roughly parallel to Bull Run, there's an elevated pasture. You have a glass?"

"I do."

"Then you ought to be able to command a view of Bull Run at some distance on either side of the stone bridge. But, as I suggested, you won't be alone. The hillside is crowded with those damned civilians—"

"Yes, I met many of them on the road from Washington."

"—including more than a few of our illustrious members of Congress." His sarcasm was evident. "One of them was in here an hour ago, waving around a pistol as a testimony to his manhood, demanding to be taken on a tour of the battlefield. I sent him off with an orderly who had orders to lose him somewhere." The major laughed then.

Dewey thanked him and rode off. It was only a few minutes at a steady trot before he came upon a wooden bridge on the turnpike built over Cub Run. He turned off the road and made his way up the hillside to the pasture the officer had recommended. He hadn't been lied to; there were all the carriages and the ladies in the summer finery and the officious-looking men and more than a few Union army officers, who had somehow escaped their duty to serve as charming guides to the assembled throng. Picnic meals were arrayed on linen cloths on the ground. The newspaperman made his way around the crowd to seek out a more private vantage point. Once it was achieved, he dismounted, tied his horse to a sapling, and propped himself against a tree to being a sketch of the scene before him.

Alternately consulting his glass and drawing on his sketch pad Dewey was meticulously bringing the scene to life with his charcoal. Bull Run meandered wildly across the landscape; at most places it was impassable, even though it wasn't a wide stream, because of its steep, rocky banks. But there were numerous fords cut across it, and there was the stone bridge on the turnpike.

He spent some time studying that bridge. The Confederates had made it difficult there for any invader. An abatis had been thrown up across the bridge on the western side, the sharpened ends of fallen trees pointed like giant daggers at any advancing foe. A battery of artillery guns were in position on the turnpike just to the rear of the abatis. Behind the battery were troops along both sides of the road. Dewey guessed several companies were involved there. For the first time he understood why McDowell had decided it best to turn Beauregard's flank; a frontal assault on the stone bridge would have been suicidal.

Another important distinguishing aspect of the terrain were the heavy woods seen on all sides of the bridge. There were some open pastures, with a few houses on the upper slopes of them, but mostly the landscape was wooded—dense enough woods to hide an army, or at least a sizable portion of one. They would have to come into play, he reasoned, as the battle progressed.

He cursed under his breath. While the high pasture was a good vantage point it was far enough removed from the fighting to make identification of specific units impossible. Also, his late arrival denied him knowledge of what units were actually being employed by the Federal army. Thus, what he saw—and what the civilian spectators saw—were armies of ants maneuvering across what open spaces there were. What movements there were in the covering woods he could not know. He realized soon enough that even uniform colors were of little value. For some time he watched a gray-clad unit move forward against an artillery battery, thinking it was a Confederate unit advancing. Then a slight breeze unfurled the flag carried at the head of the advance and it was an American flag. No doubt it was a state militia unit of some kind, uniformed in gray by the state government that financed it. Worse, some groups weren't uniformed at all, wearing only homespun. But Southern homespun or Northern homespun? He couldn't tell. Lee's ignorance angered him.

Even the sounds of the battle were of no help. Union muskets sounded the same as Confederate muskets. There were different sounds to the artillery, but those differences depended on the caliber of the weapons and not their origin.

"You draw nicely," a feminine voice said.

Startled, Dewey whirled around to find a young woman, her long hair wound in ribboned braids around her head. She was a beautiful woman, who had been looking over his shoulder. For how long he didn't know; his concentration had been on the scene before him.

"Are you a newspaperman?" she asked.

"I am."

"Then perhaps you can tell me what's happening out there." She pointed in the direction of Bull Run.

"I don't know."

"You're a tease, sir." She giggled delightfully.

"No, really, I don't know. I see what you see."

"And that's not much."

"True."

Boldly, she dropped down beside him. "If you don't mind, I'll stay with you for a time. I've had a captain as a guide for more than an hour and I'm tired of his lies. He makes great tales about those tiny figures moving about, but I know he's not honest. I fear he merely wants to . . . well, ingratiate himself with me. Some men are like that, you know."

Dewey chuckled. "So I've heard."

"But you, sir, I perceive as being honest."

He wanted to be rid of her. "Thank you—I try to be honest always. And being as honest as I can be now, I wish you'd go away. I have no time to . . . entertain a lady."

She stayed sitting on the ground next to him. "I'll be quiet," she said sweetly.

Lee sighed. "As you wish." He turned away from her, concentrating on his sketching again, consulting his glass from time to time as he tried to make sense of what was happening before him. *This is sheer insanity,* he thought.

IV

STAUNCH Dewey, near exhaustion, could not stop the muscles of his arms from quivering. He tried to raise his musket to fire again, blindly, at an enemy he had difficulty seeing, but the shaking arms would not permit him to point it properly. He was hot, even feverish, after many hours in the boiling July sun; his eyes burned terribly from the smoke of the black powder that seemed to cover the men of Hampton's Legion like a shroud. He was filthy, his nostrils picking up the scent of his own stink. Twice he had urinated in his pants, denied the opportunity for a proper method of relief. He had long since discarded his uniform jacket; his knapsack, in which his daily rations had been packed, had been dropped somewhere—where he did not know. His canteen, too, had been discarded; empty, it was useless baggage. And now his mouth was parched, his lips painfully cracked. He had his gun, a rapidly diminishing supply of powder, and only a few balls of lead. And he had his terror.

The Legion was pinned down near a farm house on a small knoll, under heavy fire from musketry and devastatingly accurate artillery fire. The soldiers had heard that the owner of the house, a widow named Henry, was bedridden in the building. If so, then she must be dead by now because the Federal battery a hundred and fifty yards in front of them was reducing the house to rubble.

They had been in action all day, marching and countermarching (in circles, it seemed) without respite, never out of the reach of danger. The Legion's second in command, Lieutenant Colonel B. J. Johnson had been killed; one moment he was grandly astride his horse urging the Legionnaires forward, and the next moment his body was crumpled on the ground. There had been nothing heroic about it, no brave last words from a dying commander. He was just . . . dead.

Now, it seemed certain to Staunch, they would all be dead. The artillery fire continued to crash about them. Once more the lad raised his musket, wanting to return fire. But his arms trembled so violently such an act was impossible. He dropped the weapon with a loud moan; more of a scream, really, than a moan.

"Staunch, are you hit?" his brother Jack yelled at him over the noise of the battle.

There was no reply. Staunch had wrapped himself into a disconsolate ball, weeping profusely, the salty tears further enflaming his eyes.

Jack dropped to his knees, cradling Staunch in his arms, frightened by the extent of his shaking. "It's going to be all right," the brother assured him. "The Legion's intact. There's no Union army that can beat us!"

As Jack held his brother, rocking him gently, continuing to whisper reassurances in his ear, the trembling diminished and then stopped finally.

Staunch was sheepish about his loss of control. "It was the heat," he said. "I don't know . . . it just seemed that the heat—"

Jack picked up his brother's musket, handing it to him. "We still have work to do."

To the right of them they could see the mounted Colonel Hampton waving his sword, seeming to be urging his men forward. Very quickly the word was passed by the sergeants through the ranks of the Legion.

"We're going to attack that battery and put it out!"

Hampton rode forward and, as one, the Legionnaires rose with a mighty yell and followed him. One yard they advanced, two, five, ten, fifteen—pouring musket fire into the Federal battery. Stopping momentarily to reload and advancing again.

Suddenly, Hampton's horse veered off its course and the colonel was slumped slightly in the saddle, unable to rein his mount.

"Hampton's hit!" the cry went up.

"Oh, God," Staunch Dewey shouted, "we're all going to be killed!"

Jack grabbed his arm, squeezing it tightly. "Not today, brother, not today." And he moved ahead, tugging Staunch with him.

V

It was late afternoon, about four o'clock, and Lee Dewey's meticulous observation of the battle from the raised pasture along Cub Run had enabled him to sort out the ebb and flow of the fighting. He was still unsure about the actual units, not being close enough to identify them, but his glass told him a pattern had been established. It seemed certain that McDowell's army, given its vastly superior artillery power, was inexorably gaining the upper hand.

Lee didn't know it, of course, but the Union general was of the same mind in the early afternoon. He had telegraphed to Washington a message suggesting the enemy was being routed.

That's the way it had looked earlier to the newspaper correspondent and he had passed that intelligence on to his constant female companion. He had learned her name; it was Mary Ellen Edgett, and she had come there with her aunt and uncle from their Maryland home. And during the long hours she had brought him cool spring water and tidbits from the picnic lunches spread on the hill by the civilian observers. When Dewey said to her, "McDowell seems to be in charge," she had spread the happy news to the ladies and gentlemen on the hill, causing a huge cheer to go up from the assembly.

Now, however, Lee was seeing something else. It seemed to him the Confederate forces were being reinforced. He wrote on his note pad: *From the railroad at Manassas?* In his glass he began to see what appeared to be stragglers from McDowell's forces recrossing Bull Run in no particular order, moving away from the fighting. The big artillery battery he had watched for several hours battering the Confederates had now gone silent. Refocusing the glass, he could see gray-clad men laboriously turning the cannon around and then he saw them fired again, this time into the backs of fleeing Union units. *Is that an isolated incident?* he asked himself.

Slowly, starting at the northern end of the battlefield and moving his glass southward, he surveyed the entire scene. When he came to the Warrentown Turnpike again, he raised his glass to take in the ground he knew still to be controlled by the Confederates and saw a large cavalry unit charge out of the woods and fall upon perhaps several companies of McDowell's army, scattering them in all directions.

He began to see supply wagons and ambulances and caissons, all with Federal markings, moving eastward (toward Washington, in other words) heading for the stone bridge crossing Bull Run. To his right, he could see infantry units moving out of the heavy woods to attack the remnants of the Union companies routed moments earlier by the cavalry attack.

"Miss Edgett," he said sternly, "I want to suggest to you that you and your aunt and uncle start to make your way toward Washington."

"Why?" She seemed unconcerned.

"Because—and I don't wish to panic you—the tide seems to be turning. The Confederates have counter-attacked and the battle is moving this way."

Her eyes opened wide. "This way?!"

The woman's doubt angered him. "Leave right now," he ordered, "before it's too late!"

His ire moved her and she raced away. Within moments the civilians on the elevated pasture were saddling their horses and harnessing their teams to get away.

Dewey turned his attention to the two bridges carrying the turnpike over Bull Run (the stone one in the distance) and Cub Run (nearest him). The Cub Run bridge was wooden and somewhat damaged by the heavy wagons that had trundled over it for nearly a week. As he watched—and it was close enough that he didn't need the glass—a wildly-whipping teamster raced onto the bridge with a supply wagon. One of its wheels broke through the wooden flooring, toppling the wagon over on its side, effectively blocking the way for all who followed.

It was a terrible scene. Other wagons piled up behind the blocking one; wagons and ambulances and caissons. Infantrymen on foot simply forded the slow-running creek at the bridge, as teamsters cut their horses lose from the harness and rode them bareback, racing away from the advancing Confederates.

Dewey heard a heavy thump of artillery and saw a shell land in the middle of the scramble on the Cub Run bridge. The panic became a general thing. Civilian carriages fleeing from the pasture hill on which Lee stood now mingled with wagons and caissons of the army, each impeding the other.

He took a quick sweep of the scene with his glass. There was no doubt any longer; it wasn't a Federal retreat, but a *rout* with all of its attendant madness. Lee rolled up his sketches and put them into his saddlebag. And then he mounted his horse, kicked it into action, moving parallel with the Warrenton Turnpike, but staying off it. He wondered whether Mary Ellen Edgett had got away safely.

Even though it looks impossible now, Dewey told himself, McDowell will likely try to hold at Centreville. And, if not there, certainly at Fairfax Court House.

VI

AN hour earlier, perhaps more than that, Jack and Staunch Dewey had wondered whether they would have the strength or the will to move forward against the artillery battery on the pasture knoll. But they had, and they had taken it, swinging it around and using it on the fleeing Federals.

Maybe that was the turning point of the battle. Or one of the turning points. Whatever the reason, the Union army was running and Hampton's Legion, under another command in light of the wounding of their colonel, was sweeping along the Warrenton Turnpike pursuing the enemy. Fatigue had melted away; victory was their stimulant.

Someone shouted: "On to Washington!" And the cry swept up and down the ranks of the Legion.

Wrecked wagons and abandoned supplies and dead bodies were commonplace along the road.

"Look at that," Staunch said, pointing to perhaps a dozen bodies of Federal zouaves, their gaudy uniforms dirtied by the realities of war, scattered along the side of the road. Laughing, the young man ran to one of them and snatched a cap from one of the bodies, holding it high like a trophy.

A shot rang out and Staunch crumpled with a scream.

Jack raced toward him and there was another shot. For just a second, the elder Dewey brother was frozen in mid-step. Then he fell in the heavy dust of the road, a hole in his forehead oozing scarlet gelatin.

"Jack!" Staunch, a wounded left leg rewarding him with excruciating pain, crawled to his brother's side. "Jack, speak to me!" He could not. Would not—ever. Staunch fell across him, the last measure of any emotional control gone.

He was not conscious of a brief firefight that ensued between some of the Legionnaires and three zouaves who had been in ambush in the woods along the turnpike. And he was barely aware of being picked up and placed beside his brother's body in the stubbly grass along the road.

"Just leave them there," an authoritarian voice said, "and an ambulance will soon pick them up."

VII

THERE had been no stand of the Federal army at Centreville or Fairfax Court House or anywhere else along the road into Washington. The rout of McDowell's army had been complete; the new Confederacy had won the first major battle of war between neighbors.

Heavy rain had begun to fall as Lee Dewey, more tired than he could ever remember, rode across Long Bridge into the capital city. Every foot of the way back to Washington had seen the signs of the defeat: soldiers without units (and not seeking to find them, either), abandoned supplies, broken wagons, even ambulances, their horses stolen, inside of which lay wounded men, discarded as certainly as thousands of muskets had been.

Now, on the streets of Washington, in the early morning darkness, there were more men of McDowell's scraggling army, some walking the muddy streets aimlessly, some trying to sleep in doorways, but all giving ample testimony to the extent of the defeat at Bull Run. Lee put up his horse at the livery stable and entered the Willard Hotel, where he lived. The lobby and bar were crowded with Federal soldiers, mostly officers, all talking loudly and all offering excuses for the defeat. Lee ignored them and wearily mounted the stairs to his second-floor room. As he approached the door, he saw someone huddled against it in the dark shadows.

"I've been waiting for you, Lee," a voice said. "I need a bed."

"Ben Turner, my God . . . where did you come from?" The man at the door was an artillery captain he knew; a capable and experienced professional soldier, hardly one he expected to see had fled the battlefield.

"I came from Virginia, where all those others downstairs came from."

"But your command?"

"Gone." There was a wry smile. "Totally gone. The guns in the rebs' hands, the men"—he shrugged sadly, sighing—"well, they just ran away. And when I realized McDowell wasn't going to make a stand anywhere short of Washington, I came here, too. And I thought of my old friend, Lee Dewey, and the soft bed he had in the Willard—"

"You're welcome to share it, of course." Lee unlocked the door, gesturing the officer inside.

"What I can't understand," the newspaperman said as he lit an oil lamp, "is that no one seems concerned about an attack on Washington."

"There'll be no direct assault on Washington," the captain said. "Not at this time anyway. The truth is, Lee, we were inflicting major damage on the rebs. Had the battle in hand, I thought."

"That was my impression, too, from my vantage point—even though somewhat removed. So, what happened?"

"The volunteers happened," Turner said as he wearily pulled off his boots. "The yahoos who have been crying for war for several years now. The patriotic civilian soldier, the tavern hero—" He stopped suddenly. "Oh, hell! What's the use? We didn't have an army in Virginia; we just had a collection of ninety-day soldiers out on a lark. I'll wager, Lee, that half of McDowell's army—maybe twelve or fifteen thousand—had entirely lost their regimental organizations. And when that happens, you don't have an army, but a mob."

"Could the Confederate forces have been any different?"

"Probably not," the artillery captain admitted. "We can't suppose that the enemy troops had attained any higher degree of discipline than our own, but they acted on the defensive—an easier position for an untrained army. Also, they were defending their . . . homeland, so to speak, giving them a more compelling reason to fight."

"What now, Ben?"

Having undressed, Captain Turner placed himself on one side of the big bed. "Maybe there will be a full-scale war. Or maybe the debacle of Bull Run will bring everyone to their senses and we'll find another way out of our difficulties. But if there is to be general war—if that's what Lincoln believes must be—then the idea of a volunteer army will have to be discarded. There will have to be conscription, as painful as that may be to the populace." He sighed deeply. "We will have to try to develop an army of . . . well, call them 'old soldiers.'"

Dewey nodded, taking notes on the conversation.

"You see, an old soldier—and I mean one properly trained, if not one old in years—gets to feel safe in the ranks, and unsafe out of the ranks. The greater the danger, then, the more . . . uh . . . pertinaciously he clings to his place in the ranks. The volunteer of three months never attains this instinct of discipline. Under danger, and even merely under excitement, he flies from his ranks, looking for safety in dispersion. And that's what happened today. And that's what will happen in the next battle, if there is to be one, unless we construct an army of old soldiers."

"You make a good point," the correspondent said.

Turner laughed wryly. "Perhaps. But remember, my friend, these are the views of a mere artillery captain, often of little consequence in the councils of war."

"I suppose. Try to get some sleep, Ben. I have dispatches to write for my newspapers before I can do the same."

VIII

STAUNCH Dewey came to consciousness slowly, his brain befogged with the heavy dose of morphine a Confederate surgeon had given him. Behind his closed eyes there was a montage of blurred pictures; of unreality. He began to remember pain, although there was none now. And then there was the sharp report of a rifle, followed by a terrible scene of his brother falling to the ground.

"Jack!" he screamed, trying to sit up.

"There, there, son, everything is all right now," a voice said to him. Strong hands were on his shoulder to prevent his movement.

Staunch's eyes opened. An older man stood over him, the white apron he wore smeared with blood. Daylight flooded through a small window and a small chorus of moans demanded his attention. He turned his head to see men stretched out in a long row, lying on blankets as he was, in a small room that had once been a sitting room.

"Where am I?" he asked the man with the bloody apron.

"In a house at Manassas Junction. You've been wounded."

"And where's Jack?"

"Jack?"

"My brother, Jack . . . where is he?"

"Son, I'm not sure." The voice was kind. "You were brought in here with another young man who was . . . already dead. But I don't know who he was."

The fog lifted entirely. The pain of remembering returned. "Jack . . . he was . . . he came to my aid when I was shot and he—" He began to cry. "Where is he now?"

The surgeon shrugged. Not with unconcern, but with the futility he felt. "The men have had to bury so many of our brave boys. I'm sorry, son, but . . ."

Staunch wailed in his grief. The surgeon moved away to attend to others in the low row, eventually returning to where the young man was struggling to control his weeping.

"Son, I'm sure you want to know that your wound, while serious, was not beyond repair. Just as soon as we can, we'll move you to Richmond where you can begin your . . . recovery."

The patient wiped tears from his cheeks. "Wounded how?"

"A musket ball shattered the left femur, the thighbone, that long bone between the knee and the hip, and . . ." He paused. "And we could not undertake the normal repair of a broken leg. We've . . . uh . . . had to amputate the leg."

The doctor stopped Staunch from looking under the covers.

"But I can still feel it!" the boy insisted, disbelieving what he had been told.

"Yes, I know. The mind—a strange and wonderful thing—hasn't come to terms yet with the . . . loss of the limb."

"Oh, God," Staunch moaned.

"But you're alive, son," the man said, trying to be cheerful. "And after a few weeks of good care in Richmond you'll be able to go home."

Home? Young Dewey could not believe he would be welcomed home. Especially now. Especially as a surviving cripple returning alone without his brother, Jack. His stiff-necked father would never be able to accept that.

31

EPOCH IN THE HISTORY OF LIBERTY! the *Nashville Monitor* trumpeted after Bull Run. Statler Dewey, greatly displeased with the somber, discursive dispatches of his uncle-correspondent Lee Dewey, preferred to reprint in full, and in larger type than normal, the congratulatory public message written to the "soldiers of the Confederate States" by victorious generals Joe Johnston and Pierre Beauregard. And while the message carried both names no one doubted the rhetoric was that of the flamboyant Beauregard.

He set the scene dramatically:

One week ago a countless host of men, organized into an army, with all the appointments which modern art and practical skill could devise, invaded the soil of Virginia. Their people sounded their approach with displays of anticipated victory. Their generals came in almost royal state; their great ministers, senators, and women came to witness the immolation of our army and the subjugation of our people, and to celebrate the result with wild revelry.

It is with the profoundest emotions of gratitude to an overruling God, whose hand is manifest in protecting our homes and our liberties, that we, your generals commanding, are enabled, in the name of the whole country, to thank you for that patriotic courage, that heroic gallantry, that devoted daring . . . by which the hosts of the enemy were scattered and a signal and glorious victory obtained . . .

[The] sustained and continued effort of your patriotism against the constantly-recurring columns of an
enemy fully treble your numbers . . .

Statler, in his role as editor, had some trouble with that
claim. Lee Dewey, in his dispatches, put the Union effective
forces at Bull Run at some 28,000, opposing a Confederate
army of 32,000. Nowhere was there any suggestion in the correspondent's stories that McDowell outnumbered Beauregard
and Johnston by a margin of three-to-one. Statler solved the
discrepancies by simply discarding Lee's reports, believing the
greater authority of General Beauregard.

. . . fully treble your numbers was crowned on the evening of the 21st with a victory so complete that the invaders were driven disgracefully from the field and made
to fly in disorderly rout . . . Soldiers . . . you have created an epoch in the history of liberty, and unborn na-
tions will call you blessed. Continue this noble devotion,
looking always to the protection of a just God, and before the time grows much older we will be hailed as the
deliverers of a nation of ten millions of people.

Only momentarily did Statler Dewey wrestle with the grim
realities of his uncle's dispatches. He could not, would not,
believe Lee's eyewitness appraisal of the battle of Bull Run.
In Statler's view, Lee had removed from his stories all heroics, all patriotism, and all emotion save despair. That was not
what Statler perceived about the Southern victory; Beauregard's words served the "cause" better.

The editor crumpled Lee's telegraphed dispatches into a
ball and tossed them into the trash bin.

II

STATLER Dewey's naive euphoria was not shared by all in
Nashville. Nor at Bon Marché. Alma May, for one, was
acutely aware that the economy of the plantation, with racing
suspended and stallion bookings nearly nonexistent, was already damaged by the regional fighting. Then, too, she was
privy to the activities of True Jackson, who was now working
day and night to prepare the Confederacy for a greater war.
He was spending large sums to set up a complex network of

spies in the areas surrounding Tennessee—to Kentucky and Ohio and Missouri. And he was urging the governor to fortify Nashville in light of the intelligence that Union forces, under a newly-appointed brigadier general named Grant, was considering a plan to strike into the western Confederacy along the Tennessee River.

Slowly and inexorably the schism between North and South widened. A month after Bull Run there was a lesser battle in Missouri, at a place called Wilson's Creek, in which the Federal troops were again badly mauled. Resolve stiffened in Washington. By November, the old Union army was being reorganized by a brilliant young man, only thirty-four, who was returning to the military after having been president of the Ohio and Mississippi Railroad. General in Chief George B. McClellan was a symbol of the Union's determination to fight. Bull Run was not to be an end, as Statler Dewey concluded, but a beginning.

Fortification of Nashville began and once more there was an impact on Bon Marché. A call went out for all slave-holders in the Nashville region to contribute the labor of their blacks to building forts on the rivers stabbing like a dagger toward the heart of the city. One, on the Tennessee, was to be called Fort Henry; another, closer to Nashville on the Cumberland, was designated as Fort Donelson. Alma May had no choice but to make the Bon Marché slaves available. To look after their well-being, however, and to make certain they would be returned to the plantation, she put Drew Jackson in charge of their labors for the state, effectively removing him from the plantation.

Thus, Bon Marché became largely a feminine place. True Jackson was rarely there; his brother, Colonel Able Jackson, was with the growing Confederate army, as were the Princess's grandnephews, Herbert, Victor, and Foster; Drew was building forts; and Statler was preoccupied with his newspapers (anyway, he had never been regarded as being of Bon Marché, the Statler Deweys preferring to isolate themselves at the adjoining Beau Monde mansion). What was left at Bon Marché, then, were women: Joy Jackson and her daughter, Honore; Hope Jackson and her unmarried daughters, Ruth, Mercy, and Dolley; Alma May herself, and her ailing, sixty-nine-year-old half-sister, Louise Dewey Schimmel. There had been a time when the families had taken dinner separately, but now the women drew together. Eight of them joined in their mutual sorrows.

A dinner gathering as November of 1861 drew to a close mirrored the quiet despair of the group.

"I have a letter from Albert," the Princess announced.

"What news is there of Jack and Staunch?" Louise asked.

"Strangely, he doesn't even mention them until the final sentences. Most of the letter is of his efforts to keep Kentucky neutral in the fighting and the farm there secure. But at the end he writes"—The Princess looked down at the letter—"'There is no word at all of the boys. We know only that they were with Hampton at one time and we can assume they might have been at Manassas. Wherever they are now they haven't chosen to inform us.'"

Joy spoke. "Well, if there had been some . . . uh . . . some trouble, Albert certainly would have been notified by now by the authorities. In this case, then, no news may be the best news."

"I suppose," Alma May sighed.

"Is it possible, do you think," Hope interjected, "that they might have been badly wounded and simply *can't* communicate? I mean, I've heard of people so badly hurt . . . uh . . . that they lose their faculties."

"Anything's possible," the Princess replied. "I prefer to believe that they're well and just don't realize, in their youth, how much unhappiness their silence is bringing to their family."

III

STAUNCH Dewey sat in a rocking chair, a shawl covering his shoulders, a book of poetry ignored on his lap, staring out of the window of the warm, comfortable Petersburg, Virginia, house where he had been taken to recuperate. A family named Williams had taken him in after he had been brought from Manassas, had fed him and cared for him.

He watched now as the Williams's daughter, Sylvia—a pretty, plumpish girl of his own age—came up the walk on the right arm of Lieutenant Jason Mills; the sleeve of the left arm of his uniform was empty, just as was the left pant leg of young Dewey. But Sylvia and Mills were laughing gaily as they came up on the porch of the house.

Staunch heard them coming in and it was only seconds before they burst into the sittingroom.

"Great news," Sylvia announced in her tinkly voice, "Jason's going home!"

"Yes, I'm leaving within the hour," the lieutenant added. "God, it's going to be good to get back to Alabama!"

"I'm happy for you," Staunch said soberly.

"Well, I've got to pack—"

"Shall I help you?" the girl asked.

"No, no, I can take care of it. I have precious little to take with me." He hurried from the room.

"Isn't this grand news?" Sylvia said to Staunch.

"Yes."

She sank down on the floor in front of him and took his hands. "Shouldn't you be thinking of home, too, Staunch?"

A frightened look came over his square-cut Dewey face.

"Oh, I mean . . . well, Daddy and Mommy say you can stay as long as you need . . . and I do, too . . . but your family must be terribly worried about you—"

"I'm not up to travel yet," Staunch insisted.

"Of course you are," the girl said reassuringly. "The doctor says you're every bit as well as Jason and he's—"

"Jason has two good legs to travel on."

"Yes, I know, but you've been doing so well on the crutches."

He reached out and touched her dark brown curls, smiling at her. "Maybe I'm not anxious to go home because it would mean leaving you."

"Oh—" She seemed startled, a slight blush evident on her cheeks.

"The prospect of my staying in Petersburg doesn't please you?"

"Of course it does," Sylvia said quickly. "These months of having you here have been very . . . pleasant."

"But you feel nothing special for me." It was a statement.

"You have become a very dear friend."

"But nothing more." Another statement.

Sylvia got to her feet. "Staunch Dewey," she said, adopting a scolding tone, "you are being very naughty!"

The young man was silent for a moment. "I was trying to say that I've fallen in love with you."

"Staunch! Stop it!" The girl was flustered. "This is not proper talk, you know. We're both much too young to be . . . well, to . . . to—"

Lieutenant Mills reentered the room carrying a small carpetbag. He held it up. "In here," he said, grinning, "is the sum total of my current assets."

"For now only," Sylvia assured him. "You have a long and prosperous life before you."

"That's my hope." He went to the rocking chair and offered Staunch his hand. "Well, old fellow, it's been nice knowing you and I hope you'll be able to go home, too, very soon."

The Kentuckian shook Lieutenant Mills's hand vigorously, smiling broadly as he did. "The best of fortune, Jason. You've inspired me, just now, to follow your lead. I've just decided I'll be leaving before the week is out."

"Good, good." He turned to Sylvia and kissed her cheek. "I'm sorry I must leave before your parents return, Syl, but please tell them of my gratitude and that I'll write."

"Be sure you do."

"You have my promise." He left the sitting room quickly.

When the door closed behind him, the girl faced Staunch again, tears on her cheeks. "I shall miss him."

"Hmmm." Young Dewey seemed preoccupied in watching through the window the departure of the lieutenant.

"Will you really be starting for home before the end of the week?"

"I'll be leaving, yes." Staunch's reply was sullen. "That's what you want, isn't it?"

"Staunch, dear, please don't believe that I *want* you to go." There were more tears now. "I've been horrid, haven't I?"

"No, don't think that," he answered quietly as he reached for his crutches. "I was selfish to think that you ought to saddle yourself with a one-legged man."

IV

TRUE Jackson shifted his weight in the saddle, contemplating for the first time he could recall the matter of his advancing age. His fifty-three years had not been of any consequence to him before, but now, after the hard ride from Nashville, most of it over difficult backcountry roads to skirt Union troop dispersals, he approached Bon Marché Lexington in an extremely sore and weary state. Of one thing he was sure: if not really old, he was no longer young.

He had made the trip as an agent—without title, command or portfolio—of the Confederate States of America. Had he been stopped and searched by Federal troops, the papers he carried would have brought a forfeit of his life. They would brand him for what he was in fact: a Confederate spy. True wasn't fearful of losing his life; he had already pledged that to the Confederate cause. It was just that it would have been most inconvenient at this time. He had a mission he believed to be of vital importance to the Confederacy and he wanted to finish it.

He recognized, although he had not really seen it before, the outer reaches of Bon Marché Lexington. The neat white fences, the gleaming thoroughbred mares in the fields, and the patrolling mounted and armed white men, told him he had reached the domain of Colonel Albert Dewey. He urged his tired horse into a spirited trot, anxious to be done with his ride. As he came upon the arched iron gate at the entrance to Bon Marché Lexington he saw four armed men in front of it. He drew abreast of them and stopped. A cocked musket was pointed at him.

"Do you have business here?" one of the men asked; the Irish brogue was unmistakable.

"I do."

"Then dismount and come forward with your hands raised!"

"I'm True Jackson of Bon Marché in Nashville," he said as he slid out of the saddle and raised his hands. "Tell your master immediately that I'm here."

"There's no master about," the Irishman said, grinning as he handed his weapon to another of the guards and began to search Jackson roughly.

"See here," True protested angrily, "there's no need of that! I'm a friend. Colonel Dewey is a cousin."

"Is he now?" The grin persisted as the guard found the visitor's Deringer in his waistband. "I'll just keep this toy until we check you out." He nodded to one of the others, who mounted a horse and galloped away down the lane.

It was only a few minutes before two riders returned. One of them was Jefferson Dewey, Albert's son.

"Cousin True!" Jeff exclaimed. "My God, what are you doing here?"

"I have a matter of some importance to speak to your father about."

"Well, mount up and we'll be there in just a minute or two."

"Is it far?" True asked.

"Just about half a mile."

"If you don't mind, Jeff, I'd prefer to walk. I don't believe I could boost myself into the saddle again."

The young man laughed. "Of course." He, too, dismounted and the two of them, leading their horses, started toward the mansion. As True passed the guard who had searched him he held out his hand and the Irishman slapped the Deringer into it.

"You'll have to excuse the men," Jeff apologized. "They're under Father's strict orders. There are all kinds of renegades about these days, some of them in uniform and some of them not."

"I understand, of course."

"You rode all the way from Nashville?"

"I did," True replied.

"Without running into any troops?" Jeff's tone was one of incredulity.

"I thought it best to deliberately avoid them."

"And how are things in Nashville? Aunt Alma May's letters tend to be . . . well . . . rosy and we learn little from them."

"Tense," True told him.

Jeff chuckled. "Just 'tense' would be welcome here. Bon Marché Lexington sits in the middle of a cauldron."

"And that's why I'm here."

The mansion loomed up in front of them. Albert, who had been standing on the veranda waiting for his son to return with the visitor, ran to them, embracing Jackson, and asking all the same questions his son had asked and getting the same answers.

"You must be exhausted," Albert commented.

"A most inadequate word, Cousin."

They entered the mansion, Albert leading the way into the library. There Albert's wife, Lillian, also greeted the visitor, as did Albert's stepdaughter, Carolina, a beautiful youngster of seventeen, and their shy son, Lance, who was now nine years old. Dr. Jamie Orr, the veterinarian, was pumping True's hand as Lillian shooed the younger children out of the room. She stayed, however, to serve bourbon to the men.

True groaned as he settled his aching body into a deep chair. He sipped the bourbon appreciatively.

"Now, True, what brings you here?" Albert asked in his no-nonsense manner. He had already guessed the reason for the visit.

"You know, of course, of my deep commitment to the Confederacy," True started.

Albert nodded.

"And I know of your equal commitment to the strict neutrality for Kentucky," Jackson went on. "I don't want to fence with you, Albert, so I'll get right to the point: I want to urge you to use your considerable influence to break the neutral stance and to bring the state into the Southern alliance, where it belongs."

"Kentucky has already made its choice," Colonel Dewey snapped.

"And it's a poor choice, because it can't work. It hasn't worked, as the Union troops on your soil prove."

"There are Confederate troops, too, damn it!" Albert's anger was rising.

"Only to protect Tennessee's safety," True insisted. "Our generals have offered to withdraw, not once but several times, consistent with a similar withdrawal of the forces of the Lincoln government. But if we stand idly by and allow a Union buildup here in Kentucky to continue, we will soon have a major force aimed right at our heart. This we cannot allow!"

The master of Bon Marché Lexington said nothing.

"I came because I want you to fully understand Lincoln's disdain for Kentucky's neutrality policy." True reached into his coat and brought out a folded document, handing it to Albert. "This will prove the rape of your neutrality."

Dewey unfolded the document, spending several minutes reading it, his reaction evident in the surprise registered on his face. "My God, True, where did you get this? Is it genuine?"

"Where or how we got it isn't important. But is it genuine? Absolutely. It's the full report of Brigadier General William T. Sherman, commanding the so-called Headquarters, Department of the Cumberland from inside *your* Louisville! Study that troop dispersal, Albert." True Jackson was racing his words. "General Cook has four full brigades encamped at Nolin, Kentucky . . . General Thomas has eight companies at Camp Dick Robinson, including cavalry and artillery . . . the Tenth Indiana is at Bardstown . . . the First Wisconsin at Jeffersonville . . . the Ninth Michigan at Salt River . . . the Thirty-fifth Ohio at Cynthiana . . . the Twenty-fourth Illinois at Colesburg . . . and others at Crab Orchard and Lebanon Junction and Nicholasville and Big Hill and Elizabethtown and Owensburg and—"

"You seem to have it memorized," Albert cut in, smiling slightly.

"I do. I thought it best to commit it to memory, should I be stopped by the Federals and need to destroy the document. And note, too, that other regiments are forming at Rockcastle and Harrodsburg and Irvine and Burkesville and Somerset." Jackson's voice rose in intensity. "You've *been* invaded! Lincoln and Sherman have spit on your vaunted neutrality!"

"Not to mention the Confederate troops in the state," Dewey commented sarcastically.

"For defensive purposes only . . . to prevent the Federals from using Kentucky as a staging area for a massive strike into the western section of the Confederacy. More to the point for my personal purposes, to save Tennessee."

"And what would you have me do?"

"Use that document. Take it to Frankfort and show it to the governor and the legislature. Show them irrefutable proof of the Union's treachery."

"Oh, they're aware of the Federal presence."

"Of course they are," True said sternly, "but the Sherman report is damning proof of the unconscionable size of the Union presence in your state. I daresay, no one in Frankfort is fully aware of the number of Lincoln's soldiers in Kentucky. So use it, Albert, to reverse the neutrality. Join Kentucky with the Confederacy and together we can drive out the invaders!"

"Scorching the very earth we treasure," Albert said.

"You're likely to have that anyway. My way, the Confederate way, at least you'll have honor. Neutrality is a coward's device."

Dewey bridled. "You zealots are all the same, True, evoking honor when all other arguments fail. Well, believe me, because I fought in one, I know there's nothing honorable about war. Yes, I want to see a neutrality policy that keeps the insanity of civil war out of Kentucky. Failing that, like any trained soldier, I have my fallback position chosen."

"And that is?"

"Bon Marché Lexington. Defending it against all incursions, from the Union or the Confederacy."

"And you'll die right here!" Jackson said coldly.

Lillian Dewey gasped and True looked at her apologetically.

"In that case," Albert commented, "it will be with real honor—defending what is *mine.*" He tossed the stolen Sherman report back to his cousin-by-marriage. "I won't be needing this."

"You're a fool."

"Perhaps."

Jackson exhaled a deep breath. "Well . . . I've made the effort asked of me. And I've also been asked to give you this." He removed from his coat this time a sealed envelope, extending it to Albert, who took it and tore it open, again reading.

"Did you know what was in this envelope?" Dewey asked.

"No."

"It's from a former friend of mine—a Captain Walter Darnell, now Colonel Darnell of the C.S.A. We served together in Mexico, where he was an adjutant to one Jeff Davis. In any event, Walter is now with Davis in Richmond as a military aide, and . . ." He paused.

"And?" True prompted him.

Albert smiled wanly. "I'm offered a commission in the Confederate army, as a brigadier of an infantry division." He glanced at his wife. "Don't worry, dear, I'm not going to accept it." To True: "Are you sure you didn't know of this?

That it's not just a ploy to get me to go along with your plans?"

"I swear to you, Albert, that I was not told what was in the envelope. My agent connected with the Richmond government simply asked me to bring it to you." Nevertheless, True saw it as another opportunity to press his point. "However, I do think you ought to reconsider. A man of your background and influence could be of great value to the Confederacy."

"No, True"—Dewey seemed weary now—"I've made war once and that's enough." He looked down at the letter from Darnell again, rereading the last sentence to himself: "If there's ever anything I can do for you, Albert, you need only ask." "I'd like to have a letter delivered to Colonel Darnell in Richmond."

"Of course," Jackson agreed quickly.

"I'm going to impose on our former friendship to try to find out what has happened to my sons."

"You haven't heard anything of Jack and Staunch?"

"Not one word, True." Tears welled up in his eyes. "And I *have* to know, whatever their fate. Not knowing has been a personal hell."

32

DREW Jackson was in a surly mood. For more than a month he had been at a site on the east bank of the Tennessee River, living in a small, damp tent, and directing the labor of Bon Marché slaves in the building of what was being called Fort Henry. He was only one of the more than a dozen white overseers—he hated the word!—who were in charge of a large contingent of blacks. The entire concept annoyed Drew.

Damn it! I'm a horseman, not a construction engineer!

On that early September morning he kept seeing the same Confederate officer, a captain, poking around the site, going from place to place among the construction, frequently shaking his head negatively, and then moving off to inspect another aspect of the incomplete fort. Army officers came here often, and with each visit there always seemed to be a change in the plans. This was another one, then. Drew groaned inwardly as the officer came toward him.

"Sir," the captain called out to him, "are you in charge of the . . . uh . . . civilian labor here?"

"A portion of it only," Drew replied, unable to hide his ill temper. "Those blacks who are from the Bon Marché plantation. I have no idea who's in overall charge here—it seems to change all the time."

"Then you're a native of this area?"

"I am."

The officer smiled; he seemed pleased that he had found someone familiar with the area. "I'm Captain Jesse Taylor," he said, extending his hand, "of the C.S.A. artillery. I'm to be in command here."

Drew dutifully shook the hand offered.

"I'd like to ask you some questions about this site," Taylor started.

"You mean because it's in the flood plain?"

The captain seemed surprised. "Then you know about that?"

"Everybody knows that," Drew said sarcastically. He pointed to a large tree nearby. "See that ring of mud about three-quarters of the way up?"

"Yes, I noticed that."

"That was the high-water mark from last February's risings. By maybe mid-February next this whole damned fort will be underwater."

"Did you make this known to the state authorities?"

"Until I was blue in the face."

"And yet you continue the work on the fort?"

Drew sighed. "Look, Captain, my family has volunteered to serve the Confederacy by providing labor for this project and for the one on the Cumberland—Fort Donelson. Now, if we pulled our hands out of here, for whatever reason, we'd be thought traitorous to the Confederate cause. And honestly, Captain, I'd rather be thought a fool than a traitor. So, I stay here and do this foolish work."

Captain Taylor shook his head in disbelief. "Incredible!" There was a pause. "No one in authority has listened to you?"

"None."

"Well, you have someone who is listening now," the officer said with resolve. "Indeed, Mister . . . uh . . ."

"Jackson, Drew Jackson."

"Indeed, Mr. Jackson, there's more wrong with this site than just the flooding potential." He pointed across the river. "Here, where the fort is being built, we're in a bottom commanded by the high hills rising on the other side. It's there that the fort should be built."

Drew nodded.

"And I intend, Mr. Jackson, to do everything in my power to fortify those hills across the way."

The Bon Marché horseman said nothing.

"Yes, sir, everything in my power," the captain repeated.

"In the meantime—" He stopped cold and shrugged mightily. "In the meantime, Mr. Jackson, try to keep the faith."

Both Taylor and Jackson knew the importance of proper fortification for Nashville, a city whose assets—its river connections, its good roads, its excellent rail lines, its native industry; all of those things proudly extolled by the citizenry— also made it a prize. In what seemed only a short period of time the city had become a vast arsenal and storehouse, the key that could unlock the door to the western portion of the Confederacy. It required no military genius to recognize the strategic value of Nashville.

For one thing, the Military and Financial Board of Tennessee had established a powder mill in the city that was the largest in the South. In addition to supplying the growing military forces of Tennessee itself, it was this mill that sent gunpowder to the Confederate soldiers at Manassas, contributing in no small measure to that glorious Southern victory. As 1861 neared a close, Nashville was producing percussion caps at the rate of 100,000 a day. Huge quantities of muskets, small arms, sabers, saddles, uniforms, blankets, and other accoutrements of war were pouring out of the city's factories, foundries, and shops. Newly established warehouses were bulging with foodstuffs. Day and night supplies were moving out on riverboats and railroad cars to garrisons at Mobile and New Orleans.

The defense of all that required keeping the Union armies off the Tennessee and Cumberland rivers, which is what Fort Henry and Fort Donelson were being built to accomplish. And now, as fall gave way to winter, there was to be a Fort Heiman, as well; a small fortification—a crude one, at best— begun on the heights on the west bank of the Tennessee, directly opposite the flood-prone Fort Henry.

Artillery Captain Jesse Taylor, Drew Jackson noted with satisfaction, had scored a singular victory over bureaucracy.

II

THERE were still scars of the battle evident, some five months later, as Lee Dewey rode across the stone bridge spanning the modest stream called Bull Run. He was on a strange mission, not as a newspaper correspondent but as a civilian—a Northerner in one sense—carrying safe-conduct papers signed by Jefferson Davis, President of the Confederacy. Perhaps Lee was on a fool's errand, seeking, as he was, a sixteen-year-old, one-legged youth who might be anywhere. Or nowhere. Staunch Dewey.

Lee carried with him an official Confederate army report, sent to his nephew Albert by Captain (now Colonel) Walter Darnell, telling of the death of Jackson and the grievous wounding of Staunch—perhaps at this very spot over which Lee now guided his horse. Memories flooded the newspaperman's brain: of Colonel Albert Dewey and his aide, Captain Darnell, tracking down the traitorous San Patricios during the Mexican War, and, fourteen years later, of the mad fighting here along Bull Run.

Lee had very little to go on. Jack, Albert had been told by Darnell, had been buried on the Manassas battlefield; exactly where was a matter of conjecture. And Staunch, who had lost his left leg, had left the Petersburg, Virginia, home of a family named Williams, telling them he planned to return home to Lexington. But he did not; Confederate authorities had lost track of him.

> I know what an imposition this is [Albert had written to Lee] but I have no one else to whom I can turn. It occurs to me that a one-legged man cannot travel very fast and that he still might be in Virginia. Maybe he is seeking Jack's grave; the two of them were very close. What I fear most, I suppose, is that Staunch believes he cannot return to his family; that their defiance of my wishes now denies him my love. Nothing could be further from the truth. We want him home, Lee, where, with our love, we can try to ease the pain of his youthful indiscretions. When you find him, please make every effort to convince him of that. And should he not be found, know that you will have our undying gratitude for having tried."

The searcher believed Albert might be correct about Staunch seeking his brother's grave, which was reason enough to begin the looking at the little town of Manassas Junction. As he approached it he spotted a small tavern, with a livery stable attached, and he rode up to it, dismounting and leading his horse into the stable.

"Can you accommodate me for a few days?" Lee asked the old man who came up to him.

"Depends," the man grunted.

"On what?"

"The color of your money."

"I have only . . . uh . . . Federal dollars," Lee told him.

The old man grinned. "That's the right answer, mister." He hurried an explanation. "Understand now, I support the Southern cause, but the Confederate money ain't worth a damn."

"I see."

"And if you want a room at the tavern, my wife will make you comfortable."

"That's fine."

The old man held out a hand. "I'll take the money in advance, mister. Three dollars a day for the horse, five dollars for yourself." He reacted to the surprised expression on Lee's face. "I gotta live, mister. These are hard times."

Lee counted out twenty-four dollars. "Three days," he said, "to start."

The money was pocketed quickly.

"Now, maybe you can help me," Lee went on. "I'm looking for a young man, about sixteen. Blond, five ten. Probably wearing a uniform, or part of one. He's lost a leg—the left leg."

The elderly gentleman shook his head sadly. "One-legged men, mister, ain't unusual no more."

Three days was enough time for Lee Dewey to canvass the town of Manassas Junction and know that Staunch wasn't there. A check with the Confederate military authorities in the area—showing the papers signed by Jefferson Davis—failed to give him the slightest hint of the whereabouts of the boy he sought.

He moved slowly southwestward then in the general direction of Culpeper, stopping at every farm he came across, asking his questions and getting no answers. In the second week of the search, as he rode into Culpeper, he was struck with the realization that Christmas was only four days away. That seemed to make him even more disconsolate; he wasn't sure why he had come to Culpeper and was even less certain where he would turn next.

He decided to indulge himself, to seek the best accommodations the town had to offer, and to have some sort of Christmas even in the sad circumstances he now found himself. Lee was surprised by the large military presence he found in Culpeper and wondered whether the Federal authorities knew of the extent of it.

Of course they do, he told himself, *the place is probably crawling with spies.*

It was a bustling little town, a market community for the surrounding agricultural area in the heart of what was known as Piedmont Virginia. A quick reconnaissance told him the Virginia Hotel was his best bet, but he found, when he sought a room there, that most of the space was taken up by officers of the Confederate army. With a bit of bluster he was able to use the Jefferson Davis papers he carried to get himself a small room in the hotel; it was a wise move because the hotel also offered hot baths, something he desperately needed after two weeks on horseback.

He soaked appreciatively in a cast-iron tub and then dressed in clean clothes and made his way to the big dining room, ordering a hearty beef roast meal. He was on his second glass of burgundy wine when a trio of young ladies entered the dining room, gaily going from table to table, obviously taking up a collection of some sort. Eventually they came to where Lee dined alone.

"And you, sir," a buxom brunette said to him, "will you help in making Christmas a bit more gay for some of our brave boys who are away from home at this season?"

"You're having a party?"

"We are, sir. The Episcopal church ladies are preparing a grand array of vittles and spirits"—she giggled—"for a couple of hundred of our boys, mostly those who have been wounded and can't yet get home to their families."

"I see. When is this to be?"

"On Tuesday—Christmas Eve."

"I'd be glad to contribute," Lee said, reaching into his pocket. "May I also offer my person to help serve the spirits—I have great experience with spirits." He laughed.

"That would be most kind, sir."

Expansively, Lee counted out fifty dollars and dropped it into the small wicker basket one of the young ladies carried.

"Oh, that's most *generous, sir.*"

"I admit, young lady, that I have an ulterior motive. Do you, by any chance, know of a young man named Staunch Dewey hereabouts? He was wounded at Manassas. Lost his leg."

"Oh, dear!" The pretty face clouded. "No, I don't know anyone of that name." She looked inquiringly at the other two, who nodded negatively. "But there are so many, sir, who have lost limbs."

"Yes, yes . . . well, I'll be happy to be part of your evening."

They thanked him again and made their way to the next table. Dewey watched them as they finished their task and applauded with the other diners as they swept out, having concluded their mission of mercy. Sighing, Lee finished his wine and went to his room, deeply depressed. *If not here, then where?*

III

COLONEL Able Jackson was an unhappy man, reflecting the mood of most of the men in the Nashville Grays. They had been at Camp Harris, named for the Tennessee governor, since June without action of any kind. They had marched and countermarched daily, they had had innumerable training exercises in marksmanship, and had even engaged in several mock battles. But they had *not* fought. They were like prisoners at the Franklin County camp, some eighty miles south of Nashville. They were bored and with the boredom came desertions; even some of the original Grays had abandoned the cause and gone home.

Able, himself, had several times thought of leaving, but his sense of duty, his command responsibilities, weighed heavily on him and he stayed, unable to explain to his men why they weren't being used. In truth, in the early winter of '61, there wasn't much war anywhere. Oh, there had been some minor skirmishes miles removed from Camp Harris, but it seemed the Nashville Grays and the other volunteers at the camp— and at other camps called Trousdale and Cheatham and Boone—were destined to just rot there.

Uncharacteristically, Able had let down his guard on this

night, two nights before Christmas. Being away from Bon Marché at Christmastime left him dispirited. He removed a bottle of Bon Marché bourbon from his officer's chest and began to drink—heavily. It was nearly nine o'clock when his son, Foster, his aide-de-camp, came into his tent with an announcement.

"Some of the young officers are going into Allisonia in a few minutes," he announced, "and I'm going with them." There was a defiant note in the little speech.

Colonel Jackson stared at his son drunkenly. "Allisonia?"

"Yes, sir."

Able took another sip of bourbon. "You know I disapprove of—" He stopped, thinking of how he had suggested to his superiors that the whores who established residence in Allisonia be driven out. And how he had been ignored. "Disapprove of such matters."

"This is to be sort of a Christmas gift to ourselves," young Jackson answered lightly.

The colonel sucked in a deep breath and just as slowly let it out. "I . . . uh . . . don't think I can . . . uh . . . let you go"— he was slurring his words—"without . . . uh . . . proper parental . . . uh . . . supervision, that is."

The son was stunned. "You mean you want to go with us?"

"Want to? No. But . . . uh . . . I see it as . . . uh . . . my duty . . . uh . . . to do so." He struggled to his feet. "Have the . . . boy saddle my horse."

Within seconds, it seemed, the word sped through the camp. "The old man's going into Allisonia!"

By the time Able had stumbled out of his tent, and was laboriously boosted into the saddle by his Negro servant, there was a crowd of fifty or more standing there, just watching the scene, unable to believe what they were seeing. Son Foster came up on horse, followed by perhaps a dozen of the younger officers. The colonel studied them through half-hooded eyes, pointed ahead in a grand gesture, and shouted drunkenly: "Forward men! Charge!"

The horsemen raised a mighty cloud of dust as the enlisted men roared their approval.

That night was to become a legend in the history of the Nashville Grays, told and retold, elaborated until the truth of it was totally obscured.

The truth of it was the mounted contingent led by the drunken colonel raced up to one of the cribs in Allisonia, the younger men rushing in and making their fleshpot selections rapidly. Able, though, after sliding out of the saddle, had trouble just getting his feet to carry him through the door.

Once inside, he bellowed: "Madame!"

The hefty woman who ran the place sidled up to him. "You called me, darlin'."

"Madame, prepare yourself for battle!"

He lunged at her uncertainly, and the madam sidestepped him. Able pitched forward on his face and passed out. The whores, laughing and making bawdy remarks about his manhood, picked up the colonel's inert form and carried him outside, dumping him by the side of the road.

Able was still there when his young officers came out several hours later. They picked him up, brushed him off, sat him on his horse, and brought him back to camp, two officers riding tight against him to keep him propped up.

And then they lied about the colonel's prowess. And everyone believed them. In a very real sense, Able Jackson was more than just the colonel of the Nashville Grays after that night. He became their leader.

IV

THE young soldier's sweet tenor voice, belying the terrible burn scars on his face, filled every corner of the meeting room in the Episcopal church of Culpeper, a room crowded at that early evening hour by other young men uniformed in gray, some without arms, some with grossly bandaged heads, some missing legs, some with unseeing eyes.

> *The years creep slowly by, Lorena;*
> *The snow is on the grass again;*
> *The sun's low down the sky, Lorena;*
> *The frost gleams where the flowers have been.*

For each warrior in the place there was a comely companion, silk and lace and scent enveloped, smiles fixed on their faces suggesting nothing was wrong there. But everything was wrong, including the beautiful, tender love song.

But the heart throbs on as warmly now
As when the summer days were nigh;
Oh! the sun can never dip so low
Adown affection's cloudless sky.

It was Christmas Eve and the young women of Culpeper were duty-bound it seemed to make believe that what had happened had not happened; that the legs and arms were whole, that the eyes could see, that the burns were rosy, healthy skin. There was a cruelty in this one-evening lie; that these young people—men and women—could, would, be normal partners on any other evening.

A hundred months had passed, Lorena,
Since last I held that hand in mine,
And felt the pulse beat fast, Lorena,
Though mine beat faster far than thine.

The lovely melody, the poignant lyrics, brought tears to many eyes, most notably the eyes of the singer. Clearly he was a professional performer—the name was Ryan and he had been on the stage before the war—and the voice was what it had always been. But the face, the grotesque mask it had become because of an inferno of exploding black powder, would keep the voice off the stage; would restrict it to audiences like the one tonight, audiences of other damaged beings.

A hundred months—'twas flowery May,
When up the hilly slope we climbed,
To watch the dying of the day
And hear the distant church bells chime.

Lee Dewey joined the others at the party in appreciative applause for the singer. He had done as he promised; he had come there to help serve the spirits at the levee. But he had his own selfish reason for it: to find Staunch Dewey, if he could be found. In the two days before the party he had combed Culpeper in his fruitless search and had very nearly decided not to come to the church that evening. It seemed unlikely that Staunch was at this place; mention of his name in a hundred different venues had brought no encouraging response.

Ryan sang another song, an instrumental trio favored the assemblage with more earthy tunes from the Southern hills, and a young lady seated at the pianoforte began to play Christmas hymns for all to sing.

Lee saw the woman first. Hers was a flawless face with all the bones perfectly positioned, an ivory skin, deep green, intense eyes with a hint of laughter in them, and a cascading flow of shiny black hair. She had come into the room first, surveying it as if looking for someone to rival her. And not finding the rival, she turned to her companion, half-hidden in the shadows of the doorway, and spoke a few words. The companion moved forward into the light of the room, propelling himself on a pair of crutches; awkwardly, tentatively, suggesting not only a difficulty with the mechanics of walking with the crutches but also a strange determination not to become comfortable with them.

Lee gasped.

It was Staunch!

And then there was a doubt. He hadn't seen Albert's son since he was a small lad, and so he took the time to study him closely: the square-cut handsome face, the blond hair, the hazel eyes, the unmistakable aura of self-assurance even in those circumstances. He was a Dewey, Lee concluded, stamped as that from the moment of conception.

The beauty who accompanied Staunch was introducing him to others in the room when Lee approached them.

"Ma'am," he said, affecting a small bow to the woman, "may I also have the honor of meeting your friend?" He recognized it was a stiff way of approaching the situation, but something told him an indirect manner was required.

"Certainly, sir," the woman said, smiling sweetly. "It's an honor to present one of the bravest of our boys—Private Mason Dupree of Hampton's Legion. The Legion, you know, played a major role in driving the invaders from our soil."

Lee was sure now. Young Dewey had taken the French name of his great-grandfather, Lee's father, in seeking anonymity in this place. "I'm honored," he said quietly, "to know you, Private Dupree." He wanted to reach out and embrace the boy, confronting him with the reality of family, but he held back.

The young man stared at him, his hands clutching the crutches with such intensity that the knuckles whitened. And then Lee saw the flicker of recognition in his eyes and the fright that recognition brought. Staunch said nothing.

"Miss. . . ?" Lee started.

"Culpeper. Alice Culpeper."

The newspaperman affected a grin. "The town is named for your family?"

She laughed gaily. "It is, and at times it's a . . . bore to be a Culpeper, believe me."

"I find that hard to believe." It was small talk now and Lee knew he had to bring the matter to a head. "Miss Culpeper, I was about to ask whether I might take charge of Private . . . uh . . . Dupree's well-being for a moment or two and get this young man a drink."

"That's very kind, sir . . . ." She hesitated. "I don't believe you've told me your name."

"Dewey," Lee said clearly, looking directly into Staunch's eyes. "Lee Dewey."

"You reside here?" the Culpeper woman inquired.

"No, I'm from Tennessee." Again he answered to Staunch.

"Well, I'm sure that Mason could use a drink. He's been very nervous about coming here tonight."

Staunch spoke for the first time. "I'd prefer to leave, Alice."

"Nonsense! It's Christmas, darling. And remember what you promised me—you're to have a gay time tonight." She kissed him quickly on the cheek. "Now, allow Mr. Dewey to get you a libation. It would be most rude, Mason, to refuse."

Lee led the way to the table where the bottles of spirits were arrayed, walking slowly to keep pace with Staunch's progress on the crutches. "Bourbon?"

The young man nodded, shifting a crutch to free a hand to accept the glass held out to him by Lee.

"Your father sent me to find you, Staunch," Lee said.

There was anger in the boy's reply. "My father doesn't want to see me again. I'm making a new life here."

"With Miss Culpeper?"

"You find that strange?" Staunch snapped.

"No, but your family wants you home. They love you and miss you."

Staunch thrust the glass at Lee, not having even tasted the bourbon. "I want you to go away . . . uh . . . Uncle Lee! Stay out of my life! I'll live it as I see fit."

"With Miss Culpeper?"

"Why do you keep asking that?" The boy's anger spilled over. "Damn you! Go away!" He turned quickly on his crutches in an awkward manner, losing his balance and crashing to the floor. All eyes turned to them.

As Lee bent to help him to his feet, Staunch screamed at him. "Go away! Go away!" He began to weep.

Alice rushed to them, dropping to the floor, cradling Staunch's disconsolate form in her arms. She looked up at Lee, her green eyes flashing accusingly. "How could you have let this happen, Mr. Dewey!"

The elder Dewey reached down to grasp Staunch under his arms, hoisting him up quickly. "I think, Miss Culpeper," he said, sighing deeply, "we should find a quiet place to be alone before I answer."

V

At Bon Marché, Alma May, too, was depressed. It was Christmas Eve like none before; a pall had fallen over the mansion. She wrote slowly in her diary: "No parties this year for the yuletide. No one wants them. The family seems to be disintegrating. Dear God, I hope that Daddy is spared knowledge of these times."

VI

It was late. The embers in the fireplace at the Culpeper estate, several miles outside the town, were dying. Lee sat in the drawing room with Alice, her parents having retired for the evening, Staunch having also been put to bed like some terrified child.

"I must take him home," Dewey said. "He needs to be with his family."

The beautiful young woman was silent.

"Don't you think he needs to be with his family?"

"Yes, I suppose." The words were barely audible. "I shall miss him terribly."

"Hmmm. Do you love him, Miss Culpeper?"

She stared at him for a moment before answering. "Of course."

Lee tried not to be cruel. "As a husband, Miss Culpeper?"

Alice continued to stare. "As a dear friend," she said finally.

"But you're aware that he's in love with you? In the deepest sense. But he's only a boy. Sixteen. Some four or five years younger than yourself, I'd guess."

"Five," she admitted.

"He's a boy. You're a woman. And he's not going to want to leave as long as he continues to see you as a wife. It's a fantasy he believes in, Miss Culpeper, and I submit to you that I'll have to drag him from this place unless you dissuade him of any truly romantic notions. You're going to have to help me . . . uh . . . Alice . . . if I'm to take him home."

She shook her head firmly. "I can't. It would hurt him too much."

"And you think he'll be unhurt when he realizes, in the months ahead, that he cannot be your lover?"

The woman frowned. "You can be quite crude, Mr. Dewey."

"I risk that, ma'am, for what I see as my family duty. In Kentucky, surrounded by the love of his family, Staunch can begin to put his life together again. Here"—he swept his hand to encompass the mansion—"he's never going to be whole unless his fantasy can be consummated. And it can't, can it?"

Alice rose, going to the fireplace, staring into the embers. "How soon?" she breathed.

"I'd like to get under way quickly. It's a long journey."

She turned back to him. "I'm going to feel like a traitor."

"To what cause?"

"The Confederacy," she answered, seeming to be surprised that he would ask. "Mason . . . uh . . . Staunch has given so much and I—" She stopped. "A woman, you know, can only give herself. Perhaps that's what I should do—"

Lee cut her off in his exasperation. "Damn it, Miss Culpeper, listen to what you're saying! The cause, as you call it, would be served *how* if you took a one-legged boy into your bed?"

"Sir!" Her pretty face reflected her shock.

"I suppose I should apologize, but I won't. I've finally said what we've both been thinking. You speak of cause. Well, I have one, too—the Dewey family. And it's in that cause that I'm going to take Staunch home."

She sank into a chair opposite him, beginning to cry. "I *hate* all of this! I hate having to hurt him. I hate . . . not . . . wanting him." A hand brushed the tears from her cheek. "Very well, Mr. Dewey, you shall have Staunch. I only hope God forgives me for what I will do in the morning."

"He will, Alice," Lee tried to assure her, "for it is the most compassionate act possible." There was a slight pause. "And, in time, Staunch will forgive you, too."

33

It was uncomfortably cold and raining heavily, and Statler Dewey swore under his breath as he lashed at the straining horse with his whip, trying to move his light carriage through the thick mud of the crude road leading to Fort Henry on the Tennessee. It was the third day of February of 1862, and when he had left Nashville on the morning of the preceding day, he had expected to be at the fort by that evening. The terrible weather, however, conspired against him. Several times he had had to leave the carriage and push it from behind as he screamed at the horse to pull ahead. He wished he had listened to the advice of his wife, Harriet, and had taken one of the Beau Monde blacks with him as a driver. But he had seen the trip somewhat romantically, as a manly, spartan enterprise in keeping with the new image he had of himself—as a war correspondent. Up to that time, his newspapering had been office-bound, dealing with the war through the dispatches received on the telegraph from others. Now, however, the war was close at hand for the first time; reports indicated the Federal forces meant to strike at the Confederacy along the Tennessee and Cumberland rivers, and he meant to be there to see, and report on, the Union army being thrown back on its bases in "neutral" Kentucky. It was clear the first such enemy assault would come at Fort Henry, very near the Kentucky border.

Several days earlier he had talked to Drew Jackson about the fort because Drew had a hand in building it, directing the Bon Marché slaves there. But he had discounted much of what his cousin told him. He was annoyed when the young man told him Fort Henry was ill-planned and poorly situated. Drew's information had come from an artillery captain named Taylor, and Statler, not willing to accept naysayers within the Confederate command, reasoned that a captain was of insufficient rank to make the kind of judgments Drew had related to him. Indeed, there were several members of the family who drew Statler's ire in these troubled times. His cousin Albert was a case in point. Alma May had showed him a letter from Albert in which he told of his son Staunch being returned to Lexington by Lee Dewey. The publisher was pleased that the brave young man had returned home and he was saddened that Staunch had lost a leg at Bull Run. But he was unalterably opposed to Albert's stand for a neutral Kentucky, and he was appalled when he learned that Albert had refused a commission in the Confederate army.

Then, too, there was the tale told him by True Jackson, who had sent an emissary to Statler's brother George Dewey Jr. in New York, suggesting George's happy coincidence of being in the heart of the Union might be of some considerable value to the Confederacy. True had asked George to provide information on troop gatherings and supply movements, and George had demurred, answering he preferred to "stay out of the mess and do what I know how to do—raise and train racehorses." Statler stopped short of using the word "traitorous" to describe the actions of Albert and George, but the word stuck in his mind, nevertheless.

He cracked the whip now over the back of the tired carriage horse. Not only had the mud deepened as Statler came closer to Fort Henry, but there was water standing everywhere in great, lakelike pools. And every hundred yards closer to the fort, the water deepened until it was up to the hubs of wheels. Then it was a flood tide as Fort Henry came in sight and the horse objected to the water licking at its belly. Only through arduous whipping did Statler keep the horse moving forward until they came to the slightly higher ground on which the fort itself sat. But it was a desolate island in the middle of the flood, the water stopping just short of the artillery guns mounted there. Statler tied the horse to a sapling and the animal stood trembling of cold, exhaustion, and fright.

The newspaperman identified himself to the guards and

asked to be taken to the commanding general. Brigadier General Lloyd Tilghman was a slim, fit man; his erect bearing made him appear taller than his measurements. He wore his hair long and affected a modish Vandyke beard. Statler was greeted in a gentlemanly manner, if not with enthusiasm.

"You must have had an arduous journey," Tilghman said matter-of-factly, his eyes taking in the newspaperman's muddy and wet condition. "But I suggest to you, Mr. Dewey, that after a night's rest and some food you make your way back to Nashville."

Statler was shocked by the suggestion. "But I've come, General, to report on the battle."

"Yes, well . . ." The general sighed. "Then I should tell you that our situation is desperate. We are ill-manned and ill-equipped. We've already seen the flood tides carry away the torpedoes we had anchored in the river as one protection against the gunboats we know are coming."

"But with your guns you'll be able to turn them back, won't you?"

Slowly, Tilghman shook his head negatively. "For a very brief time we will, at best, be able to convince them they've been in a fight. But turn them back? Hardly, sir."

"But—"

"Mr. Dewey, this fort is very poorly positioned. It has been built on the flood plain, as you can see. The fortification of the heights on the west bank—which some call Fort Heiman—is incomplete. Here no less than six of our twelve-pounders are useless. They were new and our artillery officer, Captain Taylor, suggested they appeared to be made of pot metal. So, yesterday, we test-fired two of them, with just ordinary charges. Both of them burst. Not wishing to kill our own men, the other four have been discarded. The powder we've been supplied is of inferior quality."

"But, who's responsible—?"

General Tilghman stopped him by holding up a hand in a commanding manner. "It's a matter of little consequence right now. Perhaps, when you get back to Nashville, you might ask that question of other authorities."

Statler studied the commander for a long moment. "Are you telling me all this because you want me out of the way?"

"You may stay if you wish," Tilghman said forcefully. "I

recommend against it, but you may stay. Be certain, however, that I cannot guarantee your safety. My first priority will be the safety of my men."

"I appreciate that."

"Now, get some rest, Mr. Dewey. I have other duties."

II

STATLER had slept fitfully, but he had slept. His clothes, although still mud-stained, had been dried by a fire during the night. So had his boots, but when he drew them on on the morning of Tuesday, February 4, they were stiff and uncomfortable. He checked on the condition of his horse (before retiring, Statler had fed him oats obtained from the fort's hostler) and found him reasonably content.

The rain had stopped and the temperature had moderated somewhat. Skies were still overcast, however, and a fog hung weblike over the surface of the river. The newspaperman ate some of the modest soldier's fare to break fast and sought out General Tilghman again, finding him standing on the fort's parapet gazing downriver through a glass. When he saw Statler he handed him the glass.

"You can get a good look this morning, Mr. Dewey, at our predicament."

What Statler saw first was dense volumes of smoke issuing from countless steamboats. A flotilla it was—a large one—and through the smoke and river-borne fog he could make out numerous transports and at least three gunboats. Two of them were of a type he had not seen before.

"Those odd things afloat there," the general said, seeming to read Statler's mind, "are ironclads. Little more than large rafts with iron boxes on them. What guns are hidden in those boxes I cannot say, but we must assume they have sufficient firepower to reduce this fort."

"And what's to be done?"

"I cannot say with any certainty right now," Tilghman said without a trace of emotion. "We have some men out to get a closer look. One thing I do know: that flotilla is too far removed, perhaps three miles off, to reach them with our guns right now."

The morning wore on without a change in the situation and

then, suddenly, the occupants of the fort were startled by the crash of artillery fire—loud, rapid, and continuous.

The general studied the scene through his glass once more. "They're shelling the woods on the east bank," he said to his staff. The other officers nodded.

Statler, though, required more explanation. "Why would they shell the woods?"

"To cover the debarkation of their troops from the transports. They fear we have our own troops hidden there," the general told him.

"Do we?"

Tilghman smiled wryly. "We do *not*, sir. They might have landed safely without that . . . uh . . . noisy demonstration."

Within the hour three spies the general had sent out, all dressed in civilian clothes, returned to Fort Henry. They delivered terrifying news: the transports had delivered more than 15,000 (one observer put the total at 25,000). On the river the Federals had seven gunboats, four of them ironclad, presenting an array of more than fifty big guns. The general questioned them carefully, dismissed them, and resumed a lonely vigil on the parapet, staring through his glass. Staff officers and Statler Dewey stood off from him, understanding that Tilghman was weighing his options.

It was nearly dark when he went inside the fort to be a gracious, if nearly silent, host at dinner. Near the end of it he said: "Tomorrow will bring a feint at us from the river. It's clear to me that the prolific shelling of the woods indicates that the enemy is unsure of our strength. That's a minimal advantage, which will blow away like smoke when they actually test us. We'll meet the feint, gentlemen, trying to convince them we are more than we are."

Statler stayed with Tilghman after the other officers withdrew. "What's to happen to this garrison, General?"

Tilghman sighed. "Well, Mr. Dewey, you've been here long enough to have counted them. I have less than three thousand men, most of whom will be of little value in this circumstance. They're raw infantrymen—volunteers—armed with shotguns and hunting rifles. The best equipped of the lot is the Tenth Tennessee, armed with the old 'Tower of London' flintlock muskets, weapons that . . . uh, how do I put this? . . .

weapons that did the state some service in the War of 1812. But this is 1862, is it not?" He paused in thought. "Given the enemy's vastly superior infantry numbers I won't be able, in good conscience, to use those men. My reliance will have to be on the very good artillerymen we have available."

"And the infantry?" Statler asked.

"Tomorrow, Mr. Dewey, is time enough for that decision. Yes, tomorrow—"

III

On the next day then (it was Wednesday, February 5), the Fort Henry contingent had to wait until late in the afternoon until the Federals made a move. Three of the Union gunboats, two on the west side of the river and one to the east of the fort, came into range, opening a vigorous fire on Tilghman's position. Dewey was surprised that the enemy attack was met with silence from Fort Henry.

Then one of the Union shells exploded within the fort, killing one man and injuring several others.

"Now," General Tilghman said quietly to Artillery Captain Jesse Taylor.

The huge 128-pounder Columbiad gun boomed out, followed by the lesser noise of the sixteen-inch artillery "rifle." Methodically, Captain Taylor directed the firing; the Columbiad again and then the rifle, the Columbiad and the rifle. Six shots were fired only, but even in the half-light of the leaden-sky late day it seemed the half-dozen shots had been effective. Proof came when the gunboats ceased firing and withdrew downriver, out of range.

General Tilghman, strangely exhilarated by the brief fight, immediately called his officers together. "Gentlemen, we've left a mark or two on them. But we must still face reality. We are no match for the vast superiority of troops unloaded from the transports, and we must assume that they are being moved into position to surround us."

He turned to Captain Taylor. "Can you hold out for one hour against a determined attack?"

"I can, sir."

"Well, then, gentlemen," the general said, having made his decision, "hold your commands in readiness for instant motion at first light. I want your men to make their way, in haste, cross-country to Fort Donelson, where you are to report to the commanding general."

He looked around at the small group. "Captain Taylor and the First Tennessee Artillery . . . and I . . . will cover your withdrawal." He glanced at Statler. "This order, Mr. Dewey, must also cover you."

No one slept. First light came soon enough, and the Fort Henry garrison began to make its way, under forced march, along the partially flooded marshy road that led from Fort Henry to Fort Donelson on the Cumberland River, a distance of some twenty-two slogging miles afoot. They had gone only two miles or so, and were about to enter a thickly wooded area, when the first sounds of big guns came to their ears. It was impossible to know which sounds came from the Union gunboat and which from the fort, but the giant thump of the Columbiad was distinct enough to tell that Fort Henry still resisted.

It was very slow going. Although he was in his carriage, Statler could make no better time than could the infantrymen.

Less than an hour had passed, and only a mile or two more had been covered, when a lieutenant colonel rode up to Dewey's carriage on a horse without bridle or saddle. He peered down at the newspaperman.

"Sir," he said, "may I prevail on you for a ride?"

Statler stopped the carriage and the officer slid wearily off the barebacked horse and turned him loose. He climbed, wet and muddy and disheveled, into the carriage. His face was smudged with the unmistakable black of powder smoke. Dewey recognized him as one of the officers he had seen at fort, but he didn't know his name.

"You've come from Fort Henry?" Statler asked.

"Yes . . . yes . . . all is lost, I'm afraid."

Almost as if caused by the colonel's words, the sound of artillery fire ended. The officer groaned. "I suppose the colors have been' struck."

"What happened?"

The colonel sat silently for several moments. Then: "I'm Milton Haynes," he said hesitantly, "of the Tennessee Corps of Artillery." Another long pause. "Please understand, sir, that I did *not* desert under fire."

Statler nodded.

"It was very bad," Haynes went on. "Seven gunboats were arrayed in two battle lines against us, the ironclads in the van, and when they came out from behind the cover of that small island in the river all opened fire on us as one. It was telling fire. Rapid. It was like one broad and leaping sheet of flame.

"Captain Taylor, a most capable and brave officer, directed our fire and in the first twenty minutes or so made the Federals pay for their attack. One of the ironclads—the *Essex,* I think it was—took a shot through her boiler and was disabled, dropping out of the line.

"But we were dreadfully outgunned. And when our usually effective rifle burst . . . killing the crew outright"—he winced—"the only real weapon we had was the Columbiad. It was bad. Very bad, indeed."

Once more he paused. "The toll on the men was terrible. And it seemed, as the minutes passed, that the rains of a week raised the flood level even more. In the lower sections of the fort the water was waist-deep." Colonel Haynes sighed. "In any event, I went to General Tilghman—the Confederacy owes him a great debt—and asked if he was going to surrender. 'Yes,' he replied, 'we cannot hold out. I have not enough capable men left to man two guns.' Then I said, 'Sir, I will not surrender and you have no right to include me in the capitulation as an officer of this garrison.' That may seem arrogant to you, but, you see, it was true; I was *not* a garrison officer. I had been sent there only as an observer. General Tilghman shook my hand, as the gentleman he is, and I left the fort, passing down to a stable where I found a horse abandoned without tack on him. And I mounted him and somehow made my way here . . . swimming a sheet of backwater at one point . . . and—"

Words failed the colonel momentarily as he began to weep. In time: "The Confederacy has lost everything at Fort Henry but *honor.*"

IV

It was 2 A.M. on the seventh before the Fort Henry contingent finally reached Fort Donelson, exhausted beyond belief. Just under 2,600 men had been saved by General Tilghman's judicious action, protecting their safety with an hour-and-a-quarter-long defense of his untenable position, commanding a cadre of less than a hundred loyal artillerymen.

The commanders of Fort Donelson didn't have to be told of the loss of Fort Henry. Victorious Union Brigadier General U. S. Grant had already made that public and the news had been relayed to Nashville and thus to Donelson. General Tilghman had been taken prisoner, as had the gallant artilleryman Captain Jesse Taylor. All of the quartermaster's stores were likewise in Federal hands, as well as ten pieces of heavy artillery, including the Columbiad gun, and six fieldpieces. That was ordnance the still small Confederate army in the west could ill afford to lose.

General Gideon Pillow, the nominal commander of Fort Donelson, was not there when Statler Dewey arrived from Fort Henry and he approached a lieutenant colonel named Gilmer, who seemed to be in charge at that hour. The newspaperman identified himself, asking: "Is it likely an attack on this fort is imminent?"

"Highly unlikely," the colonel replied easily. "This is *not* Fort Henry, sir. As the chief engineer of the Western Department I can tell you we are adequately prepared to drive back any Union flotilla. Further, there are sufficient troops here to repel any landing from the Federal transports." He drew himself up importantly. "There will be no Confederate colors struck at this fort, Mr. Dewey."

"Then I ought to take this respite to get back to Nashville and my newspaper," Statler said. "Is there water transportation available?"

"The steam mail launch will leave at dawn for the city," Colonel Gilmer informed him. "You are welcome to be on it."

"I have a horse and wagon outside—"

The colonel called over an orderly who was instructed to take charge of the Dewey property. "And if you can't return, sir, we'll utilize the animal as best we can."

Dewey thanked him and sat down to await the sun's rising, composing in his mind the opening sentence of his dispatch:

"Although lost to enemy action, the small Fort Henry on the Tennessee River will forever serve as an example of the honor and courage of Confederate officers and men. Fort Henry will be Tennessee's Alamo."

And he felt pride. The future, he was certain, would be glorious with Confederate victories.

34

ALMA May Dewey's Diary, Tuesday, February 11, 1862:

In the midst of our deep concerns about what this war will bring us there is some joyful news. Lady Bea and her husband, the Rev. Alston Merit, came to Bon Marché last night to tell the family they are to have a child sometime in July. Grandmother Louise, while delighted, confided in me: "I'm not so sure I want to be regarded as a great-grandmother." I am greatly worried about Louise; she has grown more frail and the palsy in her hands has become quite pronounced. Then, too, she has become preoccupied with talk of her twin, Lee, fearing for his well-being. Even the news that Lee has decided to retire—the twins are nearly seventy—from his increasingly dangerous work as a correspondent, staying now with Albert in Lexington, has not diminished Louise's dour premonitions. As for myself, I am more fearful of what might happen to those actively involved in the war. Word now is that Able and his Nashville Grays have left Camp Harris at Allisonia to join General Johnston's army; to what end we do not know. Then, too, True's sons, Capt. Herbert & Lt. Victor, were both at Bon Marché most briefly two days ago—staying less than an hour—on their way to join the cavalry forces of Col. Nathan Forrest at Fort Donelson. That assignment is the most worrisome; it seems certain the Federal forces will attack Donelson sometime soon, given their successes at Fort Henry. Statler, though, contends Do-

nelson will hold. I don't trust his evaluation. I want to,
God knows, but my common sense tells me my nephew
is suffering from a bad case of naïveté . . .

II

STATLER Dewey, in mid-afternoon of that same day, stood on
the deck of the little steam launch that was prepared to depart
the Nashville wharf just as soon as the principal passenger
came aboard. They were waiting for Brigadier General Simon
Buckner, who was to be on the command staff at Fort Donelson.

The newspaperman, although he had lived with it daily, was
somewhat astonished by how quickly Nashville had become a
wartime city; a storehouse for the necessities of battle—ordnance, supplies, provisions, all being unloaded from steamboats tied up at the docks. And elsewhere in the city, he
knew, from countless railroad cars. Clearly Nashville was vital
to the well-being of the western Confederacy, making what
would happen at Fort Donelson in the days ahead so vastly
important. And there were few secrets: it was commonly
known on the streets of Nashville that the Union gunboats
which had so quickly reduced Fort Henry had now entered
the Cumberland River. Rumors raced through Nashville. Reports of the size of the invading force varied greatly: 15,000
men some had said, 25,000 said others, one rumor Statler had
heard even put the number at 50,000.

Statler was heartened, though, by his knowledge of the
quality of the command at Fort Donelson, most notably Brigadier General John B. Floyd, who had been Secretary of War
in the cabinet of President Buchanan. Then, too, there was
Brigadier General Gideon Pillow, a former officer in the U.S.
Army in the war with Mexico. And Colonel Nathan Bedford
Forrest, regarded as one of the South's most capable cavalry
officers. And the man the steam launch now awaited: the
grandly named Simon Bolivar Buckner, also of the Old
Army. In the North, of course, all were regarded as traitors.
Indeed, General Floyd had been accused of malfeasance in
office when he was the Secretary of War, charges that had
been disproved but not forgotten.

There was a flurry of activity on Water Street as several

carriages rolled up. From them came Brigadier General Buckner and his staff. Buckner was a handsome man, his square face featuring a full mustache. But there was no beard and no modish sideburns. He had the carriage of a commander, no doubt of that.

Statler waited until the launch had cast off and was in midstream in the Cumberland before he approached the general and introduced himself.

"Ahhh, Mr. Dewey," the general said, "I've read your report on the Fort Henry incident and I commend you for your tribute to the gallant General Tilghman. His sacrifice will not be forgotten by any of those who serve the Confederacy."

"What's your evaluation, sir, of the situation at Fort Donelson?" Statler wanted to know.

"Yes . . . Donelson . . ." General Buckner lightly ran the side of his thumb over both sides of his mustache as if trying to smooth it out. "I'm sure the officers and men of Fort Donelson will give a good account of themselves."

The answer disappointed Dewey. He had expected, had wanted, something more authoritarian, perhaps something more dramatic. He pressed Buckner: "Will the Fort Donelson garrison be able to throw back the enemy?"

"War, Mr. Dewey, as much as those of us who wage it would wish otherwise, does not lend itself well to accurate prediction."

"But—"

The thumb touched the mustache again. "You'll have to excuse me, sir. I have matters of importance to discuss with my staff." He turned quickly and walked to the other side of the launch where his staff waited in a small circle.

The newspaperman stared after him, somehow disillusioned.

Fort Donelson was just south of the boundary between Kentucky and Tennessee, some fifty twisting miles from Nashville. It was an enclosure of a hundred acres crowning a plateau overlooking the Cumberland River. Statler, when he had been there four days earlier, had not really seen it; he had arrived in the dead of night and had left it just at dawn. Now, as there was still some daylight when Buckner's launch approached it, it looked to him as a fort should look. Imposing, strong; the word "impregnable" came to mind. There was nothing about it to suggest the inadequacies of the doomed Fort Henry.

Its location seemed ideal, topping a bluff some 120 feet in height on the west side of the stream, at a point where the river made a slight bend to the eastward. Three batteries faced the water: the lowest about twenty feet above the flow, the second about fifty feet above the water, the third on the summit. In all, Statler counted fifteen big guns; a deadly array. Outside the fort's walls, and stretching far along the ridges that cradled it, rifle pits had been dug, protected by logs covered with hard red clay, suggesting permanence. Still farther beyond, the hillsides were covered with felled trees, the branches tightly interlaced. Statler could visualize a division hidden behind them, ready to lay down a withering fire that would deny any incursion by a foolhardy foe.

When the launch tied up at the fort's dock, General Buckner was welcomed in a desultory ceremony and then quickly led away by a captain. *To a council of war,* the newspaperman thought. He felt a need to further familiarize himself with the surroundings while there was still light and walked slowly to the rear of the fort (which is to say the western side of it away from the river), to find there a tented city, separated into small communities representing brigades, battalions, companies. They, too, were dug in. The heights around the tents bristled with fieldpieces. At one point there were two substantial log redoubts, small fortresses in their own right, stretched along the Eddyville road almost directly opposite the rear of the main fort. Statler studied the muddy roads leading from Fort Donelson. To the south, in the general direction of Nashville, the Charlotte Road, which ran past the little village of Dover (perhaps a thousand yards removed), joined up with the Eddyville Road, forming an important junction.

Statler came upon the encampment of Colonel Forrest's cavalry and asked a trooper tending several iron pots of victuals hanging over a small fire: "Can you direct me to Captain Herbert Jackson?"

"Over there," the trooper muttered, pointing to one of the larger tents nearby.

As he came within a few yards of the tent he was challenged by a musket-toting guard.

"My name is Statler Dewey," he said. "I wish to see Captain Jackson."

The guard poked his head inside the tent and said some words Statler couldn't make out. Immediately, Jackson came out, rushing to him and embracing him. "Uncle Statler, what are you doing here?"

"Like you," the uncle replied, "I'm here on duty." That sounded good to Statler; just the proper words. "I intend to witness the defeat of the enemy."

Herbert smiled. "We all want to see that, Uncle."

"I came with General Buckner," Statler explained.

"Was General Floyd with him?"

"No."

There was a frown now. "Our leaders, it seems, are a bit . . . well, tardy."

"But the battle hasn't begun," Statler shrugged.

"But it has! True, no shots have been fired yet, but the Federals are in the vicinity."

"What!" Dewey was startled. "Less than a week ago a colonel—I can't recall his name but he was a ranking engineering officer—told me the Union forces would not be allowed to disembark from the transports on the Cumberland."

"That was never their intention, apparently," the young captain said. "Our scouts report they're coming overland from Fort Henry."

"But—?"

Herbert answered the question he knew his uncle meant to ask. "It would not do to try to interdict them. It would be too costly; at least, that's the prevailing military theory. No, Uncle Statler, the battle will be fought here, where we have the upper hand."

"How many are coming?"

"It's uncertain at this hour. Victor is out now with his patrol on reconnaissance, as are others, of course."

"And here?"

"Some eighteen thousand, I'd guess. As a lowly captain of cavalry I'm not privy to all of that intelligence. But all are thoroughly protected by what you see before you." A broad gesture encompassed the widely flung fortifications.

Statler's concern, his doubts, showed on his face. "And what about the enemy gunboats on the river?"

"As far as I know, they've not yet made an appearance in the neighborhood, but the fort is ready for them."

The uncle was soberly silent.

"Have they given you accommodations in the fort?" Herbert asked.

Dewey laughed. "My God, I never even thought of it till now."

"Then you'll stay here. My brother's patrol won't be back until morning and you can use Victor's cot."

"I might as well."

"I can offer you a very modest supper." A grin broke on Herbert's face. "And I just happened to bring along a ready supply of Bon Marché bourbon. Alma May made certain of that."

It was a pleasant respite. Night had brought an inky blackness as Statler Dewey tried to get comfortable on his nephew's field cot. And as he felt sleep coming he thought of what General Buckner had told him hours earlier: "War, as much as those of us who wage it would wish otherwise, does not lend itself to accurate prediction."

III

STATLER had slept well during the chilly night, helped by the soothing medication of the bourbon. But he had been awakened—it was not yet dawn of Wednesday, February 12—by the sound of gunfire. Not anything concerted, but quite a few shots of a sporadic nature.

"The sharpshooters are out," Captain Jackson moaned from his adjoining cot. "A strange breed, those. Free-lance hired killers, you might say—the tradition goes back to days of knighthood." He rose and started to dress. "I've heard the theory expounded that what keeps men sane in war, what makes it all tolerable, is that you don't know whom you've killed—or if you've killed anyone at all—when firing a gun as a member of a great unit. An army, made up of so many others whose shots might have been the lethal ones, saves the individual from guilt. With the sharpshooter, however, he knows whom he kills. Maybe not the name and rank, but his skills assure him that someone dies when he pulls the trigger with a forehead in the sights."

More shots were heard.

"But it's dark out there," Statler said.

"There's just the beginning of light," Herbert replied. "Right now the sharpshooters are simply limbering up their Henry rifles. Testing sights, figuring distances and windage. It's a deadly game, Uncle Statler, and they play it extremely well."

Sounds of approaching horses and muffled voices came to their ears. Within seconds, Lieutenant Victor Jackson came into the tent, his weariness evident in his eyes. He didn't even acknowledge Statler there on his cot.

"We've lost Sergeant Marshall," he said to his older brother.

"Oh, good Lord! How?"

"A shooter. Hidden not three hundred yards out from this spot. Got the horse, too, with a second shot. He must have been very close to be that accurate, but we couldn't find him."

"The enemy's that close?"

"And in force. I'd say we are well surrounded. Or will be shortly." He turned to leave. "I must report to Forrest. But I thought you'd want to know about the sergeant." He was gone.

"You'll have to excuse Victor," the brother said apologetically, "for not greeting you, Uncle. I honestly think he didn't see you there. He was close, you see, to Sergeant Marshall, an Old Army veteran. They had developed"—Herbert hesitated—"well, almost a father-and-son relationship."

"No excuses are necessary," Statler said. "My being here is of little significance." He swung his legs off the cot, starting to pull on his boots (he had slept in his clothes). He felt a fear beginning to build in him and couldn't shake it off. On the night before he had failed to see the fort's commander, Brigadier General Pillow, and he wanted to do that as soon as possible to get an official assessment of the situation before the real fighting erupted.

"I'd like to offer you hot coffee, Uncle Statler," Herbert said, "but we don't dare light any fires now. There may be some cold dregs in a pot somewhere hereabouts."

"Don't concern yourself with me." The newspaperman embraced his nephew. "Just keep yourself safe."

IV

THE interior of Fort Donelson offered log-walled quarters for the permanent cadre and it bustled with activity as the light of the early morning began to filter in from the eastern horizon. Statler stood in the middle of it wondering where he might find General Pillow.

Someone hailed him. "Mr. Dewey, sir!"

He turned to find the orderly to whom he had entrusted his horse and carriage on his earlier visit hurrying toward him.

"I was kinda hopin'," the young man said sheepishly, "thet I wouldn't see you again. But I figured, when I saw you standin' there, that I oughta be honest 'bout it. I lost your horse an' carriage."

"Lost them?"

"Well, they ain't lost, exactly. I know where they be. Colonel Palmer of the Thirty-second Tennessee has . . . well, he's usin' them, you see."

Dewey smiled slightly. "Appropriated for the Confederate cause, eh?"

"Yes, sir, you could say thet."

Statler patted the orderly on the shoulder. "Then I'm satisfied. Now, could you direct me to General Pillow's quarters?"

The young soldier, much relieved, led the civilian to one of the larger log huts. "In there, Mr. Dewey."

Generals Pillow and Buckner, surrounded by members of their staffs, were at a field desk going over a series of maps when Statler entered. Buckner introduced him.

Gideon Pillow was a full-bearded man (the beard graying) whose head seemed too small for his body. Dewey had heard he was a querulous individual, jealous of his station. At that moment General Pillow was clearly annoyed by the interruption.

"Duty commands our attention right now, Mr. Dewey—"

Statler wasn't going to be put off. "I'm told that the enemy has the fort surrounded."

Pillow's eyes narrowed as he stared at the newspaperman. "The enemy, sir, is doing exactly what was anticipated. He is moving some troops from the vicinity of Fort Henry, but we are *not* surrounded."

"Then you're going to drive him back before the area can be invested?"

"Are you a military tactician as well as a journalist, Mr. Dewey?" Pillow snapped.

"No, but—"

"Then I suggest, sir, that you allow those of us who are to get on with our work."

Statler persisted. "What of the gunboats on the river?"

"There is but one, Mr. Dewey, of no real consequence at this hour. As politely as I can, sir, I must ask you to leave."

"And General Floyd? Is he en route to take command?"

"He is. In his absence the command, I assure you, is in capable hands." Pillow turned back to the maps, dismissing Statler with his action.

The lack of the sense of urgency he felt worried Statler as he left Pillow's quarters. A light snow had begun to fall; in only a short time the fortification was covered with a white blanket. Temperatures had plunged. Dewey drew his great-coat tighter around him, but he noted that many of the Confederate soldiers in the fort were not so fortunate. They were ill-dressed and many of them were shivering as they went about their duties. There was another thing of concern: what had seemed such an impregnable place when Statler arrived with Buckner now was revealed as being unfinished. Construction work was still under way, especially on the critical river batteries.

The "war correspondent"—how ridiculous the phrase seemed now—tried to reach an independent assessment of Fort Donelson. He could not; not with any certainty. And when noon came he realized he was poorly prepared for being there. He had no quarters and he could not imagine the taciturn General Pillow would provide him any. There was the further unhappy realization that he had no provisions and he was genuinely hungry. He felt the fool.

Then, suddenly, there was a flurry of activity, with men hurrying to their stations on the guns of the batteries. Statler mounted the parapet to scan the river with his glass. Out from under the low-hung clouds he could see the ungainly silhouette of a Federal gunboat emerge, the black smoke from its stack slowly dissipating over it like a shroud. It came to within three hundred yards of the fort when there was a huge flash from a bow gun. Its projectile splashed harmlessly into the Cumberland River. But the aim was corrected and the gunboat methodically threw nine more shells at the fort—Dewey counted them aloud—all of them thudding into the earth-works surrounding the Confederate batteries, sending great showers of dirt over the artillerymen cowering behind low, protective log walls.

The only response to the attack was the echo of the gunfire reverberating over the low hills. The gunboat began to with-draw. From south of the fort Statler could faintly hear the chorused cheers of men and then the rattle of musketry, as if the gunboat's activities had encouraged the enemy infantry into action. But it, too, lasted for only a brief period of time. As Statler let himself down from the parapet he began to shake involuntarily; his exposed presence there, it flashed through his mind, had made him an easy target.

He was totally perplexed in his private fright. *Why hadn't the fort responded? The Union gunboat crew must have be-lieved Fort Donelson was abandoned. Maybe that's it; maybe General Pillow wants the enemy to so believe. But to what end?*

Statler quickly ascertained there had been no casualties from the gunboat attack and turned his attention to his own plight. He needed quarters. And rations. He sought out the one man in the fort he knew as a friend—the young orderly who had "lost" his horse and carriage.

V

ROUGH hands shook Statler Dewey awake. "Mr. Dewey," the orderly said with urgency, "Floyd is here! You said I was to make sure to tell you when he came."

"Yes, yes, I did," Statler mumbled. "Thank you." He had gone to sleep in one of the log huts, sharing it with sixteen others, including the friendly orderly. And he had eaten a modest field-rations meal of hardtack and beef jerky before retiring. He rose now, rearranging his greatcoat. There had been no blanket for him; there seemed to be not enough blankets to go around in the extreme cold. Statler ran a hand over his face, the stubble of beard annoying him. He checked his pocket watch. It was two A.M.

"Where is he?" he asked the orderly.

"In with Pillow an' the others."

"Thank you," Statler said, patting the orderly on the shoulder. "Thank you."

Outside the log cabin he found that the snow had stopped and the temperatures seemed to have moderated a bit. Hurrying to Pillow's quarters he walked into the council of war. Pillow glowered at him as Buckner once more officiated with an introduction.

Brigadier General John B. Floyd was a hawk-nosed, burly man with prominent cheekbones and deep-set eyes. He greeted Statler effusively: "I'm pleased to see you here, Mr. Dewey, because it gives me the opportunity to thank you for your published defense of General Tilghman."

"That's kind of you, sir, but I don't think General Tilghman needed a defense. The truth of his heroism at Fort Henry was real enough."

Floyd frowned. "But truth, Mr. Dewey, is often an elusive thing, as I have learned in Washington in years just past." The subject was changed quickly. "You've been given accommodations here?"

"Some of the volunteers have made room for me."

"Oh, I think we can do better than that." He turned to a captain at his elbow. "See to it. And Mr. Dewey is to be our guest at the officers' mess."

"Yes, sir."

General Pillow demonstrated his dislike of the newspaperman's intrusion by making little impatient tapping noises with his fingers on the pile of maps spread out before them.

"General Pillow," Floyd said to Statler, chuckling, "would much prefer that you didn't stay and observe our deliberations." Then to Pillow: "I think, Gideon, we can safely allow Mr. Dewey to remain, believing, as *I do,* that he has amply demonstrated his patriotism. In any event, given the hard place in which we now find ourselves, we may yet need Mr. Dewey's defense in the public print."

A warm, satisfied feeling came to Statler. He was, finally, being allowed to play what might be a significant role in the history of the Confederate States of America.

35

DAWN of Thursday, February 13, might have been regarded as an omen. The wet, cold, miserable weather of the previous week and more gave way to a premature spring. There were breezes, not winds, and balmy temperatures prevailed. Statler left his greatcoat in the new quarters assigned to him on General Floyd's orders. Enlisted men and volunteers at Fort Donelson, especially those manning the batteries overlooking the river, soon stripped to their shirtsleeves.

Scouts were busy as the warm sun came up. And Statler, enjoying the confidence of the commanding general, had a full appreciation of the situation. The movement by Union General Grant of a large force from the Fort Henry area had put Brigadier General John McClernand in command of a division taking up a position south of the fort, where Pillow would face him. Brigadier General Charles Smith was heading another Federal division investing the area on the north side of the fort, his movements—and the true strength of his army—largely screened by heavy woods; Buckner would command the resistance there.

Pillow's task seemed to be the most critical. He had to defend large quantities of supplies and ordnance held in the tiny village of Dover, only a thousand yards removed from Fort Donelson. Also, he had to keep control of the important junction of the Eddyville and Charlotte roads, the only overland connection with Nashville and the western division commander, General A. Sidney Johnston. Relief for the fort, if such should be needed, would have to come from Johnston; the road had to remain open.

Statler wondered once more why the Federals were being allowed to make their incursions without challenge. He reasoned that it might be more advantageous to the Confederate well-being to hit the enemy while on the move, before the two divisions *(and was it greater than that?)* could dig in and establish a siege position. He wanted to ask hard questions of General Floyd but was timid, not willing to make himself unwelcome. Floyd had befriended him; he meant to keep it that way. Still, he was uneasy about what seemed to be a dangerous waiting game.

First action of the day came, however, not from the growing strength of the enemy infantry, but from the river. It was just after nine o'clock when the smoke of a lone gunboat—likely the one of the day before—could be seen in the distance. From the protection of a wooded point on a bend of the Cumberland, the gunboat opened fire on the fort. And this time there was no desultory, limited shelling; this time heavy shells rained on Fort Donelson in uncountable numbers. This time the Confederate batteries answered in kind, the din making even shouted orders incomprehensible. This time there was blood.

The lowest Donelson battery, the one nearest the water, was hit hard and silenced as artillerymen, several of them with grievous, flesh-tearing wounds, abandoned their stations, struggling up the steep bluff to seek the safety of the fort. They brought with them three dead. For the first time, Statler Dewey understood the terror of war.

It soon became apparent that even the interior of the fort was not safe. At about eleven o'clock a huge shell arched high over the ramparts and fell with devastating results into one of the log buildings housing the permanent cadre. Statler rushed to the scene, helping as best he could to tear at the remains of the ruined building, searching for victims. Several were pulled out alive, but as Statler and an infantryman struggled to move one of the heavy logs they uncovered a lad, perhaps no more than sixteen, his skull crushed, the one eye still visible in his head staring up at them. Statler retched.

"Musta been a sixty-four-pounder," the newspaperman's companion commented.

Statler was without words as they lifted the body out of the wreckage and laid it gently on the muddy street, side by side with three others. The bombardment continued.

Suddenly, just before noon, the gunboat stopped firing. Tentatively, the two remaining batteries at the fort also fell silent.

"We've hit her!" someone screamed in joy. "We've knocked her out!"

Cheers reverberated throughout Fort Donelson. Statler could not join in them. That one eye staring from a pulpy, bloodied skull was not an image he'd soon forget.

II

IF the situation at Fort Donelson was desperate, it was not immediately apparent in the midnight council of war convened by General Floyd. True, there were no expressions of great confidence, but there wasn't any panic, either. Statler, as he listened to the deliberations, searched his mind for a word, a phrase, to best describe the attitude of the generals. He settled on "businesslike." Floyd, Pillow, and Buckner were men used to the business of war, capable of assessing it unemotionally. And this they did.

To Statler, though, the cumulative effect of the reports he heard delivered were a lot more devastating than the generals' calm demeanor would suggest. For one thing, the gunboat had *not* been knocked out. Maybe it had been hit by the fort's gunners, but it had returned in mid-afternoon to resume shelling of the fort; with less intensity than before perhaps, but with a persistence that lasted until nightfall. Now, a local spy (a farmer from the neighborhood, really) was on hand to tell of the arrival on the river of three more ironclads and two wooden gunboats.

"Transports?" General Floyd asked.

"Ain't seen none," the farmer replied.

Floyd thanked him for the information and urged that he remain alert for any sign of troop transports on the river.

It was the intelligence of cavalry colonel Nathan Forrest that most distressed Statler. His scouts, Forrest reported to the generals, had identified another large movement of troops from the Fort Henry area.

"Most likely under General Wallace's command. We know he was being held in reserve at Fort Henry." Colonel Forrest indicated on a map where the new troops had been deployed. "He's filled in here between Smith and McClernand, enabling McClernand to extend his line so that he's now fully across the Charlotte road."

Statler noticed that General Pillow winced.

"In what strength is Wallace?" Floyd wanted to know.

"Considerable," Forrest answered calmly. "Three brigades at least. With two artillery units, as near as we can tell."

"Then Grant must have twenty thousand before us," Floyd said.

"Yes, sir. At least that many."

Forty-eight hours earlier Statler had believed the Confederate forces at Donelson numbered 18,000. Now the Union forces had a slight numerical edge. General Floyd's concern about the possibility of troop transports on the Cumberland indicated he believed Grant was bringing up still more men.

As he left the council of war Statler was bedeviled by the persistent, unanswered questions coursing through his brain.

What hadn't there been an earlier Confederate attack when the first of the Federal troops began to arrive from Fort Henry?

Why had this latest force been allowed to invest the center of the line with virtually no opposition?

Why hadn't there been some effort to keep the enemy clear of the vital Charlotte road?

Can Fort Donelson now be relieved from Nashville if circumstances make it necessary?

He thought, too, of the additional gunboats reported on the river and he shivered. Partly because he felt some fright (he could admit that to himself) and partly because it was turning cold again.

III

THE false spring of the day before was only a memory as Friday, February 14, became a reality. Winter had returned; suddenly and vengefully. The winds had shifted around to the north with stormlike intensity, bringing with them a disagreeable mixture of rain, snow, and sleet. Statler was icy cold when he awakened from a troubled sleep. And he dressed hurriedly, drawing on the greatcoat he had tossed aside on the previous morning.

He ran through the freezing rain to the small officers' mess, glad to see a fire laid there. Glad also to see General Floyd seated alone at a rough-hewn table, breaking fast. Dewey poured some steaming water from a kettle and made himself some tea, which he carried to the table. The general seemed far away; preoccupied. It took him a moment or two to realize Statler stood there.

"Good morning, Mr. Dewey," Floyd said pleasantly enough. "Please join me, sir."

"If I'm not intruding."

The general laughed. "The whole damned war is an intrusion, isn't it?"

"It is, yes," Statler replied soberly as he sat down. He wondered what he ought to say; the questions he wanted to ask seemed impertinent when he reviewed them in his mind. Instead: "It occurs to me, General, that this severe reverse in the weather may be a godsend."

"Oh, how?"

"Won't this storm deter the enemy?"

"The enemy?" Floyd mused. "It sounds strange, doesn't it? I was once the Secretary of War for the 'enemy.'" He sighed. "No, Mr. Dewey, the weather will make no difference in what happens in these precincts today. You see, I have an advantage that most other generals in the Confederacy don't have. I know Sam Grant—most don't. He'll probably never be written down as a brilliant military tactician. Nor even an imaginative one. No, nothing like that. And because he isn't brilliant or imaginative, this . . . uh . . . sudden brigadier general isn't going to act impulsively. His attack will come when he believes he has superior advantage, both in numbers and firepower. And then his attack will be unrelenting, the weather be damned!"

Statler stared at the commanding general for a long moment. "Excuse me, sir, I mean no disrespect . . . but it sounds to me that you . . . uh . . . well, that you believe General Grant will win here."

From off in the distance could be heard the muffled boom of heavy guns, carried to them by the strong north winds.

General Floyd cocked his head listening for a few seconds
before he responded. "What I believe, Mr. Dewey, is that
this fort might have had a site that was better chosen. That it
was too hastily made, in many places . . . uh . . . injudiciously
constructed. And most damning, sir, that it is of virtually no
military significance."

Dewey was shocked by the general's candor. "But—but,"
he stammered, "there's Nashville to consider."

"Indeed, there is. And if its defense had not been left to
local political considerations—that is to say, men of no military training residing in the state government—it might be
adequately fortified by now, able to withstand much more
than we'll face here in the next day or two."

The newspaperman found it difficult to comprehend what
he was hearing. "Then Nashville is lost?"

"I would hope not, but I don't know. What I *do know,* sir,
is that Manassas and what is happening here have set the pattern of this war." He hesitated. "We will have to accept this
truth: in the future it will be the role of the North to attack
and of the South to defend. Military history tells us, Mr.
Dewey, that the advantage is most often with the attacker."

A corporal entered the room, stiffly saluting General Floyd,
extending a folded paper to him. The commander took it,
read it, and groaned.

"That gunfire we've been hearing," Floyd said, "is cover
fire being laid down by Grant's gunboats, four miles distant
. . . cover fire for the disembarking of fresh troops from a
large flotilla of transports. Our informant could only guess at
the number, so numerous are they."

He stood quickly, jammed the message into his pocket, and
added: "You'll have to pardon me. My duty now is to see to
the well-being of the brave men I brought to this place." John
Floyd hurried from the room, the corporal in his wake.

Statler stared after him, greatly depressed by what he had
been told. He thought of himself as dead or dying there hard
by the Cumberland River. His mind showed him the images
of his beautiful Harriet and of his three darling daughters.
And self-interest became a companion to his fear. *His* duty,
he concluded, was to leave Fort Donelson by the first means
available.

IV

IT was a dreadful day for Statler. Not only was the weather impossible, but he recognized that General Floyd's somber assessments of the worth of Fort Donelson were true. He knew there was general fighting all along the line behind the fort; the noise of it came clear to him. But he was cut off from knowledge of exactly what was happening in the field. It was all confusion, made more frightening by the steady arrival within the fort of wounded from the battle. Of terribly hurt men, bloody and torn, with few to care for them. Some were laid out in the streets of the fortification, left to the merciless cold and wet; they were going to die anyway. After a while, he could not look at them. Guilt brought on by his inability to help the unfortunate men sickened him.

Then, in mid-afternoon, what had become a personal hell for Statler Dewey turned worse in his eyes. There appeared on the river six gunboats; the four in the van were the ungainly ironclads. Firing on Fort Donelson began when they came within four hundred yards—from big mortars and rifled artillery guns. The fort's batteries responded vigorously and the air was thick with solid shot and exploding shells. The noise was deafening, a solid, unbroken wall of sound punctuated by the muscular thump of the fort's giant Columbiad gun, hurling 128-pounders at the advancing gunboats.

And they came closer. Three hundred yards, then two hundred. At that distance it was impossible for Donelson's gunners to miss them. Statler, his fright sublimated to his morbid fascination with what was happening before him, watched the gunboats through his glass. A huge projectile launched by the Columbiad struck one of the gunboat anchors, hoisted to the deck, literally reducing it to sparking shards of deadly metal, carrying away part of the smokestack at the same time. He could see wounded men writhing on the deck. Another well-directed shot from the fort smashed into a pilothouse, knocking the iron plating to pieces. A small launch hanging on davits on one of the ironclads was reduced to splinters by a direct hit. A violent explosion on another boat ripped a big gun to pieces, again taking an immediate human toll. One of the wooden boats was set afire. Wheel ropes necessary to steer the gunboats were shot away; two of them collided in midstream. Smoke from the boats' boilers mingled with the smoke from the black powder employed, settling a pall over the river. Strangely, the black clouds of smoke obliterated from Statler's view what was closest to him. He could not see what was happening, what toll was being taken, in the fort's batteries.

For two hours it went on. Then the gunboats began to slowly withdraw. Just as slowly the firing diminished. And stopped. An exultant cheer went up from the Fort Donelson denizens. Statler's reaction was one of disbelief; the Union gunboats which had so quickly reduced Fort Henry had been beaten back here at Fort Donelson. *Was it a victory?* It seemed so, but the newspaperman could not forget the candor of General Floyd's evaluations earlier in the day. *A victory?* He'd need confirmation.

It came a few minutes later when he sought out General Pillow, whom he found in a joyful mood.

"Ahhh, Dewey," he said with uncharacteristic friendliness, "you may want to hear what I have just telegraphed to General Johnston in Nashville." He read from a paper he had clutched in his hand. "'We have just had the fiercest fight on record between our guns and six gunboats, which lasted two hours. They came within two hundred yards of our batteries. We drove them back, damaged two of them badly, and crippled a third very badly. No damage done to our battery and not a man killed.'"

That last—was it a lie? Statler reasoned that it *had* to be, given the incessant shelling of the batteries by the gunboats. Then, charitably, he put another word to it: "exaggeration." Victory would allow, he told himself, some embroidery, some hyperbole.

V

VICTORY? Its perception was short-lived.

An after-dark council of war called by General Floyd, the fort's senior commander, put an end to any thought of victory. Certainly the gunboats had been beaten back, but the other realities of Fort Donelson were more compelling. It was a sober gathering of officers. All of the commanders of divisions and brigades, and some of their aides, were there.

"We are under stern siege," Floyd told them. "The Federal

numbers have been augmented, from the transports, to fully eighty-three regiments. I see no recourse, short of abject surrender, but to try to escape—to save the garrison, or a part of it, at least. There is one rational hope, I believe, if we act promptly, to dislodge the enemy from his position on our left. To cut through him and thus pass out people into the open country lying southward toward Nashville."

There was no dissent in the council as General Floyd outlined his strategy. Pillow's division was to strike the Union forces on the extreme left; at the same time Buckner was to command an attack near the center of the lines.

"If we act early and decisively before the enemy can fall in, perhaps while he's asleep," Floyd said, "we can surprise him sufficiently to make a hole through which we can escape. General Buckner will then hold the position as a rear guard to our departure."

Many heads nodded agreement.

"Very well, then," the commanding general added. "Three days' rations are to be issued to all. The men are to have their haversacks with them." There was a strained smile. "We don't intend to return."

Brigade commanders engaged in more specific planning of details necessary for moving out with 10,000 men or more. It was nearly midnight when the council disbanded. By that time, Statler Dewey had made his own decision.

In the group of officers was a friend he knew from earlier, happier times: Colonel John Brown of the Third Tennessee Regiment of Volunteers. Statler approached him.

"John, I need to attach myself to someone to get out of here," he said. "I hope I may join your group."

"Would that be wise?"

"I *must* go."

The colonel laid a hand on his shoulder. "It's not going to be a soiree, you know. I think you might be safer right here, regardless of the morning's outcome."

Statler shook his head stubbornly. "But I cannot stay. I don't wish to be in Federal hands."

"But Statler, you're a civilian—"

"Will that be a shield? I think not. Whatever the risk, I must try to get back to my family!"

"Of course," Colonel Brown said quietly; his face was somber. "We're to be in the van of Buckner's army. And may God keep us all."

36

GOD, it appeared, turned his face from Fort Donelson on that morning of Saturday, February 15. The weather remained dreadful with temperatures well below the freezing point and intermittent snow falling. The paths and roads the garrison of the fort would have to traverse to save itself were underlaid with ice. Confederate haversacks were full, both with the three days of provisions issued and every piece of personal property the soldiers could carry. Colonel Brown had seen to it that Statler had also received a haversack and provisions, but the newspaperman knew he could expect no more concessions; he was a nonproductive civilian intruded onto a military stage, his role meaningless in the drama to unfold. Statler thought, morosely, that he wasn't even a spear carrier. His ultimate well-being would have to be his own concern. And luck's.

As the thousands of men prepared to leave their entrenchments an eerie silence of sorts settled over the body. It would have seemed a great deal of noise ought to accompany the movements of the army: the rattle of muskets and tin ammunition boxes, the staccato beat of the shod hooves of cavalry horses on the frozen ground, the jolting and rumbling of heavy gun carriages. Yet, all of those normal sounds were somehow muffled, as if the sounds themselves were live creatures recognizing the need for not being normal. The besieging enemy was dug in close at hand, in some instances no less than one hundred fifty yards removed, and it would not do to arouse him prematurely. Surprise would have to be the garrison's principal weapon.

Orders came to move out—not shouted but passed in a relay of quiet voices—and Statler Dewey attached himself to a company of Tennessee volunteer infantrymen who were part of Colonel Brown's command. He was there in the middle of young men clad not in the gray of the Confederate officers but in the nut-brown homespun uniforms of their state units. As they went forward toward the Federal lines stretching across the escape roads Statler realized his would be a narrow, restricted view of what was to happen; he would not be privy to any Olympian overview. But he didn't care. On this day he was not a newspaperman, not the foolishly romantic war correspondent he had imagined himself to be only a few days earlier. On this day he was simply a husband and father—a frightened man—who just wanted to get away.

It was just a few minutes after five o'clock, the darkness still cloaking them, when the hoped-for retreat from Fort Donelson began. They moved steadily, but slowly, along a road lined with an overgrowth of oak shrubs, their branches intertwined into what seemed a solid mass now covered with a veneer of snow. The terrain proved to be a succession of small hills and ravines and the walking was treacherous; several times Statler misstepped on the icy roadway and nearly fell. Time lost all meaning for him. He knew only that they were coming closer and closer to the Federals blocking the road to escape.

They had gone for nearly a half hour, Statler guessed (light had appeared under heavy snow-laden clouds), covering how much ground he could not know, when suddenly the unnatural quiet was shattered by the sound of gunfire. It started with a few sporadic shots but soon built into a crescendo of noise. The sounds were coming from off to the left, from General Pillow's assigned area. The clear notes of buglers sounding the alarm indicated that Pillow's men had indeed surprised the Union troops in their cold beds. The first part of General Floyd's plan apparently was successful.

"We'll be gettin' it soon," a young private walking next to Statler muttered.

"I'd imagine so," Statler replied. Those were the first words spoken in Dewey's hearing since they had left the fort's entrenchments.

The Tennessee volunteers, part of General Buckner's com-

mand, continued to move forward as the increased volume of
sound off to the left indicated that artillery fieldpieces were
being brought into play. But the Federal forces in front of
Buckner's advance, still unseen, were quiet. A minute passed.
And another. And another. And then they came to the crest
of a low hill and down below them was the waiting enemy.
There was a frozen moment of nothingness. A single rifle shot
spoke and the young soldier directly in front of Statler pitched
forward on his face, the blood pouring out of a hole that had
been his right eye staining red the virgin snow.

Dewey gasped, falling to his knees beside the boy, wanting
to somehow help him. It was a futile gesture. The Union
sharpshooter had done his job. In only a few ticks of time his
single shot grew into volleys, the frozen dirt of the road
around Statler erupting with what seemed to be tiny explosions, just inches from him. He dived into the thick tangle of
oak shrubs, hoping they would hide him. And when he
looked back to the road he saw at least six other Confederate
bodies sprawled grotesquely.

It took him a moment or two to realize that the Federal fire
was being matched by other volleys from within the oak thickets. He could see the scarlet flashes of the muskets, but he
could not see the men firing them. He squinted his eyes to
make out mounds under the oak leaves covering the ground.
The Tennessee volunteers had buried themselves in the wet
leaves, the brown of the leaves matching the brown of their
uniforms, affording them a natural camouflage. Statler did
likewise, shivering in the bitter cold.

His concept of what was happening was limited to the few
yards immediately around him. His mind saw no big picture;
it was as though he were being forced to see everything in
miniature, not unlike the porcelain miniatures his wife collected. But those were beautiful. Dewey's mental miniatures
were not.

Statler heard the rumble of Buckner's gun carriages being
brought up. The fieldpieces, hidden behind the crest of the
hill, lofted a steady stream of shells and canister in the direction of the enemy. In return came a terrible fire of grape,
shrapnel, and shells, tearing at the oak thickets. He flattened
himself on his belly, wishing he could dig himself into the
ground, wanting to be anywhere but where he was now.

He heard an exultant shout somewhere above him. Looking up he saw a Confederate sharpshooter nestled high in a big tree not five yards removed. Apparently he had seen one of his shots take effect on the enemy and he was cheering the deadly result. The newspaperman thought of the characterization of sharpshooters expressed by cavalry Captain Herbert Jackson just a few days earlier: "Free-lance hired killers, you might say—the tradition goes back to the days of knighthood." This sharpshooter took careful aim again as Statler watched him, fascinated. The trigger was squeezed and there was another whoop of delight.

But his successes had drawn special attention to him and suddenly there was a volley of lead ripping at the tree, gouging splinters from it, cut branches tumbling earthward. The sharpshooter, crouched in a fork of the tree, straightened up stiffly, the rifle leaving his hands and clattering down through the branches. He clung for an instant to the trunk until death loosened his hold and he thudded into the cushion of oak leaves below, just a yard or two from where Statler hid.

Almost immediately Dewey's attention was diverted from the dead man to the noisy rush of cavalry on the road. The troopers raced down the hill directly toward where the enemy must be massed. Cheers rose in the thicket and men abandoned their leafy camouflage to follow in the wake of the horses.

Had an order been given? If it had, Statler had not heard it. He hesitated, then also moved forward. If he was to get out of this alive, he reasoned, he'd have to stay with the Tennessee volunteers.

II

How long the pitched battle had been going on Dewey didn't know. A long time surely, but he had no certainty of time. Once, when the forward progress had slowed, he took out his pocket watch only to find it smashed. He thought at first it might have been broken by the several times he had dived on his stomach to seek a safe refuge. But then he discovered a hole through his clothing made by a bullet or a piece of shrapnel. He had felt no impact but, without question, the missile (whatever it was) had been stopped by the watch. There was brief nausea as he contemplated his good fortune.

Not only was Statler unaware of how much time had passed since they had left the entrenchments—low-hanging snow clouds prevented his using the sun as a natural measuring tool—but he was also in doubt about how much ground had been taken in the fighting. He knew they had gone steadily forward, in numerous stops and starts, and he guessed the advance had to be measured in hundreds of yards. All dearly bought. There had been no discernible break in the battle; the noise and the terror of it had been constant. Dewey feared the mental images of it would never be erased.

The unending clangor beat at his ears and then inside his head. At one time there was the impression that tens of thousands of men were beating on empty barrels with iron hammers. Not only had the snow become crimson with life blood, but there was an accompanying constant lurid red sheet of flame from the musketry and cannon. Smoke from the black powder clung like a shroud to the underbrush and treetops— kept from dissipating by the wet winter clouds. Together cloud and smoke ofttimes screened the combatants from each other. Inability to see the enemy was not a deterrent; the firing went on unabated. And as they moved forward, there was ample proof that the shot and shell had eyes in those circumstances. Bodies littered the path of the battle, Union and Confederate alike. And those were the fortunate ones. There were others, their flesh torn open to the bitter cold; some screamed in pain, some could only mumble as the strength of young bodies ebbed. At one point Statler saw two grievously wounded horses still trapped in the harness attached to a wrecked field artillery carriage. He watched as a soldier shot them in the head, releasing them from their torture. But no such relief was available in a humane society for the human casualties. Dewey contemplated that for a moment or two and then had to try to shrug it off. *It's the way of men,* he thought, *and there can be no other course.* But he didn't convince himself.

Buckner's army now had driven to within sight of the juncture of the Eddyville and Charlotte roads, where the Federals had thrown up a crude abatis across the intersection, the sharpened ends of the newly felled trees pointing toward the Confederate attack. Statler could see it from the slightly raised plateau now in control of the Confederates, and for the first time he was in a position to take out his glass and study the situation. At first the only Federal soldiers he saw were dead ones, scattered about like so much cordwood. An artillery fieldpiece lay half on its side, the exploded barrel pointing in a crazy angle to the sky. Then a figure rose up from behind the abatis, his hands raised high—an officer of some rank (he couldn't make out what rank). Behind him other figures moved, also with hands raised. Then a few more, then a dozen, then several dozen; the number grew as Statler realized they carried tin ammunition boxes in their hands, upside down to indicate they were empty.

They're surrendering!

A Confederate officer rode up to them as the firing on that front slowly abated. Dewey was on his feet now, running toward the abatis. He meant to be a witness to this moment of victory.

When he got up to the abatis he found that the surrendering officer was a lieutenant of artillery. He heard him say something about being from Illinois.

"My men are out of ammunition," he reported to the mounted Confederate major.

"Do you surrender, sir?" the major asked.

"We do."

In this moment of high drama, the major consulted his watch and then announced loudly: "Be it noted that it is eleven o'clock on the morning of Saturday, February fifteenth, in the year of the Lord 1862, and this gentleman surrenders in the name of the United States!"

A great cheer went up from the Confederate soldiers who were now pressing forward.

"March your men out," the major ordered, "and stack your arms. You are prisoners of the Confederate States of America."

There was another cheer, drowning out the sounds of battle still going on somewhere to the left of them. A great confusion prevailed as the Union soldiers came from their hiding places and dropped their muskets on a pile. Statler conjectured that there must be three hundred or more.

A cavalry officer rode up, a captain, saluted the major and reported: "Sir, the road is open to Nashville."

Quickly the word passed through the ranks and there were more cheers.

The major scrawled a quick note on a scrap of paper, handing it to a runner who was dispatched to take it to General Buckner. Other officers were bringing some order to the confusion. Units were being put together in marching order and the line of them began to stretch along the Charlotte road. Happy men, ready to march to freedom.

Perhaps a half hour went by in the preparation.

Another cavalry officer rode up to hand the major a dispatch. Statler was close enough to hear the cavalryman say: "Orders from General Pillow, sir."

The major read it, his face in a scowl. Then he seemed to read it again. Finally, he said to an aide: "We are ordered back to the entrenchments. Pass the word and let us get moving quickly before the situation worsens again."

Statler was unbelieving. The road to Nashville was open, so why this change in plans? He knew it was useless to question the major; he was, after all, a soldier obeying orders.

But I'm no soldier, the newspaperman thought. *I'm not bound to the commands of Pillow. There's nothing to prevent me from walking out on my own.*

However, the nausea of fear he had known earlier in the day returned. He wanted to weep in his realization that he had not the courage to do alone what he desperately wanted to do. Disconsolately, he found a place again in the ranks of the common soldiers.

Dear God, I shall never see my family again.

III

Two Confederate victories, Statler Dewey knew, had gone for naught. The earlier defeat of the Union gunboats on the Cumberland River had not been followed up, and the open road to Nashville, over which the Fort Donelson garrison might escape, had been abandoned. As darkness fell on that tragic Saturday the men under the commands of Generals Buckner and Pillow were back in their icy trenches. The retreat had not been easy; Federal sharpshooters dogged their steps all the way back to Fort Donelson, taking more lives. And when the Confederate soldiers got back they found a portion of their trenches had already been invested by several Federal units and another battle ensued to try to drive them out. The insanity of it all sickened Statler.

He made his way again from the trenches into the fort and to the quarters he had been assigned earlier. The bed he had occupied before was now given up to a wounded soldier; indeed, the log building had become a makeshift hospital. Statler found a corner and curled into it; he was totally exhausted, he believed he would never be warm again, he had resigned himself to dying there. With those thoughts in his mind, he fell into a troubled sleep.

All concept of time had been lost when he awakened. Except for light moans of the wounded in the room, Fort Donelson was strangely quiet. He ached in every chilly bone and he could smell himself. Painfully hoisting himself to his feet he decided to seek some answers to the bitter questions still unanswered.

Sentries were posted on the fort's parapets in greater numbers than before, but, except for that, there seemed no sense of urgency within the fortification. Instead, it was Statler's perception that the overwhelming sensation was one of depression. Or perhaps he was just caught up in his own feelings, reflecting them back on himself. His sleep had not refreshed him; he was still very cold and his damp clothes were freezing on him now that he had left the log building.

He stopped to talk to one of the sentries: "Would you know the hour, young man?"

"Very nearly one A.M., sir,"

A new day, Statler thought. A Sunday, but with none of the new beginning, the spiritual well-being, usually associated with a Sabbath day. "The generals," he asked, "have they retired?"

The sentry stared at him, apparently trying to determine whether this civilian he didn't know should be given such information. Finally: "They're in Dover, sir, as I understand it. I heard one officer say they were meeting in General Pillow's quarters there."

Statler moaned inwardly. *Could he find his way to Dover in the bitter darkness?* He decided it was imperative that he do so; after all, the village was less than a mile removed from the fort. Thanking the sentry, he left Fort Donelson. Footing was treacherous; every step of the way was iced over. But he pressed on even when he could no longer feel his feet. He had dire thoughts of frozen feet and gangrene and eventual amputation.

Suddenly, a welcome light beckoned in the darkness. As he drew closer to it he could make out a small stone house. He tried to hurry toward it, but his feet were setting their own slow pace, not answering the commands of his brain. The remaining distance to the house took an interminable time before he was at the door of what was certainly Pillow's headquarters—no other light showed anywhere in the vicinity. As he operated the latch it came to him that he had not once been challenged. *Suppose I had been a Federal soldier intent on assassination of the enemy's generals?*

Warmth assailed him as he entered the modest parlor where a fire was laid in a large country fireplace. Generals Floyd, Pillow, and Buckner sat in a small semicircle, their backs to the fire. Arrayed around them were their staff officers. Statler's presence was acknowledged by an almost imperceptible nod from Floyd, but no one spoke to him. They were intent on listening to a colonel who stood before the generals; Statler recognized him as cavalry commander Nathan Forrest.

"My men have just returned from the reconnaissance you ordered, sirs," Forrest was saying, "without seeing any of the enemy—"

Buckner interrupted. "But Mr. Rice, who lives in these precincts, has reported to us that the enemy has reinvested the ground around us. He has seen their camp fires."

"Those fires I believe to be at old campsites," Forrest insisted. "The high winds have just fanned them into blaze again. My scouts encountered no enemy, sirs."

"Your conclusions, Colonel?" Floyd asked.

"I don't believe the Federals can quickly reinvest their old positions. They took a solid beating yesterday."

"Then you believe we can march out in the morning?"

"I do. It seems to me our troops are in good spirits, knowing we've given the enemy a whipping."

"And the condition of the roads?" Floyd wanted to know.

"Poor, of course," Forrest admitted. "At the point of the river's overflow the mud is half-calf deep and would have to be avoided. But the water, which is skirt-high to the horses, could be traversed by the cavalry." He paused, looking in turn to each of the generals. "My scouts saw none of the enemy in their old positions."

General Pillow reacted with bravado. "It's my view we can again fight our way through the enemy's lines. We can cut our way out at daylight."

Statler, who had quietly made his way to a corner of the room nearest the fireplace, found Pillow's statement incomprehensible. *Hadn't the Confederate army already done that, only to be sent back to the trenches—on Pillow's orders—without marching out to safety?*

General Buckner shook his head firmly. "Gentlemen, my men have suffered for four days, being exposed to the elements without relief. They are so worn out and cut to pieces and demoralized that they *cannot* make another fight. Any attempt to extricate ourselves in the morning is almost hopeless." He glanced up at Forrest. "Everything I have learned indicates to me that we have been reinvested. Any attempt to march out would result in a massacre." The voice rose in intensity. "It would cost my command three fourths of its number to cut its way out, and it's wrong to sacrifice three fourths to save one fourth. No officer has a right to cause such a sacrifice."

"I agree," Floyd said quickly.

Pillow stood up, clasping his hands behind his back, posturing. He proposed a new course. "Understand me, gentlemen, I'm for holding out at least today right where we are, and in that time we can get steamboats and set the command over the river to go overland to Clarksville, saving a large portion of it."

Once more Buckner shook his head disconsolately. "You know the enemy occupies the rifle pits on my right," he said wearily, "and can easily turn my position and attack me in the rear. And I'm satisfied he *will* attack me at first light. When he does I won't be able to hold my position for half an hour."

"Why can't you?" Pillow snapped. "I think you can hold your position . . . I think you can, sir!"

"I *know* my position, General," Buckner retorted. "I can only bring to bear against the enemy about four thousand men, while the Federals can bring any number of fresh troops to the attack."

"Yes," Floyd sighed, "Grant does have us badly outnumbered."

"Well, if we can't cut our way out, or fight on here," Pillow said with some anger, "there's no alternative left us but *capitulation!*"

The word fell hard on the men in the room. Statler's earlier fears returned; again he saw himself dead.

"Then we'll have to capitulate," Floyd said, making that decision as the senior commander at Fort Donelson. "But gentlemen, I cannot and will not surrender, although I must confess personal reasons control me."

Buckner frowned deeply. "Such considerations should never control a general's action."

"You know my . . . uh . . . unique position with the Federals. It wouldn't do for me to surrender; it wouldn't do at all."

Pillow turned directly to Floyd. "There are no two persons in the Confederacy whom the Yankees would rather capture than you, General Floyd, and myself. And I will not surrender myself, either. I will die first."

Dewey thought he saw a wry smile flicker across Buckner's face. But if it had, it disappeared quickly. "Then I suppose, gentlemen," he said, seeming to stress the last word sarcastically, "the surrender will fall upon me."

Floyd asked, "How would you proceed?"

"I'll send a flag asking for General Grant's quarters, that I may send a message to him. I'll propose an armistice of six hours to arrange terms."

There was a long pause.

"Am I to consider the command turned over to me?" General Buckner demanded.

"If you are put in command," Floyd said, "will I be permitted to take my little brigade out, if I can?"

"Yes," Buckner replied, "if you move your men before the enemy acts upon my communication offering to surrender."

"Then, sir," Floyd shrugged, "I surrender the command."

Pillow, the nominal second in command, seemed momentarily disconcerted. "I won't accept it. I'll never surrender."

Buckner exhaled a deep breath. "Very well, I will accept the command. But know that surrender will be as bitter to me as it could be to anyone"—he glanced from Floyd to Pillow—

"yet I regard it as a necessity of our position. I also regard it as my duty to share the fate of my men."

Colonel Forrest, who had not spoken since the generals had ignored his contention that the way was still open to remove the main body of troops, now came forward. "I think there's more fight in these men than you all suppose, and, if you'll let me, I will take out my command."

"Yes, take out your command," Pillow said cavalierly, gesturing grandly. "Cut your way out, sir!"

"Yes, take out your command," Floyd added.

Buckner waved a hand of dismissal. "I have no objection." He turned to an aide. "Fetch me pen, ink, and paper."

General Pillow coughed nervously. "Gentlemen, is there anything wrong in my leaving?"

"Every man must judge for himself on that," Floyd commented.

"Then I shall leave this place."

The new commanding general was silent as Gideon Pillow strode from the house, leaving his own headquarters to the man who now had the sad duty of surrendering Fort Donelson, its men and its supplies.

Statler's mind raced. If he was to get away, to return home to his family, he'd have to attach himself to one of three men: Colonel Forrest, General Pillow, or General Floyd. Forrest was dismissed because it seemed to Statler that the cavalryman was too much of an adventurer, likely to get himself into trouble as he tried to ride out. Pillow could not be chosen because Statler simply didn't trust him. And that left Floyd. When the former United States Secretary of War left the house, Dewey followed him.

Outside: "General, a word, please."

Floyd turned. "Ahhh, Mr. Dewey, tragic business, eh?"

"Yes. I was wondering, sir, whether I might accompany you?"

"Of course, if we can indeed find a way to leave. I believe, however, that the steamers we sent to Nashville last night with our haul of Federal prisoners will return in time to be used to take my brigade across the river. Then we might use one of the boats to make it to Nashville."

Statler nodded.

"A lot of good men have died here," General Floyd mused. "A lot more will shortly be prisoners of war. Not one of them deserved his fate. And when the blame is finally assessed— and believe me, Mr. Dewey, there *will* be blame assessed—it probably won't go where it is deserved. Donelson wasn't a military fort, sir, it was a folly!"

37

WORD spread rapidly through the defenders of Fort Donelson: surrender terms were being sought from Union
general Grant. It was news accepted stoically, perhaps with
relief. The garrison was battered and torn, the blood not yet
spilled congealing in limbs too long exposed to the cruel ravages of winter. Even the prospect of long imprisonment by
the Federals seemed not to matter. The fighting was ended;
whatever terrors might be ahead could not possibly rival those
already experienced.

No such rationalization was practiced by Statler Dewey,
however. He had only one thought: to get away. Thus, the
figure of Brigadier General John B. Floyd was never to be
allowed to be separated from him by more than a yard or two.
Statler followed him like a loyal dog.

It was not yet light when two small steamers appeared in
the river, returning from Nashville. Ironically, they carried
supplies for the relief of Fort Donelson: rations, ammunition,
weapons, blankets, warm clothing, medical supplies. Those
were quickly unloaded, piled haphazardly on the riverbank
outside the fortification. They were useless items now.

Efficiently, General Floyd directed his brigade—Virginians,
mostly—to board the steamers and there were several quick
trips across the river where, once set on the opposite shore,
the men could march out in the direction of Clarksville. They,
at least, would not be pawns in the surrender.

First light came revealing white flags fluttering from the
fort's parapet. One of the steamers, the *General Anderson,*
docked again at the fort. Some wounded were put aboard

and, as Floyd and his staff waited for that to be done, a major approached the general, saluting smartly.

"I am directed by General Buckner," he said stiffly, "to tell you that unless your steamer leaves immediately he will be obliged to direct artillery fire on it and sink it. He has said, further, that his surrender has been dispatched to General Grant and, by his honor as an officer and a gentleman, the capitulation includes all now here."

Floyd did not seem perturbed. "Please inform General Buckner, sir, that I have left." He and his staff, with Statler in their wake, quickly boarded the *General Anderson*. It shoved off.

Dewey guessed that only about fifty were aboard the steamer, while several hundred other Confederate soldiers stood disconsolately on the riverbank watching it leave. *Why weren't they allowed to board as well?*

One man rushed from his ranks, dived into the icy waters of the Cumberland, and, with powerful swimming strokes, caught the barely moving boat, grabbing a trailing rope and clambering aboard.

"Private Williford, Twentieth Mississippi," the young man reported to Floyd.

The general directed an aide to see to the well-being of the swimmer and walked to the rail, staring out over the waters. Dewey came up to him.

"Well, Mr. Dewey, we are away."

"Yes."

"It's going to be a slow trip to Nashville," Floyd added. "We must assume there are Federal gunboats on the river and we will have to engage in a game of hide-and-seek."

There was a long pause and then Dewey spoke: "May I have a moment of your time, sir?"

"Of course."

"I'm perplexed by what happened yesterday," the newspaperman said. "I was with General Buckner's division and it very clearly broke through the Union lines, opening the road to Nashville, as had been planned. Yet, within a very short time, Buckner's men were ordered back to their trenches. It made little sense to me then and it makes even less sense to me now, given what has transpired since."

General Floyd stood silently.

"Could you try to explain that to me, General?" Statler asked forcefully.

"The order to retire to the trenches came from General Pillow," Floyd said slowly, "countermanding my previous order. It was General Pillow's contention that the men were not prepared to march out."

"But—but," Statler stammered, "that's not true! The men had full rations in their knapsacks for such a march. Even I was issued such rations."

"Yes . . . yes . . . I know," Floyd sighed. "But by the time I learned of General Pillow's actions it was too late to reverse the retirement. It had gone too far." He thought for a moment. "I felt a great mortification in seeing the ground we had won by such severe and brave fighting . . . uh . . . ignominiously lost again."

"Will there be an investigation of all this?"

"Yes, I suppose. I suppose." Floyd shrugged. "I suggest, Mr. Dewey, that you do as I now intend to do—to find a place to perhaps catch some sleep. I, for one, am greatly exhausted."

He turned and walked away. Statler decided to accept his advice.

II

IT was a hide-and-seek trip back to Nashville. Every hint of smoke on the horizon, indicating another boat on the river, saw the *General Anderson* seeking protection in the heavy foliage along the bank. Sunday night was spent anchored thusly, and it wasn't until the morning of Monday, February 17, that Nashville could be seen in the distance.

Once more Statler stood with General Floyd at the rail.

"I suppose, Mr. Dewey, that you intend to write your impressions of . . . uh . . . our adventure?"

"Of course."

"And then what will you do?"

"Do?" The question surprised Dewey. "I shall do what I have always done—publish my newspaper."

"You won't be allowed, you know."

"What?"

"The Federals, once Nashville has been taken—and that is

now a certainty—will impose martial law. Civilian newspapers will not be tolerated, especially civilian newspers run by . . . rebels." He smiled slightly. "No, the Federal control of this city"—he gestured toward Nashville—"will be heavy-handed. And you, if you are caught up, will be among those most suspected of . . . uh . . . insurrection. I would venture the prediction that you will be jailed, for one imagined charge or another."

Statler was stunned. "Aren't you overstating it a bit, General?"

"Not at all," Floyd replied heatedly. "The Constitution the Federals claim to be defending in this conflict will be bent and twisted in any way necessary to achieve their ends. If I had been taken at Fort Donelson, Mr. Dewey, I would have been charged with treason, tried in a court-martial, and executed. I left before that could happen because I believe I can be of future value to the Confederacy."

The newspaperman made no comment.

"So, if I were you, sir," the general went on, "I would make myself scarce before the city is taken."

"And when might that be?" a concerned Dewey asked.

"Three days. Four. Certainly no longer than a week. Grant's army won't rush in before he's ready. He's a very methodical soldier, as I told you earlier."

The deep boom of the whistle of the *General Anderson* signaled its approach to the dock area at Nashville. As it came up to the busy area along Water Street it became clear that there was chaos on the wharf. A great throng of men—civilians, it seemed—were swarming over one government boat, pitching from it slabs of bacon to other men who were piling it into carts and trundling it away. Some of the pitches were errant and not a few of the bacon slabs were splashing into the river.

"Ahhh," Floyd said softly, "the rabble."

The *General Anderson* thudded to a stop. As soon as the gangplank was run out a lieutenant hurried up it, saluted the general, and handed him a dispatch. Floyd read it without emotion showing on his face.

"The final telegraph from Fort Donelson," he told Statler sadly. "General Grant has accepted none of the terms suggested by the Confederate command. He has insisted on unconditional surrender. It's a term I've never known to have been imposed before in war." He shook his head. "Poor Buckner—a brave and honorable gentleman."

III

STATLER took his leave of General Floyd, pushed his way through the unruly mob at the wharf, and hurriedly made his way to the office of the *Nashville Monitor*. He brushed aside a joyful welcome from his printers and began to write. Page after page came from under his pen, each page immediately set into type.

Finally: "Will that be enough to fill a single sheet on both sides?" he asked his foreman.

"It should be."

"Then print just that under this banner." He scrawled only three words on another sheet of paper: "NASHVILLE FALL IMMINENT." "Have it distributed broadside to the people," he ordered, "and don't charge for it. They deserve to know what has happened at Fort Donelson."

"Yes, sir."

"We'll do something similar tomorrow," Statler said. "And now I must see my family." Halfway out the door, he stopped. "Is the telegraph still open to our other papers?"

The foreman shook his head. "Only military traffic is permitted now."

"Well, no matter," Statler shrugged. "Tomorrow, then."

Market Square was filled with people, their faces filled with worry. *They'll soon know the truth,* he thought. He noted as he moved through the square toward the livery stable that one of the carts he had seen being loaded with stolen bacon just an hour before was now the center of much attention, the people fighting to buy from it.

Nashville itself had become a sort of battleground.

IV

HARRIET clung to him, alternately laughing and crying, kissing his stubbled face, reluctantly giving him up to more embraces and kisses from their three daughters. The Beau

Monde house servants stood around in a happy semicircle, beaming at the return of their master.

"I'm so dirty," Statler protested mildly, "and smelly, too."

"It doesn't matter, darling," Harriet insisted, kissing him again. "We were so afraid we had . . . lost you."

"Nonsense, I was in no personal danger," Statler lied.

"We must have a truly wonderful dinner for you," the eldest daughter, Faith, enthused, "and I shall direct its preparation."

The father laughed. "Then it will be wonderful, indeed. Or maybe more of a miracle. I don't recall that you've ever had any familiarity with the kitchen."

"Oh, Daddy," Faith giggled. "I'm quite capable."

"What I'd really like most right now is a bath."

Several of the servants, hearing the request, took it as an order. By the time Statler could end the family welcome, and could make his way with Harriet to their suite, the big tub there had been filled with steamy water; one of the black women had even sprinkled some drops of perfume in it.

His wife shooed the servants from the room and began to undress him.

"I can do that," he protested.

"Tomorrow, perhaps," Harriet said. "Today . . . tonight . . . I intend to do it."

He let her. And then he lowered himself into the comfort of the hot water. Harriet splashed it on him playfully and started to wash him. Slowly, gently, even sensuously.

Suddenly, Dewey thought of being cold, of the frozen precincts of Fort Donelson, of the men who had suffered through day after day exposed to the elements, of the blood freezing on the snow, of the sacrifices that had been made.

"Was it terrible, darling?" his wife asked.

Her husband didn't answer."

"Statler!"

"What?" He was genuinely startled, being yanked back from his memories of the doomed fort.

"You were a million miles away."

"Only a few miles really," Statler sighed. "But I admit that this"—he swirled his hand in the water—"seems like a million miles removed."

"Was it terrible?" Harriet repeated.

"For some, yes. For most, at best, it was dreadfully . . . uh . . . uncomfortable." *How inadequate an explanation.* But he really didn't want to tell her the truth of Fort Donelson. "Yes, it was hard on a lot of men."

"I don't want this to sound unfeeling," she said softly, "but I was concerned about only one man. And he's here with me now." She kissed him once more. "I thank God that you've been returned to me."

God? Statler wasn't sure the credit had been given to the proper source. Harriet might better have thanked General Floyd and his pervasive self-interest for her husband's survival.

By the time the bath was finished, and Statler had put on clean clothes, word of his return had spread through the slaves' efficient grapevine to the adjoining Bon Marché mansion. Alma May, accompanied by her niece (and Statler's cousin) Joy Jackson, rushed to Beau Monde.

Joy's motivation was self-centered. She tolerated for only a few minutes the second round of embracing and kissing and the Princess's damnable enthusiasm. Then: "My sons. . . ?" she demanded of Statler. "Have you seen them? Are they safe?"

"Of course they're safe," Statler assured her, not certain that what he was saying was fact. "I visited with Herbert and Victor at Fort Donelson and they rode out with Colonel Forrest's corps before the surrender was effected. I would imagine that they are right now in Nashville and that you'll be hearing from them momentarily."

Joy began to weep in her relief.

A final flourish from Statler: "You can be proud of those young men of yours, Cousin. They acquitted themselves heroically. Yes, that's the word—'heroically.'"

Alma May and Joy stayed at Beau Monde for the happy family dinner. It was a chore for Statler to get through it. There were so many questions; some he could not answer with authority, others he *would not* answer, unwilling to bring the terror of the Fort Donelson experience to the women at his dinner table.

"Is there any doubt," Alma May asked, "that Nashville is going to fall to the Federals?"

"None at all."

"And what will it mean to Bon Marché?"

Damn Bon Marché! But his answer was one of studied nonchalance: "Oh, very little, I would imagine. In time there will be a military government and I suppose it will be evenhanded. There would be little purpose served in . . . well, in the Federals imposing a harsh regime. I would guess that for rank-and-file citizens life will go on much as before. Under a different flag, of course."

It was nearly ten o'clock before the dinner and its seemingly obligatory toasts ended, and Bon Marché guests left, the daughters went to bed, and Statler and Harriet could be alone. Statler had been dreading that moment since he walked into Beau Monde. He had been fearing the renewed intimacy he could not escape, knowing it would unmask him. It did.

They made love, but it lacked the passion they usually enjoyed.

"Darling," Harriet said quietly, "what's wrong?"

"I suppose I'm more weary than I thought." He forced a chuckle. "I suppose, too, I have to admit I'm not the young buck I used to be."

His wife rolled over, propped herself up on an elbow, and looked into his eyes. "I have an advantage I've never confessed before. I always know when you're—" She stopped.

"Lying?"

"No, not that. I always know when you're trying to protect us from . . . things you think will hurt us. You always shield us from unpleasant realities. And I love you for it. But I've known for hours that you won't be able to do it this time. It's dreadful, isn't it?"

Statler was silent for a moment or two. "Yes . . . dreadful. We're going to have to leave Beau Monde."

"Statler! No!"

"The occupation of Nashville, I'm certain, will turn many lives around. Mine . . . ours . . . more than most. If I'm still here when the Federals come in, I'll be jailed."

"Why?"

"Because I'm a newspaper editor. Because the pro-Confederacy articles and editorials I've written will be regarded as insurrection." That had been General Floyd's word. "I'll be thought of as a dangerous enemy fit only to be locked up as a . . . well, a criminal."

Tears began to trickle down Harriet's cheeks.

"And that might not be the worst of it," Statler went on. "We'll have no assurance that the sordid elements of the occupying army will be held in check—and who can tell what blackguards there will be. And if I were not here you and the girls would be exposed to—" He shuddered.

"Statler, you're frightening me!"

He took her into his arms and held her close to him. "I'm sorry, my dear."

Harriet was weeping fully now and he rocked her gently, petting her.

"How soon?" she sobbed.

"Tomorrow I'll be putting out the final issue of the *Monitor;* a broadside only. And I'll make preparations to leave Wednesday."

"Statler, we can't!" his wife wailed. "There are so many things to pack. We have to have the furniture crated and—"

"That won't be possible." He hated being so firm with her, but he had to be. "You'll get together what clothing you need, your personal valuables, and we'll leave the first thing Wednesday by coach. It will be impossible to go by river steamer. The Union gunboats control the waters."

Her crying was turning to hysteria.

"I imagine we'll need two coaches," he continued. "You'll have to decide which of the servants will be needed."

"Dear God, Statler! Beau Monde!"

"The Princess will be able to keep it whole," he assured her. "And the bulk of the servants will remain here." He sighed. "It won't be forever, darling. Beau Monde will still be here for you."

"And where will we go?"

"New Orleans."

"Oh." Her doubts about that were evident.

"Times have changed, dear. Your friends will welcome you back. Your family's there, and I'll have a newspaper to run."

She freed herself from his arms and sat up, setting the muscles of her pretty face. "I won't go! Nobody's going to drive me from my Beau Monde!"

Statler tried to control the sudden anger he felt. "Your beautiful world, Harriet, will become a hell when your daughters are raped in their beds by our conquerors."

His wife stared at him hard and long; she willed herself to stop the tears. When she spoke, the words were measured, even calm. "Isn't it strange, Statler? All of these years together and I never realized before how cruel you can be."

V

ON Tuesday, February 18, Nashville was firmly in the grip of panic. Statler's ride into the city that morning was much delayed by the steady stream of carts and wagons and carriages—most piled high with household goods—clogging the roads leading south. He wondered whether there would be anyone left in Nashville when the Federal army marched in.

In Nashville itself the panic was even more evident. Mobs ruled the streets; reason had fled. At several warehouses the Confederate army was using for commissary and quartermaster stores, the doors had been broken in, unruly citizens trying to carry away everything inside: clothing, hats, shoes, harness, flour, sugar, molasses, coffee, small arms, ammunition. What could not be contained in armloads was just dropped in the dust like so much trash, to be trampled underfoot.

At one of the warehouses Statler knew to contain cured meats, he found a corps of cavalry surrounding the building, cocked carbines leveled at several hundred loud-voiced people demanding to be let inside. The newspaperman saw Captain Herbert Jackson in command of the detail. He rode toward him, waving his hat in an exaggerated manner to seek recognition; he didn't want to be shot by one of the beleaguered young cavalrymen, a finger itchy on the trigger.

"Uncle Statler!" Herbert called out to him, realizing the potential vulnerability of his relative.

"A ticklish situation, eh?"

"More like a mad one," the captain replied. "We've been here most of the night trying to save this meat for the army. So far we've managed to put about four hundred wagonloads on the road toward Murfreesboro. God knows how much of it will get through." He groaned. "There's probably again that much still inside. I hope we can finish this job before someone gets killed."

"Wouldn't it be more efficient to send it on the cars?"

"What rail traffic we have available," Herbert explained, "is being used to save the heavier stuff—artillery guns, the ammunition for them, other ordnance. Before we could get back from Fort Donelson many of the rail cars were already moved out of Nashville, jammed with civilians wanting to get away."

Statler shook his head sadly. "I don't understand how all this happens." He gestured toward the mob. "How does it get started?"

The cavalry captain laughed derisively. "More madness. The city council, hearing of the reverses at Donelson, decided to throw open the doors of the commissary depot to the public, if you can believe such idiocy! And once it was started there was no way, short of at gunpoint, to put a stop to it. Then, too, the citizens haven't had a very good example set for them by city leaders. I believe you know Mr. Stevenson, the railroad president."

"I do."

"Well, as early as Sunday, Mr. Stevenson—or perhaps I should say *Major* Stevenson," Herbert said sarcastically, "—using his position of influence, had an entire train made up for his use alone. And he steamed out of here with all of his personal baggage, furniture, carriages and carriage horses, family members, and the whole of his entourage of black servants. Lord, how we could use those cars now."

"Hasn't the city been placed under martial law?" Statler wanted to know.

"In a sense. General Floyd has been placed in command. But the truth is, order is being maintained largely by Colonel Forrest's corps, apparently because it's the only one left here with any semblance of discipline. Forrest is a rock, you know."

"Yes."

"He's over at the quartermaster depot now trying to save what he can, but most of it is gone. There are a large number of tents still in hand, and a few lots of rope, but not much else." There was an unexpected grin. "Oh, yes, there are a few loose shoes. Shoes were very popular. I suspect that

Nashville must be the best booted town in the Confederacy." It was barracks humor.

"Oh, by the way," Statler said, "I saw your mother last night and I was able to assure her that you and Victor are well."

"Thank you for that, Uncle."

"I strongly urge you, Herbert, to make every effort to spend a little time with her before you must move on."

"I will . . . we will."

"May God keep you."

They shook hands and Statler spurred his horse, turning in he direction of the state capitol building where he knew he would find General Floyd. There he learned that General A. Sidney Johnston, the western division commander, had withdrawn the bulk of his army to Murfreesboro. And that plans had been made to destroy the suspension bridge, before the city would be given up to the Federals. And then Statler rode back to the *Nashville Monitor* office to prepare the final edition of the newspaper.

He was wracked by a sense of guilt as he worked. Guilt because he now believed his edition of the day before, with its inflammatory headline—NASHVILLE FALL IMMINENT— may have contributed to the general unrest in the city. And guilt because he knew, when he was finished, that he, too, would flee.

Statler Dewey ended his days as the publisher and editor of the *Nashville Monitor* with a brief, one-paragraph editorial.

"In the uncertain days head," he wrote, "the epitome of Southern patriotism will be the strength of the calm restraint with which the citizens of Nashville face the occupying army. Let it never be said that Nashvillians are a collective of rabble . . ."

38

ALMA May Dewey's Diary, Tuesday, February 25, 1862:

Nashville, and all of Davidson County for any practical purpose, is now occupied territory in this senseless military adventure. I only pray that Bon Marché will somehow survive this madness. Mother, in her will, spoke of the "sweet day" it would be when she joined Daddy in eternity. I fear at this moment that the sweet days we have all known at Bon Marché will lengthen into bitter nights. True Jackson is just back from the city, where he heard a proclamation read by Mayor Cheatham on the public square. He told the people that he had every assurance from the Federals that their persons and their property will be safe. And he asked that all return peaceably to their regular vocations. True is not sanguine about it and neither am I. There can be no "regular vocations," no peaceable normalcy, under the circumstances in which we now find ourselves. We are, in truth, all prisoners of war. Our jails are our homes; our jailers of unknown proclivity . . .

II

THE Princess was startled from her sleep by a great pounding on the main doors of the Bon Marché mansion, followed by a series of screams (obviously from the household maids), and the heavy booted tread of someone—more than one—hurrying up the stairway to the second floor. She quickly left her bed, drawing on a robe, noting that it was not yet six A.M.

As she threw open the door to her suite she came face-to-face with perhaps a dozen blue-clad soldiers, rifles in their hands, moving rapidly along the hallway.

"What's the meaning of this!" Alma May shrieked.

The column halted suddenly and a captain turned to her, making a gesture suggesting a tip of his cap. "United States Army provost marshal," he said solemnly. "I'm sorry if we woke you, ma'am."

"How dare you enter my home in this manner!"

"Ah told 'em they couldn't come in," one of the black maids cried.

"Just hush!" the Princess snapped. "Well, Captain, I demand an explanation!"

"I am under orders to arrest and detain one True Jackson. Is he here?"

"On whose authority?"

"Believe me, ma'am," the captain said wearily, "I have all the authority I need."

"Then I suggest you tell *me* by what authority you're here," a voice said. "I'm True Jackson."

The captain whirled to find a Deringer leveled at his belly. It was a ludicrous scene: True in a red dressing gown, his feet in carpet slippers, his right hand holding the tiny gun against a dozen armed men.

"Put down the gun, Mr. Jackson," the captain ordered.

"By whose authority?" True asked again.

"By the authority of my orders, sir."

"And I don't suppose you have a warrant?"

"No, sir, I don't need one. I have my—"

"Yes, yes, I know," True interrupted testily, "you have your orders."

"Right. Now, put down the gun!"

"Have you ever heard of the Constitutional guarantees of habeas corpus, young man?"

The captain smiled. "Are *you* claiming the protection of the United States Constitution, Mr. Jackson?"

"Yes, and the Constitution of the Confederate States of America, as well."

"Sir," the captain sighed, "there are others with whom you

can make your Constitutional arguments, if you wish. But at this moment you *are* under arrest and I ask you for the final time to put down your gun. I would hate to have to order my men to fire on you with that lady standing behind you."

True glanced quickly over his shoulder to find his wife standing in the middle of the hallway, weeping. "Joy, I told you to stay in the room!"

She rushed to him, clinging to his arm, crying desperately. Catlike, the captain sprang forward, seizing the Deringer from True's hand.

"Now, Mr. Jackson, shall we go?"

"Am I to be allowed to dress properly for . . . my incarceration?"

"Of course. One of my men will help you."

"That won't be necessary."

"Oh, but it *will*. I don't need any more surprises from you this morning."

True nodded. "Would you indulge me for one more moment, Captain? I'd like to see the orders under which you came here today."

"Very well." The officer shrugged, reached into his jacket for a piece of paper, and handed it to True.

As Jackson looked at it his eyebrows rose. Then he read it aloud: "'Arrest True Jackson, Bon Marché, Nashville, and send him to Camp Douglas, Chicago. Edwin M. Stanton, Secretary of War.' Just *that*, Captain?"

"Yes, sir."

"No charge? No hearing? Just that?" True was unbelieving. "Guilty of what?"

"Please, Mr. Jackson, let's not go through all that again." The captain was exasperated. "You'll have the opportunity to discuss it with my superiors."

"Well, my dear," True said to Joy, a buoyant tone in his voice, "it's obvious some error has been made. It'll only take me an hour or two to . . . uh . . . adjudicate this matter. Please ask the maid to lay out my gray suit. The new one."

Morning lengthened into afternoon, afternoon into evening, and True Jackson didn't return to Bon Marché. His son Drew—who had missed the arrest because he had been on the other side of the plantation tending to an ailing yearling—rode to the city to try to find his father.

Officers at General Don Carlos Buell's headquarters claimed never to have heard of a man named True Jackson. At the quarters of the provost marshal, found with some difficulty because they were in a private home from which the family had been evicted, the younger Jackson was met with stony silence. It didn't help his inquiry to have to admit that he didn't have the name of the captain who had arrested his father. Dispirited, Drew rode back to Bon Marché to find his mother prostrate with grief.

And True Jackson didn't return. It was nearly eleven o'clock that night when another Federal soldier rode into Bon Marché with a message for Mrs. Joy Jackson. It was opened before the other members of the family gathered in the drawing room.

"'My darling,'" Joy read, her voice trembling, "'when you read this I will be on my way to Camp Douglas, at Chicago. Although the legal reason for my arrest remains vague, there was talk of sedition, growing, apparently, from my relationship with the League of United Southerners. All such, it seems, are to be regarded by the Federals as criminals, serving to prove that the damnable Lincoln administration has no interest in preserving the inalienable rights of free men. Like all of his ilk Lincoln spits on the very Constitution he professes to defend with his cruel war. Nevertheless, I am not being treated harshly, nor do I suppose I will be. Do not worry, then, for my ultimate safety. I can't imagine I will be held very long; how are the Federals going to jail every Southern civilian who disagrees with them? That very prospect is ludicrous. Until I return do not grieve. Keep yourself and the family safe, remembering that every darkness is followed by the inevitable light. My love stays with you and I carry your love with me to sustain me. I am told I will be permitted to correspond with you just as soon as I have reached my destination.'"

Joy looked up at the other family members, her pretty face wet with tears. "What are we to do?"

It was the Princess who answered: "We'll keep the family safe. And Bon Marché. And we'll look forward to his early return. True's right, you know. The Federal authorities will soon realize their folly in trying to keep political prisoners."

"Do you really believe that?" her niece asked.

"I do," Alma May said, taking Joy in her arms. "I believe that with all my heart."

But the Princess was remembering what she had written in her diary only a day earlier. The proclivity of their Federal jailers was unknown. The bitter night had indeed fallen.

III

RUMOR was a ruthless handmaiden of the Federal occupation. With no newspapers to report precisely what was happening, the distance between Bon Marché and Nashville—so few miles only—grew into a wide gulf. Alma May herself was responsible for much of that. She saw Bon Marché as a bastion against the incursions of the enemy forces and instituted a round-the-clock mounted patrol of the borders of the plantation by the most mature of the male slaves. There was a moment or two when she even contemplated arming the blacks, abandoning the idea when she reasoned, rightly, that they would simply be murdered by any Union soldiers who came their way. No one was permitted to travel into the city without her approval, a prohibition which even applied to the lone white male remaining at Bon Marché, an unhappy Drew Jackson.

Thus, what filtered through to the center of a Bon Marché drawn in upon itself were the rumors, some brought by allowed visitors and some by the inexplicable Negro "telegraph." And what was learned made the Princess even more determined to keep Bon Marché isolated.

There were tales, each one more lurid than the one before, of constant harassment of the citizens of Nashville by the Union troops. Stories of banks and businesses being seized, of families being driven from private homes to provide residences for generals and colonels, of public buildings being turned into barracks and hospitals, of fences being torn down (and furniture chopped up) to provide firewood, of jewelry being stolen from ladies' boudoirs, of citizens who protested being beaten, of young girls being raped. Unable to evaluate the stories, unable to separate fact from fiction by personal observation, the stories were all accepted at Bon Marché as true. At least by Alma May, who dutifully chronicled them in her diary.

A week after True Jackson had been taken away (the date was Wednesday, March 5), the plantation's isolation was invaded. It was mid-morning when a mounted slave, whipping and driving his horse from the perimeter of the Bon Marché acres, raced up to the mansion to sound the alarm.

"They's comin'!" he cried. "Miss Alma, they's comin'!"

The Princess hurried from the house. Dressed in a riding habit, she nervously rapped her crop against her thigh. "How many?" she called out to the slave.

"Lots, Miss Alma!" Fright showed in his eyes. "Mebbe a dozen on horseback. Thirty mebbe walkin' an' five, six wagons."

"Go fetch Mr. Drew."

The black spurred the horse and rode off in the direction of the brood-mare barn.

Her nieces, the twins Joy and Hope, came out of the mansion, followed by their daughters.

Alma May scowled. "Get back inside!" she ordered.

They stood dumbly, unmoving.

"Do it, damn it! Go to Louise's suite and stay there. And lock the door."

The women scurried away. Alma May walked down the steps to the veranda. Determinedly, she walked along the road in the direction the soldiers would have to come, going perhaps a hundred yards before Drew ran up to her.

"What are we going to do?" he asked.

"Follow my lead," she told him, continuing to walk forward. They had gone another hundred and fifty yards when the Union column came into view. The mounted soldiers were riding slowly at the pace of the infantrymen. The slave's report had been accurate, but Alma May counted eight wagons.

"Scavengers," she groaned. Then she stopped, planting her feet wide apart in the middle of the road. The riding crop never ceased its tattoo against her skirt.

A lieutenant urged his horse forward of the others, who halted. "Good morning, ma'am." He tipped his hat. "Do I have the honor of addressing Miss Alma May Dewey?"

"Yes, I'm Alma May Dewey." There was a flutter of fright. *How does he know who I am?* "May we know the reason, Lieutenant," she said evenly, "for this intrusion of private property?"

"Lieutenant Roger Turner, United States Army Commissary Corps," he said formally. "We're here to buy provisions."

"Buy?"

"Yes, ma'am. I'm under strict orders to give you U.S. Army vouchers for all we carry away."

She slowly shook her head side to side. "I'm afraid you've been misinformed, Lieutenant," she said sweetly, smiling at him. "We have no extra provisions here."

The young officer looked around. "It's a big place, Miss Dewey."

"Yes, it is. And we have only enough to maintain it. We're sorry, but we have nothing to sell you."

"Well," he said, heaving a sigh, "I'm required to see that for myself." He signaled for the column to move.

"See here, Lieutenant," Drew yelled at him, "you have no right to force your way in here!"

He got no reply. As the column moved forward, the Princess and Drew had to move out of the way or be trampled. They trailed along, half running, as the Union force invaded the center of the plantation. It all happened quickly. When the huge smokehouse came into view, the lieutenant signaled again and another of the horsemen went to investigate it. A wagon was whistled up and several of the infantrymen began to load it with the succulent hams from inside. Two wagons were drawn up to the several hay sheds and swiftly loaded with the best of the plantation's alfalfa hay. The granary was emptied of corn.

Rifle shots were heard, and when Alma May and Drew turned toward the sound they realized that animals were being slaughtered in the deer park. They watched as a buffalo carcass was dragged out of the park and laboriously hoisted into a wagon, followed by five dead whitetail deer. Another horseman rode into the sheep pasture, killing a half dozen of them, still in the wool. Those, too, were dumped into the wagon with the buffalo and the deer.

There was great efficiency shown by the raiders, indicating much prior experience in such matters. None of the continuing protests of Alma May and Drew were recognized. It ended as quickly as it began. Lieutenant Turner rode to the Princess and began to hand her vouchers.

"Hams, hay," he said as he gave her the papers, "corn and . . . fresh meat."

Stunned, she glanced at the figures on the vouchers. "But this—this," she stammered, "isn't half the value of what's been taken!"

"It follows U.S. Army commissary procedures," he said coldly. He turned directly to Drew. "Now, Mr. Jackson, shall we take a look at the horses?"

Suddenly, it came clear to Alma May. *Mr. Jackson? He knew my name. He knew Drew's name. The vouchers were written before they ever came onto the plantation. Someone has informed the Federals of what there is on Bon Marché. Who? Someone who knows Bon Marché very well. A friend!* The Princess was ill. She turned away from the officer, fearing she was going to vomit.

"We have no horses of remount age," Drew was protesting. "A few barren mares. Some mares in foal. Several early foals of this year. Some yearlings. But, aside from two stallions, no horses of age."

"The two-year-olds," the lieutenant said.

"Yes," Drew admitted, "there are some two-year-olds. But that's not age enough for remounts! You must know that!"

"Which barn?" the officer insisted.

Sullenly, Drew led the way, Alma May behind him. Inside the dark, cool barn Lieutenant Turner went from stall to stall inspecting the two-year-olds. "Yes, yes," he said appreciatively, "very nice." There was a gesture and blue-clad soldiers who had followed them into the barn began to open stall doors, attaching lead ropes to halters.

"But these horses haven't even been broken yet!" Drew protested.

"We have wranglers who will break them soon enough." He thrust a piece of paper at Jackson. "Your voucher, sir."

Drew glanced at it, gasping. "You must be mad! Twenty dollars a head?"

"The going price for remounts," the lieutenant shrugged.

"You thieving bastard!" Drew lunged at him, grasping his neck between his hands, thrusting his thumbs into the windpipe. The officer, caught by surprise, toppled over backward, Drew going to the tanbark with him, squeezing, squeezing. In an instant a gun butt was brought down on Drew's head, catching him behind the left ear.

There was a crunching sound as Drew shrieked in pain.

Blood flowed. Alma May screamed. The cocking of a carbine seemed to echo in the big barn.

"Hold!" the lieutenant ordered. The soldier put up his rifle as Turner struggled to his feet, rubbing his neck, coughing slightly. "Get those horses out of here." To Alma May: "I'm sorry, Miss Dewey, but we—"

Alma May was on her knees, feeling for a pulse on the prostrate Drew. It was weak. Very weak. She screamed again in her agony. From the shadows in the barn, where they had hid themselves, half-a-dozen Negroes emerged. Without orders they picked up the inert form of Drew Jackson; gently, cradling him in their arms. "Take him to the house," the Princess said.

As they came out into the light again, the Federal raiders were seen leaving Bon Marché, the fully loaded wagons rumbling, the royally bred two-year-olds at the ends of lead ropes, trotting behind the mounted Union soldiers.

Drew was carried to Alma May's suite and lowered onto her bed, his blood staining the fine linen sheets. Joy Jackson rushed in with her daughter, Honore, fainting at the sight of her grievously hurt son. The Princess felt overwhelmed, but she managed to get the housemaids to carry Joy back to her own suite and then she said to no one in particular: "Ride to Nashville as fast as you can. Fetch Dr. Thompson." Several of the blacks ran out.

With the help of her own maid, Alma May cleaned up the bloodied head of Drew, nearly retching at the sight of the depression in his skull. The pulse grew weaker.

The mistress fell to her knees by the bed, praying silently. Not to God, but to the spirit of Bon Marché, to her departed father.

Perhaps an hour went by before one of the black riders returned from the city. "Dr. Thompson ain't there no more," he reported. "He's gone 'way with the army."

"It doesn't matter." The words were only whispered. "Your master is dead."

IV

THE smell of the place came to True Jackson's nostrils before he could see it. Held close to the ground by the black rain clouds, the putrid odor—a foul combination of excrement and rotting garbage—was recognized as a terrible harbinger of his fate. The difficult Nashville-to-Chicago journey, by riverboat, rail, and now bouncing uncomfortably in an open provisions wagon, had exhausted him. He was cold, wet, and angry. Angry not only because he had been taken into custody by Federal authorities without proper charges or hearing, but because it had required only a few days to strip him of his dignity. Maybe that was the worst of it.

And then his destination came into view; Camp Douglas was a sprawling complex of rough wooden buildings surrounded by a high fence. He noted heavy stakes driven into the ground every few feet, perhaps a hundred feet removed from the fence itself.

"What are the stakes for?" he asked the soldier who was at once wagon driver and guard.

"Markers for the martial-law area," the young man explained. "Ain't nobody allowed inside 'em 'cept the guards." The driver laughed. "Same way inside, too. There's a dead line to keep the prisoners off the fence."

"Dead line?"

There was another chortle. "Any fella goin' over that line is dead, you might say. 'Course we don't really shoot 'em without warning 'em first."

True felt ill.

The wagon was driven through the gate and stopped at the first building inside the camp. The driver vaulted from his seat, an ancient musket now in his right hand, and gestured toward the door. "Inside there."

Jackson boosted himself over the side of the wagon, dropping down into a deep puddle of water. It seemed water was standing everywhere in large pools; drainage appeared to be nonexistent. And it was from the standing water that the stench was rising up.

Guard and prisoner splashed through the water to the building, which was elevated several feet above the flood on heavy blocks. Inside, at a small army field desk, sat a colonel;

an oldish man with little military bearing. The guard dropped a packet in front of the officer, stepped back, and motioned True forward. He stood there, his clothes dripping, as the colonel studied the documents.

"Damn!" he muttered. For the first time he looked directly at Jackson. "You're not a combatant?"

"No," True answered. "I suppose I'm regarded as a political prisoner."

"Do you have any idea why you've been sent here?"

"None."

The colonel shook his head. "Neither do I. Most of the men here were swept up at Forts Henry and Donelson in Tennessee. Combatants." There was a sigh. "But I was under the impression the likes of you were being sent to Fort Mackinac Island."

"Perhaps a mistake has been made," True suggested boldly, "and I should be transferred." Mackinac Island certainly sounded better than this miasmic hellhole in Chicago.

"No," the officer said, tapping the papers with his forefinger. "These orders are clear enough. You're here now and we will . . . uh . . . do our best to accommodate you. Has the guard explained the dead line to you?"

"Yes."

"There are two meals here daily—the same rations issued to Federal soldiers." The voice hardened. "Better than what is being fed to our men in Confederate prisons. Do you have any money?"

"Some."

"Put it on the desk."

True complied, dropping a small wad of bills before the colonel. It was counted, placed in a small box with other money, and note made of it in a small ledger: "$115. Confederate, Jackson, True."

"Sutlers are permitted in the camp from time to time to sell vegetables, tobacco, and the like. We issue chits against this money"—he nodded toward the metal box—"and you may spend it as you see fit, as long as it lasts. I caution you not to lose this in gambling. We try to discourage games of chance here because there are frequent fights between winners and losers, but—" A shrug.

"No hard labor is required here," the colonel went on, "but

prisoners are expected to police their areas, something which is not, unhappily, done with any relish. You may have noticed the odor."

"I have."

"That's because the prisoners seem content to . . . uh . . . wallow in their own filth." The colonel adopted a scolding tone. "But I've had to accept those slovenly Southern habits. Not approve of them, you understand, but accept them nevertheless. Perhaps you, as a more mature man of apparent breeding, will be able to exert some salutary influence along those lines. It seems you're the first . . . uh . . . *gentleman* sent to us."

There was a slight smile on the officer's face. "Strange, isn't it? More than fifteen thousand men and a single gentleman. I suppose I shouldn't be too discontented about it. It's a weakness we will exploit to crush this rebellion!"

Jackson stood silently, resenting the colonel's words.

"I am Colonel Tucker, the commandant of Camp Douglas," the officer continued, "and am frequently available for consultation on matters of significance. If such there are, of course." He consulted a pile of papers; lists of some kind. "You, Jackson, are being assigned to barracks number seventeen." There was an idle flip of the hand in the direction of the guard, indicating the interview was ended.

"Excuse me, Colonel," True said. "I was spirited away from Nashville rather hurriedly, before I could properly say good-bye to my family. Is communication with the outside permitted?"

"Of course." Colonel Tucker seemed insulted by the question. "There's a constant flow of mail out and in. We're not barbarians, Dewey. Mail is delayed only momentarily by the need to . . . uh . . . peruse it."

"You mean you *read* it all?"

The reply was defensive. "Such caution is necessary for security reasons. It wouldn't do to permit mail of a scurrilous or seditious nature." There was another flip of the hand.

Barracks seventeen was almost as much of a shock to True as was the smell. He guessed the building was ninety by twenty-four feet, part of it utilized for a kitchen of sorts. In it were jammed tiers of bunks, at some places four high, at others three. There was no heat of any kind in the building. It was late in the overcast day and there was no light, either—

no candles, no oil lamps. Some of the floor was wet; the roof leaked in several spots as the rain continued.

Men sat on the floor (there were no chairs) in groups. Some of them played checkers on rough scraps of wood on which the blocks had been scratched with a nail or a knife. Others played cards with limp and dirty decks. They were ill-dressed, all of them; some wore little more than rags. Some had blankets, some did not.

And the odor! The smell of the open sewers outside filtered through to inside, mixing with the stink of uncovered slop buckets in every corner and the unmistakable aroma of unwashed bodies.

The guard pointed to one of the tiers of bunks. "Up there—the third one."

True nodded, reaching up to boost himself into it. He was terribly weary. As his hand touched the thin layer of straw laid on the planking, a large rat skittered away. Someone laughed at his startled reaction and True swore under his breath. Nevertheless, his exhaustion motivated him to gingerly lower himself onto the straw bedding. The pervasive scent of urine in it sickened him.

He tried to force his mind to think of other things and was transported back to his youth when the study of Greek was the most trying thing in his life. Yet, even that attempt at mental escape was related to his current predicament.

Hercules—didn't he face the odious task of cleansing the Aegean stables? No, no . . . it was specifically Augeias's stables at Elis. Yes, that was it. And didn't Hercules accomplish the task by burning them? At least I believe that's what he did. Fire? Nothing short of the same kind of burning will cleanse this stinking hole.

With that on his mind prisoner True Jackson fell asleep.

V

ALMA May faced a somber reality: she was alone.

The presence of others in the big Bon Marché mansion was a cruel illusion. Her nieces Joy and Hope had retreated into their own terrors. Joy was devastated—to the point of madness, the Princess feared—by the arrest of her husband and the senseless death of her son Drew. It was made worse by having no news of True, and by the receipt of a letter from cavalrymen Herbert and Victor, her other sons, that they had joined a new Confederate "raiding" force under the command of Colonel John Hunt Morgan, suggesting further dangers for them. Hope, too, suffered because of the lack of knowledge of the whereabouts and the safety of her own husband, Colonel Able Jackson, and their son, Foster. Letters from them had been infrequent and devoid of reassuring detail. Compounding the depression was the grave illness of the mother of Joy and Hope (Alma May's half sister Louise), who was falling deeper and deeper into senility. The Schimmel wing of Bon Marché had become a reclusive place, its residents unconcerned about the well-being of Bon Marché.

The Princess felt alone. There was no communication with the farther reaches of Bon Marché: Albert Dewey's Bon Marché Lexington and George Dewey Jr.'s Bon Marché East, enterprises Alma May had begun to expand the influence of the parent plantation. And it had been months since she had had any word at all from California and Charles Dewey II.

She stood in the Dewey Room on that late March morning, fashionably dressed, and gazed at the portrait of her father, preparing to do what she believed he would have done. She shuddered as if a cold breeze had swept through the room. For the first time that she could remember there was no feeling of the presence of the founder. No sense of his ghost.

Alone. It was a dreadful word.

"Very well, then," she said aloud to the portrait, "if that's the way it must be—"

An hour later Alma May's open carriage, driven by a stiff-necked black man dressed in formal livery, came to a stop at the Tennessee Capitol. She was shocked by the changes wrought in Nashville; the city had become, in only a few short weeks, a military camp. The hill on which the capitol building stood bristled with artillery guns placed behind barricades of cotton bales. Soldiers were bivouaced on the grounds in a mushroom growth of white tents, and dozens of them were busy with the erection of a cedar stockade seemingly designed to surround the entire building.

Fort Andrew Johnson, she thought.

The Princess swept out of the carriage to present herself to an armed sentry at the main door of the Capitol. "I am Miss

Alma May Dewey," she announced imperiously. "I have an appointment with Brigadier General Johnson."

That last was a lie, but it was delivered with such conviction that the guard admitted her, politely directing her to the office where she might find the military governor. It was ten o'clock in the morning when she arrived at the Capitol; it was after two in the afternoon when she was allowed to see Johnson. Ample time to review in her mind what she knew of this man.

Johnson had been the governor of the state of Tennessee for four years in the mid-fifties. Born in rural East Tennessee, the hotbed of Union sentiment, he had not been much liked in Nashville; political, financial, and social leaders of the city had never accepted him. Election to the U.S. Senate in '57 took him to Washington, where he was the most steadfast Southerner opposing secession. Even when Tennessee joined the Confederacy, Johnson refused to surrender his Senate seat. Nashville fell and President Lincoln rewarded Johnson's fealty by making him Tennessee's military governor, with the rank of brigadier general. That had been less than two weeks earlier, but even in her somewhat isolated situation at Bon Marché Alma May had heard of the arrest of many prominent citizens who were imprisoned for suspected disloyalty. All of that churned through her mind as she waited and waited, her anger growing, her dislike of the man coming full flower.

Finally, she was allowed into his office. Johnson, in a black suit of civilian clothes, sat behind a large desk. He didn't stand when she came in; he made no effort at civility. He was a somewhat portly man, with a beardless round face, his small eyes deep-set, his large nose bulbous. His lips were set sternly, turned down at the corners.

"I can give you only a few minutes, Miss Dewey," he said.

"Very well, I'll be as brief as possible." She put on his desk the sheaf of U.S. Army vouchers she had clutched in her hand. "These vouchers, General, were acquired when a group of Union armed men came onto our property unannounced and took away several wagonloads of supplies. They also took some of our best young horses. To date, the vouchers haven't been honored, even though the arbitrary prices listed on them represent less than half of the value of what was . . . uh . . . appropriated, let us say."

Johnson only glanced at the vouchers. "If they're valid,

Miss Dewey, you will be paid in due course. Some of this paperwork takes time."

Alma May still stood; the military governor hadn't offered her a chair. But she found one anyway, and dragged it close to Johnson, sitting down. "In due course?"

"Yes."

"Will you also find a way—in due course—to compensate Bon Marché for the loss of its manager, Andrew Jackson?"

"Loss?"

"One of your soldiers killed him!"

She could tell by the expression on his face that Johnson wasn't aware of the incident. "Perhaps Mr. Jackson resisted in some manner."

"If you mean he protested the illegal seizure of our property," she said coldly, "then the answer might be 'yes, he resisted.' But if you imply he was fool enough, unarmed, to resist thirty or more armed soldiers . . . then, sir, you too are a fool!" The words came easily; she had rehearsed them over and over in the hours she had been kept waiting.

"See here, madam—!" the governor sputtered angrily.

"But I'm a realist, General," the Princess went on. "Drew Jackson is dead. That cannot be reversed. And I know I'll have to accept *your* government's evaluation of the supplies removed. But I came here today for two specific reasons, and if there is any justice at all in your administration, you'll hear me out."

"If you'll be brief, madam."

"I'll try. But not everything today can be tied into neat little verbal packages. In any event, when your young lieutenant—he identified himself as Roger Turner of the Commissary Corps—invaded Bon Marché the other day, I was struck by the knowledge he had of the plantation. Here was a man who had never been on the property before, yet he knew exactly what he would find there: the buffalo and deer present in the deer park, the number of hams available in the smokehouse, the amount of hay in storage. Everything, General!" Alma May's voice grew shrill. "My God, the vouchers he gave me had been prepared *before* he came on the plantation!"

"Your point, please, Miss Dewey," Governor Johnson insisted.

"My point, sir, is that the lieutenant would not have had that prior knowledge without someone informing to your military authorities. I want . . . to know"—she was speaking slowly now—"who it was . . . who gave . . . your people . . . that information . . . about Bon Marché."

"Really, madam, you can't expect that I would have such information—such *minor* information, I might add."

"But you could check the reports—"

Johnson's anger boiled over. "I could, but I won't! There are some citizens who have wisely cooperated with our authority. You though, Miss Dewey, would wish to stage a vendetta against those citizens. My job is to keep the peace here, not to inflame it." He stood up, seeking to dismiss the Princess.

She stayed seated. "There's another matter."

Sighing deeply, Johnson dropped back into his chair.

"I'm also here," Alma May said, "to plead for the release from prison of a civilian—True Jackson. He's been taken illegally, General. And his imprisonment has devastated the family to such an extent that I'm concerned for his wife's continuing health."

Johnson stared at her for a moment. "True Jackson." It was a statement, not a question.

"Yes."

"I know that man, Miss Dewey. And I have been long aware of his activities against the Union. His traitorous activities!" The voice rose in anger. "Were it up to me, True Jackson would be shot! He would not be permitted to . . . uh . . . loll away the war in the comfort of a prisoners' stockade."

"Comfort?" the Princess asked sarcastically.

"A great deal more comfort, ma'am, than being accorded our prisoners in Confederate camps."

"Then there's no chance for True's release?"

"None!"

"Will he be permitted to communicate with his family?"

"Of course. All those being held in Federal prisons have mail privileges."

Alma May nodded. "Then my business here is ended." She rose to leave.

"Miss Dewey," Johnson said, "may I ask how many slaves you hold at your plantation."

"More than a hundred," she replied, not willing to give him an exact figure.

"We may be required to utilize some of their labor."

"Oh?"

"Yes, there are some fortifications being planned and—"

"And you'd be willing to use *slave* labor? It surprises me, General, that the Union, so opposed to slavery, would see nothing wrong in using slaves for its own purposes."

"The exigencies of war," the military governor shrugged.

"Yes . . . yes . . ." Alma May sighed. "There are always convenient reasons to be found, aren't there?"

39

WITHIN the week the first letter arrived from True Jackson. It had a startling effect on Joy. Her melancholy just seemed to melt away. She demanded that all the family be assembled in her sitting room—the house servants, too—for her reading of it. Even Louise was taken from her bed and put in a comfortable chair next to the window where the early springlike sunshine warmed her.

Joy stood in the middle of their circle and paced a bit as she read.

"'My darling,'" she began, a tiny blush coming to her cheeks. "'I must hasten at the outset to tell you I am well. This place has none of the comforts of Bon Marché, of course, but it is adequate. There is ample, if simple, food; our treatment is evenhanded and without any hint of animosity. In sum, it is not bad at all. I am surrounded by a host of men from Tennessee. Most of the prisoners here were taken at Forts Henry and Donelson.'"

Joy looked up from the paper. "Well, at least he has found some friends." She returned to her reading. "'There is even a worthwhile task for me to do here. The commandant, a Colonel Tucker, who is quite a decent fellow, is allowing me to superintend the planning for proper sanitary facilities. As you might imagine, this suddenly built camp lacks some of the amenities. In any event, I have found some qualified civil engineers among the prisoners and we are drawing plans for sewage disposal and the like. The colonel assures me that once the plans are completed, supplies and equipment will be brought in and the men will be allowed to make the improvements. And then we shall go on to other things: proper repair of living quarters, recreational facilities—those things which will make a few months of confinement tolerable.'"

Once again Joy stopped reading. "A few months, he says, isn't that exciting! Only a few months."

Alma May felt guilty. She hadn't told Joy of her conversation with Brigadier General Johnson, of his contention that there was no chance of True's release.

The reading resumed. "'I have in mind, also, that I might organize a dramatic group to provide entertainment for the men. And, perhaps, a literary reading group for those so inclined. If it is possible, I wish you would send me a few copies of some of the more popular volumes—nothing too deep or classic, you understand.

"'This will necessarily be a short letter. I wanted to get it off hurriedly and into the post as soon as possible so that you know, my dear, that I am safe. In my haste to leave Nashville I came away without shaving instruments, but I now find that to be somewhat of a symbolic godsend. My beard is sprouting mightily and I have pledged myself that I will not shave until the Confederacy has been victorious.'

"Isn't that just like True?" Joy laughed.

There was a final paragraph expressing his love once more and reiterating there was no cause for worry.

Joy brushed a tear from her cheek. "I think we should all take a moment now, each in her own silence, to thank God for his safety." Heads were bowed; there was only the sound of breathing in the room for a few moments. Alma May couldn't help but wonder how much True had left unsaid.

Then: "Now, scour the house," Joy ordered, "for the proper books to send to him." To the housemaids: "Find a small crate in which we can pack some books."

Joy sank to the floor in front of Alma May, resting her head in her aunt's lap. "Auntie Alma, I'm going to need your help. I must tell him about Drew, of course, but I want to do it in a . . . kind way. Think, please, how I can best tell him that his firstborn son is dead." There was a sob.

"I'll try, darling," the Princess said, bending down to kiss her niece on the cheek.

Several times during that day and evening, Joy came to Alma May's suite to read her paragraphs she had written about Drew's death. The aunt made suggestions and many changes were made. It wasn't until the next morning that Joy came to her with the finished letter. Without comment she handed over the sheaf of foolscap.

The writing was tiny, even-lined:

I took a long ride over Bon Marché late yesterday after receiving your most welcome letter. Spring was in the air, it was warm and clear, and new things are beginning to grow. The winter wheat looks fine and I think will yield much. John's clover field looks splendid, better than I ever saw it at this time of the year. On the red house field plowing was under way for the corn crop. It was such a beautiful sight to see the ploughs splitting the soil, turning over the black, sweet-smelling earth in such precise rows. And who do you suppose were the plowers? Cloe's children, all six of them—about the youngest set of plowers I ever saw; they were as merry as if it were a perfect frolic, and they seemed much gratified that I had come to see them. When they got to the turn row, I stopped them to tell them I had just received a letter from you and that I intended answering it and tell you who I saw plowing so nicely. Everyone stood out and begged not to be forgotten in my writing. Jeff (Cloe's oldest boy, remember?) said, "Tell Master True howdy for me. Tell Master I am trying to make as good a crop like he was here." And now I have.

There was more of that as Joy took her husband over the acres of Bon Marché, telling him—at times in poetic phrases—of the new lambs, the foals leaping in the pastures, the delicate new fawns seen in the deer park.

It wasn't until the final paragraph that she wrote:

The fruit trees are flowering colorfully and the shade trees are putting out their incredibly tender light green "baby" leaves. Nowhere is that more noticeable, or more beautiful, than on the tulip poplars at Richie's Place where they cast lovely mottled patterns over the resting place of our sweet son Andrew. I know that I am shocking you, my darling, but Drew died in a tragic accident just a few days after your departure. Would that I

could shield you from this news, but I know you would
hate me, and rightly so, if I did. I cannot yet force my
brain to direct my hand to write in detail of his passing,
but know that it was swift with only momentary pain.
Time, I suppose, will free my hand and mercifully heal
the hurt we both must share now. Our love must console
us until you are returned to me and we can weep together our final cleansing tears. Until that merciful day I
remain your constant lover, Joy.

Sighing, Alma May put down the letter. "It's lovely, dear,"
she said.

"I feel so guilty about denying him the details."

"As we discussed, I think the knowledge that Drew was so
senselessly killed by a Federal soldier," her aunt said firmly,
"might be cause for rash action on True's part. In his current
circumstances rashness might endanger his life as well."

"Yes, Auntie Alma, I agree with you." Joy took the
foolscap from her and kissed her. "In a strange way, all of this
has forced me to be stronger and has made me aware that
Hope, too, is suffering. The lack of news of Able and Foster
is devastating her. Where can they be?"

The Princess, wondering how Joy could find the compassion
to worry about her sister when her own tragedy was so great,
tried for a reassuring tone in her reply. "She'll hear soon, I'm
certain, that both are well."

II

COLONEL Able Jackson was elated. He was finally going to
be allowed to fight.

It had been nearly a year (within a few days) since the Confederacy had declared itself at Fort Sumter, and some ten
months since the glorious victory at Bull Run, and almost two
months since Fort Donelson had fallen, and Able hadn't been
in battle. Even before all of that he had drilled the Nashville
Grays as "General" Jackson, anticipating this very day.

Frustration had been his almost constant companion in recent months. When the Army of the Mississippi was being
brought together at Corinth under the leadership of General
Albert Sidney Johnston, Able had been assigned to the supervision of Negro slaves throwing up earthworks around Cor-

inth. It had been night-and-day toil and perhaps important, but he had not seen it as his destiny. His somber mood was deepened by the lack of news of his family in Nashville; he had had no mail at all since the city had been surrendered to Federal forces.

Now, however, his depression had been lifted. He was moving forward with Johnston's army—nearly forty thousand strong—toward a place called Pittsburg Landing on the Tennessee River, in command of the Second Tennessee Infantry (including some of the old "Grays"), part of the Third Army Corps of Major General William J. Hardee. And he carried in his pocket the broadside from General Johnston that Able had read to his men before getting under way from Corinth. The words had burned their way into the colonel's mind:

> I have put you in motion to offer battle to the invaders of your country. With the resolution and disciplined valor becoming men fighting, as you are, for all worth living or dying for, you can but march to a decisive victory over agrarian mercenaries, sent to subjugate and despoil you of our liberties, property, and honor. Remember the precious stake involved. Remember the dependence of our mothers, your wives, your sisters, and our children of the result. Remember the fair, broad, abounding land, the happy homes, and ties that will be desolated by your defeat. The eyes and hopes of eight million of people rest upon you. You are expected to show yourselves worthy of our valor and lineage; worthy of the women of the South, whose noble devotion in this war has never been exceeded in any time. With such incentives to brave deeds and with the trust that God is with us your generals will lead you confidently to the combat, assured of success.

Thus buoyed, Colonel Able Jackson's spirit was not even dampened by the dreadful early April weather that slowed the march out of Corinth's encampments. Rain poured down, turning the roads into quagmires, stalling the artillery caissons, imprisoning the heavy supply wagons in sticky mud.

Able rode slowly, the good thoroughbred gelding he had brought from Bon Marché carefully picking his way along the uneven road. Water dripped off the brim of his broad hat, the poncho he wore no longer kept him dry. But he didn't care.

Grinning broadly, he looked over at his only son, Foster, a handsome young man of twenty-one. He was the colonel's aide-de-camp, but his only rank was that of private because that's the way Able had wanted it. There was to be no charge that his son was being shown favoritism. And he was proud that Foster had not objected to his lowly status. Rank was not what mattered to either one of them.

"Well, son," Able called over to the young man, "tomorrow's going to bring what we've both wanted for so long."

"Yes, sir, that's true enough," Private Jackson replied, grinning back at him.

Tomorrow, Able thought, more content than he had ever been before, *will be a day for the greater glory of the South.*

III

SUNSET of Saturday, April 5, came with cloudless skies. It was calm and clear, even beautiful. But the rain of the preceding day had slowed the advance from Corinth so much that the main body of General Johnston's Army of the Mississippi had not yet come up to the anticipated battlefield, a spot marked on the maps as Pittsburg Landing with a landmark log building designated as Shiloh Chapel in the middle of it.

Able's Second Tennessee, which had been in the van of the difficult march, stopped several miles shy of Shiloh, getting off the road and retiring to bivouac. "Tomorrow," then, was to be delayed until Sunday morning. Colonel Jackson took advantage of it, riding through his camp to make certain his men all had provisions, ample ammunition, and carefully dried and oiled firearms. He wanted nothing about the Second Tennessee to be deficient.

All day long the Confederate army came up. Scattered gunshots from a distance indicated the Federals were probing for intelligence of Johnston's forces, but every indication was that none of the probing was truly effective. One report came to Able's ears that a small Federal cavalry unit which had made contact with the regiment had been captured intact, unable to return to the banks of the Tennessee River and sound the alarm.

At dusk, the order was passed to all commanders that the plan for Saturday would be the identical plan for Sunday, and quietly Able moved his men to a position some four hundred yards from where the attack would be begun by Brigadier General Cleburne's brigade, of which Colonel Jackson's men were a part.

First light of the Sabbath Day—clear skies overhead, the air fresh, the sun rising in splendor—was the signal. Able's skirmishers drew first fire and, at a slow trot, he rode at the head of the Second Tennessee, waving his hat high in the air to elicit a wild shout from the men, running and firing simultaneously. They rushed into an enemy encampment to find it abandoned, breakfast still cooking in pots, baggage abandoned in officers' tents. The surprise had been complete and Able was astonished at how easy it had been.

Through the encampment then and into a small stand of timber, where the first resistance was met. A hail of lead cut through the trees.

"Sounds like heavy rain on the leaves," Foster shouted to his father.

"Not God's rain, son," Able yelled back, "but the Yankee devils' *lead!*"

His riflemen had taken cover behind trees and boulders, returning the fire in kind. What had been a momentary impasse soon turned again to a Confederate advantage as the Southern boys—raised as hunters from their earliest days—proved to be the superior marksmen. Slowly the Second Tennessee inched forward; just as slowly as Federal troops withdrew.

For nearly an hour the minibattle in the woods raged; Colonel Jackson felt cut off from the rest of the world. He had no idea what was happening elsewhere on the battlefield around Shiloh Chapel.

Then they burst out of the dark forest and into the bright sunlight onto a pasture sloping downward away from them and the Federals were running. Able's soldiers fell to their knees to draw beads on the fleeing enemy. Their bodies littered the pasture.

"Pass the cease-fire!" Colonel Jackson ordered his aide-de-camp. "Get me a count of the losses."

Foster spurred his horse, dashing off along the line of the

First Tennessee at the edge of the woods. In less than twenty minutes he was back: "We've lost near a hundred, Colonel," he reported formally, his face white. "Twenty-three dead, including Major Doak, Captains Tyree and Bate, and Lieutenants Cryer, Fugitt and Akers."

Able cringed. The exhilaration he had felt just a few minutes earlier, the pride of victory, left him.

"Put together a burial party," he told his son sadly. "I want none of them left to the buzzards."

The colonel dismounted, leaning disconsolately against a tree. A major rode up and saluted. "General Cleburne's compliments, sir. He wishes to know your disposition."

Able hesitated for a moment. "I've lost a hundred, Major. Fully a tenth of my command." He sucked in a deep breath. "Please tell General Cleburne the rest are still full of fight."

"In that case, Colonel, I'm instructed to tell you that the enemy is entrenched in deep woods across a ravine at the bottom of this pasture, putting heavy pressure on the general's right. Several artillery guns are operating from that point. He asks that you silence them."

"You may inform the general," Able said firmly, "that I shall renew my attack in fifteen minutes. Will that be soon enough?"

"Yes, sir. Thank you." The major saluted and rode off.

Foster still being absent with the burial party, Able himself went along the line on foot, passing instructions to his young officers. Again and again: "The enemy is dug in across a ravine at the bottom of this pasture. General Cleburne wants him out of there. On my signal you are to fire a volley and move forward ten yards. Fall down, reload, and fire again. Repeat that every ten yards until we've silenced him."

Able came upon a mounted officer. "Captain Wilkinson, have you heard of the fate of Major Doak?"

"I have, sir," the captain replied soberly.

"You, sir, are now second in command of the Second Tennessee." He repeated his orders for the attack. "I shall lead, Captain, and should I fall out in some manner, you will have to assume command and lead our brave boys to victory."

"I'll do my best, Colonel."

"As shall we all, Mr. Wilkinson, as shall we all."

Able hurried back to his horse, relieved to find that Foster still hadn't returned from his burial duty. *Maybe he'll be able to stay out of this madness.*

Positioning himself to the right extreme of the Second Tennessee, he rode twenty yards into the open pasture; there was no cover of any kind there. He raised high his hat and waved it wildly. "Fire!"

A red sheet of flame spat out from the edge of the woods and the Confederate line came out of the timber on the dead run. Ten yards-fall-reload-fire. Ten yards-fall-reload-fire. The act was repeated half-a-dozen times before there was answering from across the ravine. It came in the middle of one of the ten-yard sprints and Colonel Jackson saw many of his men fall. But he continued to wave his hat, continued to expose himself, continued to urge them on.

As they drew closer to the ravine he saw that it was a satanic tangle of thornbushes, enough to cover a whole regiment. And the fire from it continued hot as the Second Tennessee kept going forward.

"It's a damned hornet's nest!" Able swore aloud to himself.

As the next ten-yard dash began the heavier thump of artillery was heard, followed by shells exploding among the charging Tennesseans, acting as a giant scythe that came up bloody after every efficient sweep. Yet, Able knew the Federals had now repositioned their big guns to meet his charge, releasing the pressure on General Cleburne's forces. *At least that much has been accomplished.*

Another ten yards. Dearly bought.

Suddenly, a lightning strike of pain hit Colonel Jackson's right arm just below the shoulder. He screamed. For a moment he thought he was going to topple off the horse, but he pitched forward to encircle the animal's neck with his good left arm. Fighting the dizzying faintness, he dug his heels into the horse and finally got it turned and on an upward path on the pasture, away from the continuing fighting. He could not focus his eyes any longer, but he could feel the warm blood running down his right arm. Thinly, like water.

Someone grabbed the reins. "Hang on, Father, I'll get you out of here!"

Foster urged the colonel's horse into a light trot, every step jolting the wounded arm in a new paroxysm of pain. Able bit into his lower lip, tasting the salty blood. In just a few minutes they had returned to the safety of the woods at the top of the pasture.

Undoing his kerchief, the son tied a tourniquet around the wounded arm. It hung limp, raglike, as if there were no muscle, no bone. "Now, let me help you down, Father."

"No, no," Able protested weakly. "If I dismount I'll never be able to get back on. Let's just find a doctor."

Foster, fearing his father would lose consciousness and fall off the horse, removed his belt and lashed together the colonel's booted feet under the belly of the gelding.

"That ought to keep you on."

There was no reply.

"Father!" The son felt for a pulse; it was very weak. He began to pray as he hurried the horses to the rear.

IV

FOUR days later—it was Thursday, April 10—Foster Jackson dozed in a rude wooden chair he had drawn up to a cot in a makeshift hospital in a Corinth, Mississippi, Baptist church. His father had been there since Tuesday, unconscious, when he had been brought from a surgeon's tent near Shiloh, the right arm amputated. Foster was startled awake by a moan.

"Father?" he said softly.

Able's eyes opened slowly. "Foster?" The voice was weak.

"Yes, Father. You're safe in Corinth."

"And the battle?"

The son sighed. "The Federals were routed on Sunday. But the next day . . ." He hesitated. "The next day their superior strength— Anyway, Beauregard had to retire the army to Corinth."

"Beauregard?"

"General Johnston has been killed."

"Oh, dear God," Able moaned. A new thought came to his mind; there seemed to be added strength in his voice. "And what of my brave boys of the Second Tennessee?"

"Captain Wilkinson has also been wounded," Foster replied, looking around the church room crowded with hurt men. "He's here somewhere."

"But the Second Tennessee?" his father demanded.

"It, too, is back in Corinth"—once more he paused, fearing

his news would be harmful to the wounded man—"and the reports are that it has an effective strength of three hundred and sixty-five men."

Tears began. "Sweet Jesus, Foster, you mean I've lost two thirds of them?"

The son simply nodded.

"Two thirds." The words were only whispered. "How will I live with that?"

"You mustn't blame yourself, Father. Casualties were heavy on both sides."

Colonel Able Jackson wept openly now.

To the cot came the pastor of the church; a tall, gaunt individual in somber black clothes, a smile fixed on his face. "Well, Colonel Jackson," he said too loudly, "tears of joy at being spared by our gracious Lord?"

Foster groaned inwardly. *The man's an idiot!*

Able just stared at him.

"I'm Pastor Armstrong," the minister went on. "And I can assure you, Colonel, that with God's help, you will live a fruitful and long life. He will enable you to compensate for the loss of your arm."

Shock showed on Able's face. His gaze darted to where his right arm had been and then they looked up into Foster's face, pleadingly.

"I'm sorry, Father." He wanted to strike the pastor. "The surgeons . . . uh . . . had to amputate. A minié ball had shattered the bone beyond any repair and—"

"You let them do this?" Able screamed at him.

"The choice," the son tried to explain calmly, "was your arm or your life. It wasn't a difficult choice."

"Your son," Pastor Armstrong intruded, "has been in constant attention to your well-being. You are a fortunate man to have had him by your side. But the choice, Colonel, was not his—it was God's."

"God wouldn't do such a thing!"

"God guided the surgeon's hands. God spared your life, sir."

"And the lives of my brave men?" Able asked angrily.

"He notes even the sparrow's fall. The world, Colonel, is imperfect. Satan is omnipresent. But, in the sum, it is God who prevails."

"And you really believe that?" the wounded man said sarcastically.

"I must. We all must. For without God's love and mercy, what have we? It is only faith in God that will sustain us through these terrible days. When all the generals and all the armies have done their deeds what will be left is the true glory of faith."

40

ALMA May Dewey's Diary, Wednesday, May 7, 1862:

Is it never to end? Every little bit of sunshine in our topsy-turvy lives is immediately clouded over by stern reality, even tragedy. Cousin Able returned home yesterday from Mississippi (as did Foster, too, thankfully), but what was a brief moment of joy was almost immediately turned round by seeing him without his right arm. And he has turned strange; a certain madness in his eyes. Or perhaps it is the look of the zealot, because he quickly informed all of us that he would not stay at Bon Marché, that he intends to take a place in Nashville so that he might start a church—for "the *proper* worship of God," whatever that may mean. It was a decision not made with Hope or his daughters; it was simply announced at dinner, and Hope, while she may wish otherwise, dutifully makes preparations to leave. Foster, already won over to this church scheme apparently, does not defy his father although he is an adult of twenty-one! I cannot comprehend such blind acquiescence.

And so the preservation of Bon Marché falls on those of us who are to be left here: myself, Joy and her daughter, Honore, and dear Louise, of course, who is totally bedridden, requiring constant care from Joy. How long Honore and I will be able to continue the work with only a handful of Negro women and children I do not know. All of our able-bodied black males have been impressed by the Federal military government to work on the lavish fortification of Nashville. There is to be a pittance paid to Bon Marché for their labor, but it would be of more value to have them here.

I am most weary. Depressed, too, I hate to admit to myself. It's as though a black curtain has been drawn down before me: one through which no light illumines any scene, through which no sound can intrude, a terrible shade which will permit no emotion to penetrate it. I feel a prisoner behind that curtain, cut off from all those I love and who may love me still. But I hear nothing at all from Albert in Lexington, or George in New York, or Charles Two (and darling Willie!) in California. There simply is no other world outside these acres.

The Princess reread the last sentence, thinking to change it, knowing that there *was* another world of cruelty and pain outside the confines of Bon Marché. She sighed, leaving it as she had written. For it was true: there was no other world for her. And she closed the book.

II

"ARE you going to do nothing at all about this outrage?" Harriet Dewey demanded of her husband.

"Dear, I've done what I had to do." The words were spoken quietly, disconsolately. The editor and publisher of the *New Orleans Delta Recorder* was wracked with the same fear that had driven him from Nashville—the dread of being imprisoned by a Federal occupying army.

New Orleans had seemed so safe, protected, as it was, by two massive fortresses, Jackson and Saint Philip. No one had anticipated what happened two weeks earlier; Confederate leaders had not believed New Orleans could be taken. But on the Union side there was a bodacious naval officer named Farragut, who had simply sailed *around* the forts to stand off the city with his entire fleet of warships. Coming in behind him was the army of Major General Benjamin Butler, whose troops captured New Orleans without firing a shot.

Now Statler sat at a contentious dinner table in his home on this mid-May evening, being berated by his wife.

"You've done what you had to do? Statler, you've done nothing!" Her pretty face was red with anger. "You've

printed that General Butler's so-called orders without comment. You've let him get away with a gross insult!" She
picked up a copy of the newspaper, reading from it:
"'General Orders, Number twenty-eight, May fifteen, 1862.
As the officers and soldiers of the United States have been
subject to repeated insults from the women (calling themselves ladies) of New Orleans in return for the most scru-
pulous noninterference and courtesy on our part, it is ordered
that hereafter when any female shall by word, gesture, or
movement insult or show contempt for any officer or soldier
of the United States, she shall be regarded and held liable to
be treated as a woman of the town plying her avocation.' The
man's a . . . a . . . *beast!*"

Her husband was lost in thought, turning off her anger, remembering the first day of occupation; hearing again the cat-
calls and curses from the populace as the Federal troops
marched in. And seeing once more a drunken gambler kicking at the end of a rope, his eyes bulging, his tongue swelling
out of his mouth, just because he had climbed to the roof of a
building and had torn down a United States flag.

"Statler!" Harriet screamed at him.

He was startled. "What?"

"Are you going to permit this . . . this . . . blue-bellied animal to insult Southern women by calling them . . . common
prostitutes? Do you want your daughters"—she gestured to
three sober-faced young ladies seated at the table—"to be
known as *whores*?"

"You're overreacting," he insisted.

"Am I now? Well, if this order stands every woman in New
Orleans will be regarded as a prostitute and every damned
Federal soldier in the city will be unleashed to have their way
with them! Is that what you want for Faith and Charity and
Lovey? Is that what you want for me?"

Statler had heard enough. "Damn it, shut up! Have you
ever considered that Butler was provoked? Don't you think
I've heard the women of New Orleans cursing the soldiers?
Don't you think I've seen them spitting in the Federals' faces?
I suggest to you, Harriet, that if you want to be considered
ladies, you are going to have to act like ladies."

Harriet stared at him. Dead silence had fallen at the dinner
table. Then, softly but bitterly: "I've always known, Statler,

that you were a cautious man. I never before realized that you're a *coward!*"

She rose slowly, keeping her hate-filled eyes fixed on him, gesturing to her daughters to also stand. And then she led them out of the room.

Statler went to the sideboard and poured himself a bourbon, downing it quickly. He repeated the act and then rang for the butler.

"I want one of the boys to drive me to the newspaper office."

The black man was surprised. "Right now, Mistah Statler?"

"Yes, right now. I have some work to do. The boy can bring the carriage back after he delivers me."

Determination built in Statler's mind as he was driven through the dark streets of New Orleans. Once at the newspaper he set to work, writing and rewriting, discarding sheets of paper as he sought just the right words. It was perhaps three o'clock in the morning when he was finished, satisfied.

He leaned back in his chair and turned up the oil lamp a bit, reading aloud: "'There are things in life which might be regarded as sacrosanct: a mother's love, faith in God, honesty in business, charity for those less fortunate. All of those things are deeply engrained in the Southern way of life. So, too, is the sanctity of Southern womanhood.

"'That sanctity, we now charge, has been grossly violated by General Orders, Number twenty-eight, made public yesterday by Major General Benjamin Butler, the leader of the occupying Federal army. In the orders, Butler has charged that New Orleans ladies have been insulting troops. Whether or not they have is not at issue, however. What is important is that General Butler, his officers, and his men will now be regarding every comment about themselves from the lips of New Orleans ladies as being spoken by "a woman of the town plying her avocation."

"'Let us be plain about this: General Orders, Number twenty-eight, will now be regarded by our uninvited guests as giving them free rein to count every woman of our city as a prostitute, and to use them as prostitutes are used. Thus, General Butler will seek to destroy, before our very eyes, the long-held sanctity of Southern womanhood. We therefore call upon General Butler's superiors (including the President of the United States) to rescind these hateful orders and, further, to remove Benjamin from his position here as a man totally unfit for command of other men.

"'Yesterday a friend suggested to the editor of the New Orleans Delta Recorder that General Butler is a beast. The editor thought long and hard about that contention and has finally accepted it.

"'If General Orders, Number twenty-eight, are allowed to stand, with their certain consequences, the man who issued them will be long remembered in history as BUTLER THE BEAST.'"

Statler was satisfied, but his work wasn't finished. He went to the racks of type and selected a large boldface font. While he had set type in the past it was not something he usually did and it went slowly. But he persisted, finally locking up the editorial in a page form—the entire page filled with the denunciation.

The last three words were spread across the bottom in 64-point caps: BUTLER THE BEAST! The exclamation point was added as a last-minute thought.

It was dawn before he had finished and the printing crew was beginning to arrive. Pointing to the completed page form, Statler said: "That's all there will be today. Just that. Round up as many black youngsters as you can and distribute them widely." He reached in his pocket for money. "There's to be no charge. Pay each of the lads a dollar."

Two hours went by before the last of the printing was done and the final copies of the *Delta Recorder* were carried out into the streets. He paid the printers their week's wages and dismissed them, and then he paced the office, waiting.

It was about noon when he saw a squad of Federal soldiers approaching the newspaper. It was just as he had expected. Sitting down at his desk, he opened a drawer to remove his Deringer pistol. He placed it in his right ear and pulled the trigger.

Blood spattered on a note he had left for Harriet, confessing his great fear of imprisonment and guaranteeing, in death, his undying love.

III

THIRTEEN hundred miles to the north and east Statler's young brother, George Dewey Jr., faced other war-borne problems. Bon Marché East on Long Island was without money; the influx of aid he had anticipated from Nashville to keep the farm going until it became self-sufficient had been cut off by the fighting. He had no word of the fate of the mother plantation; he knew only that Nashville was occupied. Offers of modest help from his uncle Marshall Dewey, half-Negro son of the founder of Bon Marché, had been turned aside. George's pride wouldn't let him accept Marshall's largess.

He sat at breakfast with his wife, Emma, and their two sons. "I've made a decision," George announced. "I'm going to take that army job as a remount agent, buying horses for the Federal cavalry."

Quiet Emma, who rarely disagreed with her husband, raised a mild objection. "But George, you're a Southerner."

"No, not anymore. I'm just a New York horse breeder without any money. If we're to have any future I have to take what's available to me."

Emma pressed on uncharacteristically. "If you take this army job won't you be away a great deal?"

"Yes, I will," George admitted. Then he smiled. "But while I'm gone Bon Marché East will be in the hands of our two young gentlemen." He nodded toward his sons.

"We'll take care of things, Father," seventeen-year-old Harry assured him. George III, fifteen, nodded agreement.

"I know they'll handle things capably," Emma said. "But I just wish there was another way. Maybe Two—?"

"I can't ask him," George interrupted. "Two would have been the Bon Marché manager if I hadn't intruded. In a sense, Emma, my presence forced him to leave Nashville."

"But he's prospered."

"Yes . . . but he still thinks I drove him out."

On that day, at that same time, Charles Dewey II was lowering himself into his bed in his Nob Hill mansion after a long session of poker in one of San Francisco's men's clubs. His wife, Beth, half-asleep, rolled over and kissed him.

"God, you're beautiful when you just wake," Two said appreciatively.

She giggled. "Yes, Mr. Dewey, I know." Beth kissed him again. "Was the evening profitable? I mean, was it worth being away from me for . . . seven hours?"

"If you put it that way, no. But if you figure it on an hourly rate, then it was decent. I won just shy of seven thousand."

"And what do you intend to do with it?"

"Whatever you want," he told her.

"You spoil me disgracefully, Two."

"Uh-huh."

She propped herself up in bed, fully awake now. "You know, I was thinking tonight—which is what happens when you leave me alone—about our families back East and how poorly they might be faring because of the war. We're really very fortunate, aren't we?"

"Yes, but then we've worked hard for our good fortune."

"I know. But don't you wonder sometimes what might be happening at Bon Marché?"

"Often," Two admitted. "There's a lot of me, a part of my heart, still back there. Lack of news about them concerns me, of course."

"Can't we find some way to resume communications, even with the war?"

Two thought for a moment. "I'll ask Roger Weatherford to try to get some news for us. He might be able to do that from Chicago."

"I hope so."

"Me, too." He leaned over her, grinning. "Are you sleepy?"

"Not if you don't want me to be."

He reached for her.

IV

ALMA May screamed with delight. A maid had just brought word from Nashville that the first child had been born to the Reverend and Mrs. Alston Merit. The Princess's favorite grandniece, Lady Bea (née Jackson), had had a daughter, to be named Felicity. The date was Thursday, July 3, 1862.

"Felicity," Alma May chortled, "means great happiness. Isn't that just the *perfect* name?"

"Yes, ma'am," the black woman agreed, a bit taken aback by the unrestrained glee of the Bon Marché mistress.

"Now, you must wait a moment," she instructed Lady Bea's maid, "while I write a note to my darling. We're going to have the christening here, of course."

No one could resist the enthusiasm of the Princess when it got up a full head of steam, least of all the new mother. Alma May was in her element: she set the date for the christening at Saturday, July 19; she put the black children to work on building a bower of flowers under which the christening would take place; she wrote more than a hundred invitations and had them dispatched by the housemaids all over the Nashville area.

She experienced some difficulty in getting an orchestra to play lullabies during the ceremony; so many of the local musicians had gone to war. But she was indefatigable—she finally put together a string quartet, picked the music for them, insisted on hearing their rehearsals, and felt grand about it all.

And on the day assigned Alma May could marvel at the revival of the human spirit in the presence of a newborn baby. For a few brief moments at Bon Marché on that Saturday, under a bower of multicolored fresh flowers, the war would seem far away, a distant terror.

Even the immediate reality of a one-armed Grandfather Able, cradling Lady Bea's firstborn in his good left arm, did not intrude the conflict on the moving ceremonies.

As Able presented the baby, the Reverend Mr. Merit, the puffed-up proud father who was officiating, asked, "By what name shall this blessed child be known?"

Able, emotion coloring his voice, replied, "Felicity Alma Merit."

The Princess let out a startled gasp, and wept.

When the ceremony was concluded, and the housemaids were serving the last champagne in the Bon Marché larder, Alma May went to Lady Bea. "You might have told me so that I wouldn't have made such a display of myself with my tears."

Lady Bea smiled. "Alston and I love you very much, Auntie. When Felicity Alma is old enough she will hear of the goodness of the lady whose name she carries."

Alma May cried again.

It was very nearly a perfect day. There was one cloud, however. The Princess had noted, as the ceremony was under way, that Honore, Lady Bea's cousin, had arrived late, slipping into the crowd around the bower just at the conclusion. Alma May sought her out now.

"I couldn't help but notice you weren't here at the beginning of the ceremony," the Princess told her.

Blushing slightly, her eyes diverted from Alma May's, she answered, "Yes, I'm sorry, Auntie Alma. Uh . . . well, something . . . uh . . . held me up."

"Your late arrival was very rude, you know."

"Yes, and I apologize for it."

Alma May waited for further explanation. When it didn't come: "May I know what could have been more important on this day?"

"I had to meet someone."

"Oh?"

"Well, you might as well know"—there was defiance in the young woman's tone—"there's a man."

The Princess was surprised. "We work together every day and I've never—"

"We've been discreet," Honore interrupted.

"Obviously." She showed her annoyance.

"His name is Frank Westervelt from New York State. He's a captain on General Andrew Johnson's staff."

Alma May's mouth fell open. "You can't be serious!"

Honore was silent. And the silence angered her great-aunt.

"My God, Honore, haven't we had enough grief here—your father in a Federal prison, your brother killed by a Federal soldier, this place devastated by the Union occupation. If your mother learns of this it'll destroy her."

"She won't."

The Princess shook her head in disgust. "And I suppose you're in love with this . . . this . . ."

"I don't know. He's a kind man and he says he loves me."

"Now, hear me, young lady"—her anger was on the surface—"you're not to see this man again! I won't have you bringing more pain to this household!"

Once more there was silence.

"I won't have it! Do you understand me?"

"Yes, ma'am." The reply was no more than a whisper.

V

IT was a brutally hot day at Camp Douglas. The stench of its open sewers and rotting garbage was overwhelming. True

Jackson held a wet handkerchief to his nose and mouth as he made his way across the prison yard to respond to a summons from the camp's commandant.

Even when he was inside Colonel Tucker's office the smell was all-pervasive.

"Ahhh, Jackson," the colonel said. "I wanted to see you because I've had a reply from my superiors on this matter of supplying materials for the building of proper sewer facilities here."

"Yes—"

"I want you to know, Jackson, that I'm much pleased with the plans prepared by the engineers among the prisoners. And I think you've presented this matter to me with great care and concern for the men incarcerated here—"

"But we're not going to get the supplies," True interjected angrily.

"At this time, no," the commandant sighed. "But I'm . . . uh . . . pressing my superiors to reconsider and—"

"My God, Colonel, do you know how many men died here yesterday?"

"A dozen or more."

"Seventeen! Damn it, man, you can't dismiss it as a mere 'dozen or more.' It was *seventeen*—all dying needlessly because the United States Army forced them to live on an open cesspool! Are you aware that fully half of the prisoners are ill? That before the day is out there may well be another 'dozen or more'—to use your convenient phraseology—dying?"

"Jackson, I'm trying," the colonel said pleadingly.

"To no damned avail!"

"And I'm going to keep trying," Colonel Tucker insisted.

"I hope you do, Colonel," Able said quietly, "because what's happening here now at Camp Douglas is criminal." He started to leave, and then turned again to the prison commandant.

"If you allow this to continue, sir"—the words were forced through his teeth—"there will come a day when you'll have to explain it not to your superiors but to a Higher Authority, who will judge you, I pray, as the evil man you are."

VI

IT was early September before Roger Weatherford could report from Chicago to Bon Marché West of his investigation of the plight of the Dewey family. It was worse than Two had imagined it would be.

"It's a litany of disaster," he said to Willie Carstairs in the San Francisco office of the Dewey Trading Company. "Drew and Jack dead. My brother Statler, too, by his own hand. Staunch and Able grievously wounded. True in jail—"

"It's not pretty," Willie groaned.

"And what he reports of the condition of the Bon Marché farms is equally distressing." Charles started to read from Roger's letter: " 'Occupation of Nashville has had, as near as I can determine, a devastating effect on the main plantation's economy. Numerous Federal incursions on the storehouses there have emptied them. Cavalry remount demands have depleted the horse population to a dozen or so mares and a few new foals. Only one stallion remains, I am told, but I haven't been able learn what stallion that may be.' "

Two looked up. "Can you imagine what hell the Princess faces now?"

"I would guess," Carstairs commented, "that it's only her personal strength that keeps it going at all."

"I suppose." Dewey started to read again. " 'In Lexington, Albert has apparently turned the farm into an armed camp. But Federal raiders there become more and more bold. At best, the only evaluation I can give you of Bon Marché Lexington is that it survives. It cannot prosper, of course, under the current circumstances. A prudent assessment would be that survival there is only a day-to-day thing.

" 'It was easier to get a report on the New York situation of your brother George Junior. He is, after all, positioned on the *right side* of this conflict. But lack of racing and a ready market for blooded horses has depleted George's cash. We must assume that is why he has taken employment as a buying agent for the United States cavalry.

" 'As for an overall assessment of the war, you must see it as clearly as I do. Even with a few Southern victories, attributable to Northern incompetence as much as to Southern generalship, the inevitable attrition will sink the Confederacy.

It is only a matter of time and one would pray that it comes before all of the South becomes scorched earth and all hope of a revived Union is lost.'"

Two exhaled deeply. "Do you accept that assessment, Willie?"

"Absolutely."

"How does it strike you that we might help in some way?"

"Well, any money expended in Nashville or Lexington," his partner said, "would be wasted now, it seems to me. Even if we could find a way to do that—which is unlikely. Perhaps the one hope for any Dewey family . . . uh . . . survival—and that's what we're talking about, isn't it?—"

True nodded.

"Any such hope must be in New York, where Bon Marché East is not in the path of the fighting and isn't likely to be. Infusion of money there will enable George to hold himself together."

"I agree. How much should we invest?"

Banker Carstairs thought for a moment. "Oh, ten . . . twenty thousand."

"I think the latter," Two decided. "I'll write to Roger immediately and have him advance it to George." He paused. "You know, it's too bad those newspaper properties Statler had in the South are going to be lost."

"Yes, isn't it?" Willie said quietly. "But maybe someday—"

41

LETTER from Joy Jackson to True Jackson in Camp Douglas, Chicago, September 1, 1862:

I wish you could ride over Bon Marché and see the rich sea of verdure, high as my head, waving in the bright sunshine, golden and ready for harvest. It is so suggestive of "peace and plenty" one can scarcely realize that stern war, in all its sad reality, is around and about us. But I take strength in knowing that you shall return here to me one day. I have vowed to spend the intervening time seeking out an unfindable place on Bon Marché—a corner of sweet tranquility and seclusion where we can be away from everyone and everything, lost in the thrall of our love.

II

THE young couple strolled hand in hand through the Bon Marché deer park, one a golden-haired, buxom woman, the other a dark-haired, broad-shouldered man in a military uniform.

"This is a beautiful place," Captain Frank Westervelt said.

"Yes," Honore Jackson replied, "but it was even more beautiful before your men invaded it with their guns and took out all the deer and buffalo."

"My men?"

"They wore Union uniforms."

He stopped, took her shoulders into his hands, and turned her to face him. "You know that the commissary hunters

weren't under my command. They weren't *my men*. If they
had been they wouldn't have been allowed to—"

Honore put a finger against his lips, stopping his words.
"I'm sorry, darling. I didn't mean to blame you. It's just that
the Federal presence here has been . . . well, so unfair."

"There are excesses on both sides."

"I know." She reached up to kiss him. "I know, and I don't
want to spoil our being together by talking about it anymore."

They walked along slowly, silently. At a deeply shaded spot
where two large maples entwined their branches over a dark
green tiny meadow of grass, Honore laughed gaily. "I think
this spot must have been saved just for us." She ran to it,
lowering herself into the grass, and reached her arms up to
him. He knelt beside her and kissed her. And then they were
in each other's arms, lying on the sweet-smelling grass, giving
themselves up to their passion.

Frank kissed her wildly—her lips, her cheeks, her eyes, her
neck. His fingers trembled as he undid her bodice and fondled
her breasts. She let him, returning his kisses. And as he grew
bolder, she breathlessly—but gently—pushed him away.

"You overwhelm me, darling," she whispered.

"That's my intent," he admitted.

"Oh, Frank, what shall we do?" The words were sad.

"We should do what we both want."

Honore was totally sober now. "What we both want may
not be possible . . . under these circumstances."

"You know I want to marry you."

"Yes, and I you. But—" Tears filled her eyes. "But it's so
difficult. How can we find a way without . . . well, without me
turning my back on my family? I don't think I could do that.
They're too dear to me."

A tinge of anger showed on his face. "And I'm not just as
dear to you? I thought you loved me."

She was silent for a moment. "Oh, Lord, I don't want us to
argue about this. How can either one of us doubt the other's
love? I want so to express it fully, but I'm fearful."

"Of what?" he demanded.

"Of . . . of . . . carrying your child, without—"

"Damn!" he said in his frustration. Then he shouted it out.
"Damn!"

"Darling," Honore breathed, snuggling close to him again. "Could we just talk of other things?"

"Like what?"

She shook her head, indicating she had no answer. For a long time they just sat there. Finally she spoke again: "Frank, have you had a chance to look at Father's file?"

"Yes."

"Is there a chance he might be released?"

"Ordinarily in these matters an effort is made to parole noncombatant prisoners after a few months. In your father's case, however, General Johnson apparently believes him to be dangerously seditious."

"Oh, how silly," Honore said lightly. "It is true he made financial contributions to the Confederacy, but thousands of Southerners must have done that, believing in the rightness of their actions, and they haven't all been jailed."

"That's true enough."

"The release of a prisoner—how is it done?" she wanted to know.

"Orders are drawn up and signed by a senior officer."

"And in this instance, is General Johnson the only senior officer allowed to sign such orders?"

"No, there are several in Nashville with that authority."

"You know them?" she asked.

"Yes."

"Could you possibly persuade one of them to release my father?"

Captain Westervelt sighed. "It would be very difficult. I might place myself in a very poor position, indeed."

She pouted. "Then you believe a fifty-four-year-old civilian, without any military experience whatsoever, could be a danger to the Union."

"Of course not."

"Well. . . ?"

He frowned deeply. "I don't see how I could accomplish it."

"Not even for me, darling?" She leaned into him and kissed him as she had never kissed him before. The passion of an earlier moment was rekindled, its progression unimpeded. Honore gave herself to the captain there in that "unfindable

place on Bon Marché—a corner of sweet tranquility and seclusion . . ." Lost in the thrall of their love.

Or so she meant it to be interpreted.

III

COLONEL John Hunt Morgan stood on the roadway some five
miles from Lexington, Kentucky, his hands on his hips,
watching the man climb the telegraph pole. He smiled in self-
assurance, the action setting his flowing mustache to twitch-
ing; even his Vandyke beard seemed to be alive.

"Well, Captain Jackson," he said to his aide, "we shall
soon know what the situation is in Lexington."

Morgan's telegrapher attached his pocket instrument to the
wires and leaned back on his climbing belt as the instrument
chattered into action. On the ground the rapid tap-tap-tap
was barely audible.

"What is it, George?" the colonel called up to him.

"General Buell, somewhere in the field near Louisville,"
the telegrapher replied, "is messaging General Wright in Cincinnati." He called out the words of the message as they came
through. "'I suggest . . . to . . . you . . . the . . . importance
. . . of . . . placing . . . a . . . division . . . at . . . Lexington
. . . without . . . delay . . . comma . . . with . . . two . . .
regiments . . . of . . . cavalry . . . comma . . . if . . . you . . .
have . . . them . . . period.' And it's signed 'D. C. Buell, October eighteenth, 1862.'"

Morgan guffawed. "Well, we won't have to worry about
Wright today. Find out what the situation is in Lexington. Do
you know the telegrapher there?"

"His name is Taylor. Should I tell him where Morgan's cavalry is?"

"Yes," the colonel replied. "Put us in Midway, traveling
overland toward Georgetown. That ought to be sufficiently
confusing."

The telegrapher went to work on his pocket instrument,
keeping up a running commentary. "I've identified myself as
Woolums in Midway, telling him that 'Morgan's guerrillas'
have just passed through, intent on taking Georgetown. And
I've asked him whether there are any signs of rebels there. He
replies no. And I'm asking whether Lexington is capable of

stopping Morgan, should he show his face there." A pause. "He's replying: 'Home . . . guards . . . only . . . with . . . one . . . regiment . . . cavalry . . . period.'"

"Tell him Morgan has five thousand."

The message was tapped out. "He replies: 'Praying . . . they . . . not . . . come . . . here . . . today . . . period . . . Home . . . guards . . . number . . . only . . . three . . . hundred . . . period.'"

"Reassure him," Morgan ordered.

Again a message was sent. "I'm telling him Georgetown is certainly Morgan's goal and suggesting he keep cool." A pause. "He says he will and thanks me for my news. And I'm signing off."

"By God, Captain Jackson," Colonel Morgan enthused, "that George Elsworth is worth an extra regiment of cavalry! He's most clever with that telegraph machine." He grinned. "Now, let's take Lexington. It shouldn't require much effort. And when we've secured it, I want you and your brother to take a hundred good men and fan out over the farms. What better place than here to get some remounts?"

At double-quick time the 1,500-man Morgan cavalry dashed quickly into Lexington, routing the home guard without a shot being fired and trapping the local cavalry regiment in its stables at the Lexington Association racetrack. The cavalrymen taken prisoner and their horses removed from the stables, Morgan ordered the stables set afire.

Immediately, the Jackson brothers—Captain Herbert and Lieutenant Victor—left Lexington on different roads, each leading fifty troopers. It was an efficient operation, honed by experience. Very seldom was there any need for gunplay; they struck too quickly for that. And at each farm, they took what horses they wanted and dispatched ten men to take them back to Lexington. Thus, they could each raid five farms before coming to the end of their assignment.

Herbert was already down to twenty men when he came upon a well-cared-for farm, much neater than the other three they had already attacked. More barns, too, promising a bigger haul.

"Hoooo!" Captain Jackson shouted, waving his sword, and the cavalry unit raced toward the gateway of the farm.

Shots rang out and two of his men tumbled into the dust.

Herbert wheeled his horse, directing his men to retreat. One hundred and fifty yards removed, he pulled up, studying the farm with his glass. He didn't see anyone moving. Clearly, they were well hidden.

To a sergeant: "Take five men and jump that fence directly in front of you. Go in toward the barns from that angle." To a corporal: "Take another five, skirt the entrance so you're safe from whoever's hidden there, and take the fence from the other side of the barn area. I'll take the rest of the men and try to silence the guns at the gate. And for God's sake, unlimber those carbines! Go, now!"

Herbert waited until the other two groups could make their incursions and then ordered a charge at the gate. He lost two more troopers before he was through the gate, but three defenders there were quickly killed. As he came up to a larger barn on his left, an older man jumped out from behind a door, a shotgun leveled directly at him. The captain fired his carbine with his left hand, while his sword, in the right, flicked the shotgun into the air. The man crumpled.

The intruder turned to see whether anyone else was coming at him from the barn. For the first time he really saw the face of the man he had shot down. He stared, unbelieving.

"My God . . . oh, my God!"

He dropped his carbine and tossed his sword aside, dismounting to drop to his knees beside the man. "Uncle Lee!" he called. Dead eyes stared up at him. "Oh, sweet Jesus . . ." He gathered the bloody body in his arms, cradling it as he would a baby, crying out in pain.

"Stay right where you are," an angry voice demanded, "or I'll kill you without mercy!"

Herbert raised his head to look at the threat, tears streaming down his cheeks. Their eyes met; recognition was instantaneous.

"I swear I didn't know, Cousin Albert," the intruder moaned, "I didn't know."

Albert Dewey glared at him, keeping the gun aimed at his head. "Well, now you know, Herbert," he said, "that you're on Bon Marché Lexington. And may you burn in hell for what you've done!"

Morgan's other cavalrymen rode up, herding the farm's defenders—now disarmed—before them. Confederate carbines were trained on Albert.

"Hold!" Herbert ordered.

Surprised, the troopers lowered their weapons.

Veterinarian Jamie Orr rushed forward, brushed Herbert aside, and felt for a pulse on Lee Dewey. He shrugged, glancing apologetically at Albert, and then he gently closed the eyes with his fingertips.

The master of Bon Marché Lexington seemed to take no notice of his veterinarian. His hate was fixed on Herbert. "I suppose you've come to take our horses?"

Herbert wiped his face on the sleeve of his tunic. "Yes," he admitted sadly, "that was the intent."

"Then *take* them and get the hell out of here!"

The captain picked up his carbine and put it into the saddle holster and then he retrieved his sword and sheathed it. Mounting his horse, he said again: "You must believe me, Albert, I didn't know."

Albert said nothing.

Herbert Jackson turned his horse; the other cavalrymen followed his example. And Colonel John Hunt Morgan's Confederate raiders rode away from Bon Marché Lexington without their usual contraband of war.

IV

HER shrieks drew the entire household to the bedchamber of Louise Schimmel. The woman who had for weeks lain nearly comatose, who had said almost nothing, who had to rely on her daughter and the housemaids for the most rudimentary of human functions, was now madly animated.

She was sitting up in the bed, her eyes reflecting her terror, her hands tearing at the bedsheets, reducing them to shreds. And her screams were knifelike, seeming to cut through the flesh, exposing the raw nerves.

Joy, panic-stricken, rushed to her. "Mother! What is it!" She tried to take Louise in her arms to comfort her.

With uncharacteristic strength, Louise knocked her aside. Screaming, screaming, screaming.

Then, as suddenly as they had begun, the awful sounds

ended. Louise fell back onto her pillows, her frightened eyes looking up at her daughter. Her lips parted and she spoke softly. "Lee . . . dear sweet Lee." The eyes closed. Her shallow breathing was almost impossible to detect.

For nearly an hour she was like that and then even the faint breathing stopped.

Joy and Honore and Alma May stood by the bed in deep shock. One of the housemaids began to weep.

"Louise always believed in the strange communication of their twinness," the Princess said. "Lee Dewey is gone, too."

No one disputed her.

A somber group stood silently in the tulip poplar grove two days later, looking down at the fresh mound of earth. Louise's son-in-law Colonel Able Jackson had said the final words over her grave.

Now, one by one, they began to walk away. It was not a time for conversation and there wasn't any.

But there were things in their minds.

So, I'm to be the last of the children of Charles Dewey, Alma May thought. *God help me, the last holder of the dream.*

V

IT was the middle of November before there was confirmation of Lee Dewey's death. And it came from an unexpected source. Not from Bon Marché Lexington; communication with Albert seemed to be lost forever. It came instead from a nondescript rider who arrived unannounced at the Nashville plantation carrying a letter for Joy Jackson. The packet in which it came was as nondescript and tattered and dirty as the deliverer. It was obvious the letter had passed through many hands, and no one could have guessed what it contained.

Joy read it before the assembled family members:

"'My darling Mother, I must warn you at the outset that the news I have for you may prove disconcerting and I apologize for that. But all the good that might remain in me tells me I must tell you the truth about what happened on October eighteenth last at Albert's Bon Marché stud in Lexington. It was there that I, riding as part of Morgan's cavalry, caused the death of my own uncle. I shot Lee down, without initially recognizing him, when I felt threatened by the shotgun he carried.'"

Tears stopped the reading for a moment.

"My God," Alma May said, "that *was* the day Louise died."

"Yes," Joy replied, "that was." She gained control of her emotions to read on: "'I rode away from that terrible scene, determined never to fight again. And Victor and I have left Colonel Morgan's forces to go west. I suppose we are now regarded as deserters, and for our necessary safety in that circumstance, and maybe for your safety, as well, in the event anyone comes asking for us, I cannot tell you where we are. Know, however, we are safe. And believe, as we do, that the day will come when we shall be able to be reunited.'"

Again, Joy's sobbing interrupted the reading. The others sat quietly waiting for it to resume.

"'I beg your forgiveness for what I've done and I hasten to add that Victor was not a part of it. He was elsewhere at the time. But I simply didn't know, when our raid began, that I was at Bon Marché Lexington. I swear to God, I didn't know. I wasn't successful in convincing Cousin Albert of that before I had to leave there, but it's the truth: I didn't know.'"

"How terrible it must have been for him," the Princess commented.

Joy nodded, choking back her tears. "'Please ask Father to forgive me, as well. I know how distressed he will be when he learns of two of his sons having deserted the Confederate cause. But, for myself, I didn't believe I had another course. I tried to dissuade Victor from coming with me, but he, being the loving brother that he is, insisted on being by my side. I only hope he will never have to pay a penalty for his love and loyalty. But now we must try to make a new life for ourselves. We will make every effort to stay in touch with you. Your loving and contrite son, Herbert.'"

The mother dropped the letter into her lap, staring off into some distant place. Alma May could see her willing herself to gather together the pieces of her shattered life.

There was a long silence. Then words spoken so softly the others had to strain to hear them: "I don't see how God could possibly devise another test of my faith."

Alma May glanced at Honore, but the young woman avoided eye contact, her face flushed. And they both thought of Captain Frank Westervelt.

42

THE one-armed man stood on a wooden crate in the center of Nashville's market square, haranguing a growing crowd.

"Maybe we have to accept the military presence of our conquerors," he bellowed over the natural noises of the marketplace. "Maybe we have to accept the disfiguring intrusion of their fortifications on the natural beauty of our hills." He gestured off into the distance with his good left arm, a Bible clutched in the hand. "But, in the name of all that's holy, do we have to accept their satanic immorality as well?"

"Colonel" Able Jackson, wearing a farmer's broad straw hat against the rays of a hot July sun, had worked himself into a sweat with his peroration. His eyes flashed—the look of the zealot Alma May had noticed earlier—as he plied his new trade as a preacher of the word of God.

"Our city has become overrun by the harlots of the vaunted United States Army!" His sarcasm wasn't lost on the Nashvillians listening to him; many of them laughed. "Hundreds of fallen women now infest our once serene community. Yes, *infest* it! For there are more men now deathly ill of venereal disease in our conquerors' hospital at the Maxwell House than are suffering there from the honorable wounds of battle.

"All God-fearing citizens must protest this proliferation of SIN AND DEGRADATION! We must *demand* the military authorities now in command of our city remove their diseased camp followers from our midst, and allow us to breathe once more the clean, fresh air of God's glory! We MUST demand it, my fellow citizens, and we must DEMAND it *now!*"

His audience applauded loudly.

On the fringe of the crowd a comely young woman touched the blue-clad arm of a Union captain. "Take me away from this," Honore Jackson demanded. "I don't want Uncle Able to see me with—" She stopped suddenly.

"With me, you mean," Captain Frank Westervelt responded sullenly.

"Yes," she said softly. "Yes, he'd never be able to understand why I'm with you."

Frank grinned. "A preacher would certainly understand God's love, wouldn't he?"

"Don't joke about it, Frank," Honore snapped. "You know exactly what I mean. Uncle Able has made a terrible sacrifice for what he believed . . . for the Confederacy. And now I'm consorting with the enemy."

As they left the market square, the captain added, "I was under the impression we loved each other. That all of this nonsense about 'enemy' wasn't in our vocabulary."

"I do love you, Frank."

"Then why this strange attitude?"

Honore sighed. "Uncle Able isn't wrong, you know. The city is overrun with . . . prostitutes. And most of them are here because your army is here—"

"I'm not responsible for every whore in town," he said heatedly.

"No, of course not. How could you be?"

He reached for her hand and squeezed it. "Good. I'm glad I'm not being blamed for all original sin."

"Frank! Stop making fun of it!"

They walked silently for a moment or two.

"I'm not due on duty for a couple of hours," Captain Westervelt said finally. "Maybe we could . . . well, use an hour or two . . . uh . . . alone. I could get a room at the—"

"No!" Her face was flushed with anger. "I'm not your camp follower!"

"Oh, Jesus," Westervelt groaned. "I'm sorry, darling. It's just that I want to be with you so much—"

"I know."

Another silence.

"Will we meet tomorrow night again at the brood-mare barn?" he wanted to know.

"I don't think so."

He grasped her arm, turning her toward him. "You *are* blaming me for the sin your uncle keeps preaching about."

She sighed once again. "It's just that . . . well, you keep telling me you love me—"

"I do!"

"—but when I ask you for help in behalf of my father you continually make excuses. Honestly, Frank, it makes me wonder about . . . well, how much you really *do* love me."

"It's difficult."

"But not impossible?"

"No," he admitted, "not impossible."

II

GEORGE Dewey Jr. sat amused at the dinner table at Bon Marché East on Long Island. Even though his wife, Emma, may have found their guest somewhat crude, George liked the outspoken John Morrissey who had come to the farm with some good news.

"I tell ya, Mr. Dewey," Morrissey was saying, "there ain't no reason why we can't have a little racing at my place in Saratoga. I don't know why sportin' men can't have some pleasure even though there's a war. After all, the war ain't here, is it?"

"No, happily," George smiled, "the war isn't here."

"Then you'll send some horses up next month?"

"Yes, Mr. Morrissey."

"Good, good! 'Tis a fine place, sir, a fine place indeed."

Morrissey's reputation had preceded him, which was why Emma was disquieted when George had insisted on having him at dinner. He was a rough-hewn man. He had been a bouncer, a bartender, a bare-knuckle prizefighter, a gambler certainly, but he seemed to have some impeccable connections. He peppered his conversation with the names of substantial, monied New York families: Travers, Hunter, Belmont, Jerome. There was a hint of more than a little political influence; Morrissey, with all of his other accomplishments, had also been a U.S. congressman for a short period. George had heard a tale about John having once offered, during a congressional debate, to lick any man in the House of Representatives.

But whatever the reputation, Morrissey's announcement of the resumption of racing in the East was most welcome. The twenty thousand dollars George had received from Two in California had enabled him to keep Bon Marché East from financial disaster and had fortunately limited his service as a horse-purchasing agent for the Union army. But without racing he could not make a go of the farm. Racing was an absolute necessity. And Morrissey offered that.

"Got a track called Horse Haven in the woods there in Saratoga," the dinner guest reported, "an' I think we'll have enough horses for a brief meetin' . . . oh, mebbe four days."

"Bon Marché horses will be there," George reiterated.

"An' next season," Morrissey went on, "I think me an' me partners will be able to offer more. A new track, mebbe."

"That would be fine."

"Yes, sir, Mr. Dewey," the former prizefighter bragged, "me an' me friends intend to make Saratoga somethin' special, believe ya me."

                              III

ABLE Jackson stood on Water Street and watched the strange procession approaching the dock area of Nashville. A contingent of Union soldiers, some of them with fixed bayonets on their rifles, were herding before them perhaps a hundred and fifty bedraggled women, all protesting mightily. The noise of them was a cacophony of complaints and curses.

A man standing next to him, resplendent in a well-tailored long coat and a topper, spoke to the preacher: "A disagreeable group, eh?"

"Yes. A decidedly sinful lot."

"I suppose." The man in the topper looked at Able closely. "I heard tell that some preacher raised so much hell about those women, the military command here had to run them off. Would that have been you, sir?"

Jackson was surprised. "Yes, it was. But how did you know?"

"There's not many men who carry around a Bible like that"—he pointed to the book clutched in Able's left hand— "as if it were a weapon of some kind. A bludgeon maybe."

There was a smile. "I suppose I do see it as a weapon."

"Well, I wish you had kept that . . . uh . . . sword sheathed, sir."

"Oh, why?"

"Because, Preacher, that mob is being escorted to my *Idahoe*." He nodded toward the nearest steamboat. "And I'm contracted to deliver them all to Louisville. Now I know I've made a terrible mistake. The boat is new, only three months built. It's a fine passenger boat, all the furniture is new. What's she going to be like by the time we get to Louisville?"

"Then why did you contract for the job?"

"I didn't. Not really. I just offered her for charter and this is the first damned thing that came up."

"Too bad."

A young lieutenant came up to the steamboat owner. "Are you Captain John Newcomb?"

"I am."

"Well, sir, I have orders to deliver this . . . cargo to you. And we're to accompany you to your destination."

Newcomb groaned. "Get them aboard, Lieutenant, and we'll shove off immediately."

As the prostitutes were pushed past them, Able called out, his Bible raised high. "Repent, Jezebels! See this journey as a fresh opportunity to come to the Lord Jesus! Repent!"

One of the women—older and fat, her face heavily rouged—broke out of the line and came to Able, standing spread-legged and defiantly in front of him. "Grandpa," she screeched at him, "why don't you go to hell!"

"Repent!" Able shouted.

She made a lewd gesture. "*That* for your repentence, Grandpa." The obese whore made her way onto the gangplank, rocking it wildly as she boarded the *Idahoe*.

Able sighed deeply. "If only they would understand that we're concerned for their souls."

"I don't give a damn for their souls," Captain Newcomb said forcefully. "I'm concerned about my boat. By the way, may I know your name, sir?"

"Able Jackson." He tucked the Bible under the stub of his missing arm and offered his left hand.

The captain shook it. "I just wanted to know by what name you're called, because I want to be sure to condemn the right man to purgatory if those whores ruin my new furniture."

IV

IT seemed a miracle.

In mid-afternoon of Thursday, August 27, 1863, a full-bearded True Jackson rode a used-up horse along the lane leading to the Bon Marché mansion. He sat slumped in the saddle, looking unwell, his rheumy eyes taking in the ravages exacted on the plantation by the Union occupation. It had been a year and eight months since he had last seen it and he was appalled by what he saw now.

The outlying acres had been given up to weeds and brush. Fencing was missing. Some of it had obviously been torn down and some of it, without its annual coating of calcimine, was rotting. And he saw no animals; no horses, no cattle, no sheep. Even when he had passed the deer park there were no animals; no white-tail deer and no buffalo. Stranger still, he saw no hands in the fields. No blacks at all. He was perplexed.

Joy has told me none of this in her letters. They've all been so positive. But this—?

He didn't hurry the horse toward the mansion. True understood that the gallant animal was suffering. Under other circumstances he would have dismounted and led the horse, but he was so weak himself he feared he would not be able to cover the remaining several hundred yards to his home on his own two feet.

Yet, it all seemed a miracle he was there. Two and a half weeks earlier he had suddenly been paroled from Camp Douglas. He didn't know why, or by whom. He only knew he was free, and that he had somehow made his way back to Nashville, helped in his journey by the safe-conduct pass he had been given at the prison. All of the money he had at Camp Douglas had been returned to him and with it he had bought the horse he rode—an inferior animal, he thought then—at a Chicago livery stable. The horse, though, was made of sturdier stuff than he had imagined and they had been on a steady, unrelenting course from Camp Douglas to Bon Marché. Both rider and mount had not had enough to eat on the way; both showed it.

Ahead, True could see the chimneys of the mansion over the tops of the trees. There had been times at Camp Douglas when he never expected to see that sight again. And now, as he came close to it, he thought of his son Drew, who would not be there to greet him.

The mansion was now in full view of the exhausted rider. He noticed that the large front lawn had been plowed up for a vegetable garden, and for the first time he saw black workers—all women.

One of them looked up, stared at him for a moment, and then screamed: "Oh, sweet Jee-sus! Mastah True . . . Mastah True!"

The others joined the delirious chorus and then the oaken double doors of the mansion burst open; his daughter, Honore, raced down the steps to him, reaching her arms for him. He slid out of the saddle, trying to embrace the young woman, but collapsed at her feet. Honore sat on the ground beside him, placing his head in her lap. And then his wife, Joy, ran out of the house and fell to the ground beside him, kissing his bearded face. The happy tears of all three prevented words. Useless words, anyway.

Slower, Alma May came from behind the house and stood over them, smiling and crying simultaneously.

Several minutes went by before Honore pushed herself to her feet and went to the Princess. They locked arms around each other and in the embrace the younger woman whispered: "Thank God, I wasn't wrong. I knew I could get Frank to do this for me."

"Yes, darling." Alma May petted her, hoping her pretty grandniece hadn't paid too big a price for having her father freed.

V

ALMA May Dewey's Diary, Saturday, August 29, 1983:

True has been back for two days now and for the first time since his return he was out of bed at noon to have luncheon with us all. He's very weak and tells us little of his prison experience, although the terrible part of it is visible in his eyes. Joy wants him to shave the heavy beard he now wears, but he will not. "I pledged myself I would be bearded until the Confederacy is victorious," he told us. "And if I am laid to rest with this beard, that's as it must be." He knows the truth now of Drew's death and the defection of Herbert and Victor from the Confederate army, and he seems to have accepted that truth stoically. Indeed, at lunch today he began to talk about rebuilding Bon Marché, in most enthusiastic terms, and that brings a joy to my heart that hasn't been there for a long time.

The Princess closed the diary and went to the cupboard to pour herself a few drops of Bon Marché bourbon. There were only two bottles remaining and no way to know when it would be possible to brew some again. So, she savored the whiskey, rolling it around in her mouth.

Someone dropped the brass knocker at the main door and Alma May heard one of the maids hurrying to answer it.

A male voice said: "I bring a message for Miss Honore Jackson from Captain Westervelt. I'm instructed to wait for a reply."

"Bring him in here," Alma May called out.

A sergeant strode into the Dewey Room.

"I'm not sure just where Honore is right now," Alma May said. "I'm her aunt and I'll be glad to give her the message when she returns."

"I'm sorry, ma'am," the soldier said formally, "but I'm under orders to deliver the message directly into Miss Jackson's hands and to wait for an answer."

"Of course, and you must follow orders." She turned to the colored maid. "Go find Miss Honore and fetch her here. And there's no need to bother Mister True or Miss Joy about this."

The maid nodded her understanding, leaving the room.

The sergeant glanced about at the horse paintings lining the walls. "Is this a racehorse farm, ma'am?"

"It was at one time," Alma May answered sadly.

"Yes, the war changes a lot of things, doesn't it?"

"Hmmm. Are you partial to racehorses, Sergeant?"

He smiled for the first time. "Oh, in a way. Back home in New Jersey I used to like to go to the track. I hope someday I'll be able to do that again."

Honore entered and the sergeant went to her, clicking his heels as he handed her the sealed envelope. "From Captain Westervelt, ma'am. He asks that I return with your reply."

She said nothing as she tore open the message. Her face reddened as she read it. And then she handed it to the Princess.

My most darling Honore,
I am under house arrest because of my role in getting your father released from Camp Douglas. I prepared the papers and then had Brig. Gen. J. D. Morgan sign them without reading them. He's a very busy man as the commanding officer in Nashville and scrawls his name on anything put before him. But now my duplicity has been discovered and I am in a bit of trouble. Please don't be alarmed, darling, because it is not as bad as it may sound. In a sense, I've received little more than a reprimand in being reassigned back to New York. And that is really fortunate for us. When I get back to New York I intend to resign my commission and we can be married. Isn't that a lovely word? Married. But we must make haste. I'm being shipped out at 7 A.M. tomorrow (Sunday) aboard the river steamer *Foster* and I've arranged passage for you as well. Together then we can travel to a whole new life as husband and wife. Please make me the happiest man in the world by assuring me, as I know you will, that you'll be there at the docks.
Your devoted lover, Frank Westervelt.

Alma May looked up from the letter. "Will you excuse us a moment, Sergeant?" She took Honore's arm and guided her out into the foyer. "What do you intend to do?" she asked.

"Well, I'm certainly not going to be there at the docks tomorrow morning," Honore replied with anger in her voice.

"Do you believe he loves you?"

"I suppose he does."

"And you?"

"I don't love Frank Westervelt, Auntie Alma. I never have. What I couldn't tell you before was that I was using him. It's shameless, I know. But, then, he used me, too. And I've . . . uh . . . *paid* him for what he did for Father; I have no further debt. I paid him well with the only currency I had available." She blushed. "Do you disapprove?"

"How can I? I might have done the same thing in identical circumstances."

Honore kissed her. "Thank you, Princess." Suddenly, fright showed on her face. "Oh, my God . . . do you think they'll come and arrest Father again?"

"I don't believe so," Alma May replied easily. "The Union army certainly has a lot more important problems than one worn-out noncombatant named True Jackson. No . . . no . . . I think we may safely conclude that the matter is closed."

The young woman turned quickly and reentered the Dewey Room. "Sergeant, please tell Captain Westervelt," she said coldly, "that I'm unable to reply at this time."

"I regret I can't accept that, ma'am. I'm under strict orders not to return without an answer."

"Oh, very well," Honore shrugged, going to the desk in the corner of the room. She sat down and arranged some writing paper in front of her and somewhat ceremoniously dipped a quill pen into the inkwell.

"This painting, Sergeant," Alma May said, directing the soldier's attention to one of the portraits on the wall, "is of one of the best-bred horses ever to carry the Bon Marché silks. He was named Charles Dewey, after the founder of this plantation. Unhappily, he never quite reached his potential." She stopped, remembering the tragic day when the equine Charles Dewey had to be destroyed. "But that's a consequence of owning racehorses, Sergeant. You have to be prepared to graciously accept both winning and losing, with the understanding that most often it's going to be losing."

She went along the wall, giving capsule explanations of some of the other horses.

After perhaps ten minutes, Honore rose from the desk to come to the Union soldier with an envelope. The Princess noted that it was sealed with wax impressed with the Bon Marché crest.

"I'm sorry to have kept you so long, Sergeant," she said.

"Thank you, ma'am." He clicked his heels, nodded to both women, and was gone.

When they heard the big door close, Alma May asked: "What did you write to your captain?"

"Nothing," Honore answered.

"What?"

"Nothing. I sent him a blank sheet of paper. The only words I wrote were 'Captain Westervelt' on the outside."

"You have the Dewey toughness," the Princess said with a slight smile. "Always keep it, my dear. Always."

43

TRUE Jackson's return to Bon Marché did not bring a renewal for the plantation, as Alma May hoped it would. He was ill much of the time, with a fever he had contracted at Camp Douglas recurring every few weeks, each time with what seemed to be more intensity.

He did try, of course, but there was no continuity possible in his efforts. And without the male Bon Marché slaves who had been impressed to work for the Union army he seemed to lose heart; whatever enthusiasm he may have had left him.

True had attempted, with his brother, Able, as his legs and his voice, to have the slaves returned. The labor they represented certainly was needed at Bon Marché. Able spent more than a week in a frustrating search for the whereabouts of the Bon Marché blacks, being shunted from one Union officer to another. Finally, in the office of one Colonel Mansfred, the name of Bon Marché was recognized.

"Oh, yes," the colonel said, looking down at a pile of papers on his desk, "the Bon Marché contingent—more than a hundred, I understand."

Able nodded.

"Our records show that regular payments have been made to the plantation for the labor of those people."

"I suppose that's true," said Able, unaware of just what payments had been made, or if they had been made at all. "But that's not the reason I'm here. Bon Marché has suffered greatly, not only from the . . . uh . . . incursions of your commissary people, Colonel, but also because of the lack of manpower to keep it up. The three ladies who own Bon Marché,

with help from a few Negro women, have only been capable
of maintaining a small garden for food. The rest of it is decaying. It's not even providing anything for your commissaries."
He thought that last point might be of value.

"Hmmm."

"So, the reason I'm here, Colonel, is to get the males
back," Able went on. "If I'm any judge, you've completed
your fortifications and don't need the Bon Marché hands anymore."

"Yes . . . well . . ." the colonel said hesitantly, rearranging
some of his papers. "As you must be aware, Jackson, the
United States Army has become a very large organization.
And with any army of size, given the rapid growth necessary,
there are opportunities afforded for some . . . uh . . . occasional . . . well, chicanery, you might say."

Able edged forward in his chair.

"The provost marshal has under active investigation right
now charges that sundry persons, some of them military, have
been obtaining passes and permits to take Negroes outside
our lines"—the colonel was speaking very deliberately, obviously uneasy with the facts he was revealing—"and running
them South to be . . . uh . . . resold."

"Including the Bon Marché hands?" Able asked angrily.

"Unfortunately, yes."

"So they've just been stolen from your command?"

"Abducted, certainly."

Able laughed sarcastically. "I suggest, Colonel, that this is
no time for the niceties of semantics. Bon Marché property,
impressed by the United States Army, is now gone—and it
can't be expected that the hands will be returned."

"The provost marshal is investigating—"

"But with no zeal, I'll wager."

The colonel made no comment.

"And what are the ladies of Bon Marché to do now? Abandon their property and have it fall into the hands of your
thieves as well?"

The officer bridled. "You overstate the case, sir. The
United States has procedures to be followed by your ladies to
recoup losses that might be the responsibility of the army."

Able was on his feet, his face reddened in anger. "In this
life, Colonel, or the next!"

"These are difficult times, Jackson, for everyone involved."

The preacher in Able Jackson came to the fore. "Maybe God, in his infinite mercy, will be able to forgive your army its cruel excesses. But as a fallible man I hope that he doesn't!"

After True received his brother's report he stopped making suggestions to Alma May about the "resurrection of Bon Marché." He retreated within himself, spending most of his time in bed, giving himself up to his fevers and his despair.

II

TIME became a triviality at Bon Marché. Minutes and hours and days and weeks and months were no measure of the lives of those who remained at the plantation. Most things happening outside boundaries of the wounded acres filtered through to them in rumors, half-truths, hearsay—coming from a world that had become incoherent.

Christmas of '63 went unobserved. The beginning of a new year went unrecognized. But the perception that the Confederacy was steadily waning, that its days were surely numbered, was real enough. Even rumors, half-truths, and hearsay brought a sum of that.

Their isolation was not total, however. In February of 1864, there came a welcome letter from Albert in Lexington, the first in more than a year.

"We have decided," Albert wrote, "that the time has come to shake off our war-borne lethargy and to become a breeding farm again, reasoning that the war cannot last forever. Thus, all of our mares are being bred to the best stallions we can find hereabouts. We look for light down the dark road of the future, believing that the foals we conceive this year will indeed race someday under our colors."

It was July when another letter—this one from George Junior in New York—somehow made its way through to Bon Marché. It had been written two months earlier.

Alma May read it aloud to the family members and the Negro housemaids she had gathered around True Jackson's bed: "'It seems impossible, but we are going to have racing here again this year. An experiment at a little track in Saratoga last August was successful; I even managed a win there. And now I learn there's to be a full-scale meeting at Saratoga at a new track there this August that will feature a stakes race to be named for W. R. Travers, one of our most prominent racing citizens. I hope to have several Bon Marché runners capable of seeking that prize.'

"Isn't that marvelous!" the Princess enthused. Even the somber True smiled.

"'There's also to be a resumption of racing in New Jersey,'" Alma May continued to read, "'with a Jersey Derby to be run at Paterson. It's for three-year-olds, of course, at a mile-and-a-half dash, with a sweepstakes premium of one thousand dollars. I don't have anything ready for that, but I do plan to take several competitors to Paterson to run in the rest of the meeting.

"'We are all well here and, if not wildly prosperous, we are now reasonably certain of the survival of Bon Marché East until the war comes to an end.'"

Aside from the brief golden moments occasioned by the arrival of those two letters, 1864 held little promise. The news, when it came through, was almost all bad; the attrition on the Confederate army was more and more apparent. Politically, Abraham Lincoln was reelected President of the United States; in Nashville the only interest in that unsurprising development was because of the new Vice President: Andrew Johnson, the Union's former military governor of Tennessee.

III

IT was in mid-November that Able Jackson rode into Bon Marché to announce his concern for those who still remained at the plantation.

"There's every indication in Nashville," he told the assembled family members, "that John Bell Hood intends to bring the Army of Tennessee to bear against the city. He's joined up with Forrest's cavalry and it's clear he can have only one goal—Nashville itself. Certainly, the Union command believes so. Schofield's army has been brought in to reinforce Thomas, and I fear we're in for a major battle. I want to recommend that you all leave here and join us in the city. For your own safety."

"Aren't you being alarmist, Able?" Alma May wanted to know.

"I think not," he answered firmly. "If Hood does attack Nashville, it'll have to be from the south, and that means some of the fighting may be over these very acres."

The Princess was surprised when True disputed his brother's contentions, especially by the manner in which he did it.

"It's an uneven contest," True said weakly. "Good Lord, Nashville must be the best fortified city in the South. Forts Negley and Morton and Houston, and those lesser forts—I don't even know their names. Hood will have no chance here." He sighed. "Indeed, the Confederacy has no chance any longer. No, Able, I'll stay here. And I suppose here is where I'll die—in bed, like the used-up warrior I've become." There was a wan smile. "If I'm allowed to still consider myself a warrior for the cause, lost though it be."

Joy was appalled by her husband's pessimism. "Don't talk like that. Able has only our well-being at heart and I think we ought to listen to his advice."

"No," True said firmly, "I'll stay!"

But two weeks later (Alma May noted it in her diary as the evening of Wednesday, November 30, 1864), Able was back at Bon Marché, more insistent than before.

"There's been a major battle at Franklin," he reported. "With heavy casualties. Hood hoped to crush Schofield there, but he's failed. Schofield has emptied his trenches there and is falling back on Nashville. We must assume that Hood will give chase, with Bon Marché directly in his path."

"Major casualties?" True asked sadly.

"Word in Nashville is that it's more than six thousand, including no less than five Confederate generals." He thought for a moment. "Adams, Granbury, Gist, Strahl, Cleburne—all dead."

True stared at him wordlessly, wanting not to believe.

"You must leave here," Able said. "You'll be safe at our home in Nashville."

His brother shook his head slowly.

But Joy had made a decision. "You stay the night, Able, and we'll leave with you in the morning." To Alma May: "Could we use one of those old mares to draw a carriage?"

"Of course."

"First thing in the morning, then."

After a sleepless night, Alma May watched as True, in the throes of one of his sudden fever attacks, was helped into the carriage, to be followed by Joy and Honore. The Princess made no effort to join them.

"Auntie Alma?" Joy called to her.

"I'll follow later," the Princess lied. "I still have the gelding."

Joy smiled at her, their eyes meeting. "You never intend to leave, do you?"

"No, dear. Never."

IV

Alma May Dewey's Diary, Monday, December 5, 1864:

There are increasing signs that Hood's army is investing this area. I spotted some cavalry along the Richland Creek this morning, but they were not near enough to address. I told the remaining Negro women and children today that if there is fighting here, we'll hide in the root cellar. And we practiced getting into the cellar expeditiously. Poor dears, they are very frightened.

V

Alma May Dewey's Diary, Friday, December 9, 1864:

A Confederate army commissary officer rode in this morning at the head of a train of six wagons, looking for supplies for Gen. Hood's army. I told him the sad truth: that the Federals had long since stripped us of everything. Nevertheless, I invited him to search the plantation for anything of value to him. He had to leave empty-handed. The word the officer gave me, cautioning that he was not privy to Gen. Hood's exact plans, is that there will be a battle any day now. He recommended I leave the vicinity. I cannot.

VI

Alma May Dewey's Diary, Tuesday, December 13, 1864:

I have had to abandon the plan to use the root cellar as a safe haven. The Negroes simply won't go into it, fearing being buried alive. Twice during the week there have been runaways, which I am powerless to stop. My census this morning showed only seven women remaining, with three children—two females and a male. The prospect facing me is that I may soon be alone. Just me. And Daddy's spirit, of course.

VII

LOW-CLINGING fog shrouded the weed-grown pastures of Bon Marché as dawn came on Thursday, December 15. Alma May, who had slept surprisingly well during the night, awoke with the portent that this day would finally bring the fighting. The thought brought her a strange relief. She dressed hurriedly and went down for breakfast, thinking that she might have to make it herself. But there had been no further defections from the ranks of the servants. She ate heartily.

From off in the distance came the sound of gunfire, echoing first like some far-removed thunder. The Princess surmised she was hearing artillery guns in action. She quickly gathered the Negroes around her in the foyer.

"Now, we're all going to stay inside today," she ordered, "and we're going to keep away from the windows. If there is any fighting here it probably won't last very long. It will probably come and go and we won't be part of it. No one wants to hurt us. If we stay out of the way we're going to be safe."

She looked around at the worried black faces in the circle. "So right now you just go on with your household chores and don't pay any attention to those noises. But I want you all to understand this: no one is to go outside today . . . without . . . my . . . allowing . . . it! Is that clear?"

The black heads nodded. The Princess turned to make her way into the Dewey Room. When she reached the door she realized the servants were still standing in a knot in the foyer, chattering to each other. "Chores! Chores!" she chided them and they scattered in all directions.

In the Dewey Room she looked up at the portrait of her father and nodded to it. And then she went to the bookshelves and took down a volume of her favorite poetry. She pushed a chair around so that she could glance out of the window across the lawn—now cut up with the fallow vegetable garden—and from that vantage point she could see down to the deer park, the chimney tops of the Beau Monde mansion barely visible in her line of sight.

As she read, trying to keep her mind concentrating on the poetry, the sounds of the gunfire grew louder. *Closer,* she thought. But she stayed with her poetry, for the lack of something better to do.

At about eleven o'clock, she rose and went to the desk to put some of her thoughts into the diary. The battle sounds were much closer now. Several times, as she was writing, a loud thump of artillery startled her, causing her to blot the page. She swore under her breath.

"Miss Alma! Miss Alma!" one of the housemaids screamed from the second floor. "They's wagons . . . wagons!"

The Princess hurried up the steps to get a better view from the windows there, to see a Confederate supply train being brought along the Bon Marché training track and then parked behind the brood-mare and breeding barns. That done, the escort company rode away.

"They've just parked the wagons there to keep them out of the fighting," Alma May told the servants. "So maybe that's all we're going to see of the battle. I'll have my lunch," she added, "at the desk."

She wasn't really very hungry, but she wanted to try to maintain a feeling of normalcy in the house. She could understand the servants' fright; she was feeling some herself. The supply wagons parked there by the barns could be trouble.

And so she ate lunch when it was brought to her and complained a bit about the texture of the omelette. *Normalcy.* After lunch she let it be known that she would be taking a brief nap and asked to be awakened at two o'clock. *Normalcy.*

There was no sleep, though; the noise of the fighting was too persistent and too close for that. At about two she feigned sleep so that she could be "awakened" by the maid. She asked for a pan of warm water and bathed her face. And then she returned to the Dewey Room and the book of poetry.

By now, however, the lines on the page were just black smudges. She couldn't concentrate on the reading at all. Sighing, she rose and went to the big window, looking out toward the deer park. She stared intently at the chimneys of the boarded-up Beau Monde because she thought she saw smoke coming out of them. *It is smoke!* But it wasn't from the chimneys. An angry, jagged, orange-red stab of flame rose up from the roof. The smoke darkened and bellowed upward.

Beau Monde's on fire!

One of the children, the eldest of the girls, ran into the room. "Miss Alma, Mistah Statler's house is burnin'!"

"I know, dear," the mistress of Bon Marché said quietly. She went to her knees in front of the girl. "Now, I want you to go all around the house and tell everyone to stay away from the windows. Will you do that for me?"

"Yes, ma'am." The child rushed away.

The Princess returned to her vigil by the window. The Beau Monde fire had become a conflagration, one that had obviously been set. *But by whom?* As she watched she saw the first of them advancing out of the small patch of woods that separated Beau Monde from Bon Marché. Soldiers in blue uniforms moving cautiously, their guns at the ready. First only a few, then ten, twenty, thirty, and more. Several mounted officers rode into view and some orders were given, although inaudible to Alma May.

A half-dozen men, torches in their hands, rushed forward and across the training track to where the Confederate supply wagons were parked, and they were set afire. One or more of them must have contained ammunition because there were several roaring explosions, the concussion rattling the window in front of the Princess. And the explosions scattered the flames broadside onto the roofs of the brood-mare and breeding barns and they were quickly engulfed. A breeze spread the flames to the other barns—the yearling barn, the horses-in-training barns, the stallion barn. All of those magnificent, oaken structures were being consumed.

Angry beyond anything she had ever known, Alma May ran to the main double doors of the mansion and flung them open, striding out to the edge of the veranda, planting herself there. If the Union soldiers meant to also burn the Bon Marché mansion, they'd have to get by her first!

She could hear the screams of the gelding and the two old mares still in the barn as the flames reached them. Tears ran down Alma May's face, but she willed herself to stop crying.

Suddenly, from the south of the burning barns there came

rifle shots. Two of the blue-clad soldiers fell. And then bursting onto the scene were perhaps fifty Confederate soldiers, some mounted and some afoot, attacking the somewhat larger Union force, firing accurately and screaming defiance.

The Princess yelled, too, waving them on. There was a pitched battle right there just yards in front of her. Bullets clipped the shrubbery at her feet, and splattered against limestone columns of the mansion on either side of her. Still she shouted and waved, cheering even louder as the Union soldiers retreated—those of them who could. For some of them spilled their blood on the Bon Marché lawn. Others of them threw down their rifles and raised their hands high in surrender. And the others fled.

The skirmish was over almost as suddenly as it had started. And Alma May stood there, trembling.

A Confederate major rode up to her, tipping his cap. "Ma'am," he said soberly, "I've seen a lot of brave things in this damned war, but nothing as brave as you standing in the middle of that fire and cheering us on."

"What?" She seemed unable to comprehend what he was saying.

"You stood just like a goddess there," he said in admiration.

Wearily, she sank down on the steps. "Thank you, Major. You're very kind."

"It's not kindness, ma'am. It's the truth. May I have the honor, ma'am? I'm Robert Robison."

"Dewey," she replied. "Alma May Dewey."

"Alma May Dewey," the major repeated. "That's not a name I'm ever likely to forget." He saluted her and wheeled his horse. "Gamest little human being I ever did see," he said loudly to no one in particular.

VIII

ON the next day, what would be called the Battle of Nashville continued, but not again in the precincts of Bon Marché. It was late in the afternoon that Able Jackson rode in, sitting his horse and gazing in disbelief at the blackened ruins of the barns.

Alma May came out of the mansion to greet him.

"Are you all right?" he asked.

"Yes, but they burned all of that." She gestured toward the barns. "And Beau Monde, too."

"I saw that."

"They paid, though. A Confederate unit ran them off. Killed nine of them and took a dozen or more prisoners."

Able grimaced. "There wasn't any victory, however. Hood took a terrible beating. I suspect we've seen the last major battle on Tennessee soil."

The Princess made no comment on his news. "I was waiting for someone to come. My gelding was . . . lost in the fire. Do you think you could get a telegraph message out?"

"In a day or two when the military traffic slacks off."

"Would you send this for me then?" She handed him a slip of paper. "It's to Two in California."

Able took it from her and read it:

"BON MARCHÉ DEVASTATED. YOU ARE ITS LAST HOPE."

Epilogue

ENGINES driving the giant paddlewheels of the riverboat *Palestine* were reversed, then silenced, and the shallow-draft vessel drifted to a thudding stop on the earthen Nashville wharf. Passengers lined the rails waiting for the gangplank to be let out. Three fashionably dressed women stood nervously on the shore watching the arrival.

"Do you think we'll recognize him, Auntie Alma?" Joy Jackson asked.

"Probably not," the Princess chuckled. "He was a lad not ten years old when he left. And now he's a man of—what?—twenty-four. Great changes in appearance take place in that transition."

She had written in her diary that morning: "Today—Thursday, April 13, 1865—marks a new beginning for Bon Marché. Charles Dewey III arrives from California . . ."

The passengers were disembarking and Alma May, Joy, and Hope craned their necks to get a better view.

Then, Alma May gasped. "Oh, dear God—!" Tears started as she pointed excitedly. "There! Behind that tall, bearded man. He's Daddy . . . *reincarnated.*"

She indicated a sturdily built young man, with light blond hair and a square-cut face, who carried himself with a familiar air of self-assurance, with an unmistakable hint of arrogance. Alma May rushed forward to him, throwing her arms about him, kissing his face.

He laughed, his hazel eyes showing his amusement. "I expected to be welcomed, Aunt Alma, but this—"

"You're the exact copy of my father . . . your great-grand-father."

"So my father says. And since I look much like my father, I suspect there must be some truth in all of that."

"The resemblance is uncanny," Alma May said.

Clearly, Charles III had quickly tired of that subject. He turned to the twins. "The Schimmel sisters," he said. "Or should I say the Jackson sisters? But I swear I can't tell who is Hope and who's Joy."

"I'm Joy."

He cavalierly kissed her hand, then turned to the other twin. "And Hope." He kissed her hand, too.

"And this fellow, ladies"—he indicated the tall, bearded man Alma May had noticed earlier—"is my dear friend Roger Weatherford, who also happens to be the general manager of my father's Eastern newspapers." He introduced the women.

"Oh, yes," Alma May said. "As you instructed in your letter, Mr. Weatherford, I've reserved a room for you at the Nashville Inn. But I wish you'd stay at Bon Marché. We have plenty of room for you."

"I appreciate that, Miss Alma," the older man said, "but my reason for making this trip is to revive the *Nashville Monitor* and I hope to get everything under way quickly. Indeed, I intend to have an issue of sorts out on Saturday."

"That sounds impossible, Mr. Weatherford."

Young Dewey laughed. "You just don't know Roger. He's a positive genius at doing the impossible."

Weatherford then hurried off toward the inn, and the others got into an open carriage for the drive to Bon Marché. Alma May had bought two gaited horses to pull the phaeton, the first horses on the plantation since the fires of the Battle of Nashville.

As they settled down (the lone black boy at Bon Marché doing the driving), the Princess began a rapid-fire series of questions: about his father, mother, little sister Glory, Willie Carstairs and his Spanish wife, the Bon Marché West farm, the Dewey business. On and on, with Charles III giving polite answers, if not as detailed as Alma May might have liked.

They came eventually to the boundaries of Bon Marché, and the young man silenced his great-aunt with a slight movement of his hand. His eyes seemed to take in every little detail. At one point, as he surveyed the rotting fences, he asked: "You have a sawmill?"

"Yes," Alma May answered. "Little used in recent years."

"Hmmm." When they came to the blackened ruins of Beau Monde, he said, "That's not the Bon Marché mansion, I take it."

"No, that was once the grand house of Statler and Harriet Dewey, before they returned to New Orleans. Statler has since—"

He cut her off. "Yes, I know of that."

As they started into the curved driveway at Bon Marché itself, Charles III vaulted out of the carriage as it was still moving, boosting himself over the fence at the training track, kicking at the dirt of it in a rudimentary inspection. Then he walked down the row of charred horse barns, his eyes studying what remained.

When he rejoined the women who waited for him on the veranda, he said: "Those barns—we'll rebuild them of field-stone."

Alma May gestured him inside the mansion and led the way to the Dewey Room. One of the maids had poured bourbon, and the newcomer took a glass, sipped it, and smiled. "Very, very good."

"The last bottle, unfortunately," the Princess told him.

"Hmmm." The glass in his hand, he began to circle the room, looking at the paintings. As he moved slowly, he began to talk: "You should understand that I am not here for my-self, but as a representative of the Dewey Trading Company. And the Dewey Trading Company, in the legal sense, is two men—my father and"—there was a quick glance at Alma May—"Willie Carstairs."

He returned to studying the paintings as he walked. "Now, we fully understand that you three were the heirs of Matilda Dewey and, as such, are the nominal owners of Bon Marché, which includes an investment in the farm in Lexington, and full ownership of the Long Island farm. I use the term 'nomi-nal owners' because, in legal reality, Mr. Carstairs holds a substantial mortgage on Bon Marché, on which there has been no payment of either principal or interest. To effect my coming here—in response to the telegraph message—Mr.

Carstairs assigned the mortgage to the Dewey Trading Company, which, in turn, has now foreclosed on the mortgage."

"But that means—" the Princess started.

"Please," the young man interrupted her, "hear me out." He was still walking slowly around the room, his attention seemingly on the horse paintings. "Recognizing the substantial contribution all of you have made to Bon Marché over the years, the Dewey Trading Company—even though Bon Marché is foreclosed—is prepared to pay each of you fifty thousand dollars in cash. Today, if you wish. In addition, any or all of you, and your families, may continue to live at Bon Marché, as you desire, without cost . . . uh . . . until your demise.

"On the other side of the coin, the Dewey Trading Company will abide, during your lifetimes, by the provisions of Matilda Dewey's will. Which is to say that the plantation will remain whole and will continue under the ownership of those of Dewey blood—Charles Dewey II qualifying on that score. And, of course, the Dewey Trading Company will provide whatever monies are necessary to restore Bon Marché to its . . . uh . . . former greatness."

He had now completed his circuit of the room, and stood leaning on the mantel, directly under the portrait of Charles Dewey the founder. They were mirror images.

"That, in a nutshell, is what's happening," he added. "I have documents with me that need to be signed, but essentially I've told you what they contain."

There was a long silence, broken finally by Alma May. "And your role, Charles?"

"I will, of course, be managing Bon Marché from now on."

"The Prince replacing the Princess," she said quietly.

Charles III laughed. "I like that analogy, Aunt Alma. I like it very much."

II

ROGER Weatherford did manage to revive the *Nashville Monitor* for the Dewey Newspapers with a special two-page edition for Saturday, April 15, 1865.

Its boldfaced headlines proclaimed:

THE REBEL FIENDS AT WORK

**President Lincoln Shot
Secretary Seward Stabbed
John Wilkes Booth Is
President's Assassin**